Richard Williams

Montgomeryshire Worthies

Richard Williams

Montgomeryshire Worthies

ISBN/EAN: 9783337368401

Printed in Europe, USA, Canada, Australia, Japan

Cover: Foto ©Andreas Hilbeck / pixelio.de

More available books at **www.hansebooks.com**

MONTGOMERYSHIRE

WORTHIES

BY

RICHARD   WILLIAMS

Fellow of the Royal Historical Society

SECOND   EDITION

"Yn mhob gwlad y megir glew"—*Welsh Proverb*

NEWTOWN:

PHILLIPS & SON, PRINTERS, "EXPRESS & TIMES" OFFICE

Preface.

IN THE YEAR 1875 I commenced the publication in the *Mont-gomeryshire Collections* of the Powysland Club of a series of "brief "sketches of men identified by birth or long residence, property or office, "with Montgomeryshire and its borders, and whose names are still "remembered in connection with literature, religion, politics, the arts "and sciences or otherwise." In 1884, such of these sketches as had appeared up to that time were reprinted and published in a collected form; but all the copies were soon taken up and for several years the work has been out of print. In response to very numerous applications this second edition is now brought out and opportunity has been taken not only to thoroughly revise the original edition but also to make very extensive and important additions to it. From the nature of the work itself I have necessarily drawn very largely upon others for my facts, but have spared no pains to be strictly accurate, fair and impartial, and to put together in a concise and accessible form all that is known of interest or importance relating to the persons whose lives are briefly recorded in these pages.

It would be simply impossible for me to enumerate all the sources from which information has been obtained or all the kind friends who have so readily and so generously assisted me—"their name is legion" —I trust, therefore, this general acknowledgment of my gratitude will be accepted by them all, and that I may venture to hope that the same kind and indulgent reception which was given to the first edition will also be extended to this.

R. WILLIAMS.

Celynog, Newtown,
    9th August, 1894.

Montgomeryshire Worthies.

AELHAIARN.—A saint who lived in the sixth century, and a brother to Llwchaiarn and Cynhaiarn—all three being sons of Hygarfael, son of Cyndrwyn, prince of Powys, " of Llystin- "weunan in Caereinion," probably identical with the Township of Llyssyn, Llanerfyl. The parish church of Guilsfield is said to have been originally founded by Aelhaiarn.

ALO.—A chieftain of Powys and head of one of the five plebeian tribes of Wales. The others were Gwenwys, Heilyn, Blaidd Rhudd, and Adda Fawr. Why he should be placed at the head of one of the *plebeian* tribes is not clear: he was lineally descended from Iestyn ab Gwrgant, head of the Fourth Royal Tribe of Wales. For arms he bore *Or*, three lions' heads guardant erased *gules*, within a bordure engrailed *azure*.

ARDDUN BENASGELL (" the wing-headed ").—A daughter of Pabo Post Prydain. She lived in the sixth century, and became wife of Brochwel Ysgythrog, who, having succeeded to the principality of Powys, lived till after the time of St. Augustine, and commanded the reserve left to protect the monks of Bangor Iscoed against Ethelfrith, where, however, he was defeated with great loss. Arddun was the mother of St. Tysilio, and is by some herself reckoned among the Welsh saints. It is stated also that several Welsh churches are dedicated to her, but it does not appear where they were situated. Dolarddun, in Castle Caereinion, probably takes its name from her.

ARWYSTL.—A son of Cunedda Wledig, who, with his brothers, drove the Irish out of Wales in the fourth century, and settled in that part of Montgomeryshire called after him Arwystli.

ARWYSTLI, HUW.—A poet who flourished between 1540 and 1590. Some say that he lived till 1594. He is known to have written at least one hundred and fifty-five poems, most of which are still to be found in manuscript in the British Museum, at Peniarth, and in other collections. In the heading of one of them he is called Huw Arwystli " of Trefeglwys." Another curious MS. in the British Museum gives an account of him, and of the manner in which he was endowed with the poetic faculty, of which the following is a translation :—

"Huw Arwystli was a poor despised cripple, and sometimes for want of lodging was accustomed to turn aside into the church at Llandinam, in Montgomeryshire, to sleep when he came that way on his travels. And it chanced that he came that way one May eve and slept there that night, and while he was in deep slumber he in his sleep saw one coming to him and putting something into his head, and, next morning when he awoke, it happened that a maiden came by who had been gathering may and bearing an armful of may, and she said to those who were with her in passing by the window under which Huw was lying these words, 'Not one of you will give any may to this cripple; I will give him some,' and she tossed to him through the window a branch of fresh gathered may, and he thanked her in verse, who had never before composed or known how to compose a single stanza; and the song that he sang to her follows thus in this Englyn. And from this time he began to compose poetry, and made many masterly odes, and was in favour with the gentry of Wales during the rest of his life, and what he saw entering his head was the poetic faculty which God gave him, and which excelled any that existed in the age in which he lived."

Lewys Dwn, the Welsh herald, places the names of "Hugh "Arwystli and Morgan Elvael, chief musicians" among those "of the generation which I saw aged and grey-headed, and who "were perfect poets, duly authorised, and all graduated." And William Lleyn thus compliments him :—

> " Dysg ag addysg go weddol—o gywydd
> Ag awen ysbrydol;
> Odid un nad ydyw'n ol
> Huw Arwystli naturiol."

According to a British Museum MS. quoted in the *Brython* vol. iii. p. 137, he was buried at St. Asaph.

BAUGH, ROBERT, of Llandysilio, and for many years parish clerk of Llanymynech, was a clever engraver. Born about 1748, he died the 27th December, 1832, aged 84 years. Among other instances of his ability and skill as an engraver may be named the large Map of North Wales, published in 1795, by his friend and neighbour Mr. John Evans, of Llwyny-groes. In 1809 the Society of Arts awarded to Mr. Baugh their silver medal and fifteen guineas in money for a map of Shropshire. The following sketch, written by an admiring friend, appeared soon after his death in the *Cambrian Quarterly Magazine :—*

"Died aged 84, near Llanymynech, the ingenious, cheerful and benevolent Mr. Robert Baugh, well known as the accurate and perspicuous engraver of the great and small Maps of North Wales, published by the late John Evans, Esq., and of his own great Map of Shropshire, together with the vignettes that adorn these elaborate works. The sensitive affections of mind and heart in this truly good man were at all times singularly alive to the playful and pathetic, and with such rapid alternations that the writer of this short and transient tribute has seen him both laugh and weep in the same moment at a passage of Shakespeare when read by their venerable friend, the amiable and eloquent poet, Dr. Evans. He loved music in the depth of his soul most cordially, and to him the rich and varied tones of an organ were preli-bations of heaven. He rarely ever omitted his sincere and really pious doctrines of gratitude in the village church, where he presided over the psalmody which he enthusiastically accompanied on the bassoon. With happiness and length of days heaven never blessed a kinder creature. Travellers have frequently expressed surprise at the excellence of the prints and maps at the village inns of Llanymynech, and still greater when informed that they were all selected by the taste, and many etched and engraved by the ingenious talents of the parish clerk, the unassuming and merry-hearted Robert Baugh."

BAXTER, GEORGE ROBERT WYTHEN, of the Upper Bryn, Llanllwchaiarn, was the only son of George Trotman Baxter, Esq., of Hereford, and was born in the year 1815. He was a member of an old family long settled in the neighbourhood of Newtown, and claimed among his ancestry the celebrated Nonconformist divine, Richard Baxter, and Hugh Baxter of Ystradfaelog (1687) and Richard Baxter (1690), the names of the two latter being recorded as benefactors to the poor of Trefeglwys and Llanwnog. He was the author of *The Book of the Bastiles*, an attack upon the Poor Law, the " Bastiles " being the Workhouses ; *Humour and Pathos*, and several other works. He died on the 17th January, 1854, in the 39th year of his age, and a handsome marble tablet was erected to his memory by his mother in Llanllwchaiarn Church.

BAXTER, WILLIAM, the eminent philological writer and antiquary, and also nephew and heir of the still more eminent Nonconformist divine, Richard Baxter, was born at Llanllugan, in 1650, of humble but respectable parents. He first went to school at Harrow, when he was 18 years of age, and was, according to his own account, so ignorant that he knew not one letter in a book, nor understood a word of any language but Welsh. By dint of great industry and perseverance, however, he made such progress that he soon became possessed of great and extensive knowledge, more particularly in the departments of philology and antiquities. During the greater part of his life Baxter was engaged in the tuition of youth. For some years he kept a boarding school at Tottenham, Middlesex, from which he was chosen master of the Mercers' School, London. This appointment he held for over 20 years, and resigned but a short time before his death, which took place May 31st, 1723, in the 73rd year of his age. He was buried at Islington. He left two sons and three daughters. The following is a list of his principal works :—*De Analogia, seu Arte Latinæ Linguæ Commentariolus*, a Grammar published in 1679 ; a new and corrected edition with notes of Anacreon in 1695, reprinted with considerable additions and improvements in 1710 ; an edition of Horace in 1701, reprinted with additions in 1725 ; a curious and learned Dictionary of British Antiquities, under the title of *Glossarium Antiquitatum Brittanicarum sive Syllabus Etymologicus Antiquitatum veteris Britanniæ atque Hiberniæ temporibus Romanorum* (1719), of which a second edition with a fine portrait of the author was published by his son in 1733; a Glossary of Roman Antiquities published after the author's death in 1726, under the title *Reliquiæ Baxterianæ, sive*

Willielmi Baxteri opera postuma, by the Rev. Moses Williams, and republished in 1731 under the new title of *Glossarium Antiquitatum Romanarum*; Notes on Juvenal and Persius, and various critical articles on philological subjects connected with the Welsh, Irish, Northern and Oriental languages as well as Latin and Greek.

BEDO HAVESP, a poet who flourished between 1550 and 1590. He was one of those who obtained degrees at the Caerwys Eisteddfod on the 26th May, 1565. Some of his poems are, it appears, still extant.

BEUNO, one of the best known of the Welsh saints, who lived during parts of the sixth and seventh centuries. He was the son of Hywgi, or Bugi, a gentleman living in Powys at a place near the Severn called Banhenic, the identity of which it is now difficult to establish. Saint Winifred (Gwenfrewi) of Holywell was his sister's daughter, and he, according to her well known legend, took a prominent part in the alleged miracle associated with her memory. Among the churches said to have been founded by him are Berriew and Bettws in Montgomeryshire; Aberffraw and Trefdraeth in Anglesey; Clynog, Penmorfa, Bottwnog, Carngiweh and Pistyll in Carnarvonshire; Llanyeil and Gwyddelwern in Merionethshire; and Llanfeuno in Herefordshire. About a mile from the village of Berriew is a stone called Maen Beuno, whereon he probably preached. He founded a great monastic institution of clergy called Bangor Beuno—yn Nghlynog Fawr yn Arfon—where he seems to have spent most of his life. A saying of his is preserved in *Englynion y Clywed*:—

> "A glywaist ti a gânt Beuno?
> Cân dy bader a'th gredo;
> Rhag angen ni thycia ffo."

(Hast thou heard what Beuno sang?
Chant thy Pater-noster and creed;
From death flight will not avail.)

BLAYNEY, EVAN, or Ieuan Blaenan, a descendant of Brochwel Ysgythrog, and founder of the families of Blayney of Gregynog and Aberbechan. His name as "Evan Blayney of Tregenon" appears 18th on the roll of burgesses in the ancient charter of Welshpool 7th June, 7th Henry IV. He had four sons—Owain, the ancestor of the Prices of Aberbechan; Gruffydd, of Gregynog, ancestor of the Blayneys of Gregynog and of the Lords Blayney in the peerage of Ireland; Howel and Gwendlear (?) To the joint praise of Owain and Gruffydd, Lewis Glyn Cothi addressed one of his best poems.

BLAYNEY, SIR EDWARD, Knt., third son of David Lloyd Blayney of Gregynog, was from his youth a soldier in the service of Queen Elizabeth. He accompanied the Earl of Essex in 1598 to Ireland with the rank of colonel. Distinguishing

himself by his zeal and ability, he was knighted on the 29th of
May, 1603, and constituted on the 13th December, 1604,
Seneschal of the county of Monaghan with the fee of ten
shillings a day (in which he was continued by King Charles I.),
and made Lord-Lieutenant of the county; and for the furtherance of His Majesty's service there, had a lease 26th January,
1606, of the Castle of Monaghan, with the town and lands
thereto allotted for the term of 21 years, if he lived so long, and
was not in the meantime moved from that government and
preferred to some place of better profit and command, paying
yearly £3 Irish money. He subsequently had various other
grants and honours conferred upon him for his services—among
them a licence granted 26th September, 1614, to him and Henry
Blayney, Esq (his son), during their lives to make and sell
aquavitae or usquebagh at such reasonable rates as they should
think fit within the county of Monaghan, except the town of
Glaslough and all the estate of Sir Thomas Ridgeway in that
county. In both King James' Parliaments of 1613 and 1615 he
was Knight for the County of Monaghan, and on 20th May of
the last named year, being then a member of the Privy Council,
he was appointed one of the Council for the government of the
Province of Munster, and on 24th September, 1616, he was
commissioned with the Lord Deputy St. John and others for the
plantation of Ulster, and as appears from the military list
then commanded 50 Foot at ten shillings a day. And the king
taking his merits and services into consideration, by privy seal
dated at Westminster 24th January, 1620, and by Patent at
Dublin 29th July, 1621, created him Lord Blayney, Baron of
Monaghan. He married Anne, second daughter to Dr. Adam
Loftus, Archbishop of Dublin and Chancellor of Ireland, who
had previously been married first to Sir Henry Colley, of Castle
Carbery, and, secondly, to George Blount, Esq., of Kidderminster, and by her he had issue two sons and six daughters.
He died on the 11th February, 1629, and on the 23rd of the
same month was buried in the church of Castlle Blayney,
Monaghan. The barony of Blayney became extinct in 1874.

BLAYNEY, JOHN, of Gregynog, son of Lewis, and grandson
of David Lloyd Blayney, was Sheriff in 1630 and 1643, and was
a staunch Royalist. The inscription on his monument at
Tregynon says that "he faithfully served and suffered for ye
"Royal Martyr." He was one of the gentlemen named in the
list of those who were deemed to be "fit and qualified to be
"made Knights of the Royal Oak"—his estate being then
(1660) valued at £1000. This Order was intended by Charles
II. as a reward to several of his followers, and the knights of
it were to wear a silver medal, with a device of the king in the
oak pendent to a ribbon about their necks; but it was thought
proper to lay it aside, "lest it might create heats and animosities,
"and open those wounds afresh which at that time were thought
"prudent should be healed." He died in 1665.

BLAYNEY, RICHARD, second son of Lewis Blayney, of Gregynog, and Bridget, his wife. He in the Parliament of 1639 represented the county of Monaghan, of which he was a Justice of the Peace: Seneschal to the Lord Blayney; Commissioner for His Majesty's subsidies; and Captain of a Foot Company, with which on the 23rd October, 1641, the very morning that the grand rebellion broke out, he was surprised by Colonel MacMahon and imprisoned in the Castle of Carrick, whence he was removed to that of Monaghan, and after about a fortnight's confinement (by warrant from Sir Phelim O'Neile and others, procured at the instance of the said MacMahon of Glaslough, Marshal of the rebel army, then resident in Lord Blayney's house, and who afterwards died mad) he was taken fettered with irons to the back of the Castle, and thence being led to Lord Blayney's orchard in Monaghan, was hanged to a tree, stripped, and thrown into a ditch.

BLAYNEY, SIR ARTHUR, Knt., second son of the above-named Sir Edward Blayney, first Lord Blayney, as stated on the Tregynon monument, "Served ye Royal Martyr K.C. ye first in "ye post of Col of Horse," and was knighted for his conduct in the battle of Beaumaris. He married his cousin Joyce, or "Joyous," sole daughter and heiress of John Blayney, by whom he had a daughter and four sons. He was Sheriff in 1644, when, according to the Peniarth list, "Montgomery Castle and Red Castle was goten by ye Parliament." On Sunday, 21st September, 1645. King Charles passed by his house on his way from Newtown to Llanfyllin. He assisted Sir William Owen, of Brogyntyn, the Governor, in the defence of Harlech Castle for the King, and was one of the Commissioners appointed by him to sign the articles of surrender on the 13th March, 1647, under which that fortress—the last stronghold which held out for the King in England and Wales—was given up on the 16th to the Parliament forces. At the beginning of 1655 two zealous Royalists, Sir Thomas Harris, Bart, of Boreatton, and Ralph Kynaston, Esq., of Llansaintffraid, undertook to capture Shrewsbury, and it was also arranged that on the same night Sir Arthur Blayney, at the head of the Montgomeryshire forces, was to attack Chirk Castle; but the vigilance of Cromwell frustrated the Royalist design. Sir Arthur Blayney died in 1659.

BLAYNEY, THOMAS, third son of Evan Blayney, of Keel, Berriew (who was probably nearly related to the Blayneys of Ystrngwern), was, as appears by a pedigree in Ashmole's Visitation of Berkshire (Bod. Lib. Oxford) a Serjeant at Arms to King Charles II. in March, 1665, being then 43 years of age. He was married to Hester, daughter of Michael Blackwell, of Roolham, in Kent, by whom he had issue Thomas, their son and heir.

BLAYNEY, THOMAS, an excellent harpist, was the third son of Arthur Blayney, of Tynycoed, in the parish of Llanllwchaiarn, by Letitia, daughter of Mr. Owens, of Dolfor, in the same parish, and was born in 1785. At the Carmarthen Eisteddfod on the 9th July, 1819, a keen contest on the harp took place between him and Henry Humphreys (also a Montgomeryshire man), when after a variety of national airs had been skilfully performed by each, Blayney was declared the victor, and a silver harp was according to ancient custom presented to him as the reward of his triumph, together with a prize of thirty guineas, while his rival's merits were at the same time acknowledged by a gratuity of half that sum. He played at most of the Eisteddfodau of those days, and went about the country occasionally with the triple harp, on which he was an admirable player. In 1829 we find him enjoying, through the kindness of Lord Powis, the harper's corner at Walcot, a post which he well deserved, and enjoyed until his death some years afterwards. At that time he kept the inn at Lydbury North, near Walcot. His eldest brother Arthur was also an excellent player on the violin.

BLAYNEY, ARTHUR, the last of the Blayneys of Gregynog, was the youngest of eight children of John Blayney (sheriff 1716), by Anne Weaver his wife, his grandfather being Henry, third son of Arthur Blayney, Knight. He was born February 11th, 1716, and succeeded to the family estates in consequence of the death in infancy or youth of his elder brothers. He served the office of Sheriff in 1764, and was much respected as a fine specimen of a country gentleman of the old school. His finely-engraved portrait may still be met with in some old Montgomeryshire houses. Mr. Blayney died unmarried October 1st, and was buried at Tregynon October 6th, 1795, in the 80th year of his age, having devised his estates to his "Welsh" niece Susannah, wife of Henry Tracy (afterwards Viscount Tracy), of Toddington, whose daughter and sole heiress married Charles Hanbury, who afterwards assumed the name of Tracy, and was in 1838 created Baron Sudeley, of Toddington, in the county of Gloucester. The appendix to *Yorke's Royal Tribes* contains the following interesting "Character of Mr. Blayney":

"Arthur Blayney, of Gregynog, Esquire, was descended from Brochwel Yrgythrog, a Prince of Powys, in the seventh century, but he valued himself on his pedigree no otherwise than by taking care that his conduct should not disgrace it. In the early part of his life he had applied to the study of the law, not with any professional view, but merely to guard himself and those who consulted him from chicane and injustice, to which many who made the profession their livelihood were in his opinion so strongly tempted and inclined that he seldom mentioned a lawyer without expressive marks of dislike; but this could be humour only. He read much, and had a good collection of books, but was more disposed to conceal than to obtrude his knowledge. He was a firm adherent to the Constitution under which he lived, and never spared his zeal and support when the public stood in need of it. At the same time his loyalty did not preclude him from using that invaluable privilege of a British subject in severely censuring, upon proper occasions, both the measures and instruments of Government. Uncorruptible himself, he detested venality in others. He was of no party but that of honest men. Whether he supposed that the Peerage was degenerated, and that some degree of contagion dwelt near a Court, or whether he had gathered the prejudice from history, in which he was conversant; but certain it is, he was by no means partial to Lords or Placemen. No man thought more highly of Parliaments, but pertinaciously he declined the honour of representing his native county, though often invited to do so by the unbiassed suffrages of his countrymen. The active part he took in behalf of other candidates was so pure in its motives that his support gave a decided superiority over the highest rank and influence. Most of the neighbouring freeholders only awaited to know his opinion to make up their own. Few gentlemen were better qualified for the magistracy, or more sensible of its importance, but from an unaccountable diffidence he could never be prevailed upon to act in the commission, though always ready to applaud and second the just efforts of those who did. Of the established religion he was a steady member; defended its rights and respected its ministers when they respected themselves. There is scarce a church, in which he had any concern, but what in its repairs and ornaments bears witness to his munificence. His tenants, from their relation, he considered as friends, and not only allowed them ample profit from his estates, but encouraged and assisted them in every rational attempt to improvement. In his farm houses and their offices, beyond what was necessary, he was always studying convenience and comfort, according to the situation, and even taste of the occupier. He did so much in this way, and did it so well, that it is easy to trace his premises, which were very extensive, by the condition in which he left them; and although he possessed an uncommon quantity of the finest wood, he generally bought his timber. To his small tenants he was a bountiful master, and he complained of the bad state of a cottage he shewed me, which in any other place might have been thought a good one: He applied a little land to each to keep their cow in the summer, and in the winter he gave them hay to support it. Nor was it his own property that he was desirous of improving only. The country at large he looked upon as having a peculiar claim upon him, and no undertaking was proposed but met with his countenance and liberality. The roads in particular for many miles round owe their creation almost entirely to him, and when his land was wanted to widen them, he would give it on one condition only, "That they took enough." You had only to convince him of the utility of a design to be sure of his purse and protection. He always took time to consider and enquire, but from the moment he was decided he wanted no subsequent instigation. His charity was liberal and diffusive; but instead of confining it to the idle vagrant and clamorous poor, his chief aim was to put deserving objects in the way, to afford them the means of providing for themselves. There are many respectable tradesmen and gentlemen, too, whose embarrassments have been removed by his friendly assistance. He was undoubtedly an economist on system, which enabled him to do what he did. When the object of expense was a proper one he never regarded the sum; of course, nothing sordid or niggardly could be imputed to him, even when economy was most conspicuous. He would never be persuaded to keep a carriage, and very seldom hired one, performing, till his infirmities disabled him, his longest journeys on horseback. His constant residence was at Gregynog, except occasional excursions to his other house at Morvill, near Bridgnorth. One of the most prominent features in his character was his hospitality, of which there are few such instances now remaining. His table was every day plentifully covered with the best things the country and season afforded, for, unless it was to do honour to particular guests, he never indulged in far-sought delicacies, preferring the ducks and chickens of his poor neighbours, which he bought in all numbers, whether he wanted them or not, and I remember in the summer of 1793 a small pond near the house swarming with the former kind; but he was very choice in his liquors, which were the best that care and money could procure. His place, not happy in situation, was neither elegant nor ornamented, but comfortable in the most extended sense of the word; inasmuch that it would be difficult to find another house where the visitor was more perfectly at his ease, from the titled tourist to the poor, benighted, way-worn exciseman who knew not where else to turn in either for refreshment or lodging; for Mr. Blayney's hospitality reached every traveller, known or unknown, who could decently make any pretentions to it. In his conversation he was affable, polite, instructive, and cheerful; seldom brilliant, but never dull, and appeared always to enjoy the innocent sallies of humour and wit from others, though they seldom originated from himself. To his domesticks he was a kind and indulgent master; their services were easy, but expected to be prompt and exact, not only to himself, but to the humblest of his company. They always looked sleek and happy, and might grow rich if they would. In truth, no animal in his possession, from the stable to the poultry-yard, had cause to complain, and I knew him once vexed with a servant for sending, as he said, a thin dog from Gregynog. His hounds, too fat for speed, were fed and followed by a running huntsman. His partridges were set, and his woodcocks shot on the ground with a pointer and stalking-horse. Order and regularity pervaded his whole household. He was never married, but was remarkably pleased with and pleasing to the ladies who visited him, and they were not a few. He carried his notions of independence to a pitch that bordered upon excess; always ready to confer reasonable favours, he reluctantly accepted them. Several worthy Bishops of the Diocese have lamented that he would never put it in their power, to use their patronage, in favour of his recommendation. In his temper he was constitutionally warm. What true Welshman is otherwise? His resentments, generally well founded, were consequently strong, and sometimes permanent. He could forgive an injury, but if his confidence was forfeited, it was nearly impossible to retrieve it. His dress was plain, and studiously neat and becoming, and he made a London suit every year, and his constant direction to his tailor (whom he had not seen for forty years) was, that he made the present coat as the last. His shoe buckles were very small, and he had a dressed pair; they were of the old form and fashion; and he wore his breeches' garters very high. Mr. Blayney died in Gregynog, the first day of October, 1795, in the 61st—[*sic.*, but should be 80th]—year of his age, and was buried by his particular directions, very privately, in the Churchyard at Tregynon. He was universally and justly lamented, an advantage which amiable men possess over great ones."

As intimated above, Mr. Blayney left in his own handwriting the following singular

"DIRECTIONS FOR MY FUNERAL.

"It is usual for people in this Country (out of a pretended respect, but rather from an Impertinent Curiosity) to desire to see persons after they are dead. It is my earnest request that no person upon any pretence whatever may be permitted to see my Corpse but those who unavoidably must.

I desire to be buried in the North side of the Church-Yard at Tregunon, somewhere about the Centre, my Coffin to be made in the most plain and simple manner, without the usual Fantastical Decorations and the more perishable the Material the better.

I desire that no undertaker or professed Performer of Funerals may be employed; But that I may be conveyed to the Church-Yard in some Country Herse, which may be hired for the occasion: And my Corpse to be carried from the Herse to the Grave immediately, without going into the Church, by six of the Chief Tregunon Tenants, to whom I give 2 Guineas each for their Trouble. It is my Earnest request & desire to have no upper Bearers, or any persons whatever invited to my Funeral which I desire to be at so early an Hour as will best prevent a Concourse of People from collecting together. The better sort I presume will not Intrude as there is no invitation.

I have been present at the Funerals of three of my Unkles at Morvil. I was pleased with the privacy and decency, with which all things were conducted, no strangers attended. All was done by the servants of the Family. It is my Earnest desire to follow those examples however unpopular, and that no Coach, no Escutcheon & no pomp of any kind may appear. I trust that my executor will be well Justified against the clamour and obloquy of Mercenary people, when he acts in performance of the last request of a dying Friend; who solemnly adjures him in the name of God punctually to observe these directions.

AR : BLAYNEY.

I likewise give to all my Servants five Guineas each in lieu of mourning, which it is my desire no person may use on my account."

After Mr. Blayney's death a beautiful monument, by J. Bacon, R.A., was erected to his memory in Tregynon Church by Viscount Tracy. The following is the inscription upon it :—

" Sacred to the Memory of Arthur Blayney, Esq., who during a long Life passed at Gregynog, devoted his Time his Fortune and his Talents to the Good of Mankind & this neighbourhood in particular; by spiritedly and generously promoting Works of great publick Utility by the constant Exercise of liberal Hospitality, by a fatherly Attention to his Tenantry and Dependents by patiently and skilfully reconciling Differences, by largely encouraging Industry and Merit ; and by relieving most bountifully the Poor and Distressed. He died October the 1st, 1795 ; Aged 80. By his express Desire his Remains were interred in the North Part of this Church-Yard. This Monument, an humble Tribute to his exemplary Virtues, is most gratefully placed in this Church, (Itself an Object of his pious Munificence) by Henry Lord Viscount Tracy his Friend and Executor."

The Blayney arms were *Sable*, three nags' heads erased *argent*, being those attributed to Prince Brochwel Ysgythrog. It seems that at his death Mr. Blayney left no relatives except on the female side and the Lords Blayney of Ireland, which line is also recently extinct.

BLEDDYN AB CYNFYN, Prince of Powys. On the death in 1060 of his half brother Gruffydd ab Llewelyn he and his brother Rhiwallon succeeded to the joint sovereignty of Gwynedd and Powys. In 1068, however, " Meredith and Ithel, the sonnes " of Gruffyth ab Llewelyn, raised a great power against Blethyn " and Rywalhon kings of North Wales, and met with them at a " place called Mechain, where after long fight, there were slaine " upon the one part Ithel and upon the other part Rywalhon, " and Meredyth put to flight, whome Blethyn pursued so " straightlie, that he starved for cold and hunger upon the " mountaines, and so Blethyn the sonne of Convyn remained the " onlie King of Powys and Northwales "—(Powel). In the well-known words of Rhys Cain,

" Bleddyn ab Cynfyn bob cwys,
Ei hun bioedd hen Bowys."

Bleddyn was an enlightened prince, considerably in advance of
his time, who took pains to support his country's laws, and to
revise and reform them. His reign, however, was short, for in
1073 he was slain in battle, as some say, but according to others
in Powys Castle, " traitorouslie and cowardlle murthered by Rees
" ap Owen ap Edwyn, and the gentlemen of Ystrad Tywy, after
" he had worthilie governed Wales 13 yeares. This man was
" verie liberall and mercifull, and loved iustice and equitie
" in all his reigne. This Blethyn had by diverse women
" manie children; first Meredyth by Haer, daughter to
" Gylhyn, Llywarch and Cadogan by another woman, Madoc and
" Riryd by the third, and Iorwerth by the fourth "—(Powel).
None of these it appears claimed the throne at the time, but
they allowed their cousin, Trahaiarn ab Caradog, to possess it.
This prince was probably chosen by the nobility of North
Wales that they might more successfully oppose the claims of
Rhys ab Owain, whom they hated for the treacherous manner in
which he had caused the death of Bleddyn. Bleddyn's death
was avenged in the following year by his grandsons Goronwy and
Llewelyn, sons of Cadwgan, who gave battle to Rhys first at
Camddwr, and again at Gwaynyttyd, where he was put to flight,
but, rallying again, Trahaiarn brought his forces against him at a
place called Pwllgwttic, where after long fighting Rees was put
to flight, and after great slaughter of his men, he fled from
place to place (according to Powel). " fearing all things, like a
" stag that had latelie been chased, which mistrusteth everie
" noise, but at the last he with his brother Howel fell into the
" hands of Caradoc ap Gruffyth, who slue them both in revenge
" of the death of the wise and noble prince Blethyn ap Convyn."
Dolforwyn Castle is said to have been originally built by
Bleddyn.

BOUND, WILLIAM, of Garthfawr, Llandinam, near Llan-
idloes, was the author, in conjunction with John Price, of
Maesygelli, near Nantmel, Radnorshire, of *Amddiffyniad y
Bedyddwyr yn erbyn Ymosodiadau y bobl a elwir Quakers*—(A
Defence of the Baptists against the attacks of the people called
Quakers), being a reply to a book published by John Moon, a
Quaker, against Hugh Evans, a laborious, " painfull," and
successful Baptist preacher at Nantmel. Hugh Evans died in
1656 or 1657. The " Defence" was printed in London in
1658. Mr. Bound's widow married William Price, who then
settled at Garthfawr, and his descendants now live there. The
name of Bound may still be met with in that neighbourhood.

BREES, EVAN, was born at Dol Howell, Llangadfan, in
1798, and was a grandson of the well-known scholar William
Jones of that place. He spent most of his life as a schoolmaster
in different parts of the country, and was a local preacher with
the Wesleyans. He published two small volumes of poems,
consisting of carols and other religious verses. He died at
Llanerfyl, and was buried there.

BREESE, REV. JOHN, an eminent Independent minister, was born in humble circumstances at Llanbrynmair in September, 1789. He was early thrown upon the world, and had therefore but scant means of education ; in fact, he owed nearly all his teaching to the Sunday School at the Old Independent Chapel. He, however, made the most of his opportunities, and by unceasing labour soon acquired considerable proficiency in Biblical and theological knowledge. Having become a member of the Independent Church, he before long was prevailed upon to become a preacher, and began to exercise his talents as such when he was about 24 years of age. With the assistance of his friends he was at this time enabled to go to Shrewsbury, where he received instruction for some time, and he subsequently studied for three years at the Independent Academy at Llanfyllin, then kept by the Rev. Dr. Lewis. In 1817 he accepted an invitation to take charge of the Welsh Independent Church at Liverpool, which then numbered only about 60 members, and met for worship in a room in Edmund Street. Soon afterwards he was publicly ordained pastor of the church, in which office he laboured very successfully for 17 years. The church soon received many accessions, and for want of room the congregation had to remove to the Tabernacle in Great Crosshall Street. In addition to his many other labours at home and elsewhere, Mr. Breese preached four times a week to his own congregation, and his sermons were often distinguished by great ability and originality. His energy was boundless. When a Welsh cause was established at Manchester Mr. Breese frequently walked there and back to preach, and when another was started in the southern end of Liverpool he used to go there every Tuesday night through all kinds of weather to preach. He travelled much, and among the people of his own denomination was considered second only to Williams of Wern as a preacher. In 1823 Mr. Breese married Margaret, daughter of David Williams, of Saethon, Esq., and sister of David Williams, Esq., subsequently M.P. for Merionethshire, by whom he had issue seven children, of whom the third, John, was a solicitor, and Town Clerk of Pwllheli (Ob. at Oporto, 1858) ; the fourth, Jane Elizabeth, married Dr. Robert Roberts, of Portmadoc ; and the sixth, Edward, who died in March, 1881, was Clerk of the Peace for Merionethshire, a Fellow of the Society of Antiquaries, and the able and accomplished editor of *The Kalendars of Gwynedd.* The others all died young. Mr. Breese was also half-brother of the late Mr. Daniel Breese, solicitor, of Portmadoc, and afterwards of Lincoln's Inn, and of the Rev. J. Breese, M.A., of Calcott House, Bicton, Rector of Great Harwood, and chaplain of the Shropshire Asylum. In January, 1835, Mr. Breese removed to Carmarthen, and there continued in the active discharge of his ministerial duties until his death, which took place on the 8th of August, 1842, in the 53rd year of his age. His loss as one of its most popular, able, and influential ministers was deeply felt by the Welsh Independent denomination. He was distinguished as exceptionally liberal in his views as a Nonconformist, so much so that during his pastorate in Liverpool Dr. Bethell, then Bishop of Bangor, wrote offering to ordain him as a minister of the Church of England, and subsequently sent a neighbouring clergyman to Liverpool specially to endeavour to persuade him to take orders in the Church. He, however, felt conscientious scruples which he could not overcome, and remained faithful to those Nonconforming Protestant principles of which he was so able an expositor.

BREESE, REV. SAMUEL, a popular Baptist Minister, was born at Upper Cwm-mawr, a small farm in the parish of Llandinam, in 1772, where his father carried on business also as a carpenter. Owing to a diseased leg he became, when he was eight years old, lame for life, a circumstance which, however, induced his father to give him a better education than he otherwise would have done. He prepared himself by study for the duties of a schoolmaster, and for some years kept a school, first at Penrhyncoch, and afterwards at Aberystwyth. He had joined the Baptist denomination, having been publicly baptised by immersion at Dolau, in the parish of Nantmel, Radnorshire, in 1793, and while at Penrhyncoch in 1795 began to preach. He soon acquired popularity, and in 1803 accepted an invitation from the Baptist Churches at Aberystwyth and other places in that neighbourhood, and was ordained their co-pastor with the Rev. John James, June 12th, 1803. From Aberystwyth he removed to Newcastle Emlyn, where he was very laborious and successful. But in the midst of his usefulness and in the prime of his days he was suddenly cut off. On Monday, the 28th of September, 1812, while returning home on horseback from Bronorwen he was struck with paralysis, and expired that afternoon, aged 40 years. He was buried the following Wednesday, with great manifestations of sorrow, in the burial ground attached to the old Baptist Chapel at Cilfowyr, Pembrokeshire. Elegies were written on his death by the Revs. D. Saunders and Christmas Evans. The latter was reprinted in the form of a pamphlet at Llanidloes, in 1846. Mr. Breese's descriptive powers were remarkably vivid, and few preachers were more eloquent and popular. He travelled much throughout Wales and parts of England, preaching fluently in English as well as Welsh.

BROCHWEL, YSGYTHROG, Prince of Powys, was the son of Cyngen ab Cadell Deyrnllwg, and was surnamed "Ysgythrog," probably from the prominence of his teeth. In 603 he was twice defeated near Chester in attempting to prevent the destruction by Ethelfred, the Northumbrian king, of the monastery of Bangor Iscoed and the massacre of the monks. On this occasion it is stated in the British Chronicle of Tysilio that 1,200 of the "religious," who had come to pray for

Brochwel's success, were slain, and that celebrated seminary of learning, with its valuable library, was set on fire and destroyed. Soon afterwards, however, joined by Cadvan, Meredydd, and Bledrig (or Bledrus) with their forces, namely, about the year 607, he again attacked Ethelfred, and totally defeated him with very great slaughter. Above 10,000 of the Saxons were slain, and Ethelfred himself was wounded, and with difficulty escaped being taken prisoner. In a Welsh MS. printed in the "Greal" it is stated that Brochwel was killed at the battle of Chester (but this is contrary to other accounts of him), and that the King of England possessed himself of Pengwern (Shrewsbury), where, according to the author of *Historia divae Monacellae*, he had his mansion "on the spot where the College of Saint Chad now standeth." The copious fountain or spring from whence the town of Shrewsbury was long supplied with conduit or spring water, is known in records by the name of Brochwel's Spring, and to the Welsh by the name of Ffynnon Brochwel. The arms attributed to Brochwel are *Sable*, three nags' heads erased *argent*, being the Saxon white horse symbolising victory over the Saxons. Many Montgomeryshire families trace their descent from him.

BRYAN, REV. JOHN, a popular Wesleyan preacher, was born at Llanfyllin, in Market-street, in the year 1770. In his youth he entered the service of a firm of shopkeepers at Chester, named Williams, who were respectable members of the Wesleyan body. After a time he himself joined that denomination, and before long became an exhorter in connection with it. When the Welsh mission was established, he in 1801 joined it, and travelled as a missionary in various parts of Wales until 1816, being one of the first who were sent by the Wesleyan Conference. In 1816 he removed to England, and continued to preach in the English language until 1824, when he left the ministry and entered into business—first in England and then at Carnarvon—which he carried on for the remainder of his life. He was a very popular preacher and a fluent writer of prose and poetry. He translated a number of hymns (chiefly Wesley's) from English into Welsh; also, *The Life of John Haime, 1811*; *The Life of John Nelson, 1812*; *The Life of James Arminius*, and *Wesley on Universal Salvation*, 1841; and assisted in bringing out some other works. He was, moreover, a frequent contributor to the *Eurgrawn Wesleyidd*, the recognised organ of the Welsh Wesleyan Methodists, chiefly on the theological controversies of the day. He was proverbially outspoken, upright, and straightforward as a tradesman. He died at Carnarvon May 28th, 1856, in the 87th year of his age.

BYNNER, DAVID (*Dewi Cadfan*), was born at Llangadfan about the year 1838, and was Master of the National School there for a short time, afterwards a Scripture reader at Llany-mawddwy, and subsequently at Llansannan, in Denbighshire.

From that place he removed to Bicton near Shrewsbury, where he settled as an organist and teacher of music. His health, however, soon failed him, and he died of consumption at the early age of 28. He was buried at Llangadfan May 7th, 1866. He published a small volume of music.

CADVAN, the leader of one of the bands of missionaries who in the 6th century came over to this country from Brittany. He was the founder of the churches of Llangadfan in Montgomeryshire, and Towyn, Merionethshire; also the first Abbot of Bardsey Isle, where it is recorded that no less than 20,000 saints were buried.

CADFARCH, a sixth century saint, who founded the church of Penegoes, and gave his name to a well close by, noted for its efficacy in cases of rheumatism.

CADWALADR AB RHYS TREFNANT, a poet who flourished about the middle of the sixteenth century, some of whose compositions are still extant, several being odes addressed to persons living in Montgomeryshire.

CADWGAN, the son of Bleddyn ab Cynfyn, whom he succeeded as Prince of Powys in 1073. He was a brave and accomplished warrior, and shewed his skill and ability as a general by defeating the Normans in North Wales in 1094, and again soon afterwards a large body of them who had invaded North Wales. He also took and plundered Hereford, Shrewsbury and Worcester. By his marriage with the daughter of Pigot de Say he obtained Marreys, properly Marros, but now called Amroth Castle in Cardiganshire, but not far from Pembroke, and here at Christmas, 1107, he gave a magnificent feast, and invited to it the chieftains and gentlemen of the country out of every province in Wales, as well as the bards and the best minstrels (vocal and instrumental) that could be found in all Wales, to whom he gave chairs and subjects of competition "according to the custom of the feasts of King Arthur." This feast, however, led to an atrocious crime, which proved well nigh disastrous to Cadwgan. Among the guests was Nest, daughter of Rhys ab Tewdwr, and wife of Gerald de Windsor, steward of Pembroke Castle, whose beauty was "praised above all women in the land," and whose charms inspired an ungovernable passion in the breast of Owain, Cadwgan's son. Owain followed her home to Pembroke Castle, which he attacked and set fire to—Gerald escaping with difficulty —and he carried Nest and her children captive to Powys. To avenge this dishonour Cadwgan's nephews Ithel and Madog invaded his territories, although he was innocent of any participation in the crime, and at their approach Cadwgan and Owain fled, and embarking at Aberystwyth fled over to Ireland. Cadwgan returned, however, the following year, and having proved his innocence to King Henry, the latter permitted him to recover his chief possessions in Cardiganshire on payment of a

penalty of one hundred pounds, and undertaking not to permit
the return of his son Owain. " Now when Madoc saw his other
" uncle Cadogan rule the countrie he hid himself in rough and
" desert places, and adding one mischief upon another deter-
" mined also to murther him by one waie or other. Therefore
" after that Cadwgan had brought the countrie to some staie of
" quietnosse, and saw right and iustice ministred therein, and
" having ever an eie and respect to the king, he came to the
" Trallwng (now called the Poole) and the elders of the countrie
" with him, and minding to dwell there, began to build a castle.
" Then Madoc pretending nothing but mischief, hearing this
" came suddenly upon him and Cadogan thinking no hurt, was
" slain before he could either fight or flee." (Powel). This
took place where Powis Castle now stands in the year 1110.

CAIN, RHYS, an eminent poet and genealogist who flourished
in the sixteenth century. He is often supposed to have been a native
of Trawsfynydd, Merionethshire, but more probably the local
tradition which asserts him to have been a native of Llanfyllin is
correct—a family named Cain (who probably took their name
from the river Cain in Mechain Iscoed) having resided there for
generations and carried on business as flax dressers. Rhys lived
the greater part of his life at Oswestry, and was the contemporary and disciple of William Lleyn, the vicar of that parish,
many of whose books came to his possession, and to whom he
wrote an elegy. He was, besides his other accomplishments, a
clever painter, and among other subjects he painted " Our
" Saviour's sufferings on the Cross," which caused some wrang-
ling between him and some poetical censors in the neighbourhood. One of them having circulated a report that Rhys was an
idolater, the poet wrote the following *englyn* :—

> " Yr annnwiol ffol a ffy,—poen alaeth,
>   Pan welo hwn Iesu ;
> Lluniod, os gwell yw hyny,
> Llun diawl yn mhob lle'n ei dy."

(The silly ungodly man flees, when Jesus's image he sees : Let
him, if he prefers it, put up the devil's image in every part of
his house.) A neighbouring poet, having viewed the picture
also came to his friend's rescue with the following :—

> " Delw Iesu i'n prynu, pur union,—Benaeth,
>   Yw baniar Crist'nogion ;
> Buddiol, a haeddol yw hon ;—
> ' *Di-les'* medd diawl a'i weision."

(The image of Jesus who hath saved us, our Captain, is the
banner of Christians ; this is useful and deserving ; but the devil
and his servants call it *worthless.*) His Puritan opponent, however replied thus :—

> " Na wnaed yr un llun a'i law,—Duw Iesu,
>   Dewisodd i'n beidiaw ;
> Ond credu i Grist yn ddistaw,
> Wr didranc—a'i Air da draw."

(Let no one draw with his hand an image,—the God Jesus hath desired us not to do it; but silently to believe in Christ the eternal and His good word). Rhys Cain was buried at Oswestry. A manuscript collection of his poems perished in the Wynnstay fire, but many of them are still preserved in his own handwriting in the Peniarth collection.

CAIN, SION, a son of Rhys Cain, was also, like his father, an excellent poet, herald, and antiquary, and resided chiefly at Oswestry. He collected and composed a large number of poems, which are preserved in MS. in the Peniarth library.

CAMPBELL, ELIZA CONSTANTIA (afterwards Morrieson), a talented poetess, was the eldest child of Richard Pryce, Esq , of Gunley, and was born January 8th, 1796. Her mother's maiden's name was Edwards (of Pentre Hall). She married in 1826 Robert Campbell, Commander in the Royal Navy, and a first cousin of Thomas Campbell, the poet. She, with her husband, resided in Edinburgh, and had three sons, of whom one died in infancy ; another, Lewis, became Professor of Greek in the University of St. Andrews; and the younger, Robert, a barrister of Lincoln's Inn. Her husband died at Gunley, in 1832, and was buried in Forden Churchyard. A tablet to his memory was placed in the porch of Forden Church. Her husband's death left her in very straightened circumstances, but she succeeded in giving her young children a good education. In December, 1833, she published *Stories from the History of Wales* (printed by Eddowes, Shrewsbury, published by Longmans, London). A second edition was printed and published in Edinburgh in 1837, under the title of *Tales about Wales.* In 1844 she was married to her second husband, Captain Hugh Morrieson, of the East India Company's service, with whom she lived in Edinburgh till his death in 1859, and she continued herself to reside there until her own death in 1864. Campbell the poet thought very highly of his "cousin's " taste and character.

CARADOC, Archdeacon of Tyssilio's Church, at Meifod, eulogized by Cynddelw as a munificent patron.

> "Caraf i barch y harchdiagon
> Caradauc vreinauc vreise rodyon."

(I love to respect its archdeacon, Caradoc the privileged; generous his gifts).

CERI, HYWEL, a poet who flourished between 1570 to 1600, whose works are said to remain in MS. His name would imply that he was a native of the parish of Kerry.

CERI, SION, or Sion ab Bedo ab Dafydd ab Hywel, an eminent poet, who flourished between 1500 and 1530. Some of his poems are still preserved in MS., and some were lost in the great fire at Wynnstay. According to an old MS. in the British Museum, he was buried at Llanuwchllyn.

CLIVE, The Ven. WILLIAM, M.A., was the second son of William Clive, Esq., of Styche, Salop, M.P. for Bishop's Castle, by his wife, Elizabeth Clive, daughter of John Rotton, Esq. He was born on the 14th March, 1795, and was educated at Eton, whence he entered St. John's College, Cambridge, where he graduated in 1817, and proceeded M.A. in 1820. In 1818 he took Holy Orders, and for a short time held a curacy under the Rev. Reginald (afterwards Bishop) Heber at Hodnet. In 1819 he was appointed Vicar of Welshpool, which living he held for forty-six years. In 1824 he was appointed domestic chaplain to Hugh, third Duke of Northumberland, and for a short time he held, with Welshpool, the benefices of Shrawardine and Montford, Salop. In 1844 he was appointed Archdeacon of Montgomery; in 1849 Honorary Canon of St. Asaph; in 1854 Residentiary Canon, which he resigned in 1861. In 1865 he resigned the living of Welshpool, and was appointed Rector of Blymhill, in the diocese of Lichfield, on the nomination of the Earl of Bradford. He was also Rural Dean of Brewood. Upon leaving Welshpool a magnificent service of plate was presented to him by his old parishioners as a token of their affection and respect. By his marriage with Marianne, fourth daughter of George Tollett, Esq., of Betley Hall, Staffordshire (who died 16th February, 1841), he had an only daughter, Marianne Caroline, wife of the Hon. and Rev. John Bridgeman. Archdeacon Clive died at Blymhill, after a short illness, on the 24th of May, 1883, having attained the advanced age of 88 years, and on the 29th of the same month was buried at St. Mary's Church, Welshpool. He took a very active part in the carrying out of the many improvements which were effected in his parish of Welshpool during his long incumbency, especially such as related to the church and schools. The total expenditure in these matters during his incumbency, and chiefly through his instrumentality, very considerably exceeded £10,000. His pure life, his kindness to the poor, his genial courtesy to all, his energetic promotion of every movement tending to the public good, and his great devotion to his sacred duties, caused him to be universally beloved by all classes.

CLYWEDOG, IEUAN, an eminent poet who flourished between 1410 and 1450. He is supposed to have taken his name from the river Clywedog, near Llanidloes. He presided at the Glamorgan Gorsedd in 1430, and several of his poems are still extant in MS.

CLYWEDOG, SION, or Sion Ieuan Clywedog, a poet who flourished about 1580 and 1620. His poems, it is said, still remain in MS. Among them is an "Ode to the Tobacco," which appears to have been much used upon its first introduction about this time.

CLYWEDOG, WATKIN, a poet who flourished about 1600, and whose works remain in MS. The late Rev. P. B. Williams was of opinion that he was a native of Rhiwaedog, near Bala, and that he and his sons were buried at Llanfor in that neighbourhood. The learned editor of Gwallter Mechain's *Works* suggests that his birthplace may have been the neighbourhood of Mallwyd, where there is a river named Clywedog. But we venture to suggest the greater probability of his being a native of Upper Montgomeryshire, and of his having taken his name from the river Clywedog, near Llanidloes. He had three sons, William, Rowland, and Meredith, who were proficient in three languages, but all of them died in the course of one year, and upon their death he wrote some very touching and beautiful stanzas, which are printed in *Gwallter Mechain's Works*, vol I., p. 463.

CREWE-READ, Capt. OFFLEY MALCOLM, R.N., was the second son of John Offley Crewe-Read, Esq., of Wern, Flintshire, Llandinam Hall, Montgomeryshire, and Laverton, Southampton (Sheriff of Flintshire, 1839, and of Montgomeryshire, 1847), and Charlotte Prestwood, daughter of Admiral Sir W. T. Lake, K.C.B., etc. This family traces its lineage from Thomas de Crewe of Crewe, *temp*. Henry III., and from John Read of Roch Castle, Carmarthenshire who settled in Montgomeryshire in 1670, and derived his descent from Peter de Rupibus, *temp*. King John. Among its distinguished members in past times may be named Lord Crewe, Bishop of Durham; Sir Randulph Crewe, and Sir Thomas Crewe, both Speakers of the House of Commons in the reign of James I.; and James Read (Sheriff, 1696), who also was Clerk of the Peace, and held other important offices. Several others of the Reads were also Sheriffs. Bagot Read (Sheriff, 1805) died in 1816, and left his estates in Flintshire, Montgomeryshire, and in the city of Chester to his sister, Mrs. Thornycroft, for life, and then to the Rev. Offley Crewe, his nephew, being a son of Dr. Randulph Crewe, by Anne Read, his wife, a sister of the said Bagot Read, and his heirs, on condition that they should assume the additional surname and arms of Read in conjunction with those of Crewe. This injunction was complied with on the death of the Rev. Offley Crewe, in January, 1836, by his only son, John Offley Crewe, who obtained the Royal licence March 5th, 1836, to assume the name and arms of Read. Offley Malcolm Crewe-Read was born at Almington Hall, near Market Drayton, September 13th 1821, and was educated by private tutors, and at the Royal Naval College. He entered the Navy in 1835, obtaining his lieutenant's commission in 1846, and saw a good deal of service on the North American, West Coast of Africa, and Mediterranean stations. During the war with Russia, in 1854-5, he was senior Lieutenant of H.M.S. *Hecla* in the expedition to Eckness and the attack on the Hango Forts, where he was severely wounded. He was also present at the bombardment of Bomarsund. He was specially mentioned in the Admiral's despatch for his gallantry at the Hango Forts, and received the Baltic medal and pension for wounds. He was promoted to be Commander in September, 1854. After this he was for five years Inspecting Commander of Coastguard in South Wales, and for three years Commander of the Steam Reserve in the Medway. He was in comcand of H.M.S *Leander*, for the purpose of saluting the Princess of Wales on her arrival at the Nore from Denmark in 1863. He retired from the service with the rank of Captain in 1870. Having succeeded to the family estates on the death of his elder brother, Bagot Crewe-Read, in December, 1862, he, a few months afterwards, took up his residence permanently at Llandinam Hall. Captain Crewe-Read was a Deputy-Lieutenant and a Justice of the Peace for Montgomeryshire, and a Justice of the Peace for Flintshire. He was an active magistrate in Montgomeryshire, and served on most of the Quarter Sessions Committees. He was Sheriff in 1870. He was for several years chairman of the Newtown and Llanidloes Union, and in April, 1874, was chosen first chairman of the Newtown and Llanidloes District Highway Board. He was a steady friend to unsectarian education, and took a leading part in the establishment, early in the year 1871, of a School Board for the parish of Llandinam, and for seven years was its chairman. He largely improved his estate by planting, draining, and building. With the able assistance of Mr. Nesfield, the eminent architect, he erected for himself an almost perfect example of modern domestic architecture—the mansion of Plas Dinam, which, however, he did not live long to enjoy. In politics Captain Crewe-Read was an ardent Liberal. He had a leading hand in the formation, and was the first president of, the Montgomeryshire Liberal Association, an organisation which paved the way for, and eventually, in 1880, brought about, a change in the representation of the County. He also took a very active part in the borough election in May, 1877, which resulted in the return of the Hon. Fredk. S. A. Hanbury-Tracy, in succession to his brother, the present Lord Sudeley. The following November, while presiding at a meeting of the Highway Board, at Newtown, he was seized by paralysis. As soon as he was sufficiently recovered he was removed to Southsea, where thenceforward he led the life of an invalid, and where he died January 2rd, 1884, in his sixty-third year. He was buried at Llandinam on the 7th of the same month. In private life Captain Crewe-Read enjoyed, for his genuine kindness and goodness, the warm and affectionate esteem of those who knew him best. He married, February, 1848, Charlotte Lucy, daughter of Thomas Marmaduke George, Esq., and Anne his wife, by whom he had issue one son, Lieutenant-Colonel Offley John Crewe-Read. His arms were :—Quarterly, 1st and 4th, *azure*, a griffin segreant, *or*; 2nd and 3rd, *azure*, a lion rampant, *ary*. Crest: 1st, an eagle displayed, *sable*; 2nd, out of a ducal coronet, *or* a lion's gamb, *arg.*, charged with a crescent. Motto, "Sola virtute salutem." The Plas Dinam estate was sold in 1866 to the late David Davies, Esq., of Broneirion.

CUAWG, one of the sons of Cyndrwyn, prince of part of Powys. Aber-cuawg (referred to in Llywarch Hen's "Ode to the Cuckoo in the Vale of Cuawg") may have been the patrimony of Cuawg, and have taken its name from him. It is generally supposed to be identical with Dolguog, near Machynlleth. The following are some of the stanzas :—

> " Còg lafar a gàn gan ddydd,
> Cyfreu eichiawg yn nolydd Cuawg ;
> 'Gwell córawg na chybydd.'
>
> Yn Aber Cuawg y ganant Gógau,
> Ar gangau blodeuawg ;
> Gwae glaf a'u clyw yn foddawg.
>
> Yn Aber Cuawg Cógau a ganant ;
> Ys adfant gan fy mryd ;
> A'u cygleu nas clwyf hefyd.
>
> Cethlydd cathyl-foddawg, hiraethawg ei llef,
> Taith oddef, tuth hebawg,
> Cóg freuer yn Aber Cuawg.
>
> Gorddyar adar, gwlyb gro,
> Dail cwyddid, difryd difro,
> Ni wadaf, wyf claf heno."

which may be thus translated :—

> The loud-voiced cuckoo sings with the dawn,
> Her melodious notes in the dales of Cuawg ;
> " Better the liberal than the miser."
>
> By Aber Cuawg the cuckoos sing,
> On the blossom-covered branches;
> Woe to the sick, that hears their contented notes.
>
> In Aber Cuawg cuckoos are singing ;
> To my mind grating is the sound ;
> Oh, may others that hear not sicken like me !
>
> The birds are clamorous, the beach is wet ;
> Let the leaves fall, the exile is unconcerned ;
> I will not conceal it, I am sick this night !

CURIG, OR **CURIG LWYD** (" the Blessed "), the founder of Llangurig Church, was one of the British saints of the seventh century, who was also a Bishop, probably of Llanbadarnfawr. Travelling inland from Aberystwyth, where he had landed, he rested, it is said, on the top of a high mountain still called on that account Eisteddfa Gurig (Curig's seat) ; from whence he perceived, on looking round, a fertile valley, where he determined to build a church, called from

him Llangurig. Giraldus Cambrensis records that in his time
"in the Church of St. Germanus [St. Harmon's] is a staff of
"Saint Curig, covered on all sides with gold and silver, and
"resembling in its upper part the form of a cross; its efficacy
"has been proved in many cases, but particularly in the removal
"of glandular and strumous swellings; insomuch that all
"persons afflicted with these complaints, on a devout application
"to the staff, with the oblation of one penny, are restored to
"health." For many centuries, indeed, St. Curig was held in
the highest veneration by the Welsh. Lewys Glyn Cothi, in
one of his poems, states that in his time (the 15th century) it
was a common thing for mendicant friars to hawk about images
of Curig and other saints, selling them to the peasantry for
charms, in exchange for cheese, bacon, corn, wool, and other
commodities:—

> " Un a arwain yn oriog
> Curig lwyd dan gwr ei glòg;
> Gwas arall a ddug Seiriol
> A naw o gaws yn ei gól."

(One bore by turns the blessid Curig under the skirts of his
cloak, another youth carried Seiriol and nine cheeses in his
bosom).

CYDAFAEL YNAD, Judge of the Court of Powys in the
time of Llewelyn the Great, which Court was then held at
Castell Dinas Brân. On an invasion of the English, he seized a
firebrand, and passing from mountain to mountain in the district
of Cydewain, where his estates were, and of which he was lord
by right of his wife Arianwen, he gave such timely notice of the
invaders as to assemble his countrymen, who were thereby
enabled to repel the invaders. For this service Prince Llewelyn
granted him for Arms, on a field *sable* three ragged staves *or*
fired *proper*. The Meyrick family, of Bodorgan and Goodrich
Court are descended from him. He flourished about the close of
the twelfth century.

CYFEILIOG, HUW, of Cyfeiliog, Earl of Chester, was born
in 1164, and was one of the lords who agreed with the king of
England for their ancient rights and privileges. Having been
afterwards dispossessed of his estates, he joined the king of
Scotland and the Earl of Leicester in a rebellion, which proved
unsuccessful. Huw appears to have been one of the leaders,
and gained possession of the greatest part of Brittany. The
king's forces, however, gave them battle, and, besieging him at
Deal Castle, took him prisoner, carried him to Normandy, and
thence to England. The king (Henry VIII), however, pardoned
him, and restored to him his lands, which he had gained with his
sword from the Welsh in Bromfield. He was a liberal benefactor to Bardsey Monastery. His grand-daughter, Isabel, was
the mother of the celebrated Robert Bruce, the Scottish warrior.

CYFEILIOG, OWAIN, a distinguished prince, poet, and warrior, was the son of Gruffydd ab Maredudd ab Bleddyn ab Cynfyr, Prince of Powys. On the death of his grandfather, Maredudd, in 1130, Owain succeeded to a large portion of Powys (viz., the portion afterwards called Powys Wenwynwyn), including the district of Cyfeiliog, from which he took his name. In 1162 he was engaged in war with Hywel ab Ieuaf ab Cadwgan ab Elystan Glodrudd, who, however, defeated him, obtained possession of Walwern (Tafolwern) Castle in Cyfeiliog, where Owain resided, and razed it. "which thing, when it was told "Owen Prince of Northwales [Owen Gwynedd] it displeased him "wonderfullie, at the which he was so greeved, that nothing "could make him merrie, until such time as he had gathered his "power and came to Llanthinam in Arustley, and thence set great "spoiles. Then the people of the countrie came all to their Lord "Howel ap Ieuaf, who folowed the spoile to Seauerne side, where "the Princes campe was: whereof the Prince, seeing such an "occasion of revenge offered him, was right glad, and set upon "his enimies, and slew the most part of them, and the rest, with "their Lord, escaped to the woods and rocks. Then the Prince "being joifull of his revenge, built up his Castell againe, and "fortified it stronglie. The yeare following, Owen, the sonne of "Gruffyth ap Meredyth, named Owen Cynelioc, and Owen ap "Madoc ap Meredyth, got the Castell of Carrechona by Owes- "trie, and wasted it."—(Powel). In 1165, he, at the head of the forces of Powys, joined Owain Gwynedd and others in resisting the invasion of Henry II., and distinguished himself at the battle of Crogen, from which the English king retreated with great loss. In the following year he deprived Iorwerth Goch of his lands in Powys. This gave such offence to Owain Gwynedd and Rhys, Prince of South Wales, that those two princes in 1167 brought their armies into Powys, and deprived him of his lands, "and chased him out of the countrie, and gave Caereneon to Owen "Vachan, the sonne of Madoc ap Meredyth, to hold of Prince "Owen; and the Lord Rees had Walwern, because it stoode "within his countrie. But within a while after, Owen Cynelioc "returned with a number of Normanes and Englishmen to "recover his countrie againe, and laid siege to the castell of "Caereneon, and winning the same burned it to the ground."— (Powel). In 1176 he, in obedience to King Henry's summons, met him at Oxford to confer with him on the affairs of Wales. In 1188, Baldwin, Archbishop of Canterbury, accompanied by Giraldus Cambrensis, visited Wales, to urge the people "to take "the crosse, and to vow the viage against the Saracens," in other words, to preach the Crusade, and during a temporary stay of a few days at Shrewsbury we find the following note made concerning Owain :—"We also excommunicated Owain de "Cevelcoc, for he alone of the Welsh princes came not "to meet the archbishop with his people." Owen had married Gwenllian, the daughter of Owain Gwynedd, by whom he had a son, Gwenwynwyn, who inherited his estates entire, except the

Commots of Ilanerch hudol and Broniarth, which **Owain** gave to his illegitimate son Caswallon. In 1197 he died at a great age at the Cistercian abbey of Strata Marcella, near Welshpool (which he himself had founded in 1170), "having previously "taken upon him the habit of religion." Owain, who was himself a poet of a high order, was a liberal patron of the bards of his time, and of Cynddelw in particular. Two of his poems are still extant, and are printed in the Myvyrian Archaiology. One of them (*Hirlas Owain*) is well known from the able translation of it by the Rev. Evan Evans (Ieuan Brydydd Hir) included among his *Specimens of Ancient Welsh Poetry*, also from a poetical version by the Rev. R. Williams, of Vron, given in Pennant's *Tours*:—His Arms were *Or* a lion rampant *Gules* armed *Azure*; or, as some say, *Gules* a lion rampant *Or*.

CYNAN and **CYNFRAITH**, sons of Cyndrwyn Prince of Powys, who, with their brother Cynddylan, were slain in defending Trên against the Saxons, and whom the aged poet Llywarch Hên thus bewails:—

> "Llâs fy mrodyr ar unwaith,
> Cynan, Cynddylan, Cynfraith,
> Yn amwyn Tren, tref ddiffaith."

> (Slain were my brethren all at once,
> Cynan, Cynddylan, Cynfraith,
> In defending Trên, a town laid waste).

CYNAN GARWYN, son of Brochwel Ysgythrog and his successor as Prince of Powys about the middle of the 7th century. His memory is perpetuated in a satirical poem upon him wrongly attributed to Taliesin, and printed in the *Myv. Arch.* He was succeeded by his son, Selyf Sarffgadan.

CYNDRWYN, a prince of that part of ancient Powys which included the vale of the Severn about Shrewsbury, and who lived about the end of the fifth century. He had four brothers, Maoddyn, Elwyddan, Eirinwedd, and Cynon ; and eight sons, Cynddylan, Elvan, Cynon, Cynfraith, Hygarfael, Gwion, Gwyn, and Cuawg, most, if not all, of whom perished in their wars with the Saxons. They, and Cynddylan in particular, are the subjects of much pathetic lamentation by Llywarch Hen. He had also nine daughters, namely, Heledd, Gwladus, Gwenddwyn, Freuer, Medwyl, Medlan, Gwledyr, Meisyr, and Ceinfryd. He is stated to have resided at Llystinwennan in Caereinion, but the precise locality thus designated is rather doubtful. Mr. Joseph Morris suggests that the name should be written "Llystyn wernan," which would be nearly synonymous with Pengwern, *i.e.*, Shrewsbury, the ancient seat of the princes of Powys. This, however, would not agree with the statement in "Achau'r Saint" that Llystinwennan was *in Caereinion*. The probability, therefore, is that it was within the present Township of Llyssyn in

Llanerfyl. By the final concords made in May, 1290, between the sons of Griffith ap Gwenwynwyn, John was to have for life the following five vills in Caereinion, viz., Brynwaven (Bryngwaeddan), *Lestynworman*, Langadevan, Blante (Blowty), and Coythalant (Coedtalog). Mr. William Jones, however, in his "Statistical Account of Llangadfan" expresses an opinion that this was the old name for the Township of Moelfeliarth, in the parish of Llangadfan.

CYNDDELW, or CYNDDELW BRYDYDD MAWR ("the great poet"), one of the most celebrated Welsh poets of the 12th century, styled by Yorke "Our British Homer," flourished between 1140 and 1220. His compositions preserved in the *Myv. Arch.* are 49 in number. He may be supposed to have commenced his poetic career soon after 1133, when Howel, son of Owain Gwynedd, overthrew several Norman fortresses in South Wales, for which exploits he is much applauded by Cynddelw. He was bard to the princes Owain Gwynedd and Owain Cyfeiliog, the latter of whom was himself no mean poet. In 1146 he was appointed chair bard to Madog ab Maredudd, on his accession to the principality of Powys, in preference to Scisyllt, who contested the honour with him, and he appears to have lived for the most part under his patron's roof at Mathrafal Castle. Among his last poems is that called "The Battles of Llewelyn,'" in which he enumerates that prince's devastations in Powys and the Marches, and mentions his encampment at "Bryn Gwyth," near Shrewsbury. All these transactions on the borders took place during the last years of the reign of King John from 1207 to 1216, It appears, therefore, that the poet must have lived to a very great age, having composed poems during a period of between 70 and 80 years, and that period one of the most eventful in Cambrian history. The bard's repeated eulogies on the prowess of the princes of Powys and Gwynedd roused the indignation of a zealous rival for martial fame, Lord Rees of Dinevor. To appease his wrath Cynddelw wrote eight conciliatory poems, and was at last permitted to include in his final peace-offering

> "Llaesa dy vâr dy vardd wyv."
> (Slacken thy wrath, for I am thy bard.)

His style is exceedingly intricate, obscure, sententious, and abrupt, which renders it very difficult to translate some of his poems. His imagery, however, is often poetical in the highest degree. For example :—

> "Gwyrdd heli Teifi tewychai
> Gwaeddlan gwyr, a llyr a'i llanwai
> Gwyach rudd gorfudd goralwai,
> Ar doniar gwyar gonofiai—"
> (The green flood of Teifi was thickened,
> The river was filled with the blood of men,
> The blood-stained waterfowl called aloud for a glut of gore,
> And swam with toil on waves of blood.)

In addition to their poetical excellence, Cynddelw's poems are of great value for their historical references. They also show that he was a man of enlightened views (taking into account the age he lived in), and a powerful enemy of the superstitions of his time. When threatened in his mortal illness with excommunition by the Abbot of Strata Marcella, and told that in such a case he could not be buried in consecrated ground, he replied

> " Cyn ni bai ammod dyfod—i'm herbyn
> A Duw gwyn yn gwybod
> Oedd iawnach i fynach fod
> I'm gwrthfyn nag i'm gwrthod."
>
> (Since no covenant against me can be shewn
> As the price of God well knows,
> More becoming were it for the monks
> To ask than to reject my body.)

And he spurns indignantly the superstitions of the monks in language of true sublimity :—

> " Ni chymeraf gymun
> Gan ysgymun fyneich
> A'u twygan ar eu glin,
> A'm cymuno Duw ei hun."
>
> (I will not receive the sacrament
> From excommunicated monks
> With their togas on their knees;—
> I will commune with God himself.)

CYNDDYLAN, the son of Cyndrwyn, and who succeeded his father in the sovereignty of part of ancient Powys—(see CYNDRWYN SUPRA). He resided at Shrewsbury, then called Pengwern, about the middle of the sixth century. The hospitable reception which he gave to the warrior bard Llywarch Hen, when forced to flee from his own country (Argoed) in the north of England has been immortalised by the latter in his "Elegy on Cynddylan ab Cyndrwyn." Cynddylan was a brave warrior, and often led his forces against the incursions of the Saxons. On one of such occasions he fell, in defending a town called Tren, near the Wrekin, and was buried in the Church of Bassa (Baschurch). His brothers, Elfan and Cynfraith, and also the twenty-four sons of Llywarch Hen, fell in fighting against the same enemies. Llywarch Hen's elegy upon his death, already referred to, may be found in the *Myv. Arch.*, which also contains another elegy on the same subject by Meugant, an eminent contemporary poet. It is also included in the *Heroic Elegies and Pieces of Llywarch Hen*, with an English translation by Dr. Owen Pughe. It has also been published with a literal English translation by the late Dr. Guest in the *Archæological Journal*, and the *Arch, Cambrensis* for 1863; also in the *Four Ancient Books of Wales*.

CYNOG, a saint who lived in the fifth century, was the son of Brychan, prince of Brycheiniog by Banhadlwedd of Banhadla [Llanrhaiadr] in Powys. The Church of Llangynog was founded by or dedicated to him, as were also those of Merthyr Cynog, Defynog, Ystradgynlais, Penderin, Battle and Llangynog in Breconshire; Boughrood in Radnorshire; Llangynog in Carmarthenshire; and others of the same name in Monmouthshire and Herefordshire. A saying of Cynog's is preserved in *Chwedlau'r Doethion* (Sayings of the Wise):—

> " A glywaist ti chwedl Cynog,
> Sant penrhaith gwlad Brycheiniog ?
> ' Deuparth addysg yn mhenglog.' "
> (Hast thou heard the saying of Cynog
> Saint and governor of the land of Brecknock ?
> " Two-thirds of one's education is already in the head.")

CYNON was one of the missionaries who in the sixth century accompanied St. Cadfan from Brittany to Wales. He was the patron saint of Tregynon, in Montgomeryshire, and of Capel Cynon, in Cardiganshire. One of his sayings is preserved in *Chwedlau'r Doethion* :—

> " A glywaist ti chwedl Cynon,
> Yn ymochel rhag meddwon ?
> ' Cwrw da yw allwedd calon,' "
> (Hast thou heard the saying of Cynon
> When avoiding drunkards ?
> " Good ale is the key of the heart.")

CYNYW, the patron saint of Llangyniew, Montgomeryshire, and Llangeview, Monmouthshire, flourished in the earlier part of the sixth century. One of his brothers was Catwg the Wise, whose recorder he was at his College at Llancarfan.

DAFYDD LLWYD AB LLYWELYN AB GRUFFYDD,

an eminent poet, and a man of wealth and position, who flourished between 1470 and 1520. He was descended from Seisyllt, Lord of Merioneth, and lived at Mathafarn in the parish of Llanwrin. He was a partizan and a great favourite of Jasper, Earl of Pembroke, and did all in his power to promote the views of that party against the usurper Richard III., in 1480. He subsequently exercised his poetical talent in favour of Henry VII., who when Earl of Richmond stayed a night with him on the way to Bosworth in August, 1485, and consulted him, it is said, as to his probable success. He was credited with powers of divination by his countrymen, and seems to have encouraged this opinion on their part in his powers by pretending to consult the Seagull and otherwise. All his pretended prophecies and prognostications tended to the furtherance of the success of the House of Tudor, and he devoted his wealth and personal influence among his countrymen to the same cause. It is related that when the Earl of Richmond consulted him, as already mentioned, about the issue of his hazardous adventure, David was not ready with an answer; he hesitated, and promised a reply the following morning. Perplexed by the question, he passed a sleepless night. His wife learned the cause, and said, "Can you doubt what to reply? Tell him the event will be successful and glorious, and if your prediction be verified, you will receive honours and rewards; if he fails, he will never return to reproach you." This satisfied the seer, and no less so the Earl when they met again the following morning. This adventure, it is said, gave rise to the Welsh proverb, "Cynghor gwraig heb ei ofyn"—(A wife's advice without being asked for it). He was a voluminous writer, and many of his poems are interesting. His descendants resided at Mathafarn for many generations. His elegy by Dafydd ab Hywel ab Ieuan Fychan has the following couplet which appears to refer to the place of his burial:—

> " Gorwedd y mae mewn gardd Mair,
> Gwrdd geudawd y gerdd gadair."
> (In Mary's garden lies he, the bold keeper of the chair of song.)

For a list of his compositions (most, if not all, of which are still extant) see the cover of the *Greal* (No. 7) December, 1806. The following extract from his poem celebrating Richmond's victory, translated by Mr. Justice Bosanquet, will give the reader an idea of the mystic and oracular style in which the poet delighted:—

> " King Henry hath fought and bravely done,
> Our friend the golden crown hath won.
> The bards resume a cheerful strain;
> For the good of the world little R was slain.
> That straddling letter, pale and sad,
> In England's realm no honour had:
> For ne'er could R, in place of I,
> Rule England's people royally;
> Nor stem the foe with puissant hand,
> Nor in the breach like Edward stand."

The person of Richard III. expressed by the letter R, is here contrasted with the tall upright form of Edward IV., expressed by the letter I, which is the initial of the Welsh name for Edward, viz., Iorwerth.

DAFYDD LLWYD AB DAFYDD AB EINION, of Newtown, or of Cedewain, as he is sometimes described, (a lineal ancestor of the Pryces of Newtown Hall), was a man of weal h, lineally descended from Elystan Glodrudd, and a munificent patron of the bards. He flourished about the close of the 15th century. Lewys Glyn Cothi, Guto'r Glyn, and other contemporary poets have eloquently sung his praises, and the former wrote an elegy upon his death. It appears that he was in the habit on the different festivals of the church of giving splendid entertainments (or *Eisteddfodau*) when bards and minstrels from far and near were invited and sumptuously entertained, and the poor of the neighbourhood partook of the alms which he liberally bestowed upon them. His son Rhys was steward to King Edward IV., of the Lordships of Cedewain, Kerry, Cyfeiliog, and Arwystli, but was killed at the battle of Danesmore, near Banbury, in 1469. Rhys's son, Thomas, was the first of the line to be known by the surname of Pryce.

DAFYDD MEIFOD, a poet who flourished from about 1630 to 1670. He was, as his name implies, a native of Meifod. Some of his poetry is, it is said, still preserved in MS.

DAVIES, Dr. DAVID, was a son of Mr. Morris Davies, a timber merchant at Machynlleth. He was a man of considerable learning, and was for some time head master of the Grammar School at Macclesfield. He died in or about the year 1827.

DAVIES, Rev. DAVID, was born at Tynchaf, Mallwyd, September 13, 1778. He received some instruction from the Rev. Thomas Morgan, the clergyman of that parish, and afterwards at Berriew school, from which he was admitted to Shrewsbury school. There he gained a scholarship at Cambridge, and in 1798 he entered that University, and soon obtained his degree of B.A. He was ordained to the curacy of Llandyssil by Dr. Bagot, in September, 1807, at £30 a year, and subsequently officiated at Llanymawddwy. He published a treatise on *Psalmody* in 1807; one on *Peace and the Bad Harvest* in 1818; another on *The Advantage of Public Worship* in 1819; and after his decease 21 of his sermons with a memoir were published in 1823.

DAVIES, Rev. DAVID, Vicar of Dylife, was the son of Mr. Davies, a farmer, living at Clochfaen Isaf, Llangurig, where he was born in the year 1823. Having for some time been employed as clerk in a solicitor's office at Llanidloes, he determined to forsake the law and enter the church. His parents being Baptists, he had not been baptized in infancy, and when he joined the communion of the Church of England he was by his own choice baptized by immersion by the Rev. E. Pughe, then Vicar of Llanidloes. After going through the usual course of study at St. David's College, Lampeter, where he gained a scholarship, he was in 1848 ordained deacon and appointed to the curacy of Llanwnog. Here he laboured assiduously in his sacred calling, employing his leisure time in investigating the antiquities of Caersws and the neighbourhood. In 1853 he was appointed one of the local secretaries for Montgomeryshire of the Cambrian Archæological Association, and at the meeting of that Society, held at Ruthin the following year, he read a paper on *Roman Remains Discovered at Caersws*. He subsequently superintended excavations at Caersws, which led to interesting discoveries described by him in communications to the *Archæologia Cambrensis*, to which and to other periodicals, Welsh and English, Mr. Davies was a frequent contributor. While at Llanwnog he was appointed diocesan inspector of schools for the deanery of Arwystli. In 1856 he was promoted to the incumbency of the newly-formed ecclesiastical district of Dylife. He at once energetically set about improving the educational facilities of his new cure, and soon succeeded in having a substantial National schoolroom erected. His next object was to secure the building of a parsonage. In this he also succeeded, but having imprudently taken up his residence in the new house before it was sufficiently dry, he took a cold that brought on a painful and lingering illness, which terminated fatally. He died at Llanidloes, on his way to Clochfaen, on the 12th February, 1865, in the 42nd year of his age, and was buried at Llangurig. Mr. Davies was a zealous and intelligent antiquary, from whom, had his life been prolonged, his countrymen expected much.

DAVIES, DAVID, of Llandinam, was one of the most remarkable men ever bred and born in Montgomeryshire. Indeed, few more typical or successful Welshmen ever lived. Born in very humble circumstances, and almost entirely self-taught, he yet, by his rare shrewdness, great natural ability, and immense energy, fought his way to a position of great wealth and influence. With indomitable pluck and unremitting exertion he embarked during his busy life in many and various vast undertakings, conquered difficulties, and overcame obstacles before which a heart less stout than his might have quailed, and with hardly an exception it might be said that whatever he took in hand prospered. In addition to all this he was distinguished through life for his frankness, integrity, strict adherence to principle, great kindness of disposition, and princely liberality to every good and deserving cause. He was born on the 18th of December, 1818, at Draintewion, a small hillside tenement in the parish of Llandinam, on the opposite side of the valley, and in sight of Broneirion, the beautiful house which he afterwards built, and for the last twenty-five years of his life occupied. His parents were industrious and hard-working persons, but having a numerous family of nine children, of whom he was the eldest, they could not afford to keep any of them long in school. After attending the village school, then held in the parish church, until he was eleven years old, David was, therefore, kept at home to assist his father, who added to his small farming business that of a sawyer. From this time forth his life was one of hard and unremitting labour, and he very soon came to be of great help to his father. From Draintewion the family removed to a larger farm in the same parish, called Neuaddfach, where his father died. At this time he was only twenty years old, and the care and support of his mother and eight younger brothers and sisters devolved upon him This duty he did not attempt to shirk, but addressed himself to it with increased energy. He soon began to speculate in a small way. One of his earliest speculations, it seems, was the purchase of an oak-tree, which the late Capt. Crewe-Read wished to cut down and dispose of, and offered to sell to him for £5. This offer he promptly accepted, and having felled the tree and sawn it into boards, he realised £80 by it. In 1843 he took a larger farm, called Tynymaen—on part whereof now stands Plâs Dinam, the beautiful mansion occupied by his only son, Mr. Edward Davies. His mother remained at Neuaddfach until her death. In 1850 he also rented Gwernerin, a still larger farm on the opposite side of the Severn. He had meanwhile been engaged in carrying out various contracts, chiefly for the construction or repair of bridges and roads. The first of these was a contract for the making of a road and bridge at Llandinam over the Severn—a work which he carried out so satisfactorily that, on the recommendation of the County Surveyor (Mr. Penson), a sum of £15 was paid to him in ad ition to the contract money. In 1851 Mr. Davies married Margaret, daughter of Mr. Edward Jones, of Wern, Llanfair Caereinion, who survived him. The only issue of this marriage was a son, Mr. Edward Davies. The rapidity and completeness of his grasp of details, and his promptness in making up his mind, showed themselves in his early undertakings, as they did so strikingly in after life. Thus, after looking at the plans and specifications of the Oswestry Smithfield, he was asked how long it would take him to make up his mind, when he at once replied, " Five minutes," other contractors stipulating for several days. He secured the contract, and it was while carrying it out that he first became acquainted with Mr. Thomas Savin, who afterwards became his partner in several important railway undertakings. The first of these was the railway from Llanidloes to Newtown, twelve miles in length, and with no railway within thirty miles of either terminus, the nearest being at Oswestry. For this reason the plant and materials were brought chiefly by canal to Newtown, and the locomotives and carriages for working the line were conveyed by road on specially constructed waggons from Oswestry. Before this line was completed Messrs. Davies and Savin had undertaken the contract for the Vale of Clwyd line from Denbigh to Rhyl, which they completed in 1858. The Llanidloes line was completed and opened for traffic on 31st August, 1859. They then entered into a contract for the completion of the Oswestry and Newtown line (portions of which had been made by other contractors), which they finished in the summer of 1862. They also contracted for the making of the line from Newtown to Machynlleth, which was finished the same year, and (in conjunction with Mr. Ward, Mr. Savin's brother-in-law) another line from Brecon to Merthyr. They also promoted a line from Machynlleth to Aberystwyth; but Mr. Savin, not content with this, insisted, against Mr. Davies's better judgment, on embarking in extensions along the Welsh coast, via Aberdovey and Barmouth to Pwllheli, including also the erection of large and costly hotels at Aberystwyth, Borth, Aberdovey, and other places. Finding his remonstrances to be in vain, Mr. Davies dissolved his partnership with Mr. Savin. Subsequent events fully confirmed the soundness of his judgment, and justified the course he took, for they ended in Mr. Savin's disastrous failure in February, 1866. In partnership with Mr. Ezra Roberts he also made the Pembroke and Tenby line, which was opened in 1863, and subsequently, in partnership with Mr. Beeston, the line from Aberystwyth to Pencader, known as the Manchester and Milford Railway. The last railway he made was that from Caersws to the Van Mines, completed and opened in January, 1871, He was, however, for many years a director of the Cambrian Railways Company. In 1863 Mr. Davies purchased the first of his estates, comprising Trewythen and other farms in Llandinam, and the following year he erected, on a site commanding a lovely prospect of the Severn Valley, Broneirion, the beautiful residence which he occupied during the remainder of his days. In 1865 he turned his attention from railway construction to coal mining. Having secured a large tract of land in the Rhondda Valley, he, in partnership with a few of his friends, sank several pits for the purpose of working the valuable coal deposits in that valley. Mr. Crawshay Bailey, the principal owner, was, it seems, at first reluctant to part with the land " to speculators and adventurers." Mr. Davies, however, boldly replied : " I am no adventurer, but an honest trader, and for every honest guinea you will put down I will put another." This straightforward and independent spirit overcame all obstacles, and secured the land on reasonable terms. The coal turned out to be of splendid quality, probably the very best for steam purposes, and the demand for it rapidly increased. In a few years the undertaking became so important that it was found desirable to convert it into a limited company, under the name of " The Ocean Coal Company, Limited." The Ocean Collieries consisted, at the time of Mr. Davies' death, of seven pits, where from six to seven thousand persons were constantly employed, whose wages amounted to half a million pounds per annum, the output of coal being about a million and a half tons per annum. In consequence of the great demand for the coal the profits have been enormous. In the golden year, 1873, Mr. Davies's own share, which was about the half of the whole, amounted to nearly £100,000. The successful development of this great undertaking led to one of still greater dimensions. The heavy charges and inconveniences which the Company were forced to submit to at the hands of the Taff Vale Railway Company, and the Marquis of Bute, who had a monopoly of the means of transit and dock accommodation for the export of the coal, became at last insufferable. Every effort was made by the colliery proprietors to obtain better terms and facilities, but in vain. Then Mr. Davies conceived the bold idea of constructing a new dock at Barry Island. a few miles out of Cardiff, with a line of railway, twenty-seven miles in length, from the Rhondda Valley to it. A company was formed to carry out this project ; surveys were made and plans deposited, and the usual notices were given in November, 1882, and the following session the Bill was brought in. The fight over it between the monopolists on the one side, and the freighters on the other, was one of almost unexampled severity.

After twenty-six days' contest it passed Committee in the House of Commons, but was rejected by the Lords' Committee after a further fight of seventeen days It was introduced again the following year, and the battle was renewed with still greater obstinacy. The Lords' Committee sat thirty-three days on the Bill, but at length passed it, and on the 14th August, 1884, it received the Royal assent, after an expenditure of £70,000. It was Mr. Davies, by his indomitable pluck and energy, the clearness of his views, and the shrewdness of his judgment, that really piloted the Bill safely through all the perils that surrounded it. The authorised capital of the company was £2,500,000. When asked in cross-examination in Committee how this capital could be raised, Mr. Davies, with characteristic boldness replied: "If the public will not come forward, I will find the whole of the money myself"; and no one doubted his word. The first sod of the new dock was cut by Lord Windsor, Chairman of the Company, in November, 1884, and it was opened by Mr. Davies, the Vice-Chairman, in Lord Windsor's absence on the 8th July, 1889. Barry Dock is one of the finest in the kingdom, and for its special purpose of loading and exporting coal it cannot be surpassed. It has already proved an immense success in every respect. In July, 1865, Mr. Davies stood as a candidate for a seat in Parliament for Cardiganshire, his opponent being Sir Thomas Lloyd, who defeated him by a majority of 342. Both candidates were Liberals. At the General Election in February, 1874, he was elected, without opposition, member for the Cardigan Boroughs, which he continued to represent until they were merged in the county by virtue of the Reform Act of 1885. At the General Election, which followed in November, 1885, he stood for the county, but was opposed in the Conservative interest by Mr. Vaughan Davies, whom he defeated by 2,323 votes. When Mr. Gladstone a few months afterwards brought forward his Irish Home Rule Bill, Mr. Davies could not agree with his policy, but joined the new party of Liberal Unionists. At the General Election in July, 1886, which followed Mr. Gladstone's defeat, Mr. Bowen Rowlands, Q.C., was brought forward as a Gladstonian Liberal in opposition to Mr. Davies, and defeated him by a majority of nine votes only. Party feeling ran very high, and the smallness of the majority was due, undoubtedly, to Mr. Davies's great personal popularity and influence in the constituency. These secured for him hundreds of votes which undoubtedly otherwise would have gone for his opponent. He felt this defeat keenly, especially the bitterness with which his return was opposed by some who were under deep personal obligations to him, and after this he took no part in politics. He qualified as a Justice of the Peace for Montgomeryshire in 1873, and was returned unopposed in February, 1889, to represent his native parish on the County Council of Montgomeryshire. Mr. Davies was a Nonconformist of a very robust character, and a Calvinistic Methodist of a very strict type. Notwithstanding this, he

c

lived on the best terms with the clergy of his own and neighbouring parishes, and contributed liberally to all denominations, though his munificence to his own denomination was most conspicuous. Indeed, his liberality to all religious, educational, and benevolent objects was almost unbounded. He gave about £6,000 to the University College of Aberystwyth, and built at his own expense the handsome Board School and teacher's residence at the village of Llandinam. The amounts he contributed towards the erection of places of worship and the extinction of chapel debts will never be known, but must have amounted to tens of thousands of pounds. He himself stated that he made some rough calculation of the amount of his various subscriptions during one year, and found that it came to about £16,000, but he never again took the trouble to add them up. His last gift was £1,000 to the Jubilee Fund of the Calvinistic Methodist Foreign Missionary Society. Mr. Davies had, at different times, purchased several considerable estates in the parishes of Kerry, Llandinam, and Llanwnog, and at the time of his death was one of the principal landowners in Montgomeryshire. He was an excellent landlord, spending annually thousands of pounds in the erection of new buildings, in drainage, and in other improvements, while the rents remained the same, or were even lowered. This made him as popular and respected with his tenantry as he had always been with his workmen, and no man was ever more so. He would speak to the workmen as a workman, and his kind, unassuming manner won the hearts of all. Faithful to the memory of his origin, he always knew how to maintain the best relations with his workpeople. He was a man of fine physique, and on occasions when his workmen would be unable to proceed with their work through unfavourable weather, or other circumstances, he would visit them in their sheds, and go through different exercises with them, such as throwing the hammer, lifting weights, and other feats demanding strength. He was a strict total abstainer, and no intoxicants were supplied to his servants on the farm, even in harvest time. He was also a strict Sabbatarian. At all times, if in any way possible, he would return home for the Sunday, in order not to miss his class in the Sunday School. So strict, indeed, were his views regarding the commandment to "Keep holy the Sabbath Day" that he would not open letters on Sunday. While yet a young man, contracting in a small way, the road surveyor who superintended the work he had in hand, one Sunday drove from Welshpool to Llandinam, a distance of about twenty miles, to see him on some matters connected with the work. On his arrival Mr. Davies was in chapel, and a message was sent to him that the Surveyor desired to see him. The reply was that Mr. Davies would see the Surveyor on the following day. While attending to his Parliamentary duties in London he rarely failed to go down every Saturday to Llandinam to spend the Sabbath quietly with his family in simple Christian worship, returning to town again on Monday morning. With the exception of a visit to Egypt and Palestine at the time of the opening of the Suez Canal, and of another to Russia a few years later, at the invitation of the Grand Duke Constantine, who desired his advice in regard to the construction of railways, Mr. Davies spent the whole of his life in England. His life and work, remarkable as they were in many respects, presented a striking contrast to those of many self-made men who have amassed large fortunes by following devious paths and crooked ways. His high Christian character, deep religious convictions, stability and firmness of mind, were prominently noticeable during his whole life. From youth to ripe age, he was the same in kindliness of heart, in purity of motive, in faithfulness to his convictions, in fervent piety, and in the exercise of beneficence to so eminent a degree. His success depended more upon these qualities, combined with a constant and careful vigilance and cautious forethought, than upon anything else. During his younger years he was a diligent worker, and throughout his life he never shirked any laborious effort. When a young man he was noted for diligent toil and labour, and so robust and healthy was he that he was able to do with only four or five hours sleep out of the twenty-four. The rest he would devote to assiduous work; and this habit grew with him, so that he was able by his own example, to arouse the energies of his workmen to their full operation. He ever manifested a broad, generous, and unselfish spirit in all his dealings, and never did a mean or shabby thing to friend or foe. His hand was always ready to help anyone who strove honestly to succeed. The unremitting anxiety entailed in carrying out to a successful issue the stupendous commercial projects already referred to told severely upon Mr. Davies's iron constitution, and probably helped to sow the germs of the disease to which he ultimately succumbed. His health had been failing for several years prior to his death, and for some months he was more or less an invalid. The most eminent physicians were called in, but all efforts to restore him to his former health failed, and for the last fortnight of his life he was confined entirely to bed, gradually getting weaker every day. He died on Sunday, the 20th July, 1890, in his 72nd year, and was buried the following Thursday in Llandinam churchyard. His remains were followed to the grave by about 2,000 persons from all parts of Wales and many English towns. After his death steps were taken to commemorate in a suitable manner his many virtues and great public services by the erection of a statue to his memory at Llandinam. Accordingly a very handsome and life-like bronze statue, designed and executed by Mr. Albert Gilbert, R.A., which cost about £1,200 (a counterpart of one by the same distinguished artist erected at Barry Dock) was put up there, the cost being defrayed by public subscription. It was unveiled in the presence of many thousands of persons on the 15th June, 1893. As a tribute to the memory of so good a husband and father, his widow and son have also signified their intention to devote £5,000 for the following purposes :—£2,000 for scholarships in connection with Intermediate Schools in Montgomeryshire, tenable by scholars in public elementary schools within the county ; £2.000 for similar scholarships in Glamorganshire, tenable by scholars whose parents are employed at the Ocean Collieries ; and the remaining £1,000 for the erection of a Reading Room at Barry for the use of workmen employed at the dock and on the railway.

DAVIES, EDWARD (Iolo Trefaldwyn), was born at Moel-y-Froches, near Llanfyllin, in the year 1819. In his early days he worked as a miner at the Minera Lead Mines. Subsequently he lived a few years in Liverpool, where he carried on business as a coal dealer in a small way, and afterwards removed to Wrexham, where he spent the remainder of his days, chiefly employed as a canvasser for orders for books. He was a good poet, excelling in the composition of Englynion and short pieces, particularly of epitaphs. He won the chair prize at one of the Liverpool Gordofic Eisteddfodau, as well as many other prizes at similar gatherings elsewhere. Some years before his death a collection of his shorter poems was published under the title *Caneuon Iolo Trefaldwyn*. He was a good singer, and often sang *pennillion* to the accompaniment of the harp, which is now a somewhat rare accomplishment. He died at Wrexham on the 4th January, 1887, in the 68th year of his age, and was buried at the New Cemetery in that town.

DAVIES, EVAN (*Philomath*), of Manafon, the Almanack compiler and publisher, flourished between 1720 and 1750. His almanacks, which for some years were annually printed and published at Shrewsbury, contained Summer and Christmas carols, Englynion on various subjects, and other miscellaneous matters.

DAVIES, Rev. EVAN (*Eta Delta*), was born at Cefn, Llanbrynmair, about 1794. He began to preach with the Independents about 1820, and studied for a short time at Dr. Lewis's Academy at Llanfyllin. After preaching for a while at Bilston he was ordained to the ministry at Llanrwst ; thence he removed to Llanerchymedd. Here, through his exertions, a large chapel was built, which in honour of him was called "Capel Evan." From Llanerchymedd he removed to Newmarket, Flintshire, where he laboured till his death on the 1st March, 1855. He was a man of moderate abilities, but a very laborious pastor, and by means of lectures, pamphlets, and otherwise, he did much to promote the Temperance and other good movements. He also wrote several pamphlets on religious subjects.

DAVIES, Rev. JACOB, the Missionary, was born at Cefnmawr, near Newtown, of humble parents, February 22nd, 1816. He was a spinner by trade. He joined the Baptist denomination, and was publicly baptized in April, 1835. In

October, 1837, he began to preach with that denomination, and in August, 1840, entered their college at Bradford to study for the ministry. After leaving Bradford he offered himself, and was accepted, as a missionary—Ceylon being assigned to him as his field of labour. Before leaving England, namely in March, 1844, he married Miss Eliza Green, of Camberwell, and on the 25th of the following May he and his wife sailed from Gravesend, arriving in Ceylon the following September. He laboured hard and successfully in that island for five years, and applied himself with so much assiduity to the study of Cingalese that he became, according to the statement of the then Governor of the island, the best Cingalese scholar of the day. His health, however, gave way, and after a short illness he died in November, 1849, at the early age of 33.

DAVIES, Rev. JOHN, D.D., generally known as " Dr. Davies, of Mallwyd," was the son of a weaver named Dafydd ab Sion ab Rhys. of Llanferres, Denbighshire, and was born about 1570). His father was, according to Yorke's *Royal Tribes of Wales*, of the tribe of Marchudd ap Cynan ; and his mother, whose name was Elizabeth, was a descendant of Ednyfed Fychan, one of the knights of Llewelyn the Great, Prince of Wales. In a letter dated August 26th, 1623, addressed to Sir John Wynn, of Gwydir, printed in the *Cambrian Register*, he refers to Mr. R. Vaughan, of Hengwrt, as his "cousin." This shews clearly his respectable connections, and that his parents were probably well to do. He was sent to school at Ruthin. It is generally stated that this school was the one established by Dr. Gabriel Goodman there, but this must be a mistake, as that school was not established until 1595, whereas Dr. Davies had graduated at Oxford, and returned to his native country in 1593. It is also clearly an error to state that Dr. Richard Parry was his tutor in that school, for Dr. Parry became Chancellor of Bangor in 1592, and Dean of that Cathedral seven years later. That statement, it is true, is adopted by Wood in *Athenae Oxonienses*, confirmed by Bishop Humphreys in his annotations thereon, and again reiterated by Parry in his *Cambrian Plutarch*, and by subsequent biographers. Archdeacon Newcome, however, in his *Memoirs of the Goodmans*, points out that there is strong reason to doubt its accuracy. As Dr. Parry was born at Ruthin, and his biographers give no account of him between 1579, when he entered college, and 1592, when he obtained the Chancellorship of Bangor, it is very probable that during part of that time he kept a private school in his native town, and that Davies received in such school the elements of learning, as well as the benefit of Dr. Parry's friendship, which continued during their joint lives, and proved of such advantage to Davies afterwards when his old tutor was raised to the episcopal bench. It may also be gathered from his preface to his Welsh Latin Dictionary that he was for some time under the tuition of Dr. Morgan, the translator of the Bible into Welsh. In 1589 he left Ruthin, and entered

Jesus College, Oxford, where he remained and took his B.A. degree. In 1593 he left Oxford and retired to Wales, where he prosecuted his study of divinity, and the language and antiquities of his native country. The following year he entered into holy orders, but received no preferment for ten years. In 1604 he was presented by the Crown with the rectory of Mallwyd, where he resided afterwards for the greatest part of his life. The following year he became Chaplain to Bishop Parry. In 1608 he returned to Oxford, and was admitted to Lincoln College as Reader of Bishop Lombard's Sentences, having first obtained a dispensation for not ruling in arts. His second residence at the university was probably not of long duration, as we find him in 1612 elected a Canon of St. Asaph; in 1613 he had, in addition to his other preferments, the rectory of Llanymawddwy; in 1615 the sinecure vicarage of Darowen, which he gave up in order to obtain the living of Llanfor, near Bala. In 1616 he took his degree of Doctor of Divinity, and the following year exchanged his Canonry for the Prebend of Llannefydd, in Denbighshire. This was his last promotion in the church. He appears to have held at the same time the livings of Mallwyd, Llanymawddwy, Llanfor, and Llannefydd, if not also Garthbeibio. Dr. Davies rendered material assistance to Dr. Parry in bringing out his improved edition of Dr. Morgan's Bible in 1620. In 1621 he published his Latin Grammar of the Welsh language, under the title of *Antiquae Linguae Britannicae Rudimenta*, with a dedication to Bishop Parry, and a preface addressed to Archdeacon Edmund Prys. A second edition of this important work was published at Oxford in 1809, under the editorship of the Rev. Henry Parry, of Llanasa. It is also tolerably certain that the translation of the Thirty-nine Articles appended to the Welsh Edition of the Book of Common Prayer was by him, for it was published separately in 1634, being 20 years after his death, with his name attached to it. In 1632 Dr. Davies published his Latin-Welsh and Welsh-Latin Dictionary, under the title of *Antiquae Linguae Britannicae et Linguae Latinae Dictionarium Duplex*, the Welsh-Latin portion being entirely his own, and the Latin-Welsh comprising the corrected labours of Thomas ab William, commonly called Sir Thomas Williams of Trefriw, a distinguished Welsh scholar. Upon this work his literary fame, especially as an expounder of his native language, must chiefly rest. The Dictionary is dedicated to Charles II., then Prince of Wales. The learned author of *Eminent Welshmen* remarks that " having seen and compared " the original Dictionary (of Dr. Thomas Williams), which is a " most copious and elaborate work, and which, to the disgrace of " the Welsh nation, still remains in manuscript, I am enabled to " state that the Latin-Welsh Dictionary printed by Dr. Davies is " little more than a bare index of that by Dr. Williams. For " the latter has enriched his work with ample quotations from " the ancient Welsh authors, and the publication of it even now " would be a boon of the greatest value to the Welsh scholar."

The Welsh-Latin portion was re-published at Amsterdam, by Boxhorn, in 1654. The author was engaged about 40 years upon this great undertaking, as appears from a letter dated January 23, 1627, addressed by him to Mr. Owen Wynn of Gwydir, a son of Sir John Wynn (See *Cam. Register* I]., p 473). It continued to be the most valuable Dictionary of Welsh for nearly two centuries, and though now superseded by Dr. Owen Pughe's and later Dictionaries it has always been highly esteemed, and proves that the author merited the character given to him by Wood of " being well versed in the history and antiquities of his own " nation, and in the Greek and Hebrew languages, a most exact " critic, and indefatigable searcher into ancient scripts, and well "acquainted with curious and rare authors." The same year (1632) Dr. Davies published a Welsh translation of Parsons' " Christian Resolution," of which there have been three subsequent editions. He also made considerable collections of Welsh poems and proverbs, which are still preserved in MS. in the Bodleian Library, and among the Harleian MSS. in the British Museum. He was in the habit, it is said, of marking in the books he read any passages that struck his fancy. After his death a collection of such passages was made by the Rev. David Lewis, and published at Shrewsbury under the title *Flores Poetarum Britannicorum*, bound with some rules of poetry, by Capt. William Middleton. Of this several editions have been published. MS. sermons used to be shewn in the library of Ystradmeurig school, which were said to be Dr. Davies's. It is said that his books became the property of one Mr. Kenrick, a Dissenting minister at Wrexham, who on his removal to Usk took them with him, and that they still remain with some of his posterity. Dr. Davies was married to Jane, a daughter, or some say a sister, of Rhys Wynn, Esq., of Llwynon, and whose sister was married to Bishop Parry. There was no issue of this marriage, and after his death Mrs. Davies is said to have been married to Dr. Davies's Curate, a union, it is added, which proved unhappy. Dr. Davies was a magistrate, and gathered considerable wealth, much of which he applied during his lifetime in various ways for the benefit of the parish of Mallwyd and its vicinity. He built at his own cost a strong bridge near the village, called Pont-y-cleifion. This bridge is not used at the present day, though still standing, one of more lofty span having been built close to it. The letters J.D. in white pebbles on the roadway over the old bridge, however, still attest the liberality of its builder. He is also said to have built two other bridges in the same parish. Also, he rebuilt the chancel and the bell-tower of the church, on the latter of which the inscription " *Venite Cantem*: J.D." was a few years ago still to be seen. On the other side of the tower the words " *Soli Deo Sacrum Christi MDCXI*," are still visible. He also thoroughly repaired the rectory house, and the initial letters of his name were set in white stones in the pavement before the door to perpetuate his memory. By his will he gave the rent of a field called *Dold-vey* to the poor of Mallwyd parish for ever. Having no issue, as already stated, he left the remainder of his property between his own nephew and his wife's nephew. Dr. Davies was greatly beloved for his cheerful, kind, and benevolent disposition, as well as respected and admired for his great talents and profound learning. He died about 74 years of age at Mallwyd, on the 15th of May, 1644 and was interred in the chancel of the church of that parish The following inscription formerly existed on his gravestone, but is now obliterated :—" Johannes Davies, S.T.P., Rector Ecclesiæ " Parochialis de Mallwyd, Obiit 15 Die Maii et sepultus fuit 19, "A.D. 1644, in Virtutis potius quam Nominis memoria." Through the efforts of the late Rev. Rowland Williams, of Ysceifiog, a beautiful white marble monument to Dr. Davies's memory has been put up in Mallwyd Church.

DAVIES, Rev. JOHN, the missionary to Tahiti (probably the first modern Welsh Missionary to the heathen), was born at a small cottage, now in ruins, on a farm called Pendugwm, in the parish of Llanfihangel, on the 11th of July, 1772. His father was a poor weaver, but struggled hard to give his son the best education he could afford. After leaving school the latter for some time himself kept a day school at Llanrhaiadr-Mochnant, and afterwards at Llanwyddelan. At this time he was accepted by the London Missionary Society as one of its missionaries, and was in February, 1800, despatched to Tahiti, one of the South Sea Islands, where, after more than a year's voyage, he arrived on the 10th July, 1801. In consequence of the bloody wars that raged among the natives there he and his fellow-missionaries were in 1808 compelled to seek refuge in Huahine, a neighbouring island, where he remained about a year, and then left for Port Jackson, which place he reached in February, 1810. Peace having been restored in Tahiti, he returned to that island in 1811, and spent the remainder of his life there, labouring hard and with great success in his sacred calling. He continued to preach every Sabbath until the last he spent upon earth. He published several works in the native language of Tahiti among them being a *Primer* of the Tahitian language, a *Tahitian and English Dictionary*, a short essay on *Infant Baptism*, translations of the *Pilgrim's Progress*, and of the Psalms, the Gospels of St. Matthew and St. Mark, and the Epistles to the Galatians, Ephesians, Philippians, Colossians, Thessalonians, Timothy, Titus, and Philemon. He also wrote many hymns in the language of Tahiti, some of them being translations from the Welsh. He kept a life-long correspondence in Welsh with his old friend, the Rev. John Hughes, Pontrobert. His sight had partially failed him for many years, and for the last nine or ten years of his life he was totally blind. Still, however, he continued to correspond with his friends in the old country in the old Welsh language, to accomplish which he wrote his letters on a slate, sentence by sentence, his step-daughter (who was unacquainted with Welsh) copying them *literatim* on paper afterwards. His laborious and useful life was brought to a peaceful end on the 19th of August, 1855, in the 84th year of his age, and the 55th of his missionary career.

DAVIES, MORRIS, was born at Pennant-tigi, in the parish of Mallwyd, in October, 1796. His father's name was Richard Morris, but in accordance with a custom which was then pretty general, he was named after his grandfather, Morris Davies. His mother was related to Dr. Owen Pughe, the eminent Welsh scholar. He had few educational advantages in early youth, but nevertheless soon showed a taste for literature, and before he was seventeen had composed several pieces of poetry and prose, chiefly of a religious character. About the year 1818 (being then 22 years of age) he became a pupil of Mr. William Owen, of Welshpool, in order to learn English more perfectly, and qualify himself for the office of a schoolmaster. In 1819 he opened a school at Pontrobert, but remained there about three months only, removing in January, 1820. to Llanfyllin, where he followed the same avocation until April, 1822. At this time he was a regular contributor, under the feigned name of " Maen " Llwyd," to " Goleuad Cymru," a Welsh periodical then published at Chester, his contributions including, among others, a series of letters on " Punctuation." From Llanfyllin he removed to his native parish, Mallwyd, where he kept a school until the close of 1823, and thence to Syston, in Leicestershire, where he undertook the charge of the National School, under the supervision of the Rev. Edward Morgan, to whom he gave valuable assistance in the preparation for the press of his " Life of the Rev. Thomas Charles, of Bala." In September, 1825, his health failing him, he returned to Wales, and having kept a school at Llanfair Caereinion for a short period, he again accepted an invitation in 1826 to re-open a school at Llanfyllin, where he remained until 1836. In 1826 he undertook the editorship of a little Penny Magazine, published by Mr. Richard Newell, for the use of Sabbath Schools, and from this time forth his literary labours were incessant. In 1836 he gave up school-keeping, and became confidential clerk to Mr. John Williams, of Vawnog (brother of the late Mr. David Williams, M.P.) a solicitor in extensive practice at Llanfyllin. In this capacity he remained with Mr. Williams and his successor until May, 1840, when he accompanied Mr. David Williams on his removal to Portmadoc, and in November of the same year again removed to the office of Messrs. Williams and Breese at Pwllheli, and on their removal subsequently to Portmadoc he accompanied them. In May, 1844, he undertook the charge of the British School at Portmadoc, and held that appointment for more than five years. In the autumn of 1849 he removed to Bangor, where he spent the remainder of his days, occupied for the most part as Clerk at the County Court Office, and with literary work. He lived to a green old age, and died peacefully on the 10th September, 1876, aged 80 years. He was buried at Glanadda Cemetery, near Bangor. Mr. Davies during his long life contributed many scores of articles and letters to the " Drysorfa," " Seren Gomer," " Gwladgarwr," Traethodydd," and other Welsh periodicals, as well as to the " Carnarvon and Denbigh Herald," " Goleuad," and other newspapers. The following are the titles of the principal articles from his pen which appeared in the " Traeth- "odydd," an ably-conducted Welsh Quarterly Magazine:— " Thieves of Time," " Philology," "Temperance," a review of "The Christian Year," " Various Peculiarities of the Welsh Language," " Welsh Proverbs," " The Blood of the Atonement," " Proverbs of the Seasons," three articles on "John Bunyan," a critical notice of "The Life of the Rev. J. Parry, Chester," " The Moral and Religious Condition of Wales at the beginning "of the Methodist Revival," " Welsh Psalmody," " Religious "Plays," "Observations on a Tract as to the Immorality of " Wales," " Epigrams," a series of able articles on " Hymn- "ology," and several reviews. He also wrote for the " Gwydd- "oniadur " (*Encyclopædia Cambrensis*), the biographical notices of the Revs. John Phillips, Rhys Pritchard ("The vicar of Llan- "dovery"), Michael Roberts, Daniel Rowlands, Llangeitho, and Morgan Rhys, and many other articles. He also translated for publication in Welsh the following works :—(1) *A Collection of Religious Anecdotes*; (2) *Questions and Answers concerning Prayer*: (3) *What is Presbyterianism?* by Dr. Hodge, America ; (4) *The Mysteries of the Bible*: A Lecture by Dr. M'Cosh ; (5) *A Treatise on the Lord's Supper*, by Dr. King ; and (6) *Scriptural Numismatics* (Rel. Tract Soc.) Besides these, he compiled and published (1) *Jeduthun*: a Collection of Sacred Tunes ; (2) *A Collection of Psalms and Hymns*, 1832, of which subsequent editions were published in 1835 and 1837 ; an American edition at Utica in 1846 ; and an improved edition under the title *Hosanna* at Carnarvon, 1860 ; (3) a small *Collection of Hymns* for the religious Tract Society, 1832; (4) *The Life of Ann Griffiths*, Denbigh, 1865 ; and (5) *The Life and Sermons of the Rev. D. Rowlands, Llangeitho*, 1876. He also edited the *Sermons of the Rev. Edward Morgan, Dyffryn*, 1873-75. His translation of Heber's Missionary Hymn into Welsh is very well known, and he was himself the composer of about 200 hymns, some of which are of great merit. He was an accom- plished musician, and the greatest authority of his day on Welsh Hymnology. In the autumn of 1875 a testimonial, towards which £188 19s. 6d. was subscribed, was presented to him as a recognition of his valuable services to Welsh literature His last work was a volume on the *Welsh Reformers*, published by the Religious Tract Society.

DAVIES, OLIVER, an eminent harpist. He was the prin- cipal harpist at the great Welshpool Eisteddfod in September, 1824, and at the Cymmrodorion Eisteddfod held in London May 6th, 1829, he is said to have "astonished the assembly with

" his masterly execution upon the pedal harp." We find him
again at another Eisteddfod held in London in 1831 delighting
all present with his playing of " Lady Owen's Delight," and
other airs.

DAVIES, Rev. RANDOLPH, or RANDLE, M.A., was
Vicar of Meifod from 1647 to about 1695. Little is known of
him personally beyond what may be gathered from the Register
of that parish. According to this he was married at Meifod
Church to Mary, daughter of the Rev. John Williams, in June,
1648. Of this marriage 13 children were baptised at the same
Church between 1649 and 1666. He was deprived of the living
of Meifod during the Commonwealth by the sequestrators, but
was again restored to it in 1660, when Charles II. came to the
throne. He had also been Rector of Aberhafesp, Llanymynech,
and Llanfechain. During his incumbency of Meifod Quakerism
and other forms of Nonconformity had made a considerable
schism in his flock, and as an endeavour to arrest the progress
of Dissent, he published in the year 1675 a tract of 237 pages,
12mo. in excellent Welsh, with a dedication of five pages in the
same language to Edwar. Vaughan, Esq., of Llwydiarth. It
has two title-pages—Welsh and English. The first, in English,
is as follows :—" A Tryall of the Spirits, or a discovery of False
" Prophets, and a Caveat to beware of them ; or a short Treatise
" on 1 John IV., 1. Wherein is discovered, by the light of
" God's Word, expounded by antiquity, that several doctrines of
" the Papists, Presbyterians, Independents and Quakers, are
" disagreeable to the Holy Scripture, and carefully to be avoided
" by every man that loves the salvation of his soul.—Pro
" Ecclesia clamitant, et contra Ecclesiam dimicant. Cypr."
There is a tradition preserved in the parish that this Vicar's wife
had a sister living at Pentrego, and that one Sunday morning
they met at Pentreparog to cross each other's paths at right
angles, one due South towards Church, the other due west
towards the Friends' Meeting house at Coed Cowryd, near
Dolobran. After a few words of salutation had passed, the
Vicar's wife said, " If you had grace, my dear sister, you would
" come with me." A reply was instantly given, " If thou had'st
" grace thou would'st come with me." And so, both orthodox in
their own minds, they departed towards their respective places
of worship. The Register thus certifies the Vicar's burial :—
" Dom. Ranulphus Davies, Cler, de Peniarth Sepultus, 25º Feb.,
" 1695." By his will he, among other bequests, gave to his
daughter, Prudence Davies, £30 and one heifer " on condition
" she shall forsake the Quakers' meetings and resort constantly
" to some parish church for divine service and the participation
" of the blessed sacrament of the Lord's Supper. . . . If
" my daughter Prudence shall be so imprudent as to marry
" Joseph Davies the smith [probably a co-religionist] that lives
" in the village of Myfod, then I revoke all former legacies to
" her, and she shall have only one shilling paid to her by my
" executor."

DAVIES, RICHARD (the Quaker) was born in the year 1635, in the town of Welshpool, of honest parents, having a small estate there. He was brought up in the Church of England, but when quite a youth (about 12 or 13 years of age) he joined the Independents. Some time afterwards he was apprenticed with one of that sect, namely, Evan Jones, a felt-maker (hatter), in the parish of Llanfair. About the year 1657 he joined the Quakers, and in about a year afterwards went to London, and settled down to his trade of feltmaker. Here he met with his future wife in the manner thus quaintly described by himself :—

"One time as I was at Horselydown Meeting in Southwark, I heard a woman Friend open her mouth by way of testimony against an evil ranting spirit that did oppose Friends much in those days. It came to me from the Lord that that woman was to be my wife and to go with me to the country and to be an helpmeet for me. After meeting I drew somewhat near to her but spoke nothing nor took any acquaintance with her, nor did I know when or where I should see her again. I was very willing to let the Lord order it as it seemed best to himself and therein I was easy; and in time the Lord brought us acquainted one with another and she confessed that she had some sight of the same thing that I had seen concerning her. So after some time we parted, and I was freely resigned to the will of God; and when we came together again I told her, if the Lord did order her to be my wife, she must come with me to a strange country where there were no Friends but what God in time might call and gather to himself. Upon a little consideration she said if the Lord should order it so she must go with her husband though it were to the wilderness; and being somewhat sensible of the workings of God upon her spirit in this matter, she was willing to condescend in her mind to what he wrought in her. But by hearkening to one who had not well weighed the matter, she became disobedient to what God had revealed to her, which brought great sorrow and trouble upon her. I went to see her in this poor condition, and I rested satisfied with the will of God in this concern being freely resigned if the Lord had wrought the same thing in her as was in me to receive her as His gift to me, and after some time, we waiting upon the Lord together, she arose and declared before me and the other Friend who had begot doubts and reasonings in her mind that in the name and power of God she consented to be my wife, and to go along with me whither the Lord should order us; and I said, In the fear of the Lord I receive thee as the gift of God unto me. So I rested satisfied in the will of God for a farther accomplishment of it. Under a weighty consideration which way to take each other in marriage we concluded to lay our proceedings before our elders and especially our ancient Friend George Fox; (people in those days were married by a Priest, or before a Justice) and I told G. Fox we thought to take each other in a public Meeting, so he desired the Lord to be with us. And when we saw our clearness in the Lord, we went to the Snail Meeting, in Tower Street, London, in the morning; and in the afternoon to Horselydown, Southwark, and in that Meeting, being the 26th of the fourth month 1659, in the presence of God and that assembly we took each other to be man and wife."

Soon afterwards he and his wife came down into Wales and settled at Welshpool, but it was not long before he was taken before the High Sheriff (Col. Mostyn) and the Magistrates, and required to take the oath of allegiance and supremacy to the King, Charles II., who had just been restored. This he declined to do, and they good-humouredly allowed him to go without taking it. Shortly afterwards, however, a troop of horsemen came to take him to Montgomery Gaol, which was then full of Presbyterians, Independents, and Baptists, but they went away without him on his undertaking to be at the prison next morning, which undertaking he fulfilled. He remained in prison about a fortnight. Having some months afterwards gone to attend a Meeting at Edgemont, near Wem, he and about 26 others were taken prisoners and sent to Shrewsbury Gaol. The account he gives of prison life in those days is very curious. He was discharged at the next Assizes. After this he travelled much throughout England and Wales visiting Friends, and preaching their peculiar doctrines with great success for more than 45 years. In his autobiography he has left us a curious and interesting account of his wanderings, labours, and sufferings, and of those of some of his friends, and the great hardships which they suffered for conscience sake under the oppressive laws then in force. His wife died on the 1st of March, 1705, and he himself on the 22nd January, 1707-8, in the seventy-third year of his age, at his own house at Cloddia-cochion, near Welshpool. On the 25th of the same month he was interred near his wife's grave in the Friends' burial ground there. Mr. Davies himself brought down the account of his life and travels to the year 1702, and the continuation of it with the account of his death was written by his daughter Tace Endon and others. The whole was published soon afterwards under the title of *An Account of the Convincement, Exercises, Services, and Travels of that ancient servant of the Lord, Richard Davies, with some relations of ancient Friends and the spreading of truth in North Wales, &c.*—a valuable as well as useful contribution to Montgomeryshire history. A second edition appeared in 1765, a third in 1771, and several other editions have since followed. A Welsh translation was also published in 1840 by Hughes, London. Quakerism is now as extinct in Montgomeryshire as Druidism. The old Meeting house at Dolobran and a few burial grounds in out-of-the-way spots are alone the touching memorials of a sect, numbering at one time some hundreds of adherents, often wrong-headed and bigoted, but always conscientious, and who shrank not from fines, imprisonment, or even certain death for conscience sake.

DAVIES, RICHARD, better known by his bardic name *Mynyddog*, was born on the 10th January, 1833, at Dol-lydan, a farm in the parish of Llanbrynmair, and was baptized on the 8th of the following month by the Rev. John Roberts. While he was yet young, his father (Mr. Daniel Davies) removed to Fron, a larger farm in the same parish, where Mynyddog lived until shortly after his marriage. He began early to show considerable poetic talent, contributing frequently to the *Cronicl* and other Welsh magazines, and winning prizes for compositions at most of the local literary meetings. Some of those compositions are among his best. It was, I believe, at an Eisteddfod held at Dinas Mawddwy in August, 1855, that he first assumed the *nom de plume* of "Mynyddog," by which he became afterwards so widely known. Having received no better education than that of an ordinary Welsh farmer's son, he, while assisting his parents in agricultural pursuits, devoted his leisure time to mental improvement and the cultivation of music and poetry. His fame rapidly spread until he became in the course of a few years one of the most popular Welsh song writers, and his name a household word among his countrymen in all parts of the world. He also acquired the reputation of being an excellent critic and conductor at literary meetings and Eisteddfodau. For the last ten years of his life, indeed, his services were eagerly sought and considered almost indispensable at every meeting of the kind among his countrymen. In this capacity he was unrivalled, displaying as he usually did so much geniality and good humour, combined with much ability and such rare tact, as to ensure the perfect and complete success of all the meetings presided over by him. He possessed a commanding stature, a powerful voice, a pleasing countenance, a cool brain and a ready tongue, and he moved and spoke on the platform as one having authority. His wit was electric, knew no bitterness, and scorned the aid of coarseness. Mynyddog was also well-known to his countrymen as a constant correspondent and writer for many years in the Welsh newspaper and periodical press upon topics of the day, under the signatures of "Y dyn a'r baich drain" (The man with the load of thorns); "Rhywun" (Somebody), &c., his contributions being invariably distinguished for point, ability, and a genial kind of humour peculiar to himself. The last Eisteddfod at which Mynyddog acted as conductor was that held at Wrexham in August, 1876. It became evident to his friends at this time that his health was beginning to fail. Immediately after this Eisteddfod he, accompanied by his wife, proceeded to America at the urgent invitation of his countrymen there, and in the hope, also, that the voyage and a thorough change would tend to restore his health. The contrary, however, proved to be the case. The excitement and fatigue of the voyage greatly aggravated the painful disease from which he was suffering (induration of the stomach), and he was compelled to bring his tour hastily to a close and return home. The best advice was obtained, and all that medical skill and knowledge could devise or suggest was tried, but in vain. After a lingering illness he died at his own residence, Bronygân, Cemmes, on the 14th July, 1877, in the 45th year of his age. His death called forth many manifestations of sorrow on the part of his countrymen, hundreds of whom, including many from different parts of Wales and from English towns, followed his remains to the grave. He was buried on the 19th July at the burial-place attached to the Old Independent Chapel, Llanbrynmair. Mynyddog was married on the 25th September, 1871, to Ann Elizabeth, daughter of the late Aaron Francis, of Rhyl, who survived him, and subsequently married Mr. D. Emlyn Evans. He left no issue. To reciprocate in some degree the kindness and affectionate appreciation always shewn towards him by the Welsh people, and to show his desire to encourage and assist his poor fellow-countrymen in gaining a better knowledge of Welsh, English, and Music, Mynyddog, by his will, bequeathed £300 free of legacy duty to be invested after his wife's death, " for providing " a Scholarship at the University College of Wales, tenable for " three years (if the successful candidate should so long remain " at the College), to be awarded to the most successful candidate " upon an examination in the English and Welsh languages and " in Music, preference being given to natives of Montgomery- " shire, and the Scholarship to be limited to natives of Wales." The published works of Mynyddog consist of three small volumes of poetry, namely, *Caneuon* (Songs), Wrexham, 1866; *Ail Gynyg* (Second Attempt), Wrexham, 1870; and *Trydydd Cynyg* (Third Attempt), Utica, 1877, and Wrexham, 1877. Another volume, consisting of some of his earlier writings, which have not hitherto appeared in a collected form, and of compositions by him during his last illness, was intended to be published soon after his death, but has not yet appeared. His works are distinguished, as he himself was, by geniality, humour combined with frequent touches of deep pathos, sterling common sense rather than a lofty imagination, and homeliness of expres- sion rather than polished language. In these respects he greatly resembled Burns, while, unlike the Scottish poet, he was ever careful to refrain from indulging in any thought or expres- sion that might be considered coarse, rude or immoral. Some of his songs will long live in the memory of his countrymen.

DAVIES, THOMAS, Governor-General of the English Colonies on the western coast of Africa. Beyond this little is known of him. Probably he was a native of Welshpool. In 1662 he presented to Welshpool Church a golden chalice (still carefully preserved there) made of Guinea gold, in token of his gratitude to God for his preservation in that pestilential climate. It bears the following Latin inscription :—

" Thomas Davies Anglorum in Africae plagâ occidentali Procurator generalis ob vitam multifariâ Dei misericordiâ ibidem conservatam calicem hunc è purissimo auro Guiniano conflatum Dei honori et ecclesiae de Welshpoole ministerio perpetuo sacrum voluit. A quo usu S.S. si quis facinorosus eundem Calicem in posterum alienaret (quod avertat Deus) Dei vindicis supremo tribunali paenas luat. Cal Apr. IX MDCLXII."

The chalice weighs between 30 and 31 ounces. It appears to be of pure gold, and is said to be worth about £168. A shield of arms is engraved upon it bearing the following charges :—" A " lion passant between three fleurs de lis," and surrounded by a plume of feathers.

DAVIES, THOMAS, a poet who flourished about the beginning of the last century, several of whose compositions are published in the "Blodeugerdd" and other collections of that period, among them being *Ystori 'r Crys Gwaedlyd*. He is described as "Thomas Davies o Sir Drefaldwyn," which is all I have been able to ascertain of his history.

DAVIES, REV. WALTER, M.A., (*Gwallter Mechain*), one of the most eminent of the Welsh scholars, antiquaries, and poets of his day, was born of humble parents at a cottage called Wern, in the parish of Llanfechain, on the 15th July, 1761, being one of seven children. In early life he learned and for some time followed the trade of a cooper, but although his educational advantages were few and scanty, he devoted every spare moment and made the best use of every means within his reach for self-improvement. He began to write poetry very creditably before he was twenty years old. He attended and competed successfully at several Eisteddfodau held at Llangollen, Corwen, and other places before he was thirty, winning victories over poets of such renown as Dafydd Ddu Eryri, Twm o'r Nant, and Jonathan Hughes. In 1790 he won the Gwyneddigion Prize at an Eisteddfod held at St. Asaph for a Welsh essay on "Liberty." Of this he said a month or two before he died that having then looked over it he did not think he could improve upon it. His studious character and literary merit becoming known, and also his desire to enter into holy orders, he was enabled through the influence and with the assistance of some gentlemen of wealth to enter the University of Oxford. In the early part of 1792 he accordingly became a member of St. Alban's Hall, which he afterwards left for All Souls' College. The same year he became sub-curator of the Ashmolean Museum. He remained at Oxford, hard at work, during all the vacations as well as in term time for nearly four years, at the expiration of which, namely, in the autumn of 1795, he took his B.A. degree. In 1803 he took his M.A. degree as a member of Trinity College, Cambridge. He obtained deacon's orders and the curacy of Meifod from Bishop Bagot, December 6th, 1795. and was ordained priest on the 25th September, 1796. In 1799 Lord Mostyn bestowed upon him the perpetual curacy of Yspytty Ifan, and Bishop Horsley presented him with the Rectory of Llanwyddelan, May the 20th, 1803. This he resigned on being promoted by Bishop Cleaver on July 7th, 1807, to the Rectory of the adjoining parish of Manafon, where he dwelt for thirty years, that is to say until he was presented (Nov. 18th, 1837) by Bishop Carey with the living of Llanrhaiadr Mochnant, where afterwards he resided up to his death. His prize and other compositions during the above period were so numerous that space will not allow us to specify them all. Suffice it to say that he was a perfect master of the Welsh metres, and his lyrical compositions are, many of them, very beautiful. His prose writings are also no less remarkable for the clearness and liveliness of his style than for the extent and accuracy of information, and the soundness of judgment which they exhibit. Being an excellent critic, his services as adjudicator at Eisteddfodau were in great request during many years. He published in his lifetime the following works, some of them being the fruit of much labour and research :—

1. *Diwygiad neu Ddinystr : wedi ei dynnu allan o lyfr Saesonaeg a elwir Reform or Ruin; a'i gymhwyso at ddealltwriacth y Cymry.*—Oswestry, 1798, 16 mo.

2. *Eglur Olygiad o'r Grefydd Gristionogol, ac o Hanesiaeth (Histori) cyn belled ag g perthyn i ddechreuad Cristionogaeth, ac i'w chynyddiad hyd yr amser presennol. Newydd ei gyfieithu allan o waith Saesnaeg Thomas Gisborne, A.M.*—Wrexham, 1801, 8 vo. This work (*A clear view of the Christian Religion*) was translated into Welsh at the request of the Bishop of St. Asaph and the clergy of that diocese. It consists of 258 pages, besides an introductory preface of 30 pages by the translator. This translation as well as the preceding was published anonymously.

3. *A general view of the Agriculture and Domestic Economy of North Wales.* Drawn up and published by order of the Board of Agriculture and Internal Improvement, London, 1813, 8vo.

4. *A general view of the Agriculture and Domestic Economy of South Wales.* Drawn up for the consideration of the Board of Agriculture and Internal Improvement, 2 vols., London, 1814, 8vo.

5. *Anerch Caredig at y Diwyd a'r Llafurus ar Fanteision neu Fuddioldeb Banciau Cynhilo.* A translation of a small English tract on the advantages and benefits of Savings Banks.—Llanfyllin, 1817.

6. *Eos Ceiriog, sef Casgliad o ber Ganiadau Huw Morris; yn ddau Lyfr : o Gynnulliad a Diwygiad W.D.* Wrexham, 1823, 8vo.

7. *Gwaith Lewys Glyn Cothi.* The poetical works of Lewys Glyn Cothi, a celebrated bard who flourished in the reigns of Henry VI., Edward IV., Richard III., and Henry VII. Oxford 1837, 8vo. This was edited and annotated by him in conjunction with the Rev. John Jones (Tegid) for the Cymmrodorion Society.

8. A second edition, edited by him, of Capt. W. Middleton's Welsh metrical version of *The Psalms*, Llanfair Caereinion, 1827, 12mo.

The above, however, represent but a small portion of Mr· Davies's labours. He edited the "Gwyliedydd" for some years, and contributed extensively to *Yorke's Royal Tribes, Carlisle's Topographical Dictionary of Wales, Owen and Blakeway's History of Shrewsbury, Lewis's Topographical Dictionary, Bingley's Tour, The Myvyrian Archaiology, The Greal* and *Mabinogion;* and the *Cambro Briton, Cambrian Register* and *Cambrian Quarterly Magazine* contain many of his productions, besides those bearing his name. Indeed few books relating to Wales and its borders appeared during the first half of the present century without receiving the benefit of his valuable aid. Mr. Davies was married October 15th, 1799, to Mary, widow of Rice Price, Esq., of Rhos-bryn-bwa, Meifod, by whom he had four children : Cecil Leland and Amelia Cecilia (both of whom died in infancy), the Rev. Walter Cecil Davies, M.A., and Jane. Mrs. Davies died in January, 1844. Mr. Davies retained his mental energy and the full possession of his powers to extreme old age. It is said that in his 89th year he wrote a long poem on the chair subject at the Aberffraw Eisteddfod (" Awdl ar y Greadigaeth ") but did not send it for

D

competition. He died, after a brief illness of two days, on the 5th December, 1849, in his 89th year, at Llanrhaiadr, where also he was buried. In 1868 his miscellaneous works and letters were published in three vols., edited by the Rev. D. Silvan Evans, and form a valuable addition to Welsh literature.

DEVEREUX, GEORGE, was the son of Sir George Devereux, Knt., of Sheldon Hall, in the county of Warwick, by his wife Blanche, daughter and eventual heiress of John Ridge, of Ridge, in the parish of Chirbury, and Catherine, daughter of Humphrey Lloyd, of Great Hem, Forden. He acquired the estate of Vaynor, by marriage with Bridget, sole daughter and heiress of Arthur Price, of Vaynor, and was the first of his family who settled in Montgomeryshire. He was elected M.P. for Montgomery Borough on the 6th April, 1647 (being described as of Nantcribba), and supported the Parliament against the King. He was one of "the gentlemen, ministers, "and well affected of the County of Montgomery," who signed the "Resolutions and Engagements" to assist the Parliament to suppress the insurrection, dated 20th May, 1648—(see *Perfect Diurnall*, No. 252). In 1654 we find him litigating at the Assizes with respect to his succession to the Vaynor estate. He was sheriff in 1658 and 1673, and was the ancestor of the present Viscount Hereford.

DEVEREUX, PRICE, of Vaynor, grandson of the foregoing George Devereux, was member of Parliament for Montgomery Borough from 1689 to 1700, when, on the death of Edward Devereux, eighth Viscount Hereford, he, as the nearest heir male, succeeded to the title. He died in October, 1740, and was interred at Berriew on the 14th of the same month.

DEVEREUX, PRICE, his son, represented the County of Montgomery in Parliament from 1718 to 1740, when he succeeded his father as 10th Viscount Hereford. Upon his death in 1750, and failure of male issue, the title reverted to Edward, grandson of Vaughan Devereux, second son of the above-named George Devereux (baptized 25th Sept., 1712, at Berriew), who took his seat in the House of Peers, 3rd April, 1750, and married Catherine, daughter of Richard Mytton, Esquire, of Garth.

DOVASTON, MILWARD EDWARD, was born at Vyrnwy Bank, Llanymynech, in the year 1800. He was educated at Oswestry Grammar School, and afterwards proceeded to the Middlesex Hospital to be trained as a surgeon. Having duly qualified, he practised his profession with success for many years in his native village. He was an accomplished ornithologist, botanist, and antiquary; a fair musician, and poet; and was greatly esteemed for his kindness and geniality. He died at Llandrinio (where his later years had been spent) in 1852, deeply lamented by a large circle of friends and acquaintances, and was buried at Llanymynech.

DWNN, GRUFFYDD, HENRY, AND HUW, were poets who flourished between 1550 and 1600, and were probably near relatives of Lewys Dwnn, the celebrated herald, genealogist and poet.

DWNN, JAMES, was a poet who flourished in the early part of the 17th century. Lewys Dwnn had a son of that name. I have seen in MS. an ode to him by Lewis ab Dafydd ab Rhys, of Barhedyn, Darowen, dated in 1605.

DWNN, LEWYS, an eminent poet, historian, herald, and genealogist of the 16th century, was a native of Montgomery-shire, and for some time lived at Garth Gellin (probably Glan-bechan in that township), in Bettws Cedewain. He is sometimes described as "of Bettws and Berriew"; also as "of Welshpool," where, probably, he spent some of the latter years of his life. The Dwnn family were originally settled at Kidwelly, in South Wales, but David, third son of Meredydd Dwnn, grandson of Gruffydd Gethin (gentleman usher to King John), quitted Kidwelly for Montgomeryshire in consequence of being appointed steward to the Right Honourable Edward Charlton, Lord Powys, and married Angharad, daughter and co-heiress of Dackws Lloyd, of Cefn-y-Gwestydd, Llanllwch-aiarn, a descendant of Tryhaiarn, Lord of Garthmûl. It appears that his nephews, the sons of his eldest brother Gruffydd, in an affray, killed the Mayor of Kidwelly, and fled to him (David Dwnn) for protection, which his influence and position enabled him to give them. Mr. Joseph Morris, of Shrewsbury, in a letter to the *Cam. Quar. Mag.*, vol. IV., p. 390, furnishes a pedigree of the poet, which differs very materially from that given by the learned editor of the *Visitations*, in the intro-duction to the latter. From this pedigree, as well as from a statement by Ieuan Brechfa, there referred to, it would appear that David Dwnn *himself* killed the Mayor, fled to Powys, and became steward to Baron Powys. This, however, does not agree with Lewys Dwnn's account, that the David Dwnn, who, with his brothers, killed the Mayor, was one of the sons of *Gruffydd* Dwnn, and, therefore a nephew of the first-named David Dwnn. Capt. Rhys Goch Dwnn (an officer who served at Tournay, in France) was the great-great-grandson in a direct line of this David Dwnn. He is described as of Cefn-y-Gwestydd, and married Gwenllian, co-heir of Ieuan ab David, by whom he had six daughters and one son. The sixth daughter, Catherine, became the wife of Rhys ap Owain, and the mother by him of the subject of this notice, their sole issue, who took his mother's family surname. The exact date of the poet's birth is not known—probably it was before 1550. Indeed, very little is known of his private life. He, himself, gives the following outline of his education :—" And I, Lewis " Dwnn, poet, am a pupil of Owain Gwynedd's, and have been " a pupil of William Lleyn, whose pedigree tables I have com-" mitted to memory ; and I was previously the pupil of Hywel "ab Syr Matthew, many of whose books I obtained." Lewys Dwnn having been introduced and strongly recommended to Clarencieux and Norroy kings of arms as best qualified to make, as their deputy, a visitation of Wales, a patent was granted to him for that purpose on 3rd February, 1585, in which he is instructed " to record, register, and make entrances of all "discentes, mariages, funeralles, and obites of the knightes, "esquires, and gentlemen inhabitinge within the said princi-"palitie or the dominions and lordships marchers thereof; "omittinge all highe lynes dedvced from farre aboue all "memorie, which for great part ar found to be coniecturall, "vnlesse evidences, histories or matter of good credict be showed "for approbation thereof." The document (a curious one) gives other very judicious directions for the proper performance of his duties by the Deputy Herald. Mr. Joseph Morris says in the letter already quoted that he is enabled, from evidence in his possession, to state

"That Lewis Dwnn was related to the celebrated Mr. Francis Thynne, the herald, who was of the ancient family of that name, seated at Cause Castle, in this county (Salop), but close to the border of Montgomery-shire, and so much distinguished in the course of Henry VIII. and Queen Elizabeth, and from the then representative of which the present Marquis of Bath is lineally descended";

and adds that he thinks it

"very probable that to his connection with his contemporary, Francis Thynne, the herald, and the other more distinguished and courtly members of the Thynne family, Lewys Dwnn owed his appointment as deputy herald."

His labours in collecting pedigrees extended from the date of his patent until at least 1613--several of them bear that date— and probably some years later. Lewys Dwnn's experiences in making his visitations were not always of the most agreeable kind. In an " Address to the Reader," of which the following is a translation, he pathetically complains of the treatment to which he was subjected :—

"To you, courteous gentlemen readers,—I make it known that I have at all times had a predilection for this science; but I request of you, wise and learned readers, that you will not form your judgment of me by the appearance of my writing, for no one can go beyond his abilities. Besides, I wished that my work should be correct, though it be obscure and difficult to understand. It is a great accomplishment before God and man to turn darkness into light, and falsehood into truth, without any excuse for partiality. I assure you, gentlemen, had I been a person wealthy in gold, silver, land, or living stock, I would have engaged a professional copyist, before and after the occasion, for a salary, who should be a learned man that could write a fair hand easy to read in the manner I wished; but to the true God do I give thanks and praises day and night for having been able to do as I have done. Two obstruc-tions prevented my books being written fairly and elegantly; first, the hurry of some of the gentry to leave home, allowing me but a very limited time to do even a little; and next, the inhospitable dispositions of some of the gentlemen, who would neither afford me meat nor lodgings merely for working, but required money; and being far from the liberal or either a good or bad public house, I was compelled to stay a couple of hours after dinner or supper; and having at last taken down everything as they wished, I had to depart, and wend my way to the liberal, if such could be found, if not, to a tavern, as best I could. Sometimes my companions were angry with me for bearing on my back the lineage of mischievous misers; nevertheless God put in my breast hope that such a wretch who would neither give me lodgings nor any other gift would have either a liberal son or daughter. Lo, behold! true is the proverb : 'A sword will not affect the miser, while the benevolent will not lose his praise.' This made me utter the following stanzas on hope in God. [Here follow three Welsh Englynion, signed ' L. Dwnn, 1606.'] Farewell, kind reader, at this time; I could never finish giving full praise to the liberal, and enough of ill fame to the wicked miser."

The fruits of Lewys Dwnn's labours as Deputy Herald remained in MS. until 1846, when they were published by the Welsh MSS. Society in two splendid folio volumes from the Llandovery press, under the able editorship of the late Sir Samuel Rush Meyrick, and with numerous explanatory notes, nearly all of them by the late W. W. E. Wynne, Esq. The proofs of the notes unfortunately were not sent to Mr. Wynne for correction, so that he is not responsible for some errors that appear in them. The original MS. of the Visitation of the three Counties "uwch Conwy" in Lewys Dwnn's autograph is amongst the Peniarth MSS. (*not* the Hengwrt MSS.) at Peniarth. These volumes contain the pedigrees of the principal families of Wales. They are entitled:—*The Heraldic Visitations of Wales and the Marches, in the time of Queen Elizabeth, by Lewis Dwnn, Deputy Herald at Arms, from such original Manuscripts as still exist. Edited by Sir Samuel R. Meyrick, K.H., L.L.D., F.S.A., F.R.S., &c., with illustrations and numerous notes for the advantage of the English as well as the Welsh reader.* Many accomplished genealogists have borne testimony to the singular accuracy as well as the enormous labour and research shewn in these pedigrees. But the author was also an excellent poet, and poetical preceptor to the Right Rev. Dr. Richard Davies, Bishop of St. David's, and of Henry Salusbury, Esq. *Mont. Coll.* VIII., p. 123, contains a list from the Hengwrt MS. 176 at Peniarth of odes in his autograph, and mostly composed by him—one of these is dated 1616—the latest date we have of anything written by him. Lewys Dwnn married Als or Alice, daughter and coheiress of Meredydd ab David ab John ab Meredydd of Vaenor, by whom he had four sons, James, Edward, Thomas, and Charles, and two daughters, Mary and Elizabeth. Hitherto registers, manor rolls, and other documents have been searched in vain for the date of his death. It may, however, be supposed to have taken place soon after the year 1616, that being, as already stated, the latest date yet found of anything written by him.

DWNN, OWAIN, a bard, harpist, and Captain of a regiment of cavalry, who distinguished himself in Ireland about the year 1460, and is said to have been Lord Lieutenant there afterwards.

"A Chadpen llawen y llu,
Eu telyn a'u bardd teulu."
(The merry captain of the host,
Their harpist and family bard).

He is supposed to have been a member of the family to which later on the above-named Lewys Dwnn belonged.

DYFNIG, a saint of the early part of the sixth century, of whom nothing is known beyond the record in *Bonedd y Saint* (*Myr. Arch.*): "Ust and Dyfnig, the saints in Llanwrin in "Cyfeiliog who came to this island with Cadfan." Llanwrin Church, of which it thus appears he was joint founder, was afterwards re-dedicated to St. Gwriu, a seventh century saint. Dyfnig is also mentioned among the saints in an Ode to King Henry VII., printed in the Iolo MSS.

EDWARDS, Rev. GRIFFITH, M.A., F.R.Hist.S. (*Gutyn Padarn*), was a native of Llanberis, Carnarvonshire, where he was born 1st September, 1812. His father, William Edwards, was a poet well known by his bardic name, *Gwilym Padarn*, though he was but a quarryman. This occupation, after receiving a very scanty elementary education in the village school, the son pursued for some time. He, however, sought diligently after knowledge by all the means he could obtain, and was fortunate enough to receive some classical instruction from the Rev. P. B. Williams, of Llanrug, a well-known scholar and antiquary. This enabled him to enter Trinity College, Dublin, where he took his B.A. degree in 1843, and proceeded to his M.A. in 1846. Long before this, as early as 1831, he had commenced to write to the *Gwyliedydd* a series of able articles. In 1832 he was awarded the prize at the Beaumaris Eisteddfod for the best *Elegy to the Memory of the Rev. John Jenkins of Kerry*, and received it (a silver medal) from the hands of the Princess Victoria, now the Queen, who, with her mother, the Duchess of Kent, was present. In 1836 he gained a prize at the Cardiff Eisteddfod for a poem on *The Princess Victoria*; in 1840, a prize at the Liverpool Eisteddfod for an *Elegy on Sir W. W. Wynn*; in 1846, a silver medal at Bala for an *Elegy on Lady Harriet Wynn*; and a prize at Rhuddlan Eisteddfod in 1849. This was his last competition. All the above-named compositions were, of course, in Welsh. His services were in great request as an adjudicator at various Eisteddfodau, for besides being himself a good poet he was considered an excellent critic, who always discharged his duties with ability, impartiality, and general satisfaction. Besides his contributions to the old *Gwyliedydd* already referred to, he also wrote occasionally both poetry and prose to the *Gwladgarwr*, *Traethodydd*, *Haul*, and other Welsh periodicals, and for some time edited a weekly paper published at Mold, called *Y Protestant*. He published a collection of his own poetical works under the title, *Gwaith Prydyddawl Gutyn Padarn* in 1846; a volume of thirty *Sermons* in 1854; a translation of *Easy Lessons for Sunday*

Schools; and the works of his friend the Rev. John Blackwell, under the title *Ceinion Alun*, with an interesting memoir by himself. He began his ministerial career in the Church by becoming curate of Llangollen, where he remained from 1843 until 1849. He then accepted the incumbency of Minera, near Wrexham, and in 1863 was appointed to the Rectory of Llangadfan, where he laboured for nearly 20 years. During his stay at Llangadfan he wrote admirable parochial histories of Llangadfan, Garthbeibio, and Llanerfyl for the *Montgomeryshire Collections*. He was also elected a Fellow of the Royal Historical Society. A few months before his death he, in consequence of failing health and the infirmities of age, resigned his cure, and went to reside at Welshpool, where he died on the 29th January, 1893, in his 81st year. He was never married.

EDWARDS, JOHN, parish clerk of Manafon about 1740, was a poet who wrote Englynion and Carols, some of which were printed in the almanacks then annually published by his friend and neighbour Evan Davies (*Philomath*), and by William Howel, of Llanidloes.

EDWARDS, Sir JOHN, Bart., was the son of John Edwards, Esq., of Greenfields (now called Plâs Machynlleth), an attorney and solicitor, by Cornelia, only surviving child and heir of Richard Owen, Esquire, of Garth, near Llanidloes (Sheriff in 1760). John Edwards was the third son of Lewis Edwards, Esq., of Talgarth, and traced his descent from Llewelyn ab Iorwerth, prince of North Wales. The subject of this notice was born on the 15th January, 1770, and succeeded to the family estates upon the death of his father on the 3rd April, 1789. On the 28th of January, 1792, he married Catherine, eldest daughter and co-heiress of Col. T. Browne, of Mellington Hall, by whom he had no issue. On the 7th of December, 1825, he married secondly Harriet, daughter of the Rev. Charles Johnson and widow of John Owen Herbert, Esq , of Dolforgan, who had died in 1824, leaving Harriet Avarina Herbert, his only daughter and heiress. By this marriage he had an only daughter, Mary Cornelia, who was born November 13th, 1828, and in 1846 married George Henry Robert Charles William Vane Tempest, Viscount Seaham (eldest son, by his second wife, of Charles William, third Marquess of Londonderry), who, on his father's death in 1854, succeeded to the peerage (by special limitation) as second Earl Vane, and in 1872 succeeded his half-brother, who then died, as fifth Marquess of Londonderry, † Mr. Edwards was a lieutenant-colonel of the

---

† Note.—George Henry Robert Charles William, 5th Marquess of Londonderry, died 5th November, 1884, aged 63, leaving his wife, two sons, and a daughter surviving. His eldest son, the sixth and present Marquess of Londonderry, became Lord-Lieutenant of Ireland in August, 1886, and held that high office for about three years. He is a K.G.

Volunteers and local militia of the Western Division of Montgomeryshire, who were for some time quartered at Machynlleth.
In 1818 he served the office of Sheriff for the County, having
previously served the same office for Merionethshire in 1805.
At the General Election of the first Parliament after the passing
of the Reform Act of 1832 Mr. Edwards became a candidate in
the Liberal interest for the Montgomery Contributory Boroughs,
and was opposed by David Pugh, Esq., of Llanerchydol. Both
parties had been busy canvassing for nearly two years, and
political feeling ran very high. The election at last came off in
December, 1832, when Mr. Pugh was declared to have obtained
a small majority of votes, the numbers being—For Mr. Pugh,
335; Edwards, 321. The gallant Colonel was not satisfied,
however, with this decision, and shortly afterwards a petition,
signed by Edward Jones, of Rock Cottage, gentleman, and
Thomas Owen, of Vaynor, was presented against Mr. Pugh's
return, and claiming a scrutiny of the votes. The petition was
heard in the following April before a Committee of the House
of Commons, the trial lasting about a week, at the close of
which the Committee reported that Mr. Pugh had not been duly
elected, and the seat was declared vacant. The consequence was
that another contested election took place immediately, the
Conservative candidate being Mr. Panton Corbett (Mr. Pugh
having become disqualified by the decision of the Committee),
and Colonel Edwards was this time returned by a majority
of 10, the numbers being—Edwards, 331; Corbett, 321. The
Conservatives, however, petitioned against his return, but the
petition fell through on a technical point, and Colonel Edwards
retained his seat. At the election of 1835 he was again opposed
by Mr. Panton Corbett, whom he again defeated by an enlarged
majority. At the General Election of 1837 (upon the accession
of Queen Victoria) he was returned unopposed. As a reward
for his services in the Liberal cause a Baronetcy was conferred
upon him in the following year (1838), his title being, "Sir
John Edwards, of Garth, in the parish of Llanidloes, in the
County of Montgomery." The patent is dated 9th August,
1838, and the following arms were granted to the new baronet:—
Arms: Quarterly; first and fourth, quarterly gules and or, a
fesse between four lions passant guardant all counterchanged,
for EDWARDS; second and third sable on a fesse, between a lion
rampant, and a fleur de lis in base or, three snakes entwined
proper, for OWEN. *Crest*: A lion passant guardant per pale,
or, and gules, the dexter forepaw re'ting on an inescocheon of
the last, charged with a nag's head, arg. *Motto*: "Y Gwir yn
erbyn y byd" (The truth against the world). At the General
Election of 1841, Sir John Edwards was again called upon to
fight for his seat, his opponent being the Hon. Hugh
Cholmondeley, afterwards Baron Delamere, who defeated him.
During his Parliamentary career Sir John zealously supported
and voted for all the great measures of civil and religious
reform brought forward during that period by the Liberal

Governments of Earl Grey and Lord Melbourne, and actively exerted himself in promoting the local interests of his constituents. After his retirement from Parliamentary life a magnificent piece of plate, consisting of a candelabrum nearly three feet high, and weighing nearly six hundred ounces, was purchased by public subscription among Sir John's constituents for presentation to him in acknowledgment of his plucky fights (which it is said cost him over £20,000) for the "emancipation" of the Montgomery Boroughs, and of his other great public services. The following inscription in English and Welsh was engraved on the candelabrum :—

"A.D., 18 2. Presented to Sir John Edwards, Bart., of Greenfields, the first representative of popular opinions in the Montgomeryshire Boroughs, after the passing of the Reform Act, by his friends and constituents as a Memorial of their grateful acknowledgment of the spirit with which he maintained the purity of election, and supported the rights of the independent electors in three contested elections; of the fidelity and zeal with which he discharged his Parliamentary duties in five successive Parliaments : of the firm, consistent, and independent support he gave to Earl Grey and Viscount Melbourne in carrying out the great principles of civil and religious liberty and commercial freedom ; and for the important services he has rendered the local interests of his constituents, particularly in obtaining for the Borough of Newtown the privilege of an assize town."

The presentation took place amid great enthusiasm at a banquet in the Public Rooms, Newtown, on the 21st of September, 1842, to which upwards of four hundred of Sir John's admirers sat down. From 1841 to the time of his death Sir John Edwards applied himself energetically to the improvement of his extensive estates and the active discharge of his duties as a magistrate and a country gentleman. He died April the 19th, 1850, aged 80, and was buried on the 27th of that month at the parish church at Machynlleth, in the chancel of which a handsome marble tablet has been placed to his memory with the following inscription :- "Sacred to the memory of Sir John Edwards, "Bart., of Plâs Machynlleth, born January 15th, 1770; died "April 19th, 1850. He was the representative in several Par- "liaments of the Montgomeryshire Boroughs, and during a long "period spent in the County of his birth, he lived respected and "beloved as a Christian, a landlord, a husband, and father, and "died regretted and deplored by all who knew him. This "tablet is erected with every feeling of respect and affection by "his only child, Mary Cornelia Countess Vane." Lady Edwards died on the 23rd of November, 1882, having survived her husband over 32 years.

EDWARDS, WILLIAM, of Guilsfield, was a poet who flourished about 1740. Some carols of his composition are printed in the Almanacks published about that time by Evan Davies (*Philomath*) of Manafon.

EINION AB CADWGAN, a prince of part of Powys, who distinguished himself in the wars against Henry 1. In 1113 he in conjunction with others seized the territories in Merioneth-shire of his cousin or Welsh uncle, Uchtryd ab Edwin of Llys (Northope), and demolished his castle at Cymer. He died in 1121, and left his possessions to Maredydd his brother.

EINION AB SEISYLLT, lord of Meirionydd, a descendant of Gwyddno Garanhir, lived in the 12th century at Mathafarn, in the parish of Llanwrin, and was the ancestor of Dafydd Llwyd ab Llewelyn, the eminent poet, who resided at the same place in the 15th century. Owain Brogyntyn married for his second wife Marred, daughter of Einion ab Seisyllt. His arms were Argent, a lion rampant sable, between three Fleurs de lis Gules.

EINION URDD or **YRTH,** the son of Cunedda Wledig, assisted his brethren in expelling the Irish from Wales, and had for his share the district called after him, Caereinion. He suc-ceeded his father as king of North Wales in 389, and reigned until his death in 443.

ELLIS, Rev. ROBERT, better known by his bardic name *Cynddelw,* was a well-known poet and writer, and an eminent minister of the Baptist denomination. He was born at Llanrhaiadr February 3rd, 1812. He had few educational advantages in his youth, and was almost entirely self-taught, having for some years served as a farm servant. He began to preach in October, 1834, and in 1837 was ordained at Llanelian, from which place he in 1839 removed to Chirk, and thence in 1847 to Sirhowy, Monmouthshire. He remained there until 1862, when he removed to Carnarvon, where he spent the remaining years of his life. Besides being an acceptable and popular preacher, Mr. Ellis was an excellent Welsh scholar, an accomplished archæologist and lecturer upon antiquarian subjects connected with Wales and its literature, and a poet of no mean order. His *Cywydd Berwyn* (*Traethodydd,* 1875) is an excellent specimen of his poetical talent. He was also in-defatigable as a writer, and was the author of numerous works, among which may be mentioned *Esboniad ar y Testament Newydd* (A Commentary on the New Testament), in 3 vols.; *Tafol y Beirdd* (The Bard's Scale); *Darlithiau ar Fedydd a Hanes y Bedyddwyr* (Lectures on Baptism and the History of the Baptists); *Egwyddorion Deonglyddiaeth Ysgrythyrol* (The Principles of Scriptural Interpretation); *Cofiant y Parch. Ellis Evans, D.D.* (Life of the Rev. Ellis Evans, D.D.); *Cofiant y Parch. John Williams, Rhos* (Life of the Rev. John Williams, Rhos); *Geiriadur Cymreig Cymraeg)* (A Welsh Dictionary of Welsh), &c. He also annotated editions of *Gorchestion y Beirdd,* and several other works. For several years he was editor of a monthly periodical *Y Greal,* and he wrote numerous articles for many of the Welsh magazines and newspapers on his favourite subjects, the poets, poetry, and literature of Wales. On the 3rd August, 1875, he lectured on the " Poets and Poetry of Wales" at Llanrhaiadr. This was his last public appearance. On the 20th of the same month he died at Garth Eryr, in the parish of Llanrhaiadr, aged 63 years. He was buried in the graveyard attached to the old Baptist Chapel at Glyn Ceiriog. Mr. Ellis was twice married, and left four children. Besides the works above-named, he left at the time of his death others nearly ready for the press, including a volume of his own poetical compositions, which was published at Carnarvon in 1877. He was an excellent divine, remarkably conversant with the Scriptures, which, as well as ancient and modern Welsh poetry, his retentive memory enabled him to quote often to the astonishment of those who had the privilege of being in his company. It only remains to be added that he was a most genial, kindly, merry-hearted, and ready-witted companion, whose memory will ever remain green among those who knew him.

ELLIS, SAMUEL, of Irwell Works, Salford, a successful and ingenious mechanic, engineer, and ironfounder, was born at Melinrhyd Mill (now altered into a villa) near Cyfronydd, in the spring of 1803. His father, Hugh Ellis, besides keeping the mill at that place, also carried on business as a millwright and builder. He had eight children, of whom the subject of this notice was the youngest, the late Mr. Hugh Ellis, timber merchant and builder, Llanfair, being one of his brothers. He attended a school at Castle Caereinion kept by Mr. Thomas Griffiths. He was quick at his lessons, and shewed, besides a fondness for poetry (of which he committed a good deal to memory), a remarkable turn for mechanics. Indeed, while yet a mere child, his natural aptitude for mechanical contrivances developed itself in a very striking manner. It is related that when he was but nine years old he took in hand the setting right of a clock which had baffled the efforts of the local clock-maker, and that after taking it to pieces he put it together again and made it go as well as ever. Two years later he is said to have made with his pocket knife a neat model of a mill, in the construction of which he introduced ingenious contrivances which he explained to his father, who at once saw their utility, and thenceforth adopted them in the construction of mill machinery. At an early age he was placed by his father to work with his men and his other sons at the trade of a millwright. While thus employed he read voraciously everything that came in his way, and he was also very fond of sketching during his spare moments. In order to obtain greater facilities for self-improvement he felt a strong desire to go to Manchester, a project, however, which met with strong opposition from his parents. Finding it hopeless to obtain their consent, he started from home one summer morning in 1826 with seven shillings and sixpence in his pocket, and walked all the way to Manchester, where he arrived in about three days. He obtained work at once, and by his energy and fidelity he soon gained the confidence of his employers, so that in less than three years he became foreman of more than a hundred men. About this time he married Miss Fletcher, a young lady of respectable family connections. In 1832 he entered into a working partnership with a Mr. Norton as millwrights and ironfounders. This partnership was dissolved in 1838, when, with his own savings, and some pecuniary help from his wife's family, he purchased a large iron foundry known as Irwell Works, Salford, where he commenced business on a large scale on his own account. Here his genius for mechanical invention found full scope. In 1842 he made great improvements in the construction of Railway Turntables and Weighing Machines, for which in June, 1843, he obtained a Patent. The Turntables previously in use were very ricketty, unsteady, and requiring constant repair as well as causing many inconveniences. Mr. Ellis submitted his invention (the description of which is too technical to be given here) to Mr. Robert Stephenson, who at once pronounced it to be one of the greatest improvements in railway machinery that had ever come under his notice, and he introduced Mr. Ellis to a capitalist friend of his own, Mr. Kennard, who became a part proprietor of the patent, and with whose assistance Mr. Ellis was enabled to reap the benefits of his invention. Orders came so thick upon him that his business more than trebled in the course of the next six months, and all the principal Railway Companies speedily adopted the new machinery on their lines On the 12th and 13th February, 1847, an action, " *Ellis and another* v. *Ormerod and another*," for infringement of the above Patent was tried in the Court of Queen's Bench before Mr. Justice Erle and a special jury, when, after hearing the evidence of Mr. Stephenson, Mr. Bidder, and other eminent men, a verdict was taken by consent for the Plaintiff upon all the issues but one, thereby in all respects establishing his Patent, and for the Defendant on the plea of not guilty, it being admitted that what had been done by him was not an infringement of the Plaintiff's rights. About the same time (1847) Mr. Ellis perfected an invention for better adapting travelling cranes for general use on Railways, which greatly extended his already very large business. In 1848 he bought the Palace Mill in Llanymowddwy, and contemplated buying more property in that neighbourhood. He also took an active part in public affairs, and was a member of the Salford Town Council for some years prior to his death. His fame and prosperity continued rapidly to extend with his increasing business, so much so as not to allow of his taking sufficient rest and relaxation. The warnings of his physician, unhappily, were not attended to in time. After a few years of constant strain and incessant toil, his health utterly broke down, and after a lingering illness he died at his private residence, Bar Hill House, Pendleton, on the 6th April, 1852, at the comparatively early age of 49 years, leaving a widow and six children. He was buried at Pendlebury Churchyard, near Manchester. His old works are still carried on by his nephews, Messrs. H. and J. Ellis, patentees of improved Travelling Cranes.

ELLIS, THOMAS, a remarkable Orientalist, was born in Lower-street, Llanfyllin, about the year 1819. His father, John Ellis, was a shoemaker, and he himself in his youth worked at the same trade. He was a queer boy, reserved in his ways, and would not play with other boys, who did not consider him endowed with the ordinary amount of sense. He for some time attended a school kept by Mr. Morris Davies, but was not particularly clever at his lessons, and when he became a shoemaker he was it is said, like his father, a very poor workman. From Llanfyllin he went to Liverpool, where it seems he worked for some time at his trade, but like "Dick Aberdaron" (whom he appears to have resembled both as to his gifts and eccentricities), he was of a rambling turn. How or when he began to study Oriental languages does not appear, but he evidently soon developed a remarkable aptitude in that direction. The next we hear of him is that he was employed by the late Mr. Bagster about the years 1848 to 1850 in reading for the press his editions of the Hebrew Scriptures, the Syriac New Testament, the Analytical Hebrew and Chaldee Lexicon, Gesenius' Hebrew Lexicon, &c. From the beginning of 1851 to the date of his death he was employed at the British Museum in arranging and cataloguing the Museum collection of Syriac MSS.—a work, however, which he failed to complete before his death. At this time he had acquired the reputation of being a very remarkable Hebrew, Chaldee, and Syriac scholar, and as such Mr. (now Sir Henry) Layard, who had brought home some jars and bowls from the ruins of Babylon, on which were some curious ancient inscriptions, sought his assistance to decipher the latter. Mr. Layard, in his *Discoveries in the Ruins of Nineveh and Babylon* (Murray, 1853), gives a full and interesting account, extending over 16 or 17 pages, of these antiquities and the inscriptions upon them. Among other things there were some specimens of glass and several terra cotta figure lamps and jars dug out of a mound at Amran, which were considered to be of the time of the Seleucidæ or of the Greek occupation:—

"With these relics were five cups or bowls of earthenware, and fragments of others, covered on the inner service with letters written in a kind of ink. Similar objects had already been found in other Babylonian ruins. Two from the collection of the late Mr. Stewart had been deposited in the British Museum, and amongst the antiquities recently purchased by the trustees from Col. Rawlinson are eight specimens obtained at Baghdad, where they are sometimes offered for sale by the Arabs; but it is not known from what sites they are brought. The characters upon them are in form not unlike the Hebrew, and on some they resembled the Sabœan and Syriac. The bowls had not attracted notice, nor had the inscriptions upon them been fully examined before they were placed in the hands of Mr. Thomas Ellis, of the Manuscript

Department in the British Museum, a gentleman of great learning and ingenuity as a Hebrew scholar. He succeeded after much labour in deciphering the inscriptions, and I will now give in his own words an account of these singular relics." [Here follow fifteen or sixteen pages of letterpress description, partly in Hebrew characters, with eight engravings.] "As to the original use of these vessels, it is not improbable, as conjectured by Mr. Ellis, that the writing was to be dissolved in water, to be drank as a cure against disease, or a precaution against the arts of witchcraft and magic."

Mr. Layard, however, did not himself entertain this view, but thought the relics were charms buried with the dead. The inscriptions given in the woodcuts are stated to be as nearly as possible facsimiles of the originals reduced copied by Mr. Scharf under the superintendence of Mr. Ellis. Mr. Ellis had been brought up a strict Calvinistic Methodist, and retained his membership in London for some time, and occasionally attended the Welsh Chapel in Jewin Cresent up to the time of his death. Beyond this and that he once visited his native place for a short time, when he was apparently in good circumstances, very little is known of his personal history. He seems to have led a somewhat solitary life. He died in London about the end of the year 1856, aged about 37 years.

ERFYL (Saint), or ERFUL, EURFUL or URFUL, as she is variously called, said by some to have been a daughter of St. Padarn, who flourished about the middle of the 6th century. Her father's diocese of Llanbadarn comprised a large portion of Montgomeryshire, and she probably founded the church of Llanerfyl, it being in the immediate neighbourhood of Llangadfan, a church founded by her uncle St. Cadfan. Tradition states that she was buried there. A curious inscription was found upon an ancient tombstone in the churchyard some years ago, which runs as follows: HIC IN TVM LO IACIT R ST E CE FILIA PA TERNINI AN IXIII IN PA This is supposed to be Erfyl's tombstone, though it is difficult to see how the inscription can refer to her. Her feast day is the Sunday next following the 6th July. Her memory was for many years held in great veneration. Lewis Glyn Cothi speaks of

" Urvul ddoeth a Gwervul dda.!"
(Urvul the wise and Gwervul the good.)

EVAN, LEWIS, of Llanllugan, one of the founders of Calvinistic Methodism in Montgomeryshire, a man of remarkable zeal, piety, and devotion, was born in the year 1719. The first account we have of him is that he lived with his grandfather at Crugnant, where he followed the occupation of a weaver. He resided most of his life at Plâs Helyg, Llanllugan. In the year 1739 he heard Howell Harries preach at Trefeglwys his second sermon in North Wales, and was so deeply impressed that he became a changed character, and very soon began to exhort others to embrace the truth which had proved his own salvation. In that dark and corrupt age this was enought to stir up against him a storm of persecution, and he was often cruelly beaten and ill-treated. He was recognised at an Association held at Glanyrafon, Carmarthenshire, on the 1st March, 1742, as an Exhorter, it being stated that "Lewis "Evan, who exhorts at Llanllugan, is signally owned of the "Lord to be a blessing to many : several doors are opened to "him, and souls are converted under his ministry." He was therefore appointed to assist Morgan Hughes as overseer of the societies at Llanfair, Llanllugan, and Llanwyddelan. At a monthly meeting subsequently held at Trefecca, it was resolved "That the brother Lewis Evan go as far as he can into "Merionethshire and the North, according to the call there may "be for him." He was not slow to comply with this resolution, and for many years he diligently travelled through North and South Wales, in spite of many difficulties, discouragements, and persecutions. His preaching was attended with very beneficial results, and was very acceptable to many. On one occasion he was imprisoned at Dolgelley for no offence whatever, and detained for six months, but on his release he declined to prosecute for false imprisonment the magistrate who had committed him. During fifty years of incessant labour he had many narrow escapes from peril at the hands of his enemies. Though only a poor weaver, he lived a truly sublime life, and left the world better than he found it. He was short of stature, very active, and ready of speech. He died in great peace in the year 1792, aged 73 years. His nephew, James Lewis, wrote an Elegy on his death, wherein he says :—

> " Dywedai' brofiad yn bur groyw,
> Wrth un o'i frodyr cyn ei farw
> ' Tawelwch mawr, sydd yn awr,
> Trwy ddwylaw'r cawr creulon ;
> Y mae'r Iesu imi'n ddigon,
> Ffarwel myn'd rwy'i ffrydisu'r afon.' "

A handsome monument of white marble has been erected to his memory in front of Adfa Chapel, Llanwyddelan, with the following inscription : " In memory of Lewis Evan, Llanllugan, " the first preacher in connection with the Calvinistic Methodists " in North Wales. Born in 1719, A.D. Died in 1792, A.D. He " ' had trials of cruel mockings and scourgings, yea, moreover, " of bonds and imprisonment.' Hebrews xi., 36."

EVANCE, Rev. JOHN, was a member of the old Shropshire family of EVANCE, of Treflach, descended from Rhodri Mawr, king of Wales, and was born in the year 1621. In 1666 he obtained the Rectory of Newtown, which he held up to his death, a period of 22 years. In 1678 he was appointed Head Master of Oswestry School; Canon of St. Asaph in 1681 ; Vicar of Berriew in 1686 ; and Rector of Llanmerewig in 1688. He died at Llanmerewig on the 6th May, 1688, aged 67 years, and was buried near the Communion rails in the old Church at Newtown. He left a charge upon his estate of ten shillings to be paid to the oldest person in Llanmerewig twice a year. He

was succeeded in the Rectory of Llanmerewig by his nephew of
the same name who died in 1711. Another member of the same
family, WILLIAM EVANCE, was Rector of Newtown from 1732
to 1772. He appears to have been an accomplished musician,
bequeathing his " treble and tenor violin, german flute and
harpsichord and all his music" to his nephews, his only son,
the Rev. Richard Evance, having predeceased him. He left a
charge on his estate of £2 2s. 0d. to the poor of Newtown.
This family also includes Sir STEPHEN EVANCE, Knt. and Bart.,
a banker who negotiated for Mr. Pitt the sale of the " Pitt " or
" Regent " diamond to the Duke of Orleans for £125,000, now
valued at £450,000. He was member for Bridport in two
Parliaments, and died unmarried in 1711. The last descendants
of this family in the male line and bearing the arms of EVANCE
of Treflach are the children of the late CAPT. WILLIAM
DEVEREUX EVANCE, R.A., who commanded the old line of
battle-ship " Conqueror." His youngest son, Devereux Alfred
Roden Evance, F.R.G.S., author of *American Sketches*, a
pamphlet on *Emigration*, &c., now represents him at Bourton,
Dorset.

EVANS, DAVID, of Llanfair-Caereinion, a poet who
flourished about the middle of the last century. He was a
descendant of Wmffra Dafydd ab Ifan, of Llanbrynmair, a celebrated poet of the 17th century; but beyond this little is known
of him. He was a poetical contributor to the almanacks published annually by Evan Davies (*Philomath*). His brother,
Rowland Evans, of Coedbychain, was also a poet

EVANS, REV. DAVID, D.D., was born at Llangynyw. He
had the rectory of Llanerfyl in 1737, and was Vicar Choral of St.
Asaph. In 1767 he exchanged Llanerfyl for Llanymynech,
where he spent the remainder of his life, and died about 1788.
He was also buried at Llanymynech, and a marble monument
was erected there to his memory. He was an excellent scholar
and a good Welsh critic. He assisted Dr. Burney in writing
his *History of Music*, and Mr. Edward Jones in making his compilation of Welsh melodies.

EVANS, REV. DAVID, a Wesleyan minister, was born at
Aberhosan, near Machynlleth, June 2nd, 1814. He began early
to preach, and in 1836 entered the Academy at Hoxton, to
prepare for the ministry. After passing the usual examination
he was appointed to the Cardigan circuit, where he laboured with
great zeal and acceptation. Here he wrote an able treatise in
Welsh to confute the Arian and Socinian heresies, entitled,
The personal divinity of our Lord Jesus Christ. In 1838 he
removed to Mold, and the same year married Miss Elizabeth
Williams, Aberystwyth. In 1839 he was stationed at Manchester, but after remaining there about two years was obliged
in consequence of ill health to retire to Aberystwyth for some
time. In 1844 he resumed his ministerial duties at Llanidloes,

and was superintendent of the Wesleyan Bookroom there. In 1845 he was appointed editor of the *Eurgrawn Wesleyaidd* (Wesleyan Magazine), which office he held for a little over twelve months, when his health utterly broke down under his heavy labours. He bore a long and severe illness with great patience and Christian fortitude, and died September 12th, 1847, at the early age of 33.

EVANS, DAVID MORIER, a well-known journalist and author of numerous works on commercial subjects, was the son of Mr. Joshua Lloyd Evans, of Llanidloes, but was born in London in the year 1819. From an early age he was intimately connected with periodical literature. After being for some years assistant City correspondent of *The Times*, he assumed in 1857 the management of the same department of the *Morning Herald* and *Standard*, which post, and also that of general manager, he retained until the end of 1872, when he left the *Standard*, and in March, 1873, started the *Hour*, a Conservative newspaper, which proved an utter failure. In this last venture he spent his fortune, and became bankrupt on the 19th December, 1873. This event preyed on his mind and entirely broke down his health. He died at his residence in South Hackney, London, on the 1st January, 1874, aged 54 years, and was buried in Abney Park Cemetery. He was the author of numerous works, the principal of which were—*The Commercial Crisis of 1847-8; History of the Commencement of the Crisis, 1857-8; City Men and City Manners; Facts, Failures, and Frauds*, &c. He was also intimately connected with and a frequent contributor to the *Bankers' Magazine*, the *Bullionist*, the *Stock Exchange Gazette*, and other commercial papers.

√ EVANS, GRACE, of Welshpool, the quick-witted and courageous maid who so ably assisted her mistress, the Countess of Nithsdale, to effect the escape of her lord from the Tower (see HERBERT, LADY WINIFRED, *post*). Little is known of her history beyond the honourable mention made of the services of " my dear Evans " by her noble mistress, and that she lived the latter part of her life (probably as a pensioner of the Powis Castle family) at a cottage near the eastern gate to the Parish Churchyard at Welshpool, still known as " Grace Evans' " Cottage." The following entry in the Welshpool Register of Burials doubtless refers to her :—" Grace Evans, of Welsh- " Town, buried August 18, 1737." This was a little over 20 years after the escape of Lord Nithsdale.

EVANS, JOHN, Head Master of Oswestry Free Grammar School during the Commonwealth, was the son of the Rev. Matthew Evans, Rector of Penegoes, but was born at Great Sutton, near Ludlow, in or about the year 1628. He was educated at Balliol College, Oxford, but left the University sooner than he intended, because he was unwilling to submit to

E

the Parliamentary visitors. Returning to his father's home, he was ordained priest by the Bishop of St. David's in November, 1648, but soon afterwards changed his views about Conformity, and became one of the itinerant preachers for Wales. He was subsequently appointed Head Master of the Free School at Dolgelley, and in 1657 of that at Oswestry at the recommendation of Oliver Cromwell. He was ejected from this office when the Act of Uniformity came into force, and was reduced to such poverty that he was forced to sell a considerable part of a large library to obtain the means of supporting himself and his family. In 1668 he was chosen pastor of an Independent Church at Wrexham, and kept private meetings in his house through the hottest times. Being an excellent scholar, some gentlemen of considerable position sent their sons to board with him for several years, which was a help to him under the violent persecution to which he was subjected. He was repeatedly fined, and at last outlawed, and for years he was obliged for his own protection to keep his doors constantly locked. His second wife was the daughter of Colonel Gerrard, Governor of Chester Castle, and the widow of the famous Vavasor Powell. Their son, Dr. John Evans, was the author of the well-known *Sermons on the Christian Temper*. In the return of Conventicles made in 1699 by order of the Archbishop of Canterbury, John Evans is named as one of the "Teachers" of the Conventicles at Llanfyllin, Llanfechain, and Oswestry. He died on the 16th of July, 1700, in his seventy-second year.

EVANS, JOHN, of Llwynygroes, Llanymynech, was born in the year 1723. He prepared the large Map of North Wales, engraved by his neighbour, Mr. Robert Baugh, of Llandysilio, and published it in 1795. He also published some prints from sketches taken by himself, among them a large engraving of Pistyll Rhaiadr, an excellent specimen of his skill, with a description of the waterfall, and the derivation of names appended. He died in 1795.

EVANS, JOHN, M.D., son of the above, was born at Llwynygroes, July 4th, 1756, and was educated at Westminster School. He afterwards proceeded to Oxford, and then studied medicine at Edinburgh, where he took the degree of M.D. He settled at Shrewsbury, residing at the Council House, and soon acquired an extensive practice. Upon his father's death he became owner of the Llwynygroes estate, and retiring from his profession went to reside there. He married Miss Jane Wilson, of the Held, Cheshire, by whom he had five sons and four daughters. Three of the sons became clergymen; one entered the army, and the remaining one the navy. Dr. Evans spent much of his time in the study of bees and in bee culture, and wrote a didactic poem, entitled, *The Bee*, illustrated with valuable notes, philosophical and botanical. In 1802 he published an improved copy of his father's map of North Wales, for which he received a prize from the Society of Arts. He spent the last few years of his life with his son, Archdeacon Evans, at Heversham, Westmoreland, where he died in the autumn of 1846, at the patriarchal age of ninety.

EVANS, JOHN RHAIADORE, an eminent doctor, was born at Glantanad isaf, in the parish of Llanrhaiadr, about the close of the last century. He was educated at the Oswestry Grammar School, and subsequently articled with Mr. Hugh Roberts, a surgeon in good practice at Llanfyllin. He afterwards became a pupil of Sir Benjamin Brodie. After filling for a time the office of chief medical officer for the Bangor Infirmary, he was appointed Lecturer on Surgery and one of the medical officers of the Middlesex and Royal Metropolitan Infirmaries. He enjoyed for some time an extensive practice in London, and amassed a good fortune. He was the author of several medical works of acknowledged merit, among them being treatises *On the Remediable Evils attending the Life of the People ; On Irritation of the Spinal Nerves; Introductory Lectures to a course on Distortions of the Spine, Chest, and Limbs, and on Nervous Irritation;* and *The Remediable Influence of Oxygen on Vital Air.* Mr. Evans died about the year 1850.

EVANS, RICHARD, was born at Llanbrynmair in 1792, but removed at an early age to London. He carried on business for some years at Queen-street, Cheapside, and in the neighbourhood of his warehouse he gathered together quite a colony of his compatriots, comprising about twenty families, to whom he gave medicine and surgical advice at his own cost, and once a week delivered a lecture in Welsh for their instruction in manufactures, mechanics, and kindred topics. He took a great interest in all matters relating to Wales, and afforded valuable aid to many a young Welshman on his first arrival in London. At the time of his death he was President of the Cymreigyddion Society, and Curator of Welsh MSS. to the Royal Cambrian Society. He had a powerful and active mind, which overbalanced the energies of a weakly body, predisposed to consumption. He died at Old Ford, London, on the 7th of January, 1832, at the early age of 39, leaving a widow to survive him.

EVANS, ROBERT, parish clerk of Meifod in the first half of last century, was a good poet. He was the author of *Cerdd y Winllan* (Call to the Vineyard), a very popular ballad or song, which, with two other compositions of his, are published in the *Blodeugerdd.* He never debased his muse, as too many of his contemporaries did, by writing on profane subjects. He taught his Vicar, Dr. Salisbury Pryce, to read Welsh, and is said to have died in the Almshouse about 1750.

EVANS, Rev. ROBERT WILSON, B.D., was the second son of Dr. Evans, of Llwynygroes, Llanymynech. He was born in the year 1789, at the Council House, Shrewsbury, where his father at that time practised as a physician and surgeon. He was educated at Shrewsbury School, and proceeded from thence to Trinity College, Cambridge, where he greatly distinguished himself. He graduated in high honours in 1811, obtaining the place of seventh Wrangler on the Mathematical Tripos, and the second Chancellor's medal of that year. Shortly afterwards he gained his Fellowship at Trinity, and was soon appointed classical tutor of his College. In 1836 Dr. Butler, Bishop of Lichfield, whose examining chaplain he had been for some time, collated him to the important living of Tarvin, in Cheshire. Here he devoted himself with untiring energy and great self-devotion to parochial work. In 1842 he accepted from his College the Vicarage of Heversham, in Westmoreland, where he resided the rest of his life. He for some years held the Archdeaconry of Westmoreland, but resigned it in 1864 on account of advancing years. He died on the 10th of March, 1866, in the 77th year of his age. Archdeacon Evans was a man of considerable genius and learning, and the memory of his gentle, pure, and saintly life, his high spirituality, and his faithful ministry will long remain. His loving and unassuming nature secured for him many warm and faithful friends, who, when he passed away, at once took steps to raise some tributes to his memory. An endowment fund was raised sufficient to supply an annual prize at the University of Cambridge, called the "Evans' Prize," given to the most proficient student in Ecclesiastical History and the Greek and Latin Fathers. A stained glass window was put up to his memory at Heversham Church by his parishioners and other friends; a marble slab of chaste design was also erected in the chancel of the same Church by the Hon. Mrs. Greville Howard, inscribed as "A "friend's memorial of gratitude to Robert Wilson Evans"; and a memorial window for the same object has been placed in Llanymynech Church by his sister, Frances Louisa Evans. Archdeacon Evans was the author of various very well-known works. The following is a list of them:—(1) *The Rectory of Valehead* (1830), begun at Llwynygroes and finished at Cambridge, a subsequent edition of which appeared in 1831; (2) *The Church of God* (1832), a course of sermons preached by him as a Select Preacher at Cambridge; (3) *Scripture Biography*, 2 vols. (1834); (4) *Biography of the Early Church*, 2 vols. (1836), a second edition of which was published in 1859; (5) *The Bishopric of Souls* (1842), a second edition of which was called for in 1843, a third in 1844, a fourth some time afterwards, and a fifth in 1877; (6) *The Ministry of the Body*; (7) *Parochial Sermons*, 3 vols. (1845 to 1855); (8) *Tales of the Ancient British Church*; (9) *A Day in the Sanctuary*; (10) *Parochial Sketches in Verse*; (11) *England under God*; (12) *Hints on Versification*; (13) *An Exhortation to the Lord's Day*. He was also an occasional contributor to some of the leading periodicals of the day.

EVANS, THOMAS, was born at Welshpool in 1762, where he became the heir to a small property. He, with his wife (formerly Grace Sugden) and six others, were the founders of Independency or Congregationalism at Welshpool, having on the 19th December, 1794, formed themselves " into a Church on the "Independent plan." He was a man of very exemplary piety, and a friend and correspondent of De Courcy, Sir Richard Hill, Huntingdon, and others of the Evangelical clergy and laity of those days. His latter years were spent at Oswestry, where he died, but he was buried at Welshpool. A handsome marble tablet with the following inscription was in 1862 placed in the Congregational Chapel, Welshpool, to his memory and that of his first wife :—

"In memory of GRACE SUGDEN, wife of Thomas Evans, of this town, who died February 19, 1796, aged 35 years, leaving six children to lament their loss. Also of THOMAS EVANS, born in the year 1762, died at Oswestry February 21st, 1829, aged 66 years, his remains being deposited in the Churchyard of this parish in the grave that had for thirty-three years held those of his beloved wife. This tablet is erected by the surviving sons and daughters of the departed as an enduring record of filial affection, and is placed here to perpetuate the name of one of the honoured founders of Congregationalism in Welshpool. 1862."

EVANS, THOMAS, was the son of Mr. Hugh Evans, of Llanidloes, where he was born in 1773. He studied medicine, and entered the service of the East India Company as surgeon. In this capacity he distinguished himself by his skill and ability, and gained the post of superintendent surgeon to the Madras establishment. After residing for many years in India, where he realised a handsome fortune, he retired to Llanidloes, and built for himself a pretty residence close to the town, which he called Maenol. He also purchased several farms in the neighbourhood, became a Justice of the Peace, and in 1840 served the office of Sheriff for his native county. He died February 11th, 1845, aged 72, leaving his property (subject to a few legacies) to his grandniece, Margaret Eleanor Hayward, afterwards the wife of the Rev. E. O. Phillips, Canon of St. David's.

EVANS, CAPTAIN THOMAS, R.N., a distinguished naval officer, was the third son of Dr. Evans, of Llwynygroes, and was born October the 5th, 1791. He entered the Navy May 23rd, 1805, his first service being as a first-class volunteer on board the *Leda* of 38 guns, Capt. Honyman. In this frigate he assisted at the reduction of the Cape of Good Hope in January, 1806. He next served as midshipman with the troops engaged at the storming of Monte Video in February, 1807. The same year he joined the fleet sent to the Baltic under the command of Admiral Gambier, to take possession of the Danish fleet, and was present at the subsequent bombardment of Copenhagen in September, 1807. When the fleet returned to England in 1808, he was wrecked near the entrance of Milford Haven on January the 31st. The Danes having declared war against England, he was the same year called to active service in the West Indies. For twenty months he was occupied on board the *Cherub* and *Epervier* sloops under Capts. Raveushaw, Nesbit, Barclay, and Stewart. While on board the *Epervier* as master's mate he assisted in the capture and destruction of *Le Cygne* corvette, 18 guns; also of two schooners in an engagement near St. Pierre, Martinique, December 12th and 13th, 1808. From September, 1809, until the year 1811, he was employed under Sir John P. Beresford in the *Theseus* and *Poictiers* (70 guns), and in the *Royal Sovereign* yacht, along the coast of Portugal, where he found an opportunity for distinguishing himself in the boats of the *Poictiers* upon their being sent up the Tagus to harass the French lines. During 1812-13 he served in the *Impetueux*, *Stately*, and *Rodney*, flagships of Vice-Admiral Martin, stationed off Lisbon. From 1814 until the close of the war he returned to the ships under the command of Beresford. He obtained his commission as Lieutenant February 2nd, 1815, received full pay since 1810. He spent a short time at Plymouth on board the *Caledonia* (120 guns), commanded by Sir A. C. Dickson. In August, 1815, he was placed on half-pay, and was not afterwards employed on active service. Some years later he received the honorary rank of Captain. Upon his retirement from the Navy he returned to his native place, and for a few years resided at Llanymynech, where he was much respected. He died November 28th, 1853, in the sixty-third year of his age.

EVANS, Rev. WILLIAM EDWARD, was the youngest son of Dr. Evans, of Llwynygroes. He was born in 1801, and was educated at Shrewsbury School. Thence he proceeded to Clare College, Cambridge, and having decided upon entering the Church, he was ordained to the ministry, and for some time served as curate of the parish of Llanymynech. Subsequently he officiated at Criggion, and at Monkland, Herefordshire. The National Schoolroom at Llanymynech was built mainly through his instrumentality. When at Monkland he was made Precentor of Hereford Cathedral, and soon afterwards Vicar of Medley with Tiberton in that county. In 1860 he was appointed Canon Residentiary of the Cathedral. He was the author of several works, the principal of which were:—*Songs of the Birds*, *Sermons on Genesis*, and *Family Prayers*. He died in November, 1869, aged 68 years.

FFOULKES, Rev. WILLIAM, M.A., was Rector of Llanfyllin from 1660 to 1690. A Canonry of St. Asaph was also bestowed upon him in 1662, and the Rectory of Llanfihangel in 1680. He was a good scholar and edited Bishop Griffith's *Sermons* (in Welsh) *on the Lord's Prayer*. His preface to to them is dated March 2nd, 1684; the imprint is 1685. In 1688 he also published a translation of Bishop Ken's *Exposition of the Catechism*. He died at Llanfyllin, and was buried near the Church door January 9th, 1690.

GITTINS, EDWARD (*Iorwerth Pentyrch*) was born and lived all his life in the parish of Llanfair Caereinion, and was a blacksmith by trade. As may be supposed, his opportunities for mental improvement and for indulging his literary tastes were few and scanty, but he acquired some local reputation as a Welsh poet, and gained several prizes for *Englynion*, as well as a prize for a *Parochial History of Llanfair*, which subsequently appeared in the *Montgomeryshire Collections*. The latter, especially considering the disadvantages under which it was written, is a very creditable production. He died in May, 1884, in the prime of life.

GOLDSBRO' THOMAS WILLIAM JOHN, M.D., was the son of the Rev. Thomas Goldsbro', curate of Trelystan, (who also kept a private school at Welshpool), and was born at the latter place about the year 1819. He entered the surgery of Dr. Serph, who had been a French prisoner of war at Welshpool, and having established an extensive practice in that town, remained there when peace was declared, Mr. Goldsbro' went up to London in due course, and became an M.D. of Aberdeen. At the time of his death, which took place in London on the 29th of January, 1877, he held a high place in the medical profession, having been for many years Demonstrator of Anatomy at Charing Cross Hospital. Dr. Goldsbro' was an ardent Freemason, and consecrated fourteen lodges.

GOODWIN, JOHN, of Esgirgoch, Trefeglwys, was a zealous and faithful Quaker preacher in his day, for the period of 55 years. The following entry copied from the Baptismal Register for the parish of Trefeglwys refers most probably to his baptism :—"John f. Edw. Goodwin, B.P., 24 die Januarii "1685." He had intended, it seems, to emigrate to Pennsylvania, but was prevailed upon not to do so. He was the owner and occupier of Esgirgoch farm, near the hamlet of Staylittle, and built close to the farmhouse a small meeting house for the Quakers, which now forms part of the farmhouse. He also set apart a small enclosure from the farm for a Quaker "garden" or burial ground, where traces of graves may still be seen. The last person buried there was Richard Brown, a Llanidloes Quaker, who died in 1850. John Goodwin died in December, 1763, in the 82nd year of his age, and was buried on the 7th day of the same month in the Quaker burial ground at Llwyndu, near Llwyngwril, Merionethshire.

GOODWIN, JOHN, the son of John and Elizabeth Goodwin, was born at Newtown on the 14th December, 1813. He had but very few advantages of education, but by his own untiring exertions he acquired a very fair knowledge of books. At the tender age of ten he was apprenticed to the trade of a hand loom weaver, which he followed through life. He became a local preacher first with the Wesleyan Methodists and then with the Independents. He contributed to the *Oddfellows' Chronicle* and other periodicals various poetical productions, some of which possessed strong marks of poetic genius. For the last two years of his life he suffered much illness. He died April 28, 1846, in the 33rd year of his age, and was buried at the Wesleyan burial ground, Newtown. A small volume of his *Literary Remains* was in the press at the time of his death, and was shortly afterwards published, dedicated by permission to Dr. Bowring.

GRIFFITH AP GWENWYNWYN, a Prince of Powis, who in 1241 (a year after the death of Prince Llewelyn ab Iorwerth), obtained possession of Powysland, of which his father Gwenwynwyn, had been dispossessed about the year 1217. He for many years remained loyal to the English king. In 1244, he, with two other Welsh chieftains, refused to join David ap Llewelyn, then in arms against the King, and in 1247, he led an army from South Wales, crossed the Dovey, and over-ran a great part of North Wales, at that time ruled by Prince David. Llewelyn ab Gruffydd, however, in 1256, attacked him, and " wan all Powys from him save the Castell of Pole [Powys " Castle] and a little of Caereucon, and the land of Seauerne " side," and in 1259 drove him from his territory. At length, in 1263, Griffith entered into an alliance, offensive and defensive, with Llewelyn, and received back from him his territory to be held of him as Prince of Wales. The same year he took and demolished the Castle of Mold. In 1274, a rupture took place between Llewelyn and Griffith, who thenceforth returned to his allegiance to the English king, and for a time left his own land and went to England, leaving his son Owain with Llewelyn. About 1279, Griffith granted a Charter "to his beloved and faithful burgesses of Pole," [Welshpool], erecting their town into a free borough, and bestowing upon them many privileges which they continued to enjoy for five and a half centuries. Griffith died in 1286. By his wife, Hawise, the daughter of John le Strange, of Ness and Cheswardine, who survived him many years, he had six sons and a daughter.

GRIFFITH, JOHN, (*Gohebydd*), although born out of Montgomeryshire, yet by reason of family ties and residence (for a time) claims notice among its worthies. He was born at a farmhouse called Bodgwilym, near Barmouth, on the 21st December, 1821, and was the son of Mr. Griffith Griffith, by Maria, his wife, a daughter of the Rev. John Roberts, of Llanbrynmair, the eminent Independent minister. He served an apprenticeship to the grocery trade at Barmouth, and then removed to Liverpool, and subsequently to Llangynog, in this county to take charge of a shop belonging to Mr. C. Jones, Llanfyllin. About 1846, however, he found more congenial employment in assisting Sir (then Mr.) Hugh Owen, in establishing British Schools in Wales. This engagement called for his taking up his residence in London, where he mostly lived the remainder of his days. He was one of the leading laymen connected with the Welsh Independents in London, and ever took a prominent and active part in every movement, religious, political, or national among his compatriots in that great city. His letters to the *Cronicl* (a little magazine then ably conducted by his uncle, the Rev. Samuel Roberts), under the feigned name, "Wmffra Edward," attracted much attention and popularity. Mr. Gee, of Denbigh, in 1857, started *Baner Cymru*—a weekly paper—and shortly afterwards engaged the services of Mr. Griffith as its London correspondent. His racy letters from week to week referring to the principal events of the day, with such notes and comments as suggested themselves to his fertile brain, were read with the greatest avidity and secured a very large circulation for the paper in which they appeared. Mr. Griffith had for some years given up his work in connection with British Schools, and was now in business on his own account. He was not, however, well fitted for commercial pursuits, nor was he successful in that line ; so, about the year 1860 he gave up business altogether in order to devote the whole of his time to literary pursuits. He was one of the most regular frequenters of the gallery and lobby of the House of Commons during the Session. Among his countrymen he was universally known as *Gohebydd* (correspondent)—he being the first real Welsh specimen of the genus "own correspondent." The Rev. Kilsby Jones, indeed, jocularly preferred to call him "*Pobman*" (everywhere), on account of his turning up at every eisteddfod, and every meeting of importance, religious or political, of Welshmen. As Caledfryn facetiously said, Gohebydd was sure to be present on every "pig-killing" occasion. He must have attended, indeed, an immense number of public gatherings of all kinds in the course of every year. His constitution was naturally frail, his voice weak and shrill, his breathing short and asthmatic, and he had a troublesome cough,—disadvantages which effectually precluded him becoming an orator,—yet he was always listened to with attention, and his shrewd remarks often produced a great effect. His literary style was not by any means faultless, but it had the merit of being direct, striking, and picturesque ; and his letters abounded in shrewd common sense. He was an ardent patriot who fearlessly exposed wrongs and abuses wherever he found them; in politics intensely Liberal; in religion a thoroughgoing Nonconformist ; a remarkably keen observer of men and manners, and a sagacious interpreter of current events and the signs of the times. For some years prior to his death, he suffered much from ill-health, yet he travelled incessantly not only in England and Wales, but also abroad. He visited America in 1865, after the war, the Paris Exhibition, and various parts of France in 1867, and the Vienna Exhibition and various European countries in 1873. In 1875, it became necessary for him to spend the winter months at Mentone for the benefit of his health, and during his stay there he also visited Naples, Rome, and other Italian cities, and had personal interviews with the Pope, Garibaldi, and other notabilities. This last visit to the continent served to prolong his life for a while, but it soon became evident to his friends that his days were numbered. A testimonial to him in recognition of his private worth and valuable public services was therefore quietly set on foot, and a very substantial sum was raised, amounting to several hundreds of pounds. This was presented to him at a public meeting in London, attended by many of the leading men of Wales and the metropolis. The last few months of his life were spent at his brother-in-law's house, at Liverpool, where he died on the 13th of December, 1877, and on the 17th of the same month he was buried in the Llangollen Cemetery, where a handsome obelisk with a suitable inscription marks his grave. He was never married.

GRIFFITH, Capt. WALTER, R.N., a distinguished naval officer, was the second surviving son of Walter Griffith, Esq., of Brongain, in the parish of Llanfechain, in this county, where he was born on the 15th May, 1727. He was educated at the Oswestry Grammar School. At the age of sixteen he went to sea under the auspices of his relation and friend Commodore Trevor, who then commanded the *Duke* of 90 guns. He was, however, soon deprived of his patron, but continued to serve in the *Duke* till 1746, when through the interest of his friend, Mr. Pusey Brooke, and his own good conduct, he was removed to the *Hector*, 40 guns, commanded by Captain Stanhope. In this ship he remained till the general peace in 1748, during which time he distinguished himself in that memorable engagement on the 14th October, 1747, when Sir Edward Hawke fell in with a fleet of 300 sail of merchantmen, convoyed by eight French line of battle ships, six of which struck after a most bloody engagement; the rest, favoured by the night, escaped. Mr. Griffith was stationed by the Captain on the forecastle during this action, and by his coolness and regular observance of signals he gained the applause of his Captain and brother officers. On the return of peace he was made Midshipman in the *Ferigeux*, 64 guns, Sir Edward Hawke's Flag Ship to whom he so highly recommended himself by his assiduity, regularity, and propriety of conduct, that he placed him under the protection of Commodore Townsend, who was then going in the *Gloucester* Frigate, 50 guns, with a squadron under his command, to the West Indies. In a letter which Commodore Townsend wrote to a friend on the occasion he observed. "If merit had any weight in promotion "in Jamaica, Mr. Griffith would not be long unprovided for." He had not been long on the Jamaica station before he was appointed by the Commodore acting Lieutenant of the *Renown* Frigate, 36 guns, Captain Shirley, where he remained till the year 1750, when he was prevailed upon by his friends Captain Faulkner and Mr. Manning to accompany them in the *Fox* Frigate to the Havannah, and when on their return near Fort Royal harbour, they were cast away in a dreadful hurricane but the crew were saved. After this event he returned to the *Gloucester* Frigate, as the acting Lieutenant, and continued on the West India station till the return of that ship to England in

1752, when he was paid off. Mr. Griffith passed the two remaining years of peace with his friends in the country. In the early part of 1753, when the question of war or peace between the two great rival nations was drawing to a crisis, Mr. Griffith was promoted by Lord Anson to be third Lieutenant on board the *Eagle*, 60 guns, Capt. (afterwards Sir) H. Palliser, when he again signalized himself in a desperate engagement with the *Duc d' Aquitaine* ship, which had 50 guns mounted, but was taken though Mr. Griffith was knocked down by the splinters of an 18 pounder, and was supposed to have been killed. Capt. Palliser publicly thanked him for his conduct, and wished exceedingly to give him a post in the *Ripon* man-of-war, to which he had just been preferred, but Capt. Hobbs, who succeeded Capt. Palliser in the command of the *Eagle*, objected, declaring "that if he " had a brother wanting promotion he would not use his interest " for him if he were thereby to be deprived of the services of " Lieut. Griffith." However, in a short time his singular merit gained him the appointment of 5th Lieutenant of the *Royal George*, Lord Anson's Flagship, where he served under his Lordship's immediate eye, and laid the foundation for those merited rewards which soon followed. On the 4th of June, 1759, he received his commission as Captain of the *Postillion* and during the repairs that were necessary to equip her, he was requested at the special instance of Lord Anson to take the command of the *Argo* during the indisposition of Capt, Tinker, during which interval he had made several cruises to the coast of France, and having been ordered by the Commodore to watch the motions of Thurot who was then in Dunkirk harbour, he performed this service so well as to obtain the thanks of Commodore Boys who commanded on that station. About this time Sir Piercy Brett having been appointed to take the command in the West Indies, requested Lord Anson to make Capt. Griffith *Post* that he might take him there as his Captain in his Flagship, the *Cambridge*, but Lord Anson, wishing to give him something better, refused, and also recalled Captain Griffith's former appointment to the *Postillion*, giving him the command of the *Gibraltar*, in which on the 17th November, 1759, he fell in with the Grand Fleet of France, under the command of Mons. Conflans. He joined and accompanied them till the 19th in the evening, repeated all their signals, imitated all their manœuvres, bore down within gunshot of Conflans' own ship, and upon discovering that he was suspected by them he bore away to Quiberon bay, to alarm the British squadron stationed there, and dispatched his Lieutenant in a Dutch vessel to Plymouth to Sir Edward Hawke. He then set sail to the Mediterranean to communicate the information to Admiral Broderick, and though he was not present when the signal victory was gained over the French Fleet, the success was attributed to *his* enterprising and officer-like conduct for which he was raised to Post Captain of the *Gibraltar*. In the early part of the following year, 1760, the ill-fated expedition under Thurot menaced the coasts of

Ireland, and it fell to the lot of Captain Griffith to bring the first intelligence of their supposed destination to Commodore Elliot, who was then lying with three frigates in Kinsale Bay, thus enabling him to capture the enemy's whole squadron. Soon after this he was ordered to the Straits of Gibraltar, and continued cruising in the Mediterranean during the remainder of the war, where he acquired the friendship of Admiral Saunders and the Honourable Leveson Gower, and had also an opportunity of renewing his former intimacy with Admiral Sawyer, Viscount Newark and Lord Hotham. In 1762, Spain having declared war against Portugal, the Mediterranean became the scene of maritime exertions. In April, Capt. Griffith, after a long and unsuccessful cruise, fell in with *L'Etoile*, a French privateer of 10 nine-pounders and two eighteen-pounders and 137 men, who maintained a gallant resistance, nor did they strike till half her crew were killed or wounded and herself a wreck. The *Gibraltar* had five men killed and 22 wounded, amongst them Lieutenant Horton. During the heat of the action, as Captain Griffith was leaning on the binnacle, watching the motions of the enemy through the spying glass, and in the act of turning to give orders to his lieutenant, a chain shot tore off that part of the binnacle on which he had just been leaning, and severed the lieutenant in two pieces, but he escaped. Capt. Griffith, still cruising in the Mediterranean, protecting the trade of his country, having heard from a neutral vessel that the French Fleet was in the Channel of Malta, instantly left the station, and, with that promptitude and decision which ever marked his character, he ran through the Straits of Messina without a pilot, passed the French Squadron, proceeded to the Levant, prevented the sailing of the Turkish traders, landed expresses along the coast, and then proceeded to Cyprus, having heard that there were two frigates lying in the harbour, which he succeeded in blocking up for some time, but, through his stock of water failing and the Nile being out, he was compelled to quit before he could enter into an engagement. Peace being now concluded, Captain Griffith, after a period of 20 years (passed almost unremittingly at sea), retired to enjoy the society of his relations and friends, and took a house near Warrington, Cheshire, where he remained in the enjoyment of social and domestic comforts for the space of six years, when a dispute with Spain about the Falkland Islands again called him into action, and he was appointed captain of the *Namar*, 90 guns, by Sir Edward Hawke. He afterwards returned into the country, and married a Miss Nicholls, of Chester, who, however, lived but a few years, and died without issue. Not long after this a dispute arose with the American Colonies, and, his services being warmly solicited, he undertook the command of the *Nonsuch*, and sailed to America, where he was appointed by Lord Howe to bring up the rear of that vast armament which sailed at this most critical period of the war from New York to Chesapeake. Not a ship of the convoy being lost in consequence of Captain

Griffith's exertions, Lord Howe honoured him with a distinguishing blue pendant as third in command on the occasion. In the same year he, with a detachment of Admiral Byron's fleet, in co-operation with Major-General Pigot, attacked the rebels near Newport in Providence, destroyed their whole naval force, and did them irreparable damage. He was then ordered to the West Indies to join Admiral Barrington in the reduction of St. Lucia. His ship was one of the seven which, after the capture of that island, resisted ten repeated attacks of the French Fleet of thirteen heavy ships of the line. In consequence of this brilliant event, Captain Griffith was preferred to the command of the *Conqueror*, 94 guns, the *Nonsuch* being no longer fit for service. A signal being now given for a fleet between Martinico and St. Lucia, the ships were all ordered to slip their cables and chase, when Captain Griffith in the *Conqueror* took the lead, and soon succeeded in cutting off the *Hannibal*, 74 guns, notwithstanding the unceasing batteries which he had to defend himself from on the shore, and the shouts that resounded that the pilot had quitted his post. He had just declared his intention of laying the French Admiral on board that very tack when a fatal bullet from the shore glanced on an iron rod situated under the main shrouds, which altered its direction, and instantly severed his head from his body. Thus terminated the existence of this gallant and much lamented officer. Sir Hyde Parker, in his despatch to Government on the melancholy occasion, said, "The service cannot lose a better " *man* or a better *officer*." and when enclosing his will to his friends expressed himself thus :—" Give my compliments to his " nephew Walter (to whom he left the bulk of his fortune), and " tell him that in my opinion the example of his uncle's life and " death is by much the noblest part of his legacy." Captain Griffith's remains were interred at St. Lucia, where a small pedestal denotes the spot. The highest panegyric on his memory is to be found in the simple narration of his public and private life, which was spent in one continued course of active exertion and the practice of every social virtue. He possessed a greater number of excellencies and fewer faults than are the common portion of humanity. His attachment to religion was sincere and devout, founded on a knowledge of its principles and a thorough conviction of its truth. It was dignified and unaffected, without moroseness in one extreme, or puritanical enthusiasm on the other. It formed a disposition which never forsook him, either in his closet, his social conversation, in the noise of tempest or the roar of battle, and gave him an habitual presence of mind which exalted his character both as an officer and a man. When a young midshipman on board the *Duke* man-of-war, soon after he first went to sea, perceiving a sailor going into the powder magazine with a lighted candle in his hand, and, being instantly aware that if he alarmed the man too suddenly it might be attended with the most perilous consequences to the ship and crew, he beckoned to him good humouredly, as if he wished to speak to him, and, approaching him, he seized the lighted end of the candle with one hand, extinguishing it, and the man by the other, whom he immediately took to Commodore Trevor, who ordered the sailor to be punished, and handsomely rewarded the young midshipman for his dexterity. When in 1750 he was cast away on the coast of Jamaica in the *Fox* frigate, during the confusion incident to such a situation, and in the most critical period of their danger, an officer of their ship, whom Mr. Griffith had vainly attempted to convince of the existence of God, ran up to him, and, falling on his knees, exclaimed in an agony of terror, " Oh, Griffith, Griffith! what can I do to be saved ? " The other with that dignified composure which always characterized him, instantly replied—

" If you bethink yourself of any crime
Unreconciled as yet to Heaven and grace
Solicit for it straight."
Shakespeare's Othello.

Captain Griffith was also conspicuous for his high and rigid notions of honour and justice, for when it was proposed that a representation of his gallant conduct during his engagement with the *Duc d' Aquitaine* should be made to Lord Anson he rejected it with warmth, saying that he had only done his duty, and that his brother officers had all done theirs, and, as such a representation could not be made without reflecting distinctly on their conduct, he would not accept promotion on such terms. To the regard felt for him by an officer is the rescue of the whole ship's crew on one occasion attributed, for when Captain Smelt heard that the *Fox* had been seen off Port Royal in great distress, during a violent hurricane, he engaged a small vessel, and with little prospect of success sailed along the coast in search of his friend, and, after a long and laborious search, discovered him and his crew on an insulated sandbank, where, but for this succour, they must have all perished, and brought them back to Port Royal to the inexpressible joy of both parties. Captain Griffith never allowed an oath to pass without a reprimand, and it was generally remarked that his men were less addicted to the practice than those of the other ships. His courage was of the brightest kind, and evinced itself in every action of his professional life. When placed between the decks during his engagement with the *Duc d' Aquitaine* he would not allow the ports to be lowered when the guns were drawn in, saying that his men must have air and light enough, on which he received three hearty cheers, and as soon as he recovered from being knocked down and stunned by the splinters of an 18-pounder, which killed and maimed four others close to him, he cried out, " A miss is as good as a mile, my lads," and, wiping away the blood and brains of his poor comrades, with which he had been besmeared, set instantly to work again.

GRIFFITHS, ANN, the gifted Welsh hymn-writer, was born at Dolwar Fechan, a secluded farm house in the parish of Llanfihangel, in the early part of 1776, and was baptized at the parish church of that parish on the 21st of April in that year. She was the youngest daughter and one of five children of Mr. John Thomas, a respectable farmer, by Jane his wife. She received such education as was to be obtained in those days in a country village mixed school, namely, reading, writing, a little arithmetic, and a smattering of English. She grew up to be a tall, comely, rosy-faced, dark-haired, but fair-skinned young woman, with a somewhat high forehead, and an intellectual cast of countenance. Though of a delicate constitution, she was naturally of a lively disposition, fond of dancing and other innocent amusements. In her girlish days she was inclined to scoff at religious people ; and once, seeing a number of persons going to an Association at Bala, she exclaimed, "Look at the pilgrims going to Mecca!" But, about the twentieth year of her age, she was herself brought under deep religious impressions, and joined the Calvinistic Methodist Society. Henceforth her life was distinguished for its sanctity, devotional character, and religious zeal. With several of her neighbours she would frequently go on "Sacrament" Sundays to Bala—a distance of more than 20 miles of rough and hilly road--to receive the Lord's Supper from the hands of the Rev. Thomas Charles, and her retentive memory enabled her to repeat the sermons she had heard almost word for word. Her father, who appears to have been somewhat gifted with poetic talent, died in 1803, an event which so much affected her as to impair her health. In October, 1804, she was married to Mr. Thomas Griffiths, of Cefn-du, Guilsfield, who came to live with her at Dolwar. This union, however, was unhappily but of short duration. In July, 1805, she gave birth to a child who lived but a fortnight, and whom she only survived a fortnight more. She died early in August in the 30th year of her age, and on the 12th of the same month was buried at the parish church of Llanfihangel. Thus living and dying in the seclusion and obscurity of a lonely mountain farmhouse, Ann Griffiths composed some of the sweetest and most precious hymns in the Welsh language, if not, indeed, in any language. They are not numerous—all that have been preserved being only about 75 verses—and they are too often marred by faults of composition and the transgression of the simplest rules of prosody, yet many of them are so rich in poetic fancy, sublime imagery, holy sentiment, and seraphic fervour that they can never be forgotten so long as hymns are sung in the Welsh language. Mothers teach their babes to lisp them, and many a pious Christian has been heard faintly to whisper them in the hour of death. Among the most widely known are those beginning :—

> " Dyma babell y Cyfarfod,"
> '· Pechadur aflan yw fy enw."
> " Welo'n sefyll rhwng y myrtwydd,"
> "Gwna fi fel pren planedig, O fy Nuw," &c.

Her husband (who only survived his gifted and saintly wife two years and a half) also composed a few popular hymns. Ann

Griffiths, it appears, had no idea when she composed her hymns that they would ever appear in print. Her natural modesty and extreme diffidence did not permit her indeed to commit many of them to writing, and it is to Mrs. Ruth Hughes, of Pontrobert, that Wales is indebted for the preservation of nearly all that are extant. Mrs. Hughes had been for some years in service, and on terms of intimate friendship with Ann Griffiths before and after her marriage, and the hymns that have been published were nearly all treasured in her memory, and taken down from her repetition some time after Ann Griffiths's death They were first published with a preface by the Rev. Thomas Charles, at Bala, in 1806; another edition appeared in 1808; and in 1809 another at Carmarthen. From that time to the present no collection of Welsh hymns has been considered complete without including several of them. Other collected editions were published at Llanfyllin in 1817 and 1847, the latter containing a short Memoir of the Authoress, and another at Aberystwyth in 1854. In 1865 a more complete edition was published at Denbigh with Notes, and a Memoir by Mr. Morris Davies, of Bangor, and containing some of her letters and the hymns written by her husband. In 1864 a handsome obelisk of polished red Aberdeen granite was placed by subscription upon her grave, with the following simple inscription in Welsh: "In Memory of Ann Griffiths, of Dolwar Fechan. Born 1776; "Died 1805. This column was erected in the year 1864."

GRUFFYDD HAFREN, a poet, who flourished about the beginning of the 17th century. He wrote an Elegy on the death of Sion Phylip, who died in 1620, extracts from which are given in the *Brython* vol. IV. p. 142. A treatise of his on the art of poetry is said to be also still extant.

GRUFFYDD MAELOR, prince of Powys, a son of Madog ab Meredydd ab Bleddyn ab Cynfyn. He succeeded his father as lord of the two Maelors, Bromfield and Mochnant in Rhaiadr in 1159, and was renowned for his wisdom and liberality above all the princes and nobility in his time. He was also a valiant soldier, and shewed conspicuous valour at the great battle of Crogen, from which Henry II. retreated with great loss and barely escaped with his life. His wife was Angharad, daughter of Owen Gwynedd, by whom he had four sons and three daughters. His son Madog succeeded him in that portion of his dominion called after him Powys Fadog. He died in 1190, and was buried at Meifod. The *Myvyrian Archaiology* contains two poems in praise of him by Llygad Gwr, a contemporary poet.

GRUNDMAN, Rev. MARTIN, was ejected from the living of Llandyssil in 1662, for Nonconformity. " Being at London " at the time of the Plague, he was so poor that he was not able " to remove his family, and was carried off by it. He was a very " holy, humble man, and an able minister." (*Calamy's Nonconformists' Memorial*).

GWALCHMAI, Rev. HUMPHREY, was born at Dolgar, in the parish of Llanwyddelan, on the 14th January, 1788. He began to preach with the Calvinistic Methodists when he was about 17 years of age. In 1813 he settled at Llanidloes, where he continued to live for nearly 30 years. In 1819 he was ordained to the full work of the ministry. He was one of the earliest, ablest, and most ardent apostles of the temperance and total abstinence reform in Wales, and a zealous promoter of Sunday Schools. With a view chiefly of promoting these movements he in 1836 started at Llanidloes a monthly periodical called *Yr Athraw* (*The Teacher*) which he ably conducted for about seven years, but it did not prove a financial success. Mr. Gwalchmai also published several sermons and small tracts in Welsh. He was a man of considerable intelligence and ability, of a highly courteous and amiable disposition, a popular preacher and "zealous of good works." For some years prior to his death he resided at Oswestry, where he died on the 29th of March, 1847, at the age of 59. He was buried at Adfa, Llanwyddelan, on the 2nd April, 1847.

GWENDDWYN, one of the daughters of Cyndrwyn, prince of Powys, towards the close of the 5th century, and sister of Cynddylan. In his Elegy on the death of the latter, Llywarch Hen says :—

"Beloved were the daughters of Cyndrwyn,
Heledd, Gwladus, and Gwenddwyn."

GWENWYNWYN, was the son of Owen Cyfeiliog, prince of Powys, by Gwenllian, daughter of Owen Gwynedd. On the death of his father in 1197, he succeeded to the principality of Upper Powys, which henceforth was called Powys Wenwynwyn From this time forth he was constantly engaged in warfare. In 1198 he attacked the English in the open plain near Pain's Castle, but was defeated with great loss. In 1199 he took oaths of allegiance to King John, and received from him a Grant or confirmation of all the lands he had taken, or should take from the king's enemies in North Wales. In 1202 he submitted to Llewelyn ab Iorwerth, prince of Wales, and took the same oaths of allegiance to him as he had before done to the King of England, from which last he had been discharged by a dispensation from Rome. In 1204. however, we find him again at peace with the English, but in 1207 he was taken prisoner at Shrewsbury, and forced to become vassal to the King of England. During his captivity Llewelyn invaded and devastated his territories. In 1211 Gwenwynwyn joined King John in the invasion of Wales, but in the following year threw off his forced allegiance, was reconciled to Llewelyn, and recovered the Castle of Mathrafal which had been raised and garrisoned for the English king. In 1215 he assisted Llewelyn and other Welsh princes in recovering their ancient possessions and in the taking of Shrewsbury. Changing sides again in 1216 he was hunted from his dominions and driven into the county of Chester by Llewelyn,

F

who seized upon his whole territory. He died soon after without recovering his inheritance, and was succeeded by Griffith, his son, by Margaret daughter of Robert Corbet, lord of Caus, not of the Lord Rhys of South Wales as often erroneously stated. Gwenwynwyn was undoubtedly brave and skilful in the field, and was a liberal patron of religion, but whilst his versatility in changing sides so frequently cannot be altogether justified, it may be accounted for in some degree by the necessity he was probably under from the situation of his territory of temporising with the dominant party for the time being. His arms were, *Or* a lion's gamb dexterways erased *gules*, armed *azure*. He made extensive grants of land in Llanbrynmair, and other parts of Montgomeryshire to the abbey of Strata Marcella, near Welshpool. The *Myvyrian Archaiology* contains several masterly Odes addressed to him by the poet Cynddelw.

GWENWYS, of Powys, the chief of one of the five plebeian tribes of Wales. The others were Blaidd Rhudd, Adda Vawr, Heilyn, and Alo.

GWERFUL HAEL, or "the Bountiful," was born in the early part of the 15th century at Blodwel, in the parish of Llanyblodwel, Shropshire. She was the daughter of Madog ab Maredydd ab Llewelyn Ddu, of the line of Tudor Trevor. Her charities were so great as to obtain for her the title of "bountiful." She was married first to Rhys ab Dafydd ab Hywel of Rhug, by whom she had two sons—Hywel and Gruffydd; secondly, to Gruffydd ab Ieuan Vychan of Abertanat, by whom she had one only son David, heir to the Tanat estates, who was a great patron and favourite of the bards and minstrels of his time. The families of Abertanat and Brogyntyn trace their descent from Gwerfyl Hael as also do the Salisbury's of Rhug and Llewenni; Pugh, of Mathafarn; Pryse, Gogerddan; Sir W. W. Wynn; and the Godolphin family by intermarriage with the Tanat's. She was buried in the chancel at Llanfihangel in Blodwel, now called Llanyblodwel. Guto'r Glyn, an eminent contemporary poet, wrote an elegy upon her death, setting forth her many excellencies and charities, ending with the lines—

> Y bedd lle mae'i hannedd hi
> A lanwed o haelioni;
> O thelir pwyth i haelion,
> Taler ei haelder i hon.

(Charity fills the grave she now dwells in; if the bountiful are recompensed, may this one receive the recompense of her bountifulness.) Lewis Glyn Cothi, another poet of that period, also wrote her elegy describing the general lamentation that existed in consequence of her death, and that such was the excellency of her character that she was deserving of being canonized, and of pilgrimages being made to her shrine. The Abertanat estate is now the property of Henry Leslie, Esq., the accomplished musician.

GWERFYL MECHAIN, or MARY VAUGHAN, or FYCHAN, was the daughter of Hywel Vaughan, or Fychan, of Caer Gai, and flourished between 1460 and 1490. She was married to one of the Vaughan's of Llwydiarth, and was one of the best and most celebrated poets of that age. Several of her compositions are still extant, and possess very considerable merit. Guto'r Glyn, another eminent poet, wrote an elegy upon her death. She died at Llwydiarth, and was buried at Llanfihangel-yn-Ngwynfa.

GWIAWN, the son of Cyndrwyn, Prince of Powys, was one the three sentinels of the battle of Bangor Orchard, A.D. 607. A saying of his is preserved in " Chwedlau y Doethion " (The Sayings of the Wise) :—

> A glywaist ti chwedl Gwiawn,
> Dremynwr golwg uniawn ?
> Duw cadarn a farn pob iawn.
> (Hast thou heard the saying of Gwiawn,
> The observer, of accurate sight ?
> The mighty God will determine every right.)

GWIAWN BACH, a poet who flourished about 470, and was a native of Llanfair-Caereinion. A saying of his is preserved in the " Sayings of the Wise :—

> A glywaist ti chwedl Gwiawn
> Bach yn dangos deddf gyfiawn ?
> Iawn pob iawn lle bo iawn.
> (Hast thou heard the saying of Gwiawn
> Bach, teaching a just law ?
> Every claim is right where there is justice.)

None of his poetical compositions are now extant. We find also the following reference to him in the so-called " History of "Taliesin" :—" A Gwion bach mab gwreang o Lanfair yng " Nghaer Einion ym Mhowys, a roes hi i amodi y pair." (And she [Ceridwen] put Gwion Bach, the son of a yeoman of Llanfair, in Caereinion, in Powys, to stir up the cauldron.)

GWRHAI, one of the sons of Caw, a saint of the College of Deiniol, who flourished in the 6th century. He founded the Church of Penstrowed, or, as some say, was buried there.

GWRIN, the son of Cynddilig, the son of Nwython ab Gildas, a saint who flourished in the sixth century. He founded the Church of Llanwrin.

GWRNERTH, the son of Llewelyn ab Tegonwy ab Teon of Trallwng, or Welshpool, a saint who lived about the close of the sixth century, or, says Llwyd, about 610. The Red Book of Hergest contains a dialogue in verse between him and his father Llewelyn, attributed to St. Tysilio, and printed in the *Myvyrian Archaiology*. It is preceded by a head note to the following effect : —

"Llewelyn and Gwrnerth were two penitent saints at Trallwng in Powys, and it was their custom to meet together during the last three hours of the night and the first three hours of the day to say their matins, and the hours of the day besides. And once on a time, Llewelyn, seeing the cell of Gwrnerth shut, and not knowing why it was so, composed an Englyn."

GWYDDELAN, a saint whose date is uncertain, the founder of Llanwyddelan Church, also of Dolwyddelan, Carnarvonshire-Festival, August 22.

GWYDDFARCH, another saint and anchorite of the sixth century, who is variously described in Welsh Chronicles as follows :—

1.—Gwyddfarch ab Llywelyn o'r Trallwng.   Sant cf Bangor Cybi, Môn.   (Gwyddfarch, the son of Llywelyn of Trallwng. A saint of the college of Cybi, in Anglesey [Holyhead].
2.—Gwyddfarch ap Alarwt Tywyssanc y Pwyl.   Eglwys cf Meifod, Powys. (Gwyddfarch, the son of Alarwt Prince of the Pwyl). His church, Meifod, Powys.
3.—Gwyddfarch m. amalarus tywyssanc y pwyl.
4.—Gwyddfarch Erienot ap Amalarys tywyssawc o'r Pwyl.
5.—Gwyddvarch ym Meivot ap Malarys tywyssawe y pwyl.
6.—Gwyddvarch e Meinot m. Amalarus tywyssanc or Pwyl.

Some translators have rather hastily interpreted the words "tywyssawe y Pwyl" to mean "king of Poland," while others have ingeniously surmised that "the Pwyl" refers to the district of Pwyl, otherwise *Pool*, now called *Welshpool*. This latter view is, indeed, to some extent supported by the first of the above descriptions, where Gwyddfarch is stated to be the son of Llywelyn of Trallwng; but then the questions arise—Were Amalarus and Llewelyn the same?   or, Were there not two saints of the name of Gwyddfarch—one a son of Llewelyn, the other of Amalarus?   These are matters upon which antiquaries are by no means yet agreed.   It may be pointed out that *Maelrhys*, *Maclerw*, or *Meilyr* (which, probably, are but other forms of the word Amalarus) is a name which occurs repeatedly in the annals of Emyr Llydaw, to whose family many of the Armorican missionaries who came over to Wales in the sixth century belonged.   Gwyddfarch, sometimes styled "Cyfarwydd" (well-informed), founded the most ancient church at Meifod, where he ended his ascetic life.   His deathbed on the rock still bearing his name was pointed out to E. Lhuyd about the close of the 17th century.   The site of Gwyddfarch's church is fixed by tradition at the western gate of the churchyard, near a house called "the Jail," in Bridge-street.   Some years ago the foundations and some interesting relics of this ancient and long lost church were discovered nearly six feet below the surface, in excavating the foundations of the Independent Chapel at Meifod.   An interesting account of these discoveries is given by Mr. T. G. Jones (*Cyffin*), in the 14th vol. of the *Montgomeryshire Collections*.

GWYN, JOHN, of Trelydan, Guilsfield, a member of an ancient family descended from Prince Bleddyn ap Cynfyn. He was the son of Robert Powell, Gent., by Catherine, daughter of Oliver Price, of Forden, Gent., but he took the name of *Gwyn* after his grandfather, Edward Gwynne, a barrister-at-law, of Gray's Inn. He was before the Civil War a retainer in the household of Charles I., and employed in training his family in military exercises. He naturally engaged in the royal service during the great civil war as a captain in the royal Regiment of Guards, and seems to have distinguished himself by his personal courage and activity. After his royal master's execution he followed the banner of his son in the most difficult enterprises, and was with Montrose in his last unhappy attempt. He wrote *Military Memoirs of the Great Civil Wars*, which give a graphic account of many of the stirring scenes in which he took part. These were edited in 1822 by Sir Walter Scott (Edinburgh, Ballantyne and Co.).

GWYNN, RICHARD, better known in after life as *Richard White*, the Catholic " Proto-martyr of Wales," was a member of the old and influential family of Gwynn of Llanidloes, extinct now for more than 200 years. Nothing is recorded of his parentage or youth, but we are told that " he was 20 years " of age before he did frame his mind to like of good letters," after which he went to Oxford, but, not remaining there long, proceeded to Cambridge, and entered St. John's, living by the charity of the College. The change of religion brought about by the accession of Queen Elizabeth, however, caused him to leave the University and to set himself up as a schoolmaster in Denbighshire, first at Overton Madog, then Wrexham, Gresford, and Yswyd, and lastly at Overton. This occupation he pursued for about 16 years. He led an exemplary life, and became well known for his scholarship and love of learning, and his attachment to the Catholic religion. This latter brought him to trouble, and he became the object of much persecution. In July, 1580, he was cast into prison, and kept in confinement for four years, during which he was very harshly treated, being frequently tortured with the view of inducing him to forsake his religion. After several trials he was finally brought up at the Wrexham Assizes on Friday, the 9th of October, 1584, before Sir George Bromley, chief justice, Simon Thelwall, Esq., deputy-justice, and others, upon an indictment for high treason. The jury, after being locked up in the church all night, returned a verdict of guilty the following morning, and Mr. Thelwall, who then presided, in the absence of Sir George Bromley, passed the following barbarous sentence:—" Richard White shall be " brought to prison from whence he came, and thence drawn on " a hurdle to the place of execution, where he shall hang half " dead, and so be cut down alive, his members cast into the fire, " his belly ripped into the breast, his bowels, liver, lungs, heart, " &c., thrown likewise into the fire, his head cut off, his body

" parted into four quarters. Finally, head and quarters to be set
" up where it shall please the Queen. And this execution to be
" done on a Thursday; we will appoint you the day before we
" go. And so the Lord have mercy upon him." Nothing dis-
mayed at this recital of what was to be done to him, the condemned man resolutely answered, " What is all this ? Is it any
" more than one death ? " Strong efforts were made to induce
him to recant, and to acknowledge the Queen's supremacy as
head of the Church, in order to save his life, but in vain. He
remained steadfast to the last, and the sentence was carried out
in all its revolting details the following Thursday, 15th of
October, 1584. Mr. White left behind him a widow and three
children. The above account is taken from a contemporary MS.
discovered some years ago in the Mission house of the Catholic
Chapel, Holywell, and printed at full length in Lloyd's *History
of Powys Fadog*, Vol. III.

GWYNNOG, son of Gildas, a saint of the congregation of
Catwg, who lived in the 6th century. He founded Llanwnog
Church, in the north wall of which is a small window, of fourteenth century work, being probably a portion of the old chancel
window wherein he is delineated in coloured glass in episcopal
habit, with a rich mitre on his head, and a crosier in his hand,
with an inscription underneath in old English characters, which
in full ran as follows:—" *Sanctus Gwinocus, cujus animæ
propitietur Deus Amen.*" He is also the patron saint of Y
Vaenor in Breconshire, and supposed to be one of the three
founders of Llantrisant, Glamorgan. His festival is October
26th.

HAFREN was the daughter of Locrinus, by Essyllt, a beautiful
captive virgin, to whom, in order to unite himself, Locrinus had
divorced his former wife and Queen Gwenddolen. After the
defeat and death of Locrinus by his injured Queen, Hafren with
her mother was thrown by her order into a river, which has since
been called by the Welsh Hafren, and by the English Severn.
" At that period," adds the Welsh Brut, " Daniel the prophet
" governed in the country of Judea, and the nephew of Eneas in
" Italy, and Homer was reciting his poetry."

> " The guiltless damsel, flying the mad pursuit
> Of her enraged stepdame Gwendolen,
> Commended her fair innocence to the flood,
> That staid her flight with his cross-flowing course.
> The water nymphs, that in the bottom played,
> Held up their pearlèd wrists, and took her in,
> Bearing her straight to agèd Nereus' hall;
> Who, piteous of her woes, reared her lank head,
> And gave her to his daughters to imbathe
> In nectar'd lavers, strewed with ashphodel;
> And through the porch and inlet of each sense
> Dropp'd in ambrosial oils, till she revived,
> And underwent a quick immortal change,
> Made goddess of the river : still she retains

Her maiden gentleness, and oft at eve
Visits the herds along the twilight meadows,
Helping all urchin blasts, and ill-luck signs
That the shrewd meddling elf delights to make,
Which she with precious vial'd liquors heals."

Milton's " *Comus.*"

HALL, JAMES, JOHN, AND EDWARD, three brothers, were the sons of Christopher Breese Hall, tanner and farmer, Newtown, and Hester his wife. The Hall family appear to have come to Newtown early in the 18th century from Trefeglwys, where they had been settled for some generations. JAMES HALL was born December 8th, 1818; JOHN on January 13th, 1823; and EDWARD April 5th, 1825. James and John became flannel manufacturers, and for some years carried on business at Newtown and afterwards at Holywell, having been compelled to leave Newtown for a time in consequence of the hostility of the operatives to the introduction of steam power and improved machinery. After some years they returned to Newtown, about the year 1868, and carried on business separately up to their death, James as a manufacturer and fuller, and John as a wool merchant and farmer. Edward was brought up to the medical profession, and studied at St. Bartholomew's Hospital, London, for some years under Dr. Burrows. Among the lecturers were Dr. Bailey, who became physician to the Queen, and Dr. (now Sir James) Paget, who became sergeant-surgeon to the Queen. For three years he held the appointment of surgeon to Millbank Prison, Dr. Bailey being physician. The latter and Sir James Paget had the very highest opinion of Mr. Hall's abilities, and strongly advised him to set up in practice in London, but preferring to exercise his talents in his native country he settled at Newtown about the year 1849, and from that time until his death was actively engaged in his profession there. The three brothers for 40 years and upwards took an active part in all the public movements, local and political, of their time, especially such as tended to promote the social improvement and well-being of their fellow-townsmen. They were throughout life Nonconformists and strong and energetic Liberals, and, being highly gifted as public speakers, their services were in great request at public meetings, and were freely given. James was for years a member of the School Board, and a member and subsequently Chairman of the Highway Board and Board of Guardians. John was also for some time a member of the Highway Board, Local Board, and Board of Guardians. Edward was for many years medical officer of the Llanllwchaiarn District of the Newtown and Llanidloes Union, and for some time a member and Chairman of the Local Board. Upon the death of Dr. Slyman in April, 1869, he was elected unopposed to the office of coroner for the Newtown division of the county, an office which he continued to hold up to his death. He was placed on the Commission of the Peace, but never acted. John Hall died June 16th, 1882, aged 59 years, and was buried at St. David's Churchyard, Newtown, but his remains were subsequently removed to the Cemetery, where a handsome monument of polished Aberdeen granite had already been erected by subscription to his memory. James Hall died March 24th, 1888, aged 69 years, and Edward Hall on June 11th, 1889, aged 64 years. Both were buried in the Newtown Cemetery. Only five or six weeks before his death James Hall was the recipient of a public testimonial in the shape of a cheque for £126 in acknowledgment of his "life-long public services and sacrifices especially on behalf "of Liberalism." The three brothers died unmarried. In their various spheres they were especially kind to the poor, and watchful over their interests and comfort. With rare unselfishness they, indeed, always placed the interests of their fellow-citizens before their own, often to the detriment of the latter. The words inscribed on John Hall's monument may with equal truth be applied also to his two brothers. Each of them was truly "a stern foe to oppression and wrong, an unselfish "defender of the people's rights, a never-failing friend of the "poor and helpless, and an earnest advocate of freedom, justice, "and progress."

HARRIS, DAVID, an excellent musician, was the son of John and Winifred Harris, of Nantllymystyn, in the parish of Llansantffraid, Cwmdauddwr, Radnorshire—a lonesome little mountain farm, a few yards only beyond the boundary of Montgomeryshire—where he was born September 16th, 1747. There also he lived the greater part of his long life, namely, until the year 1824, when he removed to Tymawr, Carno, in this county, where his married daughter resided, and with whom he spent the remainder of his days. He died January 6th, 1834, in his 87th year. He was buried in Carno Churchyard. He composed many Psalm-tunes and anthems, among them an elaborate and at one time very popular anthem on Psalm xxv. v. 4, "Pâr i mi "wybod dy ffyrdd" (Shew me Thy ways, O Lord). He also composed and sent for competition at the Welshpool Eisteddfod in 1824 a tune called "Babell." The prize was awarded to Mr. Roger Woodhouse, but competent musicians allege that Mr. Harris's composition is by far the most skilful and artistic of the two. Mr. Harris was also well versed in Cambrian history and in the rules of Welsh poetry, and was an excellent antiquary.

HAWYS GADARN, or the "Hardy," was the daughter of Owen ap Griffith ap Gwenwynwyn (sometimes called Owen de la Pole). She was born in July, 1291. Upon the death of her brother Griffin (or Griffith) in 1309, she became heiress of Powys, while she was yet a minor and a ward of the king of England. The king (Edward II.) gave her in marriage shortly afterwards to Sir John de Cherlton, a gentleman of his bed-chamber, who in August, 1309, obtained possession of her estates, and who was summoned by writ to Parliament in the 7th Edward II. as Lord of Powys, whence a barony in fee was created, descendable to his heirs general. Hawys was a liberal benefactor (some say the founder) of the dissolved house of the Grey Friars at Shrewsbury, "where she lyith buried under a "flate marble, by Chorleton's tombe" [Leland]. She died before 1353.

HEILYN, GRONO AP, of Pentreheilyn, in the parish of Llandysilio. The Heilyns were hereditary cup bearers to the Princes of Powys, hence their name. It seems they were also pursebearers, and as such they have been charged by an old proverb with extravagance of the public money: "Hael Heilyn "o god y wlâd"—(Heilyn is generous out of the public purse). Grono ap Heilyn was one of the two commissioners chosen by Prince Llewelyn ap Gruffydd to treat with those of King Edward I. in 1277 for the concluding of a final peace which was brought about, and for a while observed.

HEILYN, ROWLAND, another representative of the ancient family of Pentreheilyn, settled in London, and eventually became an Alderman and a Sheriff of the City of London. He was a man of singular goodness, and his name will long continue to be deservedly honoured among his countrymen, for he caused the Welsh Bible (which up to that time was only accessible to them in the shape of a large and expensive folio) to be printed at his own charge, or nearly so, in a portable octavo volume for their benefit. This was in 1630. He also published the *Practice of Piety* in Welsh. He died in 1634 (or, according to Vernon, Dr. Peter Heylyn's biographer, in 1637) without male issue One of his daughters marrying a Congreve, the estate of Pentreheilyn passed into that family. Dr. Heylyn designed to re-purchase it, "and (his biographer adds) had infallibly effected it, had not "death prevented the execution of his purpose." Since his death it has passed through several hands.

HEYLYN, Rev. PETER. D.D., the historian, although not born in Montgomeryshire, was an illustrious member of the same ancient Montgomeryshire family. He was born on the 29th of November, 1599, at Burford, in the county of Oxford, was the second son of Henry Heylyn, a cousin-german to the above Rowland Heylyn. His mother was Elizabeth Clampard, daughter of Mr. Francis Clampard, of Wrotham, Kent, and through her he was descended from Peter Dodge, of Stopworth, Cheshire, to whom King Edward I. gave the lordship of Padenhugh, in Scotland, for his valour and distinguished services at the sieges of Berwick and Dunbar. He was educated first at Burford School, where he displayed much precocity, and then at Oxford under private tuition. He afterwards entered Magdalen College, where he obtained a B.A. degree in 1617. After this he read every Long Vacation until he obtained his Master's degree (in 1620) Cosmography Lectures in the Common Refectory of the College, which created a profound admiration of the learning and abilities of so young a man, and brought his admission to a

Fellowship in 1619. His father died in 1622, and was buried at Lechlade, in Gloucestershire, leaving him some property. The following year he took orders, being ordained both deacon and priest in the same year. He paid a short visit to France in 1625, and some time afterwards, as chaplain to the Earl of Danby, to Guernsey and Jersey, his observations during which he published 30 years afterwards. In 1627, he was married to Lætitia, third daughter of Thomas Heygate, Esq., a Justice of the Peace for Middlesex, and formerly Provost Marshal-General of the Earl of Essex's army before Calais, with whom a dowry of £1,000 was promised, but never paid. At this period the young divine greatly recommended himself to Laud and the Court party by his learned and vigorous exposition of their High Church views and doctrines, and ere long he was rewarded with the appointment of Chaplain in Ordinary to the King (Charles I), who also as an additional mark of his favour presented him to the rectory of Hemingford, Huntingdonshire. The Bishop of Lincoln, however, for some technical reason refused to admit him, upon learning which the King within a week afterwards gave him a Prebendship of Westminster, which had just fallen vacant by the death of Dr. Darrel. At the king's request he made a careful analysis of Prynne's *Histriomastix*, and collected together " all such passages as were scandalous or dangerous to the " king," and at the same time wrote a small tract touching " the " punishments due by law and in point of practice unto such " offenders as Mr. Prynne." For these and other services his Majesty bestowed upon him the valuable living of Houghton, in the diocese of Durham, which, however, at the King's suggestion, he immediately afterwards exchanged for that of Alresford, in Hampshire, so as to be nearer to the Court. In July, 1630, he took his degree of Bachelor and in 1633 that of Doctor of Divinity at the then unusually early age of 33. From this time forth, Dr. Heylyn took a leading and most active part on the royalist and anti-puritanical side in the bitter controversies of those days, the details of which it would be too tedious to narrate here. Suffice it to say that few of his opponents could match him either for readiness of speech or profundity of learning. He was also a very rapid writer, and hurled treatise after treatise at his antagonists in quick succession. In 1638 he obtained the living of South Warnborough in addition to that of Alresford. In 1639 he was placed on the Commission of the Peace for Hampshire, and elected Clerk of the Convocation at Westminster. On the breaking out of the Civil War, he joined the King at Oxford, and at his Majesty's command wrote " the " weekly occurrences which befel his Majesty's government and " armies," under the title of *Mercurius Aulicus*; as well as several tracts in support of the Royalist cause. For this Parliament ordered the sequestration of his estates, which reduced him and his large family to great straits. He compounded, however, for his estates after a time ; but his valuable library was irrecoverably lost to him. The composition for his Montgomeryshire

estate was £112. In the beginning of 1645, Dr. Heylyn left
Oxford, and, as Anthony Wood relates, "shifted from place to
"place like the old travels of the patriarchs, and in pity to his
"necessity some of his friends of the loyal party entertained
"him." The same year he, for a time, with his family, settled at
Winchester; thence he removed in 1648 to Minster-Lovel in
Oxfordshire; and thence again in 1653 to Lacy's Court,
Abingdon, so as to be near the Bodleian library. Upon the
Restoration he exerted himself to procure a revision of the
Common Prayer Book, and a restoration of Convocation, as well
as the enlargement of some of the privileges of the clergy, in
which he was partly successful. However, his eminent services,
like those of many other staunch Royalists, were forgotten or
passed over in silence, and the neglect and ingratitude of his
friends were a greater trial to him than the opposition and persecution of his enemies. He had, notwithstanding his great losses,
found means to contribute considerable amounts in money and
plate towards the late King's necessities, and had been the means
of getting many others to do the same. Some who knew of his
great sacrifices protested, indeed, not their wonder only, but their
grief that so great a friend and sufferer for the Royal Family and
Church " should like the wounded man in the Gospel be passed
" by both by priest and Levite, and have no recompence for his
" past services besides the pleasure of reflecting on them." He
had nothing given him but what neither law nor justice could
detain from him, namely, his former preferments in the church,
from the profits and possession of which he had been kept above
17 years. But a greater misfortune than all these unkindnesses
and neglects had latterly befallen Dr. Heylyn, namely, the loss
of his eye-sight, which happened about 1654, and appears to
have been occasioned by intense and constant study. All these
trials he bore with much patience and Christian fortitude. After
a short illness of seven days he died of a fever at Westminster
on Ascension Day, May, 1662, in the 63rd year of his age, his
last words being. "I am ascending to the Church triumphant; I go
" to my God and Saviour, into joys celestial, and to hallelujahs
" eternal." He was buried under his seat in the Abbey, and a
monument was afterwards erected to his memory on the north side
of the Abbey, over against it, with a Latin inscription, written by
Dr. Earl, Dean of Westminster, afterwards Bishop of Salisbury.
An engraved portrait of Dr. Heylyn has been presented to the
Powysland Museum by the writer of this. It is stated by his
biographer Vernon that "the whole frame of his body was
" uniform, comely, and upright, his stature of a middle size and
" proportion, his eye naturally [before his blindness] strong,
" sparkling, and vivacious." He had eleven children, two of
whom gained high positions in the Church, Dr. Henry Heylyn
and Dr. Richard Heylyn, the latter dying a Canon of Christ
Church, Oxford. A daughter of his also married the Rev. Dr.
John Barnard, who to rectify certain errors in Vernon's first life
of his father-in-law, wrote another. These " rival biographers "

of Heylyn are the subject of an amusing chapter in Disraeli's *Curiosities of Literature*. Wood, with whom Dr. Heylyn evidently was not a special favourite, hints that " the temper of the person " may have had something to do with the neglect shown towards him by King Charles II., and adds that—

" In his younger years he was accounted an excellent poet, but very conceited and pragmatical ; in his elder, a better historian, a noted preacher and a ready or extemporanean speaker. He had a tenacious memory to a miracle, whereunto he added an incredible patience in study. He was a bold and undaunted man among his friends and foes (though of very mean port and presence), and therefore by some of them he was accounted too high and proud for the function he possessed. He wrote history pleasant enough, but in some things he was too much a party to be an historian, and equally an enemy to Popery and Puritanism."

All, even his bitter enemies, agree that his moral character throughout life was blameless and unsullied. Dr. Heylyn was a voluminous writer, as the following list of his works will show : —

Spurius, a Tragedy, MS. written 1616.

Theomachia, a Comedy, MS. 1619.

Geography, twice printed at Oxford in quarto in 1621 and 1624, and four times in London : afterwards in 1654 enlarged into folio under the title of *Cosmography*.

Augustus, an essay, 1631 ; since inserted in the *Cosmography*.

The History of St. George—London, 1631 ; reprinted 1633.

The History of the Sabbath, 1635 ; reprinted 1636.

An Answer to the Bishop of Lincoln's Letter to the Vicar of Grantham, 1636 ; twice reprinted.

An Answer to Mr. Burton's two Seditious Sermons, 1637.

A short Treatise concerning a Form of Prayer to be used according to what is enjoined in the 55th Canon MS.

Antidotum Lincolniense, or an answer to the Bishop of Lincoln's Book, entitled " Holy Table, Name, and Thing "—1637 ; reprinted 1638.

An Uniform Book of Articles, fitted for Bishops and Archdeacons in heir Visitations.

De jure paritatis Episcoporum, or concerning the peerage of the Bishops, printed 1681.

A reply to Dr. Hackwell concerning the sacrifice of the Eucharist—MS. 1641.

A Help to English History, containing a succession of all the Kings' Dukes, Marquesses, Earls, Bishops, &c., of England and Wales. Written 1641, under the name of Robert Hall, but afterwards enlarged under the name of Dr. Heylyn.

The History of Episcopacy—London 1641 ; reprinted 1681.

The History of Liturgies—1642 ; reprinted 1681.

A relation of the Lord Hopton's Victory at Bodmin—Oxford, 1644.

A view of the proceedings in the West for a Pacification—Oxford, 1644.

A letter to a gentleman in Leicestershire about the Treaty—Oxford, 1644.

A relation of the proceedings of Sir John Gell—Oxford, 1644.

A relation of the Queen's return from Holland, and the siege of Newark—Oxford, 1644.

The † or Black Cross, showing that the Londoners were the cause of the rebellion—Oxford, 1644.

The Rebel's Catechism—Oxford 1644.

An Answer to the Papists' groundless clamour, who nick-name the religion of the Church of England by the name of a Parliamentary religion—1644 ; reprinted 1681.

A relation of the Death and Sufferings of William Laud, Archbishop of Canterbury—1644.

The Stumbling block of Disobedience removed—1658 ; reprinted 1681.
An Exposition of the Creed—London, 1654.
A Survey of France, with an account of the Isles of Guernsey and Jersey—1656.
Examen Historicum; or a Discovery and Examination of the mistakes, falsities, and defects in some modern Histories—1659.
Certamen Epistolare; or the Letter-combat managed with Mr. Baxter, Dr. Bernard, Mr. Hickman, and J.H., Esq.—London, 1658.
Historia Quinque Articularis—London, 1660; reprinted, 1681.
Respondet Petrus; or an answer of Peter Heylyn, D.D., to Dr. Bernard's book, entitled 'The Judgment of the late Primate, &c.'—London, 1658.
Observations on Mr Ham. L'Strange's History of the life of King Charles I.—London, 1658.
Extraneus Vapulans; or a Defence of those Observations—London, 1658.
A short History of King Charles I. from his Cradle to his Grave—1658.
Thirteen Sermons: some of which are an Exposition of the Parable of the Tares—London, 1659 ; reprinted 1661.
The History of the Reformation—London, 1661.
Cyprianus Anglicus; or, the History of the Life and Death of Archbishop Laud—London, 1668.
Aërius Redivivus; or, the History of the Presbyterians from the year 1636 to the year 1647—Oxford, 1670.
In addition to the above, several other works are attributed to Dr. Heylyn. His miscellaneous writings were published in a collected form in 1681.

HELEDD, a daughter of Cyndrwyn, prince of Powys. One of her sayings is preserved in the *Sayings of the Wise*—

"A glywaist ti chwedl Heledd,
Ferch Cyndrwyn, fawr ei rhoufedd?
Ni ellir llwydd o falchedd."

(Hast thou heard the saying of Heledd, the daughter of Cyndrwyn of extensive wealth? "Success cannot attend pride.")

In *Englynion y Clywed* another version of this saying is given—

"Nid rhoddi da a wna dlodedd."

(It is not conferring a benefit that causes poverty.)

HERBERT.—No family connected with Montgomeryshire has produced so many illustrious characters as that of Herbert. During its 370 years' close connection with and settlement in the county, its members have from time to time displayed the highest qualities, and conveyed fresh lustre on its time-honoured name.

"Proud names who once the reins of empire held,
In arms who triumphed, or in arts excelled;
Chiefs graced with scars, and prodigal of blood;
Stern patriots, who for sacred freedom stood;
Just men, by whom imperial laws were given;
And saints who taught and led the way to heaven."
Tickell.

But of these we can only notice a few of the most prominent.

HERBERT, Sir RICHARD, Knight, "of Montgomery," was the first of the Herbert family, it appears, to settle in Montgomeryshire, and which he did about the year 1520. He was a younger son of Sir Richard Herbert, of Colebroke, near Abergavenny (22nd lineal descendant of Charlemagne)—"an

"Anakim in stature," and a redoubtable warrior of whose prowess several instances are recorded. Among others it is said that at the battle of Danesmore, near Banbury, where he was eventually defeated and taken prisoner, and three days afterwards beheaded, he, with pole-axe in hand, passed and re-passed twice through the enemy's army, killing with his own hand, it is said, 140 men without receiving any mortal wound. Sir Richard Herbert, of Montgomery, was knighted by Henry VIII about the year 1510, and received a grant of Montgomery Castle and its dependencies. He is also described as Constable of Aberystwyth, and Lewis Glyn Cothi addressed an ode to him as such. His great grandson, Lord Herbert, of Chirbury, says that he

"Was steward in the time of King Henry the eighth of the lordships and marches of North Wales, East Wales, and Cardiganshire, and had power in a martial law to execute offenders; in the using thereof he was so just, that he acquired to himself a singular reputation, as may appear upon the records of that time, kept in the paper chamber at Whitehall, some touch whereof I have made in my History of Henry the eighth; of him I can say little more than that he likewise was a great suppressor of rebels, thieves, and outlaws, and that he was just and conscionable; for if a false or cruel person had that power committed to his hands, he would have raised a great fortune out of it, whereof he left little, save what his father gave him, unto posterity."

This eulogy appears to have been quite deserved, for his administration, while it was vigorous, was yet wise and liberal. He was one of the foremost among the leading gentry of Montgomeryshire to petition the king for a further diminution of the powers of the Lords Marcher, and that "the petycioners might "have theire sheriff somoned hevery yeare, as they be in the "sheires of Englunde"—a request which was afterwards complied with. He died about the year 1540, and "lyeth buried in "Montgomery; the upper monument of the two placed in the "chancell being erected for him." He was twice married; firstly, to Jane, daughter of William ap Rees, by whom he had three sons and one daughter; and secondly, to Anne, daughter of David Ap Evan ab Llewelyn Vaughan, of Trefeglwys, by whom he had five sons and five daughters.

HERBEBT, WILLIAM, Esquire, of Park, in the parish of Llanwnog, was the third son of Sir Richard Herbert, of Montgomery, by his first wife. He filled several public offices, and was the first representative in Parliament (1541-44) of the Borough of Montgomery. He subsequently represented the County of Montgomery in the two succeeding Parliaments (1545-47 and 1547-52), and was Sheriff for the County in 1547 and 1569, and for Cardiganshire in 1549. He married Jane, daughter of John ab Meredyth ab Rees, of Llandinam, by whom he had seven sons and five daughters.

HERBERT, EDWARD, Esquire, of Montgomery, was the fourth son of Sir Richard Herbert, of Montgomery, but his eldest son by his second wife Anne, daughter of David ap Evan ap Llewelyn Vaughan, of Trefeglwys. Lord Herbert, of Chirbury, in his autobiography, gives the following interesting account of him :—

"My grandfather was of a various life, beginning first at Court, where after he had spent most part of his means, he became a soldier, and made his fortune with his sword at the siege of St. Quintens in France, and other wars both in the north and in the rebellions hapning in the times of King Edward the 6xt and Queen Mary, with so good success, that he not only came off still with the better, but got so much money and wealth as enabled him to buy the greatest part of that livelyhood which is descended to me; 'tho yet I hold some lands which his mother the Lady Ann Herbert purchased, as appears by the deeds made to her by that name which I can shew : and might have held more, which my grandfather sold under foot at an under value in his youth, and might have been recovered by my father, had my grandfather suffered him. My grandfather was noted to be a great enemy to the outlaws and thieves of his time, who robbed in great numbers in the mountains of Montgomeryshire, for the suppressing of whom he went both day and night to the places where they were, concerning which the many particulars have been told me, I shall mention one only. Some outlaws being lodged in an alehouse upon the hills of Llandinam, my grandfather and a few servants coming to apprehend them, the principal outlaw shot an arrow against my grandfather, which stuck in the pummel of his saddle, whereupon my grandfather coming up to him with his sword in hand, and taking him prisoner, he shewed him the said arrow, bidding him look what he had done, whereof the outlaw was no farther sensible than to say he was sorry that he left his better bow at home, which he conceived would have carryed his shot to his body, but the outlaw being brought to justice suffered for it. My grandfather's power was so great in the countrey, that divers ancestors of the better families now in Montgomeryshire were his servants, and rais'd by him. He delighted also much in hospitality, as having a very long table twice covered every meal with the best meats that could be gotten, and a very great family. It was an ordinary saying in the countrey at that time, when they saw any fowl rise, 'Fly where thou wilt, thou wilt light at 'Black-hall,' which was a low building, but of great capacity, my grandfather erected in his age; his father and himself in former times having lived in Montgomery Castle. Notwithstanding yet these expences at home, he brought up his children well, married his daughters to the better sort of persons near him, and bringing up his younger sons at the University; . . . . . . Nothwithstanding all which occasions of expence, my grandfather purchased much lands without doing anything yet unjustly or hardly. . . . . He died at the age of fourscore or thereabouts, and was buried in Montgomery Church without having any monument made for him."

He served the office of Sheriff in 1557 and 1568, and he is also described as lord of Cherbury, one of the Justices of the Quorum, High Steward and Constable of Montgomery Castle, High Steward under the king of the hundreds of Halcoter, Kerry, Cedewain, Arwystli and Cyfeiliog, and Custos Rotulorum. He is stated to have been " Captain-general over 500 men " at the great battle of St. Quinten already referred to, which took place on the 10th of August, 1557, and to have materially aided in the suppression of a formidable insurrection in Devonshire and Cornwall in 1549. He also represented the County of Montgomery in Parliament for about 20 years, namely from 1552 to 1572. He died in 1592. He married Elizabeth, daughter of Matthew Pryce, Esq., of Newtown, by whom he had four sons (three of whom became ancestors of peers) and seven daughters.

HERBERT, MATTHEW, Esquire, of Dolguog, near Machynlleth, the direct ancestor of the present Earl of Powis, was the second son of Edward Herbert, Esquire, of Montgomery, by Elizabeth, daughter of Matthew Pryce, of Newtown. He was called to the bar as a member of the Inner Temple in 1582. His nephew, Lord Herbert of Chirbury, says that " he " went to the Low Country Wars, and after some time spent " there, came home and lived in the countrey at Dolegeog upon " a house and fair living which my grandfather [Edward " Herbert] bestowed upon him." He served in Parliament for the county of Monmouth in the 5th year of Elizabeth and for Montgomery in the Parliament that met on the 29th October, 1586, He was Sheriff for Merioneth in 1599, and again in 1610. He married Anne, daughter of Charles Fox, of Bromfield, Salop, by whom he had an only son, Francis Herbert, of Dolguog, who suffered greatly for his loyalty to King Charles I., and was one of those who compounded for their estates. Matthew Herbert's great-great grandson, Henry Arthur Herbert, was created Lord Herbert of Chirbury (second creation) in 1743, and having married Barbara, niece and heiress of William Herbert, Earl, Marquis, and Duke of Powis, was, on the 27th May, 1748, created Baron Powis of Powis Castle, Viscount Ludlow and Earl of Powis of the 2nd creation.

HERBERT, Sir EDWARD, K.C.B., the celebrated Lord Herbert of Chirbury, was the eldest son of Richard Herbert, Esq., of Montgomery, by his wife Magdalen, daughter of Sir Richard Newport. He was born in 1581 at Eyton, near Wroxeter, his maternal grandfather's seat, where he spent the first nine years of his childhood. His father he describes, in his very entertaining " Autobiography," as

" black haired and bearded, as all my ancestors on his side are said to have been, of a manly or somewhat stern look but withall very handsome and well compact in his limbs and of a great courage whereof he gave proof when he was so barbarously assaulted by many men in the churchyard at Llanervil at what time he would have apprehended a man who denyed to appear to justice ; for defending himself against them all, by the help only of one John ap Howel Corbet, he chaced his adversaries untill a villain coming behind him did over the shoulders of others wound him on the head behind with a forest bill untill he fell down, tho' recovering himself again notwithstanding his skull was cut through to the Pia Mater of the brain, he saw his adversaries fly away, and after walked home to his house at Llyssyn, when after he was cured he offered a single combat to the chief of the family by whose procurement it was thought the mischief was committed ; but he disclaiming wholy the action as not done by his consent which he offered to testifie by oath, and the villain himself flying into Ireland, whence he never returned, my father desisted from prosecuting the business any farther in that kind and attained notwithstanding the said hurt that health and strength that he returned to his former exercises in a country life and became the father of many children."

His mother was a woman of great gifts and rare piety. The subject of this notice, when he became nine years of age, was placed under the care of Mr. Edward Thelwall, of Plâsward, Denbighshire, to learn Welsh " as believing it necessary to enable me to " treat with those of my friends and tenants who understood no " other language." He made very little progress, however, in Welsh or any other study during the nine months he remained under Mr. Thelwall's roof, having suffered from tertian ague most of the time. Thence he was removed to Didlebury, Salop, and placed there under the care of a Mr. Newton, who taught him Greek and logic so successfully that at fourteen years of age he was considered fit to enter the University of Oxford. While he was at the University his father died, and family reasons induced his friends to bring about a match between him and Mary, the daughter and heiress of Sir William Herbert, of St. Julians, he being seventeen and the bride twenty-one years of age. The marriage took place on the 28th February, 1598, and soon afterwards he returned to Oxford with his wife and mother (who took a house there) and for three years applied himself closely to his studies. His mother then removed to London, and from that time until he was twenty-one he passed his time mostly between London and Montgomery Castle, having in that time several children born to him. Besides Greek and Latin he had by this time mastered French, Italian, and Spanish, and acquired a good knowledge of music. He also applied himself to the study of medicine, fencing, and " the manner of fighting " a duel on horseback," and other exercises. About the year, 1600 he made his first appearance at court, and on King James the First's accession received the honour of knighthood. In 1605, while he was yet but 24 years old, he served the office of Sheriff for Montgomeryshire. In 1608, he proceeded to the Continent with the object of seeing foreign parts, but his love of adventure induced him to join the English army then serving in the Netherlands, where he soon distinguished himself by his reckless daring and intrepidity, though some of his enterprises were of a very Quixotic character. He afterwards travelled for some time through parts of Switzerland, Italy, and France. On his return to England he was well received at Court, where he distinguished himself by his gallantry and learning, and in 1619 was appointed ambassador and commissioner to France to sign the treaty of alliance between King James I. and Louis XIII. He also received private instructions to intercede for the persecuted Protestants; and with that object in view he had an audience of the King's favourite, the Duc de Luines, Constable of France. Luines had hidden behind a curtain in his audience chamber a gentleman of the reformed religion to report to his friends, as an ear witness of the interview, how little was to be hoped from the intercession of England. But he had mistaken the character of the ambassador, who fulfilled his mission with an undaunted spirit, so that the Constable remarked that if he were not the ambassador he would use him after another fashion. Sir Edward at once replied that as he was an ambassador, so he was also a gentleman, and laying his hand upon the hilt of his sword, told him that there was that which should make him an answer. This interview being misrepresented in England, occasioned his recall in 1621, but he cleared himself so satisfactorily to the King that he was very soon sent back again to the French Court, where he remained for two years longer, being again recalled in 1624. His autobiography, containing a highly interesting and often amusing account of his adventures in Court and field, his duels and chivalrous enterprises, as well as his somewhat peculiar views of men and things, concludes before the end of his embassy His embassies, though they brought him honour, were very costly to him, for he was obliged to sell estates worth £60,000 to pay the expenses. Besides this, £10,000 of his salary remained unpaid. On his return he was created Lord Herbert of Castle Island, in the peerage of Ireland, December 31st, 1625; and Lord Herbert of Chirbury, in the peerage of England, May 17th, 1629. His conduct during the civil war has been much blamed, and indeed is scarcely consistent with the chivalrous and fearless character borne by him in his younger days, unless, indeed, we assume that his heart was with the Parliament before he thought it prudent to declare himself on that side. He, in 1644, was summoned by Prince Rupert to Shrewsbury, the latter being afraid, it would appear, of the safety of Montgomery Castle in the hands of its lukewarm and eccentric, but able, lord; but instead of going he wrote on the 23rd of August, 1644, to the Prince saying, " that though I have the ambition to kiss your " most valorous and princely hands yet because I am newly " entered into a course of physic, I do humbly desire to be " excused for the present." But a few days afterwards, on the 5th of September, 1644, he surrendered the castle, without striking a blow, to a troop of the Parliamentary army under the command of Sir Thomas Middleton, he for a short time continuing to reside in it. The castle was immediately besieged by the Royalists under Lord Byron, but after a stubborn fight was relieved by the Parliamentarians. Lord Herbert's conduct on this occasion has been much blamed, and it must be owned, has never been satisfactorily explained, though original documents lately published by the Powysland Club, tend to exonerate him from blame. Sir Thomas Middleton suddenly marched on Montgomery with 800 soldiers and captured the outworks of the Castle which commanded the entrance. The aged Lord, sick, infirm, and half blind, deserted by his panic-stricken servants, seems to have had no alternative, indeed, but to capitulate on the best terms he could secure, which were not very hard. Subsequently, Lord Herbert removed to London, where he died August 20th, 1648, aged sixty-seven, and was buried in the Church of

St. Giles-in-the-Fields. He had issue, Richard (second lord), Edward and Beatrix, who both died unmarried. Of his writings, his *Autobiography* is perhaps the best known. It is said to be the earliest instance of autobiography in the English language. It was privately printed by Horace Walpole in 1764, and several editions of it have since appeared. His philosophical treatise in Latin, *De Veritate*, first published in Paris in 1624, has been translated into several languages. An enlarged edition appeared in 1633, and another in 1645, accompanied with another work called *De Religione Gentilium*. After his death two posthumous works were published; one, *An Account of the Expedition to the Isle of Rhé* (of which a Latin translation was published in 1656, but the original work remained in manuscript until 1860, when 40 copies only were privately printed by the late Earl of Powis); the other, *The Life and Reign of King Henry the VIIIth* — considered by far his best and ablest work. His *Occasional Verses* were published in 1665 by his youngest son Edward Herbert. A new edition was published in 1881. Eleven volumes of his manuscripts are in the library of Jesus College, Oxford. There are three portraits of him at Powis Castle. Lord Herbert, though vain and eccentric, "and not exempt from passion and choler," infirmities to which, as he tells us, all his race was subject, was a man of considerable learning, as well as a profound and original thinker, and all his works display much talent and ability. His religious opinions were peculiar and not such as would be generally considered orthodox. He maintained the theory of innate ideas, and made a certain instinct of the reason to be the primary source of all human knowledge. He compared the mind to a closed volume, which opens itself at the solicitation of outward nature acting upon the senses. No man (he argues) can appeal to revelation as an immediate evidence of the reasonableness of his faith, except those to whom that revelation has been directly given; for all others, the fact of revelation is a matter of mere tradition or testimony. These views were ably controverted by Locke, Baxter, Gassendi, and others.

HERBERT, Rev. GEORGE, M.A., "the poet of the "Temple," was the fifth son of Richard Herbert, Esq., of Montgomery, by Magdalen his wife, and a younger brother of the celebrated Lord Herbert of Chirbury. He was born on the 3rd of April 1593, at Montgomery Castle, according to his biographer, the gentle Izaak Walton, but more probably at Black Hall, a quaint old family residence, described by Lord Herbert which stood between the castle and the town, but was destroyed by fire many generations ago. In his fourth year, that is in 1597, his father died, so that, with his brothers and sisters, he was left under the sole care of his mother, an admirable woman, who subsequently married Sir John Danvers, and who brought up her young family with great care. I have already noticed

Edward, afterwards Lord Herbert. Of the others Walton says, " The second and third brothers were Richard and William, who " ventured their lives to purchase honour in the wars of the Low " Countries, and died officers in that employment. Charles was " the fourth, and died Fellow of New College, in Oxford." Henry and Thomas we shall notice further on. His three sisters " were all married to persons of worth and plentiful " fortunes, and lived to be examples of virtue, and to do good in " their generations." George, about his twelfth year, was sent to Westminster School, where he acquired a good knowledge of Greek and Latin, and gained a scholarship at Trinity College, Cambridge. He entered the University on the 5th May, 1609, took his B.A. degree in 1612-13, gained a Fellowship 15th March, 1615, and his M.A. degree the following year. At the University he made himself a name for varied and sound learning, becoming proficient in French, Italian, Spanish, and Hebrew. On the 18th January, 1618-9, he was appointed Public Orator of the University—a post in those days of considerable importance, the duties of which he discharged, with some interruptions, for about eight years. He was diligent in his attendance at Court, expecting to succeed in due time, as his two immediate predecessors had done, to the office of Secretary of State. He was on terms of friendship with Lord Bacon, and many of the principal nobility; and the King, who highly esteemed him, gave him in 1623 the lucrative sinecure of Whitford, Flintshire, so as to secure his attendance wheresoever the Court was. The death of the King and of several of his powerful friends, however, affected him much, and dispelled his hopes of Court preferment, so he retired into Kent,

" Where he lived very privately, and was such a lover of solitariness, as was judged to impair his health more than his study had done. In this time of his retirement he had many conflicts with himself, whether he should return to the painted pleasures of a Court life, or betake himself to a study of divinity and enter into sacred orders, to which his dear mother had often persuaded him. These were such conflicts as they only can know that have endured them; for ambitious desires and the outward glory of the world are not easily laid aside; but at last God inclined him to put on a resolution to serve at His altar."

The conflict was, it would seem, long and severe. In the meantime the prebend of Layton Ecclesia, in the diocese of Lincoln, carrying with it the living of Leighton Bromswold, had been bestowed upon him while he was still a layman. To add to his other losses, his mother died in 1627, and this bereavement finally decided him to resign the Public Oratorship, and quit the University. On the 5th March, 1628, he married Jane, daughter of Mr. Charles Danvers, of Bainton, Wilts., a near relative of his stepfather. The romantic circumstances attending this marriage are thus related by Walton :—

" These and other visible vertues begot him so much love from . . . . Mr. Charles Danvers . . . that Mr. Danvers having known him long and familiarly did so much affect him that he often and publicly declar'd a desire that Mr. Herbert would marry any of his nine daughters (for he had so many), but rather his daughter Jane than any other, because Jane was his beloved daughter; and he had often said the same to Mr. Herbert himself, and that if he could like her for a wife, and she him for a husband, Jane should have a double blessing; and Mr. Danvers had so often said the like to Jane, and so much commended Mr. Herbert to her, that Jane became so much a Platonick as to fall in love with Mr. Herbert unseen. This was a fair preparation for a marriage; but, alas! her father dyed before Mr. Herbert's retirement to Dauntsey; yet some friends to both parties procured their meeting, at which time a mutual affection entered into both their hearts, as a conqueror enters into a surprised city; and love having got such possession govern'd, and made there such laws and resolutions as neither party was able to resist; insomuch that she chang'd her name into Herbert the third day after this first interview. This haste might in others be thought a love frenzie or worse, but it was not."

Indeed, the union proved in every respect a happy one; so happy that " there was never any opposition betwixt them, unless it were " a contest which should most incline to a complyance with the " other's desires." A few months after his marriage his kinsman, the Earl of Pembroke, obtained for him from the King the important living of Bemerton, but he was for a month or more very undecided as to accepting it owing to the apprehension he felt " of the last great account he was to make for the cure of so " many souls," for he had not yet entered the priesthood. The Bishop of London (Laud), however, so convinced him

" that it was a sin, that a tailor was sent for to come speedily from Salisbury to Wilton to take measure, and make him canonical clothes against next day; which the tailor did; and Mr. Herbert being so habited went with his presentation to the learned Dr. Davenant, who was then bishop of Salisbury, and he gave him institution immediately (for Mr. Herbert had been made deacon some years before); and he was also the same day (which was April 26, 1630) inducted into the good, and more pleasant than healthful parsonage of Bemerton, which is a mile from Salisbury . . . When at his induction he was shut into Bemerton Church, being left there alone to toll the bell, as the law requires him, he staid so much longer than an ordinary time before he returned to his friends that staid expecting him at the church door, that his friend Mr. Woodnot looked in at the church window, and saw him lie prostrate on the ground before the altar; at which time and place (as he after told Mr. Woodnot) he set some rules to himself for the future manage of his life; and then and there made a vow to labour to keep them . . . I have now [continues Walton] brought him to the parsonage of Bemerton and to the thirty-sixth year of his age, and must stop here, and bespeak the reader to prepare for an almost incredible story of the great sanctity of the short remainder of his holy life; a life so full of charity, humility, and all Christian virtues that it deserves the eloquence of St. Chrysostom to commend and declare it."

Consumption, however, had marked him for its own; and in his case the sword was too keen for its scabbard. Like his great Master, he went about continually doing good, and into a public ministry of about the same duration as His, there was crowded so much of holiness and devotion as the world has seldom witnessed. Loving hands and hearts waited upon him as he gently walked down into " the valley of the shadow of death." He died without issue about the end of February, 1632, aged 39, and was buried at Bemerton the 3rd of March following. His eldest brother, Lord Herbert, of Chirbury, describes him "as not " without passion and choler, being infirmities to which all our " race is subject "; but if this was ever the case, he had in his latter years completely conquered this infirmity. He was gifted as a musician, and sang with taste his own exquisite hymns to the lute and viol, of which he was a master. But his immortality rests upon the productions of his pen as a poet and prose writer ; particularly his famous work *The Temple*, or *Sacred Poems*, first published in 1633, soon after its author's death, and of which within a few years 20,000 copies were sold. He was also the author of numerous other poems, sacred and secular, many of them being in Latin and Greek. His prose compositions consist of *A Priest to the Temple*; or, *The Country Parson, his character and rule of holy life*; a collection of *Outlandish Proverbs*; a translation of Cornaro on *Temperance; Orations*; and *Letters*. Many editions have appeared of his best known works, but the only complete one, I believe, is that in three volumes printed for private circulation in the "Fuller Worthies Library " (1874). Izaak's Walton's *Lives*, of which that of George Herbert is one, and from which I have quoted rather freely, is one of the most charming of English classics well deserving of Wordsworth's eulogy :

" There are no colours in the fairest sky
So fair as these. The feather whence the pen
Was shaped, that traced the lives of these good men,
Dropt from an angel's wing."

Herbert, it has been well said, was " pre-eminently a poet of the " Church of England ; his similes are drawn from her ceremonial ; " his most solemn thoughts are born of her mysteries ; his " tenderest lessons are taught by her prayers "; but nowhere has he found more ardent admirers than among the Nonconformists.

HERBERT, Sir HENRY, sixth son of Richard Herbert, Esq., of Montgomery, and a younger brother of the first Lord Herbert of Chirbury, was born at Montgomery in 1595, and after receiving a good education in his own country, was sent in early youth to France, where he became master of the French language. Lord Herbert says of him, " Henry came to Court and was made " gentleman of the King's Privy Chamber and Master of the " Revels, by which means as also a good marriage he attained to " great fortunes for himself and posterity to enjoy." He was made Master of the Revels in the reign of James I. by whom he was knighted August 7th, 1623. He continued 50 years in that office, and was also one of the gentlemen in ordinary to the Court of Charles I., by whom he was much esteemed. On account of his loyalty to the King, his estates were sequestered by the Parliament, and he was forced to pay £1,350 on compounding for them On the Restoration he became Member of Parliament for Bewdley, and held his old post at Court. He married Elizabeth, daughter of Sir Robert Offley, by whom he had issue,

Henry, his son and heir, and two daughters. He died in 1673 at Ribbesford, in Worcestershire, where also he was buried. He was a good scholar, a brave soldier, and an accomplished courtier, and much beloved in the domestic and social circle, and Walton bears testimony to ' the diligent wisdom with which God had blessed " him.

HERBERT, Capt. THOMAS, was the seventh and a posthumous son of Richard Herbert, Esq., of Montgomery, having been born some weeks after his father's death in 1597. His illustrious brother, Lord Herbert of Chirbury, gives the following account of him :—

" He also being brought up a while at school, was sent as a page to Sir Edward Cecil, Lord Generall of his Majesty's auxiliary forces to the Princes in Germany, and was particularly at the siege of Juliers Anno Dom. 1610, where he showed such forwardness, as no man in that great army before him was more adventurous on all occasions. Being returned from thence, he went to the East Indias under the command of Captain Joseph, who in his way thither, meeting with a great Spanish ship was unfortunately killed in fight with them, whereupon his men being disheartened, my brother Thomas encouraged them to revenge the loss, and renewed the fight in that manner (as Sir John Smyth, Governor of the East India Company told me at several times) that they forced the Spanish ship to run a ground where the English shot her through and through so often that she run herself a ground, and was left wholly unserviceable. After which time he with the rest of the fleet came to Suratte, and from thence went with the merchants to the Great Mogull, where after he had stayed about a twelvemonth, he returned with the same fleet back again to England. After this he went in the Navy, which King James sent to Argier [Algiers] under the command of Sir Robert Mansell, where our men being in great want of money and victuals, and many ships scattering themselves to try whether they could obtain a prize whereby to relieve the whole fleet; it was his hap to meet with a ship, which he took, and in it to the value of eighteen hundred pounds, which it was thought saved the whole fleet from perishing. He conducted also Count Mansfelt to the Low Countreys in one of the King's ships, which being unfortunately cast away not far from the shore, the Count together with his company saved themselves in a long boat or shallop, the benefit whereof my said brother refused to take for the present, as resolving to assist the master of the ship, who endeavoured by all means to clear the ship from the danger ; but finding it impossible he was the last man that saved himself in the long boat ; the master thereof yet refusing to come away, so that he perished together with the ship. After this he commanded one of the ships that were sent to bring the Prince from Spain, where upon his return, there being a fight between the Low Countrymen and the Dunkerkers, the Prince who thought it was not for his dignity to suffer them to fight in his presence commanded some of his ships to part them, whereupon my said brother with some other ships got betwixt them on either side, and shot so long that both parties were glad to desist. After that he had brought the Prince safely home, he was appointed to go with one of the King's ships to the Narrow Seas. He also fought divers times with great courage and success with divers men in single fight, sometimes hurting and disarming his adversary, and sometimes driving him away. After all these proofs given of himself, he expected some great command, but finding himself as he thought undervalued, he retired to a private and melancholy life, being much discontented to find others preferred to him ; in which sullain humour having lived many years, he died and was buried in London, in St. Martin's, near Charing Cross."

In his various adventures he shewed, as Walton observes, "a "fortunate and true English valour."

HERBERT, RICHARD, second Lord Herbert of Chirbury, was a staunch Royalist and devoted adherent of King Charles I. In 1639 he commanded a troop of horse against the rebellious Scots ; and on the breaking out of the Civil War in England he was a colonel in the king's service, and at his own charge raised a full regiment of 1,500 foot and a troop of horse. In 1643 he was one of those who conducted the Queen on her arrival at Burlington from Holland to the King at Oxford. The defection of his father from the royal cause produced no change in his attachment to the king, nor did the latter cease to trust him as one of his most faithful followers. When the Parliamentary party had carried all before it, he was permitted to compound for his estates, and paid a large fine ; but on the 16th June, 1649, Montgomery Castle was ordered to be demolished. He suffered much, and was reduced to great straits through his loyalty. He died 13th May, 1655, and was buried in the chancel of Montgomery Church. By his wife Mary, daughter of the first Earl of Bridgwater, he had issue four sons and four daughters.

HERBERT, EDWARD, third Lord Herbert of Chirbury, was the eldest son and heir of the second Lord Herbert, and, like his father, was a zealous Royalist. He was one of the earliest to join the movement for the restoration of Charles II., and soon after that event was brought about he was appointed Custos Rotulorum of Montgomeryshire, and subsequently of Denbighshire also. He built Lymore in 1663, Montgomery Castle having been demolished in his father's lifetime. He appears also to have resided partly at Llyssin. He was twice married ; first to Anne, daughter of Sir Thomas Middleton, and, secondly, to Elizabeth, daughter of George, sixth Lord Chandos, but he left no issue. He died on the 9th December, 1678, in his 46th year, and was buried in St. Edmund's Chapel in the Collegiate Church, at Westminster.

HERBERT, HENRY, fourth Lord Herbert of Chirbury, was a younger brother of the third lord, whom he succeeded in the title on his dying without issue in December, 1678. He had previously followed the profession of arms, and attached himself to the party of the Duke of Monmouth. He was appointed Custos Rotulorum of Montgomeryshire December 20th, 1679. He subsequently used his utmost endeavours to promote the cause of the revolution, and on the abdication of James II. voted for the filling of the vacant throne by the election of the Prince and Princess of Orange. He married Lady Catherine Newport, daughter of Francis, first Earl of Bradford, but died without issue in 1691, whereupon the title became extinct.

HERBERT, Sir EDWARD, Knight, Attorney-General to King Charles I., and afterwards Lord Keeper of the Great Seal to King Charless II. in his exile, was the eldest son of Charles Herbert, Esq., of Aston (Sheriff in 1608), by his wife Jane, only daughter and heiress of Hugh ap Owen, of Aston. He married Margaret, daughter and heir of Sir Thomas Smith, by whom he had three sons, all of whom became famous. His eldest son Arthur became Admiral of the Fleet, and took a leading and distinguished part in the Revolution of 1688, for which he was created Baron Torbay and Earl of Torrington. His second son Edward became Attorney-General in Ireland, and then Chief Justice of Chester, and subsequently Lord Chief Justice of the King's Bench, from which for his independence he was removed, but was afterwards appointed Lord Chief Justice of the Common Pleas, and subsequently Lord Chancellor to James II. in his exile. His third son Charles was a Colonel in King William III.'s army in Ireland, and distinguished himself at the battle of Aughrim, but was taken prisoner, and barbarously murdered by the Irish. Sir Edward Herbert died at Paris in December, 1657.

HERBERT, RICHARD, of Meifod, was son of Richard Herbert, Esq., of Park (Sheriff of Montgomeryshire in 1576 and 1584), and was Sheriff in 1657. For his devotion to the Royal cause he was one of the intended Knights of the Royal Oak—his estate being valued at £700. He sold his estate in Meifod, and this branch of the Herbert family is now extinct.

HERBERT, HENRY, first Lord Herbert of Chirbury of the *second* creation, was the son and heir of the Sir Henry Herbert, younger brother of Edward, Lord Herbert of Chirbury, already noticed. He was elected Member of Parliament for the borough of Bewdley in 1676, and subsequently for the city of Worcester. He engaged with great alacrity in the cause of the Revolution, and in 1688 went over to Holland to offer his personal assistance and influence to the Prince of Orange, and returned with him to England. For these services, and being also the last heir male of the last Lord Herbert of Chirbury, who died in 1691, he was on the 28th April, 1694, raised to the peerage as Baron Herbert of Chirbury. The following year he was appointed Custos Rotulorum of Brecon, and in 1705 one of the Lords Commissioners of Trade and Plantations. He was a man of considerable ability, and distinguished for his affability and politeness. His judgment and capacity were so highly thought of in the House of Lords that he was elected Chairman of a Committee on a very critical occasion. He married Anne, daughter of Alderman Ramsay, of London, by whom he had issue Henry, his only son and heir. He died January 22nd, 1708-9, and was buried in St. Paul's Churchyard, Covent Garden, London. His son, the second Lord Herbert of Chirbury of the second creation, dying without issue in April, 1738, that title again became extinct.

HERBERT, Sir EDWARD, Knight, of Powis Castle, was the second son of the Earl of Pembroke of the second creation—his brother, the eldest son, being the ancestor of the present line of the Earls of Pembroke. His mother was sister to Catherine Parr, Queen of Henry VIII., and he inherited extensive estates in Northamptonshire and Westmoreland, which his father had acquired by his marriage with her. In 1587 Sir Edward purchased the lordship and Castle of Powys from Edward Grey, illegitimate son and devisee of Edward Grey, last Lord of Powys of that line. He married Mary, only daughter and heiress of Thomas Stanley, Esq. (Master of the Mint in 1570), of Standen, in the county of Hertford, by whom he had William, his successor, and three other sons and eight daughters. He died March 23rd, 1594, and was buried in the chancel of Welshpool Church, where in 1597 a handsome marble monument was erected to his memory by his widow, which remains there to this day. Lady Herbert and some at least of her children were Roman Catholics. In 1594 she and three of her sons and two daughters were presented at the Sessions by the Vicar and Wardens of the parish church of Pool "upon their "othes, to have been absent from the foresaide church upon the "Sondaies and Holidaies at the tyme of Divine Service for the "space of this twelve monethes last paste." Lady Herbert was again presented for the same offence in 1611.

HERBERT, Sir WILLIAM, first Lord Powis of Powis Castle, was the eldest son and successor of the foregoing Sir Edward Herbert, and was born about 1572. He was made a Knight of the Bath at the coronation of James I. In 1613 he served the office of Sheriff of Montgomeryshire, and in 1616 obtained a grant of the Manors of Kerry and Cedewain, and the borough and castle of Montgomery. He was a firm Roman Catholic, and brought up his children in that faith. He married Eleanor, third daughter of the Earl of Northumberland. There are portraits of both at Powis Castle On the 2nd April, 1629, Sir William was created Baron Powys of Powys by Charles I. During the civil war King Charles came with his army to Welshpool, where Lord Powis had the honour of receiving him under his roof, and the room in which he slept is still called King Charles's room. Powis Castle was afterwards besieged by Cromwell's forces, and forced to submit, the Castle being fortunately allowed to stand on condition that its fortifications should be demolished. Colonel Mytton and Sir Thomas Middleton had previously on the 10th of August, 1644, defeated Prince Rupert at Welshpool, and " did also face Red Castle, in which is at least " 200 Welsh and Irish Papists, which they intend to call shortly " to a strict account for all their insolencies and traitorous prac- "tices." Sir Thomas Middleton on the 2nd of October following took the castle, and sent Lord Powis prisoner to the garrison of Wem, thence to the garrison of Stafford, and thence to London upon his parol, where he remained "at his lodging in "the Strand," his estates being sequestrated, and £4 per week being allowed him for his maintenance by the Committee of Sequestrators. The *Burning Bush not Consumed* gives the following account of the taking of Powis Castle:—

"About the 6th of this instant [October, 1644] letters from Welchpool were brought to London which certified that renowned Sir Thomas Middleton had taken Red Castle, a place of very greate consequence, and one of the enemies' strongest holds in North Wales. The manner of the taking of it was to be thus:—the enemie in this castle (whereof be the lord Powis a great Papist and most desperate and devillish blasphemer of God's name, was Governor, and the owner also) did often oppose and interrupt the bringing in of provisions into our forces at Montgomery Castle; whereupon Sir Thomas Middleton summoned the whole country thereabouts to come in unto him, and presently upon it [on Monday, 30th September] advanced from Montgomery to Pool with 300 foote and 100 horse, where they quartered on the Monday and Tuesday night following, and on the Wednesday morning next at two of the clock even by moonlight, Mr. John Arundell, the master gunner to Sir Thomas Middleton, placed a petard against the outer gate, which burst the gate quite in pieces, and (notwithstanding the many showers of stones thrown from the castle by the enemy) Sir Thomas Middleton's foote, commanded by Capt. Hugh Massey and Major Henry Kett, rushed with undaunted resolucion into the enemies workes, got into the porch of the castle, and so stormed the castle gate, entered it, and possessed themselves of the old and the new castle, and of all the plate, provisions, and goods therein (which was a great store), which had been brought from all parts thereabout; they also took prisoners therein, the Lord Powis and his brother with his two sons, together with a seminary priest, 3 captains, 1 lieutenant, and 80 common souldiers, 40 horse, and 200 armes. The place is of great concernment, for before the taking of it it did much mischief to the country, and almost blockt up the passages from Oswestry to Montgomery Castle, so that now the strongest forts in all North Wales are in the possession of the Parliament; this castle being conceived to be of strength sufficient to hold out a year's siege, and to be able to keepe out at least 10,000 men for a whole twelvemonth, it having at that present sufficient provisions in it of all sorts for such a continuance of time. Besides, by this means, noble Sir Thomas Middleton hath now the command of North Wales, and can raise men there at his pleasure."

Lord Powis died 7th March, 1655, aged 83 years, and was buried at Hendon, Middlesex. He left issue behind him Percy (created a baronet in his father's lifetime), who succeeded him in the title; and two daughters, Katherine, wife of Sir James Palmer, and Lucy, wife of William Abingdon, Esq.

HERBERT, Sir PERCY, second Lord Powis, is described in the *Archœologia* as "a noble author overlooked by Horace "Walpole; a loyal sufferer unnoticed by David Lloyd; a "Welshman omitted from the useful biographical dictionary of "the Rev. Robert Williams; and a Roman Catholic apparently "unknown to Dodd." He was the son and heir of Sir William Herbert, K.B., first Lord Powis, by Eleanor, youngest daughter of Henry Percy, eighth Earl of Northumberland. He was, in February 1620-21, elected to fill one of the vacancies in Parliament for Shaftesbury caused by the expulsion of its two

members. On the 7th November, 1622, he received the honour
of knighthood, and on the 16th of the same month was created
a baronet, this being in the lifetime of his father. In 1628 he
assisted in raising the trained bands in this county; on the 12th
May, 1633, he was appointed one of the Council for Wales and
its marches; and in 1639 he was collector for Montgomeryshire
of the moneys contributed by the Roman Catholics for carrying
on the war against the Scots. He was subsequently convicted of
recusancy, and his lands were forfeited for treason, and ordered
to be sold in July, 1651. He bore this and other hardships
with great fortitude, and in 1652 published a book, now
extremely scarce, with the following title :—" *Certaine concep-*
"*tions or considerations of Sir Percy Herbert upon the strange*
" *change of people's dispositions and actions in these latter times,*
" *directed to his sonne. Deus primum, honos proxime.* London :
" Printed by E. G., and are to be sold by Richard Tomlins, at
" the Sun and Bible, near Pie Corner. 1652." [4to.] He
succeeded to the title of Lord Powis on the death of his father
on the 7th March, 1655-6. In April, 1660, the order for
demolishing Powis Castle was rescinded, " otherwise than the
" demolishing the outworks about the said Castle, to the end it
" might thereby be made indefensible in case of any trouble or
" insurrection that might thereafter happen, which, being done,
" the sayd Castle was to be at the disposall of such persons who
" had right to and property in the same " Lord Powis headed
the petition of the nobility, knights, and gentry of North
Wales, presented to Charles II. about June, 1660, praying that
the regicides and others who concurred in the death of the late
king might be brought to justice and punished. He married
Elizabeth, daughter of Sir William Craven, Alderman of
London, by whom he had issue, William, his successor, and
Mary, who married George Lord Talbot. He died on the 19th
January, 1666-7, and was buried in the chancel of Welshpool
Church.

HERBERT, WILLIAM, 3rd Lord Powis, and first Earl,
Marquis and Duke of Powis, succeeded to the Barony of Powis
on the death of his father, the second lord in 1666. He was a
zealous Roman Catholic and royalist, and a devoted adherent of
James II. in all his adversities. He married Lady Elizabeth
Somerset, daughter of the Marquis of Worcester, by whom he
had one son and five daughters. Charles II., on the 4th April,
1674, created him Earl of Powis as a reward for his loyalty.
He was generally regarded as the chief of the Roman Catholic
aristocracy in England, and, according to Titus Oates, was to
have been Prime Minister if the popish plot had succeeded. He,
however, shewed great kindness and sympathy towards Quakers
and other Nonconformists, and on several occasions used his
influence on their behalf. Richard Davies, the Quaker, refers
to him and his lady as " my particular friends." Hugh Owen,
of Bronyclydwr, another eminent Nonconformist, was confined

for some time at Powis Castle, but was treated with remarkable kindness. Lord Powis, on hearing him pray, said to his priest, " Surely this is a good Christian," and on his discharge engaged him to come to Powis Castle every Christmas. Upon Titus Oates's information, Lord Powis and four other lords were impeached for high treason and committed to the Tower, where he remained for nearly four years, that is until 1683. Soon after the accession of James II. the Earl of Powis was created Viscount Montgomery and Marquis of Powis, and Lady Powis became Lady of the Bedchamber to the Queen and her most confidential and intimate companion. In July, 1686, the Marquis of Powis was made a Privy Councillor, and by the moderate Catholics his appointment as Viceroy of Ireland was urged, but the more violent Tyrconnel obtained the post. Lady Powis was one of the witnesses present at the birth of the Prince of Wales, 10th June, 1688, and the king placed the infant Prince under the charge of the Marquis and Marchioness. By the king's direction they took him as far as Portsmouth on the way to France, but were obliged to return to Whitehall, which, after a narrow escape of capture by some of the Prince of Orange's soldiers they reached in safety. Subsequently, Lord and Lady Powis accompanied the fugitive Queen and her infant to France, and were followed a few days afterwards, on the 11th December, 1688, by the king himself. On the 12th of January, 1689, the king in his exile at St. Germains created the Marquis of Powis, Marquis of Montgomery, and Duke of Powis as a reward for his unswerving fidelity. Meanwhile his house in Great Queen-street, Lincoln's Inn Fields, was attacked by the mob; he himself was outlawed for not returning within a certain period and submitting to the new Government, and all his estates were confiscated. In 1690, the Duke of Powis accompanied king James on his ill-fated expedition to Ireland, and after the battle of the Boyne returned with him to France, where shortly afterwards he was made Lord Chamberlain and invested with the Order of the Garter. On the 2nd June, 1696, " having " broke a vein as riding from thence to Boulogne," he died at St. Germains, where also he was buried. The Duchess had died in 1692. There is something touching and truly admirable in the pure, disinterested and tenacious allegiance of this moderate and amiable nobleman to his king—one of the most bigoted, intolerant and worthless monarchs who ever sat on the English throne.

HERBERT, WILLIAM, 4th Lord Powis, and second Duke, Marquis and Earl of Powis, was the only son of the 3rd Lord Powis of that line whom he succeeded on the death of the latter in 1696. Some years before this a proclamation had been issued for his apprehension on suspicion of abetting the French in a threatened invasion of England. To prevent his outlawry he surrendered himself in December, 1696, and was committed to Newgate, where it seems he remained for half a year, after which he was bailed out. In 1715, he was committed to the Tower on suspicion of abetting the cause of the Pretender. In 1722, he obtained restitution of his estates and of all his titles except the dukedom, and was called to the House of Lords by writ on the 8th of October. He married Mary, daughter of Sir Thomas Preston, by whom he had issue two sons, William, his successor, and Edward. He died in 1745. His son William, third Duke of Powis, died unmarried in 1748, whereupon the dukedom and all minor honours became extinct. Under the will of the last duke his large estates devolved upon Henry Arthur, Lord Herbert of Chirbury of the third creation, who was the same year created Earl of Powis.

HERBERT, Lady LUCY THERESA, was the fourth daughter of William, first Duke of Powis. She was born in the year 1669, and took the veil in June, 1693, at the Convent of English Augustine Nuns at Bruges, of which she eventually became Lady Abbess. She bore a very high character for devotion and the sanctity of her life, and wrote several books of devotion of which several editions have been published. These appear to have been collected and published in 1791 under the title :—*Several excellent methods of hearing Mass with fruit and benefit according to the institution of that divine sacrifice, and the intention of our Holy Mother the Church, with motives to induce all good Christians, particularly religious persons, to make use of the same.* Lady Lucy Herbert died 14th February, 1744, aged 75 years.

√ HERBERT, Lady WINIFRED, (afterwards Countess of Nithsdale) was the fifth and most celebrated daughter of the first Duke of Powis. The date of her marriage is not known, but her husband, William Maxwell, Earl of Nithsdale, took a prominent part in the Jacobite rising of 1715, and was amongst those who were compelled to surrender at Preston. Soon afterwards he was tried and condemned to death and sent to the Tower of London to await execution. From this fate the Countess with true wifely devotion determined to save her lord at all hazards. She travelled night and day, mostly on horseback through deep snow and tempestuous weather, that she might solace him in the dark hour of his need, appeal to the king for his pardon, or if all other means of saving his life failed, plan and carry out his escape from prison. Having failed to obtain his pardon or a reversal of his sentence, she, with amazing coolness, skill, and audacity, took two women with her to the Tower, one of whom was her maid Grace Evans, of Welshpool, (see *ante.* p 65), and disguising the Earl partly in their and partly in her own clothes she most cleverly deceived the guards, and brought her husband safely out of prison on the 23rd of February, 1716, being the day before that fixed for his execution. Part of the female apparel in which Lord Nithsdale escaped was formerly in the possession of the " Ladies of Llangollen." She afterwards with much skill carried out his escape to France, where she finally joined him. They took up their residence at Rome, where the Earl died on the 20th March, 1744. His noble and heroic wife also died there in 1749, but her remains were brought to this country, and deposited at Arundel Castle. A graphic and highly interesting account of the cleverly planned and accomplished escape of the Earl was written by the Countess herself under the title of—*A Letter from Winifred Herbert, Countess of Nithsdale, to her sister, the Lady Lucy Herbert, Abbess of the English Augustine Nuns at Bruges, containing a circumstantial account of the escape of her husband, William Maxwell, fifth Earl of Nithsdale, from the Tower of London on Friday, the 23rd of February, 1716.* It was first printed with remarks by Sheffield Grace, Esq., F.S.A., for private circulation in 1827, and has been re-printed at length with a steel engraving of the Countess in the fifth volume of the *Montgomeryshire Collections*, but is too lengthy for insertion here.

HERBERT, HENRY ARTHUR, Earl of Powis, was the son of Francis Herbert, of Dolguog, and Oakley Park, by Dorothy, daughter of John Oldbury, Esq., of London. He was elected member of Parliament for Ludlow in 1727, and represented that borough in three Parliaments. On the 21st December, 1743, he was created by letters patent, Lord Herbert of Chirbury (*third* creation). On the death in March, 1748, of William, Marquis of Powis, leaving him his whole estate, he was further advanced to the dignity of Baron Powis, of Powis Castle, Viscount Ludlow and Earl of Powis by letters patent, dated 27th May, 1748. In 1745 he was appointed Lord Lieutenant and Custos Rotulorum for Shropshire, and in 1745 was one of the thirteen peers commissioned to raise each a regiment of foot to suppress the rebellion—a task which, so far as he was concerned, he completed in a very short time. On the 16th October, 1749, the King granted him the dignity of a Baron of Great Britain by the title of Lord Herbert, Baron Herbert of Chirbury and Ludlow. On the 22nd May, 1761, he was appointed Comptroller of the Household to King George III., and shortly afterwards sworn a member of the Privy Council. In October the same year he resigned the Comptrollership, and was appointed Treasurer of the Household, which he also resigned in July, 1765. On the 23rd July, 1761, he was appointed Lord Lieutenant and Custos Rotulorum of the County of Montgomery. He was also Recorder of Shrewsbury, and a Lieutenant-General. He married March 30th, 1751, Barbara, sole daughter and heir of Lord Edward Herbert, only brother of William, last Marquis of Powis. On this marriage it was arranged that the eldest son and daughter should be brought up in their father's faith as members of the Church of England, and the younger children as Roman Catholics, being their mother's religion. They had one son, George Edward Henry Arthur, and three daughters, of

whom two died in infancy, leaving one only surviving, the Lady
Henrietta Antonia, who accordingly was brought up a member
of the Church of England. Thus the family of Herbert ceased
to be Roman Catholic. Lord Powis died at Bath, September
11th, 1772, aged 70, and was buried at Welshpool. His only
son, George Edward Henry Arthur, died unmarried, January
17th, 1801, aged 46, when the titles again became extinct. The
estates passed to his only surviving sister, Lady Henrietta
Antonia, who in 1784 had married Edward, second Lord Clive,
who on the 12th May, 1804, was created Earl of Powis—the
first of the present line—and died May 16th, 1839.

HERBERT, EDWARD, K.G., second Earl of Powis of the
present creation, was the eldest son and heir of the above-named
Edward, second Lord Clive, and first Earl of Powis of the present
line. He was born 22nd March, 1785, and married 9th February,
1818, Lucy, third daughter of James, third Duke of Montrose.
On the 9th March, 1807, he adopted the surname of Herbert
instead of that of Clive. On coming of age he, in 1806, entered
Parliament as member for Ludlow, which he continued to represent until his accession to the peerage in 1839. His Lordship
displayed much public spirit and liberality in carrying out
improvements in Montgomeryshire : for instance, he built the
tower of the Parish Church, and enlarged the Town Hall at
Montgomery entirely, and the Town Hall at Welshpool mainly
at his own cost. He was President of the Royal Cambrian
Literary Institution, and of the Welsh School, Gray's Inn-road,
London, and in 1824 an Eisteddfod on an extensive and magnificent scale was held at Welshpool under his presidency, and
largely by his munificence. He also joined the Roxburghe
Literary Club in 1828, became its Chairman in 1834, and the
following year contributed to its publications a most curious and
valuable volume—English metrical Lives of the Saints by the
Monk of Clare, written in 1443. He was Lord Lieutenant of
Montgomeryshire, and Chairman of the Shropshire Union Railways and Canal Company. In 1845 the Knighthood of the
Garter was conferred upon him. But the two events for which
Lord Powis's public life will be best remembered were, first, his
uncompromising and successful opposition in 1846 to the proposed
union of the Sees of St. Asaph and Bangor ; and secondly, his
candidature in 1847 for the Chancellorship of the University of
Cambridge, in opposition to Prince Albert, who, however,
defeated him by 954 to 837 votes, a majority of 117. The
following clever epigram was written on the occasion :—

" Prince Albert on this side, Lord Powis on that,
        Have claims than which none can be slighter,—
The Prince's consist in inventing a hat,
        The Peer's in preserving a mitre.
Then why, O collegiate Dons, do ye run
        Into all this senate-house pother ?
Can it be that the youth who invented the one
        Has some share in dispensing the other ?

Lord Powis died on the 17th January, 1848, from the effects of
a lamentable accident having been shot in the thigh by one of
his own sons while shooting in the preserves adjoining Powis
Castle. His death was universally mourned, for his amiability
and gentleness, no less than his high and dignified character had
won the hearts of all who knew him. He was buried in the
chancel of St. Mary's Church, Welshpool, where a beautiful
monument was afterwards erected to his memory by the
Countess of Powis, with a Latin inscription of which the following is a translation :—" Here sleeps in Christ, Edward Herbert,
" Earl of Powis, conservator of the See of St. Asaph. He died
" the 17th day of January, 1848, in his 63rd year. Show Thy
" servant the light of Thy countenance, and save me for Thy
" mercy's sake." His lordship had issue, Edward James, who
succeeded to the title and estates, Sir Percy Egerton Herbert,
K.C.B. ; Very Rev. George Herbert, Dean of Hereford; Hon.
Robert Charles Herbert ; Major-General the Hon. William Henry
Herbert ; Lady Lucy Caroline Calvert and Lady Harriett Jane
Herbert. The Countess of Powis died in September, 1875.

HERBERT, EDWARD JAMES, third Earl of Powis of the
present creation, was the eldest son and heir of Edward Herbert,
the second Earl, K.G., by his wife Lady Lucy Graham, third
daughter of James, third Duke of Montrose, K.G., and was born
on the 5th November, 1818, at the Angel Inn, Pershore,
Worcestershire, where his mother, then Lady Clive, was taken
ill and confined on her way to London. He was educated at
Eton and at St. John's College, Cambridge, where he came out
eleventh in the first class in classics in 1840, and the same year
took his M.A. degree. His private tutor was the late Bishop
Selwyn. In 1842, he obtained the degree of LL.D., and in 1857,
he received the honorary degree of D.C.L. at Oxford. He took
great delight in the classics, the study of which he continued
throughout his life, and often corresponded with distinguished
scholars on points of classical criticism. In 1863, his University
of Cambridge elected him without opposition to the office of High
Steward. He gave annually a prize for the best copy of Latin
hexameter verses on a given subject, and in other ways was a
munificent benefactor to his College and University. On the
death of his grandfather in May, 1839, he became Lord Clive,
and in the November following came of age, when there were
great rejoicings at Welshpool and various parts of Montgomeryshire and Shropshire. At Welshpool the chief event was the
ceremony of laying the foundation stone of a church (Christ
Church) erected by subscription to commemorate the occasion.
In 1843, Lord Clive was elected one of the Members of Parliament for North Shropshire, and continued to represent the same
constituency until his father's death in 1848, when he succeeded
to the Earldom of Powis. In 1840 he joined the South Salopian
Yeomanry, and continued his connection with the regiment until
1871, when it was united with the North Salopian. He was

placed on the Commission of the Peace for Montgomeryshire, Shropshire, and Herefordshire, and took great interest and an active part in the administration of the affairs of the two former. In 1855, he was elected Chairman of Quarter Sessions for Montgomeryshire, in succession to Sir Baldwyn Leighton, Bart. He attended the Sessions with great regularity up to the time of his death, and displayed marked ability and business capacity in the discharge of his duties. On the first election of County Councils in January, 1889, Lord Powis was elected one of the Councillors for Welshpool. In 1877, on the death of Lord Sudeley, Lord Powis was appointed Lord Lieutenant of Montgomeryshire. He at all times evinced great interest in the cause of education and the study of archæology. He was a liberal supporter and the first President of the University College of Bangor, and his inaugural address was one of the most memorable of his public speeches. He was President of the Powysland Club, and a liberal supporter of it from its establishment in 1867 up to his death. He was also a patron of the Cambrian Archæological Association, and filled the office of President in 1856; also a member of the Cymmrodorion Society, and in 1885 elected its President. He was one of the members of the Committee appointed by Government to frame the Intermediate Education Scheme for Montgomeryshire, and took an active part in its deliberations. These are but a few of the many societies and organizations for promoting education and culture which owed much to his intelligent and liberal support, though quietly and unobtrusively given. But, perhaps, it was in connection with the Church of England that Lord Powis's liberality was most frequently displayed. He was a patron of 15 livings, and he every year gave large subscriptions towards the erection of new churches or the restoration of old ones, the building of parsonages and schools, and the augmentation of livings as well as to the various Church Societies in which he took a great interest. He was always an elegant and effective but not a fluent speaker—a certain hesitancy in searching for the most appropriate word, detracted from the effect of his speeches as pieces of oratory. But they always read well. At the laying of the first stone of the Great Vyrnwy Lake at Llanwddyn, for supplying Liverpool with water, he made a singularly happy use of the classical legend of Arethusa. He said—

" You will recollect that the nymph Arethusa disappeared from the middle of the Peloponnesus under-ground, and passing under a portion of the Mediterranean, bubbled up in the sacred island of Ostygia. This theme exercised the imagination of the poet Shelley. It gave to the navy, in the days when ships were not gigantic tea-kettles, one of the most dashing of its frigates, and inspired Dibdin with one of the most successful of his nautical ballads. You will recollect the first lines of Shelley's 'Ode to the Nymph Arethusa,' which I think will still typify what will soon be the triumphant progress of the nymph of the Vyrnwy to Liverpool :—

' Arethusa arose from her couch of snow
On the Acroceraunian mountains,

From cloud and from crag
With many a jag,
Shepherding her bright fountains.' "

The above is a fair sample of Lord Powis's style—a happy combination of classical lore and " modern instances." Lord Powis was the owner of about 72,000 acres of land in the counties of Montgomery and Salop, of the estimated annual value of £72,694, and he was an excellent landlord. In addition to the public offices already mentioned, he was Chairman of the Shropshire Union Railway and Canal Company; Governor of Queen Anne's Bounty; Vice-President of the Sons of the Clergy Institution; President of the Eye, Ear, and Throat Hospital, Shrewsbury; a Trustee of the Salop Infirmary and of the Shropshire Provident Society, Millington's Hospital, &c., &c. Lord Powis died in London on the 7th May, 1891, in his 73rd year, and was buried in the chancel of Welshpool Church, where a handsome recumbent statue in alabaster, resting on a plinth of black marble, has been placed to his memory. A Church House has also been erected by public subscription at Welshpool to his memory. Lord Powis was never married, and he was succeeded in the title and estates by his nephew, George Charles, the son of the late Right Hon. Sir Percy Egerton Herbert, K.C.B., by Lady Mary Petty Fitzmaurice, only child of William Thomas, Earl of Kerry, and grand-daughter of Henry, third Marquis of Lansdowne. Lord Powis, in 1860, edited and printed for private circulation among the members of the Philobiblon Society a work by his ancestor Edward, first Lord Herbert of Cherbury, entitled *The Expedition to the Isle of Rhé*. He also presented a volume of *Herbert Papers and Correspondence* to the members of the Powysland Club. By his will he directed 100 copies of his speeches and selections from his MS. Greek and Latin compositions to be printed on good paper and neatly bound in one good sized octavo volume. This has since been carried out by his executors.

HERBERT, Rev. GEORGE, M.A., Dean of Hereford, was the third son of Edward, second Earl of Powis. He was born 25th November, 1825, and was educated at Eton and St. John's College, Cambridge, where he graduated in 1848. Two years later he was ordained by the Bishop of Worcester, and appointed to the Curacy of Kidderminster, which he served for five years. In 1855, he was appointed to the family living of Clun, and the Bishop of Hereford conferred on him the Prebend of Putron Manor in Hereford Cathedral. He did admirable work as a parish priest. In 1867, Mr. Disraeli nominated him to the Deanery of Hereford, where he did much to develope the influence and popularise the services of the Cathedral. In 1863, he married Elizabeth Beatrice, fourth daughter of Sir Tatton Sykes, by whom he had two daughters. Mrs Herbert died in 1883. Dean Herbert died on the 15th of March, 1894, in his 69th year.

HERBERT, Lieut. Gen. the Right Hon. Sir PERCY
EGERTON, K.C.B., was the second son of Edward, second Earl
of Powis. He was born at Powis Castle, 15th April, 1822, and
educated at Eton, whence he proceeded to Sandhurst, and
obtained his first commission in the army as ensign in the 43rd
Regiment in January, 1840, becoming Captain in 1846, Major
27th, and Lieut.-Col. 28th, May, 1853, Colonel and Aide-de-Camp
to the Queen 29th June, 1855, Major-General in 1868, Lieut.-
General 1875, Colonel 74th Highlanders 1876. He served in the
Kaffir War in 1851-53, also in the expedition of the Orange
River Territory, and was engaged in the battle of Berea, and was
promoted for his services by the recommendation of the
Commander in Chief. He also served during the Russian War
as Assistant Quartermaster General of the Second Division of the
Army of the East from its formation to November, 1855, and
subsequently as Quartermaster General of the Army of the East
until June, 1856. During his active services he was present at
the battle of the Alma (where he was wounded), the affair of the
26th October, the battle of Inkerman and the siege and fall of
Sebastopol, where he was again wounded. On his return home
from the Crimea, his old neighbours at Welshpool, in August,
1856, gave Colonel Herbert a magnificent reception. On the
11th of the following month there was also a grand county
demonstration in his honour at Shrewsbury. There were also
great rejoicings at Ludlow, where he was presented with a sword
by his constituents. For his distinguished services in the
Crimea, Colonel Herbert was made Aide-de-Camp to the Queen
and nominated a companion of the Order of the Bath. He was
also made an officer of the Legion of Honour and a Commander
of the second class of the Sardinian Order of St. Maurice and
St. Lazarus. He received the third class of the Order of the
Medjidie, the Turkish medal, and the Crimean medal with three
clasps. He afterwards commanded the 82nd Foot during the
Indian Mutiny, and was present at Rohilcund under Lord Clyde
in 1858, and in various affairs and skirmishes at Bareilly and
Shahjohampore. He commanded the districts of Cawnpore and
Futtehpore till the spring of 1859, and a force in pursuit of
Ferozeshah, and a rebel force to the banks of the Jumna.
Shortly after his return from India, Colonel Herbert was
appointed Deputy Quartermaster General at headquarters, an
office which he filled for two years. As a campaigner probably
few officers have ever exhibited greater powers of enduring
fatigue and privation than Colonel Herbert This was especially
the case during the Crimean campaign. He was always foremost
where there was danger, and for this earned from his men (by
whom he was greatly loved) such nicknames as "Fire-ball,"
"Ball-proof," and "Danger." For nine months he was never
undressed during the night, but wore his clothes, and was booted
and spurred night and day. Many anecdotes are related of his
coolness, endurance, and personal bravery. At the battle of
Inkerman, Col. Herbert especially distinguished himself. It had

long been his habit to go out to the pickets at two o'clock in the morning, seldom returning till noon, and sometimes not until the evening. Being apprehensive of an attack, he had ordered his servant to wake him should he happen to be asleep whenever he heard any firing. He had been out the whole of the night previous to that eventful day, and had just returned to his tent about a quarter past five o'clock in the morning, when he heard the sound of firing. He immediately sprang to his charger, telling his servant to be at a particular point of the hill with another horse at a time he named, adding, "If I be alive I shall be there." He then shook his servant by the hand and galloped off, being first on the hill. He was met with a volley from the foe, who were partially concealed by the fog. He galloped back and fetched up his Division, urging them to double up as quickly as possible. Here he was joined by General Penne-father, and the two officers used their utmost efforts to get the troops into action. He remained with his division which kept retiring and advancing up the hill till half-past ten o'clock, when the Guards came to their relief. Colonel Herbert used extra-ordinary efforts to get up the artillery. His division kept a portion of the hill for hours notwithstanding that all their ammunition was expended. At one o'clock the French came up at a quick pace, and were received with loud cheers by the now nearly exhausted British troops. After this the battle was soon over. Colonel Herbert entered Parliament in February, 1854, as Conservative member for Ludlow, and continued to represent that borough until September, 1860. In July, 1865, he was elected for South Shropshire, and he sat for that constituency up to the time of his death. In spite of increasing indisposition he took an active part in the discussion of the Army Purchase Bill in Parliament, advocating vigorously the claims of the Officers of the Army. He also acted as the Representative of the various classes of Officers before the Army Purchase Commission. Col. Herbert married on the 4th October, 1860, Lady Mary Petty Fitzmaurice, only daughter of the Earl of Kerry, son of the third Marquis of Lansdowne, K.G., by whom he had issue a son, George Charles, the present Earl of Powis, and two daughters. In 1866 he was made a Knight Commander of the Bath, and in March, 1867, Treasurer's of Her Majesty's Household (an office held by him till December, 1868) being at the same time made a Privy Councillor. Sir Percy Herbert suffered much during the last two years of his life from a painful disease brought on by his arduous services, and which resulted in his death on the 7th October, 1876, in the 55th year of his age. He was buried at Moreton Say Church, Salop, where his great grandfather, Robert Lord Clive, K.B., was also buried. Of General Herbert it may with truth be said that he was a brave and true soldier, who worthily sustained the military traditions of his family, and the honour attached to the illustrious name he bore, and that dis-tinctions such as were bestowed upon him for his services have seldom been better earned or more worthily conferred.

HERBERT, JOHN MAURICE, County Court Judge of the Monmouth Circuit, was the son of John Lawrence Herbert, Esq., of New Hall, Kerry, Montgomeryshire, by his marriage with Joyce Susannah, daughter of Charles Thomas Jones, Esq., of Fronfraith, Llandyssil, in the same county. He was born on the 15th July, 1808, his father having died shortly before. His mother subsequently married Thomas Maddy, Esq., of Moreton House, near Hereford, and went to reside there. The subject of this notice was educated at the Cathedral School, Hereford, and afterwards entered St. John's College, Cambridge, where he distinguished himself by taking the Wright's Prize in the years 1828 and 1829 successively, and graduated as eighth Wrangler in 1830. He proceeded M.A. in due course, and subsequently became a Fellow of his College. During his College days Mr. Herbert was an active member of his College Boat Club, and it may be noted as an interesting fact that he was requested to steer the University boat in the first race rowed between the Universities of Oxford and Cambridge—an office which he prudently declined, because he thought it undesirable to reduce himself to the required weight. He was throughout life fond of sport, especially of fishing. Mr. Herbert chose the law for his profession, and was called to the Bar by the Honourable Society of Lincoln's Inn in Easter Term, 1835, joining the Oxford Circuit. His business, however, principally lay in London, where he practised with success for some time as an equity draftsman and conveyancer. Shortly after the passing of the Tithe Commutation Act he was appointed an Assistant Tithe and Copyhold Commissioner,—an office which he filled for some years. In 1844 he was appointed a Commisioner for enfranchising the assessionable Manors of the Duchy of Cornwall, and to enable him to fulfil his duties as such he went to reside for two years in that county. In 1847, Mr. Herbert was one of the first Judges appointed for the new County Courts established, or rather remodelled, under an Act of the previous year, and this office he continued to hold up to his death. The Circuit assigned to him comprised the towns and districts of Presteign, Knighton, Leominster, Hereford, Abergavenny, Chepstow, Monmouth, Newport, Pontypool, Ross, Tredegar, and Usk. The absence of railway communication between most of these towns in those days necessitated his driving from town to town in his own carriage, —a four-wheeled dogcart, drawn by a pair of horses called by him "Justice" and "Cottenham." In 1858, his Circuit was considerably altered, the towns of Presteign, Knighton, Leominster, and Hereford being taken away, while Crickhowell and the important town and district of Cardiff were added to it. Mr. Herbert brought to the discharge of his duties an enthusiastic disposition, great industry, and a wide and extensive knowledge of law,—qualities which combined to make him a most able judge. He was moreover a good speaker, and expressed himself with great clearness and force. His decisions were rarely appealed against, and more rarely reversed; and as shewing the estimation in which his judgment was held, trial by jury had become almost obsolete in his Courts. In an appeal against one of his decisions, the Lord Chief Justice of the Common Pleas remarked that the judgment of Mr. Herbert was a masterly exposition of the law, and that it would be an honour to his Court to have it entered upon its records. His familiarity with accounts was extraordinary, and the unravelling of mathematical problems and arithmetical puzzles was a great delight to him. He had, moreover, a keen sense of humour, and many anecdotes are related of his pleasantries and witticisms. Mr. Herbert was also a Magistrate for the counties of Hereford and Monmouth, and, I believe, also of Radnor and Glamorgan. In the first named county he for many years acted as Deputy-Chairman of Quarter Sessions. Himself an erudite scholar, he took great interest in educational and other movements for promoting the welfare of what may be called the lower middle, and poorer classes. He was a Fellow of the Geological Society, and had some knowledge of music, being himself a fairly good performer on the flute. His knowledge of agriculture and agricultural customs was very extensive. For many years he himself farmed somewhat extensively, and for the last thirty-one years of his life he was a Fellow of the Royal Agricultural Society. He was eminently social in his habits, and while himself throughout life an exceedingly moderate and abstemious man, he was always one of the leading spirits at any festive gathering he attended, ever full of fun and joke. Mr. Herbert was twice married—first, in 1840, to Mary Anne, eldest daughter of Thomas Johnes, Esq., of Garthmyl isaf, Montgomeryshire, who died in 1876; and, secondly, in 1877, to Mary Charlotte, fourth daughter of the Rev. Thomas Philpotts, Porthgwidden, Cornwall, who survived him. His last illness was very brief. He presided in the Cardiff Court, with his usual ability and with undiminished mental faculties, on Saturday, the 28th October, 1882, but he died on the following Friday, the 3rd of November, at his residence, Rocklands, near Ross (where he lived the greater part of his judicial life), and, on the 7th of the same month, was buried in the churchyard of Goodrich, Monmouthshire.

HERRING, Rev. JULINES (or JULIUS), an eminent Puritan divine and preacher, was born at Llanbrynmair in 1582. When he was but three years old his father, according to Fuller, "returned hence to Coventry, in which he was highly related; "whose ancestors for the space of nearly 200 years had been in "their course chief officers of that city." He was educated at Morechurch, Salop, and at the Coventry Grammar School, and when 15 years old his parents, "perceiving a pregnancy in their "son bred him in Sydney College in Cambridge," where in due time he proceeded M.A. Returning home, he studied divinity, and though he objected to subscription, he obtained orders from an Irish bishop, and became a frequent and popular preacher at

Coventry. He afterwards obtained the living of Calk, in Derbyshire, where he remained about 8 years, attracting so many hearers that the church would not hold them. At this time he married a Miss Gellibrand, by whom he had 13 children. This living he had to resign apparently owing to his scruples as to ceremonies. In 1618 he hired the hall of the Drapers Company at Shrewsbury for preaching, and the same year was appointed Tuesday lecturer and preacher at the Sunday mid-day service at t.S Alkmond's Church in that town. Here his Puritanism attracted the attention of Archbishop Laud, who said he " would pickle that Herring of Shrewsbury." Complaints of his Non-conformity were made to his bishop, who was unwillingly obliged to suspend him. The Vicar of St. Alkmond's, however, was said to be " no preacher," and therefore Herring's preaching appears to have been often connived at by the authorities. In 1635 he left Shrewsbury and went to reside at Wrenbury, Cheshire, where for a few months he taught from house to house, but the following year he accepted an invitation to become co-pastor with one Rulice of the English Church at Amsterdam. He had much difficulty, however, in evading the prohibition to ministers to leave the country, and he did not arrive in Holland until the 20th September, 1637. He was warmly welcomed, the magistrates of Amsterdam paying the expenses of his journey. He died there on 28th March, 1644. Fuller says of him that " he was a profitable and painsful preacher, being " one of a pious life, but in his judgment disaffected to the " English church discipline," and Samuel Clarke describes him " as a hard student. a solid and judicious divine, and in life " a pattern of good works."

HINDE, MAJOR GENERAL CHARLES THOMAS EDWARD, was the second son of Capt. Jacob William Hinde, of the 15th Hussars, by Harriet, daughter of the Rev. Thomas Youde, and granddaughter of Jenkin Lloyd, Esq., of Clochfaen, Llangurig. He was born at Plas Madog, near Ruabon, in 1820, and entered the service of the East India Company in 1840. On the outbreak of hostilities between Russia and Turkey in 1853, he volunteered his services to Omar Pasha, then commanding the Turkish army on the Danube, and was appointed a lieutenant-colonel under the name of Beyzad Bey. Shortly afterwards he acted as adjutant-general to the force under General Cannon (Bairam Pasha), which was despatched from Shumla for the relief of Silistria. He took part in the heroic defence of the latter town, and was lying side by side in an embrasure at Redout Kale with Capt. Butler at the time he received his death wound. In July, 1854, he took an active part in the passage of the Danube and the battle of Giurgevo. He accompanied the army of the Danube to Bucharest, thence to Eupatoria, and was present at various skirmishes before Sebastopol in the years 1855-56. From the Crimea he accompanied the force of Omar Pasha to Mingrelia, and was present at the battle and passage of the Ingur. For these various services he received the English Crimean medal, the Turkish medals for Silistria and the Danube, and the Order of Medjidieh, together with his brevet majority and honorary lieutenant-colonelcy. He returned to India in 1857, and was at once appointed to a command in the state of Rewah, where, during the great mutiny, he raised and organised a force of 800 men, and, at their head in January, 1858, opened the grand Deccan road by capturing six forts with forty guns and two mortars from the mutineers, for which service he received the thanks of the Governor-General in Council. Twice more during the mutiny he received similar thanks. He was promoted to the rank of Colonel in 1862, and to that of Major General in January, 1870. He married Harriette Georgina, only daughter of Capt. Souter, by whom he had issue a daughter, Harriet Julia Morforwyn, now the wife of Lieut.-Col. Verney, and whose eldest son, James Hope Verney, is heir presumptive to the Clochfaen estates. Major General Hinde died at Brussels on the 15th of May, 1870, and was buried in the cemetery of Ixelle.

HOWELL, ABRAHAM, was the son of William and Elinor Howell, of Bontdolgadfan, Llanbrynmair, where he was born on the 4th of April, 1810. He was one of a family of twelve, ten sons and two daughters. His father, who was a flannel manufacturer, found it hard work in those dear and hard times preceding and immediately following the downfall of Napoleon to bring up so large a family. He was unable to give them a better education than that afforded by the village school, and the boys had all to go out into the world at a very early age to earn their bread. Before he was ten years old the subject of this memoir had begun to earn his living at Machynlleth. Having entered the office of Messrs. Owen and Jones, solicitors in that town, his industry, intelligence, and integrity soon won the confidence of his employers, one of whom (Mr. Joseph Jones) was Clerk of the Peace for the County of Montgomery. About the year 1833 he accompanied the latter to Welshpool on his transferring his practice to that town, and there he spent the rest of his life until he took up his residence at Rhiewport, Berriew, in 1866. After some years he was articled, and in 1840 admitted a solicitor. Soon afterwards he was admitted into partnership with Mr. Joseph Jones and Mr. William Yearsley, under the style of Jones, Yearsley, and Howell. On the death of Mr. Jones in 1848 the partnership was dissolved, and he practised alone for some years. Subsequently he took into partnership his brother-in-law, Mr. Edward Jones (the present Town Clerk of Welshpool), and again his two sons, the firm being known as Howell, Jones, and Howell. Mr. Howell, in addition to a large private practice, held for many years the offices of County Treasurer, Clerk to the Turnpike Trustees, and to the Justices of the Hundreds of Mathrafal, Deuthur, Caurse and Pool Upper. Soon after he began to practice at Welshpool he was elected a member of the Town Council, and in 1848 was chosen Mayor of the town. He was again elected Mayor in 1860, re-elected in 1861, and again in 1863. During his mayoralities, and in great part through his efforts, sewerage and waterworks and a smithfield were provided, and as long as he lived he took the greatest interest in every project for promoting the welfare of his adopted town. But the chief work of his life was the promotion of the various schemes for supplying Montgomeryshire and Central Wales with railway communication. In this he took a leading and important part. The Oswestry and Newtown, the Shrewsbury and Welshpool, the Oswestry, Ellesmere and Whitchurch, the Aberystwith and Welsh Coast, and the Mid-Wales Railway Acts and the Cambrian Railways Amalgamation Act were the most important of the many Acts of Parliament which he successfully carried through in spite of enormous difficulties. Subsequently he became associated with the late Mr. David Davies, of Llandinam, and other gentlemen in the profitable development of the coal fields in the Rhondda Valley and eventually in forming the Ocean Collieries Company of world-wide celebrity. In 1874 Mr. Howell was placed on the Commission of the Peace, and in 1889 elected a member of the County Council for Welshpool, from which, owing to the infirmities of age, he retired in 1892. He was also a member of the Council of the Powysland Club. Few men possessed such an untiring capacity for work, and he retained his vigour and deep interest in public affairs almost to the last. Mr. Howell had married Mary, daughter of Mr. Edward Jones, surgeon, of Welshpool, by whom he had a family of three sons and four daughters, all of whom survive him. After a very short illness his long and laborious life came to a peaceful end on the 12th November, 1893, in the 84th year of his age. In private life Mr. Howell was greatly esteemed by all who knew him for his kind, gentle, and generous disposition, and his name will always be honourably associated with the history and progress of Montgomeryshire.

HOWELL, DAVID, was a younger brother of the above-named Abraham Howell, and was born on the 31st of March, 1816. At an early age a situation was found for him in a solicitor's office at Machynlleth. After some years he was articled, and in 1845 he was admitted a solicitor and taken into partnership by Mr. Hugh Davies. From this time until within a couple years of his death he led a very busy life in the active pursuit of his profession, enjoying a very extensive practice, and being highly respected and trusted by all who knew him. Mr. Davies died very suddenly in 1850, when Mr. Howell succeeded to his appointments as Clerk (now Registrar) to the County Court, Clerk to the Guardians, Superintendent Registrar and Steward of the Manor of Cyfeiliog. He had been for some years Secretary of the Machynlleth Savings Bank, and he held that office until the business was transferred to the Post Office Savings Bank about twenty years later. About the beginning of 1855 he was appointed Clerk to the Justices of the Hundreds of Machynlleth and Estimaner. In 1857 he promoted, and successfully carried through Parliament, a Bill for making a railway to Machynlleth from the Llanidloes and Newtown Railway at Moat Lane, and was secretary and solicitor to the Company until its amalgamation with others, in 1864, under the name of the Cambrian Railways Company. Subsequently he successfully promoted a Bill for making another line of railway from Cemmes Road to Dinas Mawddwy, called the Mawddwy Railway, and for some years acted as its secretary. In November, 1876, he was appointed coroner for the Machynlleth district of Montgomeryshire. Mr. Howell, who always took great interest in archæological matters, was a member of the Powys-land Club from its formation up to his death. In 1857 he married Isabella Jane, daughter of the late Matthew Lewis, Esq., of Llanfair Caereinion, and a niece of his former partner, Mr. Hugh Davies, by whom he had four sons and three daughters, all of whom, as well as Mrs. Howell, survive. Mr. Howell had for some years resided at Craigydon, Aberdovey, and for a considerable time his health had been gradually failing. About the beginning of August, 1890, he went to Llandudno for the benefit of his health. On Saturday, the 16th of the same month, he died very suddenly at that place in the 75th year of his age, and the following Thursday, the 21st, was buried at Penegoes, near Machynlleth. Mr. Howell, at the time of his death, owned considerable property, and he was a most kind and considerate landlord. His high integrity, kindness of disposition, and genial manner endeared him to a large circle of friends, by whom his memory will long be affectionately cherished.

HOWELL, GWILYM, or WILLIAM, was a native of Llangurig, where he was born in 1705, but he spent the greater part of his life at Llanidloes, holding the post of steward or agent of the Berthllwyd estate for many years, and at one time serving the office of Mayor of that borough. He was a poet of some merit, but is best known as a publisher of a series of Welsh almanacks or annuals, containing, in addition to the astronomical notes and other intelligence usually comprised in such publications, original poetry and other literary matter of much interest. These annuals (ten of which were published under Mr. Howell's editorship) attained great popularity, but are now extremely rare. They were printed at Shrewsbury. Several local Eisteddfodau were held under his auspices at Llanidloes. He died on the 4th of March, 1775-6, and was buried under the yew-tree near the entrance to the churchyard there. The following Englyn by himself, and composed apparently shortly before his death, is engraved on his tombstone :—

" Er gwychion|gwynion eu gwedd,—er p'lasau,
Er pleser, anrhydedd ;
Er dewrion do'n o'r diwedd
Er daued y bo'n i dy'r bedd. G. H., 1755."

HUET, Rev. THOMAS, D.D., the Welsh Biblical scholar'
was born in 1544, and was educated at Corpus Christi College,
Cambridge, where he took his B.A. degree in 1562. He became
Master of the Holy Trinity at Pontefract, and on its dissolution
received a pension. On the 20th November, 1560, the Queen
gave him the living of Trefeglwys. From 1562 to 1588 he was
precentor at St. David's Cathedral. He was a strong Protestant.
He signed the thirty-nine articles in the Convocation of 1562-3,
and in 1571 dismissed the Roman Catholic sexton at St. David's
for concealing Popish Mass books. These books he publicly
burned. Bishop Davies, of St. David's, in 1565, recommended
him for the Bishopric of Bangor, but though supported by
Parker he failed to obtain it. He, however, received the
rectories of Cefnllys and Dyserth, in Radnorshire, and about the
same time the degree of D.D. was conferred upon him. Huet
died on the 19th August, 1591, and was buried at Llanafan
Church, Breconshire, from which the author of *Llyfryddiaeth y
Cymry* conjectures that he may have been a native of that parish,
and that it was the burial place of his family. He himself
resided for some time, it appears, at Aber Dihoew, near Builth.
He was one of the translators of the Greek Testament into
Welsh, which was published by William Salesbury in 1567, the
portion done by him being the Book of the Revelation, to which
his initials, T.H.C.M., that is, Cantor Meneviæ, are attached.

HUGARFAEL, one of the sons of Cyndrwyn, Prince of part
of Powys, who lived early in the sixth century.

HUGHES, Rev. DAVID, M.A., was a native of South
Wales. He was brought up at Jesus College, Oxford, and was
an excellent scholar. In 1808 he obtained the rectory of
Hirnant, and in 1813 that of Llanfyllin, which he held for 37
years. He was one of the public examiners at his University in
1810-11, and was corrector of the University Press when the
corrected edition of the Bible was brought out in 1809. He
also published a visitation sermon, and a small volume of poems
under the title, *Pigion o Salmau a Hymnau wedi eu casglu
allan o waith amryw Awdwyr.* (Llanfyllin, 1820). He died
April 11th, 1850, and was buried in Llanfyllin Churchyard.

HUGHES, EZEKIEL, the first Welsh settler in Ohio, was
the second son of Richard and Mary Hughes, of Cwmcarnedd,
Llanbrynmair, where he was born August 22nd, 1767. His
father was a respectable freeholder, whose family had been
settled at Cwmcarnedd for more than two centuries. Ezekiel
was placed in a school at Shrewsbury for some time, and afterwards, when he was eighteen years old, apprenticed to a clock-
maker and jeweller at Machynlleth. Having served out his

apprenticeship and learnt his trade, he by the advice of his father determined to seek a home in the far West, and accordingly he in April, 1795, in company with his cousin, Edward Bebb (whose son, the Hon. William Bebb, became Governor of Ohio), set sail from Bristol for Philadelphia in the American ship *Maria*. After a stormy and adventurous voyage of thirteen weeks duration, they arrived at their destination. Ezekiel Hughes remained about a year at Philadelphia, where the American Congress was then sitting, and made the acquaintance of Washington and other leading American statesmen. After visiting several of the Welsh settlements in Pennsylvania he and his friend Bebb early in 1796 turned their faces westward, and after spending a few weeks at the infant settlement of Beulah (now Ebensburg) pushed on through the wilderness to Pittsburg, then a very small town. From Pittsburg they proceeded in an open boat, and reached Marietta in three days. After inspecting the lands in that neighbourhood the two friends pushed on in their boat to Mays Ville, Kentucky, and thence to Fort Washington, now Cincinnati. That great Ohio city, now nearly as large as Birmingham, was founded December 28th, 1788, and incorporated as a city in 1819. The first white child was born there March 17th, 1790, being only six years before Ezekiel Hughes's settlement there. Here he purchased by way of experiment 80 acres of land for two dollars and a quarter (about nine shillings) per acre, and finding the land well adapted for the cultivation of potatoes and corn he subsequently in 1801 made other large purchases. When he settled there he writes that he had three neighbours within a moderate distance. His friend Bebb settled in the fruitful valley of Paddy's Run, Ohio. In 1802 Hughes visited his native country, and married Miss Margaret Bebb, of Brynaere Mawr, Llanbrynmair, with whom he returned the following year to his log house on the banks of the great Miami river. His wife, however, died in about a year's time, and was the first to be buried in the Berea Cemetery. In 1808 he was married again to Miss Mary Ewing, of Pennsylvania, by whom he had seven children. In 1805 he was appointed by the Governor of Ohio with two others to plan and make a road from the mouth of the Miami to Hamilton, Ohio, and the following year was appointed a Justice of the Peace. President Harrison was one of his intimate friends and a near neighbour, and both laboured together as teachers in the same Sunday School. He divided his estate into large and convenient holdings, which he let out to respectable tenants on fair leases, and he so arranged that each of his children inherited a good farm. In 1820 he sustained a fall in descending the steps of a church at Cincinnati, which caused him to be lame the remainder of his days. He died on the 2nd of September, 1849, aged 82 years, having lived to see one of the largest and most important of American cities occupying the spot which fifty years before he had found almost a wilderness. Throughout life he cherished with great foundness his native Welsh language, and the religious principles of his youth. He delighted in reading Welsh books, and was always particularly kind to Welsh emigrants, hundreds of whom owed much to his timely assistance and advice.

HUGHES, Rev. JOHN, of Pontrobert, was born on the 22nd of February, 1775, at Y Figyn, in the parish of Llanfihangel. His parents were poor, and he lost his father when he was about seven years old. Like John Foster, he was brought up to the trade of a weaver, but, like him, he did not greatly prosper in that calling. He, for a time, kept a day school at various places, and having in his 22nd year joined the Calvinistic Methodists, he, in 1800, began to preach. He was ordained to the full work of the ministry at Bala, in 1814. Having had but few educational advantages in early youth, he, by dint of hard study, not only mastered the English language, but acquired some knowledge of Greek, Latin, and Hebrew. He, indeed, partly compiled for his own use a Welsh-Greek dictionary, which still remains in MS. He was long considered one of the leaders of the Calvinistic Methodists in Wales. His sermons (many of which were published) were vigorous, terse, and lucid. His appearance was uncouth and ungainly, his personal habits were slovenly and forbidding, and his voice unmusical and somewhat harsh, but, notwithstanding these disadvantages, he often displayed much power in the pulpit, and he undoubtedly possessed great influence over his brethren. He wrote and published several religious biographies, several able articles in the Welsh Quarterly *Y Traethodydd*, and also many hymns in Welsh, some of which will long retain their popularity, such as

" Bywyd y meirw tyr'd i'n plith "
" Duw ymddangosodd yn y cnawd " &c.

A small collection of his hymns under the title *Hymnau i'w canu yn yr Ysgolion Sabbothol* was published at Bala in 1821. It is chiefly to him and his wife that Wales owes the preservation of Ann Griffiths's seraphic poetry. He worked hard, and travelled many thousands of miles on horseback during his long ministerial life. In his younger days he made several journeys to London on horseback, and he used to say that each night on his way he managed to find lodging with a Welshman. He died at Pontrobert, Meifod, where he spent the greater part of his life, on the 3rd of August, 1854, in the 80th year of his age, and was buried in the chapel graveyard there, where a monument with a suitable inscription has been erected to his memory.

HUGHES, JOHN CEIRIOG, though not a native of Montgomeryshire, was born not very many miles outside its borders, and lived long and died and was buried within the county, so that on these grounds we may be allowed to claim him as a "Montgomeryshire Worthy." John Hughes, in after life universally known among his countrymen by his bardic

name *Ceiriog*, was the youngest of eight children of Richard
and Phœbe Hughes, of Penybryn, in the lonely and romantic
vale of Llanarmon, Denbighshire, where he was born on the
25th of September, 1832. · His parents were thrifty, industrious,
and highly respected among the farming class to which they
belonged. His mother, in particular, was rather superior in
intelligence and attainments to most of her neighbours, and
doubtless made up in some degree for the want of local advantages for the education of children. John attended the village
school until he was about fifteen, and then for a time assisted
his father on the farm. It soon became evident, however, that
he would never make a farmer. After trying a printer's office
at Oswestry for about three months, and a grocer's shop at
Manchester for about the same period, he found a situation as
clerk in the railway goods office at London Road Station, Manchester, where he remained for sixteen years, and finally attained
a responsible position. He was at this time of a very studious
turn of mind, and before he was twenty wrote several pieces of
poetry which attracted some attention. He won his first prize
at a literary meeting held in Grosvenor Square Chapel, Manchester. This was about 1852, and for the next fifteen or
sixteen years he was a constant competitor, and generally a
winner, at Welsh Eisteddfodau. It was, however, at the great
Llangollen Eisteddfod, in September, 1858, that he at once
secured a foremost position among the lyric poets of Wales, by
his successful pastoral poem on "Myfanwy Fychan"—an
exquisite composition of not quite 400 lines. This is generally
considered his masterpiece, and its chaste and simple beauty
cannot be matched by any other poem of its kind in the Welsh
language. In 1860 a small volume of his poetry was published
under the title *Oriau 'r Hwyr* (Evening Hours), which has
since gone through many editions In 1862 his second volume
of poems appeared under the name of *Oriau 'r Boreu*
(Morning Hours). Another volume came out in 1863 under the
title of *Cant o Ganeuon* (One hundred Songs), and this was
followed ere long by *Y Bardd a'r Cerddor* (the Poet and
Musician), and some years later by *Oriau Eraill* (Other Hours,
1868) and *Oriau 'r Haf* (Summer Hours, 1870). He also published a collection of choice extracts from his own and other
works, adapted for public recitation, under the title of *Gemau'r
Adroddwr* (the Reciter's Gems). Besides these his published
works include the librettos of a cantata on "The Siege of
Harlech," for the Swansea Eisteddfod, and another on "The
Prince of Wales" for the Carnarvon Eisteddfod, 1862. This
last led to the composition of the popular air and words, "God
Bless the Prince of Wales" As there has been some mis-
apprehension on the subject, it may not be out of place to give
here Ceiriog's own account of the circumstances :—

"The National Eisteddfod, held in Carnarvon Castle, August 26th to
30th, 1862, was brought to a close by performing Cwain Alaw's 'Prince
of Wales Cantata.' I had written this cantata at the request of the

General Council of Yr *Eisteddfod*, to commemorate the birth of the first Prince in that castle, referring to the coming of age of His Royal Highness Albert Edward, our present illustrious Prince. On the morning following the Eisteddfod Mr. Brinley Richards and myself happened to call at the same time at the offices of the *Carnarvon and Denbigh Herald* to obtain that day's paper containing a full report of the National Festival and the evening concerts. He congratulated me for having written the words of the cantata, which he stated had given him some satisfaction. I replied that my share of honour could be but small, and attributed the immense success of its performance—firstly, to the composer of the music; secondly, to the enthusiasm then existing generally throughout the United Kingdom on the advent of the coming of age of H.R.H the Prince of Wales. The ability of the choir and the historical associations of the place where the cantata was performed were also referred to. This led to further conversation, during which one of us said that His Royal Highness was not only coming of age but was reported in the papers to be married shortly to the Princess Alexandra of Denmark. The Principality since its union with England had no appropriate National Anthem, but the high tide of overwhelming enthusiasm was approaching, and we decided to have something to launch, for there was a tide for songs as well as fortunes. I then expressed a wish that Mr. Richards would kindly compose music suitable to words for a national song, which I would endeavour to furnish him. The words were forwarded in due course, and were shortly returned to me with the music. Llew Llwyfo and several friends of mine sang them in public concerts for two months before the English version was written. In fact, the song was intended to be a purely Welsh one, and the idea of obtaining an English version was an after-thought, which naturally suggested itself to the composer when he was about arranging with the publishers to buy the copyright. Mr. Brinley Richards and myself had many English versions to select from before we decided on Mr. George Linley's, and I believe Mr. Richards himself wrote the whole of the chorus part commencing "Among our ancient mountains,' &c. A writer in the *South London Press*, February, 1870, asserts the *amende* has to be made to Mr. George Linley, the real author of the words, or rather the gentleman who 'did them out of the Welsh,' and hence the reason I have entered into these details, showing that the song existed for some time purely as a Welsh one, and was becoming popular in the Principality before the English version was composed. The third verse was written at the request of the publishers, and has only appeared in their latest editions of the music."

Mr. Richards, it seems, received £10 for the copyright of the song, and, in consequence of its popularity, was subsequently presented with £100 by the publishers He presented Ceiriog with a ring, which was all he obtained for his share in it. In a similar way Ceiriog wrote a great many other songs and lyrics, some of them very charming, for old Welsh melodies, arranged by Messrs. John Owen, Brinley Richards, and other popular musicians, as well as for new compositions. About fifty of his songs are published in Brinley Richards's *Songs of Wales*, which first appeared in 1873. He thus rendered to the national airs of Wales service similar to that done by Burns to those of Scotland, and by Moore to those of Ireland. Several of his compositions appeared also in the *Traethodydd* and other Welsh periodicals. Among Ceiriog's prize compositions, not already mentioned, are an epic poem on " Sir Rhys ap Thomas," written for the Carmarthen Eisteddfod, 1867, and a love-song, *Catrin*

Tudor, for Bangor Eisteddfod, 1874. He also wrote a heroic poem on *Helen Luyddawg*. These, and a few songs, appear to be about all the poetry he wrote during the last fourteen years of his life. During all that time, much to the regret of his countrymen, his muse was nearly silent. His hitherto unpublished works were after his death collected and published in a small volume under the title of *Yr Oriau Olaf* (The Last Hours, 1888). Ceiriog was also a facile and vigorous prose writer when he liked, as his excellent article on *Dafydd ab Gwilym*, in the *Gwyddoniadur*; his frequent contributions to *Baner Cymru*, as its regular correspondent for twenty-seven years, and one article on *Dyffryn Ceiriog Folk-lore*, which appeared in the *Montgomeryshire Collections*, abundantly testify. Ceiriog married, on the 22nd February, 1861, Anne, daughter of Thomas Roberts, chemist, the Lodge, Chirk. Of this union there were two sons and two daughters, all of whom are living. Tired of city life, and longing for a home among the Welsh mountains, he in 1865 sought and obtained the appointment of stationmaster at Llanidloes. In 1870 he removed to Towyn, but did not remain long at that place. The following year he was appointed manager of the Van Railway, then just opened, and took up his residence for a short time at Trefeglwys, and afterwards at Caersws, where he spent the remainder of his days. In November, 1886, he went up to London to take part in the ceremonies attending the proclamation of the National Eisteddfod to be held there in 1887. His last public appearance was at the Holborn Town Hall, on the 11th November, 1886, when he received quite an ovation from the large gathering of his countrymen who were present. During his stay in the metropolis he caught a severe cold, which, unhappily, developed into a serious and painful illness, which finally proved fatal. He was confined to his house for several months. He died at Caersws on Saturday, the 23rd of April, 1887, and was buried the following Tuesday, at the parish church of Llanwnog. Wales has produced during the last fifty years four eminent lyric poets—Talhaiarn, Mynyddog, Islwyn and Ceiriog—but the greatest of these undoubtedly, and perhaps the greatest of all Welsh lyric poets, was Ceiriog. Some of his poems have been translated into English by himself and others; but such translations necessarily convey but a faint idea of the charm and beauty of the originals. A few months after his death the Government recognised his claims to the gratitude of the nation for his eminent services to Welsh literature, by granting to his widow a Civil List pension of £50 per annum.

HUGHES, Rev. THOMAS, a Wesleyan minister of some eminence, and the author of several works, was the son of a poor quarryman at Llangynog, where he was born during the third decade of the present century. His parents removed, when he was young, to the neighbourhood of Llangollen, and there in 1842 he began to preach. In spite of many difficulties

I

he mastered the English language, and beame an influential and acceptable minister in several important circuits. He was the author of the following works:—(1) *The Ideal Theory of Berkeley and the Real World* (1865); (2) *The Human Will, its Functions and Freedom* (1867); (3) *The Economy of Thought* (1875); (4) *Knowledge: the fit and intended furniture of the mind*; (5) *The Great Barrier, a delineation of prejudice in its different phases*; (6) *Sermons: The Divine and the Human in Nature, Revelation, Religion and Life*; (7) *Prayer and the Divine Order, or the Union of the Natural and Supernatural in Prayer*; (8) *Things New and Old relative to Life, being Sermons on different subjects*; (9) *The Condition of Membership in the Christian Church viewed in connection with the Class Meeting in the Methodist Body*, and eight or nine smaller works, chiefly sermons on special occasions. The last-named work, disapproving of the devotional meetings known among Wesleyan Methodists as "Classes," brought upon its author the displeasure of his brethren in the ministry. In his latter years he became a supernumerary, and lived at Morton, near Oswestry, where he died January 31st, 1884.

HUGHES, WILLIAM, the harpist, was a native of Llansantffraid, where he was born in 1798. He was a brilliant player on the Welsh or triple harp. He unsuccessfully competed with Benjamin Connah and others at the Wrexham Eisteddfod in 1820. At Carnarvon Eisteddfod in September, 1821 (the Marquis of Anglesey presiding), we find him again competing with Connah (his old master and nine others, and carrying off the silver harp with twenty guineas. His success was received with great enthusiasm, although it seems that some of the judges wished to award the prize to Connah. He competed again at Welshpool in 1824, but giving way to habits of intemperance he never distinguished himself again in public. At the time of his death, which took place in Liverpool in 1866, he was engaged to play the harp at an hotel there.

HUGHES, EDWARD (*Eos Maldwyn*), son of the above-named William Hughes, was also an accomplished harpist. Among many other eisteddfodic honours he won a grand Welsh harp at the Abergavenny Eisteddfod with a silver medal, presented by Lady Hall (now Llanover). He died of consumption at Liverpool on the 9th of December, 1862.

HUMFFRAY, THE HON. JOHN BASSON, was born at Newtown on the 17th April, 1824, and when a young man emigrated to Australia, where he settled at Ballarat in the colony of Victoria. Here he soon gained a prominent position, and took the lead in the town of his adoption in the constitutional struggle for political reform. He was elected the first member for West Ballarat in the Reformed Parliament, and was appointed the first Minister of Mines for the Colony of Victoria. He died at Ballarat on the 18th March, 1891, in his 67th year.

HUMPHREY, or WMFFRE DAFYDD AB IFAN, was
an excellent poet and parish clerk of Llanbrynmair, who
flourished in the seventeenth century. He was on terms of
friendship with William Phylip, of Arduawy, another eminent
poet of that age, who, it is said, on one occasion paid a visit to
the village of Llanbrynmair, and asking a lad to shew him the
house of Wmffre Dafydd, the lad led him to the churchyard,
and, pointing to a *fresh grave*, said, "This is the house of
"Wmffre Dafydd ab Ifan." This circumstance greatly affected
W. Phylip, and caused him to write his "Ode to the Grave."
Several of Wmffre Dafydd ab Ifan's poems were published in
Ffoulke Owen's *Cerdd lyfr*, published at Oxford in 1686, subsequent editions of which were published at Shrewsbury under
the name of *Carolau a Dyriau Duwiol*, by Thomas Jones in
1696, and by Sion Rhydderch in 1729. Others have appeared
in the *Gwyliedydd* and other magazines, and some still remain in
manuscript in the Hengwrt, the Ceniarth, and other collections.

HUMPHREYS, HENRY, the harpist, of Welshpool, was
the son of Henry Humphreys of the same place, an excellent
trumpet player. He unsuccessfully contested for the silver
harp with several eminent players at the Carmarthen Eisteddfod
in July, 1819, when Thomas Blayney was declared the victor.
One of the airs played by him was a beautiful one, not so well
known as it should be, called "Holl Ieuenctyd Cymru" (All ye
Cambrian youth). His father having died about this time,
leaving a widow and eight children in indigent circumstances,
this air, with Humphreys' variations, and with a monody on the
death of Sir Thomas Picton by the Rev. Walter Davies, was
published, with the assistance of the Rev. J. Jenkins, of Kerry,
for their benefit. He afterwards unsuccessfully competed on the
triple harp, with nine others, at the Wrexham Eisteddfod on
the 14th September, 1820, when he executed "Pen Rhaw" with
variations in a very masterly manner. At a bardic meeting held
at the Rev. John Jenkins' house at Kerry, on the 20th January,
1820, the Rev. Walter Davies addressed the following *Englyn* to
Humphreys :—

> "Poed heb loes hir oes a hedd—i'r ifanc,
> Er afiaeth a mawredd ;
> Bydd Harri, goleuni gwledd,
> Cywir dôn, cured Wynedd."

He won the silver harp at the Brecon Eisteddfod in 1822, and
again at Welshpool in 1824.

HUMPHREYS, JAMES, an eminent conveyancing counsel,
was born at Montgomery about the year 1768, his father being
Mr. Charles Gardiner Humphreys, a solicitor in good practice
there. He received his early education at Shrewsbury School,
after which he was articled to Mr. W. Pugh, of Caerhowell, a
solicitor in very extensive practice, father of the late Mr. W.
Pugh, of Brynllywarch, and grandfather of Mr. W. Buckley

Pugh, Dolfor Hall, and Patrington. Leaving Mr. Pugh's office, he was for a short time at that of a Mr. Yeomans, at Worcester, and then proceeded to London, where in 1787 he entered as a pupil the chambers of Mr. Charles Butler. At this period of his life he imbibed those liberal political principles to which he was a steadfast adherent ever afterwards, and which brought him into association and intimacy with Horne Tooke, Dr. Parr, Sir Samuel Romilly, and other leading men of the day. On leaving Mr. Butler's chambers, Mr. Humphreys commenced practice as a conveyancer, in which, though slowly, he established a high reputation and a lucrative business. He contributed several articles to the *Supplement to Viner's Abridgment*; but the work which at the time made him famous was one published by him in 1826 under the title, *Observations on the actual state of the English Laws of Real Property with the Outlines of a Code.* This publication produced numerous pamphlets for and against his views, one of his principal opponents being Sir Edward Sugden, afterwards Lord St. Leonards. A second edition of the *Observations* came out in 1827. This work, undoubtedly, did much to place the subject of law reform in the prominent position it occupied soon after that date, and to bring about the amendments in the law of real property afterwards made by the legislature. In 1822 he married Charlotte, daughter of Bartlett Goodrich, Esq., of Saling Grove, Essex. His health, which had long been delicate, gave way in the autumn of 1829, and his illness was aggravated by a fall from his horse about that time. He lingered, however, until the winter of 1830, when he died at Upper Woburn Place, London, aged 62 years. Shortly after his death an interesting memoir of him, written by his nephew, the late Erskine Humphreys, Esq., appeared in the *Cambrian Quarterly Magazine.*

HUMPHREYS, Rear-Admiral Sir SALUSBURY PRYCE, R.N., a brave naval officer, was a grandson of the Rev. Dr. Salusbury Pryce, who was Vicar of Meifod for the long period of 53 years. It was he who committed the bold yet, as some think, justifiable error of firing on the *Chesapeake*, American ship of war. He was the son of the Rev. Evan Humphreys, rector of Montgomery and Clungunford, by Mary, daughter of the Rev. Dr. Salusbury Pryce, and he was born in November, 1778. He was an officer of some distinction, and saw a good deal of service during his short career up to the time when he attained the rank of Captain; but will best be remembered as Captain of the *Leopard*, when in 1807 at Halifax, Nova Scotia, under orders, he boarded the *Chesapeake* American frigate, for the seizure of some naval deserters, which led to loss of life on both sides, an angry correspondence between both Governments, and to his own ultimate retirement on half-pay. He became, nevertheless, a Rear-Admiral of the White, and was made a C.B. in 1831, and K.C.H. (Knight Commander of the Royal Hanoverian Guelphic Order) in February, 1834. He married firstly, in 1805,

Jane Elizabeth, daughter and co-heir of John Tixel Morin, Esq., of Weedon Lodge, by whom he had a son, the Rev. Salusbury Humphreys, who inherited the Weedon estate; secondly, in 1810 Maria Brooke Vel Davenport, natural daughter and heir of William Davenport, Esq., of Bramall, Cheshire; and by sign manual he in 1838 assumed the name and arms of Davenport. Sir Salusbury Pryce Humphreys Davenport died on the 15th November, 1845, and was buried at Leckhampton.

HUW CAE LLWYD was probably a native of Arwystli. He was a poet who flourished from 1450 to 1480. He presided at the Glamorgan Gorsedd in 1470. There are at least eight of his poems preserved in the British Museum. One, with a translation, is printed in the second volume of the "History of Powys Fadog." He was buried at Llanuwchllyn.

HYWEL AB SYR MATHEW, an eminent poet, herald, and genealogist, who flourished between 1530 and 1560, or a little later perhaps. Lewis Dwnn wrote an elegy upon his death, dated 1581. Some of his poems are, it is said, still preserved in MS. According to a Memorandum attributed to Rhys Cain, dated about 1570, he wrote a "History of all Britain," and his books were seen by him, and pronounced fair, valuable, and intelligent. Lewis Dwnn inspected his MSS. also, and bore testimony to their great value. The latter was also a pupil of his, and had many of his books. The celebrated William Lleyn was also one of his pupils. His name would imply that he was the son of a Protestant clergyman.

HYWEL SWRDWAL, an eminent poet and historian of Cedewain, who wrote between 1430 and 1460. He was bailiff of Newtown in the years 1454-5 and 6. He is also said to have lived at Machynlleth. According to a manuscript apparently written by 'Rhys Cain about 1570, found by Mr. Edward Jones (*Bardd y Brenin*) in the possession of Mr. Evan Bowen, Penyrallt, Llanidloes, and by him translated and published in his *Relics of Welsh Bards*, Hywel Swrdwal was "a "Master of Arts, and a chief of song, wrote the history of the "three principalities of Wales from Adam to the first king in a "fair Latin volume; and from Adam to the time of King "Edward the I.; also he wrote a Welsh Chronicle, which is now "with Owain Gwynedd, chief bard, and a teacher of his "science." According to another old MS. in the British Museum, quoted in the *Brython* (vol. iii, p. 137), he was buried at Llanuwchllyn, in Merionethshire. There is in the Library of Balliol College, Oxford, a volume of Welsh poetry containing a curious English poem, "An ode to the Virgin Mary," written in the Welsh mode of alliteration and orthography by way of a challenge to certain Englishmen who alleged that no Welshman could possibly be made as good, as learned, and as wise a scholar or as skilful a versifier as an Englishman. It begins—

> " O michti lady, our loding ;—to haf
> At hefn our abeiding ;
> Yntw thei ffest everlasting
> I set a braints ws tw bring."

(O mighty lady our leading—to have
At heaven our abiding ;
Unto thy feast everlasting
I set a braynts [branch] us to bring.)

This is sometimes attributed to Hywel Swrdwal and sometimes to his son, Ieuan ab Hywel Swrdwal. It is given at length in *Arch. Camb.* vol. i. (second series), p. 304. See also *Cam. Journal* iv. 39.

IDLOES, the founder of the church of Llanidloes, was a saint living in the early part of the seventh century. He was the son of Llawvrodedd Varvog (or Varchog) Coch, and was famed for his piety. A saying of his is preserved in *Englynion y Clywed*:—

> " A glywaist ti a gânt Idloes
> Gwr gwâr hygar ei cinioes,
> Goreu cynnydd cadw moes."

(Hast thou heard what Idloes sang,
A man of a peaceful and amiable disposition ;
The best [road to] prosperity is by observing civility.)

A slightly different version is given of the saying in *Chwedlau'r Doethion* (the Sayings of the Wise), namely—

> " Goreu cynneddf yw cadw moes "
(The best quality is that of maintaining morals).

IEUAN AB BEDO GWYN, a poet who flourished from about 1530 to 1570. He lived at Llyssyn (of which he was also the owner) in the parish of Llanerfyl. Some of his poems remain in manuscript.

IEUAN AB HUW CAE LLWYD, a poet who flourished between 1470 and 1500. His compositions remain in manuscript.

IEUAN AB HYWEL SWRDWAL, a son of Hywel Swrdwal, already noticed, was also an eminent poet and historian. The manuscript already quoted describes him, too, as a Master of Arts, and states that he "wrote a fair book in Welsh "of the three principalities of Wales, from the time of "Cadwallader to that of King Henry VI., and was a primitive "bard of transcendent merit." He flourished between 1450 and 1480, and some of his poems are preserved in manuscript.

IEUAN DYFI, another eminent poet, who wrote between 1470 and 1500, and whose compositions remain in manuscript.

IEUAN TEW, otherwise called Ieuan Tew Hên, or Ieuan Tew Hynaf, was an eminent poet of Arwystli who flourished from about 1400 to 1440. He presided at the Glamorgan Gorsedd in 1420, and was buried at Llanidloes. Some of his poems remain in manuscript.

IFAN, SYR o Garno, a clergyman and an accomplished poet who lived at Carno about 1530 to 1570. A "Stanza to the "Snake" and a few other short compositions of his are found in the *Greal*. Among his other works still extant is a poetical correspondence carried on by him with his neighbour Huw Arwystli.

INGRAM, ROBERT, was the son of Mr. Edward Ingram, of Old Hall, Glynhafren, Llanidloes, where he was born about the year 1784. He was tall, finely-built, and handsome, full of restless activity, and sought at an early age congenial work for his adventurous spirit by joining the navy. On the 1st September, 1798, he went on board the *Formidable*, 98, under Captain Whitshed, then stationed in the Channel. In the following November he joined the *Triton*, 32, as midshipman; was in the *Medusa*, 32, on the home and Mediterranean stations until July, 1802, and, when in company off Cape Finisterre with the *Naiad* and *Alcmene*, witnessed the capture of the *Santa Brigada*, a Spanish 36-gun frigate, having on board 1,400,000 dollars, besides a cargo of equal value. He was also at an attack made by Lord Nelson in 1801 on the Boulogne flotilla After serving for some time in the Mediterranean on board the *Cyclops* and *Termagant* sloops, Mr. Ingram rejoined the *Medusa* in February, 1804, and on the 5th October following was present at the capture of three more Spanish frigates laden with treasure, and the destruction of a fourth off Cape St. Mary. In the course of the following year he successively became lieutenant of the *Fervent* and the *Rebuff* gun-brigs, and also of the *Favourite* sloop, stationed on the coast of Africa, where he displayed an eminent degree of zeal and perseverance in the latter vessel, during an arduous chase of three days in December, 1805, which terminated in the capture of *Le General Blanchard*, a privateer of 16 guns and 130 men. He was made full lieutenant 1st September, 1806, to the *Princess of Orange*, 74, flagship in the Downs of Vice-Admiral Holloway; and after he had been for a short time re-attached to the *Favourite*, he was in May, 1807, appointed to the *Medusa* sloop, which formed part of the force employed in the Walcheren expedition. In 1808 he left the navy and returned to his native place, where he led a prodigal sort of life, selling portions of the family estates to supply himself with money, and finally, in 1826, disposing of the Old Hall itself— the residence of his ancestors for nearly 200 years. He was then appointed to the *Gloucester*, which formed part of the fleet sent to assist the Portuguese. On the 28th October, 1829, he was advanced to the command of the *Ætna* bomb, and paid her off 26th May, 1830, after which he was not employed. Commander Ingram married 7th September, 1806, Miss Wilmot, of Portsmouth. He died on the 13th August, 1860, aged 76, at 92, St. Thomas-street, Portsmouth, and was buried at the Portsmouth Cemetery, at Southsea.

IORWERTH AB BLEDDYN AB CYNFYN, a Prince

of Powys, "the honour and comfort of Britain," ("Decus et solamen Britanniæ."—Ann. Camb.) Having in 1101 joined Robert du Belesmo, Earl of Salop, and Arnulph, Earl of Pembroke, in rebellion against the King (Henry I.), the latter

" was counselled to send prinilie to Iorwerth ap Blethyn, promising him great gifts, if hee would forsake the Earle and serve him, remembring what wrongs the Earles father Roger [de Montgomery] and his brother Hugh had doone to the Welshmen. Also the King to make him more willing to sticke vnto him, gave him all such lands as the Earle and his brother had in Wales without tribute or oth; which was a poece of Powys, Cardigan and halfe Dyuet. * * * Iorwerth being glad of these offers received them willinglie, and then coming himself to the king, he sent his power to the Earles land, which doing their maisters comandement, destroied and spoiled all the countrie for the Earle had caused his people to conveie all their cattell and goods to Wales, litle remembering the mischiefs that the ·Welshmen had received at his fathers and brothers hands. But when these newes came to the Earle to Cadogan, and Meredyth Iorwerths brethren, they were all dismaid and despaired to be able to withstand the king; for Iorwerth was the greatest man of power in Wales. * * * * After this [1102] when the king was returned home, Iorwerth took his brother Meredyth and sent him to the kings prison : for his brother Cadogan agreed with him to whome Iorwerth gave Caerdhydh and a piece of Powys. Then Iorwerth himselfe went to the kings court, to put the king in remembrance of his promise : but the king when he saw all quiet, forgate the service of Iorwerth, and his own promise, and contrarie to the same took Dyuet from Iorwerth, and gave it to a knight called Saer; and Stratdtywy, Cydewen and Gwyr he gave to Howel ap Grono; and so Iorwerth was sent home emptie. * * * * In the end of this year the king did send diuerse of his councell to Shrewesberie, and willed Iorwerth ap Blethyn to come to meete them there to consult about the kings busines and affaires. Now when he came thither, all the consultation was against him, who contrarie to all right and equitie, they condemned of treason, because the king feared his strength, and that he would reuenge the wrongs that he had received at the king's hands, and so they committed him to prison. * * * * Then [1109] also the king remembered Iorwerth ap Blethyn, whom he had kept long in prison, and sent to know of him, what fine he would paie to haue his libertie; and he promised the king 300 pound, or the worth thereof in cattell or horses : then the king set him at libertie, and gave him his land againe. * * * * [1110.] And shortlie after Madoc ap Kiryd returned from Ireland, because he could not well awaie with the maners and conditions of the Irishmen, and being arriued came to the countrie of his vncle Iorwerth, who hearing that, and fearing to lose his lands (as his brother Cadogan had done) made proclamation that no man should doo for him, but take him for his enemie. Which when Madoc understood, he gathered to him a number of unthrifts and out-lawes, and kept himself in the rockes and woods, deuising all the means he could to be revenged upon Iorwerth, for that vnkindness and discourtesie as he tooke it, and so entred friendship priuily with Lhywarch ap Trahaern, who hated Iorwert. to the death. Then having knowledge that Iorwerth laie one night at Caerenoen, they two gathered all their strength, and came about the house at midnight, then Iorwerth and his men awoke, and defended the house manfullie, vntil their foes set the same on fire : which when Iorwerths men saw, every one shifted for himselfe so that some scaped through the fire, and the rest were either burnt or slaine, or both. Then Iorwerth himselfe seeing no remedie, adventured rather to be slaine than burned and came out; but his enemies receiued him vpon sharpe speares, and overthrow him in the fire, and so he died a cruell death."—(Powel).

JAMES, JOHN, a brave soldier, at one time Colour-sergeant in the 50th Regiment of Foot, was born at Buttington Green, Welshpool, in 1774. He enlisted in the Montgomeryshire Militia in 1798, volunteered into the 63rd Regiment of the line in 1799, and went to Holland with the Duke of York, where he was wounded in the left leg. He volunteered into the 50th in 1801, to go to Egypt with Sir Ralph Abercrombie; in 1807 went to Copenhagen to take the Danish Fleet, came home and was equipped to go to Spain; was at the battle of Corunna, and present at the death of Sir John Moore; was through the whole of the Peninsular War, and wounded on July 25th, 1813, at Mayo, in the Pyrences, through both thighs, and was sent to the hospital at Vittoria to be discharged, when he was sent to England. Total years' service, 14; pension, 1s. 10d. per day. The following character was given to him by Sir Charles Napier, Lieut.-Col. 50th :—" Sergeant James is a good and brave soldier, " and has always received a high character from the officers " under whom he has served. He stood by his captain when " every other had left him or been killed ; nor did he forsake " that gallant and lamented officer till ordered to save himself " by his captain, who expired as he spoke." Lieut.-Col. C. Hill, 50th Regiment, also recommended him for a pension as " A " brave, well-conducted soldier." He wore a medal with two clasps, on which were inserted the following battles :—" Toulouse, Pyrences, Vittoria, Fuentes-d-Onor, Talavera, Vimiera." His wife, who died about a dozen years before him, was with him through the whole of the Peninsular War. She was a brave woman, and at Mayo, where he was last wounded, she found him lying on the field of battle, had his wounds roughly dressed, lifted him on a mule herself, and held him there for some miles till they overtook the army, when he was properly attended to. After his return to England, Sergt. James became lock-keeper on the Shropshire Union Canal at Pool Quay, which berth he held till about ten years before his death, when the Company granted him a pension, and he went to reside at Cefn Buttington, where he lived till his death. After his retirement from the Army, Sergeant James suffered great pains from the wounds in his thighs, and also from asthma notwithstanding which he attained the great age of more than 100 years. He died May 25th, 1875, and was buried at Welshpool.

JENKINS, Rev. JOHN, M.A., of Kerry, was the second son of Mr. Griffith Jenkins, of Cilbronau, in the parish of Llangoedmor, Cardiganshire, and was born April 8th, 1770. He received his early education at a neighbouring school and at the Academy at Carmarthen. In 1789 he was admitted a member of Jesus College, Oxford, from which after a time he removed to Merton College. After the usual lapse of time he took his B.A. degree. and the same year (1791) was ordained deacon, and became curate to his uncle Dr. Lewis, rector of Whippingham, Isle of Wight. He officiated there over six years, but in 1799

became chaplain on board the *Agincourt* man-of-war on the
the West Indies station. The fleet on that station was under
the command of Admiral the Hon. William Waldegrave, who
was the same year, for his distinguished services in the great
naval battles of St. Vincent and others, raised to the peerage
under the title of Lord Radstock. In March, 1802, Mr. Jenkins
was transferred from the *Agincourt* to the *Theseus*, which with
other ships was occupied in watching the Island of Jamaica.
Here he remained until July, 1804. In that year the blacks of
St. Domingo rose in insurrection, took possession of the island
and massacred a large number of the white inhabitants at Cape
Francis. The third day after the massacre, Mr. Jenkins with
Lieut. Muddle ventured on a mission to De-Salines, the leader
of the insurrection, with the object of interceding for, and preventing the massacre of, the remaining whites in other parts of
the island. The two arrived at the residence of the President,
and were led into a dark room, where they were kept for many
hours in suspense as to the safety of their own lives. At last
they were liberated without gaining their object, and with some
difficulty regained their ship in an open boat upon a dark and
stormy night. The information they had obtained, however,
enabled the fleet to save the lives of about a thousand of the
white population of Monte Christi, who were conveyed in safety
to Cuba. Fearlessness was, indeed, throughout life one of Mr.
Jenkins' chief characteristics. The insalubrity of the climate,
however, soon told upon his health, and in September, 1804, he
was obliged to return on board the *Bellerophon* to his native
country. When his health was sufficiently restored he in the
following summer undertook clerical duties at Manor Teivi in
Pembrokeshire. Having during his naval chaplaincy gained the
warm estimation of the Admiral, Lord Radstock, the latter
obtained for him the appointment of a chaplain to H.R.H. the
Duke of Clarence, afterwards King William IV., and he now
used his influence with Dr. Burgess, bishop of St. David's, to
obtain promotion for him, in which he succeeded, for the bishop
soon conferred upon him the valuable living of Kerry in Montgomeryshire. Mr. Jenkins took up his residence at Kerry
in 1807, and there spent the remaining 22 years of his life.
Having found the Vicarage and other buildings in a ruinous
state, he in a short time rebuilt them at considerable expense.
He soon formed an acquaintance with several gentlemen in the
neighbourhood of literary tastes including the Revs. Walter
Davies, David Richards, David Rowland, and others, who
frequently met at his house in social converse on topics relating
to Wales, its literature, and poetry. Dr. Burgess was present on
one of these occasions in August, 1818, and his interest in such
matters was greatly awakened. The result was that it was
determined if possible to revive the ancient Eisteddfodau on a
worthier scale than they had lately been held, and arrangements
were made for holding the first of a new series of such
national gatherings in July, 1819, at Carmarthen, under the

presidency of Lord Dynevor. Others were held annually for some years afterwards in various parts of Wales—of most of which Mr. Jenkins was the heart and soul. He, however, gradually became so disgusted with the Anglicising tendencies of some persons connected with the movement, and the neglect of native talent in favor of the importation of singers and musicians from England, that he did not attend the great eisteddfod held at Denbigh in 1829. The first week of every new year was observed by him as a kind of bardic festival, during which time his house and table were open to all bards and minstrels. On April 8, 1823, he married Miss Elizabeth Jones, second daughter of the Rev. Edward Jones, vicar of Berriew, and niece and heiress of Edward Heyward, Esq., of Crosswood, Guilsfield,—a lady of kindred tastes with his own. The only issue of this marriage was one son, John Heyward Jenkins (who has since exchanged the name of Jenkins for Heyward), born April 4th, 1824. Mr. Jenkins was a frequent contributor on antiquarian and other subjects to the *Cambrian Quarterly Magazine*, and under the name of *Hooker* to the *Gwyliedydd*. One or two sermons and some poetry of his were also published. He was also an accomplished musician and contributed not a little to rescue some of the old Welsh tunes from oblivion. Besides the Vicarage of Kerry, he held the Rural Deanery of Maelienydd, the prebend of Mochdre in the collegiate church of Brecon, and latterly a prebendal stall in the Cathedral of York. There is a touch of romance in connection with his promotion to the latter dignity. While he was on board the *Theseus* on the West India station a young man named Vernon, a son of the Bishop of Lichfield, who served in the same ship as midshipman, was struck down by yellow fever. His bed being in a close ill-ventilated part of the ship, Mr. Jenkins thought that unless he could be removed to a healthier part his death would be certain. He therefore interceded with the captain, but, failing in his attempt, he resolved to give up his own bed to the patient, whom he afterwards tended with affectionate care. The young man to his great joy recovered, and subsequently forsook the navy and entered the church. Mr. Jenkins had almost forgotten this incident, when in 1828 he received a letter from his old friend, Mr. Vernon, informing him that there was a prebendal stall in the Cathedral of York worth £600 a year in the gift of his father (then Archbishop of York) at his service. Mr. Jenkins went to Oxford and took his degree of Master of Arts to qualify him to hold his new office, which, however he was destined to occupy but a short time. The tropical climate of the West Indies had doubtless seriously injured his constitution. He was taken ill on the 2nd November, 1829, and on the twentieth of the same month, he died. In 1830 a marble tablet to his memory was placed in the church of his native parish, Llangoedmor, Cardiganshire, and subsequently another was placed over his tomb in the chancel of Kerry church with the following inscription :—" Sacred to the memory of the Rev. John Jenkins, M.A.,

" Prebendary in the dioceses of York and St. David's, chaplain
" to His Royal Highness, the Duke of Clarence, and twenty-two
" years vicar of this parish ; who in every relation of life, whether
" clergyman, magistrate, son, husband, father, brother, friend,
" was most exemplary. He departed this life November 20th,
" 1829, aged fifty-nine years, leaving a mournful widow, an
" infant son, and a numerous circle of relations and friends, to
" lament his loss."

JOHNES, ARTHUR JAMES, Judge of County Courts,
was the son of Edward Johnes, Esq., M.D., of Garthmyl isaf,
Berriew, by Mary, daughter of Thomas Davies, Esq., of Llifior.
He was born on the 4th of February, 1809, and at an early age
was sent to Oswestry Grammar School, of which Dr. Donne
was then Master. Thence he proceeded to the London University, where he had the advantage of studying law under Professor Andrew Amos, and in 1829 won the chief honours in the
law examination—gaining the *first* prize for law ever given by the
University. The writings of Bentham exercised a great influence
on his mind, in particular the views of that great writer as to
the fusion of law and equity. In 1834, while yet a student, Mr.
Johnes published a pamphlet entitled *Suggestions for a Reform
of the Court of Chancery by a union of the Jurisdiction of
Equity and Law*. This work, which at once attracted much
attention, he modestly inscribed to his old tutor and friend,
Professor Amos. Possibly the merit and honour of originating
the idea of the fusion of law and equity cannot be claimed for
Mr. Johnes, but must be ascribed to Bentham, or perhaps,
indeed, to Lord Mansfield. It, however, lay dormant, but Mr.
Johnes saw that it was rational and must eventually prevail at a
time when the Sugdens and Lyndhursts looked upon it as a
revolutionary folly. He, therefore, took it up, and by his pamphlet he in reality started that agitation, which brought about
the important changes effected in 1875 by the Judicature Acts. On the 30th January, 1835, Mr. Johnes was called
to the bar by the Honourable Society of Lincoln's Inn, adopting
the practice of equity and conveyancing as his special pursuit.
In 1847 he was appointed a Joint Commissioner to report on
several Bills relating to certain Gas Companies in various towns
in England. Mr. Johnes wrote much in favour of providing a
more easy method for the recovery of small debts, by reforming
and conferring additional jurisdiction upon the County Courts.
This much-needed reform was brought about by the passing of
the Act of 9 and 10 Vict., cap. 95, which came into operation on
the 15th March, 1847. Mr. Johnes was appointed one of the
first Judges under the Act—his Circuit extending at one time
from Holyhead to Hay, and comprising the whole of North-
West Wales and a part of South Wales. This office he continued to hold until within a few months of his death, but
during his tenure of it several changes were made in the area
of his Circuit. It is not too much to say that few men ever

devoted themselves with greater earnestness and singleness of purpose than did Mr. Johnes to the conscientious discharge of his duties. The wide extent of his circuit necessitated incessant toil in travelling in all sorts of weather, for except during the last 9 years of his judicial life railways were unknown throughout the whole of his district. He was not satisfied, however, with the mere discharge of the duties of his judicial office, but laboured constantly to bring about such further reforms in County Court procedure as his experience taught him were necessary. To this end he kept up for many years a correspondence with Lord Brougham and other law reformers, and published numerous pamphlets on the subject. As a Judge, Mr. Johnes was, it need hardly be said, upright, thoroughly impartial and conscientious, and his decisions were universally respected. Very few, if any, were ever reversed or even appealed against. After 23 years of judicial life he, in consequence of ill-health, retired in December, 1870, upon a well-earned pension of £1,000 a year, having the satisfaction of seeing the County Court system greatly developed and improved by the adoption of most of his own suggestions. Early in life Mr. Johnes imbibed a taste for Welsh literature, and often associated with that energetic band of Welsh clergy-men, who then lived in the immediate neighbourhood of his home—the Revs. Walter Davies, J. Jenkins, of Kerry, T. Richards, of Berriew, and others. Under their inspiration he determined to learn Welsh, and very soon acquired a critical knowledge of the language. In 1834 he published an elegant translation into English of the *Poems of Dafydd ab Gwilym*. He was also one of the promoters of the *Cambrian Quarterly Magazine* (1829-1833), and contributed several articles to its pages, chiefly under the signature "Maelog." During the first 30 years of the present century the Church of England was nowhere in so deplorable a condition as in Wales. Pluralism, nepotism, and absenteeism were rampant; many of the best livings, and those entirely Welsh-speaking parishes, were held by clergymen utterly ignorant of the Welsh language, while the incumbents of others were men of grossly immoral character. As a natural consequence, the parish churches were well nigh deserted, and the Welsh became a nation of Dissenters. Under these circum-stances, the Cymmrodorion Society offered in 1831 the Royal medal for an *Essay on the Causes which in Wales have produced Dissent from the Established Church*, which Mr. Johnes gained under the *nom de plume* of *Caractacus*. Of this essay the adjudicator (Dr. Owen Pughe) spoke in the following terms:—"No. 2, "signed Caractacus, is an elaborate and valuable treatise and "explains the real ground of dissent in a most satisfactory "manner, bringing forward proofs to awaken conviction, and "made interesting by pertinent remarks upon the history of the "Welsh church. It would be highly desirable that this Essay "should be printed by the Cymmrodorion under the sanction of "its author." In accordance with this recommendation, the Essay was soon afterwards published at the expense of the

Society. In the following year, 1832, a second edition was published with copious historical and statistical details, which, notwithstanding various attempts made through the press to impugn their correctness, were eventually accepted by unprejudiced men, whether Churchmen or Dissenters, as accurate and truthful. In 1870 Mr. Pryse, of Llanidloes, brought out a third edition. Happily, most of the abuses exposed and condemned by the writer are things of the past; but this reform was brought about in no small degree by the force of public opinion created by the publication of Mr. Johnes's essay. Some of the parties who benefitted by the abuses dragged into light by Mr. Johnes, winced under the exposure, and violently attacked him in the press. Mr. Johnes addressed an able letter to Lord John Russell on the state of the Welsh Church, and the subject was debated in Parliament. In 1837 some of the *Correspondence on the subject of the Church in Wales, with reference to "A Letter "from A. J. Johnes, Esq., to Lord John Russell"* was published in a pamphlet. By an Order in Council published in the *London Gazette*, October, 1838, the sees of St. Asaph and Bangor were to be united on the next vacancy in either, and the Bishop of Manchester was then to be created without any addition to the spiritual peers of the realm. This measure encountered very strenuous opposition on the part of the Earl of Powis and others. A deputation of members connected with the Principality (Mr Johnes acting as their Secretary) waited upon Lord John Russell at the Home Office, who undertook to investigate the subject with a view to the preservation of the revenues of the Church in Wales. The order was subsequently annulled by Act of Parliament. Mr. Johnes, for the information of his Lordship, published *Statistical illustrations of the Claims of the Welsh Dioceses to augmentation out of the Funds at the disposal of the Ecclesiastical Commissioners, in a Letter to Lord John Russell*, 1841. Mr. Johnes was a member of the Genealogical Society, the Powysland Club, and several other literary societies. He at all times took a particular interest in ethnological and philological researches, and was himself a diligent and painstaking student. In 1846 he published *Philological Proofs of the original unity and recent origin of the human race* (8vo.)—an important work, displaying a great amount of research and labour. In 1862 Mr. Johnes offered for competition at the Swansea Eisteddfod a Prize of Fifty Guineas for "the best Essay on the origin of the English nation, more "especially with reference to the question how far they are "descended from the Ancient Britons." This was eventually won by the late Dr. Nicholas, who afterwards published his essay under the title of *The Pedigree of the English people*. The uprising of the oppressed nationalities of Europe in 1848-9 aroused much sympathy among liberty-loving Englishmen ; in particular the struggles of the Hungarian patriots for the emancipation of their country from the Austrian yoke. When, after a gallant but futile struggle, Kossuth and others sought and found an asylum in England, the utmost enthusiasm was evoked on their behalf throughout the length and breadth of the land. A national subscription was got up for the Italian refugees, and Mr. Johnes issued a stirring *Address to the Inhabitants of Wales* on their behalf. In the same year the Papal Bull for the establishment of a Catholic hierarchy in Great Britain greatly exercised the public mind. Mr. Johnes, in December, addressed an able *Letter to the Rev. Lewis Edwards, M.A., on the Mutual Claims and Duties of Protestants and Roman Catholics at the present juncture.* The want of railway communication had long been severely felt in Montgomeryshire and Central Wales. At length a band of local gentlemen, among whom Mr. Johnes was one of the most active, succeeded in obtaining in 1855 an Act for making a railway from Oswestry to Newtown, and the following year one for making a line from Shrewsbury to Welshpool. Mr. Johnes was one of the first directors, and his advice and services in the early history of these undertakings were of very great value. The cause of temperance also found in him a very warm advocate. He took great pains to gather a large mass of valuable information and facts, which he made use of in evidence given by him as a witness before a committee on the subject appointed by Convocation. He also kept up for years a correspondence with other leading temperance reformers, and wrote frequently in the newspapers with a view to bring about reforms in the licensing system, and in particular the restriction of the sale of intoxicating liquors on the Lord's Day. Some of these reforms he had the satisfaction of seeing carried out in his own day; others have since been adopted. It may be said, indeed, that whatever movement was set on foot for promoting a social or moral reform of any kind, especially if it related more particularly to Wales, it was sure to find in Mr. Johnes a warm friend, and an able and untiring advocate. In private life Mr. Johnes was one of the most amiable, kind, and charitable of men, ever ready to give a helping hand to struggling merit. For many years his health had been precarious, and during last nine or ten months of his life he suffered much. He died unmarried at Garthmyl on the 23rd of July, 1871, and was buried at the parish Church of Berriew.

JONES, Sir CHARLES THOMAS, Knt., was the third son of Charles Thomas Jones, Esq., of Fronfraith, near Abermule. He was born in the year 1778, and married in 1817 the daughter of Gilbert Saltoun, Esq., collector of customs at Bermuda, by whom he had several children. He entered the navy in May, 1791, and was present in the action of 1st June, 1794; also in that of 23rd June, 1795, when he was wounded. He was knighted by the Duke of Richmond when Lord Lieutenant of Ireland in 1809, in recognition of his public services. He was a magistrate and deputy-lieutenant of Montgomeryshire, and served the office of sheriff in 1832. He became a retired rear admiral in 1851.

JONES, DAVID, (of Llansantffraid), was born at Llan-fyllin, December 2nd, 1797, and was the youngest of thirteen children of Mr. Robert Jones, a respectable tradesman. In November, 1817, he married Miss Elizabeth Griffiths, of Llan-santffraid, and in May, 1819, removed to that place, where he carried on business as a shopkeeper until his death. In 1827, mainly through his exertions, a chapel was built in the village by the Independents, with whom Mr. Jones was an active member. He at this time carried on also an extensive business as maltster; but about the year 1836, when the teetotal move-ment first began in Montgomeryshire, Mr. Jones became one of its earliest and most zealous adherents and advocates; and not only so, but at a considerable pecuniary sacrifice he gave up the malting business, and converted his malthouse into a temperance house. He travelled, spoke, and wrote much during the rest of his life on behalf of total abstinence. He was also an earnest promoter of Sunday Schools and other religious movements, and, for the last ten years of his life, an acceptable lay preacher with the Independents. He died August 6th, 1848, in his 51st year, and was buried in accordance with his own wishes, under the communion table at the Independent Chapel, Llansantffraid. He left a widow and five children. He was the author of a tract in English, entitled *A Teetotaler's Defence.* Shortly after his death a memoir of Mr. Jones was published by the Rev. Hugh James.

JONES, Rev. EDWARD, M.A., rector of Llanmerewig, from 1635 to 1643, translated into Welsh the *Churchman's Companion in the Visitation of the Sick,* of which editions appeared in 1699, 1700, and 1738. He had previously held the vicarage of Nantglyn for some time, but had been ejected.

JONES, Right Rev. EDWARD, D.D., bishop of St. Asaph, was born at Llwyn Ririd, in the parish of Forden. He was the son of Richard Jones, Esq., by Sarah, his wife (daughter of John Pyttes, Esq., of Marrington), and was baptised 24th July, 1641. He was educated at Westminster School, whence he was elected to Trinity College, Cambridge, where he was elected Fellow in 1667. He obtained a doctor's degree, became Master of the Kilkenny College, and Dean of Lismore in Ireland, and in 1682 was raised to the bishopric of Cloyne, from which, on 13th December, 1692, he was translated to St. Asaph. His promotion is said to have been entirely owing to his being a native of the country, and thereby qualified to be made a plausible competitor, in order to defeat the claims of a person in nomination of the same country, and of great learning, integrity, and experience. But this worthy person had given offence by appearing in the Convocation of 1689 against the measures of Dr Tennison, then Archdeacon of London, and afterwards Archbishop of Canterbury. The contrast between his and his eminent prede-cessor's (Bishop Lloyd) administration of his diocese was sad and painful in the extreme. That of Bishop Jones was marked by so much corruption, negligence, and oppression, that in 1697 an address, signed by thirty-eight of the principal beneficed clergy, was sent to the Archbishop, representing their complaints under no less than thirty-four heads, and praying for an inquiry. These charges the Bishop was summoned to answer on the 20th July, 1698. By his own confession he had been guilty of gross neglect of ecclesiastical discipline, not only in not punishing a case of known drunkenness, but even in promoting to a canonry one who had been accused to him of crimes and excesses; he had permitted laymen to perform the office of curates at Abergele and Llandrilio; he had been guilty of a simoniacal contract in the disposal of some of his preferments, and had allowed his wife to receive money, by way of earnest, for certain promotions. Besides which, he had been in the habit of appropriating to himself a year's profits of vacant livings, on the plea of carrying on the lawsuit for the recovery of the advowson of Llanuwchllyn—a plea never put into practice. After much delay the Archbishop's sentence was pronounced in June, 1701. It was that the Bishop be suspended from his episcopal office, administration, and emoluments for the space of six months, "et ultra donec satisfecerit." He died May 10th, 1703, at Westminster, and was buried in the parish church of St. Margaret's. He had been married to Elizabeth, eldest daughter of Sir Richard Kennedy, Bart., of Mount Kennedy, Wicklow, by whom he had several children. One of his grandsons, Richard Jones, was mayor of Shrewsbury in 1753.

JONES, EDWARD (*Hebog*), a skilful poet and musician, was born at Penygarnedd, near Llanfyllin, about the year 1825. He competed at the Tremadoc Eisteddfod in 1851 for the prize offered for an *Anthem on Habaccuc's Prayer*; and at Llangollen Eisteddfod in 1858 for *Cywydd ar y Gweddnewidiad* (Ode on the Transfiguration). In 1860 he published a long *Awdl* of about 7,000 lines on *David, King of Israel*. He also was a frequent contributor to the Welsh Wesleyan magazines. He died on the 8th December, 1868, at Llanfyllin, where he had for some years carried on the business of a draper, and was buried at Llanrhaiadr.

JONES, HUGH, of Maesglasau, in the parish of Mallwyd, was born in that parish in the year 1749. He was one of a family of 9 children, he being the fifth. In his childhood and youth he and his brothers and sisters had to walk four miles each way daily to school at Mallwyd and home again. However, by making the best use of all the means at his disposal, he acquired so fair an amount of useful knowledge, that he came to be considered among his neighbours an excellent scholar. He delighted in music, and among his closest friends there was one John Williams, of Dolgelley, also a good musician, whom he frequently visited, and on those occasions the two friends would frequently sing together all through the night, utterly oblivious of the flight of the small hours. He also taught psalmody in many of the surrounding villages, and wrote several Psalm-

J

tunes and interludes which obtained popularity in his own neighbourhood. When he was about 23 years of age he wrote his first book—*Cydymaith yr Hwsmon* (The Husbandman's Companion), consisting of meditations on the seasons and on other occasions, with songs and Englynion to relieve the monotony of the work. This was published in 1774, under his own superintendence in London, whither he had gone and obtained a situation as usher in a school, with the object of perfecting his acquaintance with various branches of knowledge. After a residence in London of about two years he returned to his native place, bringing with him for sale the printed copies of his book—a work remarkable for its pure idiomatic Welsh, as well as for the excellence of its contents. His first literary venture proving successful, Mr. Jones decided on devoting his life thenceforth to literary labour for the benefit of his countrymen. He was the author or translator of the following works: *Gardd y Caniadau* (The Garden of Songs, 1776), *Myfyrdod ar Ddamhegion a Gwyrthiau ein Harglwydd Iesu Grist* (A meditation on the parables and miracles of our Lord Jesus Christ, 1777); a Welsh work on *Arithmetic: Cysuron Dwyfol; new Addewidion gwerthfawr er anogaeth i gredinwyr* (Divine Consolations or precious promises for the encouragement of believers, 1781), *Ateb i bob un a ofyno reswm am y gobaith sydd ynom mewn ffordd o Holiad ac Ateb, gan Joseph Humphreys* (An answer to everyone who may ask for a reason for the hope that is in us, by way of question and answer, 1781), *Gair yn ei Amser, neu Lythyr-anerch i'r cyffredin Gymry, &c.* (A word in season, or an address to the common Welsh people, 1782), *Hanes Daeargryn ofnadwy a ddigwyddodd yn Itali ac a barhaodd lawer o ddyddiau yn mis Chwefror diweddaf, &c.* (An account of a terrible earthquake that took place in Italy, and lasted for several days in February last, &c., 1783), *Marweiddiad Pechod mewn Credinwyr*, a translation of Dr. Owen's " Mortification of sin in believers " (1791). He also published second editions of translations of Brooks's " Golden Apples for young people, and a Crown of Glory for old people," and of Bunyan's " Salvation through Grace," " The Strait Gate," and " Last Sermon " (1791). Most of the above works were printed at Shrewsbury, and it appears that at one time of his life the author kept a moveable day school, and sold books for the Shrewsbury booksellers. He also translated into Welsh the *Works of Josephus* and *Buchan's Family Medicine*, both of which were published; and began the compilation of a work under the title of *Crynhodeb o Hanes Prydain* (A summary of the history of Britain), but which was not published. He was the author of several of the old Welsh psalm tunes, and of that very beautiful hymn, the first two verses of which begin—

" O tyn
    Y gorchudd yn y mynydd hyn, &c."
" Pa le
    Y gwnaf fy noddfa dan y ne, &c."

For some time before his death he lived at Denbigh, where he was reader and corrector of the press at Mr. Gee's office He had made some progress with the translation of Matthew Henry's *Commentary* and Dr. Watts's *World to Come*, when death put an end to his laborious life. He died at Denbigh on the 16th of April, 1825, aged 76 years, and was buried at Henllan, near that town.

JONES, HUGH (*Erfyl*) was born at Cefnbachau, in the parish of Llanerfyl, in the year 1789, and was a nephew of Hugh Jones, of Maesyglasau. Being a cripple, and therefore unable to earn his living by physical labour, his parents gave him a better schooling than their other children to fit him for the calling of a schoolmaster. At the Beaumaris Eisteddfod in 1832 he gained a prize for an essay on the "Syntax of the Welsh language." He was a good Welsh scholar, a sound critic, and a talented poet. For many years previous to his death he resided at Chester, where he corrected the press for Mr. Edward Parry, and afterwards for Messrs. John Parry and Son. From the beginning of 1835 to the end of 1840 he edited the *Gwladgarwr* magazine. He also assisted in the bringing out of several other Welsh works. He died at Chester May 25th, 1858, aged 69, and was buried at Llanerfyl, where a monument has been erected to his and his parents' memory, with the following *Englyn* inscribed upon it :—

> "Huna isod Hanesydd,—Erfyl,
> Brif-fardd ac Athronydd;
> Gwr o ddawn, gwir Dduweinydd,
> Hyd y farn ei glod a fydd."

JOHN, REV. JOHN, Vicar of Pennant in 1719, and Rector of Llangynog from 1720 to 1744, the date of his death, published a *Letter, being a solemn and affectionate Address from a country Clergyman to his Parishioners.*

JONES, REV. JOHN, was a native of Cardiganshire, who, after serving the curacy of Mallwyd for some time, obtained in 1782 the Vicarage of Pennant, and the same year the Rectory of Llangynog, which he held for five years. He left behind him a large number of *Sermons* in MS., thirty of which were, after his death, printed at Wrexham under the editorship of the Rev. Henry Parry, Llanasa.

JONES, REV. JOHN, Curate of Llangadfan, was the author of a translation into Welsh of *The Church Catechism explained, &c.*, by the Rev. John Lewis, Minister of Margate, to which is added a *Treatise on Confirmation by Mr. Adams; Prayers, &c.* This was published at Shrewsbury in 1790.

JONES, REV. JOHN, M.A., Rector of Llanllyfni, Carnarvonshire, was born at Lledfair Hall, Machynlleth, in 1786. He was educated at Bangor Grammar School, and from thence proceeded to Christ Church, Oxford, where he graduated in due

course. He was in 1819 inducted to the Rectory of Llanllyfni,
which he held up to the time of his death. He was one of the
earliest members of the Cambrian Archæological Association, and a valued contributor to the *Archæologia Cambrensis.*
Of his contributions one at least, *An Essay on the state of
Agriculture and the progress of Arts and Manufactures during
the period and under the influence of the Druidical system*, was
republished in a separate form. He left a number of well-
written and valuable papers on archæological subjects, which
were placed by his executors at the disposal of the Association.
He also published several sermons. Mr. Jones was an excellent
antiquary, and possessed a clear judgment and a well-stored
mind. He died on the 12th of February, 1863, aged 77 years.

JONES, JOHN, of Llettyderyn, Mochdre, was born at
Craigyrhenffordd, Llanbrynmair, about the year 1760. About
the year 1826 he published a Welsh translation of *The Life and
death of the Rev. Vavasor Powell, &c.*, in five parts,—a translation of which had already appeared in 1772, but which he
appears to have been unaware of. In his younger days he is said
to have walked all the way to Bala to induce the Rev. Thomas
Charles to come to Mochdre to preach. Mr. Charles complied
with this request, and, with the permission of the incumbent,
preached in Mochdre Church. Subsequently, Mr. Jones is said
to have taken offence at the action of the Calvinistic Methodist
denomination (to which he belonged) ordaining ministers of their
own. He is said to have purchased land for the erection of a
mill at Caersws, but the project was abandoned. He died about
the year 1846, aged 86 years.

JONES, JOHN (*Myllin*) was a young poet of very great
promise. He was born about the year 1800 at Glyniau, near
Llanfyllin. He was a shoemaker by trade, and for a time
worked at Liverpool. His poetic genius early attracted the
attention and received the encouragement of the Rev. David
Richards. Llansilin, and other patriotic Welshmen of his
neighbourhood. He gained the prize at the Welshpool
Eisteddfod in 1824 for the best six stanzas of *Epitaph to Dic
Sion Dafydd*, the latter, it need hardly be explained, being the
name given by Welshmen in derision to one of their own countrymen who among strangers is ashamed of his country and
language. He also at the same Eisteddfod delivered a poetical
address, which by its fervour and eloquence took by surprise
those who heard it. This probably, had his health not failed
him, would have led to his being sent to the University to be
educated for the Church. He was a thorough master of the
Welsh metres, and his *awen* was of the highest order. He wrote
a large number of beautiful stanzas, some of which, unfortunately, have been lost, and many excellent songs. Of the latter
perhaps the best known, and certainly one of the most beautiful,
is that to *Rhianod Sir Drefaldwyn* (the Maids of Montgomeryshire)—suggested by and worthy of being placed side by side

with Mr. Lewis Morris's famous song to the *Fair Maids of
Merioneth*. Another highly poetical composition of his is
Myfyrdodau wrth wrando y Gnul (Meditations on listening to
the Tolling Bell). He excelled also in translation. *Auld Lang
Syne* and Dibdin's *Lash'd to the helm* were exquisitely rendered
by him into the same metre in Welsh—a task requiring no small
amount of genius to accomplish it. He was also a good prose
writer, and some of his essays gained prizes at the Eisteddfodau.
But a life of so much promise was destined to be cut short.
That terrible bane of our climate, consumption, had marked him
for its victim, and slowly but surely he succumbed to its insidious
attacks During his long illness, which he bore uncomplainingly,
his mind was very active. A short time before his death he was
visited by his intimate friend, the Rev. Robert Jones, of Rotherhithe, then an Oxford student, who asked him how he was. The
dying poet, in a deep tone of sadness, slowly replied in the
following exquisite Englynion :—

> Mac trwm gystudd prudd yn parhau—arnaf,
> Mal oer ernest angau;
> Egwann mac'm gewynau;
> O na chawn fy llawn iachau!

> Gan nychdod darfod bob dydd—mac'm corph;
> A mwy yw'm cur beunydd;
> Ofnaf—O bran yw 'nefnydd!
> Mai marw wnaf yn moreu 'nydd.

> Eiddigor y Pen-meddygon—eto
> All atal gofidion;
> A rhoi iechyd llwyrbryd, llon,
> Dinam, pan ballo dynion.

A few days afterwards his pure spirit took its flight. He died
on the 9th of July, 1826, having barely attained the age of 27
years. Thus was prematurely cut off, at almost its very beginning, the career of undoubtedly one of the most promising poets
ever produced by Wales. Myllin himself had, it is said, a short
time before his death collected together his poetical compositions
with a view to their publication for the benefit of his wife and
children, and had handed them to his friend the Rev. Robert
Jones, who lent them to the Rev. John Jones (*Tegid*). While
in his custody they were somehow or other lost and never could
be found afterwards. An obelisk of slate and stone has been
erected on Myllin's grave in Llanfyllin churchyard, with the
following stanzas, composed by the poet himself, engraved upon
it :—

> " Och! er cau dorau durol,—a gwylio,
> A galw gwyr meddygol;
> Llaw angau y llew ingol,
> Dwylaw neb nis deil hi'n ol.

> Nid ienctid llawn gwrid na grym,—na ffrydiawg
> Amgyffredion cyflym,
> A etyl gledd lleithwedd llym
> Y creulawn Angau crylym."

JONES, Rev. JOHN (*Idrisyn*), was born near Dolgelley on the 20th January, 1804, being, it is stated, a descendant of Ellis Wynn, the author of *Bardd Cwsg*. Early in life he was apprenticed to Mr Richard Jones, printer and publisher of *Yr Eurgrawn Wesleyaidd*, whom he accompanied to Llanfair Caereinion on his removal in 1824 to that town, and shortly afterwards to Llanidloes. There in 1830 he settled as a printer and publisher on his own account, and was for several years a member of the Town Council, being Mayor for 1852. During this time he was a local preacher among the Wesleyans, but in 1853 he joined the Church of England, when he was ordained and licensed by Bishop Thirlwall to the curacy of Llandyssul in Cardiganshire. He remained there till 1858, when he was made Vicar of Llandyssiliogogo in the same county. He resided in the neighbouring village of New Quay, where he died on August 17, 1887. In 1881 he was granted a pension of £50 from the Civil List Fund. In 1841 he published *Esboniad Hanesiol ar y Testament Newydd* (A Historical Commentary on the New Testament) ; also *Esboniad ar Bum Llyfr Moses a'r Testament Newydd* (A Commentary on the Five Books of Moses and the New Testament). He also wrote *Gwobr i Blentyn, neu Gatecism wedi ei seilio ar yr Ysgrythyrau i'w arfer mewn Ysgolion Sabbothol* (A Child's Reward, or a Catechism founded on the Scriptures for use in the Sunday Schools, Llanidloes, 1842) ; *Darlith ar Natur, Dyben, a Llesoldeb Cymdeithasau Llenyddol* (A Lecture on the Nature, Object, and Utility of Literary Societies, Llandovery, 1854) ; *Magl i ddal Haul Belydryn* Aberystwyth, 1871), a translation of Combe's "Trap to catch a Sunbeam" ; *Y Dyddlyfr Cristionogol* (The Christian Diary), and *Darlith ar y Milflwyddiant* (A Lecture on the Millenium). His best known work is a critical commentary on the Bible, *Y Deonglydd Beirniadol*, (Llanidloes, 1852), which has run into eight editions, and it is stated that 80,000 copies of it have been sold in this country and America. He also wrote another commentary in six vols. called *Yr Esboniad Beirniadol*, (Llanidloes, 1845), and a volume of sermons (Wrexham, 1886), besides numerous pamphlets, poems, and contributions to the Welsh press. He rendered into idiomatic Welsh the Queen's "Journal of our Life in the Highlands."

JONES, Rev. JOHN FOULKES, B.A., was the eldest son of John Foulkes Jones, of Machynlleth, by Lydia, daughter of Thomas Foulkes, of that town. He was born in the year 1826. Having at an early age shown an inclination to join the Calvinistic ministry, he studied for some years at the college of that denomination, at Bala, and afterwards entered the University of Edinburgh, where he graduated B.A.. He left the University in 1848. In 1849 he settled at Mochdre, near Newtown, as a Home Missionary, and subsequently removed to Berriew, where he laboured in a similar capacity. After four years thus spent he went to Liverpool, where he resided for about 12 months. He was ordained in 1856, and settled down at Machynlleth. In 1855 he visited Egypt and the Holy Land, and upon his return published an account of his travels under the title, *Egypt in its Biblical relations and moral aspects.* He also contributed several essays to the "Traethodydd," the Welsh quarterly, and to other periodicals. Mr. Jones was a popular preacher, and widely known and revered on account of his amiability and pious character. In May, 1861, he married Margaret, only daughter of Lewis Jones, Esq., of Shrewsbury, by whom he had several children. During the last few years of his life he suffered much from a painful disease, which eventually proved fatal. He died on the 14th April, 1880, and was buried on the 20th in the Cemetery at Machynlleth. His funeral was attended by some thousands from all parts of Wales and several English towns.

JONES, JOSEPH DAVID, of Ruthin, a good musician, and the author and compiler of numerous works relating to congregational singing, was born in the year 1827, at Bryngrugog, near Llanfair Caereinion. His father being only a poor weaver could not afford to give his children (of whom he had four) much instruction. Indeed, the subject of this notice had not more than a year's schooling, and his father appears to have greatly discouraged a taste for music shewn at an early age by his son Joseph. The youth, however, persevered, and before he was twenty published, under the title *Y Perganiedydd* (The Sweet Singer), a small collection of Psalm tunes, which met with a favourable reception, and the proceeds of the sale of which enabled him to enter the Training College in London, to prepare himself for the office of schoolmaster. When his funds were exhausted he walked all the way back to Towyn, where he had previously conducted a British School for some years. The second time he only remained about a year at Towyn, leaving that place in October, 1851, to occupy a similar position at Ruthin, which he held for 14 years. He was a conscientious and successful teacher, and, in addition to his daily duties as such, he laboured incessantly to promote the taste for and the cultivation of congregational singing. In 1866 he resigned the mastership of the British School, and opened a private school for boarders. This he conducted very successfully until his death on the 17th September, 1870. The following are Mr. Jones's principal works;—*Y Perganiedydd,* already noticed above; *Y Cerub* (The Cherub); *Cydymaith y Cerddor* (The Singer's Companion); *Y Delyn Gymreig* (The Welsh Harp); *Alawon y Bryniau* (Melodies of the Hills); *Cuniadau Bethlehem* (Songs of Bethlehem); *Carolau, Emynau, ac Antheman* (Carols, Hymns, and Anthems); and a Cantata entitled *Llys Arthur* (Arthur's Court); also *Casgliad o Gorganiadau* (Collection of Chorales); and *Llyfr Tonau ac Emynau* (Tune Book and Hymn Book). Besides these he published translations of *Æsop's Fables,* and of the *libretto* to the *Creation*; also a selection of pieces suitable for recitation under the title of *Yr Adroddiadur* (The Reciter). He was also a constant contributor to several Welsh magazines and newspapers, chiefly upon musical subjects. Mr. Jones married in January, 1860, Miss Daniel, of Towyn, by whom he had six children.

JONES, Rev. MATTHEW, Prebendary of Donoughmore, was born at Llwyn Ririd, in the parish of Forden, in 1654. He was a younger brother of Bishop Jones, whom he accompanied to Ireland, and there obtained and long held valuable ecclesiastical preferments. Amongst others he became Vicar Choral of Lismore Cathedral in 1681, Precentor of Cloyne Cathedral, November, 1683, and Prebendary of Donoughmore in 1687. He died 7th December, 1717.

JONES, MORRIS CHARLES, F.S.A., to whom Montgomeryshire history and archæology owe probably more than to any one else, was the eldest son of Morris Jones and Elizabeth his wife, and was born at Welshpool, the 9th day of May, 1819. He was educated at Bruce Castle School, Tottenham, under Messrs. Arthur and Rowland Hill (afterwards Sir Rowland Hill) and was in 1835 articled to Mr. Joseph Jones, solicitor, Welshpool, and admitted a solicitor in 1841. Soon after his admission he went to Liverpool, and joined the firm of Messrs R. and H. Christian, with which he continued until 1858, when he founded the firm of Jones, Paterson, and Co., still carried on by his eldest son. Mr. Jones was married in 1844 to Elizabeth, daughter of Mr. Robert Paterson, of Nunfield, Dumfriesshire, by whom he had issue eight children. He retired from the practice of his profession in 1880, and was placed on the Commission of the Peace for Montgomeryshire, making his home henceforth at Gungrog, his patrimony, near Welshpool. He had for many years taken a deep interest in the history and archæology of his native county. His first literary production, I believe, was a little *brochure* on *The Evans family*, privately printed. This was followed by an able and elaborate article in the *Archæologia Cambrensis* for 1866 on *Vale Crucis Abbey; its origin and Foundation Charters*, in which he proved that Valley Crucis was a daughter-foundation of the abbey of Strata Marcella, near Welshpool. In 1867 he succeeded in forming the Powysland Club, "for the " collecting and printing for the use of its members of the " historical, ecclesiastical, genealogical, topographical and literary " remains of Montgomeryshire." Its first volume of *Montgomeryshire Collections* was published the following year, and contained among other things a long and important article by Mr. Jones, the editor, on *The Feudal Barons of Powys*. With one or two exceptions all the subsequent twenty-five volumes of those *Collections* contain productions of his industrious pen. As Secretary of the Club and the editor of its transactions his enthusiasm, energy, tact, and courtesy, enlisted the co-operation of quite a host of others in the work he had so much at heart, the result being that the publications of the Club contain a mass of information on the history and archæology of the county, which its future historian will find to be invaluable. In connection with the Club, Mr. Jones succeeded in founding the Powysland Museum and Library in 1874, and a School of Science and Art in 1883, and in 1887, the Queen's Jubilee year, these were transferred by deed of gift to the Mayor and Corporation of Welshpool, and to ensure their adequate support the town adopted the Public Libraries Act. From the first foundation of the club down to his death, Mr. Jones continued to watch over its interests and to promote its success with unabated devotion. In 1876 a testimonial was raised by public subscription in acknowledgment of these services, the amount collected being devoted to the purchase of a fine life-size bronze group representing a scene in Welsh history, which was placed by Mr. Jones's desire in the Powysland Museum, and of a copy of the Milton shield. He was elected F.S A. of Scotland in 1864, and F.S.A., London, in 1870. Some two or three years before his death, Mr. Jones raised a small fund to enable him to lay bare the foundations of the old Abbey of Strata Marcella, near Pool Quay, and in vol. xxv., of the *Montgomeryshire Collections* will be found an interesting description of the excavations. He had warmly but unsuccessfully advocated the claims of Welshpool to be the site of the University College for North Wales. In 1884, after the College had been established at Bangor, he was nominated by the President of the College (Lord Powis) as one of its Governors. He in fact was an earnest and munificent supporter of every movement to benefit his native town—one of the last being the Church House in memory of the late Earl of Powis. Mr Jones had been failing in health for some time. He died on the 27th of January, 1893, in his 74th year, and was buried at St. Mary's Churchyard, Welshpool, the following Friday, lamented by a large circle of friends who loved him for his genial and amiable disposition and by Montgomeryshire archæologists as one whose loss it will take long to make up.

JONES, Rev. OWEN, of Gelli, Llanfair, was born at Towyn, Merionethshire, on the 16th of February, 1787. Having spent some time at a good country school at Penypark, near Towyn, he was afterwards sent by his parents to an English town to complete his education, and then apprenticed to a shopkeeper at Aberystwyth. During his apprenticeship he and another young man undertook the carrying on of a Sunday school in a neglected part of the town, and were very successful. He applied himself to the work with great energy, and carried it on every night but Saturday night. Being a good singer, and possessing much tact, pleasing manners, and great persuasive power, he soon attracted numbers, especially of the young, around him, and speedily shewed that rare excellence as a catechist for which he became distinguished in after life. He was then scarcely 18 years old, nor had he yet become a member of a Christian Church; but before long he joined the Calvinistic Methodists.

On the eve of his leaving Aberystwyth at the end of his apprenticeship, a great religious revival broke out in the Sabbath school, in which he had laboured so faithfully, resulting in the addition of hundreds of members to the Calvinistic and other Churches. From Aberystwyth, Mr. Jones went to Llanidloes, where he remained about two years, and where he threw himself heart and soul into work similar to that he had engaged 'in at Aberystwyth. His energy instilled new life into the Sunday schools which already existed in the town and neighbourhood, and he soon started several others—among them one at Rhayader, which soon numbered 240 members. From Llanidloes he removed to London, where for some time he assisted Dr. Owen Pughe in correcting for the press the first edition of the Welsh Bible published by the Bible Society. Having completed this work, he left the metropolis, and took up his residence at Shrewsbury in the autumn of 1807. Here again he established an English Sunday school to which he speedily gathered 120 scholars, and he frequently visited another school at a place called Perthi, near Pool Quay, about sixteen miles distant from Shrewsbury. He had not yet attained his 21st year, but the great success which attended his efforts induced some of his friends to urge him to visit all the schools of the county of Montgomery. This request he complied with, though it cost him very great labour and sacrifices. This naturally led him to decide upon entering the ministry, and in the year 1808 he was accepted by the Calvinistic Methodists as a preacher. The same year he married, and took up his residence at Gelli, his wife's home, near Llanfair Caereinion, where he dwelt the remainder of his days. He was ordained to the full work of the ministry in 1819. To the end of his life he continued to manifest the greatest interest in Sabbath schools, and probably no single individual with the exception of the Rev. Thomas Charles, their founder in North Wales, has done so much for the promotion of Sabbath school work in that portion of the Principality. As a preacher, Mr. Jones was earnest, impressive, and eloquent ; as a catechist, unrivalled. In 1820 he published a small *Catechism* under the title, *Arweinydd i Wybodaeth, neu, y Catecism Cyntaf i hen bobl a'r ail i bobl ieuainc* (the Guide to Knowledge, or, the first Catechism for old people, and the second for the young), which long continued in use. But in the midst of his labours his useful life was cut short. He died on the 4th of December, 1828, aged 41 years, and was buried at Llanfair on the 9th of the same month.

JONES, RICE, of Llanfair Caereinion, was a poet of the seventeenth century. He is said to have written a metrical paraphrase of the New Testament under the title of *Testament ein Harglwydd Iesu Grist wedi ei gyfansoddi yn Benhillion Cymreig trwy lafur Rice Jones o Lanfair yng Nghaer Einion* (1653).

JONES, RICHARD, was born at Black Hall, Kerry, about the year 1724, and became a Purser in the Royal Navy. By his will and codicils he bequeathed £3,000

Bank Annuities to Trustees, the dividends to be for ever applied in victualling, clothing, and educating the children of the poor of Kerry parish and apprenticing boys, the charity to be called "The Black Hall Institution." He also bequeathed the further sum of £700 Bank Annuities to the same trustees, the dividends to be for ever applied in supporting a Sunday School established by him and to be called "The Kerry Church Sunday School on the Black Hall Institution." £1,000 of the above having been redeemed by Government was advanced on Mortgage of the Turnpike Roads, and the greater part of it has been lost. Mr. Jones died at Greenwich on the 3rd of November, 1788, in the 65th year of his age. A tomb monument in marble with a bust *in relievo* of the deceased " to per-" petuate his memory and donations" has been placed in Kerry Church, towards which he bequeathed to his trustees the sum of £500.

JONES, Rev. ROBERT, B.A., for thirty-seven years Vicar of All Saints, Rotherhithe, was a distinguished Welsh scholar and author. He was born at Llanfyllin, January 6th, 1810, his parents holding a respectable middle class position in that town. He received his early education at the Oswestry Grammar School under Dr. Donne. In the year 1834 he entered Jesus College, Oxford, where he took his B.A. degree. On leaving the University, he was licensed to a curacy at Connah's Quay, Flintshire. Subsequently, he was a curate at Barmouth, where he published a small *Collection of Psalms and Hymns* in Welsh, including several of his own composition. In the year 1842 he was appointed to the district parish church of All Saints, Rotherhithe, where up to his death, he was indefatigable in the pursuit of his sacred calling. During the severe visitation of cholera in the years 1853-54, he worked hard, fearless of danger, administering medicine to the poor, and visiting the dying. He was himself struck down by the malady, but recovered. Mr. Jones during his incumbency did much for the improvement and adornment of his church—the stained glass windows, the organ, and the new pewing having been carried out by his exertions. Mr. Jones was at one time Welsh tutor to Prince Louis Lucien Buonaparte, whom he accompanied on a tour through Wales, the Prince being desirous of finding out the purest Welsh dialect spoken. It was he also who taught Welsh to Dr. Siegfried whose keen and unconcealed disappointment he well remembered on the occasion of his seeing for the first time the results of Zeuss's industry put into the tangible form of the ' *Grammatica Celtica*,' and the field he had destined for himself occupied by another. In his earlier days he had been a frequent contributor to the *Shrewsbury Chronicle* and *Eddowes's Journal* under the *nom de plume*, "Rob Roy." He was also an occasional contributor to several of the Welsh Magazines, and in later years wrote several valuable papers for the *Montgomeryshire Collections*. In 1864 he published a reprint of that rare work by Dr. John Davies, of

Mallwyd, *Flores Poetarum Brittannicorum* sef *Blodeuog waith y Prydyddion Brytannaidd*. In 1876 he brought out an excellent edition of the *Poetical Works, Life, &c., of Goronwy Owen*, enriched with valuable notes from his own pen. He also in 1877 edited another most rare and curious work, *Salesbury's Welsh-English Dictionary*, being a reprint of the original edition of 1547. In 1876 he accepted the post of Editor of *Y Cymmrodor*, being the transactions of the new Society of Cymmrodorion, which he had been the means of resuscitating. That periodical contains many abundant proofs of his scholarship, and wide and varied acquaintance with the literature and language of his native land. Among other contributions to its pages he began the printing of *The works of Iolo Goch with a sketch of his life*, but only twelve poems and part of the thirteenth, without any sketch, appeared. He had, indeed, an astonishing memory for poetry both Welsh and English, and he was moreover a great collector of books. His collection of Welsh printed books was one of the most complete in the kingdom, and comprised some unique copies not to be found elsewhere. His hospitable board was the meeting point of numbers of the Welsh *literati* who visited the metropolis, and he himself was ever foremost in promoting every movement set on foot for the social and moral well-being of his fellow countrymen, regardless of creed or sect. It is noteworthy that his last public appearance to speak was at an Anniversary of the Welsh Independents in Fetter Lane about three weeks before his death. He attended a Welsh Bible Society Meeting at Aldersgate-street a few nights afterwards, but was too ill to speak. His genial presence and cheering words have been missed and lamented at many gatherings of his countrymen. He died of bronchitis, after three weeks illness, on Friday, the 28th of March, 1879, in his seventieth year, and was buried at All Saints Churchyard.

JONES, Sir THOMAS, Knt., of Carreghofa Hall, Lord Chief Justice of the Common Pleas, was the son of Edward Jones, Esq., of Sandford, by his wife, Mary, daughter of Robert Powell, Esq., of Park, and was born in 1614. His education was begun at Shrewsbury Grammar School, and completed at Emmanuel College, Cambridge, where he took his B.A. degree in 1632-3. He had previously been entered at Lincoln's-Inn, and was called to the bar on May 17, 1634. He took up his residence at Carreghova Hall, Llanymynech, and married Jane, daughter of Daniel Barnard, Esq., of Chester. During the troubles of the Civil war he managed to keep tolerably clear of both sides, and according to one writer " his conduct spoke more of prudence " than loyalty, or perhaps of timeserving than either." He was returned as one of the members for Shrewsbury in the Parliament elected just previous to the arrival of Charles II. in 1660, and again the following year. Possessing good abilities he made his way at the bar. In 1669 he was made serjeant-at-law, and two years afterwards king's serjeant. While holding that position he was knighted, and on April 13, 1676, was made a judge of the King's Bench. He was engaged in most of the political trials that disgraced the latter part of Charles's reign and the commencement of that of James II. In 1680 the Court of King's Bench having dismissed the grand jury suddenly so as to prevent an information against the Duke of York for not going to church, the House of Commons directed the impeachment of Chief Justice Scroggs and Justice Jones, but the Parliament being soon after prorogued the proceedings were dropped. He was one of the judges who tried Lord Russell in 1683, and in June the same year he, in the absence of Chief Justice Saunders, pronounced judgment in the famous *Quo Warranto* case wherein proceedings were brought against the Corporation of London at the instance of the King with the object of putting an end to or curtailing the privileges of the citizens. The judgment of the Court was "that the liberties and franchises of the City of " London be seised into the King's hands." In three months afterwards he was rewarded for his servility by being promoted to the place of Chief Justice of the Common Pleas. He presided at several famous trials afterwards, and shewed great severity and harshness. But still he was too honest and plain-spoken for King James, and on the whole, as one of his biographers remarks, " he was a very tolerable judge for those times." He finally sacrificed his position for his integrity. The King wished to dispense with the Test Act whenever he thought fit to do so, but Jones and three other Judges declared "that the King had not " power to dispense with a statute which Parliament had enacted " for the preservation of the established religion of the country." They were immediately sent for, but they held firmly to their opinion. Being told that they must either give up their opinion or their places, Jones, " a man who had never before shrank from " any drudgery, however cruel or servile, now held in the royal " closet language which might have become the lips of the purest " magistrates in our history." He said, " For my place I care " little ; I am old and worn out in the service of the Crown ; but " I am mortified to find that your Majesty thinks me capable of " giving a judgment which none but an ignorant or a dishonest " man could give." To this the King responded, " I am deter- " mined to have twelve lawyers for judges who will be all of my " mind as to this matter." Jones replied, " Your Majesty may " find twelves *judges* of your mind, but hardly twelve *lawyers.*" He and the three other judges were accordingly dismissed from their places next morning, April 21st, 1686 Sir Thomas Jones now retired to his mansion, Carreghova Hall, where he spent the remaining years of his life. At the revolution he was called before the House of Commons to account for the judgment of the Court of King's Bench, pronounced six years before in the case of Jay *v.* Topham, the serjeant-at-arms, and with Chief Justice Pemberton was committed for the supposed breach of privilege on July 19th, 1689, both remaining in confinement till the proro- gation of Parliament. He died at Carreghova Hall, May 31st,

1692, aged 78, and was buried in St. Alkmond's Church, Shrewsbury, where his monument erected by his daughter still remains.

JONES, Rev. THOMAS, Vicar of Pennant from 1757 to 1782, Rector of Llangynog from 1762 to 1782, and Rector of Hirnant from 1782 to 1790, published in 1761 *Rheol o Addoliad ac Ymarfer Duwioldeb i'r Hwsmon*, (a translation of Archbishop Secker's Lectures on the "Rule of Worship, and Practice of Piety for the Husbandman"); *Traethiadau ar Gatecism Eglwys Loegr, gyda Phregeth ar Gonffirmasiwn*; and in 1779, *Pregeth ar Salm cxix, v. 165*. (A Sermon on Psalm 119, v. 165). The Parochial Register of Hirnant also records that he in 1784 translated into English *Drych y Prif Oesoedd* by the Rev. Theophilus Evans, but it does not appear that this was ever published.

JONES, Rev. THOMAS, M.A., a very eminent Tutor and Lecturer at Trinity College Cambridge. The following interesting Memoir of him was contributed to the *Encyclopædia Londinensis*, by his friend the learned Dr. Herbert Marsh, afterwards Bishop of Peterborough :—"The Rev. Thomas Jones was born at Berriew, in Montgomeryshire, on the 23rd of June, 1756. His education, till he entered on his twelfth year, was confined to the instruction of a common country school, first at Berriew, and afterwards in the neighbouring parish of Kerry. During the time that he frequented the latter school, the vicar of the parish, discovering in him those talents which he afterwards so eminently displayed, advised his mother (for he lost his father at an early age) to send him to the Grammar School at Shrewsbury. Here he continued nearly seven years, and was inferior to none of his school fellows, either in attention to study, or in regularity of conduct. On the 28th May, 1774, he was admitted at St. John's College, Cambridge and came to reside there in the October following. From that time the excellence of his genius became more particularly conspicuous. He had acquired, indeed, at school a competent share of classical learning; but his mind was less adapted to Greek and Latin composition than to the investigation of philosophical truths. At the public examinations of St. John's College he not only was always in the first class, but was without comparison the best mathematician of his year. His first summer vacation was devoted entirely to his favourite pursuit; and at that early period he became acquainted with mathematical works, which are seldom attempted before the third year of academical study. He remained at St. John's College till after the public examination in June, 1776; and on the 27th of that month he removed to Trinity College. To this step he was induced by the same unfortunate cause which has deprived St. John's College of many other very distinguished members, the limitation in the election to fellowships. By this limitation, which, when the college statutes were framed was intended to obviate a then existing evil, there can be only one fellow at a time from each diocese in Wales; and there being then a fellow from the diocese of St. Asaph, who was not expected very soon to make a vacancy, Mr. Jones, who was of the same diocese, had no prospect of obtaining the reward to which his talents and conduct entitled him. When he removed to Trinity College, he determined (according to academical phrase) to degrade a year; he became a member of the year below him, and thus deferred the taking of his bachelor of arts degree till January, 1779. His motive for so doing was not any design of more effectually securing to himself the first rank in academical honours (for there are few years in which he would not have obtained the same distinguished place), but solely to obviate the objection, which might otherwise have been made to him when candidate for a fellowship of Trinity College, that he had resided a little more than a year in that society, when he took his bachelor's degree. His superiority at that time was so decided, that no one ventured to contend with him. The honour of Senior Wrangler was conceded before the examination began; and the second place became the highest subject of competition. If anything were wanting to shew his superiority, it would be rendered sufficiently conspicuous by the circumstance, that he was tutor to the second Wrangler. [This was the writer himself.] And the writer of this memoir gladly embraces the opportunity of publicly acknowledging, that for the honour which he then obtained he was indebted to the instruction of his friend. In the same year in which Mr. Jones took his bachelor's degree he was appointed assistant tutor at Trinity College. On the first of October, 1781, he was elected Fellow; and in October, 1787, on the resignation of Mr. Cranke, he was appointed to the office of Head Tutor, which he held to the day of his death. In 1786 and 1787 he presided as Moderator in the philosophical schools, where his acuteness and impartiality were equally conspicuous. It was about this time that he introduced a grace, by which fellow-commoners, who used to obtain the degree of bachelor of arts with little or no examination, were subjected to the same academical exercises as other undergraduates. During many years he continued to take an active part in the senate-house examinations; but latterly he confined himself to the duties of college tutor. These, indeed, were sufficiently numerous to engage his whole attention; and he displayed in them an ability which was rarely equalled, with an integrity which never was surpassed. They only who have had the benefit of attending his lectures are able to estimate their value. Being perfect master of his subjects, he always placed them in the clearest point of view; and by his manner of treating them, he made them interesting even to those who had otherwise no relish for mathematical inquiries. His lectures on astronomy attracted more than usual attention, since that branch of philosophy afforded the most ample scope for inculcating (what, indeed, he never neglected in other branches) his favourite doctrine of final causes, for arguing from the contrivance to the contriver, from the structure of the universe to the being and attributes of God. And this doctrine he enforced, not merely by

explaining the harmony which results from the established laws
of nature, but by shewing the confusion which would have arisen
from the adoption of other laws. His lectures on the principles
of fluxions were delivered with unusual clearness; and there was
so much originality in them, that his pupils have often expressed
a wish that they might be printed. If these, as well as his
lectures on astronomy, had been published, the world would
certainly have derived from them material benefit. But such
was his modesty, that, though frequently urged, he never would
consent; and when he signed his will a short time before his
death, he made the most earnest request to the writer of this
memoir, that none of his manuscripts should be printed. But it
is a consolation to know, that his lectures on philosophy will not
be buried in oblivion; all his writings on those subjects have been
delivered to his successor in the tuition, and, though less amply
than by publication, will continue to benefit mankind. As the
admissions under him as tutor were numerous beyond example,
the labour and anxiety attendant on the discharge of his duties
gradually impaired a constitution which was naturally feeble.
During many years he suffered from an infirmity of the breast,
and it was his constant belief that this infirmity would be the
occasion of his death. But he seemed to have recovered from
this complaint, when he was attacked by another of still more
dangerous tendency. He was latterly subject to internal inflam-
mations, which at length produced one of the most singular and
distressing ulcerations in the annals of medicine. He went
immediately to London, to consult Dr. Baillie and Mr. Cline;
but the disease was soon found to be incurable. His friends,
indeed, at one time flattered themselves with the hope of his
recovery; for, when he had been in London about six weeks, he
was so far restored, after a confinement to his bed, attended with
excessive pain, that he was not only enabled to remove to a
lodging in the Edgeware-road for the benefit of the air, but to
walk several miles without apparent fatigue. The former
symptoms of his complaint gradually abated, and at length
totally ceased. But this cessation was only the prelude to
another form of the disease, which proved more immediately
fatal. A total and insurmountable obstruction ensued, and he
died on the 18th of July, 1807. It was his particular request to
be buried without pomp, and in a church-yard only so far distant
from town that his body might not be exposed to the depredation
of nightly robbers. He was conveyed, therefore, to the burial
ground of Dulwich College, followed by his relations in London,
and by some of his nearest and dearest friends. His academical
character has been already described. As a companion he was
highly convivial; he possessed a vein of humour peculiar to himself; and no one told a story with more effect. His manners
were mild and unassuming, and his gentleness was equalled
only by his firmness. As a friend, he had no other limit to his
kindness than his ability to serve. Indeed his whole life was a
life of benevolence, and he wasted his strength in exerting him-

self for others The benefits which he conferred were frequently
so great, and the persons who subsisted by his bounty were
so numerous, that he was often distressed in the midst of
affluence. And though he was Head Tutor of Trinity College
almost twenty years with more pupils than any of his predecessors, he never acquired a sufficient capital to enable him to
retire from office, and still continued his accustomed beneficence.
But he never boasted of the good which he did, not even to his
intimate friends; and it was only through incidental occurrences
that the writer of this memoir obtained the knowledge of it.
In theology and in politics Mr. Jones has occasionally taken an
active part. On these subjects, as the author of this memoir
sometimes differed from his deceased friend, he must speak with
delicacy and caution. The parties which Mr. Jones has openly
espoused are so well known, that the public can need at present
no further information; and many private opinions, both in
theology and politics, which he entrusted only to his most
intimate friend, it would be a breach of confidence to reveal. It
is sufficient to say, that in both of them his sentiments on
various speculative points underwent a material alteration.—Of
his practical theology, which remained always the same, the best
description which can be given is the description of his latter
end. He waited the approach of death with a dignified firmness,
a placid resignation, and an unaffected piety, which are rarely
equalled. Even after his eyes were grown dim and his speech
began to falter, he uttered with great fervency what he had
frequently repeated during the course of his illness, that prayer
in the Visitation of the Sick, " Sanctify, we beseech thee, this thy
" fatherly correction, that the sense of my weakness may add
" strength to my faith and seriousness to my repentance." On
these last words he dwelt with peculiar emphasis. About the
same time he said to his surrounding friends, as distinctly as the
weakness of his voice would permit him, " I am conscious, no
" doubt, of many failings; but I believe I have employed the
" abilities with which God has blessed me to the advancement of
" my fellow creatures. I resign myself, then, with confidence
" into the hands of my Maker."—He shortly afterwards expired,
without a groan or struggle. Thus lived and died one of the
most able and most amiable of men. His memory
will ever be revered, and the loss of him will be deeply
felt by all who knew him—by no one more than by the author of
this memoir, who is proud to style himself his most intimate
friend. The only things he ever published were a *Sermon on
Duelling*, and an *Address to the Volunteers of Montgomeryshire*.
The former was published as a warning to the young men of the
university, soon after a fatal duel had taken place in the neighbourhood. The latter, which he wrote with great animation (for
he was a zealous advocate of the volunteer system) was calculated
to rouse the volunteers to a vigorous defence of their country,
and was at the time extensively circulated. As above stated,
Mr Jones, who died a bachelor, was buried at Dulwich, where a

K

plain tombstone was afterwards placed over his grave to the
memory of one "eminently distinguished by his piety and
abilities." He was the owner of the farms of Trefeen, Coedy-
brain, and Ross in Kerry, and Henllys in Manafon. The former
he devised to his first cousin, Mrs. Davies, of Trefeen, who left it
to her son, Edward Davies, of Snowfields. The latter possessed
a crayon portrait of Mr. Jones; also an engraved portrait by
James Heath, from a fine painting by Gardiner, of Kendal. A
tradition, as well authenticated as such a tradition can be, is in
existence that Mr. Jones was an illegitimate son of Mr. Owen
Owen, of Tynycoed, father of Sir A. D. Owen (who did not go to
the University), and of David Owen, who was senior wrangler in
1777, and William Owen, who was 5th wrangler in 1782.
Tradition also says that Mr. Jones's mother was married to a Mr.
Jones, of Treffin, in Kerry, and that Mr. Thomas Jones was
brought up as his son. It has been said that he died of a broken
heart on learning the fact as to his birth, but there are good
grounds for believing that this was not the case, and that the
illness of which he died was neither caused nor accelerated by
mental trouble of any kind. What Bishop Marsh says about his
having "degraded" refers to a story that he did so in order to
escape competition with the distinguished Prof. Farish, who was
senior wrangler in the year above Mr. Jones.

JONES, Rev. THOMAS, the first missionary to the Khassee
Hills, North Eastern Bengal, was the second son of Edward and
Mary Jones, and was born near Tanyffridd, between Llanfair and
Meifod, on the 24th of January, 1810, and baptized at Dolanog
Chapel on the 25th of the next month. His father, Edward
Jones, was a wheelwright and carpenter by trade, and had in all
ten children. A few years after his marriage he removed to
Liverpool, but afterwards returned to Wales in consequence of
failing health. Thomas Jones at first learned his father's trade,
and worked for him some time, but subsequently he became a
miller, and was employed as such at Llivior Mill, Berriew. Here
he was brought under deep religious impressions, and having
decided on devoting himself to Missionary work, he entered
the Calvinistic Methodist College at Bala to be trained for it.
He was ordained at Bala on the 1st January, 1840. He offered
himself to the London Missionary Society for Missionary work in
India, but that Society, acting upon the report of Dr. Conquest,
its medical adviser, at first declined the offer altogether, but subsequently accepted Mr. Jones on condition that he would consent
to labour in South Africa. This he declined; and the result
was that the Calvinistic Methodists at once withdrew their
support from the London Missionary Society, established a
Missionary Society of their own, and sent Mr. Jones as their
first Missionary to the Khassee Hills. He and his wife, whom
he had lately married, sailed from Liverpool on the 25th of
November, 1840, arriving at Calcutta (where he stayed a few
weeks) on the 23rd April, 1841, and at Cherranpoonjee on the

Hills on the 22nd of June following. His first task was to learn the native language, and it turned out to be one of no small difficulty. Mr. Jones, however, with great patience and perseverance, succeeded in mastering it, and after a while translated the Gospel of St. Matthew and some other works into it. He laboured zealously and earnestly in the mission field for some years, but in consequence of some misunderstanding between himself and the Committee in Liverpool his connection with the Society was terminated, and he retired from the work. Probably he erred in judgment, but by those who knew him best his piety and integrity were not doubted. His health failed him. On the 4th of September, 1849, he arrived in Calcutta in a very bad state of health, and was received into the house of the Rev. Mr. Ewart, who treated him with great kindness. He died on the 16th of the same month, in his 40th year, and was buried the following day in the Scotch burial ground at Calcutta.

JONES, THOMAS GRIFFITHS (*Cuffin*), was a son of David Jones, of Llansantffraid, and Elizabeth his wife, and was born January 12th, 1834. From a child he suffered much from severe headaches, owing to which, and his delicate health generally, he could not attend school regularly. In consequence of this and of the death of his father when he was only fourteen years old, his education was imperfect, but by close application and with his good natural abilities, he in after life remedied this defect to a great extent. At a comparatively early age he was called upon to undertake his father's business as a shopkeeper at Llansantffraid, where he spent the whole of his life. He married, February 7th, 1871, Mary Anna, daughter of Mr. Samuel Pryce, of Gwernypant, by whom he had six children. His tastes were decidedly archæological, and he took great delight in collecting books, manuscripts and every scrap he could lay hold on of folklore or local tradition relating to Wales and Welsh literature or antiquities, and especially such as had any relation to his own native parish. He was a shrewd observer of local idioms, habits, and customs, and on these and kindred topics was a frequent contributor, chiefly under the name of *Cuffin*, to the *Brython*, *Golud yr Oes*, *Anibynwr*, *Dysgedydd*, *Dysgedydd y Plant*, and other Welsh magazines, as well as to *Mo t. Coll.* and *Byegones*. Some of his contributions to the latter were signed *Gypt* and *Borderer*. In the summer of 1861, he succeeded in founding the Powys Cymreigyddion Society, and became its first president. The objects of that Society were in many respects similar to those of the Powysland Club subsequently formed. Its term of existence, however, was short, and it died from want of funds. *Cuffin* joined in the operations of the Powysland Club soon after its formation, and contributed to the *Mont. Coll.* a valuable and interesting *History of Llansantffraid*. He subsequently contributed other papers, among them a well-written paper, on which he was engaged, and which he had not quite completed, when he died, on *Traces of Roman Roads*. etc. He was a great reader and very industrious, employing every spare moment in either reading or writing. He used to take long rambles in the country, collecting facts, traditions, and folk-lore, or picking up plants and observing the habits of birds and animals as he went along, for nothing escaped his keen eye. Of late he used to take with him his two boys, and on returning home to give a small prize to the one who wrote the best account of what they had seen. He thus instilled into them largely his own tastes and habits of observation. He was often confined to his room by illness, but was always cheerful, and his active brain and pen were never idle. One of his projects was to write a history of the Quakers, their meeting-houses and burial-places in Montgomeryshire, towards which, we believe, he had collected a mass of materials. In politics he was an ardent Liberal, and in him the Independent church at Llansantffraid lost one of its most prominent, useful, and energetic members. On Tuesday evening, the 9th of September, he was seized with an attack of apoplexy, which, in a few hours, terminated fatally. He died early in the morning of September 10th, 1884, aged fifty years, and leaving a widow and six children, as well as a large circle of friends to deplore his loss.

JONES, WILLIAM, was born in Llangadfan parish about the year 1729, and it appears he never resided a fortnight out of his native place. The education he obtained at school was of the scantiest kind; a little broken English, and the ability to write his name. He got his livelihood in early life by farming a few acres of land at Dol-howel. The leisure time which this occupation afforded him he devoted to the improvement of his mind. He thus acquired a sufficient mastery of English to write in that language with ease and elegance (although, being a red-hot Welshman, he as cordially hated the English as our ancestors did the Saxons), but in *conversation* he frequently broke down. In music and poetry he also became a proficient, and in Welsh syntax and prosody he ranked among the most profound critics. His thirst after knowledge prompted him to attempt to learn Latin, and he succeeded so far as to be able to translate some of the Odes of Horace and Ovid's Metamorphoses into excellent Welsh verse. He was much afflicted in his youth with an inveterate scrofula, and this turned his attention to the study of the art of healing. His first attempt upon himself succeeded in a complete cure. His fame soon spread among the common people, numbers of whom flocked to him from considerable distances, and he came to be considered an excellent doctor. Thenceforth he earned his living chiefly by practising as such. Those who thought themselves of the better sort despised his mean appearance, his broken English, and his want of pretension. When strangers, by his uncouth appearance, seemed to doubt his ability to cure scrofulous diseases, he used to shew them what he called his *certificate*—the scars left upon himself. Early in life he read some of Voltaire's writings, whose principles he imbibed,

Voltaire (whom in features he is said to have curiously resembled)
became his favourite tutor in politics and religion. This brought
him into disrepute with his neighbours. Churchmen could not
think of employing a Republican, nor could Dissenters expect
the blessing of heaven upon the prescriptions of an infidel. This
and an Act of Parliament prohibiting certain practitioners from
vending medicines without taking out annual licences (which he
scorned to do) interfered much with his practice as a country
doctor, and although he was now over 63 years old, he entertained serious thoughts of emigrating to America, and of founding a Welsh colony there, which he hoped might in time become a
State with laws administered in the Welsh language. The failure
of his emigration scheme, added to other disappointments, was
more than his spirits could bear; he sank and died at Dolhowel,
near Llangadfan, on the 20th of August, 1795. His *Statistical
Account of the Parishes of Llanerfyl, Llangadfan, and Garthbeibio*, published with valuable notes by the Rev. Walter Davies
in the *Cambrian Register* for 1796, proves him to have been, notwithstanding his eccentricity, a man of considerable intelligence
and natural abilities, as well as of some learning. He also made
a good collection of pedigrees, and several poems in Welsh and
a few in English written by him are still preserved. His portrait
and an interesting sketch of his life, by the Rev. Walter Davies,
were published in the second volume of the *Cambrian Register*.

JONES, WILLIAM (*Gwrgant*) was born at Brwynog in the
parish of Llanfihangel about January 1803, and was the son of
Robert Jones, a mason, and Margaret his wife. His father was
addicted to drink and neglected his family, but his mother was a
woman of high character and good abilities, to whom Gwrgant
was indebted for his early education. In after life he and his
brother John Evans Jones, a successful builder at Preston, placed
a handsome stained glass window in Llanfihangel Church to the
memory of their mother. Having attended the village school at
Llanfihangel for some time, and afterwards that at Meifod he
found a situation in the office of Mr. Evans, solicitor,
Llanfair, and afterwards in that of Mr. Thomas at Llanfyllin. Here he was articled, and in due course admitted a
solicitor. From Llanfyllin he removed to St. Asaph, where he
practised for some years, and thence to London, where for many
years he carried on extensive business. Mr. Jones at an early
age mastered the intricacies of the Welsh metres, and often
wrote to the Welsh magazines of the day under the *nom de plume*
of *Gwilym Brwynog*. He was a zealous and patriotic Welshman, and an excellent critic of Welsh poetry, but wrote comparatively little himself. He was one of the adjudicators at the
Rhuddlan Eisteddfod. He published a work entitled *Gwreiddian
yr Iaith Gymraeg* (the Roots of the Welsh language). Gwrgant
married a lady who owned some property at Greenwich, where
he resided at the time of his death. He died in 1886.

LANGFORD, Rev. WILLIAM, M.A., Vicar of Welshpool, was born April 12th, 1602, and having received some schooling at Gresford and Ruthin, was admitted a Commoner at Brazenose College, whence he removed to Hart Hall, Oxford, where he took his degrees of B.A. and M.A. in due course. After leaving the University he became first usher, and in 1626 head master of Ruthin School. This appointment he held for about two years. Subsequently he became rector of Heneglwys in 1630, vicar of Welshpool in 1632, rector of Llanerfyl 1637, Canon of St. Asaph 1639, and sinecure rector of Llanfor 1644. He was however deprived by the Committee of Sequestrators of all these preferments save Llanfor, which he appears to have retained through the influence of Mr. Edward Meyrick. Upon the restoration of Charles II. he was restored to Welshpool in 1660, and obtained the rectory of Castle Caereinion in 1664. In his Will dated 1668 (shortly before his death) he gives a short autobiography, wherein he complains of the conduct not only of Vavasor Powell and the sequestrators, but also of Lord Powis and his lady, and their tenants, whose refusal to pay the legal tithes had reduced his income to less than £40 a year. Yet he acknowledges that "God's providence hath marvellously and mercifully delivered "me out of ye gripings of unreasonable men." The *Autobiography* of Richard Davies, the Quaker, contains many allusions to Mr. Langford, " the priest of Welshpool." Having had a dispute with him as to " Easter reckonings," which was amicably settled, R. Davies adds, " He was very friendly afterwards, and "never sent to me more for Easter reckonings. And as for the "Tithe, in time of harvest, he charged his servants to take from "me no more than their due, nor so much. I was informed he "should say, he knew not why he should take anything from me, "seeing I had nothing from him. He lived here among us many "years, a good neighbour; and though in the time of great "persecution, yet he had no hand in persecuting any of us." He died on the 17th, and was buried on the 20th January, 1668, in his 66th year.

LEWIS AB MAREDYDD AB IEUAN VYCHAN, of Llanwrin, was a generous, wealthy, and influential person, a warrior, and an esquire of the body guard to Henry VI., to whom Lewys Glyn Cothi has addressed a spirited Ode. He was a nephew of Sir Richard Gethin, a brave and warlike knight, who fell at one of the sieges of Roan, in Normandy.

LEWIS AB JOHN AB JENKIN, Vicar of Darowen, was one of the bards who are recorded as having attended the great Eisteddfod at Caerwys in 1567.

LEWIS LANG, or as he was sometimes called " Lewis Gig Eidion," was a humorous poet who flourished between 1580 and 1620. Some of his compositions are said to remain in manuscript. There is a Powysian adage commemorative of his wide sprea l renown for buffoonery—" Bydd cymaint o sôn am danåt ag am Lewis Gig Eidion." (You will be as much talked about as Lewis Gig Eidion).

LEWIS, LODOWICK, of Dolgwenith, Llanidloes, was one of the Commissioners appointed in 1650 for Montgomeryshire, for levying money for the maintenance of the forces raised for the service of the Commonwealth. He married Mary daughter of John Pryce, Esq., of Park, and sister of Matthew Pryce, Esq., M.P. for the Boroughs, by whom he had three daughters.

LEWIS, Rev. MATTHEW, was born at Llanidloes about the year 1817. Originally a weaver by trade, he at an early age attracted attention by his abilities and gifts as a speaker. Having joined the Independents, he was encouraged to become a preacher with that denomination. His kindly nature and refined intelligence won the esteem of all with whom he came in contact. After a few years residence in Anglesey in the double capacity of a schoolmaster and pastor of a small church, he removed to Bangor to undertake the pastoral care of a church at that place, and soon gained a high reputation for eloquence and a peculiarly charming manner. In a few years he accepted a call to become the pastor of the Independent Church at Holywell, where his chapel was constantly crowded and his fame rapidly increased. His wife, a daughter of the Rev. David Griffiths, formerly a Missionary to Madagascar, died some time after his removal to Holywell. Her death affected him greatly, his spirits became depressed, and unfortunately he sought to drown his sorrow in the use of intoxicating liquors. His conscience, however, was still too tender to allow him to hold his ministerial office at the same time that he was guilty of intemperance. Suddenly and without warning he gave up his charge at Holywell, and went over to Liverpool, where for some years he battled with the enemy—sometimes conquering, but oftener conquered. For a time he was sub-editor of the *Amserau,* a Welsh newspaper then published at Liverpool, to the columns of which he contributed two original tales of great merit, entitled *Rhydderch Pryddrech* and *Y ddwy Lili* (The Two Lilies). He also wrote several able and interesting articles for the Welsh quarterly, Y *Traethodydd,* one being an Essay on the *Wedding Ring,* another entitled *Gwyr Ieuainc Llanllenorion,* a descriptive account of the literary efforts and aspirations of Llanidloes youth about 50 years ago. He was for some time Minister of the Welsh Congregational Church at Newtown. At last he became a slave to drink, and enlisted as a soldier in a Regiment of Foot, which he accompanied to China. Here his talents soon raised him to the rank of a sergeant, but he was struck down by disease, and died in that distant country in 1860, aged 43 years--a sad example of brilliant talents, a refined intellect and a promising career in a sacred calling, all shipwrecked through intemperance.

LEWIS POWYS, a poet whose name appears among those who attended the great Caerwys Eisteddfod in 1567, but of whom little else is known.

LLAWDDEN, or IEUAN LLAWDDEN was a very eminent poet of the 15th century. He was born at a house called Glyn Llychwr, near Pontardulais, in the parish of Llandilo Talybont, Gower, South Wales, about the year 1430, and is said to have been of illegitimate birth. Some expressions in his poems have led to the supposition that he occasionally resided in Radnorshire, but the greatest part of his life was spent at Machynlleth as curate or parish priest. He was present at and appears to have been one of the chief promoters of the great Eisteddfod held at Carmarthen in 1451 under the patronage of Sir Gruffydd ab Nicholas, to whom he was related. When Sir Gruffydd asked what was the proper colour for bards to wear, none but Dafydd ap Edmund and Llawdden appear to have been able to answer in poetic verse as all questions at an Eisteddfod should be answered. Llawdden's answer to the effect that blue was the proper colour, was an extremely clever bit of versification, and was as follows :—

> "Gwn glâs oll yn lâs, a'r lliw'n lân—ysgawn,
> Glas esgid, a chapan,
> Gloyw ei sas, a glas hosan,
> Glas i gyd, glwys yw ei gan.

Llawdden obtained the highest bardic honours of his time. In his old age he retired to the place of his nativity, and wrote the following stanzas, in which he compares himself to the *Gleisiad* (Sewin)—the vulgar belief as to which, in that neighbourhood, still is that it returns from the sea into the same river from which it first went forth :—

> "Y gleisiad, difrad yw ef—i'w ddichwain,
> Fe ddychwel i'w addef,
> 'Nol blino treiglo pob tref,
> Teg edrych tuag adref.
>
> Adref y daw ef a deufin—ei gerdd
> At ei gar a'i orsin ;
> Adref i'w dref gynefin,
> Addef a hawl fawl o'i fin.
>
> Miniaw bydd, mae'n oi ben—y cyfawd
> Lle cafodd ei awen,
> Lle addug a gar *Llawdden*
> Yw Gwyr ym Morganwg wen."

Llawdden died at Glyn Llychwr, and was buried at Llandilo Talybont. Many of his poems are preserved in MS., and some have been printed.

LLONIO LAWHIR, the founder of Llandinam Church, was the son of Alan an Armorican, who was son of Emyr Llydaw. He flourished during the early part of the sixth century, was a member of the college of Illtyd, and afterwards dean of the college of Padarn at Llanbadarn-fawr. He was buried at Bardsey.

LLOYD, CHARLES, of Garth, was Member of Parliament for the Montgomery boroughs from 3rd September, 1654, to April, 1660. He had previously in 1650 served as one of the Commissioners appointed for levying money for the maintenance of the forces raised for the service of the Commonwealth.

LLOYD, Sir CHARLES, Knt., son and heir of Brochwel Lloyd, of Leighton, was a distinguished and loyal soldier of Charles I. In the early part of that king's reign he held command as "Colon'll of a Reg'mnt of Ffoott," and for his services received an augmentation of arms. On the 6th April, 1639, the king by letters patent granted to him the important command of General in Chief of Engineers, and Quartermaster General of all fortifications in England, Scotland, and Ireland, "with ye sallary "and entertainment of 13s. 4d. per diem." In these capacities he distinguished himself by his activity, faithfulness, and personal courage during the whole period of the civil war. He was Governor of Devizes, where he had a garrison of from 300 to 400 Welshmen, when that town was besieged and forced to capitulate to Cromwell and Fairfax, on 23rd September, 1645. After the death of the king he followed the banner and fortunes of his exiled son. Upon the Restoration, although he had cheerfully sacrificed all for his master's sake, he, like many others, experienced nothing but neglect and ingratitude from Charles II., who was too much occupied in gratifying his own selfish and sensual desires to bestow a thought upon those brave and noble men who had endured so much for his cause. In September, 1660, a few months before his death, Sir Charles Lloyd petitioned in vain for the continuance of his salary, and although he had sustained great losses, and spent not only his own fortune, "but all that ever could be raysed by creditt of friends" for the king's interest, he was suffered to die after a lingering illness in want it would seem almost of the ordinary requirements of life. He died in March, 1660-1, and was buried on the 14th of that month at St. Margaret's Church, Westminster.

LLOYD, CHARLES, the Quaker, was the eldest son of Charles and Elizabeth Lloyd, of Dolobran, in the parish of Meifod, where he was born on the 9th of December, 1637. His father was a County Magistrate, descended from an ancient Welsh family, which held its patrimonial estates for more than a thousand years. Charles Lloyd, the subject of this notice, was educated at Jesus College, Oxford, where he graduated in medicine. Upon the death of his father in August, 1657, he succeeded to the family estates, and was beloved and respected as his father was before him. On the 1st January, 1661, he married Elizabeth, daughter of Sampson Lort, Esq. (High Sheriff of Pembrokeshire in 1649), by whom he had six children, four of whom died in their infancy. His wife died on the 7th April, 1665, and was buried on the 10th of the same month in the

Friends Burial Ground at Cloddian Cochion, near Welshpool. While a student at Oxford he became favourably impressed with the doctrines promulgated by George Fox. In September, 1662, he attended a public meeting of Friends at the house of Cadwallader Edwards, near Dolobran. Richard Moore, a minister of the persuasion, was also present. The next morning, both Edwards and Moore visited Mr. Lloyd, who "tenderly " received them." About the middle of October, seven of those who attended the meeting were arrested, and required to sub- scribe to the oath of allegiance and supremacy. This they refused to do, although a more loyal subject than Charles Lloyd did not exist in the Kingdom. The prisoners were committed to Welshpool jail. Here Edward Evans, a fellow sufferer, died of distemper. Notwithstanding at this time Mr. Lloyd was a County Magistrate, and in nomination for the Shrievalty, the penal and oppressive laws against Sectarians were enforced against him with the utmost rigour. He was detained a prisoner in Welshpool for a period of ten years; his possessions placed under praemunire, his cattle sold, and the Dolobran mansion partially destroyed. For a long period he was confined in a "little smoky room, and did lie upon a little straw himself "for a considerable time." His wife, who had been tenderly nurtured, "was made willing to lie upon straw with her dear " and tender husband," and shared with him the many dis- comforts unfamiliar to prisoners of a later period. It was probably after his release from prison that Charles Lloyd built the Friends' Meeting house at Dolobran, which is still standing. There is some reason for believing that the famous William Penn (who was an intimate friend of Thomas Lloyd, the brother of Charles Lloyd) worshipped, and not improbably preached in this old chapel. Portions of its oak panelling have been carried across the Atlantic by descendants of the family, and are pre- served by them as precious relics. He afterwards suffered a good deal of persecution, and accompanied Richard Davies on several journeys to visit Friends in various parts of the kingdom. Richard Davies, among many other references to Charles and Thomas Lloyd, gives an interesting account of a discussion between them and Bishop Lloyd, of St. Asaph, which lasted three days; also of a visit by Charles Lloyd, Thomas Wynn, himself, and several others to the Palace at Whitehall, in the early part of 1682, and their interview with Lord Hyde and Sir Leoline Jenkins, Secretary of State, in behalf of many suffering Friends imprisoned at Bristol. At this interview Charles Lloyd, in reply to Sir Leoline, said: "If thou did'st ask my friend " the question aright, he had answered thee right, for there is " English, Welsh, Latin, Greek, and Hebrew for Quaker." So the Secretary said, " Sir, I understand Welsh pretty well, and " English, and Latin, and Greek, but if you go to your Hebrew " I know not what to say to you." Again, Sir Leoline said, " I " am sorry that one of the stock of ancient Britons, who first " received the Christian faith in England, should be against

" those who have received the true Christian faith in this day."
Some time after, Charles Lloyd conveyed the remnant of his
estates to his eldest son, and himself removed to Birmingham,
where he became an Iron-master, and the founder of Lloyd's
Bank, and a very wealthy family. He married, secondly, in
1686, Ann Lawrence, of Lea, in the county of Hereford, but it is
not recorded that he had any issue by her. He died 27th
October, 1698, at the house of his brother-in-law, John
Pemberton, Esq., of Bennett's Hill, Birmingham. Many of his
numerous descendants attained high positions in various departments of the state. After his death the Dolobran estate passed
through several hands, but it is satisfactory to state that of late
years the principal portions have been repurchased by, and are
once more in the possession of members of the Lloyd family.
The following is a description by a contemporary of Charles
Lloyd :—

" He was a comely man in person, of an amiable countenance, quick of
understanding, of a sound mind, and would not be moved about on any
account to act contrary to his conscience, very merciful and tender, apt to
forgive and forget injuries (even to such as were his enemies), and did
good for evil, hated nothing but Satan sin and self. His usual familiar
expression was 'Lord! lead me in a plain path!' He was no man-pleaser
or temporiser, but delighted to deal plainly with all people of all degrees
and conditions; which made some hypocrites and such as love flattery to
think sometimes hardly of him,—but the faithful, sincere, and upright-
hearted loved him unfeignedly, and his memory will be had in esteem,
when the memory of the wicked will rot." He is termed in the
Philadelphia Friend, " a noble and valiant champion of the truth, and an
eminent instrument in the hands of the Lord for strengthening and confirming many in the holy faith,"—

a character well justified by his exertions, sacrifices, and sufferings on account of his religious principles.

LLOYD, CHARLES, the intimate friend of Charles Lamb, the
essayist and so often mentioned in his early letters, and also the
friend of S. T. Coleridge, Southey, and Wilson, was the eldest
son of Charles Lloyd, a wealthy Birmingham Banker, and the
great-great grandson of Charles Lloyd, the Quaker. He was
born February 12th, 1775. In due course he entered the
University of Cambridge, where he was attracted to Coleridge
by the fascination of his discourse, and was introduced by him to
Lamb. It had been intended that he should assist his father in
his banking business, but his attachment to Coleridge induced
him to relinquish his connection with the bank, and to enjoy the
enviable privilege of Coleridge's conversation he took a house at
Kingsdown, near Bristol, and induced Coleridge to come and live
with him there. This was in 1796, but Coleridge did not
remain with him long. The same year appeared the *Poems of
Charles Lloyd* (8vo.), followed soon afterwards by a *Poem* in
quarto. The following year another volume of the joint poetical
productions of Coleridge, Lamb, and Lloyd was published, to
which Coleridge, in a letter to Cottle, the publisher, thus refers :

" The volume is a most beautiful one. You have determined
" that the three bards shall walk up Parnassus in their best bib
" and tucker." In the year 1798 the blank verse of Lloyd and
Lamb, which had been contained in the volume just referred to
was, with some addition by Lloyd, published in a thin duodecimo,
under the title of *Blank Verse by Charles Lloyd and Charles
Lamb*. Both had a little while previously spent a fortnight
together as Southey's guests in Hampshire. Through his literary
association with Southey, Lamb, and Coleridge, Lloyd found
himself caricatured by Gilray in the very first number of the
Anti-Jacobin Magazine and Review, in which Coleridge and
Southey were introduced with asses' heads, and Lloyd and Lamb
as toad and frog. Talfourd, in his description of Lamb's famous
supper at his chambers in the Temple, refers to Lloyd as dis-
coursing on abstruse topics with Leigh Hunt, and " you will
" scarcely know which most to admire, the severe logic of the
" melancholy reasoner or its graceful evasion by the tricksome
" fantasy of the joyous poet." On the 24th April, 1799, Mr.
Lloyd married Sophia, daughter of Samuel Pemberton, Esq., of
Birmingham, and shortly afterwards removed to Brathay, Westmoreland. By this lady he had nine children. Among his
nearest neighbours and most intimate friends at Brathay were
Southey, Wordsworth, Coleridge, Wilson, Whittaker, and other
famous personages. De Quincey thus notices Mr. Lloyd:—" He
" was a man never to be forgotten. * * He had in conversation
" the most extraordinary power for analysis of a certain kind
" applied to philosophy of manners * * and his translation
" of ' Alfieri,' together with his own poems, show him to have
" been an accomplished scholar." Even before his marriage,
however, symptoms had appeared of that malady of the mind
which gradually took a deep hold upon him. Delusions of the
most melancholy kind thickened over his latter days, yet left his
admirable intellect free for the finest processes of severe reason-
ing. At a time when like Cowper, he believed himself the
especial subject of divine wrath, he could bear his part in the
most subtle disquisition on questions of religion, morals and
poetry, with the nicest accuracy of perception, and the most
exemplary candour; and, after an argument of hours, revert with
a faint smile to his own despair. Mr. Lloyd died January 16th,
1828, in his 53rd year. Besides his *Poems*, Mr. Lloyd published
in 1798 *Edmund Oliver*, a novel in 2 vols.; *A Letter to the Anti-
Jacobin Reviewers* in 1799; *Duke of Ormond*, a tragedy; *Beritola*,
a tale; *Poetical Essays on the character of Pope*; the *Tragedies
of Vittorio Alfieri*, translated from the Italian, 13 vols.; *Nugæ
Canoræ*, poems, 1819, and *Desultory Thoughts in London*; *Titus
and Gisippus*, with other poems, 1821. Talfourd thus sums up
his merits as a poet:—

" He wrote, indeed, pleasing verses, and with great facility,—a facility
fatal to excellence; but his mind was chiefly remarkable for the fine
power of analysis which distinguishes his *London*, and other of his later
compositions. In this power of discriminating and distinguishing—

carried to a pitch almost of painfulness—Lloyd has scarcely been equalled; and his poems though rugged in point of versification, will be found by those who will read them with the calm attention they require, replete with critical and moral suggestions of the highest value."

LLOYD, The Very Rev. DAVID, Dean of St. Asaph, was born at Berthlwyd, near Llanidloes, about 1598. When he was but 14 years of age, that is, in Michaelmas term 1612 he became Clerk or Chorister of All Souls College, Oxford, where he was elected Probationary Fellow in 1615, perpetual Fellow the next year, and in 1628 he "proceeded" in the Civil Law. Afterwards he became Chaplain and Comptroller of the household to the Earl of Derby. On the 2nd December, 1641, he was instituted to the Rectory of Trefdraeth, Anglesey, which he resigned on being instituted to Llangynhafal, Denbighshire, in July, 1642. On the 21st of December following he obtained the Vicarage of Llanfair Dyffryn Clwyd, and the Wardenship of Ruthin. He was an ardent and active Royalist, on account of which he was ejected out of all his preferments by the Long Parliament, and endured a long imprisonment. Upon the restoration, he recovered all his preferments, and was promoted to the Deanery of St. Asaph, being installed September 24th, 1660. Soon afterwards he was also presented to one of the comportions of Llansannan. About the same time he had a Prebendship of Chester bestowed upon him. He died September 7th, 1663, at Ruthin, where he was buried without any inscription or monument. Having by his generosity and loyalty run himself deeply into debt, some wag, or as some say he himself wrote the following "Epitaph" on him:

> "This is the Epitaph
> Of the Dean of St. Asaph,
> Who by keeping a table,
> Better than he was able,
> Ran into debt,
> Which is not paid yet."

He was esteemed "an ingenious man, of great spirit, and well beloved of the gentry," and was a good poet. His best known work was *The Legend of Capt. Jones* in two parts, 8 vo., first published in London in 1656, and frequently afterwards reprinted. This work was a good burlesque written in imitation of a Welsh poem called "Awdl Richard Sion Greulon." He was also the author of many songs, sonnets, and elegies, some of which are printed in several books.

LLOYD, Sir EDWARD, Knt., of Berthlwyd, Llanidloes, was the son and heir of Jenkin Lloyd, (Sheriff 1588 and 1606), by Dorothy his wife (daughter of Edmund Walter, Esq., Chief Justice of South Wales). He was in 1606 deputy Sheriff to his father, whom he succeeded in his estates in 1627-8. He was admitted of the Inner Temple in 1619, and in 1629 served the office of Sheriff. During his year of office he had the Assizes held at Llanidloes. The following year 1630 he received the honour of knighthood. He was an ardent Royalist, and upon the Restoration in 1660 he was one of the eight Montgomeryshire gentlemen " deemed fit and qualified to be made Knights of the Royal Oak"—an Order intended (but never established) to reward those who had suffered in the royal cause. His estate was valued at £1,200. He died and was buried at Llanidloes in 1666.

LLOYD, HUMPHREY, of Leighton, was the *first* Sheriff of Montgomeryshire. He served that office for the year ending Michaelmas 1541. He was a grandson of Sir Griffith Vaughan, Guilsfield, Knight Banneret (who was knighted as is alleged on the field at Agincourt, and who in 1447 was decapitated by Henry Gray, lord of Powys), and a descendant of Brochwel Ysgythrog. Prior to the dissolution of the Abbey of Strata Marcella, he held (in 1523) the appointment of steward or judge of the Abbey Court, and subsequently that of receiver of the abbey lands. He was also Ringild, or crown receiver of rents of assize, of the Crown demesnes of Tregynon, Llanllwchaiarn, Kerry, Egville, and Teirtref, and in 1553 was high constable or steward of the barony of Caus. His name appears on the roll of magistrates as late as the 2nd Eliz. (1560). He was the ancestor of the Lloyds of Leighton, Talgarth, and Forden, and other Montgomeryshire families.

LLOYD, JACOB YOUDE WILLIAM, generally known as the Chevalier Lloyd, of Clochfaen, Llangurig, was the son of Jacob William Hinde, of Langham Hall, Essex, by Harriet, daughter and co-heir of the late Rev. Thomas Youde, of Clochfaen and Plasmadoc. He was born in 1816, and through his mother claimed descent through Tudor Trefor from Gwrtheyrn Gwrtheneu or Vortigern, lord of Erging Ewias and Gloucester. He was educated at Wadham College, Oxford, and on the 12th December 1868 received her Majesty's licence to assume the old name of Lloyd of Clochfaen in lieu of that of Hinde, and also to bear the arms of Lloyd. In early life he entered into holy orders, and for a time was curate of Old Chapel, Llandinam, but before long he went over to the Church of Rome, and when he succeeded to his mother's property in 1856, on her death, he expended a large portion of it on the Church of his adoption. Some years afterwards he joined the Pontifical Zouaves in defence of the temporal power of the Pope, serving as a private. In 1870 he was created a Knight of the Order of St. Gregory the Great by Pope Pius IX. He felt himself unable, however, to accept the new Papal dogmas soon afterwards promulgated, and in 1875 he, for a time, discarded the title of Chevalier, but it continued to be given to him by others, and he was always known as the Chevalier Lloyd. During the latter years of his life he became gradually estranged from the Roman Catholic Church. In 1877 he returned to Clochfaen, where he continued to reside up to his death, and where his catholicity of spirit, his kind and genial disposition, and his unstinted benevolence and generosity, gained for him the esteem and affection of all around him. Among other proofs of his munificence may be cited the restoration in 1878, at his sole charge, of the ancient parish church of Llangurig, at a cost of £11,000, and this although he was not a member of the Anglican Communion. "As a mark of gratitude and esteem for his unbounded liberality, extraordinary charitableness, and his restoration of the parish church," his tenants and friends in 1885 erected a handsome obelisk in his honour in the village of Llangurig. The Chevalier was also devoted to antiquarian pursuits, and a contributor to the *Archæologia Cambrensis* and the *Montgomeryshire Collections*. He greatly assisted Mr. Edward Hamer in compiling the "History of Llangurig," which appeared in the latter, and was afterwards reprinted and published in a handsome volume. But his chief literary work was the *History of Powys Fadog*, which came out in six volumes octavo. This work, it is true, contains much that might have been with advantage omitted, but the mass of pedigrees and old Welsh poems, with translations and other valuable materials illustrative of the genealogy and history of the district to which it relates, gathered at great trouble and expense, supplies a rich quarry for local historians and genealogists. The Chevalier died, after a short illness, at Ventnor, in the Isle of Wight, whither he had gone for the benefit of his health, on the 14th October 1887, aged 71 years, and was buried at Llangurig on the 21st of the same month. Having died unmarried, his estates passed on his death to his niece, Harriet Julia Morforwyn, the wife of Lieut.-Colonel George Hope Verney.

LLOYD, JOHN, a younger brother of Charles Lloyd, the Quaker, of Dolobran, already noticed, was born in 1638. He received a liberal education, and became one of the Six Clerks in Chancery. He married Jane, daughter of Sir Thomas Gresham, the munificent founder of the Royal Exchange. Dr Lloyd, bishop of Oxford, was one of his descendants. It was he (not his grandfather of the same name as is sometimes erroneously stated) who presented the Communion plate to Meifod Church. This and other circumstances lead us to assume that, unlike his brothers Charles and Thomas, he remained loyal to the Established Church.

LLOYD, LUDOVICK, or LUDWICK, fifth son of Oliver Lloyd, of Marrington, was sergeant-at-arms to Queen Elizabeth, a distinguished herald, spoken of by Lewys Dwn as a high authority, and a voluminous writer. Anthony Wood mentions Lodowyke Lloyd as one of the contributors to Richard Edwards' *Paradise of Dainty Devises* (London 1578), qu.). The following is a list of his works:—

"(1) *The Consent of Time*, disciphering the errours of the Grecians in their Olympiads, the uncertain computations of the Romanes in their Penteterydes and buildinge of Rome, of the Persians in their accompt of Cyrus, and of the vanities of the Gentiles in fables of antiquities, disagreeing with the Hebrews and with the sacred histories in consent of

time. Wherein is alsoe set down the beginninge, continuance, succession, and overthrowe of kinges, kingdoms, states, and governments (1590);
(2) *Diall of Daies* (1590); (3) *Triplicitie of Triumpas* (1591); (4) *A Briefe
Conference of Divers Lawes* (1602); (5) *The Stratagems of Jerusalem* (1602);
(6) *The Practice of Policy* (1604); (7) *Pilgrimage of Princes* (1586, 1607, and
1653); (8) *Linceus Spectacles* (1607); (9) *Tragi-Comedie of Serpents*
(1607); (10) *The Jubile of Britaine* (1607); (11) *The Choyce of Jewels*
(1607); (12) *The Order, Solemnitie, Pomp, etc., of Emperors* (1612); (13)
Marrow of History (1653). There is also in the Myvyrian collection in
the British Museum a curious poem by the same author entitled *The
most ancient and comendable siecle sonet of British Sidanen applied by a
Courtier to the princelye prayse of the queens maiestie* printed in Mont.
Coll. xxii., p. 239. On the 13th May, 1587, Queen Elizabeth by letters
patent "did graunt and to fearme sett (for 40 years) unto Ludovick Lloyd
esquire, then one of her Maiesties seriant-at-Arms, amongst other things,
All that then Chapel of FFording al's FForden * * * * all manner
of Tythes of corne and hey and all other tyethes in great Heme, little
Heme, Kelekewith, FFording, Nantereba, Penylan, Brinkendrithe, Akley,
Llettinwynwarethe, some'ymes belonging unto the late Priory of
Chirbury".

LLOYD, MEREDITH, of Welshpool, was an eminent lawyer,
and an intimate friend and relative of Mr. Robert Vaughan, of
Hengwrt, the antiquary. Having become the owner of the valuable collection of MSS. formed by Sir Thomas ab William, or
Dr. Thomas Williams, of Trefriw, he presented the greater part
of it to Mr Vaughan. Some of his correspondence with the
latter in the years 1654-5, on antiquarian subjects, was published
in the *Cam. Reg. and Cam. Briton.*

LLOYD, Rev. MAURICE, of Aberhavesp, is mentioned by
Calamy among the clergy who in 1662 were ejected for Nonconformity, but his name is not given in the list of Rectors in
Thomas's *History of St. Asaph.* He appears to have afterwards
conformed.

LLOYD, OLIVER, L.L.D., a younger brother of Dr. David
Lloyd, the Dean of St. Asaph, was sometime Fellow of All Souls,
Oxford, out of which he was ejected by the Parliamentary
Visitors in 1648, but restored in 1660, and afterwards made
Warden of Manchester College. He died near Doctor's Com-
mons, in London, about the 17th March, 1662, and was buried
there.

LLOYD, Rev. ROBERT, M.A., Rector of Hirnant. The
earliest account we have of him is that in 1680 he was preferred
to the living of Eglwysfach, near Conway, but which he was
force l by Bishop Jones to resign for a vicar choralship in 1697
to make way for the Rev. John Humphreys, who had an estate
in the parish. The following year (1698) he published a translation into Welsh of a small work on the keeping of the
Sabbath ("Trefn am dduwioldeb ar ddydd yr Arglwydd") by
Dr. William Ashton, of Beckenham, a second edition of which
also appeared in 1768. In 1717 he was preferred by Bishop
Wynn to the Rectory of Hirnant, which he held for many years.
The parish Register contains the following curious entry in his

handwriting: "1730. A memorable year, wherein I am "oppressed and injured by certaine persons, whom I freely for- "give. However, I made of this Parish this year 4 Score "pounds. All glory to God alone. R. Lloyd." He lived to a great age, but the exact date and place of his death are unknown. He was succeeded in the Rectory of Hirnant, in 1757, by the Rev. John Edwards.

LLOYD, ROGER, of Talgarth, was descended from Sir Gruffydd Vaughan, who was bannereted at Agincourt in 1415. He was one of the intended Knights of the Royal Oak (*temp.* Charles II.) His estate was valued at £800.

LLOYD, REV. THOMAS, Rector of Llanbrynmair, in the time of Charles I. and the Commonwealth (1644– 1661) On account of his royalist principles he was, according to Walker (*Sufferings of the Clergy*) "totally "dispossessed for the space of three years, after which he "recovered it, and made a shift to keep it, but with much "trouble." He had previously been Vicar of Llannefydd 1638 ; Rector of Llansannan 1642 ; and Vicar of Berriew 1643. After the Restoration he became Rector of Llangynyw 1661 ; and Vicar of Caerwys 1666.

LLOYD, THOMAS, of Dolobran, the first Chief Magistrate of Pennsylvania, under the Proprietory Government of William Penn, was born at Dolobran, in the parish of Meifod, on the 17th February, 1640. He was the third son of Charles Lloyd (of Dolobran) and his wife Elizabeth, a descendant of Sir Rowland Stanley, brother of Lord Strange. Thomas Lloyd was like his elder brother Charles educated at Jesus College, Oxford, where he became distinguished for learning and ability. He left Oxford to visit his brother in prison, and " became his champion "and embraced his faith," He vainly sought to effect his liberation through interviews with such Justices as had partici- pated in the prosecutions. The details of some of these efforts are given in Richard Davies's Autobiography, who quaintly adds that " he received the truth, and was obedient to it, took up his "daily cross, and followed Jesus, came to be his disciple, was "taught by him, and went no more to Oxford for learning." This was in 1662. Thomas Lloyd himself was imprisoned the next year, but soon released. Subsequently at the request of Mr. Corbet, a magistrate, he accompanied Richard Davies to a place of public worship, and briefly addressed the congregation. In 1664, he was arrested with others, while quietly travelling on the highway; and, for refusing to subscribe to the oath of allegiance and supremacy, was again imprisoned. According to a brief account published in the *Philadelphia Friend.* he was detained a prisoner eight years. He had married Mary, daughter of Gilbert Jones, of Welshpool, a short time before his incarceration. In 1672 the Friends in Welshpool Jail, with others throughout Great Britain, detained under ecclesiastical laws, were discharged

L

from confinement by letters patent. Thomas Lloyd after his release, resided at Maesmawr, near Welshpool. On the 7th March, 1675, David Maurice, of Penybont, a Justice of the Peace, visited the Friends' Meeting House at Cloddian Cochion, with fourteen or fifteen armed men. The Friends, who were sitting in silence, were ordered to depart, but Thomas Lloyd desired that they might be permitted to remain fifteen minutes longer. To this the Justice assented, and he and his followers sat down in the meeting. Availing himself of this opportunity, Thomas Lloyd proceeded briefly to define Friends' principles and defend their mode of Worship. The Justice then fined him £20, the House £20, and each person present five shillings. On the 15th April the stock on his farm was distrained upon, and several of his cattle driven away. In 1677, Walworth, one of the Counsel against George Fox, was made Judge of part of North Wales. He opened his circuit in Merionethshire, and, causing certain Friends to be arrested, tendered to them the obnoxious test oath. To this they refused to subscribe; whereupon he informed them he did not intend to proceed by praemunire, but they should be tried for high treason at the next Assizes, and the men hanged and the women burned. The Friends, throughout Wales, were greatly alarmed. Thomas Lloyd proceeded to London, and enlisted the sympathy and efforts of Counsellor Corbet, whose legal ability the Friends held in high estimation. The Counsellor expressed much concern, for it was evident that Walworth had the law on his side, and was inclined to do mischief. He and Mr. Lloyd represented the matter to certain members of Parliament, as fraught with great dangers likely to arise, if the law remained as it then stood. So thoroughly were they convinced, that the law was repealed the same session. Walworth, therefore for a time, discontinued the prosecution. In 1681, Dr. William Lloyd, Bishop of St. Asaph, who sought to convince Dissenters by argument rather than force, held a public discussion with Charles and Thomas Lloyd in the Town Hall of Llanfyllin, where according to authentic accounts, "the debate was conducted with great credit to both parties." The Town Hall was crowded with people. A MS. statement, prepared by the Clerks appointed by the Bishop, is entitled "An Account of a Conference between the Right Reverend Bishop of St. Asaph and Mr. Charles and Mr. Thomas Lloyd." One of those who took part in the argument against the Lloyds was Dr. Humphreys, afterwards Bishop of Bangor. "They had no previous notice of what matters they would argue, and at the last day, Thomas Lloyd was obliged to reply to about twenty-eight syllogisms; all written down as they disputed, to be answered extempore." Proud, the historian, who had seen the MS. account, says : "It is a learned and ingenious dispute marked with moderation on both sides, chiefly in syllogistical method on baptism and the Lords' Supper, with divers Greek quotations, and explanations from the New Testament." It is said "The Bishop highly commended Thomas Lloyd." The Lloyds also

"had much discourse with the Chancellor and Henry Dodwell.
Also with the Dean of Bangor, afterwards Bishop of Hereford."
Thomas Lloyd accompanied by his family, joined William Penn's
colony in Pennsylvania, in 1683. They took passage in the ship
America, Captain Joseph Wasey, and after a voyage of eight
weeks, landed at Philadelphia, which then consisted of three or
four little cottages, nearly surrounded by a dense forest.
Thomas Lloyd's devoted wife died soon after their arrival in
Philadelphia, and was the first person interred in the Friends'
(Arch Street) burying ground. Watson, the Annalist of Philadelphia, terms her a very pious woman, and says that William Penn
spoke at her grave much commending her character. The elder
daughter, Hannah (who afterwards became distinguished as a
Minister), took charge of the household affairs. At that time she
was seventeen years of age. Watson says : " Thomas Lloyd was
Deputy-Governor as long as he would serve,—a man of great
worth as a scholar, and a religious man. * * * His family
was respectable and ancient in Wales ; he himself was educated
at the University, talked Latin fluently on shipboard with
Pastorius [a learned German fellow-passenger]. He exercised
as a public minister among Friends in this country, and in his own
person suffered imprisonment for truth's sake." Watson also
states : " Having established his Colony on the broad principles
of Christian Charity and Constitutional freedom, he (Penn) left
the Executive power in ths hands of Thomas Lloyd, an eminent
Quaker. Bowden, in his work on the " Early Friends of
America," says : " Although Thomas Lloyd, from his first
arrival, took an active and conspicuous part in civil affairs, it was
nevertheless contrary to his natural inclination, and so far from
deriving any pecuniary advantage from devoting so much time
and superior talents to the affairs of the Colony. it is asserted
that his temporal interests suffered in consequence." William
Penn, recognising Thomas Lloyd as a man of education and
probity, at once advanced him to honourable and responsible
positions in the Province. He is first mentioned as Foreman of
the Grand Jury in 1683, and in the Minutes of the Council of
State, of October the same year (the year of his arrival), it is
recorded " Ye Governor was pleased to appoint him (Thomas
Lloyd) Master of the Rolls, who doth solemnly promise to officiate therein with diligence." On the same date Penn
empowered the Provincial Council " to act in the Government in
his stead, Thomas Lloyd being President of ye same." Also,
was read a commission for Thomas Lloyd to keep the Great Seal.
At a meeting of the same body, 9th June, 1684, the Great Seal
was delivered to Thomas Lloyd and two others to sign Patents
and grant Warrants. Again, on the same date, Present,
Thomas Lloyd (President), Samuel Carpenter, and others of the
Council. Penn's Commission under the Broad Seal was read,
appointing Thomas Lloyd as one of the Deputy Governors.
Penn left for England on the 12th of June, 1684. In December
1686, the Council was superseded in the government by five

commissioners, of whom Lloyd was again President until December 18th, 1688. These were superseded in the latter year by Captain John Blackwell, Deputy Governor, who was relieved of duty in January, 1690. At a meeting of the Council held 2nd, 11th month, 1689-90, Thomas Lloyd was once more elected President, an office which he held until March 1691, when he became Deputy Governor. According to Proud's *History of Pennsylvania*, " in 1691, the Province preferring the choice of a Deputy Governor, contrary to the minds of the territories " (i.e., New Castle, Kent and Sussex), and Thomas Lloyd being preferred to that office (which he appears to have accepted, with some reluctance), the Proprietory commissioned him Governor, and the Secretary William Markland. In the Spring of 1693 the Crown of England took possession of the province of Pennsylvania. On the 26 April, 1693, Benjamin Fletcher having been appointed Captain General and Commander-in-Chief of the Provinces of New York, Pennsylvania, and the country of New Castle, and the territories and tracts of land depending thereon in America (after the Surrender of Penn's Proprietory to the Crown), his Excellency having sent for Thomas Lloyd the late Deputy Governor, did offer unto him the first place in the Council, which he did decline." In 1684, Thomas Lloyd married Patience Storey, whose maiden name was Gardiner. She was the widow of Robert Storey, a wealthy merchant of New York, and conspicuous as a member of the Society of Friends. She had issue by her first marriage, but not by her last. After his marriage, Thomas Lloyd resided in the City of New York several years, but continued in the discharge of his official duties in Pennsylvania. It is stated in *Chalkley's Journal*, that when in Philadelphia, Governor Lloyd used sometimes in the evening, before retiring to rest, to go in person to public houses and order the people he found there to their own homes, till at length he was instrumental to promote better order, and did in a great measure suppress vice and immorality. Thomas Lloyd was the father of ten children by his first wife, who died in 1680, of whom Hannah married John Dalaval (her second husband was Richard Hill; all of her children died unmarried); Rachel in 1688, married Samuel Preston; Mary married Isaac Norris; Thomas married Sarah Young, and Deborah married Mordecai Moore, all leaving heirs. Mordecai, John, Elizabeth, Margaret, and Samuel were unmarried. In addition to his official and ministerial duties, he was also a physician, and " had great " knowledge and experience therein, having generally good " success ; and he was conscientiously careful over his patients " whether rich or poor." He was seized with a malignant fever 5th July, 1694, and died on the 10th of the same month, aged fifty-five years, and was interred in the Friends' burying ground, Philadelphia. The Friends of Haverford Meeting, Pennsylvania, recorded their memorial of Thomas Lloyd in the following affectionate terms :—

"His sound and effectual ministry, his great patience, temperance, and humility, and slowness to wrath, his love to the brethren, his godly care to the Church of Christ, that all things might be kept sweet, savoury and in good order ; his helping h nd to the weak, and gentle admonitions, we are fully satisfied have a seal and witness in the hearts of all faithful Friends, who knew him both in the land of his nativity and these American parts. We may in truth say he sought not himself nor the riches of this world, but his eye was to that which was everlasting, being given up to spend and be spent for truth and the sake of Friends. He never turned his back on the truth, nor was weary in his travels Sionwards, but remained a sound pillar on the spiritual building * * * * He reviled not again, nor took any advantage ; but loved his enemies, and prayed for them that despitefully abused him. His love to the Lord, his truth and people, was sincere to the last. * * * The remembrance of his innocent life and meek spirit, lives with us, and his memorial is, and will remain to be sweet and comfortable to the faithful."

The following testimony from the Quarterly Meeting at Dolobran, 30th November, 1711, is also interesting:—

"Though we may truly say with the Apostle Paul that not many wise men after the flesh, not many mighty, not many noble are called, yet it hath pleased the Lord in his mercy to visit and to reach unto some few who have been acknowledged men of wisdom and learning, and they have received the blessed truth in the love of it, and continued faithful thereunto until the end of their days, through all their sufferings, tribulations, and exercises of many kinds. Amongst the number our honourable friend Charles Lloyd, of Dolobran, and this our friend Thomas Lloyd, his younger brother, may be accounted, who were esteemed wise and learned men by the wise and learned of the age. Both of said brothers were men of natural and acquired parts, and ingenious men, as the enemies and adversaries of Truth, who knew them, were obliged to confess and acknowledge. They were both brought up scholars in some of the best schools, and under the care and tutorship of some of the most able school masters that were in these parts, whereby they profited very much in their learning. From whence they were sent to the University of Oxford, where they continued students for some years, and informed themselves much, and were accounted men of extraordinary parts. Our friend Charles Lloyd was convinced of the Truth about 8th month, 1662, in the five-and-twentieth year of his age, by the ministry of our worthy and dear Friends, Richard Moore and Richard Davies. He was a noble and valiant champion for Truth, and an eminent instrument in the hands of the Lord for strengthening and confirming many in the most holy faith, and was an able and faithful minister of the Gospel of our Lord Jesus Christ. He had a living, powerful, and searching Ministry. He was the first of that family who received the Truth, and was instrumental in the convincement of his brother, our said friend Thomas Lloyd and others. He departed this life in peace with the Lord, the 27th of 9th month, 1694. Our dear friend Thomas Lloyd was convinced of Truth about the year 1663, and he gave up in all faithfulness and obedience thereunto, and after some years he had a gift in the Ministry committed unto him, and he was very serviceable to Truth and Friends in many places He practised physic and had great knowledge and experience therein, having generally good success, and he was conscientiously careful over his patients, whether rich or poor. He had a great practice, whereby it was often his lot to be amongst many of account in the world, and he was much loved and respected by them, yet being a man of tender spirit, their company became bitterness to his soul, and he went many days mourning on his way, because their life was on that which crucified the Just. He was very charitable to the poor, and compassionate unto such as were in affliction and distress, doing good freely to all. He had a notable way of softening harsh spirits, and begetting mildness in them towards Friends and their sufferings. He was a man of extraordinary temper, very obliging, humble, and courteous in his behaviour and deportment. He had a good utterance and could express himself eloquently, and was very instructive in his discourse, and pleasant and cheerful in his conversation, so that his company was very desirable, being a man of good and savoury life. Much might be written concerning him, but it is not our desire to set up or exalt man, who is but a creature. All praise and honour belong to our Creator, yet when outward wisdom is sanctified by the Lord, it may be and is serviceable in its place. Our said friend suffered cheerfully the spoiling of his goods rather than he would disobey the Lord. He had many considerable offers from some noted men, who had power to bestow great places, if he would have been prevailed on to change his religion. But he was firmly established on the true and sure foundation even the Rock of Ages, Jesus Christ, so that neither the frowns or smiles of men or devils could move or shake him from his foundation. In the year 1681, his brother Charles Lloyd and himself held a public dispute for the most part of two days with William Lloyd then Bishop of this Diocese, now Bishop of Worcester and the Dean of Bangor and Hereford, at the Town Hall, in Llanfyllin, in this County of Montgomery. Our friend Thomas Lloyd managed the dispute most of the time with great reputation. But it was agreed betwixt both parties that the said dispute should not be published. Our said friend continued among us for many years in great love and unity, and was a very serviceable man, and left a great savour behind him. His first wife Mary Lloyd, was a woman of good life and conversation and well beloved in these parts, by whom he had many children, both sons and daughters, who went over into Pensylvania. We desire the Lord may raise up many more faithful and serviceable labourers, who may work in the harvest for the gathering of many to the Lord, that they may at last receive a Crown of Righteousness, as we firmly believe this our worthy friend with many more of the servants of the Lord Jesus Christ in our age have received, who are gathered into rest with the Saints of glory."

To his educational attainments were united great benevolence of disposition and probity of character. His steadfast adherence to religious convictions, his great desire for the spiritual and temporal welfare of his fellow men, and devotion to what he deemed the Truth, impelled him with the spirit of a martyr to submit to irksome imprisonment, the sequestration of property, and the severance of family relations. Still unconquered and undismayed, he determined to enjoy that liberty of conscience elsewhere, which was denied him in his native land ; and embarking with his devoted family, crossed the ocean with little else in prospect than what must have seemed a choice between starvation and the scalping knife in the wilds of America. Notwithstanding the heroism which enabled him to encounter and overcome all this, those who knew him best both in Wales and Philadelphia testified that " his life was pure and innocent," and " characterized by a sound and effective Ministry, great " patience, temperance, humility, and slowness to wrath." While Wales reverences and cherishes the memory of Thomas Lloyd as one of her ablest and purest champions of freedom of conscience, Pennsylvania, the Key-stone of a mighty Commonwealth of English-speaking States, not the less regards her first Chief Magistrate, to whose exemplary character, teachings and executive ability, she is in a great measure indebted for those germs of civil and religious liberty which evolved in free thought, free man, and direct spiritual accountability to God. The Declaration of Independence first promulgated in the city of Philadelphia, was simply an outcome of the principles contended and suffered for by Thomas Lloyd.

LLWCHAIARN, a saint who flourished in the sixth century, the son of Hygarvael ab Cyndrwyn, and the brother of Aelhaiarn, and Cynhaiarn. He founded the churches of Llanllwchaiarn and Llanmerewig in this county; also those of Llanychaiarn and Llanllwchaiarn in Cardiganshire.

LLWYD, DAFYDD, or DAVID LLOYD, was a son of Dafydd ab Einion, of Mochdre and Kerry, the founder of the Pryce family of Newtown Hall and Glanmiheli, and was lineally descended from Elystan Glodrudd, founder of the fourth Royal Tribe of Wales. He flourished about the middle of the 15th century, and was a man of great wealth and influence. He was also a liberal patron of the bards, several of whom addressed Odes to him. Among them is one by his contemporary Lewys Glyn Cothi, considered to be one of that poet's best efforts. The bard compares his readiness to go and see him to that of the hawk to return to the falconer, and dwells fondly on his kindness, amiability, and devotedness to religious duties, and generosity. He was, it is stated, in the habit, on the different festivals of the church, of giving splendid entertainments (in the nature of Eisteddfodau it would seem) when bards and minstrels were invited and sumptuously entertained at his mansion at Newtown; and the poor partook of the alms which he liberally bestowed:

"Ei arfer ydyw, wyr Faredydd,
I rai odidawg roi diodydd;
Rhoi cardawd i dlawd hyd ei wledydd,
Rhoi llety i wawdwr, wr llwyd dedwydd,
Ac i wan torth gan gynnydd—gwlad Bowys,
Ac i ail Baradwys galw ei brydydd."

David Lloyd, among numerous offices, held that of farmer of the tolls of Newtown under Richard Duke of York. Among the poets whom he specially patronised was Hywel Swrdwal, who was Bailiff of Newtown in the years 1454-5 and 6, but died before him. Lewys Glyn Cothi, however, survived his patron, and wrote his elegy in which he represents death as having gone like a foe to Cedewain, and carried away in triumph from thence a rich treasure. David Lloyd was succeeded by his son Rhys.

LLWYD, RHYS AB DAFYDD, or REES AB DAVID LLOYD, of Newtown, succeeded his father Dafydd Llwyd at Newtown, being thirteenth in lineal descent from Elystan Glodrudd. He was esquire of the body to king Edward IV., and was a staunch Yorkist. Edward rewarded him for his services by appointing him governor of Montgomery Castle. He was also steward of the lordships of Montgomery, Cedewain, Kerry, Cyfeiliog, and Arwystli. Lewys Glyn Cothi in an Ode addressed to him describes him as a powerful and distinguished warrior. He did not live long to enjoy his honours, for he fell in 1469 on the bloody field of Danesmore, near Banbury, where 5,000 Welshmen were, it is said, left dead on the field, and their leaders, the Earl of Pembroke, Sir Richard Herbert, and many other eminent persons were taken prisoners and beheaded. Rees left two sons, Thomas ap Rees, or Pryce, of Newtown, and Meredydd ap Rees, or Pryce, of Glanmihely, Kerry. From their time all the somewhat numerous branches of this family bore the surname of Pryce.

LLYWELYN, the son of Tegonwy ab Teon, and brother of Mabon, a saint of the sixth century, who founded a religious house at Trallwng or Welshpool. He died at Bardsey monastery. The *Myv. Arch.* contains a dialogue in verse between him and his son Gwrnerth attributed to Tyssilio.

LLYWELYN AB GRUFFYDD, of Llanwrin, father of the more celebrated Dafydd Llwyd ab Llywelyn of Mathafarn, was bard to Henry Tudor, afterwards Henry VII., and appears to have composed a poem to him when he was a babe in his cradle.

LLYWELYN AB GUTYN, a poet of considerable merit, who flourished about 1460 to 1500. He was a performer on the *Crwth* to that other eminent poet and chieftain already noticed, Dafydd Llwyd ab Llywelyn. Some of his poems are still preserved in manuscript.

LLYWELYN, son of Madoc ap Meredydd, prince of Powys, was a young chieftain of great promise, but who was slain in 1159. He is styled " the only hope of all the men of Powys." The *Myv. Arch.* contains Englynion in his praise (attributed to Llywarch Llaety, but which, according to both Stephens and Price, were more probably written by Llywarch Llew Cad), reckoned by Stephens among " the most interesting pieces of " the twelfth century,"

" In the whole range of our literature, we have not as lively a portrait of a chieftain; the minutest features are noticed, without the *tout d' ensemble* being lost sight of, and Llywelyn ab Madoc stands as palpable before us, as if his portrait had been painted on the canvass. In the easy flow of the language, the minuteness of the description, and the spirit of the whole delineation, we have a collection of merits not frequently to be met with in the works of the bards, and the prince described seems so deserving of being the idol of a poet's fancy, that the poet and his subject share an unbounded admiration."

The poem opens with the question—

"Govynnwys nebun ny raen gan rei &c."

The following is a translation of the first twelve stanzas :—

" Does no one ask,—are men so unconcerned
   Before unsheathing their swords,
Who is yon mail-clad youth ?
Who is the haughty warrior before us ?

A glorious prince full of intelligence,
    None will be allowed to lead him,
He is a prince, valiant, powerful and war-loving,
Llywelyn the enemy of Gwynedd.

Whose swift moving shield is that,
    And bright shining spear?
Who is the determined warlike chief,
Who holds it by its armlets?

It is the shield of Llywelyn the brave
    Protector of his country's rights;
A shield with a man's shoulder behind it;
A shield which carries terror before it.

Whose is the flashing sword which cuts the air,   .
    A sure wound-inflicter;
An emblem of honour it will be,
And in that right hand will destroy enemies.

He who handles it is the defender of his country,
    Renowned for downward strokes ;
A courageous soldier in the day of battle,
Is the hero of Mechain,—his country's pride.

Whose is that red helmet of battle
    Surmounted with a fierce wolf?
Who is the rider of the fierce white steed?
What is his name? how wonderful his appearance!

He is called long-handed Llywelyn,
    The irresistible leader of conflict,
Commander of men of the terrible shout,
Devastator of England ; faultless and perfect is he.

Whose is the suit of complete armour ?
    He will not fly from the battle field.
Who is this hero of princely race ?
I ask you all, whence sprang he?

He is a renowned and valiant prince,
    Famed for bravery and slaughtering;
The majestic Chief, dreadful in the fight,
Is the son of Madoc ab Meredydd.

Whose is the war-steed, fastest in the race,
    Which so haughtily paws the ground?
Who the prince so loved by his army,
With the spear which pierces without warning?

He is a known, ambitious chief,
    Who, as long as God supports him,
Will be famed as conqueror, brave and glorious—
Worthy of the men of Tysiliaw."

LLYWELYN MOEL Y PANTRI, an eminent poet who flourished in the parish of Llanwnog from about 1400 to 1480. He was of good family, and evidently occupied a high social position. On his mother's side he was descended both from Celynin of Llwydiarth, and from Brochwel Ysgythrog, prince of Powys—his mother, according to a pedigree in Lewys Dwn s *Visitations*, vol. II., p. 277, being Lleuku, daughter of Deio ap Jenkin, by Maddevus, daughter of Gruffydd Deuddwr. Guto'r Glyn wrote an Elegy on his death, printed in the *Cymmrodorion Transactions* (1843) vol. II., in which he says—

" Cwn mawr yw acw'n y Main
A mwy uchod yn Mechain.
  *   *   *   *   *
Ni chyrch nag oes na chôg
O Lwyn Onn i Lan Wynog
  *   *   *   *   *
Marmor yn y Côr a'i cudd
  *   *   *   *   *
Cafodd yn emyl y Cwfaint
Urddas Adda Fras a'i fraint,
Y gwr y sydd yn gorwedd
Dan allawr faenawr a'i fedd."

(Great is the cry yonder in Main, and greater up in Mechain.   *   *
Neither nightingale nor cuckoo will resort from Llwyn Onn to Llan-
wynog.   *   * Marble covers him within the choir.   *   * The
dignity and privilege of Adda Fras were conferred upon him in the
border of the Convent, his resting place and grave are beneath a stone
altar.)

The references to Main (Meifod) and Mechain are explained by
the fact of Llywelyn's mother being a sister of Ieuan Teg of
Dolobran; and the Llwyn Onn alluded to was probably the
poet's residence in Llanwnog. Formerly an old mansion so
named stood on land now held with Nenoddnewydd (the New
Hall) probably built in substitution for Llwynon. Part of the
old Llwynon residence stood and was occupied as cottages about
70 years ago. It was probably a black and white timber
building, its panels being filled with lath and plaster. The last
four lines of the elegy quoted above refer to the poet's burial in
the abbey of Strata Marcella—an honour conferred only upon
persons of very high rank. Several of Llywelyn's compositions
are preserved in manuscript in the Hengwrt collection at
Peniarth, and in other collections. His son, Owen, was also a
poet. Among other things he wrote an ode in praise of David
Lloyd Vaughan of Hafodwen (Marrington), which is also to be
found among the Hengwrt MSS.

MADOG AB MEREDYDD AB BLEDDYN was the eldest
son of Meredydd ab Bleddyn, Prince of Powys, which from
him was afterwards called Powys Fadog, the other division
being called Powys Wenwynwyn, from Gwenwynwyn, the
grandson of his brother Gruffydd. Madog entered into an
alliance with Henry II. in 1158, and during that monarch's first
and successful campaign in Wales he took the command of the
English fleet, and invaded Anglesey, where he was defeated
with great loss; nor was he more fortunate against his countrymen at the battle of Consyllt. He was a prince of an amiable
character and more than ordinary talent Powel's testimony
is that he was " ever the king of England's friend, and was one
" that feared God and relieved the poor." Cynddelw, Gwalchmai, and other contemporary poets composed several poems in
his praise, highly extolling him. These are printed in the
Myv. Arch., and an elegant translation of Gwalchmai's Ode will
be found in the Cambro Briton, vol. 2, p. 460. He built the

castles of Oswestry, Caereinion, and Overton, in which latter he
resided. He married Susanna, the daughter of Gruffydd ab
Cynan, prince of North Wales, by whom he had three sons,
named Gruffydd Maelor, Owain, and Elise, and one daughter,
Marred, who became the wife of Iorwerth Drwyndwn, and
mother of Llewelyn the Great. He had also three illegitimate
sons, Owain Brogyntyn, Cynfrig Efell, and Einion Efell. He
often resided in England, and died at Winchester in 1160 (or
1161, according to the *Annales Cambriæ*), whence his body was
conveyed and buried in the church of Tysilio at Meifod. He
bore for arms, *Argent* a lion rampant *sable*, armed and langued
gules, according to the *Visitations of Salop*, but in the Lingen
pedigree his arms are thus emblazoned:—Paly of six *Or* and
Gules, over all a lion rampant *sable*. If the account of his
death given in the *Cae Cyriog M S.* be correct, he must have
been twice married. That account states that he married
Matilda Verdown, or Verdun, an Englishwoman, and entailed
the lordship of Oswestry upon her and her heirs by him
to be begotten ; and because they could not agree to cohabit
together, she made her complaint to the King of England, who
sent for Madog, and it was concluded that Madog should come
to Winchester and refer the case to the decision of arbitrators,
and that neither party should bring more than twenty-four
horses in their retinue ; consequently Madog brought twenty-
four horses and twenty-four riders, and the lady met him with
twenty-four horses and two men on every horse, so Madog's
party was overpowered by this treachery, and he was apprehended and imprisoned in Winchester, and compelled to entail
the lordship of Oswestry on her and her heirs by *whomsoever*
begotten. Madog dying in prison, Matilda married John
Fitz Alan, Earl of Arundel and Lord of Oswestry. In this
manner the English became possessed of that lordship. Mr.
William Jones, of Llangadfan, the translator of the *Cae Cyriog
MSS.*, adds, "It is beyond all doubt that Madog was murdered
"at Winchester by the instigation of his loving wife: his
"elegy by Cynddelw Brydydd Mawr, which I have by me, con-
"cludes thus :—

> " Ae ddiwedd ys bi can bu y leith
> Y ddiwyn y cam cymeint y affeith
> Yg golender seint ig goleudeith
> Y goleuad rhad, rhydid perffeith."

"Thus literally :—' Since he lost his life may he in recompence
"for the flagitious injustice remain in the glorious hierarchy of
"saints, in the presence of grace, in perfect bliss.'"

MADOG AB RHIRYD, the grandson of Bleddyn ab
Cynfyn, prince of Powys, was a turbulent character, who,
during the six years from 1108 to 1113, was constantly engaged
in deeds of violence and slaughter. Cadwgan and his son Owen
having been deprived of their lands in Powys, in consequence of
the outrage committed by the latter upon Nest, the wife of

Gerald of Pembroke, Madog and his brother Ithel divided them
between them. Owen, however, soon afterwards returned from
Ireland (whither he had fled for refuge), and Madog, having
quarrelled with the English Lieutenant of the Marches, sent for
him, and, as Powel says, " desired his friendship, whose greatest
" enimie he was before; and by this meanes they were made
" freends, and swore either to other that none of them should
" betraie the other, nor agree by himselfe with the king or with
" his officers, without the other ; and thereupon they burned and
" spoiled the lands of such as they loved not, and destroied all
" things that they met withall." Before long, however, he was
obliged to make his escape to Ireland, but he soon returned,
" because he could not well awaie with the manners and con-
" ditions of the Irishmen, and being arrived came to the
" countrie of his uncle Iorwerth." The latter issued a proclamation that every man should "take him for his enemy."
Madog, understanding this,

'gathered to him a number of unthrifts and outlawes, and kept himselfe
in the rockes and woods, devising all the meanes he could to be revenged
upon Iorwerth, for that unkindnes and discourtesie as he tooke it, and so
entred freendship privily with Llywarch ab Trahaern, who hated
Iorwerth to the death. Then having knowledge that Iorwerth laie one
night at Caerneon, they two gathered all their strength and came about
the house at midnight, then Iorwerth and his men awoke, and defended
the house manfullie untill their foes set the same on fire : which, when
Iorwerth's men sawe, everie one shifted for himselfe, so that some
scaped through the fire, and the rest were either burnt or slaine, or both.
Then Iorwerth himself, seeing no remedie, adventured rather to be
slaine than burned, and came out : but his enemies received him upon
sharpe speares, and overthrew him in the fire, and so he died a cruell
death."—(Powel.)

His other uncle Cadwgan having made his peace with the king,
and regained his lands, Madog

"hid himselfe in rough and desert places, and, adding one mischiefe
upon another, determined also to murther him by one waie or other.
Therefore, after that Cadwgan had brought the countrie to some staie
of quietnesse, and saw right and iustice ministered therein, having
ever an eie and respect to the king, he came to the Trallwng (now called
the Poole), and the elders of the countrie with him, and minding to
dwell there, began to build a castell. Then Madoc, pretending nothing
but mischiefe, hearing this, came suddenlie upon him, and Cadwgan,
thinking no hurt, was slaine before he could either fight or flee."—(Ibid.)

This career of wickedness was, however, destined to be cut
short. Meredydd ab Bleddyn, determined to avenge the death of
his two brothers, sent a number of men to seize him.

" These men, as they passed through the country of Madoc in the night,
they met a man which belonged to the said Madoc, whome they tooke,
and examined him where his maister was, and he first said that he could
not tell; but being put in feare of death, he confessed that he was not
far from thence. Therefore they laie quietlie there all the night and in
the dawning they came suddenlie upon Madoc and his men, where they
slew a great number of them, and taking Madoc prisoner, they brought
him to their lord, who was right glad thereof, and put him in safe
prison, till he had sent word to his nephew Owen, who came thither

streight, then Meredith delivered Madoc unto him. And albeit he had slaine Owen's father, being his owne uncle, yet Owen remembering the freendship and oth that had been betwixt them two in times past, would not put him to death, but putting out his eies let him go. Then Meredyth and Owen divided his lands betwixt them, which was Caereneon, Aberhiw, and the third part of Deuthwr "—(Powel.)

This was in 1112, and we hear no more of him. He left a son named Meurig.

MADOG DANWR ("Ignifer") a descendant of Tudor Trefor, was a faithful and brave soldier who served under Gwenwynwyn, lord of Powys, who, as a reward for his services, bestowed upon him the lordship of Llangurig, with an addition to his coat of arms. He bore, according to Mr. Joseph Morris, *argent* a lion rampant *sable* within a bordure *gules*, in which six lions passant *argent*, one of them in chief another in base. The new arms, which he had the privilege of bearing in augmentation of his paternal coat, were a bordure *gules* charged with eight mullets *argent*. He married a daughter of Idnerth ab Meredydd Hen, lord of Buallt, by whom he had three sons, Meredydd, Idnerth, and Gruffydd. He resided at Clochfaen, Llangurig, and was the progenitor of the Lloyds of Clochfaen, one of the oldest and, at one time, most powerful of Montgomeryshire families.

MANUEL, DAFYDD, a poet, who lived in a cottage called Byrdir, on Gwernafon farm, Trefeglwys, and who flourished about the year 1700. A poem of his, entitled "Bustl y Cybyddion,"—a satire upon Avarice—was published in the *Blodeugerdd*, and many of his carols and compositions were published in various collections about the beginning of the last century. Some have also appeared in print for the first time in Lloyd's *History of Powys Fadog*. He was present at an eisteddfod at Machynlleth in the summer of 1701, when he composed an englyn, which may be found in the *Gwyliedydd* for 1836. Some traditions of him may also be found in *Y Brython* vol. V., p. 209. The Peniarth MSS. include a large number of his compositions. Mr. Nicholas Bennett, of Glanyrafon, has also about thirty of them in MS. dated between 1689 and 1719, some displaying considerable merit Dafydd Manuel ("Yr hen Fanuel o'r Byrdir," or "Yr hen Fanuel y Prydydd" as he was generally called) lived to an extreme old age, being, it is said, 101 years old when he died. The parish register of Trefeglwys contains the following entry of his burial :—"David Manuel "sepult. fuit 16 die Maii 1726."—His wife Margaret had died before him in 1699. They left three children—a son David, usually called "Deio," and two daughters, Mary (Malen) and Anne. The daughters were excellent poets, and several of their compositions in MS. are in Mr. Bennett's possession. Mary was especially noted for her ready wit and power of repartee, and as a Pennillion singer with the harp—a mode of singing which to be effective, demands very great skill, a quick ear, and a retentive memory. In Bardd Alaw (Parry)'s *Welsh Harper*, vol. 2, we have a melody associated with her name, namely, " Hoffedd Merch " Dafydd Manuel," (The delight of David Manuel's daughter.) Other members of the same family have attracted attention on account of their precocity, genius, and attainments. *John Manuel*, who joined the army in 1798, and fought in Egypt under Sir Ralph Abercromby, could not read a line at the time of his enlistment, but became in an exceedingly short time an excellent reader of both Welsh and English, as well as thoroughly conversant with French His daughter, *Sarah Manuel*, was quite illiterate up to her 30th year, when she joined a Sunday school class, learned to read fluently at once, and became well acquainted with the current literature of the day. *Thomas Manuel*, a sawyer, grew up to manhood illiterate, but accidentally becoming possessed of a French Testament he determined to master that language, which he did in a remarkably short time. In the year 1834, the Rev. Thomas Price, the well-known Welsh scholar and historian, took great interest in *William Manuel*, a wonderful boy, the son of Thomas and Mary Manuel, and a member of the same gifted family. This child, then only four years old, read Welsh, English, Hebrew, Greek, and Latin, and naturally read backwards or upside down with the same ease that other persons would read in the ordinary way. Mr. Price first became acquainted with him at the Cardiff Eisteddfod, and afterwards frequently visited his mother's cottage when she resided in the parish of Llanover, and also near Crickhowel Through the kindness of Alderman Thompson he was at the age of eight years placed in Christ's Hospital, where, after a most successful career, he died of consumption when only twelve years old. This extraordinary child had two brothers also who possessed great natural gifts. *Thomas*, the eldest, was an excellent Welsh, Latin, Greek, and English scholar ; and while daily engaged as a clerk in a lawyer's office he, in the last year of his life, wrote during the night for a prize (which he won), an essay under the bardic name of " Efrydydd " on " Wales as it is, &c." He died in early manhood, of decline in 1851. *Edward*, the youngest child, gave promise of even more extraordinary abilities than William. He could read English, Welsh, German, Latin, Greek, and Hebrew when he was only four years old, but he also died of consumption before he was five. Their mother (herself a remarkable woman) being mistress of Welsh and English, and perceiving the extraordinary thirst for learning evinced by her children, taught herself to read and translate Latin and Greek for the sake of assisting them.

MARCHELL, (Lat. *Marcella*) the daughter of Arwystli Gloff by Tywanwedd or Dwywannedd daughter of Amlawdd Wledig was a British saint (not canonised by the Church of Rome) who flourished between 566 and 600. She is the reputed original foundress of Ystrad Marchell, or Strata Marcella, near Pool Quay, where the famous Cistertian abbey bearing that name was afterwards established ; also of Capel Marchell, near Llanrwst.

MATTHEWS, OLIVER, was a member of an old and respectable family, settled for many generations at Park, in the parish of Llanwnog, where it appears he was born about the year 1520, He removed to Shrewsbury, where he became a prosperous mercer, being a resident in that town in the year 1576, where he also carried on the trade of an apothecary. After retiring from business he settled, according to the *Heraldic Visitations* of Shropshire, at Bishop's Castle. He married Jane, daughter of Edward Broughton, of Broughton, who was buried at Bishop's Castle 9th January, 1611. On the 18th March, 1615 (being then 95 years old), he wrote a letter "to his 2 lovinge freends of the cittie of Bristowe," namely, "Mr. Phillip Jenkins, my naturall countreyman, and Mr. "Thomas Taylor, my loving and faithfull frind," in which, after having at some length shewed them his

"knowledge and judgement, as touchinge the Antiquitie and Foundation of your famous cittie of Brennus Towne, which was built abouts 369 yeres before Christ's Incarnation by Brennus, that noble Brittaine,"

He concludes thus:—

"I, being aged 95 yores, and by reason thereof decayed in memorie, praie you, to have me excused, yf I have not performed to the full your expectacion herein. And nowe, not ever thinckinge to see you in this transitory World, I take my last and *ultimum vale* of you both, bequeathinge unto you, and to that famous Cittie of Brennus, and to Mr. Maior, with the Magistrates and Commynaltie thereof, my best love, wishinge yt with all my harte all prosperity and happiness. Dated at Snead neere Bu [shops] Castle the xviiith daie of March, *anno Domini*, 1615. Your old Frind and Brittaine, OLIVER MATTHEWS."

The following May (1616) he wrote " *An Abbreviation of divers* " *most true and auncient Brutaine Cronicles*, brieflie expressing " the foundation of the most famous decayed Cittie Caer Souse " or Dinas Southwen, most auncient in Brutaine, (Troy Newyth " onlie excepted) and of some other famous Citties in Greate " Brutaine," to which is added "The Cause of the Brittaines " Captivity." The first appeared in print in Hearde's *History and Antiquities of Glastonbury*. Lastly, he wrote an account of " *The Scituacion, Foundation, and auncient Names of the* " *famous Towne of Sallop*, not inferiour to manie Citties in this " Realme, for Antiquitie, godlie Government, good Orders, and " Wealth. The Lord so continue yt, to his good pleasure and " theire good. Amen. By Oliver Matthews, gen. Julie, 1616." The exact date of his death I have not been able to ascertain, but his Will was proved 2nd April, 1618. A reprint of all these quaint and curious compositions was issued in 1877 by Messrs. Bickley and Son, Shrewsbury.

MEISIR, one of the daughters of Cyndrwyn, prince of Powys, and who resided at Llystinwennan, in Caereinion, about the close of the fifth century. She was a sister of Cynddylan, in whose Elegy Llywarch Hen thus refers to her:—

" Eryr Eli gorthrymed heno,
Dyffrynt Meisir mygedawg
Dir Brochwael ; hir rygodded."
(The eagle of Eli let him oppress this night
The valley of Meisir, the celebrated
Land of Brochwael ; long has it been afflicted.)

" The valley of Meisir," her patrimony, is said to be identical with Maesbury, near Oswestry, and her palace gave name to the Township now called by the Welsh *Llys Feisir*. There is also an old mansion in Berriew parish called *Bryncaemeisir*.

MELANGELL (*St. Monacella*), a virgin saint, daughter of Tudwal ab Ceredic, by Ethni the Irishwoman, who flourished about the beginning of the seventh century. Her legend relates that her father, who is there stated to have been an Irish monarch, but who was probably a prince of. the Strathclyde Britons, had determined to marry her to a nobleman of his court, but that she having vowed celibacy fled from her father's dominions and took refuge among the hills in Pennant, called after her Pennant Melangell, Montgomeryshire, where she lived fifteen years without seeing the face of man. Brochwel Ysgythrog, prince of Powys, being one day in 604 hare hunting in that neighbourhood, pursued his game till he came to a great thicket, where he was amazed to find a virgin of surpassing beauty engaged in deep devotion with the hare he had been pursuing under her robes boldly facing the dogs, who had retired to a distance howling, notwithstanding all his efforts to make them seize their prey. Brochwel having heard her story, gave to God and her a parcel of land to be a sanctuary to all who fled there, and he desired her to found an abbey on the spot. She did so and died an abbess, having passed her solitary life for 37 years in the same place, where also she was buried. Her hard bed is still shewn in the cleft of a rock. From the above incident the hares of the district were placed under her protection, and were called *Wyn Melangell* (St. Monacella's lambs), and so strong a superstition prevailed, it is said, until the early part of the last century that no person would kill a hare in the parish, and when a hare was pursued by dogs it was firmly believed that if any one cried *Duw a Melangell a'th gadwo* (God and Melangell preserve thee), it was sure to escape. Her festival is May 27th.

MEREDYDD AB BLEDDYN, prince of Powys, succeeded his father Bleddyn ab Cynfyn as such in 1072. In the year 1101 Robert de Belesme, Arnulph Earl of Pembroke and Iorwerth, Cadwgan, and Meredvdd (Bleddyn ab Cynfyn's three sons) rebelled against the king of England, Henry I. The following year, however, Iorwerth made his peace privately with the king, and betrayed his brother Meredydd, who was taken and cast into the king's prison, where he remained four years. He then broke out of prison, " and came home, and gat his owne " inheritance againe, and enioied it quietlie." He also obtained possession of the territories of his brothers Iorwerth and Cadwgan, both of whom were slain in 1109—the one at Caereinion, the other at Welshpool. In 1118 the king invaded Wales, when Meredydd defended the passes into Powys with great ability and success, and the king himself narrowly escaped with his life. Peace was afterwards made between them. Meredydd was a prince of undoubted abilities, but his ambition to re-unite under his own rule the various divisions of Powys led him to commit or sanction many acts of cruelty even towards his nearest relatives. He was twice married—first to Hunydd, the daughter of Eunydd ab Gwernwy, by whom he had several children; secondly, to Eva, daughter of Bledrws ab Ednowain, and granddaughter of Ednowain Bendew, by whom he had a son named Iorwerth Goch, who was father to Sir Gruffydd Vychan, lord of Criggion and Burgedin. With regard to the time of his death, various dates are mentioned. "Brut y Tywysogion" gives 1124 as the date, adding that he died "in his old age, a thing not often "witnessed in the family of Bleddyn ab Cynfyn." "Brut y "Saeson" and another copy of "Brut y Tywysogion" give the date as 1129, and the latter speaks of the death of Meredydd, "the ornament and safety of all Powys, and its defence, after "taking upon his body salutary-penance, and in his spirit pure "repentance and the communion of the body of Christ and oil "and fasting." Powel, however, gives the date as 1133, speaking of Meredydd as "the greatest lord and cheefest man in "Powys, as he that had gotten his brethren and nephews lands "by hooke and by crooke into his owne hands." Upon his death, Powys was again divided between his eldest son Madog (whose share was thenceforth called Powys Fadog) and his grandson Owain Cyfeiliog, whose moiety descended to his son Gwenwynwyn, and was from him called Powys Wenwynwyn. His arms were *Or* a lion's gamb in bend *Gules*, armed *Sable* and erased.

MEREDYDD AB ROTPERT, lord of Cedewain, a descendant of Tegonwy ab Teon, was a chieftain of power and note during the struggles of Llewelyn ab Iorwerth (Llewelyn the Great) for the liberty of his country. He resided chiefly at Dolforwyn Castle. In 1211 his name appears among the list of Welsh chieftains who opposed the invading army of King John. In 1223, during the minority of Henry III., the castle of Kinnerley, Salop, having been ransacked and demolished by Llewelyn's forces, Llewelyn afterwards engaged upon his corporal oath to make satisfaction for the damage then done, Meredydd ab Rotpert being his surety for the performance of the treaty. According to Lewys Dwn, Meredydd was a "nephew" (more properly a cousin's son) of the Welsh prince who gave him the lordship of Cedewain, which upon his death without an heir again reverted to Llewelyn, but this latter statement is clearly wrong. Llewelyn died in 1240, while we find Meredydd in 1241 doing homage for his lordship to Henry III.,

M

who confirmed him in it. "Brut y Tywysogion" alleges that Henry gave him the lordship as a reward for his treachery to prince Llewelyn by doing homage to himself at Shrewsbury. In the same year, 1241, he was one of the intercessors with the king for the release of Gruffydd ab Llewelyn from his brother prince David's custody. He was a great benefactor of the Nunnery of Llanllugan, to which he gave considerable lands by a Charter still extant. It was probably he also who gave to the abbey of Strata Florida extensive lands at Court, Brynderwen, and other places near Dolforwyn, which the monks of that abbey long held. Meredydd ab Rotpert, "the chief counsellor "of Wales," took the religious habit at Strata Florida Abbey, and died and was buried there in 1244. He married Eva, daughter of Meredydd Fychan, of Abertanad, and Lucy his wife, by whom he had five sons and several daughters. . His arms were *Argent*, a lion salient *Sable*, crowned *Or*, armed and langued *Gules*.

MEREDITH, REV. BENJAMIN, a popular Nonconformist minister, ordained at Llanbrynmair in 1733 as pastor of the Independent Church there, but who, the following year, was requested to resign his charge because his views concerning several important doctrines were not considered orthodox. He was succeeded by the celebrated Lewis Rees. He translated into Welsh Bunyan's *Jerusalem Sinner Saved*, and the translation was published at Hereford in 1721, and subsequently in 1765 at Chester.

MEREDITH, LEWIS (*Lewys Glyn Dyfi*), was the youngest of seven children of Thomas and Jane Meredith, and was born on the 22nd March, 1828, at Ffridd Factory, near Machynlleth, where his father carried on business as a flannel manufacturer in a small way. About 1840 his parents removed to Cwmllinau Factory, Cemmes. When he was only 13 years of age he joined the Wesleyan Methodist Society, and before he was 20 he commenced to preach with that Connexion. About the same time he began to contribute poetry to the *Cronicl*, *Eurgrawn Wesleyaidd*, and *Traethodydd*, some of his compositions evincing much taste and true poetic feeling. His thirst for knowledge was very great, and he read with avidity, and thoroughly mastered the best literature that he could get hold of. A spinal complaint confined him to his bed for some years, during which he whiled away the time partly in storing his mind with such literary riches as lay within his reach, and partly in the composition of poetry. In 1852 he published by subscription a small volume of poetry under the title *Blodau Glyn Dyfi*, produced during his long and wearisome illness On his recovery he sought for admission to the Wesleyan ministry—the great object of his ambition—but by this time he had passed the limited age according to the rules of the Conference, and his application failed. This was a heavy blow to him, and a disappointment which he very keenly felt. After this he laboured for two or three years as a missionary among his countrymen at Witton Park, Durham, and subsequently emigrated to America, where he was soon afterwards admitted to the ministry by the Black River Conference of Episcopal Methodists. In 1869 he removed to the Rock River Conference, and acquired much popularity as a preacher. In 1887 he undertook the charge of the Welsh Wesleyan cause at Chicago. He was a frequent contributor to American Welsh periodicals, and was the author of several essays and tracts on theological subjects. His poetry is marked by a love and a knowledge of nature which strongly remind one of Wordsworth, and by a purity of diction and chasteness of expression too rarely met with. His health was always delicate, and ultimately consumption took a strong hold of his weak frame. After long languishing, he died at Oak Park, Chicago, on the 29th September, 1891, aged 63 years.

MEREDITH, RICHARD (*Caradog*), an elder brother of the above-named Lewis Meredith, was born about the year 1826, and was a young man of great promise. He also was a local preacher with the Wesleyan Methodists, and wrote several able articles for the *Traethodydd* and other periodicals, as well as some poetry. He died at Cwmllinau, Cemmes, in the summer of 1856, about 30 years of age.

MEREDITH, THOMAS, of Coedyrhos, Mochdre, was one of the earliest in Montgomeryshire to join the great Methodist movement, and about the year 1745 was appointed an exhorter and superintendent over some of the small societies in the neighbourhood of his home. He was a man of great zeal and courage, and in attempting, with Mr. Evan Roberts, of Bronllan (the writer's great-grandfather), to put down the riotous licentiousness and immorality which then prevailed in Mochdre, he met with a good deal of ill-usage, and on more than one occasion, it is said, barely escaped with his life. When the unhappy differences arose between Howell Harries and Daniel Rowlands, the two Methodist leaders, which led to their separation, Meredith adhered to the former, and went to Trefecca, as many others of his followers did, to live with him. How long he remained there is not stated, but during his stay there he adopted mystical and Antinomian views, and with a number of others seceded under the leadership of one Thomas Sheen. On his return into Montgomeryshire he attempted to win converts to his views, and in some measure succeeded. With that object in view he published in 1770 *The Scourge for the Assyrian the great oppressor, according to the slaughter of Midian* a work by the Rev. William Erbury, together with letters of Erbury and Morgan Llwyd, and a poem by John Cennick. The same year he also published a small work of his own :—*Some Observations on passages of Scripture, and Letters.* The religious views of his latter years paralysed his own spirit, and greatly weakened his influence among his neighbours.

MILLS, EDWARD, was the eldest son of Edward and Mary Mills, of Llanidloes, where he was born in the year 1802. In his earlier years he was of an unsettled disposition, but after his marriage he applied himself to study, and, being possessed of considerable natural abilities, he acquired a very fair knowledge of several of the sciences, more particularly of astronomy and geography. He constructed an *Orrery*, with which he travelled through various parts of Wales, illustrating by its means lectures delivered by him on his favourite science. He also published an excellent work, Y *Darluniadur Anianyddol* (The Illustrator of Science), being an exposition of the principles of Astronomy, Geography, Geology, &c., an octavo volume of 254 pages, with eighty illustrations all engraved on wood by himself and his son. The last fifteen years of his life were spent at Denbigh. He died in 1865, aged 63 years.

MILLS, Rev. JOHN, F.R.G.S., F.R.A.S., &c., was the youngest of five children of Edward and Mary Mills, of Llanidloes, where he was born on the 19th December, 1812. His father carried on, in a small way, the business of a flannel manufacturer, and the subject of this notice, after receiving such school instruction as was then available at Llanidloes, was in his fourteenth year placed to work at the loom. Such, however, was his thirst for learning, that in order to gratify it he contrived a frame which he attached to his loom to hold a book so that he might read at the same time that he plied the shuttle, and another to serve him during his wakeful moments in bed. He was wonderfully industrious, seldom allowing himself, at this period of his life, more than three hours' sleep. Without any assistance he made considerable progress with the study of Hebrew and Greek. In 1838 he made his first appearance as an author with *Grammadeg Cerddoriaeth* (a Grammar of Music), a work which has done more probably to promote a knowledge of music in Wales than any other. The same year also he married, in May, Miss Lewis, of Llanidloes, and in the following October he made his first appearance as a preacher with the Calvinistic Methodists. He also took a leading part in the Temperance movement then lately begun. In 1839 he wrote and published the first edition of *Hyfforddwr yr Efrydydd* (The Student's Guide)—partly founded upon Todd's work of that names), and in 1840 Y *Geirlyfr Ysgrythyrol* (Scripture Dictionary. In August, 1841, he removed to Ruthin, where in 1843, in addition to his many other labours, he wrote and published Y *Perl Ysgrythyrol* (The Scriptural Pearl), and in 1845 undertook the editorship of Y *Beirniadur Cymreig* (the Welsh Critic)—an ably-conducted periodical then published at St. Asaph. In 1846, assisted by his brother, Richard Mills, he published Y *Cerddor Eglwysig* (The Church Musician) ; in 1848 *Elfenau Cerddoriaeth* (The Elements of Music) ; and in 1851 Y *Canor* (The

Singer). In December, 1846, he left Ruthin for London to labour as a missionary among the Jews under the auspices of the Missionary Society of his own denomination. In that capacity his prudence, discretion, patience, and gentlemanly bearing, together with his determined perseverance, obtained for him admission into the most exclusive Jewish circles, and did much at any rate to break down and diminish Jewish prejudice. In 1847 he published *Y Salmydd Eglwysig* (The Church Psalmist), and in 1849 *a Lecture on Welsh Music* delivered in Crosby Hall. He was ordained at Carnarvon in 1848 to the full work of the ministry. In 1852 he published *Iuddewon Prydain* (The British Jews), which appeared also in English in an enlarged form in 1853, and is still regarded as a work of high authority. Mr. Mills paid two visits to the Holy Land— the first in 1855, an account of which he published in 1858, under the title *Palestina*; the second in 1859—60. Soon after his first visit he resigned his position as a missionary, but never ceased during the remainder of his life to take great interest in the work. In 1861 he published *Daearyddiaeth Ysgrythyrol* (Scripture Geography). During his second visit to Palestine he spent several months at Nablous in investigating the history and religious rites of the Samaritans. The result he embodied in a work of great ability, entitled *Nablûs, and an Account of the Modern Samaritans* (London, 1864). He also succeeded in establishing a Mission to the Arabs of Palestine, under whose auspices his friend and pupil Yohannah El Karey became a Christian missionary to his own people. The remaining years of his life were spent in London in the discharge of ministerial duties, and in active literary work and researches. Besides contributing several articles to the *Traethodydd* Welsh Quarterly, and other periodicals, and to the *Gwyddoniadur* (Encyclopædia Cambrensis) he wrote seventeen articles for Cassell's *Bible Dictionary*, eleven to Dr. Fairbairn's *Imperial Bible Dictionary*, and several to the *Journal of Sacred Literature*. He also published in 1872 a lecture on the State Church and the Bible under the title Yr *Eglwys Wladol a'r Bibl*. In his younger days he shewed considerable skill in versification according to the rules of Welsh prosody. His poetical efforts appeared for the most part under the feigned name *Ieuan Glan Alarch*. Had he persevered in this line he would doubtless have made his mark and attained a high position among Welsh poets. His literary labours obtained for him a distinguished position among the *savants* of the metropolis. He became a Fellow of the Royal Asiatic Society, and of the Royal Geographical Society, and was also the honorary secretary of the Anglo-Biblical Institute. Thus he was brought into correspondence and communication with many of the profoundest and most eminent scholars of his day, among whom also he himself occupied a very high position as one of the best Biblical scholars. It may be said of him that he was in every respect a refined Christian gentleman, and that he left behind him a noble example. He died in London, after a lingering illness, July 28th, 1873, in his 61st year. His London friends erected a handsome monument over his grave, with the following inscription :—" In memory of the Reverend John Mills. " F.R.G.S. Born 19th Dec., 1812. Died 28th July, 1873. " His heart's desire and prayer to God for Israel was that they " might be saved. He laboured as pastor of the Welsh Church " in Nassau Street for 15 years. He was dearly beloved and " very highly esteemed as a man, as a Christian, and as a " Minister of the Gospel. He died as he had lived, in faith, " hope and love. Felly y rhydd Efe hun i'w anwylyd."

MILLS, RICHARD, was a son of Henry Mills, of Tynewydd, near Llanidloes, by his second wife, and was born in March, 1809. From early youth he displayed a considerable share of musical talent, and before he was sixteen years old composed several psalm tunes of sufficient merit to gain admission into the columns of *Seren Gomer*. He subsequently composed many anthems and congregational tunes, which are still and probably for a long time will continue to be popular in Wales, the best known among them being " Duw sydd Noddfa," " Ai gwir yw?" " Fy anwyl fam fy hunan," " Pwy yw ? " " Heber," &c. Some of these were prize compositions. He was also a successful competitor and gained two prizes at the Cymreigyddion Eisteddfod at Llanidloes in 18??, one being for an Essay on *Llythyreg yr Iaith Gymraeg* (Welsh Orthography); the other an *Elegy on the Death of Dr. Owen Pughe.* These, with another short essay on *Dyledswydd y Cymry i goleddu eu Hiaith* (The duty of the Welsh people to foster their language), were published in 1838. He was also the author or compiler of the following works —*Caniadau Seion*, sef Casgliad o Donau ac Anthemau at wasanaeth Crefydd (Songs of Zion : a Collection of Tunes and Anthems for the service of religion) 1840 ; *Arweinydd Cerddorol*, Rhan I, sef Gwerslyfr ar Gerddoriaeth (Guide to Music, Part I, a Lesson Book of Singing), 1840 to 1842 ; *Arweinydd Cerddorol*, Rhan II, yn cynnwys Tonau ac Anthemau Crefyddol a Moesol (Guide to Music, Part II, consisting of Tunes and Anthems, Religious and Moral), 1843 ; *Arweinydd Cerddorol*, Rhan III (Guide to Music, Part III), 1845. The author died before completing this last work, which was of a miscellaneous character, like Part II, and it was brought out through the Press by his nephews, the Rev. John Mills and Mr. Richard Mills. By these works and by his personal services as a teacher of choral and congregational singing, Mr. Mills did more than probably any other man before his day to guide, elevate, and refine the musical taste of his countrymen. His services as a teacher were in great request far and near. While engaged in this work in Merionethshire in September, 1844, he was suddenly taken ill. He hurried home, but fell into a rapid consumption, and on Christmas Eve in the same year died at the early age of 35.

MORGAN AB CADWGAN, a son of Cadwgan, prince of Powys, a wild and ferocious character, who in 1122 slew his brother Meredydd with his own hands. For this atrocious deed he appears to have repented bitterly afterwards, and to expiate his crime "carried the Cross to Jerusalem." According to the British Chronicle, "after having a strong hand in the work of "killing, and pulling out of eyes, he took to himself his con- "science; and in his repentance went on a pilgrimage to "Jerusalem, and on his return he died at Cyprus in the Grecian "sea," in the year 1126.

MORGAN, Rev. DAVID, of Llanfyllin, a well-known Independent Minister, was a native of Cardiganshire. He was born at Dolwen in that county, December 27th, 1779, his father being a respectable freeholder. In his youth he was placed on trial in a shop at Machynlleth, but after six months' probation his aversion to trade was so great that the idea of bringing him up to it had to be given up, and he returned home to his parents. He remained there until he was about 26, when he married and took a farm in the same neighbourhood. His wife was Mary, eldest daughter of John Hughes, Esq., of Llwynglas, a County Magistrate. During his short stay at Machynlleth he had been brought under the influence of the Rev. John Roberts, of Llan-brynmair, which eventually led him to leave the Church of England, in which he had been brought up, and to join the Independents, in the year 1807. He was naturally gifted with great fluency of speech, readiness, and clearness of expression, gifts which his neighbours and fellow church members were not slow to discover, and at their earnest solicitation he was induced to enter the ministry. In 1813 he was ordained at Towyn as pastor of several churches in that district. The following year he accepted a call from the Independent Church at Machynlleth to become its pastor, and he laboured in that capacity with much ability and success for 22 years. He was the means of building five chapels in the immediate neighbourhood, and of adding 500 members to the churches under his care. His stipend during the whole time was only £30 a year. In 1836 he removed to Manchester to undertake the pastorate of the Welsh Independent Church there. Having held that office three years, he accepted an invitation to undertake a similar charge at Llanfyllin. He took up his residence in that town in 1839, remaining there 18 years, that is, until October, 1857, when old age and its infirm-ities compelled him to resign his charge. A small annuity having been secured for him through the exertions of a few of his numerous friends, he retired to Oswestry to spend his few remaining days. He was not destined, however, long to enjoy his well earned rest, for in three weeks time after his removal to Oswestry, namely on the 14th June, 1858, he died, and on the 18th of the same month he was buried in the burial ground of Pendre Independent Chapel, Llanfyllin. Mr. Morgan had a striking presence and was an excellent preacher. His sermons displayed much ability, but his delivery was rapid and monotonous—a defect which prevented his attaining very great popularity. He was intensely Nonconformist in principle, and a sturdy advocate of religious equality, a great reader, a hard student, and an incessant writer, as well as a hard working pastor. He was for years in the habit of getting up to his studies at three o'clock in the morning. His principal works are:—1, *Hanes yr Eglwys Gristionogol*, (History of the Christian Church) 2 vols., 1830 ; 2, *Dyledswydd yr Eglwysi at eu Gweinidogion yn cael ei ystyried mewn pregeth*, (The duty of churches to their ministers, considered in a sermon), 1830 ; 3, *Pregeth ar Ymneilldduaeth* (A Sermon on Dissent) ; 4, *Traethawd ar Ymneilldduaeth* (An Essay on Dissent), 1835 ; 5, *Pregeth ar Ddiwygiad Crefyddol*, (A sermon on religious revivals) ; 6, *Hanes Ymneilldduaeth*, (History of Nonconformity), 1855, not completed ; 7, *Darlithiau ar Lyfr y Datguddiad*, (Lectures on the Book of Revelation), and 8, *Cyflwr gwreiddiol, cwymp, a chynyrchiolaeth Adda*, (Adam's original state, fall, and representative character). All these works displayed no less the clear and acute intellect than the great research and industry of their author. He also wrote a great deal for the *Dysgedydd* and other magazines.

MORGAN, Rev. EDWARD, of Dyffryn, Merionethshire, an eminent minister with the Welsh Calvinistic Methodists, was the son of Edward and Elizabeth Morgan, and was born at a small hamlet called Pentre, near Llanidloes, on the 20th September, 1817. He was one of a family of eleven children, his father being a small farmer and flannel manufacturer, who in 1829 removed to Llanidloes, where in addition to the manufacturing business he opened a retail shop. His mother died in May, 1831. About this time he joined the Cymreigyddion Society at Llanidloes, which no doubt gave an impulse to his literary tastes and aspirations. He had but little schooling, but an ardent desire for knowledge was kindled within him, to gratify which he made the best use of every means and opportunity. He served an apprenticeship to the drapery business with his brother, and was for some time afterwards an assistant with Mr. E. Cleaton. During this time it was his habit to sit up until two o'clock in the morning or later to study such books as came within his reach. When about 18 years of age he made his first appearance as a public speaker on behalf of total abstinence, and his talents were speedily recognized. In 1839 he entered the College at Bala in order to qualify himself for the ministry with the Calvinistic Methodists, but only remained there a few months, leaving Bala to undertake a day school as Dyffryn. Here towards the close of 1840 he began to preach, and early in 1842 he returned again to Bala, which the following year he left again to resume his scholastic duties at Dyffryn. About the beginning of 1846 he studied theology for a few months at New College, Edinburgh, then conducted by Dr.

Chalmers and other eminent professors. He was fully ordained as a minister at Bala in 1847, and soon afterwards undertook the pastoral care of a church at Dolgelley. On the 19th July, 1849, he married Janet, daughter of the Rev. Richard Humphreys, of Dyffryn, where soon afterwards he took up his residence. From July, 1854, to December, 1856, he edited with considerable ability and taste a small Magazine called *Y Methodist*. Mr. Morgan's talents as a preacher, and his tact, energy, and administrative ability, soon won for him great influence and a leading position in the denomination to which he belonged. In 1870, his brethren by electing him Moderator of their General Assembly, conferred upon him the highest honour within their power. Although endowed with a weakly frame and a very fragile constitution, and for the last sixteen years of his life a great sufferer from bronchial affections, Mr. Morgan in addition to his pastoral labours undertook and brought to a successful issue undertakings before which many stronger men might well have quailed. About the end of 1856 he undertook the collection of an Endowment Fund of £20,000 for the denominational College for North Wales at Bala. In this he succeeded so well that at the end of five years the Fund amounted to £26,000, in addition to which he subsequently collected £7,000 more towards the Building Fund of the new College, which was completed and opened in 1867. In acknowledgment of these services he was presented with a well-deserved Testimonial of 220 guineas in money, and a handsome tea and coffee service of the value of 50 guineas. Mr. Morgan also took a very active part in his own county in the political struggles of his day, which ended in the return of a Liberal Member for Merionethshire—a result which probably he, by his eloquence and personal influence, did as much at least as any single individual to accomplish. His active and laborious life was brought to a close in his 54th year, on the 9th May, 1871, and on the 16th of the same month he was interred in the burial ground attached to Horeb Chapel, Dyffryn, his funeral being, it is said, the largest ever seen in Merionethshire. His wife and eight children survived him. Since his death two volumes of his *Sermons* have been published, characterised by purity of diction, chasteness of expression, glowing eloquence and great fervour of feeling, and many of them displaying considerable depth and originality of thought.

MORGAN, The Ven. HUGH, M.A., was the second son of Hugh Morgan of Machynlleth, merchant, and Catherine his wife, and was born in the year 1826. Being destined for the church he entered Jesus College, Oxford, where in due time he took his Master's degree. He was ordained Deacon in 1849, and Priest in 1850. After serving one or two curacies he, in 1855, succeeded the Rev. Evan Evans, the well-known poet *Ieuan Glan Geirionydd*, as Incumbent of Rhyl, where he continued to labour up to the time of his death. As a parish clergyman he was very hard working and conscientious in the discharge of his duties. In consequence of the rapid growth of Rhyl, it became necessary to provide additional Church accommodation, chiefly for its English inhabitants. This Mr. Morgan set about doing with great zeal, and owing principally to his exertions St. Thomas's Church, a handsome edifice in a central position, was built at a cost of upwards of £13,000. Mr. Morgan and his wife contributed themselves upwards of £1,500 of this. Mr. Morgan also succeeded in getting the National School greatly enlarged and improved in 1857, at a cost of over £1,000. Trinity Church in the same town was also enlarged and improved in 1869, and an organ was set up in it with the following inscription :—" Rhodd Hugh Morgan. Ficer Rhyl, mewn diolchus " gôf am garedigrwydd ei gyfeillion, pan ar feddwl ymadael i " blwyf Llanrwst. Nadolig, 1867," (The gift of Hugh Morgan, vicar of Rhyl, in grateful remembrance of the kindness of his friends when he thought of leaving for the parish of Llanrwst. Christmas, 1867.) This refers to an offer made to him by the Bishop of the valuable living of Llanrwst, worth over £900 per annum, whereas Rhyl at that time was not worth £200 a year. Mr. Morgan, greatly to his honour, declined the offer, preferring to continue at work where his labours were so useful and so highly appreciated. In 1877 he was appointed Canon and Archdeacon of St. Asaph, honours he was not permitted to enjoy long. He died at the Canonry, St. Asaph, June 8th, 1878, aged 52 years.

MORGAN, JENKIN, though neither a native of Montgomeryshire, nor for long resident within the County, deserves honourable mention among its Worthies, for it was he who established, and in Montgomeryshire, the first Sunday School in Wales. He was a native of Cardiganshire, and was master of one of Madam Bevan's circulating day schools, and also a lay preacher with the Calvinistic Methodists. For a time he kept school at Tynyfron, near Crowlwm, Llanidloes, where Mr. Owen Brown then resided, but as none but children could attend he determined to establish a night school on Wednesdays for the benefit of grown up persons. This proved so great a success—that shortly afterwards he determined to open a school also on *Sunday* afternoon or evening. This step greatly increased the popularity of his school, and multitudes flocked to it from distances of five miles and more, and in all sorts of weather. Besides the Bible, it appears that Vicar Pritchard's *Canwyll y Cymry* (the Welshman's candle), was also used as a text book. This was in the year 1769, being at least 12 or 13 years before the establishment of Sabbath Schools at Gloucester by Mr. Raikes. It was the same Jenkin Morgan, I believe, who 29 years before was the means of introducing Methodism in the neighbourhood of Bala, and stood by Howell Harries, and shared his ill-treatment by the mob in that town when Harries barely escaped with his life.

MORGAN, Rev. JOHN, M.A., rector of Matchin, Essex, was the author of *Myfyrdodau ar y Pedwar Peth diweddaf, sef Angeu; Barn, Nef ac Uffern,* (Meditations on the four last things, death, judgment, heaven, hell). The author had been curate at Llanfyllin, and as a token of his esteem the preface, which is dated Matchin, May 6th, 1714, is addressed to the inhabitants of Llanfyllin. Five or six editions appeared in the course of the last century.

MORGAN, JOHN BICKERTON, F.G.S., was the son of Mr. Arthur J. Morgan, of Welshpool, and was born on the 26th of June, 1859. He at an early age evinced a fondness for the study of geology, and took the first prize for Collections of Fossils at the Cardiff Eisteddfod in 1883, and at the Carnarvon Eisteddfod in 1886. In 1887 he became Assistant Curator of the Powysland Museum at Welshpool, and re-arranged and labelled the geological specimens there. An interesting article from his pen on *The Land and Freshwater Shells of Montgomeryshire* appeared in the *Mont. Coll.* for 1887 and 1888. In 1889 he was elected a Fellow of the Geological Society, and the following year he read a paper on *"he Geology of the District"* before the British Association at Leeds. In 1892 he obtained a free studentship at the Royal College of Science, London, where he distinguished himself by his close application to study. In the examinations at the close of the Session he took the first place, and was awarded the Murchison medal and prize. He was subsequently elected demonstrator of geology for elementary teachers, also a member of the Council of the Glacialists' Association, and a member of the Geologists' Association and of the Conchological Society. But his incessant labours and devotion to his work proved too much for his constitution, and his health gave way. In the winter of 1893-4 he went to the Isle of Wight in the hope of re-establishing his health, but it was of no avail. He died at Ventnor on the 8th of March, 1894, in his 35th year. Thus terminated all too early a career of much promise.

MORGAN, The Right Rev. ROBERT, D.D., an eminent Bishop of Bangor, was born in 1608 at Fronfraith, in the parish of Llandyssil. He was the third son of Richard Morgan, of that place (who represented Montgomery in Parliament in 1592-93), by his wife Margaret, daughter of Thomas Lloyd, of Gwernybuarth, in the same parish. He received his school education under Mr. Lloyd, the father of Archdeacon Simon Lloyd, who lived near, and was afterwards admitted to Jesus College, Cambridge, where in due course he graduated M.A. On the elevation of Dr. Dolben to the see of Bangor, he became his chaplain, and was by him promoted first to the vicarage of Llanwnog, in 1632, and then to the rectory of Llangynhafal, Denbighshire. Upon the death of Bishop Dolben he returned to Cambridge, and settled at St. John's College, where he took

the degree of B.D. Upon the promotion of Dr. William
Roberts in 1637 to the bishopric of Bangor, he returned to
Wales as his chaplain, and received from him the vicarage of
Llanfair Dyffryn Clwyd. He resigned Llangynhafal, and in
1642 was instituted to Trefdraeth, Anglesey. The same year he
resigned Llanfair, and was instituted to Llanddyfnan, Anglesey
—a living then worth only £38 per annum, the tithes having
been leased for 99 years to the Bulkeleys of Baron Hill prior to
the Statute of Limitation. Mr. Morgan, at a cost of about
£300, bought out the remainder of the term, being about 15
years, and this enabled him to keep this preferment, when he
was deprived of his other livings, during the Commonwealth ;
and he subsequently left it to the Church free of charge. He
suffered much during the Civil War and the Commonwealth,
and resided chiefly at Henblas, in Anglesey. On the Restoration of Charles II. he was restored to his preferments, made
archdeacon of Merioneth, and obtained the degree of D.D. In
July of the same year (1660) he was made comportioner of
Llandinam. Upon the death of Dr. Robert Price, he was
elected Bishop of Bangor, and consecrated July 1st, 1666. On the
death of Archdeacon Mostyn, of Bangor, in 1672, he took that
archdeaconry *in commendam*, and secured it in the same manner
for his successor, who so enjoyed it, and had it annexed to the
bishopric by Act of Parliament. He performed the sacred
duties of his office with exemplary diligence and conscientiousness. He died September 1, 1673, and was buried in the
Cathedral, on the south side of the altar, in the grave of Bishop
Robinson. He married Anne, daughter and heir of the Rev.
William Lloyd, rector of Llanelian, Anglesey (uncle of Dr.
William Lloyd, Bishop of St. Asaph), by whom he had four
sons and four daughters. He did much to improve and repair
the interior of the cathedral, and, with some assistance from the
neighbouring gentry, furnished it with an excellent organ. He
had written several compositions for publication, which he left
behind him, but because, as he said, they were ill transcribed,
he forbade them to be published. It is said of him that " he
" was a man of great prudence in business, good learning, and
" eloquence in preaching, both in the English and in his native
" tongue, and he perfectly spent and wore himself away by his
" constant preaching." There is a portrait of Bishop Morgan
at Cefn, near St. Asaph.

MORGAN, The Right Rev. WILLIAM, D.D., bishop of
Llandaff and St. Asaph successively, and to whom as the first
translator of the Bible into Welsh we owe an eternal debt of
gratitude, was the son of John and Lowry Morgan, of Tymawr,
Gwybernant, in the parish of Penmachno, Carnarvonshire, where
he was born in the year 1541. Descent is claimed for him from
no less than three noble tribes in Wales. It is said that he was
taught as a boy by a papist refugee of distinguished learning.
Subsequently, through the influence of the Wynn family, of

Gwydir, he entered as sub-sizar St. John's College, Cambridge, February 26th, 1564-5 and proper sizar June 9th, 1565, and took his B.A. degree in 1567-8, his M.A. in 1571, B.D. in 1578, and D.D. in 1583. He was Vicar of Welshpool from 1575 to 1578, when he obtained the Vicarage of Llanrhaiadr yn Mochnant, which he held for ten years. It was during this period that he undertook and completed his great work—the translation of the Bible into Welsh—at the urgent request, it is said, of Archbishop Whitgift, who had a high opinion of his attainments and qualifications for the task, and who, it is said, appointed him as one of his chaplains. His moral character was unblemished (which, unfortunately, was the exception not the rule among the Welsh clergy of those days), and Strype, in his *Annals*, records that in 1587 Dr. Morgan was one of the only *three* clergymen in the diocese of St. Asaph who resided upon their livings, the others being Dr. Powell of Ruabon, and the clergyman of Llanfechain, an old man of about eighty years old. Dr. Morgan completed his translation of the Bible and presented a printed copy of it to Queen Elizabeth in 1588. In 1579 he obtained the Rectory of Llanfyllin, which he held till 1601; and in 1588 the sinecure rectory of Pennant Melangell, which he held till 1595. In 1594 he also obtained the sinecure rectory of Denbigh, which he held until 1596. On the 30th June 1595, at the express command of Queen Elizabeth, he was elected Bishop of Llandaff, and was consecrated on the 20th July following. On the 21st July, 1601, he was translated to the see of St. Asaph. He died at St. Asaph on the 10th September, 1604, at the age of about 63 years, and was buried the following day in the Cathedral. He shewed an independence of spirit, and a conscientiousness and high regard for the interests of the church, during his brief episcopal career, that were as highly creditable to him as they were rare in those days, as appears from his correspondence with Sir John Wynn, of Gwydir, published in Yorke's *Royal Tribes of Wales*. His life was indeed one of great devotion, pious study, and marvellous industry and perseverance—the great object of it being to provide the whole Word of God for the Welsh people in their own tongue. Before his translation was issued there was no complete Bible in Welsh, nor was there any provision in the church service for any of the Old Testament being read, except a few fragments connected with the Sacraments. Salesbury's New Testament had, it is true, been published twenty-one years before, but its idiom was so stiff, and so many obscure and little-used words were embodied in the text, that it was found necessary to append a glossary to it. The Welsh people were accordingly, as might have been expected in the absence of the Bible in " a language understanded of the people," sunk in gross moral, and spiritual darkness, and the importance of the work accomplished by Dr. Morgan can hardly be over-estimated. His translation was printed by the Deputies of Christopher Barker, in London, and Dr. Morgan resided in the metropolis for a year, while he was superintending its printing. It is a small folio of 555 leaves, printed in black letter, and perfect copies are extremely scarce. He also published in Welsh a *Sermon at the Funeral of Sir Yevan Lloyd, Knt.* (1587); and *The Psalms of David* (4to. 1588), and he had also revised and again corrected his version of the New Testament, which was ready for the press, when he died. Sir John Wynn states that " he repaired and slated the chancel of the Cathedral " Church of St. Asaph, which was a great ruin. He died a poor " man. He was a good scholar, both a Grecian and Hebrician," Two years ago a handsome monument was unveiled at St. Asaph to the memory of this " incomparable man for piety and industry, " zeal for religion and his country, and a conscientious care of " his church and succession." A stained glass window has also been put up in the parish church of Penmachno to perpetuate his memory.

MORRIS, DAVID (*Bardd Einion*), was born at Tanybryn, Llanfair Caereinion, about the year 1792, and lived there all his life. He was originally a weaver, but during the latter years of his life a gardener by occupation. He was well versed in Welsh history and poetry, and could recite from memory from beginning to end some of the masterpieces of Goronwy Owen, Dewi Wyn, and other poets. He also attained some excellence as a composer of *Englynion*. At an Eisteddfod held at Llanfair on Christmas Day, 1856, he recited many of these, and to him, out of more than forty competitors, was awarded the prize for the best *Englyn i'r Gwynt*. It is as follows :—

> " Organ Ior yn telori—yw y gwynt,
>   Per gantor y llwyni;
> Awel rwydd yn ail roddi
> Bywyd a nawdd i'n byd ni."

Caledfryn, the adjudicator, objected to the use of the term " organ," and suggested that " nerth " instead of " nawdd " in the last line would have been an improvement. The Rev, Walter Davies (*Gwallter Mechain*) and Mr. Robert Jones (*Bardd Mawddach*) assisted him in his earlier attempts by correcting his compositions He was of a taciturn and reserved disposition. His only daughter went to America many years ago. The death of a grand-daughter who lived with him troubled him much, and it is supposed hastened his own, which took place April 10th, 1868. He was then 75 years of age.

MORRIS, EDWARD ROWLEY, F.S.A., was the eldest son of Edward Rowley Morris and Eleanor his wife, and was born at New Hall, Kerry, on the 22nd of April, 1828. He was originally intended by his parents for the Church, and received his early education partly at the Collegiate Institution, Liverpool, and partly under private tuition. In 1846, at the age of 18, he was studying at Capel Curig with his cousin, the incumbent of Bettws-y-coed, and the Bishop of Bangor held a confirmation in Welsh in the old Capel Curig Church, at which he was a candidate. After the service the Bishop, having noticed that he did not respond, asked him the reason why, to which he replied that he could not speak Welsh. He was thereupon confirmed the second time in English. In 1851 he went to America, but did not remain there long, and on his return he settled down to business at Newtown with his father as a woolstapler. About the year 1862 he became general manager of a Coal and Lime Company at Welshpool, where he resided for nearly ten years. In the early part of 1872 he removed to Newtown, where, on the Company going into liquidation, he carried on a similar business on his own account for some years. During this time he took a prominent part in the public affairs of the town ; he was a director of the Gas and Waterworks Companies, and for some time a member and Chairman of the Local Board. But he chiefly delighted in antiquarian researches. He was one of the earliest members of the Powysland Club, and one of the most valued contributors to its *Collections*, illustrative of the past history of Montgomeryshire. His principal contributions include a *History of Kerry* ; *Royalist Composition Papers* ; and summaries and notes on *Early Montgomeryshire Wills*, &c. In 1881 Mr. Rowley Morris removed to London, where proximity to the British Museum, the Record Office, the Probate Registry, Lambeth Library, &c., afforded him opportunities of which he fully availed himself to prosecute his favourite work, and thus he acquired an acquaintance with Montgomeryshire history which was perfectly unique. His familiarity with the vast stores of local information contained in the various London depositaries of public records, and his patience, skill and industry in transcribing or noting their contents were truly marvellous. Besides what has been already published, Mr. Rowley Morris left in manuscript a large mass of notes and transcripts from Gaol Files and other records, which has been secured by the Powysland Club for publication. He was also a constant contributor to *Byegones*, the well-known antiquarian publication, his communications being often of great interest and value But his labours were not confined to Montgomeryshire records alone. He transcribed for the Record Society of Lancashire and Cheshire the Royalist Composition papers for those two counties. A few weeks before his death he was elected a Fellow of the Society of Antiquaries. In 1857 Mr. Rowley Morris married Mary, daughter of Mr. Richard Morris, of the Bank, Pool Quay, by whom he had issue four sons and four daughters, five of whom survive. In the early part of 1893 he had a serious illness, from which he rallied for a time, but in July he suffered a relapse, and on the 24th of that month he died at his residence in London, at the age of 65. On the 28th he was buried at St. David's Churchyard, Newtown. By Mr. Rowley Morris's death Montgomeryshire archæology has sustained a loss which is well-nigh irreparable.

MORRIS, SHON THOMAS, or John ap Thomas ap Morris ap John, the Quaker, was a native of Llanwddyn. His father, Thomas ap Morris ap John, was a freeholder of good standing, whose name appears on the second Jury List at the Great Sessions held at Pool, 11th October, 43 Eliz. He was at an early age sent to school at Shrewsbury, where he made such progress that at twenty-one years of age he was said to be one of the best scholars in his native county. He, however, soon fell into habits of dissipation, and having heavily mortgaged his property, he went over to America, where some time afterwards he became the owner of some land in Pennsylvania. He had by this time joined the Quakers, and after his settlement in Pennsylvania he wrote and published an account of that sect in Montgomeryshire, where at that time its adherents were rather numerous. After an absence of about 30 years from his native land, he returned to Llanwddyn, where, having paid off the mortgage on his property, he settled down, and spent the remainder of his life in peace and happiness. An old couplet—

"Ai Shen Thomas Morris hunanol ei hunan
Yw'r garw foneddwr goreuaf ei gyfran."

is supposed to refer to the fact of his having never been married.

MORUS BERWYN, a poet, who flourished between 1560 and 1590, some of whose poems are said to be still preserved in manuscript.

MORYS AP DACIN AB PRYS TREVOR, of Bettws Cedewain, a poet and genealogist of the sixteenth century, named by Lewys Dwn among those works he had consulted. Many of his books and MSS. after his death came into the hands of Rhys Cain, of Oswestry, another distinguished genealogist.

MYLLIN, a British saint, whose date is uncertain, but who is classed by Rees (*Welsh Saints*) among those of the seventh century. He founded the church of Llanfyllin. His feast is June 17th.

MYTTON, RICHARD HERBERT, of Garth, Guilsfield, was the only son of the Rev. Richard Mytton, LL.B., of that place by Charlotte daughter of John Herbert, of Dolforgan. The Mytton family resided for several generations at Pont-is-Cowryd in the parish of Meifod—the first of the name who lived there being John, fourth son of Richard Mytton, of Halston. His descendant, Richard Mytton (Sheriff in 1674) by his wife Bridget, daughter of George Devereux, of Vaynor, left a son and heir Richard Mytton, who married Dorothy heiress of Brochwel Wynn, of Garth (of the line of Brochwel Ysgythrog), which thenceforth was preferred as the family mansion. The latter was Sheriff in 1730, and died in 1772, and the above named Rev. Richard Mytton was his great grandson. Mr. Mytton, the subject of this notice, was born on the 2nd December, 1808, and was educated at Eton and Haileybury College. On the 30th April 1827, he entered the Bengal Civil service. The following are the dates and particulars of his appointments in India during the subsequent 25 years:—1828, Extra Assistant to the Registrar of the Sudder Dewanny and Nizamut Adawlut. 1830, Registrar and Assistant to the Magistrate of Jessore. 1831, Officiating Judge of Jessore. 1831, July, Third Assistant to the Magistrate and Collector of Jessore. 1832, Acting Joint Magistrate of Baraset. 1833, Joint Magistrate and Deputy Collector of Baraset. 1835, Acting Magistrate and Collector of Nuddra. 1835, August, Magistrate and Collector of Sylhet. (In 1838, Mr Mytton came to England on furlough.) 1842, January, Magistrate of 24 Pergunnahs and Superintendent of Allipore Jail. 1849, Judge of Ditto. 1849, Commissioner of Revenue and Circuit Dacca Division. 1852, Officiating Judge of the Sudder and Nizamut Adawlut. The following year (1853) he retired on an Annuity and returned to England. Mr. Mytton was well acquainted with the native laws, usages, and customs, as well as with several of the languages of India, and discharged the judicial and other functions of the various important offices which he held with distinguished ability and credit. Upon his return to England he, in 1854, by virtue of a Deed of arrangement with his mother, took possession of the Garth estates, and thenceforth resided at Garth up to his death. He found the property heavily mortgaged, but was able before his death to pay off all the incumbrances. He was placed on the Commission of the Peace, and appointed a Deputy Lieutenant for Montgomeryshire, and in 1855 was elected Deputy Chairman of Quarter Sessions. The important judicial and administrative duties of this office he discharged with great zeal and ability for thirteen years, that is, until January Sessions 1868, when failing health compelled him to send in his resignation. Upon this occasion the following Resolution was passed by the Court :—

"Resolved that the Magistrates assembled in Quarter Sessions have received with great regret the communication made by Mr. Mytton, to the Chairman, that he is unable from the state of his health to continue to preside over the judicial business of the Court and the trial of prisoners, and that he consequently desires to resign the office of Vice-Chairman. That the Magistrates desire to express their sense of the advantage which the Court and the County have derived from Mr. Mytton's judicial experience and constant attention to the business of the County, and they trust that they may still have the benefit of his assistance as Chairman of the Police Committee."

Mr. Mytton also served the office of Sheriff in 1856. He married May 15th, 1830, Charlotte, third daughter of Major General Paul Macgregor, Auditor General of the Bengal army, by whom he had a large family. His eldest son and heir, Devereux Herbert Mytton, late Captain 85th Light Infantry, is Chairman of Quarter Sessions for Montgomeryshire, and of the Pool and Forden Highway Board, and served the office of Sheriff in 1873. Mr. Mytton died on the 12th May, 1869, in the 61st year of his

N

age, and was buried at Guilsfield Churchyard. His arms were : Quarterly : 1st and 4th per pale *azure* and *gules* an eagle displayed with two heads *or*, within a bordure engrailed of the last ; 2nd and 3rd *argent* a cinquefoil *azure*. Crest; a ram's head couped *argent*, horned *or*.

NAYLOR, JOHN, of Leighton Hall, was the second son of John Naylor, of Harford Hill, Cheshire, and Dorothy his wife, and was born in April, 1813. He was educated at Eton and Trinity College, Cambridge, and became head of the banking firm of Leyland and Bullen, Liverpool. In 1846, he married Georgina, daughter of John Edwards, Esq., of Ness Strange, Shropshire, by whom he had issue ten children. Having come into possession of considerable estates at Leighton and Kerry he, a few years after his marriage, took up his residence at Leighton, where he lived the remaining 40 years of his life. There he built a fine mansion, where he brought together a splendid collection of paintings and other works of art. He also erected a beautiful church and extensive model farm buildings, and carried out various other improvements on a large scale which in a few years quite transformed the appearance of the estate. He also expended large sums in the development and improvement of the Bryllywarch estate in Kerry. He was one of the promoters of the Oswestry and Newtown Railway in 1855, and subscribed £20,000 to that undertaking. He was also the principal subscriber to the short line of Railway some years afterwards made from Abermule to Kerry. Mr. Naylor was a Justice of the Peace and Deputy Lieutenant for Montgomeryshire, and served the office of Sheriff in 1853, but he took little part in public life. He died at Leighton Hall on the 13th July, 1889, and on the 17th of the same month was buried at Leighton Church.

NEWELL, RICHARD, was the son of a respectable farmer of that name, and Bridget his wife, and was born at Alltyffynnon, Aberhavesp, on the 23rd of March, 1785. From 1803 to 1831 he lived at the Old Hall Farm, Manafon. In February, 1811, he married Elizabeth Griffiths, of Cefndu, Guilsfield (a sister of the Rev. Evan Griffiths, Meifod), by whom he had nine children. For some years he was High Constable for the Berriew district, and in that capacity took energetic steps to put down interludes, Sunday wakes, and other forms of rowdyism, which at that time were prevalent in that neighbourhood. He prosecuted several of the ringleaders at the Quarter Sessions, and there was very soon a very marked increase of order and propriety throughout the district. In May, 1831, he removed to Meifod parish, living for some years successively at Plasbach and Cwm. He died at the latter place June the 22nd, 1852, aged 67 years. For the last 32 years of his life he preached with the Calvinistic Methodists. His abilities were small, but his great earnestness, zeal, and faithfulness on behalf of Sunday Schools, Temperance, tract distribution and catechising, and other good movements went far to compensate for his lack of talent. He was one of the earliest of the Calvinistic Methodists to labour among the English on the borders of Montgomeryshire. For the benefit of the young he for some years brought out a little Welsh publication, *Pethau Newydd a Hen neu Drysorfa i'r Ysgol Sabbothol*, (Things New and Old ; or a Treasury for the Sunday School, 1826, &c.)—probably the first of its kind in Welsh specially addressed to children and young persons.

OLIVER, ROBERT AB, was the third son of Oliver ab Thomas, of Neuaddwen, Llanerfyl, by Catherine, daughter of Morris ab Ieuan, of Llangedwyn. He lived at Cynhinfa, in the parish of Llangynyw, about the middle of the seventeenth century. During his residence there he built a stone bridge across the Owddyn (*Vyrnwy*), for the public convenience, which was named and is still called *Pont-Robert ab Oliver*, or shorter, *Pont-Robert*. That also is the name given to the adjacent hamlet. In 1670 his daughter Jane was married to Rees ab Evan, of Bryn Bwa, in the same neighbourhood. Dying without issue, their estates descended to a second niece, who married Owen Vaughan, of Llwydiarth, and through him came into the possession of the Wynnstay family.

OLIVERS, REV. THOMAS, was the son of Thomas Oliver and Penelope his wife, and was born at the village of Tregynon in the year 1725. He was baptized September 8th, in that year. His parents were respectable, and owned a small estate. His father died in December, 1728, and was buried at Tregynon on the 31st of that month, and his mother in the March following. He was then taken charge of by his father's uncle (a man of some property), who, at his death, left him a small fortune, and also placed him under the care of his grand-daughter, Elizabeth Tudor, who, being unmarried, committed him to the care of her father, Thomas Tudor, a large farmer in the parish of Forden. Here he was boarded and sent to a local school until he was 18 years of age, when he was bound apprentice. He was at this time of a particularly gay and lively disposition, fond of dancing and company, for in his *Autobiography* he states " that out of " sixteen nights and days, he was fifteen of them without ever " being in bed." Some years afterwards he went to Shrewsbury, where he lived for some time, and thence to Wrexham and other places. At Bristol he went to hear the celebrated Whitefield preaching, whose sermon he ever afterwards considered the means of his conversion. Thenceforth his whole demeanour and conduct were entirely changed. Leaving Bristol he went to Bradford in Wiltshire, where he joined the Wesleyan Methodist Society, and was admitted a lay preacher. When he had been a local preacher for about twelve months he had the small pox in its most virulent form. On his recovery he paid a short visit to his native county " to receive his fortune, which had remained so long in Mrs. Tudor's hands." With the money he bought a horse, " and rode far and near paying all he owed in his own country," which seems to have rather astonished the people, and especially Lord Hereford, who in fact sent him to the stocks because he had turned Methodist. Having paid every farthing he owed in his own country he went to Shrewsbury and did the same. From Shrewsbury he went to Whitchurch to pay sixpence, and thence to Wrexham, and satisfied every one there. He also visited Chester, Liverpool, Manchester, Birmingham, and Bristol—preaching wherever he went—and finally returned to Bradford. Having paid about 70 debts (which he could not accomplish till he had sold his horse, bridle, and saddle) he, with the small remains of his money, and with a little credit, set up in business. Before, however, he was half settled he, at Mr. Wesley's request gave it up, sold all his effects and went to Cornwall—setting out on foot from Bradford, October 24th, 1753—preaching on his way; and for the next 24 years he devoted himself entirely to itinerant preaching in various parts of England, Scotland, and Ireland. His preaching appears to have been of an earnest convincing character attended with much success. About 1758 he was married at Whitehaven, "after consultation with Mr. Wesley," to a Miss Green. In 1764 he paid another visit to his native county, and preached at Montgomery, Newtown, Llanidloes, Tregynon, and other places. About 1777 he undertook "the care of Mr. Wesley's printing," superintending among other things the publication of the *Arminian Magazine*. This office he held for 12 years, but the work was not altogether satisfactorily done, as the following entry in Mr. Wesley's Journal, under the date of August 9th, 1789, shews:—" I settled all my temporal business, " and, in particular, chose a new person to prepare the *Arminian* " *Magazine*; being obliged, however, unwillingly, to drop Mr. " O—, for only these two reasons :—1. The errata are un- " sufferable. I have borne them for these 12 years, but can " bear them no longer. 2. Several pieces are inserted without " my knowledge, both in prose and verse. I must try " whether these things cannot be amended for the short residue " of my life." This affair, however, does not seem to have in the least disturbed the friendly relations which previously existed between Mr. Olivers and the great leader of English Methodism. Mr. Olivers continued to reside in London, where he exercised his ministry, as the infirmities of age permitted, until his death, which took place somewhat suddenly in March, 1799, in the 74th year of his age. His remains were deposited in Mr. Wesley's tomb behind the City Road Chapel. Mr Olivers was certainly a man of considerable natural abilities, and besides being an argumentative and sometimes a powerful preacher he took a prominent, though a somewhat too bitter part in the theological controversies of those days. He was the author of several excellent hymns printed in most hymn-books—the best known being that commencing

"The God of Abraham praise."

He was also the composer of *Helmsley* and other sacred tunes, which were at one time very popular. With regard to *Helmsley*, however, Mr. Chappell, in his *Popular Music of the Olden Time,* says that it was taken from the old air "Guardian Angels" in the *Golden Pippin* :

"Guardian angels now protect me,
Send to me the youth I love."

The following is a list of Mr. Olivers' publications :—1. A *Hymn on the last Judgment,* set to music by the Author. 2. A *Hymn of Praise to Christ,* to which is added a Hymn on Matt. v,, 29, 30. 3. A *Hymn to the God of Abraham,* adapted to a celebrated air sung by Leoni in the Jews' Synagogue. 4. *A Letter to Mr. Thomas Hanby,* occasioned by the sudden death of several near relations. 5. *Twelve reasons why the people called Methodists ought not to buy or sell uncustomed goods.* 6. *An Answer to a pamphlet entitled* " A few thoughts and matters of " fact concerning Methodism, offered to the consideration of the " people who attend, encourage and support Methodist teachers," in a letter to the author. 7. *A full reply to a pamphlet entitled,* "An answer to a late pamphlet of Mr. Wesley against Mr. " Erskine." 8. *A Letter to the Rev. Mr. Toplady,* occasioned by his late letter to the Rev. Mr. Wesley. 9, *A Scourge to Calumny,* in two parts, inscribed to Richard Hill, Esq. Part the first, Demonstrating the absurdity of that gentleman's Farrago. Part the second, Containing a full answer to all that is material in his Farrago Double-distilled. London, 1774. 10. *A full defence of the Rev. John Wesley* in answer to the several personal reflections cast on that gentleman by the Rev. Caleb Evans. 11. *A Rod for a Reviler ;* or an answer to Mr Rowland Hill's Letter to the Rev. Mr. John Wesley. 12. *An account of the life of Mr. Thomas Olivers,* written by himself. 13. *A full refutation of the doctrine of Unconditional Perseverance.* A Welsh translation of this was also published. 14. *A Defence of Methodism.* 15. *A descriptive and plaintive Elegy on the death of the late Rev. John Wesley.* 16. *An Answer to Mr. Mark Davis's Thoughts on Dancing :* to which are added. Serious considerations to dissuade Christian parents from teaching their children to dance.

OWAIN AB CADWGAN AB BLEDDYN, Prince of Powys, was a wild, turbulent, and dissolute character. At Christmas, 1107, Cadwgan gave a banquet at Cardigan, where he then resided, to which he invited all the lords of the country, and among them his son Owain. At this feast the beauty of Nest, wife of Gerald de Windsor, constable of Pembroke Castle, was extolled above that of all the ladies in the land, and Owain's curiosity to see her was strongly excited. Under colour of friendship and relationship (she being his cousin german) he obtained admittance to the castle, and finding that her beauty and elegance far exceeded the reports he had heard, his passion was inflamed, and, going away, he returned secretly with a number of his wild companions the same night, set fire to the castle, and carried away Nest and her children to Powys, Gerald himself escaping with the greatest difficulty.

When Cadwgan heard of this he was much grieved, and at his and Nest's entreaty the children were returned to Gerald, but nothing would induce Owain to part with Nest. To avenge this atrocious act the English king induced several Welsh chieftains to gather a force and march into Cadwgan and Owain's dominions and lay them waste, and bring him the two princes alive or dead. When the country people heard this, some fled to Arwystli, some to Maelienydd, some to Ystrad Tywi, and some to Dyfed, and a great number were killed. Cadwgan and Owain fled by ship from Aberystwyth to Ireland. Cadwgan, however, shortly afterwards returned to Powys, and satisfied the king of his innocence, and Owain secretly followed him. For various mischiefs he was again obliged to seek refuge in Ireland, but upon his father's death in 1110 he succeeded to part of Powys, and was received into the King (Henry I.)'s favour, whom he accompanied into Normandy, where he was knighted. He is stated to have been the first Welshman that received this honour from a King of England. On his return to England he was sent by the king to take or kill Gruffydd ap Rees in Ystrad Tywi—a commission which greatly pleased him, and which he hastened to execute. Ravaging the country, he was met in a wood with only 100 men by Gerald and a large number of Flemings. Instantly, although he also was in the king's service, the idea of revenge rushed on Gerald's mind for the insults his honour had received by the outrage Owain had committed on his wife. Owain refused to fly, but with much spirit called on his men to support him, telling them that though their enemies were seven to one they were but Flemings, and such as feared their names, and were good for nothing "but to emptie cuppes," and with that set upon them courageously. However, on the first onset, he was struck by an arrow to the heart and slain. This, according to Powel and the *Annales Cambriae*, was in 1116, but Canon Williams dates it two years earlier, probably a mistake.

OWAIN VYCHAN AB GRUFFYDD AB IEUAN LLWYD, of Llanbrynmair, was a chieftain of Cyfeiliog, to whom his contemporary. Lewys Glyn Cothi, has addressed a highly eulogistic Ode. He is described as a generous friend of the bards, who ever delighted to hear the dulcimer and harp, and was himself a skilful musician, as well as accomplished in other respects, and well versed in the laws and customs of his country. From him descended the Owens of Rhiwsaeson and Ynysymaengwyn.

OWEN, ANNE WARBURTON, of Glansevern, Berriew, widow and relict of William Owen, Esq., K.C., of the same place, was the daughter and only child of Thomas Sloughter, a Captain in the 16th (General Burgoyne's) Regiment of Light Dragoons, by Anne, his wife, daughter of Thomas Warburton, Esq. She was born January 22nd, 1782, and was married first in February, 1806, to the Rev. Thomas Coupland, of Preston, who died a few months afterwards at Lisbon, where they were both staying on a continental tour. She afterwards, in 1823, was married to William Owen, Esq., K.C., of Glansevern, who died November 10, 1837. There was no issue by either marriage. Mrs. Owen, during a residence in Montgomeryshire of over 52 years, and especially during her second widowhood, which lasted 38 years, took an active interest in public affairs, and in all matters tending to the social and moral improvement of her poorer and less fortunate neighbours. Like her second husband, she was a staunch advocate of political reforms, and to her latest day took the liveliest interest in the promotion and passing of Liberal measures. She also came out nobly in aid of the efforts made to provide railway communication with the rest of the kingdom. She subscribed £10,000 towards the Oswestry and Newtown Railway, being one of the first subscribers to that undertaking, and considerable sums to the Llanidloes and Mid-Wales lines. For this reason she was selected to take the leading part in the opening ceremony of the Newtown and Llanidloes Railway on the 31st August, 1859, the first railway opened for traffic in Montgomeryshire, and she occupied a similar position on the opening shortly afterwards of the Oswestry and Newtown Railway to Welshpool. Mrs. Owen was a lady of considerable shrewdness and ability, and of rather uncommon business capacity, and paid great attention to the welfare of her numerous tenantry in Berriew and Llangurig, and in Lancashire, and the development and improvement of her estates. Her Montgomeryshire estates, by virtue of a Deed of Settlement executed in her lifetime, became vested upon her death in Arthur Charles Humphreys (a great grand-nephew of her late husband), who thereupon took the name and arms of Owen in pursuance of a clause in the same Deed, and is Chairman of the County Council, and M.P. for Montgomeryshire. Mrs. Owen lived to a very great age. She died January 5th, 1876, only seventeen days short of completing the 94th year of her age. On the 11th of the same month she was buried beside her late husband at Berriew Church.

OWEN, Sir ARTHUR DAVIES, Knight, of Glansevern, was the eldest son of Owen Owen, of Cefnhafodau, Llangurig (Sheriff 1766), by Anne his wife, daughter and heiress of Charles Davies, of Llivior, Berriew. He was brought up to the profession of the law, and became an able and active magistrate, one of the deputy-lieutenants of the county, and for many years Chairman of Quarter Sessions. From the formation of the corps of Montgomeryshire Yeomanry Cavalry in 1803 to the time of his death he was second in command of it. He served the office of High Sheriff in 1814. He was married to Mrs. Pugh, a widow (the mother of David Pugh, Esq., M.P. for many years for the Montgomery Boroughs) whom he survived without having issue. He died October the 18th, 1816, aged 64, and was buried in Berriew Church.

OWEN, Rev. CHARLES, a Nonconformist divine of some celebrity, was born in Montgomeryshire in 1654. He was educated at a private academy at Shrewsbury, and was subsequently privately ordained minister of a congregation at Bridgnorth; but the persecutions he endured compelled him at last to leave the people of his charge and seek shelter in London, where he remained until the King (James II.) granted toleration to Nonconformists. He then returned to Bridgnorth, and afterwards removed to Ellesmere, where he continued to officiate until his death, which took place in 1712. He was the author of several tracts advocating Nonconformist doctrines.

OWEN, Rev. DAVID, M.A., was the second son of Owen Owen, of Cefnhavodau, Llangurig. He was educated at Trinity College, Cambridge, and in 1777 became Senior Wrangler of that University. He was elected a Fellow of his College, and subsequently ordained priest. Eventually he settled in the island of Campo Bello, in Passamaquoddy Bay, New Brunswick, which belonged to his family, where he died unmarried in 1829. His remains were, in accordance with his own request, brought over to England, and deposited in the family vault in Berriew Church.

OWEN, Rev. EDWARD, M.A., the elegant translator of Juvenal, was the third son of David Owen, of Cefnhavodau, Llangurig, by Frances his wife, from whom also descended the Owen's of Glansevern. He was born about the year 1728, and was educated at Oxford. He obtained the living of Crosby in 1753. In 1757 he was appointed Master of the Grammar School at Warrington, and in 1767 he became rector of that place. He was an elegant scholar, and of a peculiarly benevolent disposition, and was the author of numerous works on ethical, classical, and political subjects; among others, *Ffaringdon's Sermons; a Latin Grammar* (1770); *The original text of Juvenal and Persius, with copious explanatory notes and introductory essays,* &c. (2 vols., 1785). The latter work passed through many editions. The celebrated Welsh poet, Goronwy Owen, while a curate at Walton, made his acquaintance, and subsequently received some kindness at his hands. He is spoken of by the poet in 1795 as " his dear friend and fellow country-" man." Years after Goronwy had left for America Mr. Owen instituted inquiries after him, and was the means of elucidating more of his later history than anyone else. He died in the year 1807, aged 79 years, and was buried in Warrington Church, where formerly a marble slab with a Latin inscription marked his grave. During a recent " restoration " of that church this seems to have disappeared.

OWEN, Sir EDWARD WILLIAM CAMPBELL RICHARD, G.C.B., K.H., and Vice-Admiral of the Red, was a son of Capt. William Owen, youngest son of Mr. David Owen, of Cefnhafodau, Llangurig, and was born in 1771. He was educated at Hanway School, Chelsea, and entered the Navy August 11, 1785, became a lieutenant November 6th, 1793, and post captain November 30th, 1798. After the peace of Amiens he was stationed with several sloops and smaller vessels under his orders on the coast of France, and by his activity and zeal kept the enemy in a constant state of alarm, at one time driving their ships on shore, and at another bombarding the towns of Dieppe and St. Valery. Subsequently, in 1806, Commodore Owen (having then hoisted a broad pendant) superintended a very successful attack on Boulogne, and in 1809 accompanied the expedition to Walcheren, where his ability and energy in the discharge of his arduous duties gained for him warm commendation. In 1815 he was made, for his distinguished services, Knight Commander of the Bath; in 1821 he was appointed a Colonel of Marines; and in 1825 advanced to Flag rank. From 1828 to 1832 he held the chief command on the East India Station, and from 1841 to 1845 that in the Mediterranean. He was a member of Parliament for Sandwich from 1826 to 1829; became Surveyor-General of Ordnance in 1827, and was a member of the Council of H.R.H. the Duke of Clarence, Lord High Admiral. He was a great favourite with H.R.H., who, after his accession to the throne as William IV., conferred upon him in 1832 the insignia of the Grand Cross of the Hanoverian Guelphic Order, and it is said proposed to confer a peerage upon him, but for some reason or other this proposal was not carried out. In 1834-5 Sir Edward held office again as Clerk of the Ordnance. In January, 1846, the Grand Cross of the Order of the Bath was conferred upon him, and a Grant of Supporters was made to him, and recorded at the College of Arms on the 26th of that month. His arms are therein described as—Per saltire _sa._ and _gu._ a lion _rampant or_, surrounded by the motto, "Tria juncta in uno." Crest on a wreath of the colours, A stag _argent_, billetty, tripping. Motto, "Flecti non Frangi." Sir Edward married, in 1829, Selina, daughter of Capt. J. B. Hay, R.N. He died October 8th, 1849, at his residence, Windlesham House, Surrey, aged 78.

OWEN, The Ven. HUGH, M.A., was the son of Pryce Owen, of Bettws. He became the incumbent of St. Julian's, Shrewsbury, Archdeacon of Salop, Prebend of Lichfield and Salisbury, and portioner of Bampton, Oxfordshire. He was a man of considerable learning, and of great eminence as an antiquary and historian. Besides numerous contributions to the _Gentleman's Magazine_ and other periodicals, chiefly on historical and ecclesiastical subjects, he published, in 1808, _Some account of the ancient and present state of Shrewsbury_; and he was also the joint author with Mr. Blakeway of that very valuable work, _The History of Shrewsbury_, published in 1825. He died December 23rd, 1827, and was buried in St. Julian's Churchyard, Shrewsbury.

OWEN, Rev. HUMPHREY, D.D., was the son of Humphrey Owen, of Gwaelod, in Nantymeichiaid, in the parish of Meifod. On the death of Dr. Thomas Pardo, in 1763, he was appointed Principal of Jesus College, Oxford. He was succeeded in this office in 1768 by Dr. Joseph Hoare.

OWEN, JOHN, was a native of Machynlleth, where he was born in the year 1757. He carried on business there for many years as a grocer and merchant, and was a partner with Mr. Hugh Williams (the late Mr. Cobden's father-in-law) in the Dylife Lead Mine. He was also interested in the Dyfngwm and Esgairgaled Mines. From early life he was a great reader, especially of theological and astronomical works. He was a man of a poetical and imaginative temperament, and possessed a knowledge of general literature far in advance of most of his neighbours. He married Elizabeth, daughter of Captain (Master Mariner) Paul Jones, of Aberdovey. He had joined the Calvinistic Methodists when a very young man, but always retained his affection for the Church of England, and in his latter days strongly objected to the distinct separation of the Methodists from the established church. He was the author of several poetical and prose works of considerable merit, viz. :— I. *Troedigaeth Atheos* (the Conversion of Atheos), a poem written in imitation of the well-known *Golwg ar Deyrnas Crist* of Williams, of Pantycelyn. The author carried this imitation a little beyond fair limits, his numerous notes being for the most part copied almost *verbatim* from a work published in 1725 by the Rev. David Lewis, under the title *Golwg ar y Byd*. *Troedigaeth Atheos* was first published at Carmarthen (J. Daniel) in 1788; a second edition appeared in 1818, and a third edition (Liverpool) in 1871. II. *Difrifol Ystyriaeth, sef 1. Pa beth yw Dyn. 2. A pha beth yw Duw, &c.* (Serious Considerations. I. What is man. 2. What is God, &c.) 1789. III. *Tair Gerdd Newydd* (Three new songs), 1795. IV. *Golygiadau ar Achosion ac Effeithiau'r Cyfnewidiad yn Ffrainc* (Views on the Causes and Effects of the Revolution in France). "Weigh others' woes "and learn to bear thine own," Machynlleth (Pritchard) 1797. V. *Golygiad ar Adfywiad Crefydd yn yr Eglwys Sefydledig oddeutu y flwyddyn* 1737 (A view of the revival of Religion in the Established Church about the year 1737), 1818. VI. *Golygiad ar Athrawiaeth y Drindod, ac ar Berson Crist* (A View of the Doctrine of the Trinity and on the Person of Christ), 1820. After the death of his wife, Mr. Owen removed to Llangyndeyrn, Carmarthenshire, where he died in 1829, aged 72.

OWEN, Rev. OWEN, was born at Machynlleth in 1806, and was educated for the Independent Ministry at the Carmarthen and Highbury Colleges. He was minister for some time at Newport (Monmouth), Liskeard, and Manorbeer, but later in life he joined the Established Church, and emigrated to America, where he practised medicine at Chicago till his death in

1874. He married Mary Anne, daughter of David Beynon, Esq., and grand-daughter of John Beynon, Esq., of Trewern, Carmarthenshire, Sheriff of Cardiganshire in 1783. He wrote and published several works under the *nom de plume Celatus*, each of them containing an acrostic giving his name, and sometimes his address also. The following is a list of them :—1. *The Modern Theme.* A work on education (1848 and 1854). 2. *The Taper for lighting the Sabbath School Lamps.* A series of lectures to Sunday School teachers. 3. *A glass of wholesome Water.* A plea for Total Abstinence. 4. *The Shepherd's Voice.* 5. *The Working Saint.* A Sermon (1843). 6. *The sources of Science*; or the Pierian Springs laid open. Lectures on the benefits arising from Scientific Institutions (1854). 7. *The Public Pearl*; or Education, the People's right and a Nation's glory (1854). The ideas contained in these works are many of them excellent, and in advance of the time in which they were written, but the style is unattractive, hazy, involved and sometimes ludicrous. The author was, however, evidently a man of good parts but an enthusiast. He is said to have spent his own and most of his wife's fortune in various well-intentioned but ill-managed efforts for the public good. His wife, a talented and educated lady, also published in 1852 a small illustrated volume of dialogues and poems for the young, entitled *The Early Blossom*, under the *nom-de-plume, Celata.*

OWEN, Rev. RICHARD, D.D., was the son of the Rev. Cadwaladr, Owen, B.D., some time Fellow of Oriel College, Oxford, and rector of Llanfechain from 1601 to 1617. He was born at Llanfechain in 1605, and at the age of fifteen was entered at Oriel, of which college he was made Fellow in 1627, being then Bachelor of Arts. Afterwards he proceeded in that faculty, and having taken his Master's degree, he entered holy orders, became rector of Llanfechain in 1634, and in 1635 was presented by the University of Oxford to the vicarage of Eltham in Kent. In 1638 he resigned his fellowship, and the same year took the degree of Bachelor of Divinity. On Sept. 2nd, 1639, he also became Rector of St. Swithin's, London. In the beginning of the Civil War he adhered to the Royalist cause, and was deprived of his livings by the Parliamentary Committee, that of St. Swithin's being lost to him in 1643. For seventeen years he suffered much for the Royalist cause, but on the restoration of King Charles II. his preferments were restored to him, and he had afterwards the Prebend of Reculverland in St. Paul's, and the living of St. North Cray, in Kent. He also became Doctor of Divinity. He died about the end of January, 1682-3, and was buried in the chancel of the church of Eltham. Wood says that " he was in high esteem for his holy " life and conversation, for his orthodoxness in judgment, con- " formity to the true ancient doctrine and discipline of the " Church of England, and in the former revolutions for his " loyalty to his sacred Majesty." He wrote and published—I.,

A *Sermon on the 2nd Cor.*, 8, 18, preached at St. Mary's, Oxford, on St. Luke's Day, 1637, of which Wood says, "I have seen "this in manuscript, which for its rarity went from hand to "hand, but whether ever made public I know not." II. *Paulus Multiformis, Concio ad clerum Londinensem*, in I. Cor., 9, 22, published in 1666, quarto. III. A translation of *Juvenal's Satires*. He also wrote some controversial tracts.

OWEN, RICHARD, of Rhiwsaeson, Llanbrynmair, was one of the gentlemen upon whom the Knighthood of the Royal Oak was intended to be conferred by King Charles II. He was the son of Athelstan Owen, of Rhiwsaeson. His estate was valued at £1,000 per annum. He served the office of Sheriff in 1653. The Rhiwsaeson estate was sold in 1750, and is now the property of Sir Watkin Williams Wynn, Bart.

OWEN, ROBERT, the *Socialist*, was the son of Robert Owen (a native of Welshpool), saddler, ironmonger, and post-master at Newtown, and Anne his wife, who lived where Messrs. Park and Son's shop now stands in Broad-street, near the Cross. He was born on the 14th of May, 1771, and was the youngest but one of seven children. At a very early age he evinced quite a passion for reading and study. In consequence, as he believed, of his having while very young hastily swallowed some flummery that was scalding hot, his health was ever after-wards delicate. When he had attained the age of ten, he left Newtown for London, "with my habits of reflection and extreme "temperance," as he says, "not liking the habits and manners "of a small country town." In London he remained a few weeks with his eldest brother William, a saddler, in Holborn, after which he obtained a situation with a Mr. McGuffog in a respectable drapery establishment at Stamford, Lincolnshire, where he very happily spent three years. He then stayed for a few months in London with his brother, and after paying a short visit to his relatives in Wales, again returned to London to a situation in a haberdasher's shop on Old London Bridge. Here he did not remain long, but went to Manchester to occupy a similar position, where he became acquainted with a mechanic named Jones, who persuaded him to become a partner with him in the manufacture of mules for spinning cotton. The partner-ship, however, proved unsatisfactory, and was dissolved, and for some time Mr. Owen carried on himself the business of spinning cotton yarn or thread. Soon, however, and before he was twenty years of age, he became manager of a large cotton mill, where 500 persons were employed, belonging to one Mr. Drink-water, who took to all his machinery at cost price, and agreed to give him a salary of £300 a year. When he entered upon this responsible office he was almost entirely ignorant of the business, but he set about acquiring a thorough knowledge of it so ener-getically and so discreetly that he not only mastered it, but brought the mill into superior order. At the end of six months his employer was so pleased with his conduct that unsolicited he offered to increase his salary the second year to £400, the third year to £500, and the fourth year to take him into partnership with himself and his two sons. The mill he was now managing was the first that had ever been erected for fine cotton spinning by machinery, and it is worthy of note that Mr. Owen was the first to manufacture thread from Sea Island North American cotton—an article which afterwards came so much in demand. His name soon became known as the first fine cotton spinner in the world. At this time he became acquainted with Mr. (afterwards Dr.) Dalton, Coleridge, and other literary characters, and joined the Manchester Literary and Philosophical Society, thus obtaining an introduction to the best society. He appears to have at this time largely imbibed materialistic views, and was the one who, in the discussions which took place at the Society's meetings, generally opposed, " the religious prejudices " (as he terms them) of all sects. Having one night laid it down that all the universe was one great laboratory ; that all things were chemical compounds, and that man was only a complicated chemical compound, he acquired thenceforth the *soubriquet* of " the philosopher who intended to make men by chemistry." The account he gives of the circumstances under which he left Mr. Drinkwater's service is very characteristic. One day Mr. Drinkwater sent for him and told him, " I have sent for " you that I may explain unexpected changes which have taken " place lately in my family. The celebrated Mr. Oldknow is to " become my son-in-law. You know he is the first British " muslin manufacturer, and he is becoming a great cotton " spinner. He has expressed a strong wish that the entire " business of both families should be retained in the family, but " you are entitled by our agreement to become a partner in my " mills next year, and this agreement obstructs his extensive " views and arrangements. He wishes me to ascertain from you " on what conditions you would retain the management of my " mills, and give up the agreement for a partnership in our " business. If you will give up your claim to the partnership " you may name your own salary. You have now £500 a year, and " whatever sum you will name you shall have." He appeared very anxious to hear Mr. Owen's reply, who said, " I have brought " the agreement with me and here it is, and I now put it into " the fire, because I never will connect myself with any parties " who are not desirous to be united with me ; but under these " circumstances I cannot remain your manager with any salary " you can give " ; and the agreement was consumed before him. It was in vain that Mr. Drinkwater endeavoured to change his determination—he would only consent to remain until a new manager could be found. He then formed a partnership with several influential men under the firm of the " Chorlton Twist Company." Under his superintendence a large factory was built in the neighbourhood of Manchester, where the business was, under his management, afterwards successfully carried on. During a business visit to Glasgow, he became acquainted with Miss Dale, the daughter of "an extensive manufacturer, cotton spinner, merchant, banker, and preacher," whom he afterwards married. Mr. Dale had mills at New Lanark, about thirty miles from Glasgow, which he happened to be desirous of giving up. Mr. Owen, as a means of introducing himself to him, and eventually of obtaining his consent to his union with his daughter, entered into a negotiation with him for their purchase. Terms were agreed upon (namely, a payment of £60,000 by 20 annual instalments of £3,000), and the New Lanark establishment thus passed from Mr. Dale into the hands of Mr. Owen and his partners, Messrs Barton and Atkinson, under the name of "The New Lanark Twist Company." This occurred in the summer of 1797, Mr. Owen being still but 26 years of age. On the 30th September, 1799, he married Miss Dale, whom he took to Manchester. They did not reside there long, however, it being found necessary for him to take the superintendence of the New Lanark Mills, his partners looking after the Lancashire business. So he returned to Scotland, and about the first of January, 1800, entered upon the " government " (to use his own term) of New Lanark. The population at this period consisted of about 1,300 settled in the village as families, and about 400 or 500 pauper children, procured from various parishes, whose ages were from seven to 12. Their moral and social condition is described as very low. Having disposed of his interest in the Manchester business, he took measures to carry out an experiment which he had long thought of, the object being no less than " to change " the fundamental principle on which society has heretofore been " based from the beginning," his own principle being " that the " character is formed *for* and not *by* the individual, and that " society now possesses the most ample means and power to well " form the character of everyone by reconstructing society on " its own true principle, and making it consistent with the " fundamental principle in all its departments and divisions." He built a new village for his workpeople at New Lanark, and governed the community upon principles partly republican and partly patriarchal. In 1806 in consequence of differences between the United States government and ours, the former laid an embargo on their own ports, and no cotton was allowed to be exported. Prices immediately advanced so rapidly and so high that manufacturers stopped their machinery rather than continue to work the material at the high price it had attained, and run the risk of a great and sudden fall in the price should the embargo be removed. Mr. Owen, however, stopped his machinery, but retained the people and continued to pay them their full wages for only keeping the machinery clean and in good working condition as long as the embargo was maintained. During this period, which was of four months' duration, the New Lanark population received more than £7,000 for their unemployed time, without a penny being deducted from the full wages of any one. This proceeding overcame the prejudices, and won the confidence and the hearts of the whole population. Some of his partners being unable to acquiesce in his operations, Mr Owen purchased their interest in the New Lanark establishment for £84,000, and became the sole proprietor of it for a short time. Having afterwards admitted fresh partners into the concern, these began very soon in every possible way to obstruct his plans, particularly his project for establishing infant schools, and formed a deep-laid scheme to get the whole business into their own hands at a great sacrifice to Mr. Owen. He, however, shrewdly defeated their tactics and once more became the purchaser at £114,000,—made up of thirteen shares, of which Mr. Owen held five, the others being held by six philanthropic gentlemen (the celebrated Jeremy Bentham and several Quakers being among them), who had become interested in his plans for the amelioration of society, the partnership being formed on the condition that the surplus gains over five per cent. were to be expended for the education of the children and the improvement of the workpeople at New Lanark, and for the general improvement of the condition of the persons employed in manufactures. He appears to have owed his introduction to his partners by the publication by him, in 1812-3, of four essays entitled *New Views of Society*, and on *The Formation of Character*,—works which also brought him into favour with the Archbishop of Canterbury, Lord Liverpool, Wilberforce, Macintosh, Malthus, and other leading men of the time. The new partnership was formed in 1814, and Mr. Owen directed his energies to carry out measures not only for the extension and profitable conduct of the business (in which he was eminently successful), but also for the promotion of the comfort, education, and well being of the large number of persons employed by the firm. He also exerted himself to rouse public opinion to consider the lamentable condition of young children and others employed in factories, in which he encountered strong opposition from interested millowners. At that time children were admitted into cotton, woollen, flax, and silk mills at six and sometimes even at five years of age ; the time of working, winter and summer, was unlimited by law, but usually it was fourteen hours a day, in some fifteen, and even occasionally sixteen hours ; and in many cases the mills were artificially heated to a degree most unfavourable to health. Mr. Owen prepared a Bill, which he induced the first Sir Robert Peel to introduce into Parliament, for the purpose of regulating the employment of children in factories and providing for their education. This Bill proposed to limit the time of working to ten hours a day, and the age of admission to twelve ; to provide for the instruction of children before their admission and for the keeping of factories clean and well ventilated. After some delays it was referred to a Select Committee, but encountered such strong opposition from the manufacturers that although it finally became law it was in such a mutilated form as to be of very little good. Meanwhile the establishment at New Lanark grew into one of vast proportions, until the population reached 2,500 persons, all acting entirely under Mr. Owen's direction.

Infant and other schools were in active operation, and all the wants of the community were supplied on the "co-operative" principle, which of late years has become so general in its application. "This institution for the formation of character," as he himself preferred to call it was considered, he assures us "by the "more advanced minds of the world one of the greatest of "modern wonders." Certainly, while it remained under his immediate direction it was eminently successful and attained a a world-wide celebrity. Among the thousands of distinguished persons who visited it were the Grand Duke Nicholas, afterwards Emperor of Russia, with several of his nobles and attendants, the Grand Duke of Oldenburgh, Princes John and Maximilian of Austria, and numerous other foreign princes and nobles. But his experiments and reflections led him to·advocate Communism, and to take up an attitude of antagonism to religion, which eventually ruined his prospects as a social reformer. In the summer of 1817, Mr. Owen held a series of crowded public meetings at the London Tavern for the purpose of expounding his schemes for the amelioration of the human race, and for governing the affairs of men. Having at one of these meetings denounced all religions as injurious to mankind, most of his former friends withdrew from him their countenance and support, and he at once lost much of his influence and popularity. After this he visited France, Switzerland, Frankfort, and other parts of the Continent, where he was well received by Cuvier, Louis Philippe, Oberlin, Humboldt, and other eminent men. On his return to England he found that by his attacks on religion he had forfeited to a great extent his popularity, and was looked upon by many as an avowed infidel. He, however, found a powerful friend in the Duke of Kent, who kept up a long correspondence with him, became Chairman of a Committee formed for the promotion of his "new views of society," presided at public meetings held for the same purpose, and in other ways supported and encouraged him until his death, which occurred about three years afterwards. Mr. Owen subsequently visited Ireland to expound his views and plans for the regeneration of mankind. All this time New Lanark had continued to prosper financially, but Mr. Owen's partners, who were religious men, and had joined him from purely philanthrophic motives began to doubt whether they could longer conscientiously continue their connection with the apostle of infidelity, and the professed enemy of all religion. Some of them therefore determined to introduce certain regulations of their own in the carrying on of the establishment; but he resented such interference and finally determined to retire from the concern. It was not, however, until 1829 that he broke off all his connection with New Lanark In 1824 Mr. Owen made a voyage to the United States, having determined to make a trial of his plans in another hemisphere, where he could buy an expanse of country at so small a cost as to be within his own means, and thus be free from all claims on the part of others to dictate laws for his guidance. He accordingly purchased in April, 1825, 30,000 acres of fertile land in Indiana and Illinois, on the river Wabash. The purchase was made from the community of German Socialists who called the place Harmony and themselves Harmonians. Here he established a communistic colony under the name of New Harmony —which eventually developed into ten societies. After giving them a fair start he himself paid a hurried visit to England, but returned before the end of the year. Mr. Owen on his return found that things had not gone on well in his absence and ere long, to his grievous disappointment, his plans utterly broke down and he was forced to abandon his fondly cherished scheme. In the summer of 1828, a few months after the breaking up of the experiments at New Harmony, Mr. Owen met with what appeared another opportunity of carrying his views into practice in Texas, the Mexican Government, to which that country then belonged, having proposed to make a grant of several millions of acres for the purpose of colonization to certain persons who sought his assistance. To secure this concession and promote the establishment in this vast territory of " communities on the social system," he visited Mexico, where he was cordially received, but before the grant was confirmed a change of government took place and the whole project came to nothing. From Mexico he proceeded by way of the West Indies to the United States, to fulfil an engagement he had made to enter on a discussion of his principles with a Rev. Mr. Campbell. The discussion took place at Cincinnati ; and, as often happens, both sides claimed the victory. From Cincinnati he travelled to Washington, " to proceed with the mission of peace between " Great Britain and the United States." Soon afterwards he returned to England " to continue his mission." He found that his partisans had, during his three years' absence, increased in number, and as his partnership at New Lanark had now determined, the society at New Harmony had ceased to be inviting, a similar community, established by his aid at Orbiston in Scotland, had passed from his hands, and the magnificent Mexican project had proved an abortion, he resolved to devote himself to the instruction of the working classes in London, to prepare them for the mighty changes he still hoped to effect. To this end he held public meetings, delivered lectures, established a penny weekly paper called the *Crisis* (the first number of which appeared on the 14th of April, 1832), and an " Equitable Labour Exchange." This latter came to a disastrous close about the end of 1833 ; there being a confessed deficiency of £2,500, the whole of which Mr. Owen paid himself. From this date, for nearly twenty years, little was heard of him. His ambitious and Utopian scheme for " the reconstruction of society " had proved a failure, and gradually his existence was almost forgotten by the world outside the rather small circle of co-operators or Socialists, as they came to be called, who still looked to him as their prophet, and from time to time assembled to do him honour

He never took much interest in any political reforms. He crossed the Atlantic several times, and was still busy as ever with tongue and pen, but the leading newspapers took no note of his proceedings and his publications were not to be seen on the counters of respectable booksellers or newsvendors. Lord Melbourne, however, presented him at Court in 1840,—a proceeding which drew forth from the redoubtable Bishop of Exeter (Dr. Philpotts) one of his bitterest philippics. During this period Mr. Owen also published a work called *The Book of the New Moral World, containing the Rational System of Society*, with a dedication to King William IV. About the year 1853 he became a convert to spiritualism—a defection upon which his disciples looked with shame and confusion. For forty years and more he had denounced Christianity and all the other religions of the world, as unfounded and mischievous; had dissuaded men from spending their time and efforts in preparing for the next life; had declared it absurd to offer God services which could not possibly benefit Him; had even doubted the existence of a personal divinity; had denied the Bible and classed Jesus of Nazareth with Mother Lee and other imposters;—but now in the last years of his long life he, who had done all this, had become extremely credulous—a firm believer in apparitions and spirit rapping. He asserted that he received frequent visits from the spirits of the Duke of Kent and others of his old friends—that he had been specially selected by them to reveal their secrets to a wretched world, to convince it of error, and to save it from that chaos into which it had fallen. In alleged obedience to an urgent recommendation from the spirit world he, in December, 1856, commenced to write an account of his own eventful life, of which two volumes were published in the author's lifetime, entitled, *The Life of Robert Owen, written by himself, with selections from his Writings and Correspondence.* 2 vols. (London: Effingham Wilson, 1857). Of this work there is a copy in the Powysland Library at Welshpool, with the following characteristic inscription in the autograph of the venerable author:—" Presented to his Excellency the Saxon " Ambassador to Great Britain by the author, who has written " these works with a view to open a new Book of Life to man and " a greatly superior existence to the human race.- Sevenoaks " Park, Sevenoaks, 20 April, 1858." The Museum also contains an engraved portrait of Mr. Owen. His last public appearance was at a meeting of the Social Science Congress in Liverpool in October, 1858. He was very feeble at this time and after the meeting was for a fortnight confined to his bed at the Victoria Hotel. He and his secretary (Mr. Rigby), however, paid a hurried *incognito* visit to Newtown, arriving one day and departing the next, not above one or two persons knowing who they were. They returned again in about a fortnight arriving at Newtown on the 8th November, and putting up at the Bear's Head Hotel

" And as an hare, whom hounds and horns pursue,
Pants for the place from whence at first it flew,"

so Mr. Owen this time came fully resolved to spend his few
remaining days in his native town and to die there. This
happened sooner than he or his friends anticipated. He died on
the 17th of the same month (November, 1858) aged 87 years.
By his own desire, his body was placed, awaiting burial, in the
room where he was born at Mr. David Thomas's, where hundreds
of persons went to see it. The funeral took place in a few days,
and was attended by twelve chief mourners, and twelve of the
oldest men in the town, two of whom had been his schoolmates.
Then came twelve little boys, after whom came twelve tradesmen
of the town, followed by any others who wished to join the procession—nearly the whole population of the town lining the
streets to witness the funeral. He was buried in the old Churchyard. The day of the funeral was one of the foggiest and
darkest ever known at Newtown—a phenomenon considered by
not a few to be one of ominous significance. Thus after a long
life of nearly 88 years spent mostly far from his birthplace,
Robert Owen was permitted to spend the last nine days of his
eventful life, and to die within a few yards of where he was born,
and to have his ashes mingled with those of his own kindred, in
the old churchyard of his native town. Besides *The New Views
of Society and on the Formation of Character* already referred to,
first published in 1813, and which subsequently passed through
several editions, Mr. Owen also published *An address delivered
to the Inhabitants of New Lanark on the 1st Jan.*, 1819, *at the
opening of the Institution established for the Formation of
Character* (1819); *A Letter to the Archbishop of Canterbury on
the Union of Churches and Schools* (1818); *Observations on the
Cotton Trade of Great Britain, and on the late Duties on the
Importation of Cotton Wool* (1803); *Observations on the Cotton
Trade* (1815); *A Bill for regulating the hours of work in Mills and
Factories* (1815); *Observations on the effect of the Manufacturing
System* (1815); *Letter to the Earl of Liverpool on the Employ-
ment of Children in Manufactories* (1818); *Letter to British
Master Manufacturers*, on the same subject (1818); *Two
Memorials on behalf of the Working Classes* (1818); *An address
to the Working Classes* (1819); and several other tracts and
addresses on these and kindred topics. By his wife, who pre-
deceased him many years, Mr. Owen had eight children. His
eldest son, Robert Dale Owen, at one time had a political
appointment under the United States Government at one of the
EuropeanCourts, and wrote *Debateable Land between this world
and the next: Twenty-seven years of Autobiography—threading
my way;* and other works on Spiritualism and kindred subjects.
Proposals have been made on several occasions by Robert Owen's
admirers to erect a monument to his memory at Newtown, but
these have been coldly received by the inhabitants, whose
religious sensibilities have been shocked by his outspoken
scepticism. In 1861, a plain tombstone of blue flag was placed

over his own and his parents' graves, enclosed within a neat
railing, with the following inscriptions :—" In memory of Robert
" Owen, the philanthropist. Born at Newtown, May 14th,
" 1771; died at Newtown, November 17th, 1858. Erected by
" public subscription, 1861.— Robert Owen, father of the philan-
" thropist, died March 14, 1804. Aged 65 years. Anne Owen,
" mother of the philanthropist, died July 13th, 1803. Aged 68
" years." Robert Owen possessed, undoubtedly, rare abilities as
an administrator ; and as a man, as a citizen, and as a thinker,
it is but justice to say that he had many excellencies. He was
the founder of infant schools, and practically of co-operation in
commercial undertakings, and some of his political projects and
schemes which in his day were condemned as visionary, impractic-
able, and revolutionary, have been adopted. But as a theorist
his views on religion were crude and pernicious and he was a
most erratic, unsafe, and dangerous guide to those who took him
for their leader on religious and moral questions. No one has
ever doubted his utter unselfishness and honesty of purpose, the
sincerity of his convictions, or the disinterestedness of his
motives ; but his openly confessed infidelity destroyed his
influence and baffled his schemes. But while he disbelieved and
denounced all his life what the generality of his countrymen
believed and held sacred, he, in his own person, offered to the
world another remarkable instance of a man rushing from one
extreme to another — from openly avowed infidelity to that most
absurd and infatuated of all superstitions — Spiritualism.

OWEN, Capt. WILLIAM, R.N, was the fourth and
youngest son of David Owen, of Cefnhavodau, Llangurig, by
Frances, daughter of John Rogers, of Cefnyberain, Kerry. He
entered the Royal Navy, in 1750, when very young. He was
present at the battle of Plassey, June 23rd, 1757, and in the
year 1760, while yet but a midshipman, greatly distinguished
himself at the taking of Pondicherry from the French, losing
his right arm in the action. He was a lieutenant in 1766, and
about 1770 was promoted to the command of H.M.S. *Cormorant*,
in which he again distinguished himself. Capt. Owen was
bringing home despatches when he lost his life by an accident
at Madras in 1778. He was the father of two distinguished
naval officers—Admirals Sir Edward W C. R. Owen and
William F. Owen. He kept a very full and interesting diary
of his adventures by sea and land between 1750 and 1771, very
full extracts from which have been published in the *Montgomeryshire Collections*, and in *Byegones.*

OWEN, Vice-Admiral WILLIAM FITZWILLIAM, was
the younger son of the above-named Captain William Owen,
and was born at Manchester in 1773. Having been educated
with his brother at Hanway School, Chelsea, where he attained
the first rank, he entered the Royal Navy, in the Summer of
1788, on board the *Culloden*, 74 guns, commanded by his

relation, Sir Thomas Rich, and was present at the great battle of the 1st June, 1794, Shortly afterwards he sailed in the *Ruby* (64) for the Cape of Good Hope, where he witnessed the capture of a Dutch squadron of three sail of the line and six frigates and sloops in Saldana Bay, in August, 1796. Returning to England after this exploit he joined the *London* (98), bearing the flag of Admiral Colpays, with whom he quitted that ship during the mutiny at Spithead in May, 1797. For his firmness on that trying occasion he was in the following month promoted to the rank of lieutenant, and placed in command of the *Flamer* gunbrig. In this and other vessels he saw much active and harassing service till the close of the first French revolutionary war. At the commencement of hostilities he was among the foremost to offer his services, and in July, 1803, he was appointed to the command of the *Sea Flower*, a brig of 14 guns. Very shortly afterwards he sailed for the East Indies, where he was employed upon various missions by the Commander-in-Chief. In 1806 he captured *Le Charle*, a French vessel, and by the exploration of several of the channels between the eastern islands, contributed greatly to the improvement of the charts. Towards the close of the same year he piloted Sir Edward Pellew's squadron through an intricate navigation into Batavia Roads. Here his bravery and skill were conspicuous in the command of a division of armed boats at a successful attack on a Dutch frigate, seven men-of-war brigs, and about twenty armed vessels, for which he was honourably mentioned in the *Gazette*. The following year he assisted in the capture and destruction of the Dutch dockyard, stores, and fleet at Griessik, in Java. In 1808 his ship, the *Sea Flower*, was captured by the French in the Bay of Bengal, and he himself taken prisoner, and carried to the Isle of France, where he was detained until June, 1810, when he was exchanged. In May, 1809, the rank of Commander was conferred upon Mr. Owen, and on his liberation and return to India he assisted in organising the expedition against the Isle of France, which was taken in December, 1810. He subsequently commanded the *Barracouta*, and took part in the operations which led to the surrender to the British forces of Batavia in August, 1811, having in May of the same year been advanced to post rank. After acting in command of the *Piedmontaise* for a short time, he was appointed Captain of the *Cornelia*, 32 guns, in which he sailed from Batavia Roads in March, 1812, with a small squadron to take possession of the commissariat depôt at the Eastern end of Sumatra. Having accomplished this, he returned to England in charge of a valuable convoy from China in June, 1813. In addition to his other arduous services, Capt. Owen materially assisted his friend, Captain Horsborough, in compiling his well-known *Oriental Navigator*, and employed his leisure time in correcting charts, and translating from the Portuguese Franzoni's *Sailing Directions*. In March, 1815, he was appointed to the corvette *Leven* (24 guns), in which, accompanied by the *Barra-*

couta, he was for four years employed on the west and east coasts of Africa, and during that period rendered effective aid to General Turner in the Ashantee war. In February, 1827, he was commissioned to the *Eden* (26 guns), for the purpose of forming a settlement in the island of Fernando Po, and to complete his surveys of that coast, which occupied him until the close of 1831. He then retired on half-pay, but continued his labours in correcting charts and improving the means of maritime surveying. He and his brother, Sir Edward Owen, having on the death of their relative, the Rev. David Owen, become owners of the island of Campo Bello, in Passamaquoddy Bay, New Brunswick, and desiring to settle there, Sir Edward surrendered to him his portion. Capt. Owen accordingly brought his wife and two daughters there, and for some time energetically occupied himself in the improvement of his estate. He represented the island in the House of Assembly at Fredericton, where he exposed various abuses, and shewed himself to be a staunch reformer. Being still anxious to pursue his hydrographical labours, he was appointed to the *Columbia*, a fine steam vessel of 100-horse power, to survey the Bay of Fundy, and the coast of Nova Scotia. In December, 1847, he was promoted to flag rank, and continued the rest of his life on half-pay. Vice-Admiral Owen had been for many years prior to his death an active Fellow of the Royal Astronomical Society. He was in conduct and bearing firm of mind, shrewdly sensible and unostentatious, his manner sometimes bordering on the eccentric; a man of steady resources and unremitting zeal; and a fluent, though blunt, speaker. He died at St. John's, New Brunswick, on the 3rd of November, 1857, at the advanced age of 84 years.

OWEN, WILLIAM, King's Counsel, of Glansevern, was the third son of Owen Owen, of Cefnhavodau, Llangurig, and was born in the year 1758. He was educated at the Free Grammar School, Warrington (then conducted by his uncle, the Rev. Edward Owen, M.A.), from which he proceeded to Trinity College, Cambridge. In 1782 he took his degree of B.A., and was fifth wrangler. Among the members of his own college who graduated at the same time were Professors Porson and Hailstone, Drs. Raine and Wingfield. Mr. Owen and these four gentlemen were afterwards elected Fellows of Trinity College. He subsequently entered upon the study of the law, and was called to the Bar by the Honourable Society of Lincoln's Inn, of which eventually he became a bencher. For several years he travelled the Oxford and Cheshire Circuits, but afterwards confined his practice chiefly to the Courts of Chancery and Exchequer. He was appointed Commissioner of Bankrupts and (7th August, 1818) a King's Counsel. About the year 1821 he relinquished his practice, and retired into the country to reside upon his estate at Glansevern inherited from his brother, Sir Arthur Davies Owen, where he became a magistrate and

Deputy Lieutenant. During the rest of his life he took an active part in all the public business of the county, and generally presided as Chairman of Quarter Sessions. Mr. Owen was chiefly instrumental in abolishing the Great Sessions and the old system of Welsh judicature by the important evidence he gave on the subject before a Committee of the House of Commons in 1817 and 1820, and otherwise. He was a staunch Whig (or what would be now called a Liberal) in politics, and took a leading part in Montgomeryshire in the great reform agitation which preceded the passing of the Reform Bill in 1832. The County of Montgomery was the first to petition in support of that Bill. He stoutly opposed the original proposal to give the representation of the Montgomery Boroughs to Llanfyllin alone, and it was in a great measure through his exertions that Newtown, Llanidloes, Machynlleth, and Welshpool were admitted to share the representation with Llanfyllin and Montgomery. In 1823 Mr. Owen married Anne Warburton, only child of Captain Sloughter, and relict of the Rev. Thomas Coupland, of the Priory, Chester, but there was no issue of the marriage. Mr. Owen died on the 10th of November, 1837, aged 79, and was buried in Berriew Church. A handsome marble monument was there erected to his memory by his widow, testifying that " he left behind him a name without reproach." The following Grant of Arms was made 3rd April, 1838, to Mrs. Owen " to be " placed on any monument or otherwise to the memory of her " late husband, the said William Owen deceased " :—*Sable* a tilting spear erect *or*, the head *proper* imbued *gules*, between three scaling ladders *argent*, on a chief ermine a fort triple towered also *proper* ; and for a crest, on a wreath of the colours a wolf salient *proper*, supporting a scaling ladder as in the arms. Motto, *Toraf cyn plygaf.*" (I will break before I bend.)

OWEN, WILLIAM (*Gwilym Ddu Glan Hafren*), a talented schoolmaster, poet, preacher, and musician, was the son of Owen Williams, of Wern Dwn, Llangybi, Carnarvonshire, his mother being a descendant of the Rev. Edward Samuel, of Llangar, well known as a Welsh poet and translator. He was born about the year 1788. Having received what was then considered a good education, he for a few years kept school in various parts of South Carnarvonshire, one of his pupils being Ebenezer Thomas, who afterwards became an eminent poet known as *Eben Fardd*. Before he was thirty he opened a school at Welshpool, to which young men from all parts of the county flocked, for he was an excellent teacher. Some years afterwards he removed to Newtown, where he spent the remainder of his days, and where he died on the 8th October, 1838, aged 49 years. For many years he was an acceptable lay preacher with the Calvinistic Methodists, both at Welshpool and Newtown, but had ceased to be so for some time prior to his death. He was a very good poet, and many of his productions may be found in the Welsh magazines of those days. He competed at the

Welshpool Eisteddfod of 1824 with his old pupil Eben Fardd
for the prize offered for the best *Awdl ar Ddinystr Jerusalem*
(Ode on the Destruction of Jerusalem), and the adjudicator, the
Rev. Walter Davies, is said to have admitted that in some
respects his *Awdl* was decidedly the best, but that unfortunately
after "destroying" Jerusalem he proceeded to "re-build" it,
which was outside the limits of the competition, and consequently he had forfeited his claim to the prize. He was also
one of the best musicians of his day in Wales. In 1828 he
published *Y Caniedydd Crefyddol* (The Sacred Songster), an
elementary work on music dedicated to the Rev. John Jenkins,
of Kerry. He also published in Welsh a *Memoir of Mr. John
Bebb, jun.*, a highly promising young medical student, of a well-
known Welshpool family, whose life was prematurely cut off. This
little volume contained among others the following beautiful
Englyn, which shews what a gifted poet Mr. Owen was :—

> " Angau ddaw a braw'n ei bryd,—O ! gwylia
> Ei golyn dychrynllyd !
> Tro dy fyw, trwy dy fywyd,
> Fore a hwyr i farw o hyd,"

OWEN, WILLIAM, was the son of poor parents living at
Meifod, his father, of the same name, being a plasterer. He
was brought up to the same trade, and up to the age of seventeen knew no Latin, but being an intelligent youth he attracted
the notice of the Vicar (the Rev. Hugh Wynne Jones), who took
him in hand. He first had him instructed by the Curate, and
then sent him for two years to Bangor, under the charge of the
Rev. Morris Williams (*Nixander*). He used to walk to and
from Bangor, and during the vacation he gave lessons to John
Evan Davies, the present Rector of Llangelynin, Merionethshire.
He was next sent, through the generosity of Mr. Wynne-Jones,
to Oswestry School, under the Rev. Dr. Donne, and from thence
to Shrewsbury, under Dr. Kennedy, where he became Captain of
the School, and was distinguished for the elegance of his
scholarship, especially his Latin verses. From Shrewsbury he
went to St. John's College, Cambridge, of which he became a
scholar. In 1848 he was St. John's Port Royal Latin Exhi-
bitioner ; in 1849 he won the Camden medal for a Latin heroic
poem, and was proxime accessit for the Craven. In 1850 he
gained the "Porson"— the blue riband of the University. In
those days it was necessary that in order to take honours in
Classics honours should first be taken in Mathematics also, and
as he hated Mathematics he only took a plain B.A. degree in
1851. But a career which had opened so brilliantly and so full
of promise was soon afterwards clouded and ruined by the
demon of intemperance, and the last years of his life were
spent in Colney Hatch Asylum, where he died on the 26th of
May, 1892, at the age of 68. He was buried on the 31st of the
same month in the Great Northern Cemetery, London.

PALMER, ROGER, Earl of Castlemaine, was the eldest son of James Palmer, of Dorney, Bucks, of the ancient family of the Palmers of Sussex, by Katherine, daughter of William, first Lord Powis, and was born at Dorney, 3rd September, 1634. He spent his childhood chiefly with his mother in Montgomeryshire, owing to the civil war troubles, but returning home in 1647 he was the following year sent to Eton, and thence at Lady-day, 1652, to King's College, Cambridge. In 1656 he was admitted to the Inner Temple. On the 14th April, 1659, he married, and the following year was elected to represent Windsor in Parliament. In 1661 he was created Earl of Castlemaine and Baron Limerick, and for some time travelled abroad. His wife became notorious as King Charles II.'s mistress, and was by him created Duchess of Cleveland. Castlemaine himself is charged with having purchased his title by his wife's dishonour and his own. On the 2nd November, 1679, Lord Castlemaine, who was a Roman Catholic, was committed to the Tower, on the information of Titus Oates and his confederates, on a charge of having been concerned in the alleged Popish Plot. He was tried at the Old Bailey on the 23rd of May following, but was acquitted. In 1685 he was sent by King James II., Ambassador to the Pope—the object being to try to reconcile this kingdom to the Church of Rome, and to demand a Cardinal's hat for Father Petre. He was well acquainted with Rome, and, for a layman, deeply versed in religious controversy. His salary was fixed at a hundred pounds a week, but the embassy was carried on in so costly a manner that Castlemaine declared that thrice that sum would hardly suffice, and that he was a loser by it. He was accompanied by several young gentlemen of the best Roman Catholic families in England, and was sumptuously lodged in a stately palace in Rome. He was early admitted to an interview with Pope Innocent, but the public audience was long delayed. Castlemaine's preparations for that great occasion were indeed on so large a scale that though commenced at Easter, 1686, they were not complete till the following November, and then the Pope had, or pretended to have (for his feelings towards James and his ambassadors were anything but friendly), an attack of gout, which caused another postponement. The following is Macaulay's account of the public ceremony :—

" In January, 1687, at length, the solemn introduction and homage were performed with unusual pomp. The state coaches which had been built at Rome for the pageant were so superb that they were thought worthy to be transmitted to posterity in fine engravings, and to be celebrated by poets in several languages. The front of the ambassador's palace was decorated on this great day with absurd allegorical paintings of gigantic size. There was Saint George with his foot on the neck of Titus Oates, and Hercules with his club crushing College, the Protestant joiner, who in vain attempted to defend himself with his flail. After this public appearance Castlemaine invited all the persons of note then assembled at Rome to a banquet in that gay and splendid gallery, which is adorned with paintings of subjects from the Æneid by Peter of Cortona. The whole city crowded to the show, and it was with difficulty that a company of Swiss guards could keep order among the spectators. The nobles of the Pontifical state in return gave costly entertainments to the ambassador; and poets and wits were employed to lavish on him and on his master insipid and hyperbolical adulation such as flourishes most when genius and taste are in the deepest decay. Foremost among the flatterers was a crowned head. * * * Christiana, the daughter of the great Gustavus. * * She now composed some Italian stanzas in honour of the English prince who, sprung like herself from a race of kings heretofore regarded as the champions of the Reformation, had like herself been reconciled to the ancient church. A splendid assembly met in her palace. Her verses set to music were sung with universal applause, and one of her literary dependents pronounced an oration on the same subject in a style so florid that it seems to have offended the taste of the English hearers. The Jesuits, hostile to the Pope, devoted to the interests of France, and disposed to pay every honour to James, received the English embassy with the utmost pomp in that princely house where the remains of Ignatius Loyola lie enshrined in lazulite and gold. Sculpture, painting, poetry, and eloquence were employed to compliment the strangers. * * * * In the midst of these festivities Castlemaine had to suffer cruel mortifications and humiliations. The Pope treated him with extreme coldness and reserve. As often as the ambassador pressed for an answer to the request which he had been instructed to make in favour of Petre, Innocent was taken with a violent fit of coughing, which put an end to the conversation. The fame of these singular audiences spread over Rome. Pasquin was not silent All the curious and tattling population of the idlest of cities, the Jesuits and the prelates of the French faction only excepted, laughed at Castlemaine's discomfiture. His temper, naturally unamiable, was soon exasperated to violence, and he circulated a memorial reflecting on the Pope. He had now put himself in the wrong. The sagacious Italian had got the advantage, and took care to keep it. He positively declared that the rule which excluded Jesuits from ecclesiastical preferment should not be relaxed in favour of Father Petre. Castlemaine, much provoked, threatened to leave Rome. Innocent replied with a meek impertinence which was the more provoking because it could scarcely be distinguished from simplicity, that his Excellency might go if he liked. 'But if we must lose him,' added the venerable Pontiff, 'I hope that he will take care of his health on the road. 'English people do not know how dangerous it is in this country to ·travel in the heat of the day. The best way is to start before dawn, and 'to take some rest at noon.' With this salutary advice and with a string of beads, the unfortunate ambassador was dismissed. In a few months appeared, both in the Italian and English tongue, a pompous history of the mission magnificently printed in folio and illustrated with plates. The frontispiece, to the great scandal of all Protestants, represented Castlemaine in the robes of a Peer, with his coronet in his hand, kissing the toe of Innocent."

On his return he was sworn a member of the Privy Council. After King William's accession he was arraigned before the House of Commons in 1689 " for high treason in going as an "ambassador to Rome," He made a long speech in his own defence, and to account for his not surrendering sooner he explained that as soon as the King (James II.) first left Whitehall he

" thought it decency to go out of town, and therefore three days after I took coach for Montgomeryshire where of late I used to reside in the summer time. On the borders of that county, at a small Corporation called Oswestree, I was stopped by the rabble, and afterwards detained by a strong guard at my inn by the Mayor, though nobody he confessed made any oath against me, and though he had no orders as he said from London for it; nay after a month's restraint he denied me my liberty upon bail notwithstanding two neighbouring lawyers, whom I sent for, assured him he could not justify the refusal by law. * * * After a confinement of seven weeks, I was sent for up and brought hither by a party of horse."

The trial resulted in his discharge. After this he led a retired life, part of which was spent at the Hall, Llanfyllin, the residence of the Prices "the Papists." By his will dated 30th November, 1696, he expressed his desire " as to the place of my buriall, if I " die in Wales, 1 may be buried in ye parish churche of Pole, " near my unkle Powis and others of my mother's family." He died at Oswestry, July 21st, 1705, in the 71st year of his age, and was buried in Pool "chapel" amongst his mother's relations. His portrait is at Powis Castle.

PARRY, HARRI, an eccentric bard, was born at Craigygath, near Dolanog, Llanfihangel, in 1709. Few of his compositions have been printed. Sion Prys's Almanack for 1744 gives an account of an Eisteddfod at Llansaintffraid Glyn Ceiriog, the proceedings being opened by Parry with the following *Englyn* :—

> Eisteddwch, ceisiwch ein cân—llu clauar,
> Lle clywir ymddiddan ;
> Gosodiad fel gwe' sidan
> Cu rwym glos—y Cymry glân.

He greatly disliked the Methodists and all Dissenters. In W. Howel of Llanidloes's Almanac for 1774, there are 19 Stanzas by him under the title *Ceryddiad difrifol i'r Methodistiaid, &c.* (A Serious Reproof to the Methodists, &c.) As for himself, he said—

> Nid a Harri Parri pêr—i wrando
> Ar Ronndhead na Chwacer ;
> Y dynion sydd dan y sêr,
> Yn peidio dweyd eu pader.

He was of diminutive stature, and was a sawyer by occupation. The celebrated Walter Davies finding him in his old age at this laborious work, thus addressed him :—

> Teithiais anturiais at Harri,—mi wela'
> Wr penlas yn poeni ;
> O resyn, ar ol hir oesi,
> Wel'd hen wr llwyd yn tynu'n y lli'.

To which he replied :—

> Walter heb gymhar, fel Gomer,—Dafis
> Llawn dyfais a doethder ;
> Rhaid i Harri Parri pêr
> Capio lle byddo'r cwper.

During the last 30 years of his life he was in the habit of going about the country *clera*, that is to say, singing and vending songs, carols, and other poetical effusions of his own. In April each year he began to sing his May Carol recounting the events of the past twelvemonth. He died at Llanfyllin, and was buried at Llanfihangel. At the time of his death he was nearly 90 years of age.

PARRY, ROBERT, a poet of considerable merit, was the son of a clergyman of the same name, and was born near Machynlleth. During his childhood he removed with his parents into Denbighshire, his father having been promoted in 1810 to the Vicarage of Eglwysfach, in that county. He received a university education, being intended for the church, but preferring the life of a farmer, he relinquished the idea of taking Orders, and passed the greater part of his life as a respectable farmer at Plas Efenechtyd and Plas Towerbridge, near Ruthin. He died at the latter place in 1863, and was buried at Eglwysfach. His poem on *Belshazzar's Feast*, the Chair subject at the Denbigh Eisteddfod of 1828, was adjudged to be second best. It is printed in *The Gwyneddion*, being an Account of that Eisteddfod, and many of his compositions may be found in the Welsh magazines of those days.

PARRY, THOMAS, the third son of Edward Parry, of Leighton, near Welshpool, and Anne his wife, was born in the year 1768. At the age of 21 he went to Madras, in the East Indies, and for about four years held Government appointments, being at one time private secretary to the Governor, General Meadows. In 1792 he embarked upon the business of a merchant in the shipping of produce from Madras to this country, and founded the eminent mercantile firm of Parry and Co., which remains to this day. His active interest in the affairs of the native princes rendered him obnoxious to the authorities at the fort, and for a time he was banished from Madras. He is said to have been an accomplished man of unblemished character, who might have amassed an enormous fortune had he been unscrupulous in the mode of making wealth ; as it was, it would appear from his will (of which a copy was published in *Mont. Coll*, XIX., p. 247) that he died a rich man. In the month of February, 1824 (being only six months before his death) the native inhabitants of Madras presented him with a gold cup, accompanied by an address expressing their warmest gratitude for the interest he had taken in the welfare of the natives during a protracted career in India of 36 years. While travelling between Porto Novo and Cuddalore he was attacked by cholera, and died on the 14th August, 1824, aged 56 years. He was buried at Cuddalore. At Madras a handsome monument by Chantry, with a finely-executed figure of a Hindoo, was erected to his memory in St. George's Cathedral.

PICKMERE, JOHN RICHARD, was born in 1794 at Warrington, where he practised as a solicitor for many years. He purchased the Mount, in the parish of Llanfair, in 1852, and resided there until his death. He was the author of a work bearing the following strange title :—*Being, analytically described in its chief respects and principal truths, in the order of this Analysis, fully stated, with a detail of man's spiritual and chief relations.* He died May 11th, 1875, and was buried in Llanfair churchyard.

PIERCY, BENJAMIN, the eminent Civil Engineer, from whose surveys and plans nearly every mile of railway in Montgomeryshire and Mid-Wales was made was born at Trefeglwys, on the 16th of March, 1827. He was the third son of Robert Piercy, of Chirk, a well-known commissioner, valuer, and surveyor in the inclosure of commons and waste lands, and extensively engaged in the construction of public roads and other works, and in surveys and valuations under the Poor Law and Tithe Commutation Acts. He at an early age entered his father's office, and soon became actively engaged upon important surveys and other work of varied description. About 1847, he became chief assistant to Mr. Charles Mickleburgh, of Montgomery, a surveyor, land agent, and inclosure-commissioner with a large practice, with whom he remained four or five years. After that Mr. Henry Robertson, sometime M.P. for Shrewsbury, and subsequently for the county of Merioneth, engaged him to assist him in making the parliamentary surveys for the Shrewsbury and Chester Railway. So much energy and attention did he devote to the work that he was the means of preventing the loss of a year in obtaining the Act for that line. He was afterwards employed under Mr. Robertson upon the plans and sections for the first Bill for a Railway from Oswestry to Newtown. That Bill was not passed. Application was made to Parliament in a subsequent session, and Mr. Piercy was again engaged in the engineering, but upon that occasion, too, the Bill was not passed. It was in 1852, when he became the Engineer for the Rea Valley Railway from Shrewsbury to Minsterley and Newtown, that Mr. Piercy's independent practice commenced. With characteristic energy and skill he had within a very limited time prepared the parliamentary plans for deposit, but they were surreptitiously removed from a room which he occupied at a hotel in London, so that it was impossible to proceed with the Bill in the then ensuing session. In the following year, however, he duly deposited the plans for a railway from Shrewsbury, with a branch to Minsterley. Although strongly opposed at every stage, he succeeded in carrying the Bill through both Houses, and it received the Royal assent. It was in the Select Committees on this Bill that he first made his reputation as a witness in Parliamentary Committees. After this he was engaged in nearly all the projects for introducing independent railways into Wales, all of them meeting with fierce opposition; for several days consecutively, he was as a witness under cross-examination by the genial Mr. Serjeant Merewether and other eminent counsel, but so little headway were they able to make against Mr. Piercy, that upon one occasion, when a Committee passed a Bill of Mr. Piercy's, Mr. Merewether held up his brief-bag and asked the Committee whether they would not too give that to Mr. Piercy? Amongst the numerous railways in this country of which he was engineer are the following:—The Oswestry and Newtown, and its Llanfyllin and Kerry Branches, the Llanidloes and Newtown, the Newtown and Machynlleth, the

Oswestry, Ellesmere, and Whitchurch, the Welsh Coast Railways, extending to Aberystwyth and Pwllheli, the Vale of Clwyd,
the Carnarvonshire, the Denbigh, Ruthin and Corwen, the
Bishop's Castle, the Mid-Wales, the Hereford, Hay and Brecon,
The Kington and Eardisley, the Hoylake, and the Wrexham,
Mold, and Connah's Quay, with its extensions and branches
Among the most important engineering works upon the above
railways were several important river bridges, comprising the
crossing of the Vyrnwy and three crossings of the Severn. In
these cases, the railway was carried over upon iron-plate girders
of large span, resting upon iron cylinders sunk to a great depth
and filled in with concrete. There were also two fine stations,
one at Oswestry and the other at Welshpool. The construction
of the Newtown and Machynlleth Railway, owing to the
mountainous nature of the country, involved some heavy work,
e.g., an open cutting about 120 feet deep at Talerddig, and
several long skew bridges over mountainous torrents, constructed with unusually massive masonry, firmly bedded in solid
rock foundation at great depth. Upon the Welsh Coast Railway was the crossing of two great estuaries, exposed to the
sea, with tides of 16 feet range. One of these at Barmouth,
about two miles wide, was crossed with iron girders resting
upon screw piles, with an opening bridge to admit of the
passage of sea-going vessels. The other estuary crossing was
near Portmadoc. Originally it was intended to cross the Dovey
from Ynyslas to Aberdovey, which would have entailed the construction of a long and costly viaduct across the estuary. The
plans were all prepared by Mr. Piercy, who himself considered
them at that time his masterpieces. The project, however, was
abandoned in favour of the present deviation line from Glandovey
junction. At this period Mr. Piercy resided for some years at
Welshpool, and then removed to London. In 1862 Mr. Piercy
was consulted by the Concessionaires of Railways in the Island
of Sardinia with reference to the construction of the railways,
for which they had obtained the concession comprising about
250 miles of lines. The plans and sections which had been
prepared by Italian engineers, involved the construction of about
20 miles of tunnels and many heavy works, so that it
was found impossible to get contractors who would be willing
to build the railways within the limit of time allowed by the
concession, and at the cost within the amount of funds available.
Mr. Piercy re-surveyed the whole of the projected railways, and
changed their proposed course, reduced very considerably the
tunnelling and other heavy work, and he succeeded in designing a
system of lines capable of construction at a practicable cost within
the prescribed time. The Royal Sardinian Railway Company was
thereupon successfully formed, having first obtained the adoption
and acceptance of Mr. Piercy's plans by the Italian Government,
and a contract was entered into with Messrs. Smith, Knight and
Co. for the construction and completion of the railways accordingly. The works progressed, and some of the easier sections

of railway were nearly completed when the war broke out between Italy and Austria, and stopped all further operations. Everything remained suspended until 1869. During the interval the works sustained considerable damage from floods and otherwise. Mr. Piercy was again called in by the Railway Company to re-survey the lines, and prepare new estimates for their completion. When these were finished he negotiated on behalf of the new Convention with the Italian Government. By this Convention, which came into force in August, 1870, an increased annual kilometrical guarantee was obtained for the Company, and it was agreed that the railways should be divided into two series, one called the "lines of the first period," the other, the "lines of the second period." The "lines of the first period" comprised only the lines of the plains left unfinished in 1865, of a total length of 197 kilometres; the "lines of the second period" were the more difficult lines over and along mountains, 194 kilometres. The time allowed for completing the "lines of the first period" was extended to the 31st of December, 1874, after which the Company was to decide whether it would construct the "lines of the second period" or whether it would sell the undertaking to the Government. Mr. Piercy lost no time in taking energetic action on this new convention. For some months he carried on the construction of the railways on behalf of the Company, but subsequently the works were again let to a contractor, Mr. Piercy acting as engineer-in-chief, and early in 1872 the "lines of the first period," excepting one section of about 45 kilometres, were opened for public traffic, leaving only the construction of that section to fulfil the Company's obligations under the Convention of 1870. The Convention of the "lines of the second period" was subsequently proceeded with, and after almost endless difficulties from various causes the junction of the "lines of the first period" with the "lines of the second period" was effected in June, 1880, and the whole were formally accepted, approved by the Government, and opened throughout early in 1881. As an acknowledgment of the great national service rendered by Mr. Piercy, he was created a Commendatore of the Crown of Italy, and the freedom of various cities in Sardinia was conferred upon him. Subsequently it was decided to construct an extension of the system from the extreme north-eastern terminus of the line at Terranova to the Golfo di Aranci, a splendid natural harbour directly facing Civita-Vecchia, the port of Rome. The construction of this extension—about 27 kilometres was also entrusted to Mr. Piercy. The work involved a heavy cutting of more than half a mile in length, and over 40 feet deep, through difficult strata. The cutting was completed within ninety days, and the whole line within seven months. Mr. Piercy also designed a mole and other harbour works at the Golfo di Aranci, which are now being constructed to his plans. Supplementary to the main lines of railway in Sardinia, which are all of the standard 4ft. 8½in. guage, Mr. Piercy took advan.

tage of his long residence in the island to study several series of subsidiary lines of the metre guage to be feeders to the main system. His studies extended to nearly 2,000 kilometres of narrow-gauge railways, passing through difficult mountainous districts at an altitude, in several instances, of from 3,000 to 4,000 feet. For several of these lines his plans were accepted by the Company and approved by the Government, and they are now in course of construction. It was not in railways only that Mr. Piercy interested himself in Sardinia. He gave great attention to effecting agricultural improvements in the island. Deserts and swamps were converted by him into perfect gardens by extensive drainage works, and the planting of many thousands of eucalyptus and other trees, so that places, formerly noted as hot-beds of fever, were rendered perfectly healthy. He also planted vineyards and orchards on a large scale. He acquired large estates, which he stocked with cattle, horses, and sheep, of all of which he so improved the breeds that his stock attained the reputation of being far superior to any other in the island, and he gained many medals awarded by Government as well for horses, cattle, and sheep, as for agriculture. He, moreover, did a good deal towards instructing the natives in good husbandry, which was before in a very primitive state. In short, Mr. Piercy's hand was pre-eminently visible in all improvements, and he was universally looked upon as a public benefactor throughout the period of his connection with Sardinia, which extended over twenty-five years. During Mr. Piercy's residence in Italy he was an intimate friend of Garibaldi, who paid him frequent visits in Sardinia, and one of the great Italian patriot's sons (Ricciotti) was for some time his pupil. In addition to the Sardinian railways, Mr. Piercy was employed upon other public works in Italy, notably a project for the canalization of the Tiber. He also prepared the plans for the Acqua Marcia, the great Company by which Rome is now supplied with water. In France, he was the Engineer-in-chief of the Napoleon-Vendée Railway, a line which has been constructed and in operation many years, about 160 miles in length, from Tours, _via_ Bressuire, to Sables d' Olonne, a well-known port and seaside resort on the Bay of Biscay. In India, he was the engineer for the lines, about 90 miles in length, of the Assam Railways and Trading Company Limited, passing through the tea plantations in Assam, and connecting Dibrugarh, on the River Brahmaputra, with the coal fields at Makum, in the Naga Hills, near the frontier of Burmah, where the Company is working extensive collieries. These collieries were opened up under Mr. Piercy's direction, and he was engaged at the time of his death in taking measures for the working of the valuable petroleum deposits also belonging to the Assam Railways and Trading Company. He also took an active part in projecting an extension of the Assam Railway across the Burmah frontier, through the Naga Hills, south-eastward, to meet the railway now being constructed in Burmah, northward of Mandalay. To revert to the year

1881, when the Sardinian "lines of the second period" were completed, Mr. Piercy then again took up his residence in Great Britain, and purchased the Marchwiel Hall Estate, near Wrexham, with the intention of devoting himself to the resuscitation of the railways in North Wales, of which he had been the engineer before he went to Italy. He took them in hand financially as well as in the capacity of engineer ; consolidating and re-arranging their capital accounts, and planning extensions, branches, and improvements, so as develope the valuable mineral resources of the districts through which they passed, and to bring to the lines their fair share of traffic. He found a ready ally in Mr. Henry Robertson, who had, before Mr. Piercy's departure for Italy, occupied a position antagonistic to the latter's Welsh railway projects, and the two became cordially associated in the common object of improving the industries of North Wales. Parliamentary powers were obtained by the Manchester, Sheffield, and Lincolnshire Railway Company for connecting the Wrexham, Mold and Connah's Quay Railway with Birkenhead, Liverpool, and Chester on the north by a bridge across the Dee at Connah's Quay, and powers were obtained for connecting the Wrexham line with the Cambrian Railways on the south by an extension to Ellesmere, thus completing the North Wales Railway system, and providing a new through continuous route, uniting Liverpool, Manchester, and the north with all parts of Wales, south as well as north. Mr. Piercy was a member of the Institution of Civil Engineers, and a Justice of the Peace for the County of Denbigh, his assistance in matters of County Government being highly appreciated for its eminently practical and original character. In private life Mr. Piercy's tastes were simple, healthy, and intellectual. He was a most agreeable companion, and much esteemed by his intimates for his generous and amiable disposition, but his great characteristics were thoroughness, a habit of bestowing regard upon things which those around him would consider trifles, infinite capacity for taking pains, an extraordinary power of premeditation and forethought, thinking things out to the end, and mentally working out the result of even the smallest matter to which he put his hand, coupled with indomitable and unceasing perseverance and persistence in all which he undertook, but at the same time modest and unassuming to an unusual degree. His life, as will be seen from the above record of the numerous and important undertakings in which he was engaged, was one of unceasing activity and hard work. Few men, indeed, have accomplished so much in a comparatively short life. He died in London after a very brief illness on the 24th of March, 1888, aged 61 years, and was buried in the Kensal Green Cemetery on the 29th of the same month. Mr. Piercy was married in 1855 to Sarah, second daughter of the late Mr. Thomas Davies, of Montgomery, by whom he had three sons and six daughters, who survive. At the time of his death Mr. Piercy had amassed considerable wealth.

PIERCY, ROBERT, an elder brother of the above-named Benjamin Piercy, and his partner and associate in his Montgomeryshire undertakings, was born at Trefeglwys on the 26th January, 1825. After spending some time in his father's office at Chirk and elsewhere, he was appointed Engineer to the New British Iron Company at Ruabon, in whose service he remained for 10 years. He carried out all the Company's lines in and about their Collieries and works, including the Plas Madoc branch, and had charge of the underground Colliery surveys, &c. His experience during this period proved of the greatest value to him in after life. Having joined his brother in partnership during the construction of the Montgomeryshire lines he resided for some years at Welshpool, and thence removed to London. It fell to his share chiefly to superintend the office work. He was essentially a practical Engineer and a first rate Surveyor and Leveller, well up in locating lines and possessing a thorough knowledge of the details of engineering works, but he was of a retiring disposition, and therefore less known to the general public than his more celebrated brother Benjamin. About the year 1874 he married Miss Valleria, by whom he had one son and two daughters, who survive him and reside in Switzerland. From 1879 to 1884 he was in India constructing the Assam Railways, and opening the rich and important Collieries at Margherita from which a large trade is carried on with Calcutta by means of the Railway and the flotilla on the Brahmaputra River. His residence in India materially affected his health, but before he left he had put both the Railway and works on a good and satisfactory footing. He was an old member of the Institution of Civil Engineers, and was held in high repute as an able and practical Engineer, notably in dealing with treacherous foundations for bridges. He had numerous works of this class without practically a single failure. He died on the 29th January, 1894, aged 69 years, at Celyn, Caergwrle, and was buried at the parish church of Chirk.

POWELL, THOMAS, the Chartist, was a native of Newtown. His father, Richard Powell, was the son of William Powell, of Cilgwrgan. His mother's maiden name was Blayney, and she was related to the Blayneys of Gregynog. Richard Powell, in his younger days, served in the American War of Independence, and was wounded at Bunker's Hill. For some years prior to his death, at an advanced age, in 1835, he lived in lodgings at the Grapes Inn, Newtown. Thomas Powell was educated at Welshpool. Subsequently he was apprenticed to Mr. Watkins, an ironmonger at Shrewsbury, and at the expiration of his apprenticeship he obtained an appointment in a wholesale house in Upper Thames Street, London. During his residence in London, his Radical proclivities brought him into acquaintance and fellowship with those who afterwards became leaders of the Chartist movement. In 1832 he removed to Welshpool, having purchased an extensive ironmongery business there formerly carried on by Mr. Pryce Bowen. He was, it is said, an excellent tradesman, and did a large business, but expensive habits and the expenditure of large sums in the furtherance of his political opinions, landed him in pecuniary difficulties which compelled him to compound with his creditors. Mr. W. J. Linton, in an interesting article on *Who were the Chartists?* in the *Century Magazine* relates the following incident of this period of Powell's life :—

"Some words I must spare for Thomas Powell, whom I knew when he was a shopman with his friend Hetherington. He, a fiery little Welshman, had more of the rebel in him, albeit a sensible man, clever and wary,—a man who might have led an insurrection. * * * What quality he had, how trusted and trustworthy he was, one little anecdote will shew. When Hetherington was indicted for selling Haslam's *Letters to the Clergy*, he made up his mind to suffer imprisonment rather than pay a fine. He had been mulcted enough in former days, and this time 'they should take it out of his bones.' A friend (Chartist also, Hugh Williams, a Carmarthen lawyer, Cobden's brother-in-law) lent him a sum sufficient to purchase his whole property, books, presses, household stuff, &c. This he handed to Powell, the property being valued by a broker to make the sale legal. Powell bought all, paying the ready money for it. Hetherington returned his friend's loan, and coming out of prison (he was not fined) received back his own from Powell. There were no vouchers or receipts passed to vitiate the transaction. So these Chartists trusted one another."

Henry Hetherington was a printer, bookseller, and news agent in London. He attended meetings at Newtown and Llanidloes during the Chartist agitation in the winter of 1838. He died of cholera in 1849. Hugh Williams was a native of Machynlleth. He wrote and published a Collection of Chartist songs, and was the solicitor who got up the defence of the Llanidloes rioters at the Welshpool Assizes in July, 1839. He practised for many years at St. Clears, Carmarthenshire, where he died. Powell, having gone out of business, devoted all his time and energies to the Chartist agitation, and was its ablest advocate in Montgomeryshire. On Christmas Day, 1838, a great demonstration was held at Newtown and Caersws, at which Powell was one of the principal speakers. His speech on this occasion, as reported, contains little that would now be considered reprehensible, but much that is sensible and just. It, however, brought him into trouble—he was tried for using seditious language, and sentenced to twelve months' imprisonment. During his confinement he devoted much time to teaching his fellow prisoners at Montgomery. When the Chartist movement collapsed, Powell engaged with a Colonial Company to go with a party of emigrants to Trinidad, where he settled, and it is said married a woman of colour, by whom he had several children, and where after a few years' residence he died.

POWELL, VAVASOR, an eminent Nonconformist preacher of the seventeenth century, although born out of Montgomeryshire, was closely connected with the county by descent and marriage, as well as residence within it for some years, and is intimately associated with the early history of its Nonconformity. He was born at Knucklas, Radnorshire, in the year 1617. His father, Richard Powell, belonged to an ancient Welsh family who had lived in that neighbourhood a hundred years before him. His mother was of the Vavasors, a family of great antiquity that came from Yorkshire into Wales. His bitter enemies (of whom his sturdy and energetic Nonconformity produced many) have endeavoured to throw discredit upon his origin, as well as upon every action of his life. Thus Anthony Wood, in his *Athenæ Oxonienses*, with ill-concealed spite, says :—

"Vavasor Powell having often told his friends and the brethren, not without boasting, that he was once a member of Jesus College in Oxon, I shall therefore upon his word number him among these writers. Be it known, therefore, that this person, who was famous in his general tion for his ill name among those that were not of his opinion, was born in the Borough of Knucklas, in Radnorshire, son of Richard Howell, an Ale-keeper there, by Penelope, his wife, daughter of William Vavasor, of Newtown, in Montgomeryshire. He was brought up a scholar, saith the publisher of his Life, but the writer of *Strena Vavasoriensis* tells us that his employment was to walk guest's horses, by which finding no great gain at such a petty Ale-house, he was elevated in his thoughts for higher preferment, and so became an Hostler (I would say Groom) to Mr. Isaac Thomas, an Innkeeper and Mercer in Bishop's Castle in Shropshire."

The above statement as to the occupation of Powell's father, and the other depreciating remarks which follow, are copied from *Strena Vavasoriensis*, or *Hue and Cry, &c.*, a scurrilous book written by one Alexander Griffiths, and published about 1652 while Powell was in prison. It is almost entirely a tissue of calumnious falsehoods, to refute which Charles Lloyd of Dolobran, the Rev. James Quarrell, and others, in 1653, published *Examen et Purgamen Vavasoris*. The author of the *Strena* describes Powell's father as "a poor Ale-man and Badger of Oatmeal." His grandfather, William Vavasor, was the son of Andrew Vavasor, sheriff of Montgomeryshire in 1563, and was himself High Constable of the Hundred of Newtown, 39 Eliz. (1596). Walker (*Sufferings of the Clergy*) says that Powell became "a Schoolmaster, and at length a preacher at Clun," and charges him with having entered the church by means of forged orders, —a charge for which there seems not to have been a particle of foundation. The truth appears to be that after spending some time at Oxford he was employed by his uncle, the Rev. Erasmus Powell, to be his curate at Clun, where he also kept a School. He had always been from his childhood, as he himself says in his *Autobiography*,

"very active and forward in the pursuit of the pleasures and vanities of this wicked world, * * * only drunkenness I much hated," encouraging the sports and pastimes that were then common on the Sabbath. "Being one Lord's Day," he says, "a stander by and beholder of those that broke the Sabbath by divers Games, being then myself a Reader of Common Prayers, and in the habit of a foolish Shepherd, I was ashamed to play with them, yet took as much pleasure therein as if I had, where-

upon a godly, grave Professor of Religion (one of those then called
Puritans) seeing me there came to me, and very soberly and mildly asked
me, Doth it become you, Sir, that are a Scholar, and one that teacheth
others, to break the Lord's Sabbath thus?"

This reproof caused him to resolve not to transgress again in
that manner, and soon afterwards a sermon of the celebrated
Puritan preacher, Walter Cradock, deeply impressed him. He
forsook his former companions and took to Puritan ways, travelling much in Radnorshire and Breconshire especially preaching,
until the persecution he met with caused him in August, 1642,
to leave Wales and go to London. His enemies, however, assert
that he was never ordained, and that being indicted at Radnor
for " Nonconformity, forging of Orders, and seditious doctrine,
" he was with much ado reprieved from the gallows." After
passing two years in London, preaching whenever he had an
opportunity, he was called to Dartford in Kent, where he was
very successful in his ministry for two years more. In 1646,
Wales having been reduced under the power of the Parliament,
he wished to return thither, and accordingly applied to the
Assembly of Divines then sitting "for the trial of public
preachers " for a certificate. After some demur about ordination,
they gave him the following :

"These are to certify those whom it may concern that the bearer hereof,
Mr Vavasor Powell, is a man of a Religious and blameless conversation,
and of able gifts for the work of the Ministry, and hath approved himself
faithful therein; which we, whose names are under-written, do Testify :
some of our own knowledge, others from Credible and Sufficient information :
And therefore he being now called, and desired to exercise his Gifts in his
own Countrey of Wales, he also having the Language thereof, we con-
ceive him fit for that Work, and worthy of encouragement therein. In
Witness whereof, we have subscribed our Names—Sep. 11, 1646.

Charles Herle, Prolocutor:

Henry Scudder,	Phillip Nye,
William Greenhill,	Stephen Marshall,
Franc. Woodcock,	Jer. Whitaker,
William Strong,	Arthur Salwey,
Joseph Caryl,	Peter Sterry,
William Carter,	Henry Prince,
Thomas Wilson,	Christopher Love,
Jer. Burroughs,	Tho. Froysell,
	Robert Bettes."

This document is interesting as showing that although born at
Knucklas, Welsh was Powell's native tongue, and that at that
time it was the language generally spoken in Radnorshire. The
Rev. Jonathan Williams, in his *History of Radnorshire*, says
that, even in 1747, divine service was performed in all its
churches in the Welsh tongue alone. Now there is not, I
believe, a single place of worship belonging to the Established
Church in Radnorshire where the service is ever conducted in
Welsh, and it would probably be hard to find in the whole
County 1000 persons who can speak Welsh. On his arrival in
Wales he renewed with great energy his former labours,

" Preaching the word in season and out of season * * * * * insomuch that there was but few, if any, of the churches, chapels, Town halls

in Wales wherein he did not preach Christ, yea very often upon mountains, and very frequent in Fairs and Markets, it was admirable to consider how industrious he was by his often preaching in two or three places a day, and seldom two days in a week throughout the year out of the pulpit, nay he would sometimes ride a hundred miles in a week, and preach in every place where he might have admission both day and night."

His enemies, of course, called this fanaticism. It is said that he often preached twenty times a week. The pocket Bible used by him is now in the possession of the writer. It is a copy of the Welsh bible published in 1630 by Heylyn and Middleton. Sometimes he spoke and prayed for three, four, nay six and seven hours together!—and

"He had a ready wit, was well read in history and geography, a good natural phylosopher and skilled in physick, which greatly furthered his invention, but above all very powerful in prayer, much indued with the Spirit, and an eloquent man, mighty in the Scriptures, which was so admirably imprinted in his memory, that he was as a Concordance where ever he came. * * * * * He was exceeding hospitable, the feasts that he used to make were not for the rich, but the poor and aged, whom he often supplyed with Clothes, Shoos, Stockings, and all other necessary accommodations. He was very free in the entertainment of strangers * * * and great resort was to him from most parts of Wales and many from England, and was so free harted that he would use to say, he had room for twelve in his beds, a hundred in his barns, and a thousand in his heart."

In 1647, Powell accompanied as Chaplain a portion of the Parliamentary forces into Anglesey, where he narrowly escaped being killed. His name is among those who on the 20th May, 1648. subscribed "The Resolutions and Engagements of us the Gentlemen, Ministers, and well-affected of the County of Montgomery" to assist the Parliament to suppress the insurrection. At this time he lived, it appears, on his property at Goitre, Kerry, in this county, where he had built a "fair and sumptuous house," and continued to reside there until his imprisonment in 1660. It was mainly through his instrumentality that in February, 1649-50 the celebrated "Act for the Propagation of the Gospel " in Wales" was passed, and he was named one of the examiners or approvers appointed to carry it out. This Act lasted but for three years, namely until 1653. Under it a great number of the clergy were ejected "for ignorance, scandal, &c., yet not all (he "says) as it was falsely reported; for in Montgomeryshire, the "county where I lived, there were eleven or twelve never ejected." After deducting from the list of 330 given by Walker, those who were pluralists and are named twice, and those who were unqualified for the ministry, but were employed by the Commissioners as schoolmasters, the actual number is reduced in all Wales to about 150. His enemies charged him with having received enormous sums from the sequestered benefices, but this he indignantly denied, saying " Let me deal freely and truly with "all the world in that particular; I never received by salary, "and all other ways put together, for my preaching in Wales " from Christians and from the states since the beginning, which

" is above 20 years, but between six and seven hundred pounds
" pounds at most." Fired with apostolic zeal, he and his fellow
itinerants, besides preaching incessantly, in the short space of
14 years presented their countrymen with three editions of the
New Testament in Welsh, and one edition of 6,000 copies of the
whole Bible. In 1652, Powell " supposing himself able," as
Wood says,

" to encounter any Minister in Wales, did after his Settlement there,
send a bold challenge to any Minister or Scholar that opposed him or his
Brethren, to dispute on these two questions. (1) *Whether your calling or
ours (which you so much speak against) be most warrantable and nearest
to the word of God ?* (2) *Whether your mixt ways, or ours of Separation,
be nearest the word of God ?* This challenge being sent flying abroad
11th of June 1652, it came into the hands of Dr. George Griffith, of Llanymynech, in Shropshire, who looking upon it as sent to him, he returned
an answer in Latin two days after, with promise, on certain conditions, to
dispute with him, either in private or public. On the 19th of the same
month, Vav. Powell returned a reply in Latin from Redcastle, but so full
of barbarities, that any Schoolboy of 10 years of age might have done
better. After this the Doctor made a Rejoynder in elegant Latin, wherein he corrected Powell for his false Grammar, Barbarisms and Solecisms,
and did set a day whereon they should meet to dispute on the aforesaid
Questions: but the time, place, and method, with conveniences, being
discussed and delayed from time to time, the Disputation was not held
till the 23rd of July following. At that time both parties meeting in the
company of their Friends, Powell's cause fell to the ground, meerly, as
'twas conceived, for want of Academical Learning, and the true way of
arguing. So that he being then much guilty of his own weakness,
endeavoured to recover it in his Reputation by putting a Relation of the
Dispute in the News Book called the *Perfect Diurnal*, as if he had been
the Conqueror. Which relation redounding much to the dishonour of the
Doctor, he the said Doctor did publish a Pamphlet entitled, *Animadver-
sions on an Imperfect Relation in the Perfect Diurnal, &c.*"

The disputation above referred to took place near the New
Chapel, Penrhos, and excited great interest at the time. Dr.
Griffith became afterwards Bishop of St. Asaph. Powell was a
staunch republican, and in 1653 and 1654 he spoke against
Oliver Cromwell to his face, preached publicly against him, and
wrote letters to him blaming him for assuming the Protectorship,
for which he was more than once imprisoned. For joining with
others in a letter of protest against Cromwell's usurpation, he was
apprehended by a party of horsemen " from a day of fasting and
" prayer at Aberbechan " (Llanllwchaiarn), and taken before
Major Gen. Berry, at Worcester, who, however, received him
kindly, and did not detain him long. The latter end of 1654, he
at the head of a party of " fanatics," quelled a rising of the
Cavaliers at Salisbury, and took an active part in preventing
risings in Wales. In 1656 his views upon Baptism were changed,
and he was immersed. From that time he must therefore be
reckoned as a Baptist, but his views were not extreme and he
continued on friendly terms with those who differed from him,
saying " In this of Baptism as in many other cases, difference in
" persuasion and practice may well consist with brotherly love
" and Christian communion." In 1657 he was at Oxford,
where on the 15th July we find him preaching in the pulpit of

All Saints. Being known to be an irreconcileable enemy to the monarchy, he was, upon the approach of the king's restoration, namely, the latter end of February, 1659-60, seized and imprisoned at Shrewsbury, and his lands and tenements that had been purchased by him were taken from him. He was very soon removed from Shrewsbury into Montgomeryshire, and there kept in close custody, and upon his refusing to take the oaths of allegiance and supremacy he was removed to the Fleet Prison in London, where he remained two years. During twelve months he was so closely confined that he was not suffered to go out of his chamber door; this and the offensive smell arising from a dunghill which stood right under his window so impaired his health that he never afterwards quite recovered it. In 1662 he was again removed to Southsea Castle, near Portsmouth, where he was closely confined five years. In 1667 he was removed by Habeas Corpus and being set at liberty he retired to Wales, where he again preached to vast multitudes, but before ten months end he was again committed to Cardiff gaol, and in 1661 again removed to Karoon House (the then Fleet Prison) in Lambeth. It seems that he was allowed to preach occasionally, and had some measure of liberty here. The last sermons he preached were on the 25th September, 1670, many being admitted to hear him. A day or two afterwards a violent attack of dysentery, from which he never rallied, confined him to his bed, and after a month's illness he died peacefully at four o'clock in the afternoon of the 27th of October, 1670, in the 53rd year of his age and the 11th of his imprisonment. Powell was buried at the lower or west end of the burial place in Bunhill Fields, " in the presence of innumerable Dissenters that "then followed his corps." Over his grave was soon afterwards erected an altar monument of free stone, on the "plank" of which was engraved the following epitaph composed by his friend and biographer, Mr. E. Bagshaw :—

" Vavasor Powell, a successful teacher of the past, a sincere witness of the present, and an useful example to the future age, lies here interred, who in the defection of so many, obtained mercy to be found faithful; for which being called to several Prisons, he was there tried, and would not accept deliverance, expecting a better Resurrection. In hope of which he finished this Life and Testimony together, in the eleventh year of his imprisonment, and in the 53rd Year of his Age, Octob. 27, an. 1671 (sic, should be 1670).
        " In vain Oppressors do themselves perplex,
        To find out Arts how they the Saints may vex,
        Death spoils their Plots, and sets the oppressed free,
        Thus Vavasor obtain'd true liberty —
        Christ him releas'd, and now he's joyn'd among
        The martyr'd Souls, with whom he cries, How long !
                                        —Rev. 6, 10."

Vavasor Powell was twice married, but left no children. His first wife was the widow of Mr. Paul Quarrell, of Presteign. His second wife, a woman of high intelligence and great abilities, was Katherine, daughter of Col. Gerard, Governor of Chester

Castle. By his will (a copy of which appeared in *Mont. Coll.* xxvi., 221)) he gave her all his property subject to a few small legacies. After his death she became the wife of the Rev. John Evans, of Wrexham, an eminent Nonconformist, and by him the mother of Dr. John Evans, author of *The Christian Temper*. Powell was the author of several works, all written in English, although more than one have been erroneously recorded in *Llyfryddiaeth y Cymry*, as written in Welsh. The following is a list of them :—

1. *Disputation between him and Joh. Goodwin*, concerning universal Redemption, held in Coleman Street, Lond., 31 Dec, 1649. (London 1650 quarto).

2. *Scriptures Concord :* or a Catechism compiled out of the words of the Scripture, &c. Lond., 1647, Octo ; 2nd ed. 1653),

3. *Several Sermons, as (1) Christ exalted by the Father, God the Father, g'orified, and Man's Redemption finished*, preached before the Lord Mayor of London. (London, 1649, quarto., &c.)

4. *Christ and Moses Excellency, or Sion, and Sinai's Glory*. Being a Triplex Treatise, distinguishing and explaining the Two Covenants or the Gospel and Law ; and Directing to the right understanding, applying, and finding of the Informing and Assuring Promises, that belong to both Covenants. (London, 1650, octavo.)

5. *A Dialogue between Christ and a Publican, and Christ and a Doubting Christian.*

6. *Common Prayer Book no Divine Service:* or 27 Reasons against forming and imposing any human Liturgies or Common Prayer Book, &c., Lond., 1661, quarto.

7. *Arguments to prove that Lord Bishops, Diocesan Bishops, &c. and their Authority, are contrary to the word of God, and so consequently unlawful, &c.* Also a discovery of the great disparity between Scriptural and Congregational Bishops, and Diocesan Bishops. London, 1661, quarto. 2nd ed. corrected and much enlarged.

8. *The Bird in the Cage chirping, &c.* Lond., 1661, 2nd Oct. Written in prison.

9. *The Sufferer's Catechism.* Written also in prison.

10. *Brief Narrative concerning the proceedings of the Commissioners in Wales against the ejected Clergy.*

11. *The Young Man's Conflict with the Devil.*

12. *Sinful and Sinless Swearing.*

13. *An Account of his Conversion and Ministry.* [" 'Tis a canting and enthusiastical piece."—*Wood.*]

14. *A Confession of Faith concerning the Holy Scriptures. Some gracious, experimental, and very choice Sayings and Sentences. Certain Hymns, and his Death-bed Expressions.* London, 1671.

15. *A new and useful Concordance of the Bible :* with the chief acceptations and various significations contained therein. Also marks to distinguish the commands, Promises and Threatnings. London, 1671, and 1673, 8vo. Mostly done by V. Powell, but finished by N. P. J. F. &c.

16. *Collection of those Scripture Prophecies which relate to the Call of the Jews, and the glory that should be in the latter days.* Printed at the end of the Concordance—A second edition in 1673 contained nearly 9,000 additional references ; with the addition of Scripture Similes, &c.

17. *Saving Faith. or the Candle of Christ.* (1653.) Also published in Welsh.

Wood adds, " The most ingenious Mrs. Kath. Phillips of the Priory of Cardigan hath among her Poetry a *Poem upon the double Murder of King Charles I.* in answer to a libellous Copy of Rhimes made by Vav. Powell,

but in what Book those Rhimes are, or whether they were printed by
themselves, I cannot tell."

In the year 1671, being that which followed his death, his
biography (written it is said by his friend E. Bagshaw) was
published under the title,

"*The Life and Death of Vavasor Powell, that faithful Minister and
Confessor of Jesus Christ.* Wherein his Eminent Conversion, Laborious,
Successful Ministry, Excellent Conversation, Confession of Faith,
Worthy Sayings, Choice Experiences, Various Sufferings, and other
Remarkable Passages in his Life and at his Death, are faithfully Recorded
for Publick benefit. With some Elogies and Epitaphs by His Friends."

This work contains many curious and interesting particulars of
his life, persecutions, sufferings, and escapes from peril. Among
the latter it is related that on one occasion

"one came to a Meeting where he preached at *Newtown*, with a full purpose to kill him. but was at that time convinced and converted by the
Word, and confessed and begged pardon for his wickedness. . . . .
Another time a man of *Welsh Pool* entered into an oath to kill him, and
designed to attempt it at *Guilsfield*, where he was also at the same
instant converted by the power of the Word. . . . . Another time a
woman came with a knife to kill him as he was preaching in a Market
place at *Machynlleth*, but was prevented. . . . . A soldier shot a
Brace of Bullets at him looking out of his Prison Window in *Montgomery*,
but God preserved him."

A Welsh translation of this *Life* was published at Carmarthen
in 1772, and another about 1826 by Mr. John Jones, of Llettyderyn, Mochdre. Powell's biographer says that gentlemen of
the best rank in the Counties of Salop, Radnor, Montgomery,
&c., saluted him as their kinsman. We also learn that as to his
personal appearance he was

"in stature mean, yet meek, content," and that "he had a body of steel
made as of purpose for his never resting indefatigable spirit." Wood
also tells us, "I have been informed by M. Ll., who knew and was
acquainted with Vav. Powell. . . . that when he preached a mist or
smoak would issue from his Head, so great an agitation of spirit he had,
&c., and therefore 'twas usually reported by some, especially those that
favoured him, that he represented the Saints of old time that had Rays
painted about their Heads."

In calmly surveying his character after the lapse of two centuries,
while admitting that some of his doctrines and theories were
extreme and visionary, and that

"Failings he had, but where is he
From more and greater that is free?"

it is but simple justice to say that his moral character, notwithstanding the foul aspersions of his enemies, was unblemished,
his courage undaunted, his zeal and energy fervid and untiring,
that he was earnest, sincere, and self sacrificing to a remarkable
degree, and that by his incessant labours he left an impression
upon Wales so deep and lasting that upwards of two centuries
have failed to efface it.

PRICE, The Very Rev. DANIEL, M.A., was the second
son of Lewis Price, by Mary Sheinton, of Pertheirin, Llanwnog,

and was born about the year 1650. He was educated at Westminster School, and Trinity College, Cambridge, was appointed to the living of Aspenden and Westmill, Herts, in 1685, and subsequently became Dean of St. Asaph, and sinecure rector of Llansaintffraid-yn-Mechain. He was a relation of Bishop Jones, and being found guilty of simony in procuring this last benefice was deprived of it. He died and was buried at St. Asaph in 1706.

PRICE, HUGH, was the son of Austin ap Rees, of Carno, a descendant of Brochwel Ysgythrog, by his second wife, Ales, daughter of Hugh Sheinton, of Llanwnog. His name first occurs as bailiff of the Hundred of Llanidloes, 9th, Charles I. (1633-4). On the outbreak of the Civil War he took the side of the Parliament, and became a colonel in the army. As such he held Powis or Red Castle for the Parliament, and was Sheriff in 1654. He died in November, 1657, and was buried at Montgomery.

PRICE, OWEN, was a native of Montgomeryshire. In October, 1648, he was entered a Scholar of Jesus College, Oxford, by the Parliamentary Visitors, where he remained four years, and afterwards was appointed master of a public school in Wales, and in that capacity took much pains to impart Presbyterian principles to his pupils. In 1655 he returned to the University, and became a student of Christ Church, and the following year took his degree. Soon afterwards he became master of the free school near Magdalen College, "where by his "industry and good way of teaching he drew many youths of the "city, whose parents were fanatically given," as Wood puts it, "to be his scholars." Upon the Restoration he was ejected for Nonconformity, and after that kept school, in which he much delighted, in various places in Devonshire and elsewhere, "became useful among the brethren, and a noted professor in "the art of Pedagogy." He was the author of the following works:—1. "The Vocal Organ; or a new art of teaching "Orthography by observing the instruments of pronunciation and "the difference between words of a like sound whereby any out- "landish or meer Englishman, woman, or child, may speedily "attain to the exact spelling, reading, writing, or pronouncing of "any word in the English Tongue, without the advantage of its "fountains, the Greek and Latin." (Oxon. 1665, 8vo.) 2. "English Orthography: teaching (1) The letters of every sort of "print; (2) All syllables made of letters; (3) Short rules by "way of question and answer for spelling, reading, pronouncing, "using the great letters and their points; (4) Examples of all "words of like sound, &c." (Oxon. 1670, 8vo.) He died at his house near Magdalen College, Oxford, on the 25th of November, 1671, and was buried two days afterwards near the door leading to the belfry of St. Peter's in the East, Oxford.

PRICE, THOMAS, of the Hall, Llanfyllin, was an eminent antiquary of the seventeenth century. He was a Roman Catholic, and the family to which he belonged were called "Prices the Papists." He formed a large collection of Welsh and other MSS., which he is said to have sent to the Library of the Vatican in Rome He was frequently presented at the Great Sessions for recusancy.

PRYCE, MATTHEW, or *Matthew Goch*, of Newtown, was a grandson of Rhys ab David Lloyd (see *ante*), of Newtown Hall, who was killed at the battle of Danesmore, near Banbury. His father was Thomas ap Rhys, of Newtown ; his mother, Florence, daughter of Howell Chun, of Clun. He was Sheriff in 1548, and joined Sir Richard Herbert and others in petitioning the King (Henry VIII.) for an assimilation of the laws of Wales to those of England. His sister Gwenllian was married to Humphrey Lloyd, of Leighton, first Sheriff of Montgomeryshire. He himself was twice married; first, to Jane (or Elizabeth) daughter of Llewelyn Vaughan, a grandson of Sir David Gam, by whom he had a daughter, Catherine, who became the wife of Thomas Tannatt, Sheriff in 1570 ; secondly to Joyce, daughter of Ieuan Gwyn, of Mynachdy, Radnorshire, by whom he had two sons, namely John (his heir) and Arthur (of Vaynor), and four daughters, Elizabeth, ancestress of Lord Herbert, of Chirbury, Margaret, Joyce, and Catherine. The author of *The Sheriffs of Montgomeryshire* states Joyce to have been Matthew Pryce's first wife, but this probably is an error.

PRYCE, JOHN, of Newtown Hall, eldest son of the abovenamed Matthew Pryce, was twice Sheriff of Montgomeryshire, namely in 1566 and 1586. He also sat in Parliament for the Borough of Montgomery in the Sessions of 1558-9, 1562-3, and 1567-8, and for the County in the Sessions of 1572 and 1581. In right of his mother he had property in Cardiganshire, and served the office of Sheriff for that County in 1568. By his wife Elizabeth, daughter of Rees ap Morris ap Owen, of Aberbechan, he had issue four sons (Edward, Matthew, Richard, and Arthur) and four daughters (Bridget, Mary, Margaret, and Joyce). He died about the year 1602.

PRYCE, EDWARD, of Newtown Hall, eldest son of the above-named John Pryce, was Deputy-Sheriff to his father in 1586, bailiff of Newtown in 1594, and Sheriff in 1615. The Shrewsbury bailiffs' accounts for 1601 thus refer to an important visit of his to that town :—"Bestowed on Mr. Price of "the New Towne and other gentlemen of worshipe having occa- "sions with Mr. Bailiffs in the Bothehall a potell of Muscadell, and "three fine cakes 2s. 6d." He married Juliana, daughter of John Owen Vaughan, of Llwydiarth, by whom he had a son, John, who was created first baronet in 1628, and a daughter, Jane.

PRYCE, SIR JOHN, the first Baronet, of Newtown Hall, was the son of Edward Pryce (Sheriff 1615), by Juliana, daughter of John Owen Vaughan, of Llwydiarth. He was sixth in descent from David Lloyd (see *ante*), the founder of the Pryce family, of Newtown Hall, and Glanmiheli. He was created a Baronet on the 15th August, 1628, and married Catherine, daughter of Sir Richard Price, of Gogerddan, and widow of James Stedman, of Strata Florida. He represented Montgomeryshire in the Long Parliament which assembled 3rd November, 1640, at Westminster. He was one of the 118 members who, at the king's summons, formed the short-lived " mongrel " Parliament at Oxford, which met there on the 22nd January, 1644-5, and separated on the 16th April, 1645, having done nothing beyond voting subsidies which could not be collected, and inditing a long letter (to which we find Sir John Pryce's name appended among others) to the Earl of Essex in favour of peace. For attending this Parliament he was for a time " disabled " by the Parliament at Westminster from sitting there. Towards the middle of September, however, Sir John suddenly changed sides, and went over to that of the Parliament. *The Kingdom's Weekly Intelligencer* thus announces the change :—" Sir John Price, a Parliament man " (whose heart was always with the Parliament, but was so over- " mastered by the enemy that he durst not appear), writes that " the country do come in cheerfully. They only want arms " to defend themselves, and he hopes to help his neighbours' " counties in Pembrokeshire." Sir Thomas Myddelton speedily recognized the importance of his adhesion to the Parliamentary cause by appointing him Governor of Montgomery Castle, which had recently fallen into the hands of the Parliamentary forces. Sir John's influence, indeed, soon made itself felt. Sir Michael Ernley, writing from Shrewsbury to Prince Rupert on the 21st of September, states that " since the disaster at Montgomery " the edge of the gentry is very much blunted—the country's " loyalty strangely abated. They begin to warp to the enemy's " party." Archbishop Williams also writes to the Marquis of Ormond that Myddelton was " quietly possessed of Montgomery- " shire by the help of Sir John Price." Sir John was assiduous in his new office, but six months afterwards Colonel Gerard, pushing his way triumphantly through North Wales, routed him at Llanidloes, and sent a detachment from Newtown under Sir Edmund Cary to scour the country as far as Shrewsbury, and to attack Sir Thomas Myddelton. His career for some years after this is involved in some obscurity. It was alleged against him by his enemies that his loyalty to the cause of the Parliament was not sincere, which probably was true, and that taking advantage of his office of Governor of Montgomery Castle he endeavoured to betray it to the enemy. For this, or some other reason, he was excluded from Parliament, and his estate sequestered and ordered to be sold. After this he served in the Parliamentary army in Scotland and at Worcester, and the sequestration was taken off. In 1654 he was again elected to represent the county of Montgomery in Parliament, but exceptions against him were laid before the Protector, which, for some months, prevented him from taking his seat. Thes·exceptions were:—

"1. He was an M.P. in 1612, but deserted and sat in the Junta at Oxford. 2. He came not in until after the memorable battle at York, and when Montgomery Castle was taken, and he would else have been sequestered, as his whole estate lay there. 3. By his plausible pretences Sir Thomas Myddelton, then Major General of North Wales, made him Governor of the Castle, which he endeavoured to betray to the enemy. Being excluded from Parliament, and his estate ordered to be sold, he then took himself to the army. Query, whether he should be considered a man of integrity and fit to be a M P."

In reply to these Sir John presented the following Petition to the Protector and Council:—

"I was elected by Co. Montgomery to serve in this Parliament, and returned by the Sheriff; but coming to London I find my name omitted in a List returned to the Crown Office of members approved by you, and am told that objections are made against me as unfit to serve as a member. Now, these allegations I have already cleared myself of, and proved my affection by service in Scotland, and at Worcester fight, &c., which the late Parliament noticing took off the sequestration of my estate. Though I am within the meaning of the instrument of the Government, I have forborne for modesty to go to the House, lest I should offend you, but having signed the recognition I beg admission, that my County may not be deprived of a member."

This petition, it is supposed, proved successful, and Sir John continued to represent Montgomeryshire in Parliament until the year before his death. That event took place June 18th, 1657. He was succeeded in the title and estates by his second son, Lieut.-Col. Edward Pryce, distinguished by his valour in several actions, having died unmarried in his lifetime, at Gogerddan, on the 29th November, 1645, having been killed, it is said, in endeavouring to appease a tumult. Besides these sons, Sir John Pryce had issue two daughters, Mary, who died unmarried, and Elizabeth, who married Edward Clun, of Clun.

PRYCE, Sir MATTHEW, the second Baronet, of Newtown Hall, was the second son of Sir John Pryce, the first Baronet, whom he succeeded in the title, his elder brother, Edward Pryce, having died in his father's lifetime. He served the office of Sheriff in 1659-60, at the time of the Restoration, and was a zealous Royalist. During his Shrievalty he issued warrants to apprehend Vavasor Powell, Capt. Price, and other leading Nonconformists, upon frivolous charges of sedition, rebellion, and had them cast into prison. He and his successor in office were so zealous in this work that the prisons at Welshpool and Montgomery were so full of Nonconformists that there was no room for thieves and felons, but some had to be sent, as Richard Davies the Quaker says, "to the upper garrets." He married Jane, daughter of Henry Vaughan, of Cilcennen, Cardiganshire, by whom he had issue John, Vaughan, Edward, Jane, and Anne. He died in 1674.

PRYCE, Sir JOHN, the third Baronet, of Newtown Hall, was the eldest son of the above-named Sir Matthew Pryce, whom he succeeded in the titles and estates. He was baptized September 24th, 1660. He married Anna Maria, daughter of Sir Edmund Warcup, Knt., of English, in the County of Oxford, and had surviving issue four daughters, Anna Maria, Elizabeth, Penelope, and Juliana. Having thus no male issue, the baronetcy at his decease devolved upon his brother. He died about 1691.

PRYCE, Sir VAUGHAN, the fourth Baronet, of Newtown Hall, was the second son of Sir Matthew Pryce, and succeeded his brother, the last-named Sir John Pryce, in the title. He was born in 1663. He married Anne, daughter of Sir John Powell, of Broadway, Carmarthenshire, one of the judges who tried the seven bishops, by whom he had issue five sons and one daughter, namely, John (his heir), Arthur, Matthew, Edward, Vaughan, and Mary. He served the office of Sheriff in 1709. He died April 30th, and was buried May 5th, 1720.

PRYCE, Sir JOHN, the fifth Baronet, of Newtown Hall, was the son of Sir Vaughan Pryce, Bart. (Sheriff in 1709) of the same place, by Anne, his wife. He was born about the year 1698, and succeeded to the title and estates on his father's death, April 30th, 1720. He married, firstly, his first cousin, Elizabeth, daughter of Sir Thomas Powell, of Broadway, Carmarthenshire, who died in childbed April 22nd, 1731, leaving issue a son and two daughters, namely, John Powell, Anna Elizabetha (who died October 18th, 1736), and Diana. Sir John Pryce erected in the Old Church at Newtown a handsome marble monument to the memory of his first and second wives, which, upon the dismantling of that Church, was removed to the new Parish Church, and placed against the north wall. The following is the inscription to the memory of his first wife:—

" To the Pious Memory of Dame Elizabeth Pryce Wife to Sr. John Pryce Bart. Daughter to Sr. Thomas Powel, of Broadway in Carmarthen-Shire Bart. by Elizabeth Daughter to Thomas Mansel, of Briton Ferry in Glamorganshire Esq. (a Lady of great Vertue and Merit) and Grand-Daughtr. to Sir John Powel Knt. one of the Justices of the King's Bench in the Reign of King James IInd. who eminently Signaliz'd his Integrity and Resolution, in the Delivery of the 7 Bishops out of the Tower. She was a Lady of Singular Piety, Goodness & Charity, without the least Ostentation of either: one who chose rather to be, than to appear to the World, a good Christian & a true genuine Member of the Church of England. She behaved her-Self in all the Social & Relative Duties of Life with a religious Exactness, being a most dutifull Daughr. a most Affectionate Wife, a most tender Parent, a most kind endearing Relation & a most sincere Friend. She was Civil & obliging in her Deportment towards her Equals ; of great Affability, Courteousness. & Condescension towards her Inferiours ; of a most tender, compassionate temper to all in Distress. All which good Qualities were joyn'd to an uncommon Degree of Modesty & an humble Opinion of her-Self which added a Lustre to all her other Vertues & pro-cured her the general Esteem & Respect of all that knew her. She Dy'd

A pr. 22d 1731 in the 33d year of her Age: and left Issue, John Powel, Anna Elizabetha and Diana Pryce."

Sir John also erected a neat marble monument to his little daughter, Anna Elizabetha. It is now placed against the wall near the western door of Newtown Church. The following is the inscription upon it :—

" Here underneath lieth the Body of Anna Elizabetha Pryce Eldest Daughter of Sr. John Pryce Bart. and Dame Elizabeth his first Wife, who exchanged this Mortal for a Better Life on Monday the 18th Day of October, 1736. Aged 8 years 5 months and 17 days.

> Short was thy Term on Earth, translated hence,
> In the first Bloom of Virgin Innocence,
> Thy dawning Vertues like the Morning bright
> But just appear'd, and sunk in endless Night.
> Had Heav'n propitious but prolong'd thy Days,
> To emulate thy Vertuous Mother's Praise,
> Then had the rising Age rejoyc'd to see
> Her bright Example copy'd out in Thee."

Sir John married, secondly, Mary, daughter of Mr. John Morris, of Wern Goch, Berriew, a farmer. Tradition says that Sir John first met her whilst taking shelter under a tree during a storm, and taking a fancy to her married her. She died August 3rd, 1739, leaving issue two daughters, Mary and Elizabeth. The inscription to her memory is as follows :—

' To the Pious Memory of Dame Mary Pryce, Second Wife of Sr. John Pryce of Newtown Hall in Montgomeryshire Bart. and Eldest Daughter of Mr. John Morris of Wern Goch in the parish of Berriew & Mary his Wife Daughter of Mr. Oliver Jones of Gwern yr Ychen in the Parish of Llandysul in the same County. She was a Lady whose incomparable Beauty & fine Proportion, was the true Index of her sweet disposition of Mind, which shone through all that cloud of Infamy which had been cast upon her Character by Envious & Malicious persons; & forced even her Inveterate & most Cruel Enemies to confess (soon after her decease which was most unfortunately occasioned by their unjust Aspersions) that she was the Reverse, in every Character of Life, to what she was so undeservedly, & so injuriously represented. She excelled in all ye Social & Relative Characters of Wife, Parent, Step-mother, Daughter, Neighbour and Friend : nor was she less eminent in her Religious, than in her Moral Life ; being from her Infancy a constant Attendant on Divine Worship in ye Church of England, of which she was a most sincere & pious Member. She was extreamely Modest, Chaste, & Vertuous; adorned all her life long, with ye Resplendent Robe of Innocence & those inestimable Iewels, a a meek and quiet spirit. She was very compassionate towards ye Poor, the Afflicted and Distressed; especially towards Orphans and Children, that were deprived of either Parent. The advancement of her Fortune was not attended with the least exaltation of her Mind; neither did she seem conscious of these & many other innate perfections, which wanted nothing but ye advantages of a more refined Education to render them illustrious in ye Eyes of all her acquaintance. She dyed August 3d 1739, Aged 24 years 1 month, & two days; and left Issue, Mary and Elizabeth Pryce."

It has been surmised from some expressions in this epitaph that owing to Lady Pryce's humble origin Sir John while she lived kept his marriage with her a secret ; that therefore it was generally supposed and stated that she was only a concubine ; and that " the unjust aspersions " and the " cloud of infamy " referred to such statements which so preyed upon the poor wife's mind that she died of a broken heart within two years of her marriage. On the 6th July, 1741, Sir John addressed the following singular letter to the Rev. William Felton, Curate of Newtown, who was then lying dangerously ill, and who died the very next day :—

" Dear Mr. Felton,—I waited an opportunity yesterday of confering a little while with you in private ; but, not finding the room in which you sat clear a minute, I am forced to communicate this way my thoughts upon the subject I then intended to speak upon ; & I desire you will not suspect from what I am going to say that I look upon your case to be desperate, but yet, on the contrary, I approve some symptoms in your disorder as prognosticks, I hope, of your recovery out of. Neither do I give you this caution as tho' I was apprehensive of your being in the least troubled at the thought of whatever may befall you in the conclusion, for I have been credibly informed that it is quite otherwise with you, but only because I would not have you think that I imagine it worse than I really do. But as God Almighty may dispose of you in a manner contrary to either my wishes or expectations, and as I have abundant reason to believe from my own as well as other people's observation of your conduct that you will immediately enter upon a happier state whenever you make an exchange forth, as the reward of a wellspent life, I desire that you will do me the favour to acquaint my two Dear Wives, both of which you will be sure to find within those happy Regions, and questionless within the same mansion too, that I retain the same tender Affections and the same Honour and Esteem for their Memories which I ever did for their persons, and to tell the latter that I earnestly desire, if she can obtain the Divine permission, that she will appear to me, to discover the persons who have wronged her and to put me into a proper method of vindicating those wrongs which robbd. her of her life and me of all my happiness in this world, that since she left me I never knew what joy or comfort means, and that probably I never shall, at least not within many degrees of that which I enjoyed whilst she was with me, till it please God to give us a happy meeting in a better world ; that the consideration and hopes and expectations of that happy time are all my support under this great and unparallel'd affliction ; that her enemies, & perhaps the very worst, even the Ringleader of them all have since her death, as she herself predicted, declared that she deserved not the least of all those calumnies which Envy and Malice had besmeared her with ; that I have several other weighty things to tell her of and several important questions to ask her, and that you will tell her that I think, tho' I am not very sure, that she promised me an appearance after death if it should be permitted her. The reason I desire this of you is that it is a matter of uncertainty to me whether the dead are conscious of what we say and do on earth, tho' I must confess that I have been long accustomed to an imagination that they do ; and the more I ruminate upon that subject, the more strongly I am inclined to think that I am in the right, and that for several reasons, which I forbear to give you because I must have sufficiently tired your attention already. I desire no answer in writing ; your distemper will not allow it. If I live till Sunday, I intend just to speak to you upon these heads. In the meantime, I heartily wish you the Divine protection and assistance in conjunction with the means used for your recovery, and am,

Your Friend & Humble Servant,
Jon Pryce.

New Town Hall, July 6th, 1741.
P.S.—I have sent you a Bottle of Mint Water, which, if you find too strong, you may dilute with Spring Water to what size you please."

Sir John also wrote an elegy of a thousand lines to his second

Q

wife, in which he affirmed that with his latest breath he would "lisp Maria's name." Ere long, however, he forgot his vow, and was smitten with the charms of Eleanor, widow of Roger Jones, Esq., of Buckland, Breconshire. He had embalmed his first two wives, and kept them in his room, one on each side of his bed, but this lady declined the honour of his hand till her defunct rivals were committed to their proper resting places. He married her at the parish church of Llansaintffraid, Breconshire, on the 19th December, 1741. The *Gentleman's Magazine* in announcing the marriage adds her fortune, as was usual in those days, namely, "with £150,000." A year or two afterwards, Sir John appears to have quitted Newtown, and taken up his residence at Buckland. After 1743, his signature as church-warden is not to be found on the parish books. An old MS, diary of an inhabitant records that "The Organs," which had been "opened to play with" in July, 1731, and had been presented to Newtown Church by Sir John, "were taken down "in ye year 1745, and carried to Buckland, in Brecknock shire by "the orders of Sr John Pryce of Newtown." The following entry also occurs: "A Charytie Scool Being erected by the "Honourable Sir John for the poor of the parish of Newtowne. "The entring day is August the 10 in the year 1730." The third Lady Price died in 1748. At that time multitudes resorted to a woman named Bridget Bostock, "the Cheshire Pythoness," who undertook to heal all diseases by prayer, faith, and an embrocation of fasting spittle, which she supplied. Sir John, who was very credulous and eccentric, but otherwise a very worthy man, seems to have entertained full confidence in this impostor. He accordingly wrote to her the following letter, requesting her prayers for the restoration to him of his third wife recently deceased :—

"Madam,—Being very well informed by very creditable people, both private and public, that you have done several wonderful cures, even when Physicians have failed, & that you do it by the force and efficacy of your prayers mostly, if not altogether (the outward means you use being generally supposed to be inadequate to the effects produced), I cannot but look upon such operations to be miraculous, & if so, why may not an infinitely good & gracious God enable you to raise the Dead as well as to heal the Sick, give sight to the Blind, & hearing to the Deaf? for since He is pleased to hear your prayers in some cases so beneficial to mankind, there's the same reason to expect it in others, &, consequently, in that I have particularly mentioned, namely, raising up the Dead. Now, as I have lost a Wife whom I most dearly loved, my Children one of the best of Stepmothers all her near Relations a friend whom they greatly esteemed, and the poor a Charitable benefactress, I intreat you for God Almighty's sake that you wou'd be so good as to come here if your actual presence is absolutely requisite, or if not, that you will offer up your prayers to the throne of Grace on my behalf that God would graciously vouchsafe to raise up my dear wife, Dame Eleanor Pryce, from the Dead,—this is one of the greatest acts of charity you can do, for my heart is ready to break with grief at the consideration of the great loss—this wou'd be doing myself & all her Relations & friends such an extraordinary kindness as wou'd necessarily engage our daily prayers for your preservation as the least gratuity I cou'd make you for so great a benefit, tho' were any other compatible with the nature of the

thing, & durst we offer & you accept it we"shou'd think nothing too much
to the utmost of our abilities, & I wish that the bare mention of it is
not offensive both to God and you.

" If your immediate presence is indispensably necessary, pray let me
know by return of the Post, that I may send you a Coach & Six & Servants to attend you here, with orders to defray your expences in a
manner most suitable to your own desires. If your prayers will be as
effectual at the distance you'r from me, pray signify the same in a letter
directed by way of London, to, good Madam,

" Your unfortunate afflicted petitioner & hble. Servt,
"JOHN PRYCE.

" Buckland, 1st Dece'r 1748.

" P.S.—Pray direct your letter to Sir John Pryce, Bart., at Buckland,
in Brecknocksh., South Wales. God almighty prosper this undertaking
& others intended for the Benefit of mankind, & may He long continue
such a useful person upon earth, and afterwards crown you with Eternal
Glory in the Kingdom of Heaven thro' Jesus Christ   Amen."

In compliance with this invitation, Mrs. Bostock is said to have
visited Buckland, and to have exerted all her miracle working
powers, but without effect.   How long Sir John Pryce resided at
Buckland after his third wife's death is not known, but in his
Will, a long and very curious document, dated the 20th of June,
1760, he is described as of Haverfordwest.   At that time he
appears to have intended a *fourth* marriage to a lady whom he
described as " that dearest object of my lawful and best and
" purest Wordly affections, my most dear and most entirely
" beloved intended Wife Margaret Harries of the parish of St.
" Martin in the said Town and County of Haverfordwest,
" Spinster."   Subject to legacies of £1,000 to his daughter
Elizabeth, and £600 to his daughter Mary, he gave to this lady
" all his Castles, Manors, Lordships, Messuages, Mills, lands,
" tenements, and hereditaments whatsoever* * * * within
" the several Counties of Montgomery, Carmarthen, or elsewhere
" or anywhere in or upon this Globe of earth and waters, and
" appointed her his sole Executrix and residuary legatee." He had,
however, it seems previously executed a Settlement of most of his
Montgomeryshire property upon his son John Powell Pryce, and
the rest was apparently very heavily mortgaged at the time of his
death.   He gave his Organ to St, David's Cathedral, where also
he desired to be buried, " with the burial service composed by
" the late William Croft, Doctor of Musick," but his wishes
were not carried out.   He died the 28th of October, 1761, at
Haverfordwest, and on the 31st of the same month was buried at
the church of St. Mary's in that town   Hulbert states that at
the time of Sir John's death his estates produced a rental of
over £40,000 a year, evidently a gross exaggeration.   He must
have been, indeed, comparatively poor.   Miss Harries was
therefore induced to renounce Probate, and to accept probably a
moderate lump sum for all her interest under the Will.
Elizabeth and Mary Pryce each accepted £500 in lieu of their
£1,000 and £600 legacies.   On the 7th December, 1761,
Administration with Will annexed was granted to his son Sir
John Powell Pryce, and his daughters Diana Evors, Mary Pryce

and Elizabeth Pryce. The chapter of St. David's renounced their claim to the Organ. Sir John Pryce's portrait or what purports to be such, was sold by auction with the other family portraits and furniture many years ago. Some of the pictures were bought by Mr. Herbert, and taken to Dolforgan, and are said to be now at Rood Ashton, Wiltshire. Sir John's portrait was purchased in a very dilapidated state by Mr. John Gittins, flannel merchant, who had it "restored." After his death it was sold by auction to the late Major Drew, of Milford Hall.

PRYCE, Sir JOHN POWELL, the sixth baronet, of Newtown Hall, was the only son of Sir John Pryce, the eccentric fifth baronet, by his first wife, Elizabeth, daughter of Sir Thomas Powell. A few years after his father's third marriage, in December, 1741, he, by Deed of Settlement or family arrangement, was admitted into possession of the Newtown Hall estates, and became the occupier of the mansion, and a County Magistrate. He married Elizabeth, daughter of Richard Manley. Esq., of Carleigh Court, Berkshire. His ancestors had large estates, not only in Montgomeryshire, but also in the counties of Brecon, Carmarthen, Berks, Wilts, Chester, Oxford, and Flint. Some of these had been squandered away or heavily mortgaged before his time, and he managed to get through a good deal of what remained· He succeeded to the title on the death of his father in October, 1761. His fate was a melancholy one. Having by some accident severely injured his eyes, his wife was induced in the hope to facilitate his recovery to apply some powerful spirit or acid which entirely destroyed his sight. Yet he is said to have been accustomed, though blind, to follow the hounds, and seldom to be the last in the chase. Want of prudence, litigation, and accumulated misfortunes also deprived him of the bulk of his fortune, and he died in the King's Bench Prison, where he was imprisoned for contumacy, on the 4th of July, 1776 He was buried at Newtown, but not, it seems, until nearly *six weeks* after his death. His wife also spent many years with him in prison. She had been, apparently, a good and faithful companion to him, but he rewarded her constancy by bequeathing to her *one shilling.* She died in London in very reduced circumstances in 1805. There is at Newtown Hall an oil painting, supposed to be her portrait, dated 1752. After Sir John Powell Pryce's death most of the property was sold under a Decree in Chancery—the park fencing having previously been taken down, and the deer sold.

PRYCE, Sir EDWARD MANLEY, the seventh and last baronet, of Newtown Hall, succeeded his father, Sir John Powell Pryce, in the title, and what remained of the property. He was an officer in the Guards, and squandered a good deal, and was fleeced by Bill brokers of the remnant left to him of the once fine estate of his ancestors. He was found dead in a field at Pangbourne, near Reading, on the 28th of October, 1791, and was buried there He is said to have died in great destitution, having left not even the means to pay the expense of his interment; and his body consequently remained unburied for forty-five weeks, when at last some benevolent persons had it buried at their cost. Some say that he had married a daughter of a Mr. Flinn, of Norfolk Street London, and had by her an only son, who died an infant in his father's life-time. At any rate some years after his death a coffin, enclosing the remains of a child, was discovered over the ceiling in the roof of a house at Chiswick, with the following inscription on a plate nailed to it :—" Edward " Manley Powell Pryce. Esq., only son and heir of Sir Edward " Manley Pryce, of Newtown Hall, Montgomeryshire, Bart., died " the 28th of April, 1788, aged five years and a half." Yorke, however, says he died unmarried. The title became extinct at his death. Early in the present century the Rev. George Arthur Evors, a son of Diana, second daughter of Sir John Pryce, the fifth baronet, came to an agreement with the creditors, and obtained possession of the small portion that remained of the Newtown Hall estate, which, by careful management for many years, he greatly improved in value. At his death, in September, 1844, it passed under his Will to his nephew, Arthur Brisco, Esq., in whose family it remains. The arms of the Pryce family were :—*Gules* a lion rampant regardant *or*.

PRYCE, MAJOR JOHN, was the son of John Pryce, of Gwestydd, Llanllwchaiarn, by Anne, his wife, (widow of. . . Meredith, of Munlyn, previously " Anne Baxter of the Bryn.") Having entered the army he distinguished himself at the battle of Dettingen (1743), became a Major, and was killed at the battle of Fontenoy in 1745. His estate of Gwestydd became vested on his death without issue and intestate in his three sisters, Jane, wife of John Pryce of Penygelly, Elizabeth, wife of Richard Baxter, of the Bryn, and Anne, wife of Andrew Owen, of Gellidywyll, Llanbrynmair, as coparceners.

PRYCE, MATTHEW, M.P., of Park, Llanwnog, was the eldest son of John Pryce, of the same place, who represented a junior branch of the Pryces of Newtown Hall, and was born in the year 1639. He sat in Parliament for the Borough of Montgomery from 1678 to 1685. He married Hester, twelfth daughter of John Thelwall, Esq., of Bathafarn, Denbighshire, but left no issue. He died on the 23rd of January, 1699—the tradition being that he was drowned in Afon Garno in going home to Park from Penstrowed Hall. A handsome marble monument was placed to his memory by his widow in Llanwnog Church, with the following long inscription :—

" Here lieth interr'd the Body of Mathew Pryce of Park-pen price in the county of Montgomery Esqr who was the Eldest Son of John Pryce of Park aforesaid Esqr (by Mary, daughter of William Read of Castle Bromshill in the County of Gloucester Esqr) who was only Son of Matthew Pryce of Park Esq (by Catherine Eldest daughter of Lewis

Gwynne of Llanidloes, Esqr) who was second Son of John Pryce of Newtown Hall in ye County of Montgomery, Esqr.

As He had the Happiness to be descended from an Antient and Worshipfull Family, so he took Care to improve ye Advantages of his Birth & Fortune, that he might be able to distinguish himself No less by his own personal Worth and Merits than by the Dignity and lustre of his Ancestors. His known Abilities & Integrity recommended him to the Service of his Prince & Country. In several Imployments and Important Trusts at ye Barr an Able & Learned Councellour, on ye Bench an Upright and Vigilant Justice of ye Peace. In ye Militia a Loyal & Active Deputy Livetenant & Captain of ye County Troop. And in Parliament where He had the Honour to serve as Burgess for Montgomery, In ye two last Parliaments of Charles ye Seconds' Reign. He shew'd himself a good Patriot & True Lover of his Country In all these Honourable Trusts He acquitted himself with Inviolable Fidelity to his Prince with eminent Care & zeal for ye good and Prosperity of his Country & with Singular Duty and observance to his Mother ye Church of England, of which he always approved himself A True & obedient Son & A zealous and steady Defender of her Rights & Constitution. Nor was He less Exemplary in ye Vertues that adorn a private Life in respect of which he Worthily sustain'd ye Character of A Wise and truly Honest Man & of A Sincere & Hearty Christian.

He married Hester Thelwall ye Twelfth Daughter of John Thelwall of Bathavern Park in ye County of Denbigh Esqr. who surviving Him and desireous to transmitt His deserved Character to Posterity at her sole Charge Erected this Monument as well to be a Publick & lasting Mark of that true Love & Affection She had for him when alive, as for ye Respect & Veneration She retains for the memory of her deceas'd Husband.

He died ye 23rd of Jan., A.D., 1699.   Annoque Ætat. suæ 60."

This monument was originally placed against the southern wall of the Church over the *piscina*. On the so-called restoration of the Church, some thirty years ago, it was taken down and cast into the churchyard, where it lay neglected for some time, and small portions of it were chipped off. At last John Pryce Davies, Esq. (a descendant of Matthew Pryce's sister and co-heiress, Mary, wife of John Edwards, Esq., of Melinygrug). took charge of it, and had it removed to Bronfelen, and subsequently carefully put up again on the left side of the altar, where it now is. The Benefaction Table has the following inscription :—
" Hester Pryce widow and Relict of Matthew Pryce of Park
" Esqr. gave A Large Silver Challice and salver to the use of this
" Church in ye year of our Lord One Thousand seven Hundred
and seven." There is a similar inscription on the Cup itself.

PRYCE, Capt. RICHARD, of Gunley, was the son of Edward Pryce, of Gunley, and Bridget, his wife. He became an active and distinguished officer in Cromwell's army, and was Sheriff of Montgomeryshire in 1651-2. He demolished Montgomery Castle by warrant, dated 16th June, 1649, and was one of the Commissioners who sat at Ruthin to assess the amount of an indemnity to the inhabitants of Montgomery for their losses in the Civil War. He was twice married, but left no issue, and was succeeded at Gunley by his brother, Edward Pryce, of Pont-y-perchyll. His portrait is at Gunley.

PRYCE, ROBERT DAVIES, was the eldest son of Pryce Jones of Cyfronydd, and Jane his wife, daughter of John Davies, E·q., of Aberllefenni, Merionethshire, and was born on the 25th December, 1819. He was twenty-sixth in direct male descent from Bleddyn ab Cynfyn, Prince of Powys. He was educated at Rugby, whence he proceeded to St. John's College, Cambridge, where he graduated B A. in 1842. In 1849 he married Jane Sophia, daughter of St. John Chiverton Charlton, Esq., of Apley Castle, Shropshire, by whom he had issue four sons. On the death of his father in 1858 he succeeded to the family estates, and resumed the old family name of Pryce in lieu of Jones. He was a justice of the Peace for the Counties of Montgomery and Merioneth, and was Sheriff for the latter County in 1849, and in 1884 was appointed Lord-Lieutenant of the same County. He was also for some years a Captain in the Montgomeryshire Yeomanry Cavalry. He was one of the promoters and first directors of the Newtown and Machynlleth Railway, and on the amalgamation of that Company with the Cambrian Railways Company in 1864 he was elected a director, and in 1868 was appointed Deputy-Chairman, and in December, 1884, Chairman of the Cambrian Company. Capt. Pryce was an active county magistrate, and took a prominent part in promoting the Liberal cause (of which he was a staunch adherent) in the county and boroughs, especially during the ever-memorable election of 1880, when Mr. Stuart Rendel (Liberal) was elected M.P. for the county by a majority of 191 votes over the former member, Mr. C. W. W. Wynn. He was an original Vice-President of the Montgomeryshire Liberal Association, and in 1878 became its President, a post which he held until 1886, when failing health compelled him to resign it. He died at Aberystwyth on the 21st August, 1891, in his 72nd year, and was buried at Castle Caereinion Church. His arms were :—Quarterly 1st and 4th or a lion rampant *gules*, 2nd and 3rd *argent* three bears' paws *proper*; Crest, a lion rampant *gules*. Motto : " Heb Dduw heb ddim ; Duw a digon."

PRYSE, JOHN, was born in Radnorshire, but lived nearly all his life at Llanidloes. He was apprenticed a shoemaker, but forsook that trade for the more congenial one of book-dealer, to which he subsequently added that of printer. He was an enthusiastic lover of Welsh literature and lore, and published numerous reprints of books relating to Wales, such as *Evans's Specimens of Ancient Welsh Poetry, Evans's View of the Primitive Ages, Johnes's Causes of Dissent in Wales*, and several original works, as *Rowlands' Cambrian Bibliography, Breezes from the Welsh Mountains, Welsh Interpreter, Handbook to the Radnorshire and Breconshire Mineral Springs, Jenkins' Poetry of Wales*, and others. In 1859, he started the publication of the *Llanidloes Telegraph*, a weekly newspaper, price one penny half-penny, afterwards reduced to one penny. This in point of date was the *second* newspaper printed, or partly printed, in Montgomeryshire, the first being the *Montgomeryshire Herald*, published for a few weeks at Newtown in 1835. Its publication was discontinued a few months before its proprietor's death. Mr. Pryse was twice married, his first wife being the widow of Mr. Richard Mills, the musician. He died on the 19th of October, 1883, aged 57 years.

PUGH, DAVID, of Llanerchydol, for many years Member of Parliament for the Montgomery Boroughs, was the son of Charles Pugh, and Jane his wife, who married secondly Sir Arthur Davies Owen, of Glansevern. He was born August 14th, 1789, and succeeded to the Llanerchydol estates under the Will of his great uncle David Pugh, Esq., of London (Sheriff 1793), on the death of his widow in October, 1819. Mr. Pugh joined the Local Militia, in which he became Captain in December, 1819. In 1828 the old regiment was disbanded, but in February, 1831, a new corps of Yeomanry Cavalry was formed with the Right Hon. C. W. W. Wynn, M.P., as Lieut.-Colonel, and Mr. Pugh as Major, a post which he resigned in January, 1844. He was Sheriff in 1823, and in 1830 was appointed Recorder of Welshpool, an office which was abolished by the operation of the Municipal Corporations Act. Mr. Pugh was also a Justice of the Peace and Deputy-Lieutenant for Montgomeryshire. At the first general election after the passing of the Reform Act of 1832, which took place in December that year, Mr. Pugh was elected Member of Parliament for the newly-constituted District of Montgomery Boroughs in the Conservative interest. He was opposed by Col. (afterwards Sir John) Edwards, the Whig or Reform candidate, whom he defeated by a majority of 14, the number of votes recorded being for Pugh 335, Edwards 321. A petition was, however, immediately lodged against his return, which was heard the following April, and resulted in his being unseated. He did not again seek the suffrages of the electors until the general election of 1847, when he entered the field as an opponent of the sitting member, the Hon. Hugh Cholmondeley (afterwards Baron Delamere). Party feeling ran very high, and the contest was so exceedingly close that it resulted in a double return, the number of votes on each side being equal. The Indenture returning Mr. Cholmondeley was, however, taken off the file by order of the House of Commons, dated February 14th, 1848, and Mr. Pugh retained the seat. At the general election of 1852, Mr. George Hammond Whalley, of Plasmadoc, came out as a Free Trader and Liberal to oppose him, but was defeated by a considerable majority. At the general election of 1857, the seat was not contested, and Mr. Pugh continued to represent the Boroughs until his death. He never, it is believed, took part in the debates in the House of Commons, but faithfully supported his party with his vote. Mr. Pugh was one of the promoters and first Directors of the Oswestry and Newtown Railway, and was also an active and useful County Magistrate, and as a kind and courteous country gentleman was much respected by all who knew him, irrespective of political differences of opinion. He died April 20th, 1861, and was buried at Welshpool parish church. Mr. Pugh, by his wife Anne, daughter and heiress of Evan Hugh Vaughan, Esq., of Beguildy, Radnorshire, whom he married July 11th, 1814, and who died October 8th, 1863, had five children, namely (1) David, born April 24th, 1815, died un-married Sept. 23rd, 1857; (2) Margaret Anne, born in 1818, married Capt. Willes Johnson, R.N. (a brother of Lady Edwards, the relict of Sir John Edwards, Bart., and M.P. for the Montgomery Boroughs in succession to Mr. Pugh), died November 25th, 1881, leaving three daughters; (3) Charles Vaughan, Capt. 90th Light Infantry, born May 19th, 1819, married Felicia Harriet, only daughter of Captain Gosling, R.N., died without issue December 28th, 1874; (4) Mary Jane, married Peter Audley Lovell, Esq., of Cole Park, Wilts, who died March 18th, 1869, leaving one son, Peter Audley David Arthur Lovell, Lieut. Coldstream Guards; (5) John Cadwalader, Lieut. 1st Royal, born May 30th, 1826, died unmarried July 19th, 1851. Mrs. Lovell, by Royal Licence, took the additional name of Pugh in accordance with the provisions of her father's Will.

PUGH, ROWLAND, of Mathafarn, in the parish of Llanwrin, was a descendant of Dafydd Llwyd ab Llewelyn, of the same place, a celebrated poet of the fifteenth century, and a man of great wealth. He was the son of Richard Pugh, by Gaynor his wife, and studied the law at the Inner Temple, of which he was entered a member in 1598. His grandfather of the same name was Sheriff for Merioneth in 1575, and represented the Borough of Montgomery in Parliament in 1572, and again in 1588-9. In 1602 the subject of this notice became Steward of the lordship of Cyfeiliog, and in 1606 a Magistrate. He was also twice Sheriff, namely, in 1609 and 1626, and for Merioneth in 1631. He was twice married; first, to Elizabeth, daughter of Sir Richard Pryce, of Gogerddan, by whom he had two daughters; and, secondly, to Mary, widow of Thomas Jones, of Llanbadarn, by whom he had a son and heir, John Pugh. He was a staunch Royalist, and for his zeal in that cause his house was on the 20th November, 1644, burnt down by a troop of Parliamentary soldiers. He died in less than a month after that, namely, on the day after Christmas, and was buried at Conway. His arms were, *argent* a lion passant *sable*, between three fleur de lis *gules*.

PUGH, JOHN, of Mathafarn, was the son and heir of the above named Rowland Pugh, by Mary his wife, and was like his father a devoted Royalist. Upon the restoration of Charles II. his name was included in the list of gentlemen who were deemed fit and qualified to be made Knights of the then intended but subsequently abandoned Order of the Royal Oak, as a reward for their fidelity to the Royal cause. His estate was then (1660) valued at £1.000. His grandson of the same name represented the Borough of Montgomery in Parliament from 1708 to 1727. The Mathafarn estates were sold in 1752 to Sir W. W. Wynn, Bart., for £33,400, and now form part of the Wynnstay property.

PUGH, WILLIAM, of Brynllywarch, was born at Pennant Berriew, on the 26th December, 1783, and was the only son and heir of William Pugh, of Pennant, afterwards of Caerhowel, by Frances, his wife, eldest daughter of Richard Lewis, of Welshpool. His grandfather owned Kilthrew and Brynllywarch in Kerry, which had been in the family possession as far back as 1500, and was Sheriff in 1767. His father was one of the leading attorneys in Montgomeryshire, and accumulated a considerable property. He also served the office of Sheriff in 1813. He died the 13th November, 1823, aged 75, and was buried at Kerry. The subject of this memoir was at an early age sent to Rugby School, where he remained until 1802. He then entered Trinity College, Cambridge, and pursued his studies there, taking his B,A. degree in 1806, and his M.A. in 1812. During his university career, he secured the acquaintance and friendship of several gentlemen who, in after life, attained great eminence, among others Lord Palmerston and Sir Robert Peel. On leaving College, Mr. Pugh proceeded to the study of the law, and entered as a student at Lincoln's Inn, on the 5th February, 1805. He became a pupil of Mr. Humphreys, a Chancery barrister and conveyancer of high standing, and was called to the bar on the 11th February, 1813, but never practised, his object in studying the law and procuring a call to the bar having been to better qualify himself for the position he was destined to occupy as a magistrate and country gentleman. He was appointed a Deputy-Lieutenant in December, 1807; Captain in the Royal Western Regiment of Local Militia, 25th April, 1809, and Major, 21st May, 1813; and a Justice of the Peace, 17th April, 1817. On the 5th June, 1816, Mr. Pugh married Beatrice Matilda, youngest daughter of Richard Dennison, Esq., M.D., Brighton, and great grandchild of Mrs Jane Buckley, of Dolfor. By his marriage the Dolfor estate came into Mr. Pugh's family. After his marriage, Mr. Pugh resided for some time at Mellington, Churchstoke, whence he removed to the old family mansion at Brynllywarch, Kerry. In 1829, after his mother's death (13th January, 1828), he sold the Caerhowel estate, comprising the mansion and several valuable farms—in all upwards of 439 acres —and rebuilt and enlarged Brynllywarch. His wife died on the 26th of June, 1829, aged 38, leaving by him five children, namely Frances Matilda (who died unmarried at Beverley, Worcester, in September, 1843), William Buckley, Pryce Buckley, Laura Seraphina (married to Dr. W. M. Beddowes, of Shrewsbury), and Geraldine Hannah, the second and last named of whom still survive. Soon after attaining his majority, Mr. Pugh began to take an active and leading part in the public affairs of Montgomeryshire, and in the setting on foot and promotion of various important movements, enterprises, and improvements—some of the chief of which, indeed, owe their origin, prosecution and successful completion, almost entirely to his public spirit and energy. Besides performing with exemplary zeal his duties as a magistrate, he was an active trustee of Kerry School, and took an energetic part in the carrying out of the Kedewen and other Inclosure Acts, the improvement of turnpike roads, and the obtaining of the Montgomeryshire Turnpike Act, the building of a new bridge over the Severn at Newtown, and various other local and public improvements. He invested over £7,000 in Montgomeryshire Roads Bonds. He was also mainly instrumental in making the new road from Newtown through Radnorshire to Builth, completed and opened for traffic in June, 1823—a work of very great public utility, to which he devoted much labour and energy, and in which he invested over £10,000, the greater portion of which the South Wales Roads Commissioners subsequently, for some reason, declined to recognise. But the most important, perhaps, of all the undertakings he engaged in was the Western Branch of the Montgomeryshire Canal, being an extension of the canal system from Garthmill to Newtown. It is not too much to say that Mr. Pugh was the life and soul of this enterprise, and in it he held (as appears from a statement made out in 1841) shares to the amount of £26,000 and mortgage bonds for £25,000, besides £1,700 which he had paid towards the expenses of an Act of Parliament in 1834 (total £52,700), of which, practically, he never saw a farthing again, and received but little in the shape of interest or dividends. The Branch Canal was begun in 1819, and completed in 1821, at a cost, up to that time, of £56,232 8s., subsequently increased to £83,416 10s 7d. up to 1846. The immediate result was a reduction of at least 80 per cent. in the price of coal and lime, and a very considerable reduction in the price of other commodities. It is difficult to over-estimate the advantages derived from this extension by the manufacturing and agricultural classes of Newtown, Llanidloes, and the surrounding districts. It led to Newtown becoming the centre of the flannel manufacture of Wales, and in the course of fifteen years, to an increase of its wealth and population at least sevenfold. On the opening of the canal to Newtown, the following resolution was passed by the proprietors, at a meeting held at the *Rock* on the 4th of August, 1821 .

" Resolved, that the Proprietors cannot receive the information communicated by the report now read, of the successful results arising from the completion of the Canal, without expressing and recording in the strongest manner their sense of the important advantages derived from the unremitting assistance and superintendence of Mr. W. Pugh in the execution of the work. The Proprietors are assured not only that the Canal could not have been completed in the excellent and perfect manner in which it has been made without that superintendence; but that it would at this time have been, in a great and most important part, unfinished, unless the difficulties that have attended its progress in its various details had been met by his active, skilful, and judicious exertions. That the warmest thanks of the Proprietors be presented to Mr. William Pugh for the great and valuable assistance he has so kindly and so usefully afforded throughout the whole progress of the Canal, together with a piece of Plate of the value of One Hundred Guineas, in testimony of the sincere regard and high respect they entertain for him."

The plate, presented with the above resolution, consisted of three large tureens and other articles. On two of the tureens the following inscription was engraved:—

"This piece of plate was presented to William Pugh, Esq., by the Proprietors of the Western Branch of the Montgomeryshire Canal, on the 3rd of August, 1822.

On the other:—

"As a grateful, though inadequate testimony of their sense of his foresight and activity in promoting the beneficial measure of extending the line of Canal to Newtown, as well as his indefatigable exertions for the interests of the Company during the progress of the works, the Proprietors of the Western Branch of the Montgomeryshire Canal presented this piece of Plate to William Pugh, Esq., on the 3rd day of August, 1822."

A valuable piece of plate, consisting of a silver chandelier or epergne, purchased by public subscription, was also presented to Mr. Pugh, which bore the following inscription:

"Presented to William Pugh, Esq., by the Inhabitants of Newtown, as a token of their esteem and gratitude for the very great and successful exertions made by him to promote the prosperity and the trade of that place."

The whole of these articles were sold with Mr. Pugh's other effects in 1836. Mr. W. B. Pugh, after his return to England in 1843, saw in the window of a silversmith's shop in London, strange to say, several of them on sale, which he subsequently purchased, and they are now in his possession. At an early period of his life, when country squires were, as a rule, either Tories or moderate Whigs, Mr. Pugh attached himself to the then unpopular school of advanced Liberals, and soon came to be recognized as one of the leaders of his party in Montgomeryshire. He was a strenuous supporter of the great movement which resulted in the passing of the Reform Act of 1832. Montgomeryshire largely partook of the intense excitement of those days. Chiefly through Mr. Pugh's exertions, county and other public meetings in favour of Reform were held, and petitions signed by upwards of three thousand persons were sent up to both Houses of Parliament. Newtown and its neighbourhood especially took up the cause with great zeal, where the public excitement and irritation of the working classes were, unfortunately, increased to a dangerous degree by the following untoward incident. A few days before Christmas, 1830, six men from Newtown, in consequence of the stagnation of trade in that place, went round the neighbourhood to solicit charity, and amongst other houses called at Glansevern, the seat of William Owen, Esquire, who immediately gave them in charge to a constable, and directed them to be taken before a neighbouring magistrate, where Mr. Owen attended and charged them with highway robbery! On this charge they were remanded to gaol, to be brought up again for examination on the 1st of January, 1831. Exasperated at this, a mob of three or four hundred men and boys went from Newtown in a body to Glansevern on the 31st December, 1830, threatening Mr. Owen with vengeance. So peremptory were they in their demand for the liberation of the prisoners, that they compelled him to mount his horse and accompany them to Montgomery to release them. This proceeding came to the ears of Mr. Pugh, who hastened from Newtown to the scene. Near Montgomery he met the rioters bringing home the released prisoners in triumph. He at once ordered the procession to stop, and alighting from his carriage addressed the crowd, pointing out to them the egregious folly and illegality of their conduct, and peremptorily demanded that the released prisoners should be given up to him. Mr. Pugh, it should be stated, had some years previously earned the gratitude of the Newtown operatives by collecting and distributing amongst them £400, to keep them from starving when out of work. This, and other acts of kindness, had made him extremely popular with the working classes. The men, therefore, knowing with whom they had to deal, immediately complied with his demand, and delivered up the prisoners to him. He directed them to enter his carriage, and then drove them to Newtown and thence to Kerry, where he kept them at his own house that night. They were not locked up, but were treated like his own servants. Early next morning he drove them over to Montgomery, and lodged them safely in the county gaol. The same day they were brought before the Lord Lieutenant and a full bench of magistrates for examination, when they were all discharged. Several of the rioters were subsequently apprehended, and committed for trial at the assizes, when all pleaded guilty, and one of them (who had carried a flag in the procession) was sentenced to six months, and the others to shorter terms of imprisonment. The above episode shews not only Mr. Pugh's popularity and almost unbounded influence over the working class, but also his strict impartiality and love of justice. So excited were the populace of Newtown at this time that it was considered necessary to swear in many hundreds of special constables—(351 were sworn in the adjoining parishes of Kerry and Mochdre)—and to hold the cavalry in readiness. However, owing in a great degree to the moderate counsels and firmness of Mr. Pugh, serious breaches of the peace, though feared, were happily averted. On the dissolution of Parliament in April, 1831, Mr. Pugh was urged by a large number of freeholders in the neighbourhood of Newtown, to contest the seat for the county against the old member, Mr. C. W. W. Wynn. This he declined. Mr. Joseph Hayes Lyon, however, came forward, and was proposed by Mr. Pugh, but was not successful. The expenses of Mr. Lyon's candidature amounted, it seems, to £1,813 18s., towards which Mr. Pugh contributed £536 6s., and

Colonel Edwards a similar sum. In 1833 Mr. Pugh was again urged to allow himself to be put in nomination for the Boroughs, in the event of the sitting member, Colonel (afterwards Sir John) Edwards, being unseated on petition, a contingency, however, which did not arise. Mr. Pugh took a great interest in the prosperity of the staple trade and manufactures of Newtown, and was one of the most prominent of those to whose exertions were due the removal of the flannel market from Welshpool to Newtown, the building of the Public Rooms, and the introduction of Gas at the latter place—to all of which he contributed considerable sums of money. He also exerted himself much between 1833 and 1835, in endeavouring to introduce steam power and improved machinery for the manufacture of flannels into Newtown; but the want of enterprise among the masters, and the short-sighted opposition of the operatives prevented this being fully accomplished during his life-time, and for some years after his death. He also took the lead in and mainly through his energy brought to a successful issue the movement for removing the summer assizes from Welshpool to Newtown. Petitions and counter petitions, signed in the aggregate by over 11,000 freeholders and others, together with a mass of evidence, were got up on behalf of the rival towns, and at last an Order of the Privy Council was obtained in June, 1835, complying with the prayer of the petitioners, as soon as a proper court and lock-up house should be provided. Various delays, however, took place and the assizes were not actually held at Newtown until the 15th July, 1840, Lord Denman being the judge on that occasion. Hitherto no newspaper had ever been published in Montgomeryshire. Mr. Pugh, and a few other like-minded with himself, felt that the time had come when an effort should be made to establish a local journal; and in a very great measure through his exertions, and in consideration of his personally indemnifying the publisher against loss to the extent of £300, the *Montgomeryshire Herald* was started. The first number was issued at Newtown by John Williams the publisher, on Monday, the 15th of June, 1835, price sevenpence, and it came out weekly for several months, but was discontinued for want of support. In consequence of the large sums expended by Mr. Pugh in promoting various enterprises, and particularly of the large amount of his capital that was locked up in the Montgomeryshire Canal, several Montgomeryshire turnpike roads, the new road into Radnorshire, and several other undertakings, none of which proved such remunerative investments as he had expected they would be, his estates became much encumbered, and his income considerably diminished. He had, for several years, been endeavouring, in vain (owing to the hostility and obstruction of two or three individuals on the Canal Board), to obtain a settlement of his claims, or even securities from that Company, for his own money and many thousands of pounds which he had borrowed of others for the use of the Company, and which had been applied for its purposes, but for which he, unfortunately, had made himself personally responsible, and paid interest out of his private estate. These, and other creditors, now became very pressing, and although he had still the utmost confidence in the Canal and other undertakings as valuable properties and a good investment, the continual drain upon his private resources, and the increasing clamour of his creditors, made it evident that he could no longer hold out against his growing embarrassments. He, therefore, determined at once to realize his property in order to pay his debts; but in the meantime he found it necessary for his personal safety to leave the country, and seek a refuge in France from the importunities of his creditors. In June, 1835, therefore, he took up his residence with his children at Caen, where he spent the remainder of his days in close retirement. In October, 1835, the Brynllywarch estate and some of the Montgomeryshire Canal shares were brought under the hammer, and, the following spring, the farming stock, furniture, and other effects were sold. The auctioneer (the celebrated George Robins) in his advertisement thus describes the property in his usual florid style :—

" A singularly important and very eligible Freehold estate which it is believed will not yield in its influence and great advantages to any property that has been introduced this season to the consideration of the monied world. It is situate in a County where the last year's experience has demonstrated that the wealthy prefer the certain tenure of Terra Firma to the more equivocal enjoyment of funded property. The influential power, which will necessarily appertain to the possessor of this vast domain of most excellent meadow, pasture, and arable land, needs hardly to be the subject of remark; the situation gives to it a most important qualification. . . . . The estate under consideration includes 27 Freehold Farms, exceeding 3,500 acres, tenants unexceptionable, contented and affluent, ... The London Mail passes daily through this vast territory of the fruitful produce of a rich soil (sic). . . . . These are only a few of the advantages that appear to be almost exclusively the inheritance of the possessor of this fine property. . . . The present low rental is about £4,000 a year."

The bulk of the property was sold to Mr. Bullen, a wealthy Liverpool banker, from whom the late John Naylor, Esq., derived it. Some, we are sorry to say, of those who, in the time of his prosperity, had availed themselves of Mr. Pugh's friendship and support, now turned their backs upon him, and even exhibited some vindictiveness towards him. To make up, in some measure, the loss of his income, a Bill in Mr. Pugh's interest was, with the concurrence and support of the majority of the proprietors of the western branch of the Canal, introduced into Parliament in 1838, to increase the tonnage dues on the Canal. The Bill was, to their honour, warmly supported by the most influential traders and agriculturists in Newtown and neighbourhood, who could not forget their immense obligations to Mr. Pugh in connection with the Canal, and who deeply sympathised with him in his misfortunes, but it met with determined hostility from other quarters, and, in March, 1838, was thrown out on the motion for its second reading by a majority of 77 to 3. This was a grievous blow and a severe disappointment to Mr. Pugh, but in his exile and misfortunes he was greatly comforted by the receipt of the following address from his old friends and neighbours, the merchants, manufacturers, and other inhabitants of Newtown:—

"Sir,—Although a period of some years has unfortunately separated you from us, we consider the present time opportune to publicly address you.

"We do so for several reasons. First, from a high personal respect for you. Secondly, from the deep sense of obligation and gratitude we owe you as an indefatigable public benefactor, whose valuable time, energetic talents, and independent fortune have ever been devoted, with ceaseless perseverance, to extend the commerce of our town, to improve the agriculture of our county, and to maintain the poor in industrious (although humble) independence. And, thirdly, that your mind may be relieved from the distressing impression, that while you have thus, by your restless anxiety, effected the great objects of your patriotic endeavours, we fear lest our silence may cause you to imagine that the inhabitants of Newtown remain, with remorseless and callous ingratitude, unaffected spectators of your great exertions in our favour, or unfeeling observers of your undeserved misfortune. We beg to assure you, with the most earnest and unfeigned seriousness, that we have never heard of any disappointment or circumstance which was likely to cause your unhappiness without feeling the most poignant sorrow; nor have we ever been made acquainted with any occurrence likely to promote your interest or to gratify your feelings, without gladly and deeply entering into its merits.

"Twelve months ago we received your address relative to the propriety of raising the tonnage on the Canal, as an act of justice to yourself due by the public. In that desire we fully acquiesced, although we were not unconscious of the consequences likely to accrue; but our minds were too strongly imbued with the justice of your desire to cause us to imagine that we ought to participate in the expenditure of your large capital without your obtaining an equitable remuneration; and we entertain no doubt that it will be *especially* gratifying to you to learn that the operative and industrious classes entered most zealously into the subject, from a just sense of your sacrifice, and a thankful remembrance and appreciation of your integrity as a magistrate.

"We lament that the disposal of your estates should have become a matter of necessity; but having known for some time that it has been an object of your desire, we beg to congratulate you on the result, which we trust will prove as satisfactory to you as we sanguinely anticipate.

"Our sympathy and regret have, in common with a great mass of our fellow-townsmen, been powerfully excited in your favour by the unjust and cruel persecutions to which you have been subjected; and our minds have been naturally led to dwell on your sufferings, which are the result of your anxieties for the benefit of your native county; and while we admire your moral and manly resignation, and rejoice to see your lofty character displayed, we can but hold in utter detestation the rancorous fatuity of your open, disguised, and malignant enemies, comprised of men who, individually and collectively have benefitted thousands by your efforts, and from whom no gratitude could be too munificent.

"Gladly, indeed, would we have avoided recurrence to this subject, but we feel it due to ourselves and fellow-townsmen to enter our protest against such violent and ungentlemanly behaviour, which induces the melancholy conviction, that the love of justice and the good of this county are not the objects which influence those on whose proceedings we have thus commented.

" During the eventful period of your public intercourse with this town, never did its inhabitants more require your assistance than at the present time, not only as a country gentleman, but most distinctly and especially as a public magistrate; and, although we now address you as an inhabitant of a foreign land, most fervently do we pray that you will shortly return to your native county, and that your useful and patriotic life may long be spared to enjoy in repose and in the bosom of your sincere friends the fruits of your unparalleled exertions and sacrifices."

[Here follow the signatures of several hundreds mentioned at the end of the address]. To this Address Mr. Pugh replied as follows :—

" GENTLEMEN,—I feel unable to find words sufficiently strong to express the pleasure and gratification I have received from your address.

" I beg to assure you, that so far from regretting, in the smallest degree, any sacrifices which I have made in forwarding the completion of the public works in your neighbourhood, I would most cheerfully, under similar circumstances, again incur the same, being assured by you that my humble exertions have been beneficial to my native county, and that my conduct has met your approbation.

"Notwithstanding the extraordinary opposition to your wishes, and consequent failure of the Canal Bill last session of Parliament, I trust, nevertheless, at no very distant period, that I shall have the gratification of personally thanking you for the great kindness you have expressed to me on this and on all other occasions,

And am, Gentlemen, your sincerely obliged,

" Caen, 22nd October, 1838."   W. PUGH.

It will be seen that Mr. Pugh still cherished hopes of being able to make arrangements with his creditors which would enable him to return to his native county—hopes, alas! which were never realised. Though debarred from personally taking part in them, he still watched closely through the " loopholes of retreat," and with his pen actively supported the anti-corn-law agitation, and other public movements of that day ; and, in an especial manner, took deep interest in everything calculated to promote the welfare and prosperity of his much loved Montgomeryshire. From the first introduction of railways, he was keenly alive to the superior advantages of that over all other existing modes of conveyance and communication, and was anxious that Montgomeryshire should early participate in its benefits. In the spring of 1840, a Government inquiry was held with the object of ascertaining the best route for railway communication between London and Ireland, towards which the Chancellor of the Exchequer had announced the willingness of Government to grant a subsidy of two millions. The commissioners were Sir Frederick Smith and Professor Barlow. While the inquiry was going on, and the Commissioners were engaged in examining the claims of the proposed North-Western route, via Shrewsbury and Chester to Holyhead, of which Mr. Robert Stephenson was the engineer ; and a rival route from Birmingham via Shrewsbury, Bala, and Dolgelley, to Porthdinlleyn, surveyed by Mr. Vignoles ; Mr. Pugh, although so far away, succeeded, with the aid of a committee formed at Worcester, in having the inquiry extended to a third route, commencing by a junction at Didcot with the Great Western Rail-

R

way, and proceeding through Oxford, Worcester, Ludlow,
Newtown, and Dolgelley to Porthdinlleyn. Mr. T. G. Newnham, a
local surveyor and engineer to the Canal Company and others
were employed (Mr. Pugh, out of his then limited means, contributing a large portion of the cost), to make careful surveys of
the Montgomeryshire route, and to get up evidence in its favour.
Mr. Pugh, by correspondence, directed the fight before the
Commissioners with his characteristic energy; and Messrs.
Stephenson, Brunel, Vignoles, and other engineers and scientific
men of great eminence were examined as to the merits of the
rival routes. Eventually, however, the Commissioners reported
in favour of the Holyhead line, which in course of time was completed. Mr. Stephenson originally proposed to cross the Menai
Straits by a *wooden* bridge. As to the Porthdinlleyn line, it
was proposed to cross the Severn, near Newtown, along a high
viaduct or embankment, 136 feet above the level of the canal!
But one of the principal objections to that route was a tunnel of
more than three miles in lengh, through solid porphyry, which
would have to be made between Dinas Mawddwy and Dolgelley,
at an estimated cost of £330,000, and as to which Mr. Newnham
complacently wrote: " Sir Frederick came to the conclusion that
"it would require 20 years to make it, but Mr. Brunel will, I
"think, be able to make it appear that it may be completed in
"10 years"! Mr. Newnham's proposed viaduct over the
Mawddach was to be 169 feet high, but Mr. Vignoles's was to be
200 feet high! Mr. Pugh had never indulged in any expensive
tastes or habits, but had always lived very quietly and frugally
so far as his personal and domestic expenditure was concerned.
His Caerhowel and Brynllywarch estates—a very fine property,
produced a rental of at least £5,000 a year—and his furniture
and effects, produced a very large amount; his eldest son gave up
also half the settled property towards paying the creditors; yet
for all this the latter were not paid in full. Mr. Pugh's return
to his native land was therefore delayed month after month, and
year after year, until the " hope deferred " made his heart very
sick. It has never been satisfactorily shewn what became of all
the money, for even after taking into account all the expenditure
above referred to, on the Canal, the Montgomeryshire and
Radnorshire roads, elections, and other matters, there must have
been a very large surplus unaccounted for. One thing is certain
it never came into Mr. Pugh's hands, nor into those of any
member of his family. At last, enfeebled and worn out by
anxiety and disappointments, and grieved by his long exile from
the Montgomeryshire he loved so well, and for whose prosperity
he had sacrificed everything, Mr. Pugh's naturally vigorous constitution became an easy prey to disease; he was struck down by
paralysis; and on the 4th March, 1842, he died, in the fifty-
ninth year of his age, at Caen, where also he was buried. His
family immediately returned to England. The arms of Pugh
are 1st and 4th *Argent*, a lion rampant *sable*, between three
fleurs de lis *gules* for Pugh. 2nd and 3rd *sable*, three spears'

heads *argent* 2 and 1 for LEWIS. Crest, a dolphin embowed *proper*. The arms of Buckley are *Argent* on a chevron *sable*, 5 roundels *argent* between three stags couchant. Crest, a stag's head couped *proper*, pierced with an arrow.

RAVENS, REV. NATHANIEL, was Vicar of Welshpool "in Oliver's time," but was ejected after the Restoration for Nonconformity, and was succeeded by the Rev. W. Langford. The value of the living at that time is stated at £46 18s. 9d.

REES, REV. ABRAHAM, D.D., F.R.S., the eminent encyclo-pædist, was born at the Old Independent Chapel House, Llanbryn-mair (the site of which now forms part of the burial ground), in the year 1743, and was the son of the Rev. Lewis Rees, pastor of the Independent Church. He was educated for the ministry at the Carmarthen Academy, then conducted by Dr. Jenkins, whence he proceeded to that at Hoxton, London, then jointly conducted by Drs. Jennings and Savage. On the death of Dr. Jennings in 1762, Dr. Kippis was appointed classical tutor, and Mr. Rees, although he was so young, became mathematical tutor, an appointment which he held with great distinction for 22 years. In 1766 he was ordained minister of a Presbyterian Church in the parish of St. Thomas's, Southwark. Here he laboured for 15 years, during which his literary attainments procured for him from the University of Edinburgh at the express desire of Dr. Robertson the historian, the degree of Doctor of Divinity. In 1781 he removed to the Old Jewry, where his ministry prospered so greatly that his congregation found it necessary to build for him a larger chapel in Jewin Street, where he continued to preach as long as the state of his health permitted. About 1777 he undertook the editorship of *Chambers's Cyclopædia*, a task which cost him immense labour. The work came out in numbers extending over nine years, and was completed in 1786 in four large folio vols. The matter was more than half of it new, and furnished by himself, and the pro-found ability and learning which the work displayed caused it to be immediately translated into several Continental languages, and procured for its learned editor the honour of being elected a Fellow of the Royal Society. Many foreign literary and scientific bodies also paid him the compliment of enrolling him among their members. The Hoxton Academy was broken up about 1785, and in 1786 a new one was established in its stead at Hackney, with which Drs. Kippis, Price, and Priestley were at first associated, but eventually the whole weight of its manage-ment fell upon Dr. Rees. Political and doctrinal differences arose among the subscribers, and after a few years' chequered existence this Academy also was broken up. In 1802 he pub-lished the first half-yearly volume of his great undertaking, commonly known as *Rees's Cyclopædia*—a work of stupendous magnitude, which he brought to a successful termination in 45 vols. quarto. Although he had many able assistants in this great work, a large proportion of the articles were written by himself, and the plan and arrangement of the whole was entirely his own.   His other publications were :—*Economy illustrated and recommended*; *Antidote to the Alarm of Invasion*; *The Principles of Protestant Dissenters stated and vindicated*; and several volumes of Sermons.   Dr. Rees was one of the earliest members of the Linnæan Society.   He was also for many years President of the Presbyterian Board in London, a director of Dr. Williams's Fund, and of the Library founded by him in Redcross Street, one of the chief directors of the City Road Orphan Working School, and an active member of most of the charitable institutions of the metropolis.   He at all times took a leading part in most of the religious movements of those days promoted by the Nonconformists of London.   He was an able preacher, though his religious opinions, which were Arian or Unitarian of the old school, were not acceptable to many of his co-religionists.   In politics he was a firm friend of religious and political liberty, but opposed to all resort to violence or rioting.   On the 3rd of May, 1820, he headed a deputation of 89 dissenting ministers to present King George the 4th with an Address on his accession to the throne.   It was remarked that he was the only one present, who had also been present, when a similar Address was presented to the late King in 1760.   He was a great favourite of the Duke of Sussex, who associated his portrait with that of Dr. Parr to ornament his principal library at Kensington Palace.   He died on the 9th of June, 1825, aged 82 years, after a long and laborious life, in the full possession of his faculties, and was buried in Bunhill Fields.

REES, Rev. LEWIS, of Llanbrynmair, an eminent Independent minister, and father of the above-named and still more eminent Dr. Abraham Rees, was the son of Rees Edward Lewis, of Glyn Rhiwdre, in the parish of Glyncorwg, Glamorganshire, where he was born March 2nd, 1710.   His grand father was a clergyman of the Church of England, and held the living of Penderyn, Breconshire, but his parents were Presbyterians, and he himself joined that denomination at an early age.   He appears to have received a fairly good education for those days, and for some time studied at the Academy of Mr. Vavasor Griffiths, at Maesgwyn, Radnorshire.   His piety and talents attracted the notice of several ministers, one of whom, the Rev. Edmund Jones, of Pontypool (whose name is still well-known and revered in connection with the early history of Welsh Nonconformity), induced him to accompany him to Llanbrynmair, where a small Independent Church, meeting for worship at Tymawr, was in great need of pastoral care.   Here he accordingly settled about the year 1734, and about four years afterwards, namely, April 13th, 1738, he was ordained at Blaengwrach (his old home in South Wales) minister of the Church at Llanbrynmair.   When he first came to Llanbrynmair the religious state of North Wales generally was most deplorable,

There was but one Dissenting chapel in Montgomeryshire, that is, at Llanfyllin, but through Mr. Rees's exertions one was built at Llanbrynmair in 1739. Mr Rees threw himself into his work with great zeal, not confining his labours to the neighbourhood of his home, but travelling much throughout all the counties of North Wales, often at great personal risk. It was at his invitation that the celebrated Howell Harries, one of the founders of Welsh Methodism, paid his first visit to North Wales the beginning of the year 1739, and Llanbrynmair was the second place in North Wales in which he preached, In 1740 Mr. Rees married Esther, daughter of Abraham Penry, of Penderyn, Breconshire. It is related that when he sought Mr. Penry's consent to the union his future father-in-law asked him what fortune he had, to which he, taking up a Bible, replied, " This is my chief fortune." Mr. Penry was well satisfied with the reply, and readily gave his assent. There were six children of the marriage—Josiah, Abraham, Mary, Isaac, Jacob, and Ebenezer During his residence at Llanbrynmair Mr. Rees established new churches in various parts of Montgomeryshire and Merionethshire, and visited, it is said, every Dissenting church in North Wales once or twice every year. He was on very friendly terms with the Methodist reformers, and gave much assistance to the Methodist movement. Being himself a duly licensed preacher, he escaped some of the persecutions to which the Methodist exhorters (who refused to acknowledge themselves Dissenters and to apply for licences) were exposed. In 1745, he, for family reasons, removed for a while to Maesyrouen, Breconshire, near his wife's native place, but still visited Llanbrynmair once a month, and in three years' time, namely in 1748, he returned there once again, and continued to labour among his old friends for eleven years more. In 1759 he accepted a call from the Independent Church at Mynyddbach, near Swansea, where he laboured with much success until the infirmities of old age compelled him to give up his charge. The death of his wife, September 5th, 1794, aged 78 years, after a happy union of 54 years, affected him greatly. The following year he resigned the pastorate, and, after a short residence at Swansea, went to live with his married daughter and son-in-law, the Rev. John Davies, Llansamlet, where he spent peacefully his remaining days Notwithstanding his great age, he continued to preach until a very short time before his death. That event took place March 21st, 1800, he having then just completed the 90th year of his age, and having preached the Gospel for the long period of 70 years. Mr. Rees was a sound, practical and earnest preacher, very powerful in prayer, an excellent and laborious pastor, and his private life was pure and holy. These qualities, combined with a handsome and dignified presence, exercised a considerable influence on all who came within his reach. He also published the following works: (1) *Rhai Rheolau a Chyfarwyddiadau a gynygiwyd er cynnyddu Cyfeillach Grefyddol ymhlith Crist'nogion yn nghyd a Hymn ar*

Dymmer Lonydd. (Some Rules and Directions offered towards
promoting Religious Fellowship among Christians, with a Hymn
on a Quiet Temper, Carmarthen, 1771.) (2) *Y mawr bwys o
fod ein tybiau mewn Crefydd yn gyson a'r Ysgrythyr, &c.* (The
great importance of our religious opinions being consonant with
the Scriptures; a Sermon preached before an Assembly of
Ministers at Ringwood, July 29, 1788. By the Rev. David
Bogue, of Gosport. Translated from the second edition in
English, and published for the benefit of the Welsh. To which
are added a few Hymns on evangelical subjects by E. ap James
Davies, Carmarthen, 1793.) Mr. Rees was himself a somewhat
strict Calvinist, and it is said that it was in consequence of the
Arian views of his eminent son, Dr. Abraham Rees, that he was
induced at the advanced age of 83 to translate and publish this
little book.

RHIWALLON AB CYNFYN, on the death of Prince
Gruffydd ab Llywelyn in 1062, became joint sovereign with his
brother Bleddyn of Powys and North Wales. In 1068, however, Meredydd and Ithel, the sons of the late prince, raised an
army to recover possession of their sovereign rights, and a severe
battle was fought between the contending hosts at Mechain,
when Rhiwallon on the one side and Ithel on the other were
slain—the result being that Bleddyn became sole sovereign of
Powys and Gwynedd—Meredydd being "put to flight, whome
"Blethyn pursued so straightlie, that he starued for cold and
"hunger vpon the mountaines."

RHYDDERCH, JOHN OR SION, a poet, grammarian, and
printer, was a native of Cardiganshire, being the son of
Rhydderch Dafydd ab Gruffydd, of Cwm Du, near Newcastle
Emlyn. He settled in Shrewsbury as a printer about 1708, and
carried on business there for twenty years, printing and publish-
ing many Welsh books. He for about 10 years published
annually a Welsh *Almanack*, containing besides the usual
information original Odes, Carols, and other poetical compositions, some of them written by himself. He was also the
author of a Welsh Grammar (*Gramadeg Cymraeg*, 1728), and
an *English and Welsh Dictionary* (1725). A second edition of
this work was published in 1731, and a third edition in 1737.
Some years before his death he quitted Shrewsbury, and resided at Caetalhaiarn, Cemmes. He died there in November,
1735, and was buried at the Parish Church of Cemmes on
the 27th of that month. He sometimes spelt his own name
Hydderch, Rhydderch, Roderick, and Rogers.

RHYS o GARNO, SIR, an eminent poet and priest who
flourished between 1440 and 1470. He is supposed to have
been a native of Carno, but resided most of his time at or near
Corwen. He is also sometimes called Syr Rhys of Drewen,
and Syr Rhys ab Hywel Dyrnor. Some of his poetry is still
extant.

RHYS, DAVID, THOMAS, and MARY, of Penygeulan, Llanbrynmair, were brothers and a sister, and were all gifted as poets, or at least rhymesters and minstrels. DAVID was born about the year 1742, and was a carpenter by trade. He composed many very popular carols and songs, some of which are still remembered. He was also a good musician, and led the church choir. He died in March, 1824, aged 82 years. THOMAS was born in 1750-51, and was a joiner, but was of a more wandering turn than his brother David. He was very witty, and his songs were pungent and telling. He died in March, 1828, aged 77 years. A daughter of his died at Corris in December, 1883, aged 94 years. MARY was also a poet, but excelled as a singer. She was rather eccentric, delighting in fishing, basket-making, ploughing, and other masculine employments rather than housework. She generally wore a red coat over her other habiliments. She died in December, 1842, at the extreme age of 98 years. These were about the last survivors in Montgomeryshire of the old school of wandering minstrels and carol singers.

RICHARDS, REV. DAVID (*Dewi Silin*), was born at Darowen in 1783, and was the second son of the Rev. Thomas Richards, vicar of that parish. He was educated at Ystradmeurig School, then conducted by the Rev. John Williams, father of Archdeacon Williams, and was admitted to orders and licenced to the curacy of Llansilin, and subsequently, in 1819, promoted by Bishop Luxmoore to the vicarage of that parish, which he held until his death. As a clergyman, Mr. Richards performed his sacred duties with conscientious zeal and devotion, exhibiting towards those whose opinions differed from his own that tolerance and intelligent appreciation which ever distinguish a mind truly great and generous from one that is cramped within the limits of a bigoted creed. His kindliness of disposition was proverbial, and his preaching was evangelical and earnest. But he became more widely known among his countrymen as an accomplished poet and antiquary, and a friend, associate, and patron of literary men—with whom he was more familiarly known as *Dewi Silin*. He was one of the adjudicators at the Carmarthen Eisteddfod in July 1819, and the following October, on the establishment of the Powys Cymreigyddion Society, he became its secretary. He adjudicated at the Wrexham Eisteddfod in 1820, and at most of the Eisteddfodau held during the remainder of his life, including that held at Welshpool in 1824. He was at that time, indeed, one of the most active and able promoters of this ancient institution. Llansilin during his time was frequented by bards, minstrels, and literary characters from every part of Wales, and the genial vicar's name is still mentioned with reverence and esteem. He died at Llansilin on the 4th December, 1826, aged 43 years. His four brothers also were well-known and highly-respected clergymen of the Church of England, namely, the

Revs. Richard Richards, of Caerwys, and subsequently Vicar of Meifod; Thomas Richards, curate of Berriew, and Master of Berriew School, and afterwards from 1820 until his death in 1856 Rector of Llangynyw; John Richards, Perpetual Curate of Llanwddyn; and Lewis Richards, Rector of Llanerfyl.

RICHARDS, Rev. RICHARD, eldest son of the Rev. Thomas Richards, Vicar of Darowen, was born November 15th, 1780. Like all his brothers, he was brought up to the Church. He received the first elements of education at home, his father having generally several young men under his care preparing for Orders. Afterwards he was sent to Dolgelley Grammar School, and then to Ystradmeurig. He was ordained Deacon by Bishop Burgess, of St. David's. His first curacy was Nant-cwnlle and Llanddeiniol, Cardiganshire, the two Churches being 9 miles apart. His stipend was only £25. He also occasionally kept school at Nantcwnlle. Thence, after a stay of three years, he removed in 1811 to Llanbrynmair, where he served as Curate and Schoolmaster for two or three years, and thence to Caerwys, in Flintshire, where, having served as Curate for 11 years, he was in 1826 promoted to the Rectory, which he held for 23 years. During that period he distinguished himself for his zeal and activity as a parish clergyman of the evangelical school, and for his eloquence as a preacher, acquiring the reputation of being the best preacher connected with the Established Church in North Wales. In 1849 he was promoted by Bishop Short to the Vicarage of Meifod, which he held until his death, which took place April 3rd, 1860, in the 80th year of his age. He was buried at Llangynyw. He published a Welsh translation of Leigh Richmond's *Dairyman's Daughter*; also, some Sermons and Tracts.

RICHARDS, Rev. THOMAS, Rector of Newtown from 1713 to 1718, and of Llanfyllin from the latter date to 1760, was a native of Cardiganshire. He was an excellent classical scholar, and was said by Dr. Trapp, Professor of Poetry at the University of Oxford, to have been the best Latin poet since Virgil. He is best known as the author of *Hoglandia*, written in answer to a satirical poem under the title *Muscipula*, written by Holdsworth in 1709, the latter being an illiberal attack upon the Welsh. The *Cambrian Plutarch* gives the following account of the circumstances which led to the writing of *Hoglandia*:—

"The famous Dr. Sacheverell, who seems to have been influenced by some unaccountable antipathy against the Welsh, had prevailed upon a person of the name of Holdsworth to write a satire on the nation which gave birth to the well known *Muscipula*. Upon the publication of the work, Sacheverell, with a malicious pleasure, presented a copy to Llwyd [the antiquary], saying, 'Here, Mr. Lloyd, I give you a poem of banter upon your country, which I defy all your countrymen to answer.' The Welshman, naturally irritated by this, resolved to take up the cause, and had recourse to Mr. Thomas Richards, then a student at Jesus College, and afterwards Rector of Llanfyllin, to enter the lists against Holds-worth; at the same time suggesting the subject and supplying him with hints for the treatment of it. Richards, in the course of about a week, produced the *Hoglandia*, the merit of which has been generally admitted. It underwent the revision and correction of Llwyd, who also wrote a caustic preface to it in elegant Latin. But as he died before it was published, the preface was suppressed on account of its severity, and the one which now accompanies it substituted. In the composition of this Mr. Richards was assisted by Mr. Anthony Alsop, of Christ Church."

He also wrote an *Elegy on the death of Queen Caroline* in Latin Hexameters (folio), dedicated to Bishop Madocks, private Secretary to Her Majesty, which was much admired ; and made happy translations into Welsh of several popular English songs, such as *Sally in our Alley*, *Lovely Peggy*, &c., which were long favourites with his countrymen. Besides the above, he published two sermons—one on *Christmas Day* ; the other, *A Sermon preached at Newtown April 28th, 1732, being the Anniversary of the Funeral of Lady Pryce, wife of Sir John Pryce, of Newtown Hall, Bart.* He was a personal friend of the eccentric Baronet, who held him in high esteem, and referred to him in his Will. He also wrote a letter, published in the *Philosophical Transactions* of the Royal Society, on the fire in Harlech Marsh in 1694, and was a corresponding member of the old Cymmrodorion Society. He died and was buried at Llanfyllin in 1760.

ROBERT DYFI, a poet who flourished from about 1590 to 1630. Some of his poems are, it is said, preserved in manuscript.

ROBERTS, CADWALADR, a poet contemporary with and a friend of Huw Morus. He lived at a farm called Cwmllech-ucha, of which he was also the owner, in the parish of Pennant Melangell. He died February the 12th, 1708. Two or three of his compositions are printed in " Blodeugerdd Cymru." One of these, *A Song to the Small Pox*, concludes thus :—

" Os daw'n fanwl ymofynion
Pwy a wnaeth y gerdd mor gaeth i'r Frech yn ffraeth ffrwythlon :
Dinerth fesur dyn wrth faesa
A gwedd gethin a gadd y gwaetha."

These lines shew that the poet himself had suffered from that terrible and loathsome disease.

ROBERTS, Rev. GEORGE, of Ebensburg, Pennsylvania, was born at Bronyllan, in the parish of Mochdre, Feb. 11, 1769. His parents were Evan and Mary Roberts, who, after a long life of piety, ended their days at Bont-Dolgadfan, Llanbrynmair. George Roberts was a brother of the Rev. John Roberts, of Llanbrynmair. On May 20, 1795, he married Jane Edwards, of Cwmderwen, Llanerfyl ; on the 11th of the following July they, and some of their kindred and friends, arranged to emigrate to the United States of America. Their friend, Ezekiel Hughes, of Cwmcarnedd Ucha, one of the company, had engaged the *Maria*, a Bristol ship for the voyage, and they walked all the way from Llanbrynmair to Carmarthen to meet the *Maria*, but

as it could not at that time sail up the Carmarthen river they
engaged a smaller ship to take them to Bristol, but that smaller
ship was closely watched by a press gang and to evade the
horrid danger of being taken and "pressed" to the army, the
husbands resolved to walk all the way from Carmarthen to
Bristol, leaving their courageous young wives and their luggage
to come after them in the little ship of William Hugh. As that
little ship was slow in spreading its sails to start, the women
became uneasy, and resolved to walk after their husbands
towards Bristol. Their husbands and the captain of the *Maria*,
confident that they should meet the small ship of William Hugh,
sailed towards America, and they did meet Hugh's ship, as
expected, but, to their great sorrow, their wives were not there,
and W. Hugh would not deliver up their luggage but in the
Bristol Custom House. Consequently, they had to return to
Bristol, where they happily found their wives alive, but in sorrow
and distress. Their joy on meeting, after such trials and confusion, cannot be expressed. It is painful to reflect on the
anxieties and troubles and expenses caused unto them, and many
others, by the cruel oppressions of the barbarian press gangs of
those bloody days. The partners of George Roberts were
Ezekiel Hughes, of Cwmcarnedd Ucha, and Edward Bebb, who
had married Margaret, a sister of George Roberts, and Rev. Rees
Lloyd, and William and Morgan Gwilym, and David Francis
and their families, and some others. They were very dear
friends, but after laborious movements in America they settled
in different localities. George Roberts started the Cambria
Settlement in Pennsylvania. Edward Bebb settled in the fruitful valley of Paddy's Run, Ohio, and Ezekiel Hughes bought a
large tract of rich land at Cleves, near Cincinnati, and became a
friend and neighbour of President Harrison. Bebb started a
flourishing settlement at Paddy's Run. His son William was
elected Governor of Ohio, and filled afterwards several offices
under the United States Government. They all at first sustained
many hardships and privations, but lived to see their small
clusters of pole cabins develope into flourishing cities. George
Roberts was very highly esteemed in the various callings which
he followed. He was handy at the loom in weaving warm clothing for his family and neighbours; earnest and practical as a
Christian minister; keen and impartial as one of the judges of
the county. He was a regular and very affectionate correspondent, especially with his brother and other relatives in Wales,
was intimate with Mr. Rush, the then United States Ambassador
to London, and was always anxious to strengthen all feelings of
good-will and co-operation between England and the United
States. After speaking of Loretto, a Catholic town founded by
Prince (afterwards Father) Galitzin, who came thither as a
priest in 1799, and died in 1840, Mr. Lathrop in an interesting
article on "The Heart of the Alleghanies," which appeared in
Harper's Magazine, says: "Ebensburg, near by, was settled by
"Welsh Dissenters. 30 years ago Cymric was heard commonly

"on the street, and the Welsh women walked about with babies
"on their backs, knitting while they walked. But Father
"Galitzin was always on good terms with the Welsh pastor, Mr.
"Roberts, and they were wont to talk over their respective flocks
"together." George Roberts, in 1834, published at Ebensburg
A View of the Primitive Ages, being a translation of *Drych y
Prif Oesoedd*, by the Rev. Theophilus Evans. This translation
was reprinted at Llanidloes some 30 years ago. George Roberts
died at Ebensburg in November, 1853, in his 85th year. Among
his children were Thomas, an able and popular preacher, who
died young; Edward, a successful merchant at Ebensburg; and
another son well known in America as *Judge* Roberts. He had
also three daughters. Many of his descendants occupy good
positions and are held in high esteem as active, loyal, and high-
minded citizens of the United States.

ROBERTS, Rev. JOHN, of Llanbrynmair, an Independent
minister whose name is still greatly revered, was the son of
Evan Roberts, Bronllan, Mochdre, where he was born on the
25th February, 1767, and was a brother of the above named
George Roberts. He was one of twelve children. His parents
were religious people, who carefully brought up their children,
and were both members of the Independent Church at Llanbrynmair, but chiefly in connection with the branch of it meeting
at Aberhafesp. His father was a member for upwards of seventy
years, that is from the age of fifteen to that of eighty-six, when
he died. John Roberts, when he was seventeen years old, went
to live with some relatives at Allt-y-ffynnon, Aberhafesp, where
he remained two years, and then removed to Llanbrynmair,
where he spent the rest of his life, except the period of his stay
at the Academy. On the 29th October, 1786, he joined the
Independent Church at Llanbrynmair, and in January, 1790,
was induced to begin preaching, his first attempt being made at
Tybrith, Manafon. The following March he entered upon a
course of study at the Academy at Oswestry, then presided over
by the celebrated Dr. Edward Williams, afterwards of Rother-
ham. He followed his studies afterwards at various other
places, and in January, 1795, he accepted an invitation of the
Church at Llanbrynmair, to become co-pastor with their venerable minister, the Rev. Richard Tibbot. He was ordained in
August, 1796, and upon Mr. Tibbot's death in March, 1798, he
became the sole minister, which office he filled with
remarkable zeal and ability until his death—a period of
more than thirty-six years. He was married January 17,
1797, to Mary Brees, of Coedperfydau, and became the
father of three sons and two daughters. In addition to his
ministerial labours, Mr. Roberts kept a day school, and through
his exertions six school houses, where occasional services and
Sunday Schools were held, were built within a radius of four or
five miles of the old chapel. He wrote several able pamphlets
upon controversial theological subjects both in English and

Welsh, and though he was often bitterly assailed, his moderation, gentleness, meekness. and seraphic piety gained for him the
deep and lasting regard of friends and foes alike. He was also
a frequent contributor to the *Evangelical Magazine* and other
periodicals, English and Welsh. He died on the 21st of July,
1834, aged 67 years, and was buried at the parish church of Llanbrynmair. His Memoir, with an engraved portrait, appeared
shortly afterwards in the *Evangelical Magazine*, and his life was
also published in Welsh by his sons. The following were the
principal pamphlets or tracts written by him:—1. *A friendly
address to all who desire to know the truth as it is in Jesus
Christ.* (Welsh 1806); 2. *A friendly call to the Arminians to
consider who hath made the difference between them and others.*
(Welsh, 1807). 3. *Directions and Counsels to Believers to
make their calling and election sure.* (Welsh, 1809). 4. *A
friendly address to the Arminians.* (1809). 5. An English
version of No. 2. 6. *A second address to the Arminians* in
answer to Mr. Brocas (of Shrewsbury)'s reply to the first
Address. 7. *The Life of the Rev. Lewis Rees.* (Welsh, 1812).
8. *A humble attempt to explain the truth taught us in the
Scriptures conserning the general and particular objects of the
death of Jesus Christ.* (Welsh, 1814). 9. *A Serious Call to
seekers after the truth to consider the testimony of the Scriptures
concerning the extent of Christ's Atonement.* (Welsh, 1820).
10. *The Bee; a collection of short anecdotes.* (Welsh, 1816).
11. *A short defence of the right of children in general to the
ordinance of Baptism.* (Welsh). His opinions were moderately
Calvinistic, and his writings were intended to counteract the
Arminian doctrines then lately promulgated in Wales by the
Wesleyans on the one hand, and the hyper-Calvinistic views
taught by some of their opponents on the other.

ROBERTS, REV. JOHN (J.R.), of Conway, was the second
son of the above-named Rev. John Roberts and Mary his wife,
and was born at the Old Chapel House, Llanbrynmair (the
birthplace also of Dr. Abraham Rees), November 5th, 1804, and
was educated chiefly at home by his father. He was 25 years
old before he commenced to preach. In March, 1831, he was
admitted a student at the Independent Academy at Newtown,
where he remained a little over three years. Upon the death of
his father, he was in 1835 ordained co-pastor, with his brother
Samuel, of the independent Churches at Llanbrynmair, Carno,
and Beulah. Having married a lady from Llansantsior, near
Conway, he, in 1838, removed to that place, and took charge of
the Independent Churches at Llansantsior and Moelfra, but in
about a year he returned again to Llanbrynmair. In 1848 he
removed to Ruthin, thence in 1857 to London, and thence in
1860 to Conway, where he continued to reside and to discharge
his pastoral duties up to the time of his death. Mr. Roberts
was an eloquent and very popular preacher, and wrote much for
the Welsh magazines and papers. He also published in 1854 a

volume of Essays, Sermons, and Dialogues (*Traethodau, Pregethau, ac Ymddyadanion*); and some years later another volume of *Sermons*, besides several minor works and pamphlets, and edited the *Croniel*, a small Welsh magazine for 27 years in succession to his brother, the Rev. Samuel Roberts—that is, from 1857 up to the time of his death. His style as a writer was clear, terse, and highly descriptive; but sometimes, it must be owned, he was too bitter in controversy, though in private life a more amiable man than Mr. Roberts could scarcely be found. He continued to labour to the end, and preached at Rhyl the very last Sunday of his life. He died at Conway, after a very short illness, September 7th, 1884, aged 79 years.

ROBERTS, JOHN (*Telynor Cymru* OR *Alaw Elwy*), an excellent harpist and Penillion singer, was born at Llanrhaiadr in the year 1816. Gipsy blood (of which he was proud) ran in his veins, and he could converse freely in the Romany or Gipsy language. He began life as a drummer in the 23rd Regiment (Welsh Fusiliers), in which regiment he remained nine-and-a-half years. After that he bought his discharge, and took up the study of music, and especially harp playing. He settled at Newtown, where he lived up to his death, a period of over 50 years, and was one of the first to introduce musical instruments into Newtown, which now possesses probably the finest band in North Wales. He won many medals and prizes at Eisteddfodau for harp playing and penillion singing, among others a prize harp at the Abergavenny Royal Eisteddfod, 1842, the chief prize at the Abergavenny Royal Eisteddfod, 1848, and the prize harp at the Cardiff Eisteddfod, 1850. Lady Llanover and others also presented him with an ancient Welsh harp as a token of their esteem for his exertions in adhering to the national instrument of his country. Besides the harp, he was an excellent player on the violin and other instruments. He had a large family of 18 children, most of whom became, like himself, excellent players of stringed instruments. He and his nine sons often gave concerts together. On the occasion of the Queen's visit to Wales in 1889, he had the honour of giving a concert before Her Majesty at Palé Hall, in which he and his talented family solely took part, the Queen expressing great pleasure with the performance. He also had the honour of playing before the Prince and Princess of Wales, the Empress of Austria, the Queen of Roumania, and other royal personages. About a year before his death, overtaken by the infirmities of age, he sent his old triple harp (believing he would not be able to play it again) full strung and having on its comb three medals to his friend and patron, Mr. Nicholas Bennett, of Glanyrafon, for his acceptance. Mr. Bennett has had a recess built for it, where he has also placed a portrait of the old harper done in oil on an old oak panel, playing on his favourite instrument. Mr. Roberts died after several months' illness on the 11th of May, 1894, aged 78 years.

ROBERTS, MARIA, an accomplished harpist, was the eldest daughter of a respectable farmer near Llanfyllin, and was born about the year 1777. In infancy she was attacked by small-pox, which destroyed her eyesight, and her father having died while she was yet young, in reduced circumstances, she was left without any provision for her maintenance. At the age of sixteen she was taught to play the harp, and soon acquired such proficiency that she was able to instruct others. She played with great skill and taste, and occasionally accompanied the instrument with her own voice, which was peculiarly sweet. Having, after some years, met with an accident which disabled a finger of her left hand, she was incapacitated from following her profession, and appears to have felt the pangs of poverty. An appeal for pecuniary assistance for her was made in the *Cambrian Quarterly Magazine* for January, 1830.

ROBERTS, RICHARD, an eminent mechanic and engineer, was born at Llanymynech, April 22nd, 1789. His father, William Roberts, was a poor shoemaker and toll collector, whose house was built on Offa's Dyke, and stood on the very border line of the Counties of Salop and Montgomery—the front door opening in one county and the back door in the other county. His parents were both Welsh speaking persons, and he himself could also speak Welsh and was proud of it. He appears as a boy to have shewn a turn for mechanics, and among other things he is said to have made a spinning wheel for his mother. But desiring better opportunities of indulging his tastes than were afforded him in his native place he went to the Staffordshire ironworks, where he found employment as a pattern maker in the service of Mr. John Wilkinson, Bradley Ironworks, Bilston, and afterwards at the Horsley Ironfoundry in the same neighbourhood. Having been drawn for the militia in his native county, he, to escape service, went to Liverpool, thence to Manchester and Salford, working a short time at each of these places as cabinet maker, turner, or lathe and tool maker. From Manchester he proceeded to London, where he was fortunate enough to find employment with Mr. Maudsley, the founder of the great engineering firm of Maudsley and Co. This was in 1814. In 1816, however he determined once more to try his luck in Manchester. He accordingly left London and took a small house in Water Street, Manchester, where he informed the public that "he was prepared to execute mechanical "work and screw cutting upon reasonable terms." His workshop at this time is thus described:—"His fly "wheel was in the cellar, and his lathe up stairs in the "bedroom. The strap passed through the living room of the "ground floor, and the power that turned the wheel was his "wife." His ingenuity and industry brought him more and more business until he found it necessary to remove to larger premises and erect more efficient machinery in New Market Buildings. His services in fitting up new or improving old machinery were in great demand, and about this time he also invented the sector used for taking the size of wheels, and some improvements in the lathe used for screw cutting. On the first introduction of gas, he, in 1817, was applied to by the borough-reeve of Manchester to furnish a meter which would correctly measure the consumption of gas—the result being his invention of the wetmeter worked by a water lute. He also the same year produced the improved slide lathe, the slotting machine and the planing machine, and subsequently the wheel-cutting engine, the broaching machine, and the scale beam capable of indicating the fifteen-hundredth part of a grain. In 1822 he took out patents for various inventions for improving the working of looms for weaving plain or figured cloths. About this time Mr. Sharpe (the founder of the eminent firm of Sharpe, Stewart & Co., of the Atlas Works, Manchester) commenced the manufacture of machinery, and recognizing Mr. Roberts's great inventive genius, took him into partnership. Here he was thenceforth busily employed in the production of tools and locomotives, wheel-cutting engines, and turret clocks. He patented many improvements in the construction of locomotives and paid special attention to the construction of turret clocks. In 1845 he presented an exquisitely-made clock to his native parish of Llanymynech, estimated to be worth 100 guineas. In 1825 he patented his greatest invention, the self-acting mule, a wonderful triumph of genius to which our country owes a large measure of its success in the cotton manufacture. He subsequently greatly improved this machine, and thenceforth was often appealed to for help in mechanical questions connected with manufacturing. In 1826 he was sent for to Mulhouse in Alsace and was for two years engaged there in designing, arranging, and setting agoing a large establishment for the manufacture of spinning and other machinery—thus contributing largely to the success of the French cotton manufacture. In 1834 he took out patents for machinery required in spinning and doubling cotton, silk, flax, &c., and for grinding corn. Mr. Sharpe died in 1843, and Mr. Roberts commenced business as "Richard "Roberts and Co." at the Globe Works. After a short time the firm became "Roberts, F the gill, and Dobinson." In 1844 he obtained patents for spinning and preparation machines, and in 1847 for punching and printing metal and for beetling and mangling machines, also for two different kinds of spinning machines to complete his self-acting mule. In 1848 he invented the Jacquard punching machine—a self-acting tool of great power—for punching in bridge or boiler plates any required number of holes of any pitch and to any pattern with mathematical accuracy, and the same year he took out patents for turret clocks, especially as regards the manner of winding them. Almost every year, indeed, he took out several patents for improving machinery of the most diverse kind. Thus in 1860 he seized upon an American machine for making cigars and so improved it that it is said a boy could make 5,000 cigars in a day.

One remarkable contrivance he commenced, but did not complete —a sewing machine working with forty-four needles. During the Crimean War he had formed a plan for the destruction of Sebastopol by gunpowder, but England would not countenance such a wholesale slaughter of her enemies. The Emperor Napoleon, however, sought his advice as to the construction of armour clads and turret ships, and many of his suggestions were adopted in the French navy. The Emperor Nicholas of Russia not only consulted him, but also invited him to take up his residence at St. Petersburg. The American vessel *Flora*, which played a part in the war of secession was built from his plans. He was an active promoter of the first Mechanics' Institution in Manchester, and was also one of the first members of the new Corporation of that city, and served for some years as a Town Councillor. He was also a zealous promoter of the Manchester Literary and Philosophical Society. In 1860 Mr. Roberts removed to London, where he spent the remaining years of his life, acting as a consulting engineer. In his prosperity he did not forget his native place, but often visited it. He unfortunately spent the whole of his savings with speculators, who reaped the benefit of his inventions, and in his latter days he was comparatively poor. When this became known a subscription list was opened, and several hundreds of pounds were promised, but he died before the generosity of his old friends could avail him anything. He died in London on March 11th, 1864, in his 75th year, and was buried at Kensal Green Cemetery. His chief power as a mechanician lay in his marvellous memory and great capacity for combining forces, and he is considered by some the greatest mechanical inventor of the nineteenth century.

ROBERTS, RICHARD (*Gruffydd Rhisiart*) was the youngest child of the Rev. John Roberts the elder, of Llanbrynmair, and Mary his wife. He was born at Diosg, November 5th, 1810. He was brought up a farmer, and had but few educational advantages beyond the teaching of his own father. Like many members of the same family, he shewed a taste for literature and literary pursuits. He wrote a good deal both of prose and verse for the *Cronicl, Dysgedydd*, and other magazines, and in 1855 he published a Welsh novel under the title *Jeffrey Jarman y Meddwyn diwygiedig* (Jeffrey Jarman, the Reformed drunkard). His articles were always timely, and of a practical character. His style was lucid and racy, characterised by point, simplicity, and considerable humour. His *Cân y Glep* (Song to Gossip) is good specimen of satirical poetry. There was nothing he disliked more than affectation or high-sounding verbosity. He married February 3rd, 1853, Ann Jones, of Castell bach, Rhayader, Radnorshire, by whom he had issue—one child, a daughter. In 1856 he and his family emigrated to America, and for fifteen years lived in East Tennessee, where he cultivated a large farm. During the great civil war he suffered many trials, and was often exposed to much danger, but through all he maintained his usual calmness and cheerfulness. He was an excellent farmer, and very ingenious in devising mechanical contrivances when required. He was faithful to the Union throughout the war, though sometimes in danger from Confederate soldiers and sympathizers. In 1872 he returned to his native country, and took up his residence with his two brothers, the Revs. Samuel and John Roberts, at Conway, where he continued to live up to the time of his death. In his latter years he often preached with the Congregationalists, the denomination to which he belonged. His sermons were very practical and original in their style, his constant aim being usefulness. He died July 25th, 1883, in the 73rd year of his age.

ROBERTS, Rev. SAMUEL (s.r.), was the eldest son of the Rev. John Roberts the elder, and Mary his wife, and was born on the 6th March, 1800, at the Old Independent Chapel House, Llanbrynmair. He was taught first by his father, and subsequently at a school at Shrewsbury kept by Mr. Bagley. After this he spent several years at home, assisting his father on the farm at Diosg. Having commenced preaching when he was 19 years of age, he went to Dr. Lewis's Academy at Llanfyllin, and followed it on its removal to Newtown. In April, 1826, he accepted a call from his father's church to become assistant pastor to his father, and was ordained to the work of the ministry on the 15th August, 1827. He also had the oversight of the churches at Carno and Beulah. His father died on the 20th July, 1834, and thereupon a considerable increase of pastoral work fell to his share. He had now nine churches or branch churches, under his charge, namely, Carno, Beulah, the Old Chapel, and the six branches belonging to it, namely, Cwm, Pandy, Tafolwern, Aber, Talerddig, and Bont. With these he continued to labour for thirty years--that is, until his emigration to America in 1857. His brother John became his co-pastor in 1835, and remained with him in that capacity until 1848. Mr. Roberts's labours, however, were not confined to the work of the ministry. He wrote for the Welshpool Eisteddfod, in 1824, an essay *On the Beauty of the Welsh Language*, which gained a prize and very high commendation, but the medal was given to the Rev. John Blackwell. At the Carmarthen Eisteddfod, in 1825, his essay *On the History of the Britons before the time of Julius Cæsar* was adjudged the best. The prize medal was awarded to the second best, S.R. not being a member of the Society or a native of Carmarthenshire, as required by the rules of the competition; but he obtained the money prize. The same year he gained a prize at the Ruthin Eisteddfod for an essay on *The cruelty of plundering wrecks*. In May, 1826, he won the medal of the London Cymmrodorion for an essay on *Calondid* (Courage), and won afterwards their medal for an essay on *All Good from God*; and at the Denbigh Eisteddfod, in

1823, his essay *On the necessity for Law to support Good Manners* was declared to be the best out of twelve compositions sent in for competition, and the prize was awarded to him. He sent to the Eisteddfod at Beaumaris, in 1832, an essay on *Agriculture*, which was characterised by the adjudicators as "perhaps the most beautiful composition in any language," yet the prize was given to Mr. Aneurin Owen for a very inferior production. It is not to be wondered at that after such treatment he soon ceased to compete at Eisteddfodau, but resolved to employ his pen in other ways. All the above Essays were in Welsh. In 1830 he published a small collection of moral and religious songs or ballads, under the title *Caniadau Byrion*, which became very popular, and has passed through many editions. Several of the songs were against slavery, which at that time still flourished in our West Indian colonies as well as in America; and against this iniquitous traffic in human flesh he wrote much both of poetry and prose. He was throughout life an irreconcilable enemy of Church establishments. In 1834 he wrote and published an able essay on *The Injustice and Evil Tendency of State Religious Establishments*. The Anti-Corn Law movement also found in him an early and an ardent advocate. So early as 1827 he began to advocate a system of penny postage, many years before the idea was taken up by Sir Rowland Hill, who is often erroneously supposed to have been its originator. He was also a warm supporter of the Peace Society, and attended the great Peace Conference at Frankfort in 1850. He was indeed indefatigable in his efforts through the press on behalf of every great reform— social, political, or religious. Hence the Reform Bill of 1832, the temperance movement, the abolition of religious tests and of Church rates, the improvement of roads, the introduction of railways into Montgomeryshire, tenant rights, the adoption of more intelligent and scientific methods of cultivating the soil and of sanitary improvements—all these subjects he earnestly advocated with his powerful pen. Some of his letters on these subjects were a few years before his death printed in a collected form under the title, *Pleadings for Reform*. He also travelled much and laboured hard in collecting money towards payment of chapel debts, and was thus a great benefactor to many weak and struggling Independent Churches. He had for twenty years and more been a constant contributor to the *Dysgedydd*, the *Evangelical*, and other magazines, but in 1843 he started a small monthly magazine of his own under the title *Y Cronicl*, which soon attained a large circulation, and was very successful under his editorship until his departure for America. He also published a *Collection of over 2,000 Hymns*, in Welsh, for the use of Congregational Churches. Among the large number of tracts and pamphlets which emanated from his prolific pen, we may especially refer to *Diosg Farm* and *Farmer Careful*, as written in his happiest vein. His principal prose writings were published in a collected form in 1856, under the title, *Gweithian*

Samuel Roberts. During his thirty years' pastorate hundreds of his friends and neighbours had crossed the Atlantic and settled in the United States. In 1856 his brother Richard and a number of other friends emigrated to Tennessee, where they planted a small colony, and where, the following year, Mr. Roberts joined them. His numerous admirers in Montgomeryshire, of all parties and denominations, presented him at Newtown with a purse of £160 and a gold watch and chain. His friends at Llanbrynmair had some years previously testified their esteem for him by presenting him with £50. This American enterprise, however, turned out a disastrous affair. The great Southern rebellion broke out, and the little colony became the fighting ground of contending military parties, Unionists and Confederates. After eleven years of great hardship and danger, Mr. Roberts returned to this country in 1868. He received a warm welcome from his old countrymen, which took the practical form of a national testimonial of £1,245, presented to him at Liverpool soon after his arrival in England. Shortly after this he recommenced his literary labours. While in America he published a volume of *Sermons, Addresses, and Songs*, which soon afterwards (1865) was republished in Wales. In 1865 he published another volume of *Sermons and Lectures.* In 1869 he undertook the editorship of a weekly paper published at Dolgelley under the name of *Y Dydd* (The Day). Having occasion a few months afterwards to revisit America on business, a change of editors was effected during his absence. On his return to England a second time he took up his abode at Conway with his brother, the Rev. John Roberts, where he continued to reside until the time of his death. In 1875 he published his autobiography under the title, *Helyntion Bywyd N.R.* In 1878 he started *Y Celt*, a weekly newspaper, and through the press and in the pulpit he laboured unceasingly to the last. He died, after a short illness, on the 24th September, 1885, in his 86th year, and was buried on the 29th of the same month at the Conway Cemetery. He was never married. As a preacher Mr. Roberts was homely and simple, but often very effective. As a writer his style was idiomatic, graphic, terse, nervous, and sometimes extremely caustic. In private life he was the gentlest, tenderest, and most amiable of men.

ROGERS, REV. HUGH, Rector of Newtown, was ejected for Nonconformity in 1662 Philip Henry gives him the following character :—

" Mr. Hugh Rogers, a worthy, faithful minister of Jesus Christ, turned out for Nonconformity from Newtown, in Montgomeryshire, was buried at Welshpool, March 17th, 1680. He was looked upon as Congregational, but his declared judgment was—' That ministers ought to be ordained by 'ministers, and to give themselves wholly to that work; and that none 'but ministers have authority to preach and govern in a constituted 'church; and that Christ's ministers are His Ministers in all places; and 'that where the word of Christ is preached, and His sacraments adminis-'tered, there is a true Church.' He was a man of excellent converse, and whose peculiar felicity lay in pleasant and edifying discourse."

ROWLAND, JOHN, of Machynlleth, a poet of the early part of last century, some of whose compositions are printed in the *Blodeugerdd*. He was a son of Rowland Jones, and a grandson of John David Jones, of the same place.

ROWLANDS, JOHN, "the Unitarian," was a native of Machynlleth, where also he resided the greater part of his life, keeping a small shop in Penyrallt Street. He wrote several pamphlets in defence of Unitarian doctrines:—1, *Y Cyff Athrawiaethol; yn nghyd ag amrai o'i ganghenau mewn naw o benodau anerchiadol at Drindodwyr y Byd* (1870); 2, *Telyn yr Oes; neu Gân ar y Beibl mewn amryw gysylltiadau pwysig i'r byd a'r eglwys, wedi eu dosbarthu yn dair pennod, yn cynwys dros gant ac wyth o linellau* (1877). He died January 12th, 1888, aged 72 years.

SELYF, the son of Cynan Garwyn, and grandson of Brochwel Ysgythrog, prince of Powys—one of the "three grave slaughterers" of the Isle of Britain.

"Tri arfeddawg ynys Pryd. Selyf mab Cynan Garwyn, ac Afaon mab Taliessin, a Gwallawc mab Lleënawc. Sef achaws y gelwit hwynt yn arfedogion wrth ddial eu cam oe oc bed." (The three grave slaughterers of the Isle of Britain, Selyf the son of Cynan Garwyn, Afaon the son of Taliesin, and Gwallawg the son of Lleenawg. The reason why they were called grave slaughterers was because they avenged themselves on their foes from their graves.)

SION WYN AB GRIFFRI, or, GRUFFYDD, "of Mont-"gomeryshire, Gent., wrote the History of all Wales; and his "books are, as far as they go, good authorities to all Wales; I "[Rhys Cain] have some of them that may be seen." He flourished about the beginning of the 16th century.

SLYMAN, WILLIAM, M.R.C.S. and L.R.C.P., was the eldest son of John Slyman, of St. German's, Cornwall, and was born June 28th, 1807. He was brought up to the medical profession. In 1829, the Committee of the Dispensary, then lately established in Severn Street, Newtown, advertised in the *Medical Gazette* for a qualified Apothecary and Dispenser, and Mr. Slyman was appointed. He soon afterwards became a Member of the Royal College of Surgeons, and was taken into partnership by Mr. William Lutener, of Dolerw, who had at that time the largest medical practice in Newtown or the neighbourhood. In three or four years afterwards Mr. Lutener retired from practice. In 1838, Mr. Slyman was joined in partnership by Mr. Richard Jones then commencing practice. A few years terminated this partnership, and Mr. Slyman qualified as a Licentiate of the Royal College of Physicians, London, continuing in good practice up to the time of his death. When Asiatic cholera broke out in Newtown in November, 1832, Mr. Slyman exerted himself to the utmost, attending every case with the most fearless devotion, and published a small pamphlet, which was also translated into Welsh and widely distributed, containing much useful advice as to the treatment of cholera patients and some general sanitary instructions. Previously to 1844 there were but two Coroners in Montgomeryshire, namely, Mr. Hugh Lloyd for the Machynlleth District, and Mr. Charles Milward Dovaston Humphreys (who succeeded Dr. Edward Johnes) for the rest of the County. Mr. Humphreys died in 1844, and thereupon his district was divided into two districts, called Welshpool and Newtown. The late Mr. Robert Devereux Harrison was elected for the Welshpool District, but a very severe and expensive contest took place in January, 1845, for the Newtown District between Mr. Slyman and Mr Thomas Edmund Marsh, solicitor, Llanidloes, which resulted in Mr. Slyman's election. The votes recorded were:—Slyman, 1657; Marsh, 1440; majority for Slyman, 217. At the close of the Election he was publicly chaired through Newtown. He also became Surgeon to the Yeomanry Cavalry and, on its reorganization in 1852, to the County Militia. When the latter Regiment was embodied in 1855 for garrison duty, he accompanied it in February, 1856, to Pembroke Dock, where it remained nearly four months. Subsequently he also became Surgeon to the Volunteer Rifle Corps. Dr. Slyman took an active part in the early part of 1852 in bringing about the purchase from Lord Powis, as Lord of the Manor, of the Old Market Hall, which stood in the middle of Broad Street, Newtown, and of the Tolls at Fairs and Markets, which resulted in Newtown becoming a free Market town The old Dispensary having for some years failed for want of funds, and the want of such an Institution being greatly felt, Rev. H. J. Marshall, of Bettws, publicly intimated that he would start a subscription with £10 towards again setting up a Dispensary or Cottage Hospital. Elated with the idea, Dr. Slyman again came forward, and in conjunction with Mr. Marshall, so energetically advocated and promoted it that the result was the establishment in 1868 of the Montgomeryshire Infirmary, at Newtown. Both gentlemen while they lived did their utmost to ensure the success of this admirable institution, and its friends have placed in the vestibule a handsome stained glass window with their medallion portraits, and a suitable inscription to testify that the Infirmary owes its origin and establishment mainly to their exertions. Dr, Slyman was exceedingly fond of the chase, and it was a standing joke against him that he always had a patient in the neighbourhood of the meet. He was a bold rider, and frequently rode hurdle races at the close of the Cavalry Meetings. He was occasionally eccentric in his ways, but always extremely kind, charitable, and benevolent towards the poor. Having in early life been a pupil of Dr. Abernethy, he acquired some of that eminent practitioner's impetuosity of manner and readiness to adopt novel appliances. Few medical practitioners ever gave so much gratuitous advice or attended all classes with such prompt alacrity. This made him especially popular among the working classes, over whom he possessed considerable influence. He died a bachelor, after a short illness, April 17th, 1869, aged 61 years, and on the 22nd of the same month was buried in St. David's Churchyard, Newtown. His funeral was one of the largest ever seen in Newtown, thus testifying to the great esteem in which he was widely held.

STEPHENS, EDWARD, was the son of Edward Stephens, of Stone Street. Newtown, and was born in the year 1819. He was almost entirely self taught, and was employed in a flannel warehouse until rather late in life. He was for many years the local correspondent of the *Shrewsbury Chronicle*, and for some time of the *Oswestry Advertiser*. He spent a few years in America. On the 17th January, 1860, Mr. Henry Parry issued at Newtown the first number of the *Newtown and Welshpool Express*, a weekly newspaper of four pages, at the price of one penny half-penny, and partly printed in London. Mr. Stephens acting as reporter and assistant-editor. From July, 1864, this paper was printed wholly at Newtown, and it was enlarged to eight pages. In April, 1871, the price was reduced to one penny. For some years before this Mr. Stephens was sole editor, and on the death of Mr. Parry in November, 1875, he became, with the late Mr. John Edwards, joint proprietor both of the paper (then for some years called the *Montgomeryshire Express*) and Mr. Parry's extensive printing business. Mr. Edwards died in October, 1888, leaving Mr. Stephens sole proprietor. In consequence of failing health, Mr. Stephens sold the whole concern in June, 1890, to Messrs Phillips and Son, the present publishers. During the whole 30 years of his editorial career, Mr. Stephens. taking into account the disadvantages under which he laboured from the want of a good education and early training, filled the post with marked ability and success. Although he had never learnt shorthand, a peculiar system of his own, together with a very retentive memory, enabled him to furnish very full and accurate reports of public meetings. His journal was an unflinching and steadfast advocate of sturdy and advanced Liberal principles. He died on the 19th March, 1892, aged 73 years, and was buried in St. David's Churchyard on the 23rd of the same month.

STURKEY, HENRY GEORGE, M.D., was the third son of Roger Hudson Devereux Sturkey, of Fachwen, Tregynon, an eminent medical practitioner, and was born on the 23rd February, 1824. He was educated chiefly at home by his mother, and at the village school. Being of an unbending and determined will, he left home when he was about twenty years of age for London, where by perseverance and hard work he gained entrance into the medical profession. He afterwards settled in practice at Wisbeach, in Cambridgeshire. where he was successful in his profession, and acquired some property. He was also the author of several works, among others, *The Heir of Maberley*, a novel in two vols. (London, Saunders and Otley, 1867). He died at Wisbeach, April 6th, 1875, aged 51 years, and was buried at Tregynon, on the 13th of the same month.

SYPYN CYFEILIOG, whose real name was Dafydd Bach ab Malog Wladaidd, was a poet contemporary with Owain Glyndwr, towards the close of the 14th century. He wrote many pieces of aphoristical poetry, some of which is preserved in manuscript, among others a poem in triplets descriptive of every part of Wales, the character of the inhabitants, &c. The bards of that age gave out their pieces under fictitious names for reasons that are sufficiently obvious; hence this poet was also known as Dafydd Maelienydd, Ieutyn Cyfeiliog, Bach Buddygre, and Cnepyn Gwrthrynion—all of which indicate that he was a Montgomeryshire man.

TEON, of Guilsfield, the son of Gwineu da'i Freuddwyd was a saint of the college of Illtyd, who flourished in the middle of the fifth century. He was the ancestor of Llewelyn o'r Trallwng, and was first a bishop of Gloucester, and afterwards an archbishop of London, from whence he was driven by the Pagan Saxons and obliged to retire to Armorica. From him the Stiperstones on the borders of Shropshire are to this day called by the Welsh *Carneddi Teon.*

THOMAS, EVAN, was the son of John Abel, or John Thomas of Wtra Wen, in the parish of Llanfair, and was born in the year 1732. He was brought up a printer, and was an accurate and quick compositor, and a good Welsh scholar, which caused his services to be sought and appreciated in English printing offices, where Welsh books were printed. From Shrewsbury, where he was employed 1765, he removed to Chester, thence about 1767 to Carmarthen, where he remained some years, and among other works corrected the press for an edition of the Welsh Bible. He was then one of the principal contributors to the *Eurgrawn Cymraeg*, the first Welsh Magazine ever published, which came out about 1770, under the editorship of the Rev. Peter Williams, and was printed by Mr. John Ross, of Carmarthen, where Thomas was employed. His father, John Thomas, also contributed some poetry to the Magazine. In 1781, he was a compositor in the office of Mr. T. Wood, the first publisher of the *Shrewsbury Chronicle*. He was married to a lady of very respectable connections, being a sister of Mr. Richards, of Caerynwch. Unfortunately he gave way to drink, and became of a somewhat loose character in his later years. He had given up his occupation as a printer, and set up as an astrologer, conjurer, and foreteller of future events to such as would listen to him,—and towards the end of his life had become a wanderer so poor and needy that he had often to beg for his daily bread, and at last was glad to find refuge in the House of Industry at Shrewsbury, where he died on the 12th of January, 1814, aged 80 years—a pitiful end for a man of his literary tastes and abilities. He was a good poet, many of his productions being published under the bardic name of *Ieuan Fardd Du.* Besides various works of other authors, which were brought out of the press under his editorship and superintendence, he wrote or translated the following:—1, *Anfeidrol werthfawrogrwydd Enaid dyn, &c.*" (The infinite value of man's soul, &c.), 1767 ; 2, *Helaethrwydd o ras i'r penaf o bechaduriaid* (Grace abounding, &c.), by John Bunyan, a new translation, 1767 ; 3, *Barnedigaethau ofnadwy Duw ar blant creulawn, drwg ac annfudd i'w rhieni* (God's terrible judgments on cruel, wicked, and disobedient children), a translation, 1767 ; 4, *Traethawd ar Fywyd Ffydd* (A Treatise on a Life of Faith, by the Rev. W. Romaine), a translation, 1767 ; 5, *Hymnau cymmwys i addoliad Duw o waith y diweddar Barch, Jenkin Jones, yn nghyda'i Farwnad* (Hymns adapted to the worship of God, by the late Rev. Jenkin Jones, with his Elegy), 1768. He also for some time published an Almanack in his own name, price sixpence.

THOMAS, GEORGE, the writer of a good deal of Hudibrastic or mock-heroic poetry connected with Montgomeryshire, was the son of James Thomas, woolstapler, and Margaret his wife, of Newtown, where he was born about the year 1791. James Thomas having been unfortunate in business and sustained severe losses, removed to Shrewsbury, when George was about 10 years old, and the latter was educated at Park's School. From Shrewsbury he (James Thomas) removed to Welshpool, where he built the Upper Mill Factory (subsequently converted into a brewery), and carried on the manufacturing business for some years. George for some time acted as clerk to his father, but subsequently took the Windmill, where he carried on the business of grinding corn on his own account for some time. About the year 1816 he married Bridget Stokes, of Llandyssil, and went to live there. He at this time and for many years acted as clerk to Mr. William Lloyd of Cilgwrgan. About the year 1820 he was employed by the directors of the Forden House of Industry to put their books and accounts in order, and subsequently was appointed their clerk and accountant, an office which he held for over 20 years. For many years before the death of Mr. Evors in September, 1844, he also assisted him in keeping the books of the Newtown Hall estate. Soon after Mr. Evors's death he held a farm at Llandyssil for a short time. After this he spent some time at Liverpool, returning again to Llandyssil, where for the remainder of his days he kept a school and the Post Office. His chief productions were:—1. *The Otter Hunt ; 2. The death of Roman* (sometimes called Old Towler) ; 3. *The Welsh Flannel,* a poem which went through at least 6 editions, perhaps more ; 4. *History of the Chartists and the Bloodless Wars of Montgomeryshire ; 5. The death of Rowton* (an eccentric character who lived at Cefnycoed, Llandyssil) ; and 6. *The extinction of the Mormons,* besides a large number of smaller compositions, such as epitaphs and epigrams. The above poems contain a good deal of humour, and some of them became very popular, especially *The Welsh Flannel* (which was translated into Welsh), and *The Bloodless*

Wars of Montgomeryshire. Of the former the following lines may serve as a sample :—

> " Welsh flannel far does all the rest excel,
> It's downy soft, without offensive smell.
> All others do a grating feel disclose,
> And sulph'rous scent, offensive to the nose.
> When wash'd the merits of the whole are known,
> *Hur* rivals shrink, but *Shenkin* stands *hur* own.
>
>   *   *   *   *   *   *
>   *   *   *   *   *   *
>
> Man owes a double debt to Flannel white,
> His vest by day, his blanket warm by night ;
> The prop of life in each succeeding stage ;
> The nurse of youth and comforter of age ;
> His first best garb when hurried from the womb,
> And his last robe to shroud him in the tomb."

The History of the Chartists and the Bloodless Wars of Montgomeryshire is dated March 25th, 1840, and consists of (1) The History of Toolly Loolly. (2) The Battle of Abermule. (3) The Battle of Heniarth. (4) The Battle of Caersws. (5) The Battles of Newtown and Llanidloes. These were chiefly meant to satirize the Yeomanry. The following is a fair specimen :—

> " The courage of Welsh sergeant Webb
> Sunk down to valour's lowest ebb.
>
>   *   *   *   *   *
>
> Hur vow'd ere hur was take lead pill,
> Hur'd with good things hur belly fill
> And then sit down to make her will,
> For hur life's blood began to freeze,
> And thicken like cold toasted cheese.
> The tears wass trickle down her cheek
> Although her brow wass wear no leek,
> A coward her was bid two shilling,
> To brave the battle prov'd unwilling,
> And worse than that the low-bred elf
> Said, ' You Welsh wedder go yourself.'
> Hur went to inn and called for toddy,
> And fiss call'd soles to feed hur body ;
> ' Porter, hur said, when on the wing,
> ' If there's no fiss, fress herrings bring.
> ' And waiter mind hur stomach chooses,
> ' To have cook'd nice, two little gooses.' "

George Thomas died about the year 1872, aged 81 years.

THOMAS, Rev. JOSEPH, of Carno, one of the most popular preachers of his day, was the son of Edward Thomas, a quarryman, and Mary his wife, and was born at the Old Toll Gate, Llangynog, on the 17th September, 1814. Having joined the total abstinence movement when he was 22 years old, he gained much popularity as a temperance advocate. He soon afterwards joined the Calvinistic Methodist body, and was induced to prepare himself for the ministry. Accordingly he, in March, 1841, entered the College at Bala, where he remained and made the best of his time for about three years. Up to the time he went to College he had followed his father's occupation of quarryman. On leaving College he was appointed to labour as a missionary among the Welsh residents at Birmingham and Bilston, where he remained until the end of 1846. After this he laboured at Llanfyllin, Llanrhaiadr, and the surrounding districts for about a year. On the 4th February, 1848, he married Margaret, only child of Mr. Edward Owen, of Penybont, Carno, where he at once took up his residence and lived the remaining 40 years of his life. During this time he acquired very great popularity as a preacher, and a wide reputation for shrewdness, common sense, tact, and ability—qualities which gained for him the highest honour his denomination could confer upon him—the Moderatorship of its General Assembly. He travelled much, his services being eagerly sought in all parts of Wales, and the large English towns where Welshmen are numerous. None of the great gatherings of his people were considered complete without his genial and venerable presence. Notwithstanding a thickness of utterance, and a degree of harshness of voice, his natural and homely style, anecdotical, humorous, and at the same time earnest and practical, had a peculiar charm which never failed to make the vast audiences which flocked to hear him spell-bound under his preaching. After an illness of several months, he died on the 14th of January, 1889, aged 74 years, and on the 18th of the same month was buried in the parish churchyard of Carno, where a handsome monument has been erected to his memory.

THOMAS, WILLIAM, of Llanidloes, was the eldest son of a small farmer, and was born at Bryncoch, Llanwyddelan, in or about the year 1823. He at an early age shewed considerable mechanical aptitude and skill, and having served an apprenticeship to the trade of a wheelwright, he subsequently established a small iron foundry in the neighbourhood of Trefeglwys, where he made agricultural implements, and machines for some of the neighbouring lead mines. In 1851 he removed to Llanidloes, where he greatly extended the business, and gained a wide reputation for the manufacture of machinery used in lead mining and dressing, not only in Wales, but in distant parts of the world. He also supplied large quantities of iron castings from his foundry for several of the Welsh railways. He was for many years a member of the Town Council, and at the time of his death an Alderman of the Borough of Llanidloes, of which he had also been Mayor six times. He was also a County Magistrate. He was a consistent Liberal and Nonconformist, and for 40 years took a prominent part in the political, commercial, and municipal life of his adopted town. He died on the 3rd of August, 1893, aged 70 years, and was buried in the Dolhafren Cemetery, Llanidloes.

TIBBOTT, REV. RICHARD), an eminent Independent minister, was born at Hafod-y-bant, a little cottage on the hill-side at Llanbrynmair, now in ruins, on the 18th January, 1719. His parents were pious persons, but very poor, and had a family

of six children, of whom the subject of this notice was the
youngest. He was brought up very religiously, and was taught
to repeat the whole of the Westminster Catechism before he
was seven years old. Before he was fifteen he was admitted
into full Church membership, and about the year 1738, when he
was scarcely nineteen, he began to preach. His religious impressions were deep and strong, and his thirst for knowledge
was intense, though his opportunities for gratifying it were
extremely few. By dint of great perseverance and application,
however, he managed to acquire a fair amount of general knowledge; and in order to further fit himself for the work of the
ministry, he, about the year 1741, placed himself for some time
under the tuition of the Rev. Griffith Jones, of Llanddowror, in
South Wales, a very eminent evangelical clergyman of the
Church of England, whom Mr. Tibbott ever afterwards regarded
as the most godly man he had ever known. After this he
appears to have kept a day school in the neighbourhood of Llanddowror for a short time. He joined the early Calvinistic
Methodist reformers, Whitefield, Harries, and Rowlands and
became intimately associated with them in the early stages of
that great movement. At their first Association held at Wat-
ford, Glamorganshire, on the 5th and 6th January, 1743 (the
Rev. G. Whitefield, Moderator), it was agreed among other
things "that Richard Tibbott shall be the general visitor of the
"bands or private societies," in the Counties of Radnor and
Montgomery, and Mr. Whitefield strongly urged him to "con-
"sider the unanimous call of his brethren as the call of the
"Lord." At a Monthly Meeting held a month later at Llan-
ddeusant, Carmarthenshire, it was resolved "that the brother
"Richard Tibbott open a school in Pembrokeshire." At
another meeting held at Longhouse, in Pembrokeshire, June 8th,
1743, it was resolved "that brother Richard Tibbott work until
"he can get a Welsh school." At a Monthly Meeting held at
Nantmel, Radnorshire, April 18th, 1744, the following resolution
was passed :—"That brother Richard Tibbott be requested to
"give himself entirely to visiting all the societies in Mont-
"gomeryshire once every week." Unhappily this excellent work
did not supply his bodily wants, and hence we find that at
another Meeting held the following October, it was agreed "That
"brother Richard Tibbott go to brother John Richard to learn
"the trade of a bookbinder." As the Methodist revival extended
throughout North Wales, so his "diocese" became larger. For
fifteen years and upwards it was his custom to visit each of the
societies in the Counties of Montgomery, Merioneth, Carnarvon,
and Denbigh once in three months, and every question of
importance was submitted to his decision. In this laborious
work he often met with persecution and ill-treatment, and sometimes imprisonment. Having for twenty-three years laboured as
a Methodist exhorter and visitor, he accepted the call of the
Independent Church at Llanbrynmair to become its pastor, and
in November, 1762, he was ordained as such. For the remainder

of his life—a period of thirty-five years and more—he laboured with great zeal and success in that capacity, still preaching with the Methodists as before when circumstances permitted, and doing all he could to help them and promote their cause. His pastoral care was not confined to the parish of Llanbrynmair, but extended over nearly the half of Montgomeryshire. During his pastorate he received into church membership at Llanbrynmair 496 persons. On one occasion, 18th February, 1787, twenty-two persons were so received at the same time, among them being Mary Roberts, the writer's grandmother, who remained in church membership to the day of her death—a period of seventy-four years! It was Mr. Tibbott's custom to travel once a year throughout the Principality, preaching wherever he went, and in any chapel, whether it belonged to Methodists, Independents, or Baptists. In his younger days he invariably walked—often doing on foot a distance of from thirty to forty miles a day, and preaching three times. Several times he walked from Tanybwlch, Merionethshire, to Llanbrynmair, a distance of about forty miles, without staying to take refreshment until he reached home. On one occasion he walked all the way to Edinburgh to see and hear Erskine, the Scottish preacher, returning also on foot, having walked nearly sixty miles a day! Owing to his incessant labours it has been said that there was at one time scarcely a Nonconformist or Methodist in all Wales to whom he was not personally known. He was a man in whom a fiery zeal for the essentials of religion was combined with a moderation and tolerance of the views of others, and an absence of party zeal in a remarkable degree. He could not be considered a great orator, but his discourses were practical and to the point, and his earnestness and zeal, together with the saintliness of his character, had greater weight than any amount of mere eloquence. His influence was very considerable, and may be distinctly traced, even at this day, in the various localities where he more particularly laboured. He was thrice married, and was the father of fifteen children. He died on Sunday, March 18th, 1798, in the eightieth year of his age, and was buried the following Thursday at the parish church of Llanbrynmair.

TRACY, CHARLES HANBURY, 1st Baron Sudeley, was the third son of John Hanbury, of Pontypool Park, M.P. for the County of Monmouth (a member of a very ancient Worcestershire family), by Jane, daughter of Morgan Lewis, of St. Pierre, in that County. He was born at Pontypool in 1777, and was educated at Rugby. On the 15th December, 1798, he assumed by license the name and arms of Tracy, being the maiden name of his grandmother Jane, daughter of the fifth Viscount Tracy, as well as that of his future wife. On the 29th of the same month he married his cousin Henrietta Susan, only surviving child and heiress of Henry, eighth Viscount Tracy, to whom also Arthur Blayney, Esq., of Gregynog, devised his extensive estates.

On coming into these estates in right of his wife, Mr. Tracy took an active part in Montgomeryshire affairs; more especially in the promotion of the Montgomeryshire Canal, the improvement of the Turnpike Roads, and the political agitation attending the passing of the Reform Act and the enfranchisement of the Montgomery Boroughs. He represented Tewkesbury in Parliament from 1831 to 1837, and was a firm and consistent supporter of Lords Grey and Melbourne; by the latter of whom he was raised to the peerage on the 12th July, 1838, by the title of Baron Sudeley, of Toddington, in the county of Gloucester. On the death of the Earl of Powis, K.G., on the 17th of January, 1848, Lord Sudeley was appointed Lord Lieutenant of Montgomeryshire. Lady Sudeley died 5th June, 1839. Lord Sudeley died 10th February, 1858, aged 81 years. There was issue of their marriage six sons, namely, Thomas Charles (2nd baron), Henry, John Capel, Capel Arthur, William, and Edward; and three daughters, Henrietta, Frances, and Laura Susanna. The Tracys were lords of Sudeley and Toddington in Gloucestershire, certainly before the middle of the 12th century, and probably much earlier than that date. Arms:—Quarterly 1st and 4th *or* an escallop in the chief point *sable* between two bendlets *gules* for *Tracy*; 2nd and 3rd *or* a bend engrailed, *vet*, plain, cotised *sable* for *Hanbury*. Crests:—On a chapeau turned up *ermine* an escallop *sable* between two wings *or* for *Tracy*. Out of a mural crown *sable* a demi lion rampant *or* holding in the paws a battle axe *sable*, helved *gold* for *Hanbury*. Supporters:—On either side a falcon, wings elevated *proper* beaked and belled *or*, Motto, " Memoria pii æterna."

TRACY, THOMAS CHARLES HANBURY, 2nd Baron Sudeley, was born in the parish of Marylebone on the 5th February, 1801, and married 25th August, 1831, Emma Elizabeth Alicia, second daughter of the late George Hay Dawkins Pennant, Esq., of Penrhyn Castle, Carnarvonshire, by Sophia Mary his wife. He assumed the surname of Leigh by sign manual in 1806, but resumed his patronymic by another licence dated in 1839. On the death of his father on the 10th February, 1858, he succeeded to the title and estates, and was also appointed Lord Lieutenant of Montgomeryshire. He had issue six sons, namely Sudeley Charles George (3rd baron) Charles Douglas Richard, Algernon Cornwallis Henry, Alfred, Francis Algernon, Frederick Stephen Archibald, and Hubert George Edward; and six daughters, Juliana Sophia Elizabeth, Georgiana Henrietta Emma, Adelaide Frances Isabella, Alice Augusta Gertrude, Gertrude Emily Rosamond, and Madeleine Emily Augusta. He died at Pau, the 19th February, 1863, aged 62 years.

TRACY, SUDELEY CHARLES GEORGE HANBURY, 3rd Baron Sudeley, was the son of the above-named Thomas Charles, second Baron Sudeley, and Emma Elizabeth Alicia, his wife, He was born April 9th, 1837, and was educated at Harrow. He afterwards entered the Grenadier Guards as Ensign and became Lieutenant in 1854, and Captain in 1857, but retired from the army in 1863. In 1861, on the death of Mr. David Pugh, Captain Tracy came forward as the Liberal candidate for the Montgomery Boroughs, but did not go to the poll, and Captain Johnson, R.N., was elected in the Conservative interest. In June, 1862, when Colonel Wynn, the county member, was killed by a fall from his horse, Captain Tracy contested the County seat in the Liberal interest with Mr. Charles Watkin Williams Wynn, Conservative, but was defeated by the latter by 1267 votes to 960 votes—a majority of 307. It appears that the Wynn family at one time scarcely expected such a result. Miss Charlotte Williams Wynn in a letter to Baroness Bunsen thus refers to the Election:—"Then came the terrible " accident that killed my cousin Colonel Williams Wynn, and in " consequence my brother's election. It was a hotly contested one, "and I had no hope that he would gain it, so that a majority " of nearly 300 was the more astonishing. Our happiness at "it was more extreme, for it had long been one of my most "earnest wishes that he should get into Parliament." On the death of his father in February, 1863, Captain Tracy succeeded to the title and estates, and became Lord Lieutenant of Montgomeryshire. His feeble health prevented him from taking any very active part in public affairs, but he quietly and unobtrusively assisted every effort for promoting the well-being of the County in which by his large possessions and high office he held so important a position. His well-stored and cultured mind, and the frank kindliness of his manner endeared him to all whose privilege it was to make his acquaintance. After several months' illness he died at Toddington, on the 28th April, 1877, aged 40 years, and was succeeded in the title and estates by his brother, the Hon. Charles Douglas Richard Hanbury Tracy (who had represented the Montgomery Boroughs in Parliament since 1863) the present peer.

TRINIO, the founder of Llandrinio Church, was a British saint who flourished in the early part of the sixth century. He was the son of Divwng ab Emyr Llydaw, and accompanied St. Cadfan, his cousin, to Bardsey.

TUDOR, OWEN DAVIES, barrister-at-law, and the author of several well-known legal works, was the eldest son of Robert Owen Tudor, a Captain in the Royal Montgomeryshire Militia, and Emma his wife, a daughter of John Lloyd Jones, of Maesmawr, and was born at Lower Garth, Guilsfield, on the 19th of July, 1818. He was educated at Shrewsbury School, and choosing the Bar as his profession, he entered as a student at the Middle Temple in April, 1839, and was called to the Bar in June, 1842. For many years he successfully practised in London as an equity draftsman and conveyancer. In 1864 he was appointed Joint Registrar of the District Bankruptcy Court at Birmingham, the business of which he conducted with great ability. He continued in office until its abolition by the Bankruptcy Act, 1869, and after winding up the business of the Court in a most efficient manner, he, in 1872, retired on a pension. Mr. Tudor was a legal writer of considerable repute. His most important works (which have gone through several editions) are: *A Treatise on the Law of Charitable Trusts*, *Leading Cases in the Law of Real Property and Conveyancing*, and *Leading Cases in Mercantile and Maritime Law*. He married, in September, 1849, Sarah Maria, eldest daughter of the Rev. David James, vicar of Llanwnog, by whom he had two sons and three daughters. Mr. Tudor died at his residence in South Kensington, London, on the 14th November, 1887, aged 69 years, and on the 18th of the same month was buried in the Brompton Cemetery. In private life Mr. Tudor's cultivated and well-stored mind and his genial disposition endeared him to a large circle of friends.

TUDUR, the founder of Darowen Church (where also he is stated to have been buried), was a saint who lived about the close of the sixth century. He was one of the sons of Arwystli Gloff, by Tywynwedd, daughter of Amlawdd Wledig, and was the brother of Tyfrydog, Twrnog, and Twrog. The Church of Mynyddislwyn is also dedicated to him. His festival was held October 15th, when a curious custom formerly prevailed, called "Curo Tudur." A young man was carried about on the shoulders of his comrades, others of whom beat him with rods and staves—probably representing similar treatment suffered by the saint.

TYDECHO, another saint who lived in the early part of the sixth century, was the son of Amwn Ddu ab Emyr Llydaw, and came with his cousin, St. Cadfan, from Armorica to Wales. He settled with his sister, Tegfedd, in the district of Mawddwy, and founded the Churches of Llanymawddwy, Mallwyd, Cemmaes, and Garthbeibio. Formerly a chapel called Capel Tydecho also existed at Llandegfan, Anglesey. The sanctity of his life became known far and wide, but Maelgwn Gwynedd, then a dissolute young man, offered him many wrongs and insults, which proved harmless to the saint owing to the miracles which he was able to perform. Maelgwn was brought to his senses, and made ample reparation by gifts and immunities. Cynon, another chief, also who carried away his sister, Tegfedd, was compelled in like manner to restore her unhurt, and to make amends by the grant of lands in Garthbeibio. These and other particulars as to the astounding miracles said to have been performed by him are given at length in the legend of St. Tydecho, written in the form of a *Cywydd* or *Ode* by Dafydd Llwyd ab Llywelyn ab Gruffydd, of Mathafarn, the eminent poet, about the year 1450, and which is printed in the *Cam. Reg.*, vol. ii., p.

375; also in Jones's *Bardic Museum*, with notes by Lewis Morris. His festival is December 17th.

TYSILIO, an eminent saint, poet and chronicler, who flourished about the middle of the seventh century, was the son of Brochwel Ysgythrog, Prince of Powys, by Arddun, daughter of Pabo Post Prydain. He was a first cousin of St. Asaph, whom he is said to have succeeded as bishop of the see named after him. *Brut Tysilio*, one of the ancient Welsh Chronicles printed in the *Myvyrian Archaiology*, is attributed to him, though how much of it was really written by him it is now impossible to say. He was also a poet of a high order, but the only remnant of his poetry is a "Dialogue between Llewelyn and Gwruerth" of Welshpool, printed in the *Myvyrian Archaiology*. He was a firm supporter of the independence of the British Church against the arrogant pretensions of the Roman Pontiff, put forth by his emissary, Augustine the monk. He founded and is the patron saint of the following churches :— Meifod and Llandysilio in Montgomeryshire; Llandysilio and Bryneglwys, in Denbighshire; Llandysilio, in Anglesey ; Llandysilio, in Carmarthenshire ; Llandysilio-gogo, in Cardiganshire; Sellack and Llansilio, in Herefordshire. He was commemorated November 8th.

TYSUL, the son of Corun ab Ceredig ab Cunedda Wledig, a saint who lived in the sixth century, He founded the churches of Llandysul in Montgomeryshire and Llandysul in Cardiganshire. His festival is January 31st.

UST and DYFNIG were two saints of the early part of the sixth century, who founded the Church of Llanwrin. They came to Britain with St. Cadfan from Armorica.

VAUGHAN, EDWARD, of Llwydiarth, Member for the County in several Parliaments, was the son and heir of Howell Vaughan, of Glanllyn, Merionethshire, and the adopted heir of Edward Vaughan, of Llwydiarth, and was descended from Ririd Flaidd, of Penllyn. As stated on the monument erected to him and his wife Mary, the daughter of John Purcell, Esq., " by the "addition of so Plentifull an Estate and his own endowments he "was soon pitched upon by ye County of Montgomery and con- "tinued to be their Representative in severall Parliaments, which "trust he discharged with prudence and Fidelity." He sat in Parliament as member for the Borough of Montgomery with his father-in-law, John Purcell, of Nanteribba, as member for the County at the Restoration in 1660 On the death of the latter he sat uninterruptedly for the County during the reigns of Charles II., James II., William III., Queen Anne, and George I., until his death in 1718, a period of 58 years. The Duke of Beaufort, Lord President of Wales, during his progress through Wales in 1684, visited him at "Lloydyarth," attended by Lord Worcester, and Sir John Talbot, and several gentlemen of the country "where a noble enterteinment was provided with good standing and provisions for above 90 horse," and where they stayed a night. The printed account of this "Progress" contains a curious woodcut representing Llwydiarth in 1684. Edward Vaughan was Sheriff in 1688. He died at an advanced age December 5th, 1718. By the marriage of his daughter and eventual heiress, Ann, to Sir Watkin Williams Wynn, Bart., the estates of Llwydiarth, Glanllyn, and Llangedwyn passed to the Wynnstay family.

VAUGHAN, Sir GRIFFITH (or *Sir Gruffydd Fychan*), Knight Banneret, Lord of Burgedin, Trelydan, Garth and Gaerfawr in Guilsfield, and knighted, it is said on the field of Agincourt, was the second son of Gruffydd ap Ieuan ap Madoc ap Gwenwys, and so to Brochwel Ysgythrog, Prince of Powys. He probably commanded the quota sent to France from his own district in the general levy from Wales, and as he received the honour of knighthood at Agincourt (1415) in the company of Sir David Gam and his brave relatives Sir Roger Vaughan and Sir Watkin Lloyd, who died on the field of battle, it may be presumed that Sir Griffith shared with them in the exploit of rescuing their Sovereign (Henry V.) from a very perilous situation. About the latter end of 1417, two years after the battle of Agincourt, we find Sir Griffith Vaughan and his elder brother Ieuan engaged in a work which redounded little to their credit, though probably they acted on the occasion in obedience to the command of their lord paramount. Henry V. having basely given up Sir John Oldcastle (Lord Cobham) his old companion and faithful soldier, to the rigour of the law against the Lollards, he was arrested near Guilsfield under the direction of Edward Charlton, the last Lord Powys of that name, and taken to London by Sir John Grey, his son-in-law, where he was put to a cruel death. The two brothers, Ieuan and Griffith Vaughan, were the active agents in making the arrest, which was evidently considered a service of danger. On the 6th July, 1419, Edward Charlton, by a charter still preserved at Garth by Captain Mytton (a descendant through the female line of Sir Griffith Vaughan), in consideration of their unremitting diligence "in "the capture of John Oldcastell, a heretic, perverter of the "Catholic faith, and a traitor to the king, pardoned them all "felonies and misdemeanours perpetrated by them, and of his "special grace, and in consideration of the aforesaid good work "and fidelity," granted and confirmed unto them all their lands in the lordship of Strata Marcella, freed from all rents and services, reserving that they should render annually one barbed arrow at the feast of St. John the Baptist. On the 4th March, 1421, the two brothers signed a formal acknowledgment that "our said lord of Powys hath compownyd with us and fynely "accorded so that we and everych of us ben fully satisfied" as to their share of the king's bounty for the capture. In his old age Sir Griffith Vaughan was himself put to death by Henry

T

Grey, Lord Powys. Having refused to perform some feudal service, he was summoned by Henry Grey to his presence and offered a safe conduct, but this was treacherously violated, and Sir Griffith was beheaded. This was done, it is said, in the courtyard of Powis Castle. Dafydd Llwyd ab Llewelyn, of Mathafarn, an eminent contemporary poet, wrote a pathetic elegy to his memory, wherein he speaks of him with affection and respect, and, apostrophising his lifeless head, proceeds :—

> " Pen ni werthid er punnoedd
> Pen glân fal pen Ifan oedd
> Pen teg werth ei anrhegu
> Pen rhaith ar Bowys faith fu
> Pen dedwydd pen llywydd llwyd
> Pen dillin hyd pan dwyllwyd
> Pan oedd frwnt y saff kwndid
> Pan las y pen hwn o lid
> A dorres Iarll dau eiriog
> Harri Grai gaffo hir grôg."

(A head that would not be sold for pounds, a fair head it was like John [the Baptist?] 's, a fair head worthy to be rewarded, a head that had been adjudicating in Powys, a happy head, the head of a hoary leader, a head that was an ornament until he was foully betrayed by the safe conduct, when out of revenge this head was cut off by a double-tongued Earl, Harry Grey, may he hang long.)

His death was also mourned for in an elegy by Lewis Glyn Cothi. Sir Griffith's three sons sued the king for their rights, who restored to them again both their honour and arms. His eldest son was David Lloyd, of Leighton; his grandson, Humphrey Lloyd, the *first* Sheriff of Montgomeryshire and the progenitor of several of its chief families. Sir Griffith Vaughan was beheaded in or about the year 1447.

VAVGHAN, MARGARET, was the second daughter of Richard Herbert, of Montgomery, and sister to Edward, first Lord Herbert of Chirbury. She was married to John Vaughan, son and heir to Owen Vaughan, of Llwydiarth, by which match, Lord Herbert in his autobiography observes, " some former " differences betwixt our house and that were appeased and " reconciled." At her request Edward Morris, of Perthillwydion, translated into Welsh *The Christian Monitor*, and it was published in 1689, at her expense, under the title *Y Rhybuddiwr Cristnogawl*. For this Huw Morris the poet composed Englynion in her praise, which are reprinted among his collected works in *Eos Ceiriog*.

VAUGHAN, REES, or RICE, a learned barrister of Gray's Inn, and author of *Practica Walliæ*, printed in 1672 (after his death), was the second son of Harry Vaughan, of Gelligoch, Machynlleth, by his wife Mary, daughter of Maurice Wynn, Esq., of Glyn, Merionethshire. His elder brother Harry having died without issue, he became heir of the Gelligoch estate, and is so described in 1654. The *Practica Walliæ* was a guide to the proceedings of the Great Sessions in

Wales, and included Abridgments of the principal Statutes relating to Wales, with tables of fees, &c. In July, 1653, he was appointed Prothonotary for the Counties of Denbigh and Montgomery, and he is said to have stood as a candidate at an election for the County of Merioneth. Gelligoch has additional interest from being the birthplace of Mrs. Cobden, or at least the place where she spent the earlier part of her life, and where her father and grandfather long resided.

WALTON, JAMES, of Dolforgan, Kerry, was remarkable for his inventive genius. Like Brindley and Arkwright and other great leaders of industry who have established the supremacy of England as a manufacturing nation, he was a man of marked individuality of character, clearness of mental vision, strength of will, and steadfastness of purpose, and has left behind him a long roll of original ideas, many of which, carried into practice, have assisted greatly in increasing the productive powers of the great cotton spinning trade. He was the son of Isaac Walton, a merchant and friezer of woollen goods, and was born at the Stubbins, Ripponden, Yorkshire, April 15th, 1803. While working with his father he noticed the defects of the somewhat primitive friezing machine then in use, and set to work to improve it. He was then from 18 to 20 years of age. To enable himself to carry out his experiments he removed to a small workshop near the North Bridge, Halifax, where he constructed the first improved friezing machine. About 1824 he removed to larger premises at Sowerby Bridge. To meet the demand that arose, he built a considerable number of these machines for the supply of the then famous Petersham cloth, and for two years, that is, while that cloth continued in fashion, they were kept continuously working day and night. This first success brought him a considerable fortune, but, not satisfied with it, he continued his experiments, the result being that in 1834 he invented a series of machines for raising the pile of woollen cloth by means of wire cards in place of the vegetable teazers formerly employed for that purpose. He also constructed at Sowerby Bridge the largest planing machine which had up to that time been attempted in this country. About 1836 he went to Manchester, and entered into partnership with Messrs. Parr and Curtis, the owners of the original American card setting machine, who carried on the business of patent card making in Store Street, London Road, and subsequently in Ancoats. Mr. Walton invented several beautiful and ingenious contrivances for the improvement of the card setting machine which he brought to a high state of speed and perfection. It was, indeed, for a long time one of the most interesting and attractive sights in the cotton industry of Lancashire. Amidst all the wonders of mechanical science it stood almost unrivalled as an example of rapidity and precision of mechanical action, and many watched its movements and stood lost in wonder at the almost sentient activity of this little automaton which hour after hour

worked on with unvarying certainty of action. About this time
he also invented and patented an improved foundation for the
backs of wire cards, namely layers of cloth and India rubber
connected together in lieu of leather. This invention was contested and became the subject of long and expensive litigation
(Walton v. Potter and Horsfall), which extended from 1839 to
1843. Mr. Walton then made a vow that he would never afterwards enter a Court of Justice—a vow which he religiously
observed even when he was High Sheriff of Montgomeryshire.
The rubber as then manufactured by the process of mastication
proving defective, Mr. Walton again set to work, and remedied
the defect by the invention of a series of ingenious machines
and processes which enabled him to produce an endless sheet of
rubber without mastication. Having succeeded, he would not
trust himself again to the uncertain protection of the patent
law of the time, but selected trustworthy men to work in these
departments, which he kept strictly under lock and key for about
ten years, during which and before the secret leaked out he was
able not only to recoup himself the great cost of the previous
patent trials but to accumulate a large fortune out of the
advantage his cards possessed over those of other manufacturers.
His process became almost universally adopted as the most
perfect method of making wire cards for cotton spinning. After
some time Mr. Walton's partnership with Messrs. Parr and
Curtis was dissolved. In 1853 he established the large manufacturing concern at Haughton Dale, near Manchester, the
largest of its kind probably in the world, where he and his sons
effected many other important improvements which greatly
reduced the price of cards, the cotton spinner of to-day paying
about one fourth of the prices formerly charged. Among
numerous other inventions by Mr. Walton not already mentioned
may be named the machines for cutting and facing the various
tappets and double twill wheels, the first practical wire-stop
motion for machines, a new system of wire-drawing, wire-
testing and wire brush-making, and the patent rolled angular
wire—all of which attest the fertility of his inventive genius.
It is satisfactory to be able to add that he himself was permitted
to reap the reward of his own patient toil, talent, and industry,
and that he amassed a large fortune. He resided some years at
Compstall, in Derbyshire. Subsequently, about 1864, he purchased the Cwmllecoediog estate, Mallwyd, and took up his
residence there. In 1868 he purchased the mansion and estate of
Dolforgan, Kerry, where he principally dwelt the rest of his life,
having retired from active business some years prior to his death.
He was appointed Sheriff of Montgomeryshire for 1877, but in
consequence of the vow already referred to his duties were performed by deputy. Mr. Walton was of a very quiet retiring
disposition, and could never be induced to appear as a public
man. He was a very liberal benefactor to institutions of a
religious, educational, and charitable character, and often gave
away large sums anonymously. He erected a large day and

Sunday school at Haughton, and in 1876 he and his son, Mr.
William Walton, founded and endowed a church at the same
place at a cost of £4,000. A little before his death he contributed £1,000 towards the restoration of Kerry church. He
died at Dolforgan, November 4th, 1883, aged 80 years, and was
buried in Kerry churchyard. Mr. Walton's sons, William and
Philip, inherited some of their father's inventive genius —Mr.
Philip Walton having originated and established the important
industry of linoleum floor-cloth, as well as that of Lincrusta-
Walton wall decoration.

WARING, EDMUND, of Aberhafesp Hall, was a devoted
adherent to King Charles I., and was one of those who at one
time were intended to be made Knights of the Royal Oak as a
reward for their loyalty. His estate was then valued at £700.

WHITE, RICHARD,—see GWYNN RICHARD, *ante*, p. 85.

WILLIAMES, RICE PRYCE BUCKLEY, of Pennant, in
the parish of Berriew, was the eldest son of John Buckley
Williames, of the same place (Sheriff 1820), by Catherine his
wife, daughter and heiress of Rice Pryce, Esq., of Glyncogau.
The Williames family traced its descent from Ednyfed Vychan,
from the Pryces of Newtown Hall, and from the Buckleys of
Dolfor. He was born in 1802, and educated at Shrewsbury
School under Dr. Butler. Through the influence of the Right
Hon. C. W. W. Wynn, M.P., he obtained a good appointment in
the office of the Board of Control, in London, which he held for
many years, and which he eventually gave up with a super-
annuation allowance. A few years after he had gone to London
Mr. Williames had a chief hand in originating the *Cambrian
Quarterly Magazine*, the first number of which appeared in
January, 1829, and for some time he acted as its editor. He
was a Cornet in the Old Montgomeryshire Volunteer Corps from
September, 1819, until it was disbanded in 1828. Upon the
formation of a new Corps of Yeomanry Cavalry in January,
1831, he joined it, and March 15th was gazetted as Lieutenant.
He was subsequently promoted to a captaincy, and May 4th,
1847, to be Major. This he resigned in August, 1859, when he
was presented by his brother officers on his retirement with a
handsome sword of honour. Major Williames was a Magistrate
for Montgomeryshire. He married in 1854 Anna Frances
Parslow, eldest daughter of Humphrey Rowland Jones, Esq., of
Garthmyl, by whom he had one child, a daughter, who pre-
deceased him. He died March 23rd, 1871, and was buried at
the parish church of Bettws.

WILLIAMS, EVAN, parish clerk of Llanfihangel in the
early years of the present century, was a poet of some genius.
His compositions were chiefly carols, but little of his work has
been published. He was a joiner by trade. He had some
unhappy differences with his satirical contemporary, Twm o'r
Nant.

WILLIAMS, HENRY, of Ysgafell, Llanllwchaiarn, near
Newtown, was one of the sturdiest Nonconformists of Montgomeryshire during the evil days of Charles II., and suffered
very much for conscience' sake. He was a contemporary of
Vavasor Powell, being about seven years his junior, and was,
it is said, converted under his ministry. He was born about
1624, at Ysgafell, of which his father was both owner and
occupier, and where his family had been settled for generations.
In the autumn of 1654 a bold remonstrance against Oliver
Cromwell's assumption of supreme power was prepared by
Vavasor Powell, and sent to the Proctector by " several churches
" and divers hundreds of Christians in Wales, and some few
"adjacent." It was subsequently published under the title
A Word for God, or a Testimony on Truth's behalf, and led to
Vavasor Powell's being taken prisoner at a prayer meeting at
Aberbechan. Among the subscribers the name of Henry
Williams occurs together with those of Richard Baxter, Lewis
Price, &c. Immediately on the restoration of Charles II. a series
of cruel persecutions against Nonconformists began. In Montgomeryshire, the High Sheriff, Sir Matthew Pryce, of Newtown
Hall, was particularly active, and in July, 1660, obtained an
Order in Council to take into custody some of their leaders.
Vavasor Powell and Lewis Price were at once taken and sent to
prison without trial, and for the remaining ten years of his life
the former languished in confinement. Mr. Williams was one of
the members of Powell's congregation, and when a minister
would come he would write down the heads of the sermon, and
when they had no minister he read to the people what he had
written of the sermon and then would go to prayer with them.
Being a young man of good parts he was encouraged to engage
in the ministry and to preach among the people. This, after
repeated and pressing solicitations, he undertook to do. In
Powell's absence, Mr. Williams, who was a Baptist, was looked
upon as the Nonconformist leader in Montgomeryshire. Unlike
Powell, who was a stern unflinching Republican, he seems to
have eschewed politics, but this did not avail to save him or his
flocks from persecution. The Conventicle Act, which came into
operation in the summer of 1664, imposed a penalty of £5 or
three months' imprisonment on any one frequenting a Conventicle,
for a first offence ; £10 or six months' imprisonment for a second
offence ; and for a third offence a fine of £100, or transportation
beyond the seas. The prisons at Welshpool and Montgomery
were soon filled to overflowing with Nonconformists, so much so
that there was no room for thieves or felons, but some had to be
sent as Richard Davies the Quaker says, " to the upper garrets."
Dr. Calamy, who wrote in 1713, describes Henry Williams as
" an itinerant preacher," and says that he was " disabled from the
" public exercise of his ministry in 1662, but continued to preach
" more privately in several parts of this county as he had oppor-
" tunity. He was an upright man, very active for God, and a
" lively preacher. He suffered much for the sake of a good con-

" science, both by imprisonments and spoiling of his goods ; but
" he endured all patiently, and went on doing the work of the
" Lord in the most difficult times. He subsisted on a small
" estate of his own, and preached the Gospel freely to such as
" were willing to hear it." Mr. Williams was one of the most
amiable men that ever lived, but was one of the greatest
sufferers. He was in prison from time to time about nine years.
At one time a party of soldiers beset the house suddenly,
greatly alarming the family. Mr. Williams's father then lived
with him. The old gentleman stood on the top of the stairs
with the object of preventing the plunderers coming upstairs,
but the bloody men with halberts and other weapons of cruelty
killed the good man on the spot. Mr. Williams himself had run
out to hide some property, or it was thought he would have been
killed also. There was no remedy then for innocent blood thus
shed. At another time when they set the house wantonly on
fire, and burned it to the ground, Mr. Williams was in prison.
His wife was near her confinement. She took one child in her
arms and another in her hand intending to cross the Severn to a
friend's house to save her own life and the lives of her children,
and leave everything else to the mercy of the persecutors. One
would have thought her condition was enough to melt any heart
with pity, but one of the soldiers with dreadful oaths cocked his
pistol at her and said, " Where are you going ? " But with that
his officer saw and heard him, and instantly knocked him
down, saying " You villain ; she has trouble enough already
" without your insulting her." So the officer humanely sent a
guard with her and gave strict charge to see her safe across the
Severn, and guard her to her friend's house without any molesta-
tion. Another time, when Mr. Williams was preaching, the
enemies rushed in upon him, insulted, beat, and greatly abused
him, then dragged him out and left him apparently dead like
Paul at Lystra. At last they seized the stock upon the land,
and seemed resolved to leave nothing behind them for the
future subsistence of the family. There was, however, a
field of wheat then just sown which the unfeeling wretches
could not carry off and probably did not think worth their while
to destroy. That field thrived amazingly. All the winter and
spring its appearance struck every beholder, and the crop it produced was so very abundant as to become the common talk and
wonder of the whole country. Nothing like it had been known
in those parts. In short the produce of that field amply repaid
him for all the losses of the preceding year. It is not stated how
many stalks were on each root, but there were six, seven, and
eight full ears upon each stalk. Two stalk heads have been
preserved and are in the possession of Mr. John Thomas, Craig-
fryn, Carno. One has seven ears, and the other eight. Many
years ago some of the grain contained in them was sown in a
corner of a field, but strange to say the wheat grown from it was
of the ordinary kind. The field where this extraordinary crop
was grown is known to this day as Cae'r Fendith—" the field

" of the blessing." After Mr. Williams's death a curious and interesting Elegy was published, entitled *Wales's Lamentation*; or an *Elegy on the worthy and very much lamented Mr. Henry Williams, Minister of the Gospel in North Wales*, which refers to this " miracle " in the following terms :—

> " Let us not pass that wondrous field of corn,
> (To poise his loss, nor miracles forborne),
> His earth was healed of her ancient curse,
> The sums he gave for Christ to reimburse ;
> The clods, divinely bid, their strength release,—
> The grains entombed ten thousand fold increase ;
> And when the earth to the whole land was wild,
> To him alone was easy, kind, and mild ;
> And though pale famine threatened all the land,
> An army of joyful corn for him did stand,
> In monstrous thickness 'fore the winds do sail,
> Waving their double, triple heads, each gale.
> Their heads with blessings bowed, revered their God,
> And offer to His servant all their load."

This remarkable phenomenon, so like a direct interposition of providence, together with the untimely and awful end of some of Mr. Williams's most bitter persecutors, had such an effect upon the inhabitants of the surrounding country, that ever afterwards he was comparatively free from ill-treatment. Two of those persecutors were justices of the peace. One of them died suddenly while eating his dinner; the other, as he was returning home drunk from Newtown, fell into the Severn and was drowned. Another (the High Sheriff or his deputy), who plundered Mr. Williams of his stock, fell off his horse in a small brook, in sight of Mr. Williams's house, and broke his neck and was drowned at the same time. Probably his body pounded up the water and that this circumstance gave rise to the report that he died a double death at once. Henry Williams died the end of March, 1684, aged 60 years, and was buried the 2nd of April following, in his own garden as the following entry in the parish register of Llanllwchaiarn records:—" Henricus Williams horto suo " sepultus fuit. Aprilis 2o., 1684." The Ysgafell property was sold by his descendant about 1784 to Mr. Athelstan Hamer, and now belongs to Mr. E. A. Herbert.

WILLIAMS, MATTHEW, a tragedian, was born at Welshpool about the middle of last century. He made his debút at the New Theatre, Birmingham, on the 27th July, 1778, as Hamlet. After a probation at Bath, he was engaged at Drury Lane in 1779, his weekly salary being £5. Anthony Pasquin's *Children of Thespis* (1789) thus refers to him :

> " To Decency dear, and to Merit long known,
> See Williams advance to Calliope's throne.
> Tho' the tones of his voice are restrain'd within bounds
> They form a sweet concord of heavenly sounds ;
> If to greatness unequal, each essay prevails,
> For his diffidence aids where ability fails,
> As encircled he stood in the Temple of Fame,
> 'Twas himself that alone had a doubt of his claim."

But probably Williams's name would have been forgotten long ago but for his fatal duel with Quinn. Dr. Doran (*Their Majesties' Servants*) thus describes the occurrence :—

"It was Quin's hard fate to kill two actors—Bowen and Williams who was Decius to Quin's Cato. Williams, in delivering the line, 'Cæsar sends health to Cato,' pronounced the last name so like 'Keeto' that Quin could not help exclaiming, 'Would he have sent a better messenger!' This irritated the little Welsh actor, the more that he had to repeat the name in nearly every sentence of his scene with Cato, and Quin did not fail to look so hard at him when he pronounced it that William's irritation was at the highest, and in the green-room the irescible Welshman attacked Quin on the ground that he had rendered him ridiculous in the eyes of the audience. Quin treated the matter as a joke, but the Welsh actor would not be soothed. After the play, he lay in wait for the offender in the Piazza, where much malapert blood was often spilt. There Quin could not refuse to defend himself, and after a few passes Williams lay lifeless on the flagstones, and Quin was arrested by the watch." As he had only defended himself he was, of course, acquitted.

WILLIAMS, Rev. RICHARD, of Liverpool, was the second son of Richard and Mary Williams, of Winllan, afterwards of Weeg, Llanbrynmair. He was born at the former place on the 31st of January, 1802. His father was a flannel manufacturer in rather a small way, to which business he some years after his marriage added that of a farmer. His mother was a sister of that eminent minister of Christ, the Rev. John Roberts, of Llanbrynmair. Both were persons of very high moral character, and brought up their children, of whom they had ten, with great care. He received his education at a school kept by his uncle Roberts, and when he was 16 years old was placed for three months only under the tuition of Mr. William Owen, who then kept school at Welshpool, to obtain a better knowledge of English. When he was about twenty he began to preach with the Calvinistic Methodists. He also about this time wrote a few pieces of poetry, which are still well known. In 1826 he spent four months at Birmingham, and three months at Wrexham, partly in preaching and partly in improving himself in English Grammar, and other branches of knowledge. He read with avidity every good or useful book that he could get hold of and was a very hard student. He intended going to Cheshunt College about this time to prepare himself for the ministry, but was persuaded by some of his friends to go in the first instance to a good school at Liverpool for a year or two before going to College. He accordingly entered a superior school there, at which he remained for eighteen months, but his funds falling short he opened a school himself for his own support. This was in the beginning of 1830. In the summer of that year he married Mary, daughter of the Rev. Thomas Hughes, of Liverpool. In July, 1834, he gave up school-keeping so that he might devote himself more exclusively to the work of the ministry, which during the remainder of his life he did with great zeal and devotion—more especially in connection with the church assembled in Mulberry street Chapel, Liverpool. He was ordained to administer the sacraments in June, 1835. He took an active part in the Total Abstinence movement, which was set on foot about this time. In 1838 he began to write a series of able essays on doctrinal points for the *Drysorfa* in the form of dialogues between a preacher and his hearer. These dialogues immediately attracted much attention, and were considered the ablest exposition and defence of Calvinism hitherto published in Welsh. An urgent demand arose for their publication in a collected form, which was complied with. The first edition of the work under the title *Y Pregethwr a'r Gwrandawr* (The Preacher and his Hearer) appeared in the spring of 1840. Thousands of copies of this able treatise were sold in the course of a few months, and a second edition was called for which came out in the early part of 1842. A third edition with a Life of the Author appeared in 1861. Besides this, he also commenced in the *Athraw* a series of dialogues between *Y Methodist a'r Llanwr* (the Methodist and Churchman) on ecclesiastical questions, which were reprinted in pamphlet form, but their completion was prevented by his illness and death. He was also joint editor with the Rev. Joseph Williams of a collection of *Hymns*, and of a serial publication called *Y Pregethwr*, being Sermons by the leading Welsh preachers. He worked with great energy on behalf of all connexional movements, and was one of those who were instrumental in establishing in 1840 the Welsh Calvinistic Methodist Foreign Missionary Society, the operations of which have hitherto been confined to Brittany and the Khassee Hills, (North Eastern Bengal), but have been in the latter crowned with very marked success. Mr. Williams's constitution, never strong, became a prey, during the last two or three years of his life, to rheumatic gout and consumption, to which he finally succumbed. His active and useful life was terminated by death on the 30th of August, 1842, in the 41st year of his age. His widow survived him many years, but he left no issue. He was buried the following Friday, the 2nd of September, at Low Hill Cemetery, Liverpool, where a handsome monument was shortly afterwards raised to his memory by subscription among his Liverpool friends and admirers.

WILLIAMS, Rev. ROWLAND, M.A., Rector of Ysceifiog and Canon of St. Asaph, was the son of Richard and Catherine Williams, and was educated at Ruthin Grammar School, whence he proceeded to Jesus College, Oxford, where he gained a Scholarship, and took his B.A. degree in January, 1802, and his M.A. degree in January, 1805. After leaving the University he was appointed second Master of Bangor Grammar School, and Incumbent of Llandegai, and in the course of a short time Chaplain to Bishop Cleaver. He was the means of establishing at Bangor a Society for the publication of small books or tracts on religious subjects, such as Bishop Griffith *On the Lord's Prayer*, which proved very beneficial, and in other ways he actively laboured as a good and faithful Minister of Christ. Dr. Cleaver, on his translation to St. Asaph, gave Mr. Williams in 1807 the Vicarage of Cilcain, Flintshire, from which in 1809 he was promoted to the Rectory of Halkin in the same county, and in the same year he was appointed a Canon of St. Asaph. In 1819, Bishop Luxmoore gave him the Vicarage of Meifod, Montgomeryshire, which he held for 17 years. In 1836 he was again promoted to the Rectory of Ysceifiog, which he held until his decease on the 28th December, 1854. He was an accomplished scholar and writer, and was appointed one of four by the Welsh Bishops to edit a new edition of the Welsh Prayer Book. He wrote the *Lives* of the Rev. Peter Roberts the antiquary, and of Bishop Griffith, and contributed many able articles to the *Gwyliedydd* and *Cambro Briton*. He was a Justice of the Peace for the Counties of Merioneth, Flint, and Montgomery, and was greatly esteemed by rich and poor alike for his many excellent qualities. He married Jane Wynne, daughter of the Rev. H. Wynne Jones, of Treiorwerth, Anglesey, by whom he had several children.

WILLIAMS, Rev. ROWLAND, D.D., second son of the above named Rev. Rowland Williams, of Ysgeifiog, was born at Halkin, Flintshire, on the 16th August, 1817, a few months before his father's promotion to the Vicarage of Meifod, where the subject of this notice spent his earlier years. He himself used often to say, "I always consider Meifod, rather than Halkin, the "place of my birth." His father gave him lessons, and brought him up with great care under his personal supervision until he was ten years old. At that age he took him to Eton, where he was admitted a scholar, not on the foundation, on the 21st April, 1828. He was elected on the foundation on the 28th of July, and received into the college the 15th of September the same year. He was from a child a very diligent student, and sometimes surprised his father's guests and visitors by taking part in the discussion of questions supposed to be far beyond his years. At Eton the general opinion among his schoolfellows was that he was one of the ablest boys that had ever been there, and it was a common saying that "his Essays were so learned "and his answers so profound in the Newcastle examination "examination when he gained the Medal (1835), as to be quite "beyond the capacities of his examiners." He was noted for his tenacity in argument, never giving in unless he was thoroughly convinced that he was wrong. He was, moreover, a very religious boy, and had the courage of his convictions, so that he dared to bend his knees in prayer morning and evening in the "long-room," when to do so too often provoked sneers and scoffs from the other boys. He left Eton with a very high reputation, and on the 8th of November, 1836, was admitted into King's College, Cambridge, where he gained the Battie scholarship. In Michaelmas term, 1838, he took pupils at Cambridge, and during the summer vacation of 1839 he became private tutor to Capt. Burton, of Dunstall Priory, Kent. He was always a most patriotic Welshman. In the summer of 1840 we find him taking part at an Eisteddfod held in the Amphitheatre, Liverpool, and urging the maintenance of that national institution by Welshmen. A few months afterwards, in consequence of the delicate state of his health, he set out on a tour through France, Switzerland, and Italy. On his return to England he somewhat reluctantly accepted an Assistant Mastership at Eton in January, 1842, having previously in 1841 taken his B A. degree at Cambridge. But he only for a short time held the office. An attack of inflammation of the lungs caused him under medical advice, to leave Eton and return to Cambridge. The following autumn he received deacon's orders from the Bishop of Lincoln, and was ordained priest by the same prelate the following year. He held no living but gave his services free to relieve some of the overworked clergy of Cambridge and the neighbourhood. He always preached without notes, and this with his earnestness and masterly style produced a great impression especially on the farmers and labourers who flocked to hear him. In July, 1843, he was appointed classical tutor at King's College, on the 10th of October entered upon his duties, which he continued to perform for six or seven years with great assiduity. At the meeting of the British Association at Cambridge in June, 1844, he read a paper *On local and hereditary differences of complexion in Great Britain with casual references to the Cimbri.* In the spring of 1846 he published *Lays from the Cimbric Lyre,* under the *nom de plume* " Goronva Camlan." He won the University prize of £500 for an Essay which, after many additions had been made to it, was published under the title of *Christianity and Hinduism,* and is considered one of his ablest works. It was dedicated to Prince Albert, who greatly admired it for the erudition and research it displayed, as well as its argumentative power, and offered the author as a token of his appreciation the post of Chaplain in India, which however he declined. In October, 1848, he tried for the office of Public Orator, but was defeated by Dr. Bateson, of St. John's College. He spent the Long Vacation of 1849 on the Continent. Just before leaving England he wrote an article for the *Quarterly Review* on *Methodism in Wales,* which attracted much notice. Before the end of the same year he was elected Vice-Principal of St. David's College, Lampeter, in succession to the Rev. Harold Browne, who had resigned the office, and the Bishop of Llandaff at once asked him to become his Chaplain. In the following Spring (1850) he took up his residence at Lampeter, and entered upon his duties as Vice-Principal and Professor of Hebrew. These he fulfilled with zeal and ability for 12 years. In December, 1851, Mr. Williams was appointed Select Preacher to the University of Cambridge, and on the first Sunday in Advent he began the delivery of a series of sermons— but after he had preached two he was summoned to the bedside of his father at Ysgeifiog in what proved to be his last illness. March 25th, 1855, he was appointed to preach the Memorial sermon at King's College commemorative of its foundation, and the following May these, with about 20 other sermons preached at Lampeter, were published under the title of *Rational Godliness*, and created a deep impression in England and Wales. They and their author were unmercifully attacked as enunciating sentiments concerning inspiration, revelation, and prophecy, which were opposed to the orthodox teaching of the church. The clergy of the diocese of St. David's were particularly loud in their denunciation of him, and lodged with the bishop a formal remonstrance against his theological opinions, which induced the bishop to recommend him to resign his office, while at the same time leaving it entirely to his own discretion. Mr. Williams felt, however, that to resign would be to yield to ignorant popular clamour, thereby condemning himself on points which he conscientiously believed, while at the same time he could not see that the interests of the College would gain, but would as he believed rather suffer, by his resignation,—and gradually the conviction grew upon him that it was his duty to remain. On the 11th of June, 1857, the degree of Doctor of Divinity was conferred upon him, and about the same time he became senior Fellow of his College. In accordance with the usual custom on such occasions he preached a sermon at St. Mary's. Soon afterwards Dr. Williams on his marriage with Ellen, daughter of Charles Coksworth, Esq., R.N., accepted the College living of Broadchalke cum Bowerchalke and Alvedistone, which had become vacant by the death of the Rev. S. Hawtrey. In the early part of 1860 the famous *Essays and Reviews* appeared— the joint production of seven eminent men, namely, Dr. Temple, Dr. Williams, the Rev. Baden Powell, the Rev. H Bristow Wilson, the Rev. C. W. Goodwin, the Rev. Mark Pattison, and Professor Jowett, and a loud outcry at once arose against the alleged heretical doctrines contained in this volume. Dr. Williams and Mr. Wilson were prosecuted in the Ecclesiastical Courts on account of their contributions to it. Dr. Williams's paper was a review of *Bunsen's Biblical Researches*, and he was charged among other things with having asserted that the Bible is not the Word of God, a direct revelation from Him, and that its writers were not inspired by His Spirit in any other sense than as every holy desire, all good counsel, and every perfect deed proceed from Him alone,—that with two or three possible exceptions the Old Testament contains no element of divinely inspired foretelling of future persons or events—that Jonah was not an actual historical person, and that the book bearing his name was not written by him,—that the book of Daniel was not written by Daniel, but by some other person, that the Book of Revelation, the Epistle to the Hebrews, and St. Peter's Epistles are not parts of the Holy Scriptures,—that Scriptural accounts of historical facts may be read figuratively, and in a sense totally opposed to their evident literal meaning,—that Christ did not suffer or die to reconcile men to the Father and to be an atonement for their Sins,—that the incarnation of our Lord Jesus

Christ was spiritual only, and that he did not take upon him human nature in the Virgin's womb, &c., &c. The Court of Arches gave its decision against Dr. Williams and Mr. Wilson, but on an appeal to the Judicial Committee of the Privy Council this decision was reversed. The latter judgment in favour of the appellants caused a profound sensation and general astonishment. When the excitement of these proceedings had somewhat subsided Dr. Williams resumed his literary labours, and proceeded with his translation of the Hebrew prophets—one of his principal works. The first volume was published in his lifetime, but he died before the second was completed. He also composed a drama on *Owen Glyndwr*, to defend that patriot against the charge of having promised to assist Hotspur in his rebellion against Bolingbroke. His last work was *Psalms and Litanies, Counsels, and Collects*. In 1869 he suffered much from ill-health and a little before Christmas took a very severe cold, from which his enfeebled frame never rallied. He died on the 18th of January, 1870, at Broadchalke Vicarage, in his 53rd year. Whatever may be said of the orthodoxy, or otherwise, of some of Dr. Williams theological opinions, his deeply religious and devout character impressed itself on all who knew him. He was a man of great natural abilities, which his untiring industry enabled him to turn to the best use, and to win for him a very high position among scholars. He was an earnest seeker after truth, and hesitated not to declare publicly what he was convinced of whatever the result might be as regarded his own personal prospects in life. He was also of a most kind, obliging, and charitable disposition, and a warmhearted, patriotic Welshman, to whom the prosperity and well-being of his beloved country were objects of constant solicitude and study.

WILLIAMS, THOMAS (*Eos Gwnfa*), was born at Tyffwrn in the parish of Llanfihangel. He was a weaver by trade, whose life was spent in a long struggle with poverty to bring up a large family, but he wrote a good deal of meritorious poetry—chiefly of a sacred character. He published (1) *Telyn Dafydd* (David's Harp), a metrical version of the Book of Psalms (1820); (2) *Ychydig o Ganiadau Buddiol ar amrywiol a gwahanol achosion* (A few useful songs on various and different occasions), 1824; (3) *Newyddion Gabriel, neu Lyfr Carolau* (Gabriel's News, or a Book of Carols), 1825, of which a second edition came out in 1834; (4) *Manna'r Anialwch* (Desert Manna), Llanfair, 1831. Some of his carols are esteemed as among the best in the Welsh language. His last published work came out when he had reached his seventy-seventh year, and he died at a very advanced age at Llanfihangel in or about the year 1848.

WILLIAMS, WILLIAM (*Gwilym ab Iorwerth*) was an excellent poet, although his life was spent, the greatest part of it, in very humble circumstances, and in a hard and continual struggle with poverty. He was born at a cottage called Esgirgadwyth-fach, in the parish of Darowen, about the year 1800. His father was a labourer and molecatcher, and in his early youth he himself assisted him in that humble but useful occupation. He had but very little schooling, but Mr. Pugh, of Esgair, Llanbrynmair, the Rev. Thomas Richards, vicar of Darowen, and Miss Richards interested themselves in him, and kindly taught him Welsh and English grammar, a little arithmetic, and other useful matters. This was all the instruction he had, but he made the best use of it and of the poor and scanty opportunities for self-improvement that fell to his lot. After some years spent in service at various farmhouses in his native neighbourhood, he went to Cardiganshire, where he married a young woman in a position in life similar to his own, and by whom he had seven children. He had by constant practice acquired a fairly good handwriting, but his poverty was so great that he had sometimes to obtain ink by mixing the juice of blackberries with some other ingredients. During the latter years of his life he kept a school for some time at Melinbyrhedyn, Darowen. From that place he went to Carno to look after the turnpike road under the late Mr. Penson, the surveyor. Afterwards he resided for some time at the Clatter Turnpike Gate, near Pontdolgoch, and subsequently at Llanidloes. From thence he removed to Llawryglyn, where for some time he kept a day school. Lastly he removed to Rank-y-Mynydd, near Dylife Mine Works, in the parish of Darowen, where he died in the month of February, 1859, aged 58 years. He was buried in Dylife churchyard, on the twelfth of that month. His earliest literary efforts appear to have been some letters to the *Gwyliedydd*, on the right of the Clergy to the Tithes, and in defence of Archdeacon Prys's version of the Psalms, both of which attracted attention; also Elegies on the Rev. T. Richards, Darowen, Miss Richards and others, and many excellent Englynion. My friend, Nicholas Bennett, Esq., has also a large MS. collection of his unpublished poetry, which by his kindness I have been enabled to peruse. Among the longer pieces are three *Awdlau* on *Y Diluw* (The Deluge), *Plaau'r Aipht* (The Plagues of Egypt), and *Heddwch* (Peace)—really masterly compositions, displaying a refinement of taste, a choiceness of expression, and a cultivation of the poetic faculty very far indeed beyond what might be looked for in far higher walks of life than the humble one in which it pleased Providence to place the subject of this brief notice. One one occasion he but narrowly missed the chair prize at an important Eisteddfod, his composition being adjudged the second place in the competition.

WILLIAMS, WILLIAM (*Gwilym Cyfeiliog*) was born at Winllan, in the parish of Llanbrynmair, on the 4th of January, 1801, and was the eldest of a family of ten children. His father, Richard Williams, was a flannel manufacturer and farmer; his mother, Mary Williams, was a sister of the Rev. John Roberts, of Llanbrynmair, the well-known Independent minister. His brother Richard became a popular Calvinistic Methodist minister at Liverpool, and the author of several works (see *ante*) At an early age he was placed in school with his uncle, the Rev. John Roberts, and subsequently with Mr. William Owen, an excellent poet and musician, at Welshpool, from whom it is probable he imbibed that fondness and taste for poetry which distinguished him in after life. After leaving school he pursued his studies with great diligence, making the most of every minute of leisure time. After working all day with his father and the servants on the farm at Weeg, where he then lived, he would in the evening shut himself up for hours with his books. These, though few in number, he thoroughly mastered, and his very retentive memory enabled him to treasure up in his mind their contents. He committed to memory the four Gospels, a large number of the Psalms, and an immense amount of poetry. Of English poets he was, like John Bright, an admirer of Young. He was an excellent grammarian, and his natural aptitude for arithmetic and mathematics was such that probably with greater advantages he would have attained some eminence in those branches. He thoroughly mastered the somewhat difficult and complicated rules of Welsh prosody, and when he was about 20 years of age began to compose on the Welsh metres. He was a frequent poetical contributor to the *Goleuad Cymru*, *Seren Gomer*, *Y Drysorfa*, and other magazines of those days. One of his earliest productions was an *Awdl ar sefydliad Coleg Dewi Sant* (An Ode on the Establishment of St David's College), which gained the second prize at the Carmarthen Eisteddfod in September, 1823, the chief prize being awarded to the Rev. Daniel Evans (*Daniel Ddu*). He also competed at the Welshpool Eisteddfod the following year on an Ode, subject, *Goresgyniad Ynys Fon gan Suetonius Paulinus* (The Subjugation of the Isle of Anglesey by Suetonius Paulinus), but the prize was awarded to Mr. W. E. Jones (*Cawrdaf*). His ode was, however, spoken very highly of, and judged to be of sufficient merit to entitle it to be printed with the prize compositions. This ode was accidentally omitted from his collected works published after his death. His poetical efforts attracted the notice and secured for him the friendship of the Revs. Walter Davies, J. Jenkins, of Kerry, David Richards, Evan Evans (*Ieuan Glan Geirionydd*), J. Blackwell, and others of the principal Welsh literary characters of those days, and for some years he regularly attended and competed at the Eisteddfodau. In the winter of 1825 he paid a visit to London—the only one in his lifetime, and there composed an *Awdl ar yr olygfa o ben Clochdy St. Paul's* (an Ode on the view from the top of St. Paul's). He won the prize at the Llanfair Caereinion Eisteddfod 1st March, 1826, for *Englynion i'r Wybren Serenog* (Stanzas to the starry heavens). For some reason or other he never had much to do with Eisteddfodau after this time, but appears to have become disgusted with their management. But he still continued as long as he lived to encourage and help both as

adjudicator and by competing himself, competitive literary
meetings in his native county. He was generally considered
one of the best *Englynwyr*—or composer of Stanzas on tho
peculiar alliterative Welsh metres—of his day. It cannot be
said that he was equally successful with ordinary or " free "
metres, though some of his compositions in this line are
deservedly much admired. His hymn on *Yr Iawn* (The Atonement), commencing—

    " Caed trefn i fadden pechod, Yn yr Iawn, &c.,"

is well known, and often sung, and has even been translated
into Khassee—one of the languages of North-Eastern Bengal,
where the natives often sing it with much unction. Many others
of his hymns and temperance verses are very well known.
After his death his poetical works were in 1878 published in a
collected form under the title *Caniadau Cyfeilioy.*   Mr.
Williams lived on a small freehold property of his own at Bont-
dolgadfan, Llanbrynmair, where for 40 years and upwards he
carried on a small manufacturing business and a shop, and held
several parochial and other public offices.   He was thrice
married—first to Anne, daughter of Mr. Morris Evans, Min-
ffordd, Llanbrynmair, by whom he had one daughter ; secondly,
to Mary, daughter of Mr. Richard Morris, of Dolgwyddyl,
Trefeglwys, by whom he had two sons and a daughter ; and,
thirdly, to Mary, daughter of Mr. Evan Evans, of Tynllwyn,
Llanbrynmair, by whom he had two sons and four daughters.
He was a staunch Nonconformist and an ardent Liberal. He
died after a few hours' illness on Saturday, the 3rd of June,
1876, and was buried the following Thursday at the parish
church of Llanbrynmair. An immense concourse of persons
from far and near followed him to the grave, so testifying to
the great respect in which he was held by all who knew him.

WILSON, RICHARD, the great landscape painter, and one
of the most illustrious of Montgomeryshire Worthies, was born
at Penegoes, August 1st, 1714, and was the third son of the Rev.
John Wilson, rector of that parish, by Alice, his wife.   His
father's family had been connected with Trefeglwys parish for
some generations previously. His mother was a Flintshire lady,
of the family of Wynne of Leeswood. They had six sons and a
daughter, all of whom died unmarried. The eldest son, John,
became Collector of Excise, and was buried at Mold, 28th
January, 1785, aged 75. The second was a clergyman who
obtained good preferment in Ireland. The third, as already
stated, was the painter. The fourth was a tobacconist at Holywell, who afterwards emigrated to Pennsylvania where he died.
The youngest, (Peter), when a little boy four years of age
was accidentally killed at Mold whilst playing, and was buried
there. The daughter became an attendant on Lady Sandown, a
lady of the bed-chamber to Queen Caroline. The Rev. John
Wilson, the painter's father, died August 31st, 1728, at Penegoes,
and was buried at Trefeglwys, September the 4th in the same

U

year. His mother was interred at Mold, July 5th, 1765, aged 81 years. Richard received a good classical education and gave very early indication of the natural bias of his mind, for with a burnt stick he covered the walls of his father's house and the stone fences of the fields with rude figures in outline. His sketches attracted the notice of his relative, Sir George Wynne, who persuaded his father to place him under proper instruction. Accordingly young Wilson proceeded to London with Sir George in 1728 (probably after his father's death), and was apprenticed to a portrait painter named Wright, whom, however, he soon outstripped. Dr. Abraham Rees tells us that

"After a lapse of six years he commenced professor under the patronage of Dr. Hayter, bishop of Norwich; he soon afterwards had the honour to paint the portraits of the Prince of Wales and the Duke of York, both then under the tuition of the bishop; he continued to practise portrait painting some time in London, but with no great success, and at length went to Italy to cultivate his taste; even there he continued to practise it still unacquainted with the genuine bias of his genius, although occasionally exercising his talents and employing his time in studies of landscape. At Venice, Wilson painted the portrait of Mr. Lock of Norbury Park, one of the most creditable of his performances in that branch of his art, and it was there that accident opened his eyes to his own peculiar qualifications, and led him into that path, by pursuing which he obtained a name among the worthiest in art."

He was at this time about thirty-five years old. The "accident" referred to was the following circumstance. Having waited one morning till he grew weary, for the coming of Zucarelli the artist, he painted to beguile the time, a scene upon which the window of his friend looked with so much grace and effect, that Zucarelli was astonished, and enquired if he had studied landscape. Wilson replied that he had not. "Then I advise you, (said the other) to try, for you are sure of great success." The counsel of one friend was confirmed by the opinion of another—Vernet a French painter of high reputation. One day while sitting in Wilson's studio, he was so struck with the peculiar beauty of a newly finished landscape that he desired to become its proprietor, and offered in exchange one of his best pictures. The offer was gratefully accepted and Vernet placed his friend's picture in his exhibition room, and when his own productions happened to be praised or purchased by English travellers, the generous Frenchman used to say, "Don't talk of my landscapes "alone, when your own countryman Wilson paints so beauti-"fully." Thus Wilson was induced to relinquish portrait painting, and devote himself thenceforth to landscape painting. His reputation grew so fast that he soon obtained several pupils, and his works were so highly esteemed, that Mengs out of regard for his genius painted his portrait, for which Wilson in return painted a landscape. After remaining abroad about six years he, in 1755, returned to England, and took up his residence in London. His fame had preceded his arrival, and his elegantly furnished apartments in the Piazza, Covent Garden, were the resort of the leading men of the day. According to

Cunningham these were the apartments "wherein Lely, Kneller, "and Thornhill had lived and laboured." Smith (*Life of Nollekens*, II., p. 215) describes them as the front apartments of what were formerly Robins's Auction Rooms, but used in 1856 as breakfast rooms by the proprietor of the Tavistock Hotel. He dressed also in a style corresponding with the expensiveness of his furniture—his favourite suit being green, braided with gold lace, in addition to which he wore a portentous wig, with a club tail and a three cocked hat. His tall muscular frame thus embellished gave him a commanding appearance. He several times changed his residence. He lived at one time in Charlotte Street, Fitzroy square; then in Great Queen Street, Lincoln's Inn Fields; in Marylebone; the corner of Foley Place, Great Portland Street; No. 24, Norton Street, Portland Row in 1777-8; in 1779 he lived at No. 85, Great Tichfield street, and the following year "at a mean house" in Tottenham Street, Tottenham Court Road, in which he occupied the first and second floors almost without furniture. This was his last abode in London. To the first Exhibition of 1760, Wilson sent his celebrated picture of "Niobe," and in 1765 he exhibited with other pictures a "View of Rome," which was much admired. At the institution of the Royal Academy, Wilson was chosen one of the founders. During his residence in London, he painted a large number of very fine pictures Wright, his biographer, furnishes a list of 119, of which nineteen were destroyed in the great fire at Belvoir Castle, October 26th, 1816. He, however, met with but little success in their sale, and many of them were offered to brokers and dealers for as many pounds as they would now bring hundreds. He was doomed, in fact, to encounter the galling indifference of a tasteless public and the wretched intrigues of zealous rivals, and even the great Sir Joshua himself entertained feelings anything but friendly towards him which he took no trouble to conceal. As has been well observed,

"The name of this extraordinary man is a reproach to the age in which he lived; the most accomplished landscape painter this country ever produced, uniting the composition of Claude with the execution of Poussin; avoiding the minuteness of the one, and rivalling the spirit of the other With powers which ought to have raised him to the highest fame, and recommended him to the most prosperous fortune, Wilson was suffered to live embarrassed, and to die poor. Conscious of his claims, however, he bore the neglect he experienced with firmness and dignity; and though he had the mortification to see very inferior talents preferred in the estimation of the public, yet he was never seduced to depart from his own style of painting, or to adopt the more fashionable and imposing qualities of art, which his superior judgment taught him to condemn, and which the example of his works ought to have exposed and suppressed."

Possibly a certain abruptness of manner and want of conciliatoriness may have had something to do with his want of success. Cunningham says of him that he

"loved truth and detested flattery, he would endure a joke but not contradiction. He was deficient in courtesy of speech, in those candied civilities which go for little with men of sense, but which have their effect among the shallow and the vain. His conversation abounded with information and humour, and his manners, which were at first repulsive, gradually smoothed down as he grew animated. Those who enjoyed the pleasure of his friendship agree in pronouncing him a man of strong sense, intelligence, and refinement. * * * As the fortune of Wilson declined, his temper became touched; he grew peevish, and in conversation his language assumed a tone of sharpness and acidity which ill accorded with his warm and benevolent heart. * * * * He was abstemious at his meals, rarely touching wine or ardent spirits; his favourite beverage was a pot of porter and a toast; and he would accept them when he refused all other things."

Many anecdotes are related of the straits to which he was driven by poverty. His fine picture of "Ceyx and Alcyone" was painted it is said for (others say from) a pot of porter and the remains of a Stilton cheese. Poverty caused him on the death of Hayman to solicit the office of librarian of the Royal Academy, that Academy of which he was so bright an ornament. This post, the whole emoluments of which amounted only to about fifty pounds a year, he obtained and retained until his retirement into Wales. Small as the income was it helped to keep him from positive starvation. He seems to have had a clear and confident presentiment that posterity would do him justice, and often told Sir William Beechey, his intimate friend, that he would live to see great prices given for his pictures, when those of Barrett, which were then in high esteem, would not fetch one farthing—a prophecy which has been amply verified. He had long quitted his elegant lodgings, and disposed of his furniture to the last chair to buy necessary food of which he was often in want. At this time distress often compelled him to sell his drawings at half a crown a piece, and his residence was known only to a few. His last abode in London, as already stated, was in Tottenham Street, where an easel, a brush, a chair, and a table, a hard bed with a few clothes, a scanty meal, and the favourite pot of porter were all that he could call his own—a lasting disgrace to an age which lavished its tens of thousands on mountebanks, dancers, and Italian opera singers. A correspondence between Wilson and a relative, Mrs. Catherine Jones, of Colomendy, Llanverres, near Mold, resulted in an arrangement that the infirm artist should go down to her residence to recruit his health, and he turned his back on London for ever. A few shillings purchased all the implements and relics of his art and property. This was probably in 1781 though the exact time is not recorded by his biographers. Mountain air and the attention of kind friends could do little towards curing the broken heart of Wilson, his strength was gone, yet he crawled about viewing with silent gratification and enjoyment the beauties of his native country. He rapidly sank, his steps became more and more feeble, and his emaciated frame convinced his friends that the end was not far distant. One evening having partaken of a little food, he had with extreme difficulty tottered as far as a wood where at his request a rustic seat had been placed. It was in the month of May, 1782, and he had gone out to observe the beautiful tints of the evening sky, that sky in the delination of which he had never been excelled, when it pleased Providence suddenly to stretch him helpless on the ground, and to withdraw from him the power of contemplation. How long he remained in so pitiable a state cannot be known, but a dog which had followed him returned alone; this caused his friends to be alarmed and to proceed in search of him, when he was found as described. He rallied a little, but in a few days expired in the sixty-ninth year of his age. He was buried in Mold Churchyard at the back of the church, close to the path, where a tomb has been erected over his grave with the following inscription: "The remains of "Richd. Wilson, Esq., Member of the Royal Academy of "Artists, Interr'd May 15th, 1782, Aged 69."

"O foren 'i yrfa eirian,—rho 'i olen
Ei athrylith allan,
Darlnniai dilynai 'n lân
I'r linell ar ol anian.

"Yn llaw ei oes bu yn llesol,—dyg iddi
Deg addysg gelfyddol ;—
A'i gywir waith geir o'i ôl,
A synna 'r oes bresennol."

WOOSNAM, MAJOR-GEN. JAMES BOWEN, was the second son of Bowen Woosnam, solicitor, Llanidloes, and Elizabeth his wife, and was born 28th January, 1812. He entered Addiscombe College as a military cadet in July, 1827. Passing into the Artillery he was appointed second lieutenant 12th December, 1828, and sailed for Bombay in the following March, serving chiefly with the Horse Artillery until 1855. He served with the Bombay Column of the army in Scinde and Afghanistan in 1839, and was present at the storming and capture of Ghuznee and Khelat. He served in the Punjaub in 1848-9, and was present at the siege and surrender of Mooltan. In 1855 he was appointed agent for the manufacture of gunpowder, and was subsequently advanced to be principal Commissary of Ordnance. In July, 1863, he retired from the service as Inspector General of Ordnance with the rank of Major-General. He married Agnes, daughter of William Bell, Esq., of Bell View, Queen's County, Ireland, by whom he had issue two sons and six daughters. He died at Weston-super-mare on the 14th October, 1875, aged 63.

WOOSNAM, RICHARD, of Glandwr, Llanidloes, was the third son of Bowen Woosnam, solicitor, Llanidloes, and Elizabeth his wife, and was born 9th April, 1815. He was educated at Gonville and Caius College, Cambridge, where he took his M.A. degree. He then studied for the medical profession, and went out as an army surgeon to India and other places. In 1841 he was appointed surgeon and subsequently private secretary to Sir Henry Pottinger during the Chinese war of 1842, and he was present at most of the combined naval and military actions which led to the conclusion of the treaty of peace signed before Nanking on the 29th of August, 1842. For his services he received a medal, and was appointed Assistant Secretary of Legation to Her Majesty's Mission. From that date till 1854 he filled successfully the appointments of Deputy Colonial Secretary of Hong-Kong, and Secretary to Her Majesty's High Commission to the Cape of Good Hope entrusted to Sir Henry Pottinger in 1846, and during the six years of Sir Henry's governorship of Madras he acted as his private secretary. About 1861 he returned to this country, and, after a short residence at Cheltenham, took up his abode at Glandwr. He had also another residence at Tynygraig, near Builth. Shortly afterwards he qualified as a magistrate, and took an active and prominent part in all county and political affaiss. For some years he was Chairman of the Board of Guardians, and at the time of his death he was Chairman of the Llanidloes Bench of Magistrates, the Llanidloes combined School Boards and the Newtown and Llanidloes Highway Board. Whatever duties he undertook he discharged them with great conscientiousness, sparing no pains to study and master all the details of matters that came before him. Mr. Woosnam married Margaret, daughter of William Bell, Esq., of Queen's County, Ireland, who pre-deceased him, and by whom he left three sons and three daughters He died on the 27th November, 1888, aged 73 years, and was buried in the Llanidloes Cemetery.

WORTHINGTON, Rev. WILLIAM, D.D., an eminent divine and author of numerous works, was the son of Thomas Worthington, of Park, in the parish of Llanwnog, where he was born in the year 1703-4. His baptismal entry in the parish Register is dated April 4th, 1704. Canon Williams in his *Eminent Welshmen*, Dr. Hook, and other biographers have erroneously stated Merionethshire to have been the County of his birth. He was educated at the Oswestry Grammar School, and on the 9th of May, 1722, entered Jesus College, Oxford, describing himself in the College and University books " as the " son of Thomas Worthington, of Aberhavesp, in Montgomery- " shire." His industry, talents, and scholastic attainments soon brought him into notice. After leaving College he became for a short time an usher or tutor at the Oswestry Grammar School. In 1727 he took the degree of M.A. at Cambridge, and was afterwards incorporated at Jesus College, Oxford, July 3rd, 1758, and proceeded B.D. and D.D. July 10th the same year. His high abilities as a scholar attracted the notice of Bishop Hare of St. Asaph, who in 1729 gave him the vicarage of Llany-blodwell. In 1737 he obtained the sinecure rectory of Darowen, and in 1745 the vicarage of Llanrhaiadr yn Mochnant. A Canonry of St. Asaph was also conferred upon him in 1731. He exchanged Darowen for the sinecure rectory of Hope in 1751, and that again for the rectory of Llanfor near Bala in 1774. He was made a Prebendary of St. Asaph in 1773, and when Bishop Drummond, to whom he had been chaplain for several years, was translated to the see of York, he presented Dr. Worthington to a prebendal stall in that Cathedral. His learning and high position caused him to be selected as Boyle Lecturer for three years, namely, 1766, 1767, and 1768. He was eminently charitable, and led a pure and blameless life in a profligate and corrupt age. He promoted energetically many public improvements in the parish of Llanrhaiadr, where he chiefly resided for about thirty-three years. Dr. Worthington was a prolific theological writer, the following being a list of his works :—1. *An Essay on the Scheme and Conduct, Procedure and Extent of Man's Redemption*; designed for the honour and illustration of Christianity. To which is annexed a Dissertation on the design and argumentation of the Book of Job (1743). Of this a second edition was afterwards published. 2. *The Historical sense of the Mosaic account of the Fall proved and vindicated. 3. Instructions concerning Confirmation. 4. A Disquisition concerning the Lord's Supper. 5. The use, value, and improvements of various readings*, shewn and illustrated in a sermon preached before the University of Oxford at St. Mary's on Sunday, October 18th, 1761. 6. *A Sermon preached in the parish church of Christchurch, London, on Thursday, April 21st,* 1768; being the time of the yearly meeting of the children educated in the charity schools in and about the cities of London and Westminster (1768). 7. *The evidences of Christianity,* deduced from facts and the testimony of Sense, throughout all ages of the church to the present time ; in a series of Discourses preached for the Lecture founded by the Hon. Robert Boyle, Esq., in the parish of St. James, Westminster, in the years 1766, 1767, 1768 ; wherein is shewn that upon the whole this is not a decaying but a growing evidence (1769, 2 vols). 8. *The Scripture theory of the Earth,* throughout all its revolutions, and all the periods of its existence, from the creation to the final renovation of all things ; being a sequel to the Essay on Redemption, and an illustration of the principles on which it is written (1773). 9. *Irenicum* ; or the importance of unity in the Church of Christ considered, and applied towards the healing of our unhappy differences and divisions (1775). 10. *An impartial enquiry into the case of the Gospel Demoniacs* ; with an appendix consisting of an Essay on Scripture Demonology (1777). This was a vigorous attack on the opinion set forth by Mr. Hugh Farmer, a dissenting divine, in his *Essay on the Demoniacs* (1775), and produced a spirited reply in 1778, to which Dr. Worthington prepared a rejoinder, published, by the express directions of his Will, after his death, under the title of *A further enquiry into the case of the Gospel Demoniacs,* occasioned by Mr. Farmer's on the subject (1779). It appears also that Dr. Worthington was one of three (Dr. Henry Owen and the Rev. John Evans being the other two) appointed as a Committee to collate and settle the orthography of the Welsh edition of the Holy Scriptures published by the Christian Knowledge Society in 1769. Dr. Worthington received perhaps a larger share of preferment than any other Welsh clergyman of his day, but his eloquence, his extensive intellectual attainments, and his exemplary Christian life, eminently fitted him for a still higher sphere. It is probable that political considerations prevented his being raised to the episcopal bench—a position which his great gifts, as well as his intimate knowledge of the Welsh language, peculiarly fitted him to occupy to the great advantage of the Church. He was simple and abstemious in his habits, but very hospitable, and his social qualities caused his society to be much sought. He was visited at Llanrhaiadr by Dr. Johnson, Sir R. C. Hoare, Pennant, and other eminent literary men, who highly appreciated his society. He interested himself much in a scheme for connecting the counties of Merioneth and Carnarvon by means of an embankment across the estuary of Traethmawr, and obtained promises of subscription to the amount of £29,000 towards it, but owing to the opposition and selfish conduct of some of the landowners, it had to be abandoned. Dr. Worthington was never married. An orphan niece, Isabella Kendrick, whom he carefully educated, resided with him for many years, but owing to some unhappy differences she left him, and subsequently during a visit to London became a Wesleyan Methodist, and married Dr. Alexander Mather, the friend of Wesley. She was a woman of superior abilities, and Dr. Worthington left her a handsome legacy. He also bequeathed legacies to the Christian Knowledge Society (of which he was a zealous friend) ; to the Society for the Propagation of the Gospel; to the Dublin Society for promoting Protestant Schools in Ireland ; to Dr. Bray's Associates for the Instruction of the Negroes in the British Plantations; towards raising missionaries for the Colonies according to certain proposals published by him ; towards providing America with Protestant Bishops; to the Fund for the relief of the Widows and Children of Clergymen in the Diocese of St. Asaph ; to the Bishop, Dean, and Chapter of St. Asaph towards fitting up a room over the old Chapter House belonging to the Cathedral as a library ; and sums of money to be divided within a month after his decease among the poor of Llanrhaiadr, Llanfair, and Llanarmon-mynydd-mawr. He had in his lifetime given a field in Llanrhaiadr towards supporting a school there. Dr. Worthington died, greatly lamented, of a fever at Llanrhaiadr on the 6th October, 1778, aged 74 years, and was buried there on the 10th of the same month. His portrait, copied from an original painting by Sir Joshua Reynolds (supposed to have been by this time destroyed) is in the possession of Mr. Evan Powell, of Powelltown, West Virginia, a distant relative of Dr. Worthington.

WYNN, The Right Honourable CHARLES WATKIN WILLIAMS, deserves a prominent place among the Worthies of Montgomeryshire, with which county his long political career was closely associated. He might be designated as the statesman of the influential family of the Wynns, and was an offshoot of the great political stock of the Grenvilles, whose qualities he inherited, and whose fortunes he shared. He was conspicuous for his patronage of literary talent, capacity in debate, aptitude for the details of business, and devoted attachment to the honour and institutions of his country. He held at different times, and under repeated administrations, some of the highest offices of the State, and was deemed by his friends a suitable candidate for the chair of the Speaker of the House of Commons, and competent to discharge the arduous and responsible duties of Viceroy of India. Charles Watkin Williams Wynn was second son of Sir Watkin Williams Wynn, fourth baronet, of Wynnstay, and Charlotte, daughter of the Right Hon. George Grenville, sister of the Marquess of Buckingham, and aunt of the first Duke of Buckingham of the present creation. He was born on the 9th of October, 1775, and married, on the 9th of April, 1806, Mary, eldest daughter of Sir Foster Cunliffe, Bart, by whom he had issue two sons and four daughters. He was sent in early life to Westminster School, where he cultivated the friendship of Robert Southey, which was improved by subsequent intimacy at Oxford, and continued through the joint lives of the statesman and the poet. Southey frequently owned his deep debt of gratitude to his friend, and was enabled to take up his residence in London, and to commence the study of the law, through the kindness of Mr. Wynn, from whom he received for some years an annuity of £160. This was an act of rare friendship, twice honourable,

"To him that gives, and him that takes it,"

bestowed with pleasure, received without any painful feelings, and often reverted to as the staff and stay of those years. Mr. Southey showed his sense of the obligation by aptly dedicating to Mr. Wynn, in 1805, his poem on "Madoc," as a token of 16 years' uninterrupted friendship. It was intended to be the pillar of his reputation, and the greatest of all his works and a national epic for the Principality, prized and studied through future ages. Southey once wrote—"Perhaps all my writings are "owing to my acquaintance with Wynn. He saw the first, and "I knew the value of his praise too much to despise it." Thus Wales is indebted in a great measure to Mr. Wynn for the noble poem "Madoc," illustrative of its manners, customs, and history in the twelfth century, and exhibiting to our notice its chief warriors and poets in the stirring pages of its glorious independence. The affection of Mr. Wynn for the friend of his youth was exhibited by unabated interest in his voluminous works, and we find the entry in a letter to the Marquess of Buckingham, dated March 17th 1818, "I want to ask a copy of "the Stowe collection for Southey, who is going to review the "Rerum Hibernicæ Scriptores for the Quarterly." Mr. Wynn was returned to Parliament in the first instance for Old Sarum,

but on the death of Mr. Francis Lloyd, M.P. for Montgomeryshire in 1799, he obtained a seat in Parliament for the county of
Montgomery, and thus established a connection, which lasted
for the long term of fifty-one years. He stood amid the ranks
of the Opposition with Earl Grey and Lord Grenville on the
subject of the forcible annexation of Norway to Sweden, and
contended that British policy never sustained a deeper shock,
nor British character a deeper stain, than in the conduct which
had recently been pursued in regard to Norway. At a subsequent period he took a prominent place among the third party,
or Grenvillites, a sort of flying squadron between the Ministerial-
ists and Liberals, and capable of turning the scale on some
eventful occasions in favour of the side which they were
inclined to espouse. "The object whi h we had in view," Mr.
Wynn wrote to his cousin, the Marquess of Buckingham, Feb.
2, 1818, "of forming a third party can only be the work of
"time, and the effect of steering a steady course without con-
"nection, or coquetting with either party. If we only wait we
"shall, I am convinced, find many of the Opposition who are
"indisposed to Brougham, Romilly, Burdett, and Lambton, and
"inclined to join us." Of this section Mr. Wynn and Mr. W.
H. Fremantle took an advanced position, and in due time
attracted the attention of the Government, and Dr. Phillimore,
M.P. for Mawes, wrote Feb. 22, 1819, " Indeed, Charles Wynn
" seems now the person most looked up to by the House, and has
" not, I think, voted without having his opinion backed up by at
" least 20 votes." In 1817 a contest arose about the appointment of a Speaker of the House of Commons. Sir J.
Nichols proposed, and Mr. Littleton seconded, Mr. Charles
Manners Sutton, the Judge Advocate General, for the
coveted distinction. Mr. Dickinson proposed Mr. Wynn, on
whose peculiar fitness for the office he expatiated. Sir Matthew
White Ridley seconded the motion. Mr. Wilberforce spoke in
favour of Mr. Wynn. Both candidates addressed the
House, but Mr. Manners Sutton, being supported by
the whole strength of the Government, obtained a considerable
majority, the votes being—For Sutton, 312; for Wynn, 152.
In 1821 it was deemed indispensable by the Government to look
out for fresh supporters, and the Grenville party, who had
hitherto acted for the Whigs, presented the fairest prospect of
an alliance. Proposals were made accordingly, and accepted.
Lord Grenville, the head of the party, was disabled by infirmities from taking an active part in public life; but the Marquess of Buckingham was made a duke; Mr. Wynn, President
of the Board of Control; and his brother, Mr. H. Wynn,
Envoy to the Swiss Cantons. The Grenville party were favourable to the Roman Catholic claims. In the following year Mr.
Canning, the Secretary of Foreign Affairs, imagined that the
Speaker might be persuaded to go as Governor-General to India,
and that Mr. Wynn might accept the speakership, and that the
India Board, with its emoluments and patronage, might be

opened to Huskisson. The negotiation failed through the ambition of the Duke of Buckingham, who conceived that one of his immediate friends should be in the Cabinet, and insisted, in the event of Mr. Wynn's appointment to the Speakership, on his own admission to it; but the Ministry refrained from complying with his demands. In 1827 Mr. Wynn was one of the chief functionaries who represented the Cabinet at the funeral of the Duke of York, although previously, as a member of the Government he had openly avowed his anxiety for despatch, lest his Royal Highness's accession to the Throne should render Roman Catholic emancipation impossible. At the appointment of Mr. Canning to the Premiership, April 10th, 1827, Mr. Wynn faithfully adhered to his former colleague, notwithstanding many defections from among his recent associates, and retained his office at the India Board. It was at this time that he was a second time offered, and again refused the Governor-Generalship of India. At the formation of the cabinet of the Duke of Wellington in 1828, some difference unfortunately arose between Mr. Wynn and his noble relative, the Duke of Buckingham. The Duke, who was insatiable in his demands for high office, thought that Mr. Wynn stood in his way. An estrangement ensued between the two, of which the Duke of Wellington was perfectly aware, and Mr. Wynn was not included in the new administration. When, in 1829, Mr. O'Connell claimed his seat for Clare County, Mr. Wynn, supporting Mr. Brougham, contended that O'Connell was entitled to be heard either at the table or the bar; but the arguments of the great Irish orator were fruitless, and the House, adhering to its previous decision, ordered the Speaker to make out a new writ for Clare. On the 16th November, 1830, it was evident to all the world that the downfall of the Wellington Ministry was at hand, and, when the Chancellor of the Exchequer moved in common form that the House do resolve itself into a Committee on the Civil List, Sir Henry Parnell moved an amendment that a Select Committee be appointed to take into consideration the estimates and accounts printed by command of his Majesty, regarding the Civil List. The debate was a short one, but it was distinguished by a significant circumstance. Three old Conservatives—Mr. Wynn, Mr. Barnes, and Mr. Holm Sumner—spoke in favour of Sir Henry Parnell's motion, and against the Government, and on a division there appeared 233 for the amendment and 204 against it, giving a majority of 29 against Ministers, who consequently resigned. When Earl Grey accepted the post of the First Lord of the Treasury in 1830, the Grenvillites were propitiated by the appointment of Mr. Wynn to the Secretaryship of War, without a seat in the Cabinet; but subsequently he stated that, unless the propositions of Lord John Russell, in respect of disfranchisement, underwent a modification greater than he had reason to expect, he could not give them his support, and he retired from office, March 5th, 1831. When the Reform Bill went into Committee, and the case of each individual borough, which it was proposed to disfranchise, came under consideration, Mr. Wynn moved a general resolution that the consideration of the schedules should be postponed, avowedly for the purpose of taking advantage of the new census, the report of which might be expected in a few weeks. The House, however, by a majority of 118, determined to proceed, making the census of 1821 the rule. After two nights' debate the bill was read a second time by 302 votes to 301, and Mr. Wynn voted in favour of the Government. But when shortly afterwards Mr. Gascoigne, the member for Liverpool, proposed a preliminary resolution that the number of representatives in England and Wales should not be diminished, Mr. Wynn ventured on opposing Government, and the Ministry was defeated by 299 votes to 291. In 1835, Sir Robert Peel undertook the arduous task of forming an Administration, and offered the Chancellorship of the Duchy of Lancaster with a seat in the Cabinet to Mr. Wynn, and he once more undertook the seals of office in that short-lived Government. But he was now desirous to retire from the foreground of politics. His voice was less frequently heard in debate, or the Privy Council chamber; and his vigour of mind was less conspicuous in the engrossing avocations of Parliamentary business, but his opinion was frequently sought on points of procedure. He had intended voting for the admission of Baron Rothschild into the House of Commons, but was prevented by ill-health. The sunny glades of Llangedwyn afforded him greater pleasure than the stormy strife of St. Stephen's, and the quiet routine of domestic life imparted to him unruffled happiness. Literature and Art still retained their charms for him. He had become a Doctor of Civil Law, a Fellow of the Society of Antiquaries, and a Privy Councillor. He resigned in 1844 the command of the Montgomeryshire Yeomanry Cavalry, which regiment he had raised in 1803, and commanded for 41 years. The venerable statesman greatly enjoyed in the bosom of his family the furlough which he had won by a long life of arduous toil, and prized the delightful haven, whither he loved to retire from the storms of political animosity. He could reflect with pride on the sentiment of our great dramatist—

> ' I have done the state some service, and they know it.'
> —*Othello Act* 5, *Sc.* ii.

Mr. Wynn died on the 2nd September, 1850, aged 75 years, universally regretted, and was buried at St. George's Chapel, Bayswater, London. At the time of his death he was the "father" of the House of Commons, having sat uninterruptedly for Montgomeryshire for 53 years. He was succeeded in his estates by his son, Charles Watkin Williams Wynn, of Coedymaen, M.P. for Montgomeryshire from 1862 to 1880, a D.L., and formerly Lieut.-Colonel of the Montgomeryshire Yeomanry Cavalry, Deputy Chairman of Quarter Sessions and Recorder of Oswestry.

WYNN, CHARLOTTE WILLIAMS, was the eldest daughter of the Right Hon. Charles Watkin Williams Wynn, M.P., and of Mary his wife, the daughter of Sir Foster Cunliffe, Bart. She was born in January, 1807, at Llangedwyn, near Oswestry, where she mostly spent her childhood. Her father's high position in political life and his intimate friendship with Heber, Southey, Hallam, Mackintosh, and others brought her at an early age into contact with some of the most eminent men of the day, and bred within her a taste for literary pursuits and an interest in political affairs seldom to be found in ladies of her age. In 1836 her father was ordered to Wiesbaden for the benefit of his health, and she accompanied her parents thither. At this time she formed lasting friendships with several distinguished foreigners—among others, with Baron Varnhagen von Ense, Baron Bunsen, and M. Rio, as well as with Mr. Carlyle, the Rev. F. D. Maurice, and others of her own countrymen—with whom she corresponded for many years. Her letters display a cultured and well stored mind, a broad and catholic spirit, as well as very great shrewdness and keenness of observation, and are very pleasant reading. Her theological views and sentiments appear to have been most in accord with those of her friend Mr. Maurice. She travelled a good deal on the continent. During the later years of her life her health failed her, and she had to spend part of every year abroad. She died at Arcachon, April 26th, 1869, and was buried there. In 1877 extracts from her diary and correspondence were published under the title *Memorials of Charlotte Williams Wynn*, edited by her sister Mrs. Lindesay. A second edition of this work was called for in 1878.

WYNN, Captain ROBERT, of Maesmochnant, Llanrhaiadr, was an officer who saw much service abroad under the great Duke of Marlborough. He was descended from Owain Gwynedd in the same line as the Wynns of Gwydir. Huw Morus, the poet, addressed to him Stanzas of gratitude for visiting him on his sick bed. He died without issue 1st May, 1717.

Addenda.

BENNETT, GEORGE WATSON, was the son of William Bennett, and Ann, his wife, of the Cross Guns Inn, Newtown, where he was born on the 29th April, 1823. Having served an apprenticeship to the ironmongery business at Newtown he went to Liverpool, and while there entered into an engagement with a business firm to go to Demerara for seven years, which he fulfilled and afterwards embarked in business on his own account for about two years longer. He then obtained a government appointment and eventually attained a responsible position as Colonial book-keeper, from which he retired on a pension in 1879, and came over to England, (to which he had previously paid several short visits) to spend the remainder of his days. Mr. Bennett was a man of scientific tastes and extensive reading, and had acquired very considerable skill as a photographer. During his residence in Demerara he compiled and published a valuable and interesting *History of British Guiana* (Georgetown, Demerara, 1866), in a large handsome royal 8vo. volume; of which a second edition reduced in size appeared in 1875. Both contain numerous excellent illustrations mostly from photographs taken by himself. Mr. Bennett married in 1852, Miss Charlotte McGee, of Aberystwyth, by whom he left a son (holding a government appointment in Demerara) and a daughter (Mrs. Strathearn) surviving. He died rather suddenly at Whitehaven on the 7th December, 1884, in his 62nd year.

HUMPHREY, OR WMFFRE DAFYDD AB IFAN (*ante* p. 131) is said to have been the first to introduce into North Wales the metre known as "Tri Tharawiad," which afterwards became a great favourite with Welsh ballad writers. (*Brython*, 1860, p. 314).

JONES, REV. JOHN, an eminent Baptist Minister at Newtown, was born at Llandrindod, Radnorshire, in the year 1782. Having joined the Baptists in his 21st year he soon began to preach, and was placed for about a year under tuition at Leominster. He afterwards married and settled down near his wife's home at Newbridge, Radnorshire, for about three years. Thence he removed to undertake the pastorate of the Baptist Church at Newtown, where he laboured with eminent success for the remainder of his life— a period of 21 years, during which hundreds of members were added to the church, and the chapel was enlarged several times owing to the increase of the congregation. Mr. Jones was one of the most popular Baptist ministers in Wales, and his amiable and unblemished character caused him to be universally beloved. On the 27th May, 1831, he went to Shrewsbury to undergo amputation of the left hand for cancer with which he had been afflicted for several years. The operation was successfully performed, but after three or four days alarming symptoms supervened, and on the 4th of June he died in the 49th year of his age. The body was at once brought by road to Newtown, where the sad event produced the most profound sorrow. All the factories and shops were closed, and nearly all the inhabitants were clothed in mourning, the funeral procession to Rhydfelin burial ground comprising from five to six thousand persons.

JONES, JOSIAH (*Josiah Brynmair*), was born at Braich-odnant, Llanbrynmair, on the 4th July 1807. In August, 1850, he and his family emigrated to America, and settled at Gomer in the State of Ohio, where he died, aged 80, on the 15th October, 1887. Both in Wales and in America, Mr. Jones was a frequent contributor, chiefly of poetry, to the Welsh magazines, and some of his Hymns are deservedly esteemed and included in the Collections of S.R. and others.

MELANGELL (*ante* p. 192), Col. Heyward, of Crosswood, owns a very old stick on the ferule of which are engraved the following words :--

    " Engyl a ffon Melangell
      Trexant vlin vyddin y Vall "

(The angels and St. Monacella's staff will overcome the fierce army of hell.)

List of Subscribers.

Andrew, Mrs. Mary Anne, Oakley Cottage, Hurst, near Twyford, Berks
Ashton, Mr. Charles, Dinas Mawddwy
Ashton, Mr. John, Old Church-street, Newtown
Ashworth, Mr. J. C., New-road, Newtown
Astley, Mr. George, Hafren House, Newtown
Beddoes, Mr. Richard, Cefnperfa, Kerry, Mont.
Bennett, Mr. N., Glanyrafon, Trefeglwys
Breese, Mr. R. Birmingham
Bumford, Mr. Edward, Llanfair-road, Newtown
Bunford, Mr. David, 42, Broad-street, Newtown
Cardiff Free Libraries
Chapman, Mr. Henry, The School, Dolfor
Churchill, Mr. C. E. Kerry-road, Newtown
Clarke, Mrs. C. T., The Bent House, South Shields
Clayton, Mr. W., 47, Bryn-street, Newtown
Cooke, Mr. Fred W., Short Bridge, Newtown
Corbett-Winder, Major, Vaynor Park, Berriew
Cuthbert-Keeson, Mrs. Elynor, 40, Loudoun-road, St. John's Wood, London, N.W.
Daniels, Mr. D. R., Four Crosses, Carnarvon
Davies, Rev. Evan, Trefriw, R.S.O.
Davies, Mr. Edward, Plas Dinam, Llandinam
Davies, Mr. John, Dolgoch, Llanbrynmair
Davies, Mr. Edmund, Chapel-street, Newtown
Davies, Mr. Evan, 41, Pelham-road, Gravesend
Davies, Mr. Matthew, Garthbwt, Caersws
Davies, Mr. Robert William, Newtown
Davies, Mr. John Francis, Madras
Davies, Rev. John, Springfield, Berriew
Davies, Mr. R. (Tafolog), Oak Hill, Worthen, Salop
Davies, Mr. Richard, Nautygeifr, Llanidloes
Davies, Mr. Alfred, Tynyfawnog, Llanfair-Caereinion
Edmunds, Rev. David B., Tregynon
Edwards, Mr. Thos., Abermule
Edwards, Mr. Evan, 1, Millwood-street, North Kensington, London
Edwards, Rev. Ellis, M.A., The Theological College, Bala
Edwards, Rev. T. C., M.A., D.D., Theological College, Bala
Edwards, Mrs., Post Office, Llanbrynmair   [2 copies]
Evance, Miss Bourton, Dorset, via Bath   [3 copies]
Evance, Mr. D. A. R., F.R.G.S., Bourton, Dorset   [6 copies]
Evans, Mr. D. Emlyn, Cemmes, Mont.
Evans, Mr. David, Belle Vue, Trefeglwys, Caersws   [2 copies]
Evans, Mr. D., Machynlleth
Evans, Mr. Edward, Bronwylfa, Wrexham
Evans, Miss M. J., Bedwgwilym, Newtown
Evans, Rev. Thomas, 64, Victoria Park-road, South Hackney, London. N.E.
Evans, Mr. Charles ("Siarl Trannon"), Trefeglwys, Caersws
Fisher, Rev. J., B.D., Vale View, Ruthin
Forster, Mr. T. Ashbrook, The Laurels, Newtown
Francis, Mr. John, Nythva, Wrexham
Francis, Mr. Robert. Llwynaire, Llanbrynmair   [2 copies]
Francis, Mr. Wm, Belle Vue, Newtown

Gardener, Mrs., 41, Canal-road, Newtown
George, Mr. Richard, Glandwr Villa, Llanidloes
Gittins Mr. J. C., The Elms, Newtown   [2 copies]
Gittins, Mr. R. (Dolanog), Dolanog, Llanfair
Goodwin, Mr. R., Crescent-street, Newtown
Goodwin, Mr. R. Nettleton, *Wiltshire Times* Office, Warminster
Gowan, Dr. Charles, M,D , 199, Chester-road, Manchester
Griffiths, Rev. Edward, Meifod
Grovenor, Mr. Thomas, Caersws
Hall, Miss, Newtown
Hamer, Mr. David, 7, Wesley-street Newtown
Hamer, Mr, Wm., Moelfre Board School, near Oswestry
Harrison, Col., Caerhowel, Montgomery
Herbert, Mr. Edward A., Upper Helmsley Hall, York
Howell, Mr. Daniel, Llanbrynmair   [2 copies]
Howell, Mr. C. E., Rhiewport, Berriew
Howell, Mr. H. Llewelyn, 121, Canfield Gardens, West Hampstead,
    London, N W.
Hughes, Rev. Jonathan, Caersws
Hughes, Mr. John, Park-street, Newtown
Hughes, Mr. Robert Wm., Llwyn Onn, Newtown
Hughes, Mr. Edward, Kerry
Hughes, Mrs. Ceiriog, 7, Sydenham Terrace, Newcastle-on-Tyne
Hughes, Mr. Rowland, 5, Park-street, Swansea
Hughes, Mrs, Bazaar, Newtown
Humphreys-Owen, Mr. A. C., M.P., Glansevern, Berriew
Ingram, Mr. Richard, Llanidloes
James, Mr. W. G., Montgomery
Jehu, Mr. John, Brynavon, Llanfair
Jehu, Mr. Richard, 33, Mark Lane, London, E.C.
Jenkins, Mr. Edward, Gwalia, Llandrindod
Jenkins, Mr. W., 11, Severn-street, Newtown
Jones, Miss, Orchard Villa, Caersws
Jones, Mr. R. W., Holly Bank, Garston
Jones, Mrs., Llwyn Cottage, Montgomery
Jones, Rev. Owen, B.A., Ivy Grove, Llansantffraidd
Jones, Rev. D. Lloyd, M,A., Llandinam
Jones, Mr. Richard, Pertheirin, Caersws
Jones, Rev. Robert, Bodarwel, Rhosllanerchrugog
Jones, Mr. John Hamer, Pantmawr, Bettws
Jones, Mr. R., Big Brimmon, Newtown
Jones, Mr. T. Simpson, M.A., Gungrog Hall, Welshpool
Jones, Mr. J. Llanfyllin
Jones, Mr. E. Maurice, Westwood, Welshpool
Jones, Mrs. S. L., 25, Trafalgar-terrace, Swansea
Jones, Mr. E. O., Mayor of Welshpool
Jones, Mr. Wm., Bryn Goronwy, Llanwrin
Jones, Rev. D. Tafwys, The Manse, Berriew
Jones, Rev. Evan, 27, Segontium-terrace, Carnarvon,
Jones, Rev. Francis, Abergele
Jones, Mr. A. H., Crescent Villas, Newtown
Jones, Mr. Thomas H., Lima, Ohio, U.S A
Jones, Rev. W., Sylvanus, M A., Machynlleth
Jones, Mr. David, Clinton, N.Y.
Jones, Mr. John Howard, Kerry-road, Newtown
Jones, Mr. Francis Griffith, Maesmawr, Caersws
Jones, Mr. J. Parry, Oswestry
Jones Mr. Edward, Trewythen, Llandinam   [3 copies]
Jones, Mr. Edwin, The Board School, Llandinam
Jones, Rev. R. Evan, M.A., Vicarage, Llanllwchaiarn
Jones & Son, Messrs. William, Shrewsbury

Kirkham, Rev. W. Gillmore, M.A., Blackwood, Monmouthshire
Lambert, Mrs. W. H., The Cross. Newtown
Lewis, Rev. W. Dickens, M.A., D.D., Shrewsbury
Lewis, Rev. D., Llangyniew Rectory, Welshpool
Lewis, Mr. Hugh, M.A., Glanhafren, Newtown
Lewis, Mr. Edward, London House, Newtown
Lewis. Mr. E. Jones, 9, Severn-square, Newtown
Lewis, Mr. John, Severn-square, Newtown
Lewis, Mr. David, Meirion House, Newtown
Lloyd Mr. R. H., 17, Kerry-road, Newtown
Lloyd, Mr. D., 9, Broad-street, Welshpool
Lloyd, Mr. John Edward, M.A., Tanllwyn, Bangor
Lloyd, Mr. Richard, Mount Severn, Newtown
Lowe, Mr. William, Old Church-street, Newtown
Marpole, Mr. D. W, 46, Chancery-lane, London, W.C.
Marsh, Miss, Carno
Marshall, Mr. J. D. Chirbury, Shropshire
Meredith, Mr. Edwin, Batavia, Kane County, Illinois, U.S.A.
Mills, Mr. Richard, Bryndwr, Llanidloes
Miller, Mr. Samuel, The Court, Abermule
Milnes, Mr. James M., Kerry
Morgan, Mr. David, 29, High-street, Welshpool
Morgan, Mr. T. J., Beechwood, Wellingborough
Morgan, \ r. W., 12, Finsbury Pavement, London, E.C.   [2 copies]
Morgan, Mr. David, Llanidloes
Morgan, Mr. Rd, Bahaillon, Kerry
Morris, Mr. T. R., Welshpool
Morris, Mr. Thomas, Bodlondeb, Llanidloes
Morris, Mrs. E. R., Weylea. Cecil-road, Harlesden, London   [6 copies]
Morris, Mr. A. J., Trade Hall, Llanidloes
Mytton, Capt. D. H., Garth, Welshpool
Oliver, Mr. Ll. S., Gas-street, Newtown
Owen, Mr. John, Llandinam Hall
Owen, Rev. Elias, M.A., F.S.A., Llanyblodwell Vicarage, Oswestry
Owen, Rev. Thomas, Christchurch, Wellington, Salop
Owen, Mr. Morris, Carnarvon
Owen, Dr. Isambard, 40, Curzon Street, London, W.
Owens, Mr. John, Broad-street, Newtown
Owen, Rev. O. Lloyd, Llanwyddelan
Owen, Mr. Rufus, Tafolwern Mill, Llanbrynmair
Palmer, Mr. Joseph, The Cross, Newtown
Park, Mr. M. E., The Cross. Newtown
Parry, Rev. Edward, M.A., Newtown   [6 copies]
Parry, Rev. G., D.D., Dolafon, Carno
Parry, Mr. David, 78, Granby-street, Prince's-road, Liverpool
Phillips, Mr. Llewellyn, Plasyndre. Newtown
Phillips, Mr. Lloyd, 46, Mulgrave Street, Liverpool
Powell, Mr. Edward, Plasybryn, Newtown
Powell, Mr. Evan, Powelltown, Virginia, U.S.A.
Price, Principal John. M.A., Normal College, Bangor
Pritchard, Mr. Wm. Garthmyl, Mont.
Pritchard, Mr. John, Broad-street. Newtown.
Pryce, Mr. Thomas, New-road, Newtown
Pryce, Mr T. Davies, 39, Peachy-terrace, Nottingham
Pryce, Mr. D. Gaerfawr, Welshpool
Pryce, Mr. John, Pool Road, Newtown
Pryce, Mr. John. Highgate, Bettws
Pryce-Jones, Lady, Dolerw, Newtown
Pugh, Mr. W. B., Patrington, Hull   [3 copies]
Pugh, Miss, 69, Morpeth-street, Spring Bank, Hull   [2 copies]

Redman, Mr. Wm , Gas Works, Newtown
Rees, Mr. Thomas, Canal Shop, Newtown
Rees, Mr. John, junr., Goron, Newtown
Rees, Mr. Edward, Machynlleth
Rees, Mr. Richard, (Maldwyn), Machynlleth
Reese, Mr. E., 23, Woodville-road, Cardiff
Roberts, Mr. T. D., Penrallt, Newport, Mon.
Roberts, Mr. T. F., Manchester House, Machynlleth
Roberts Mr. J. H., Llawr Penegoes, Machynlleth
Rowlands, Rev. Daniel, M.A., Normal College, Bangor
Rowlands, Mr. B. B , Severn Square, Newtown
Rowlands, Mr. T., The Cross, Newtown
Rowlands, Rev. David, M.A., Memorial College, Brecon
Ruck, Mrs. M. A., Pantlludw, Machynlleth
Shuker, Mr. Charles, Havelock House, Welshpool
Smith, Mr. Henry Lester, Llanbrynmair
Spencer, Mr. J. D., Ladywell-street, Newtown
Stable, Mr. D. Wintringham, L.L.B., Llwyn Owen, Llanbrynmair
Story, Mr. W., Llanfair
Swain, Mr. A., High-street, Newtown
Swift, Mr. W. H. B. Crescent House, Newtown
Taylor, Mr. T. Mark, Rock, Newtown
Taylor, Mr. Cecil T. M., Crescent-street, Newtown
Taylor, Mr. H. Carl, Bridge-street, Newtown
T' eological College, Bala
Thomas, Ven. Archdeacon, M.A., F.S.A., Llandrinio
Thomas, Mr. J. Evans, Crescent Villa, Newtown
Thomas, Mr. T. S., New-road, Newtown
Tilsley, Mr. Richard, Caersws
Trevor, Rev. Canon, M.A., Machynlleth   •
Tudor, Mr. A., Ocean Collieries, Ton Pentre, Pontypridd
Tudor, Mr. R., Chapel-street, Newtown
Vaughan, Mr. E., Staylittle
Vaughan, Mr. T. H., Hafod, Llanerfyl
Wace, Mrs. F., Linden House, Abbey Foregate, Shrewsbury
Watkin, Mr. Isaac, Nantmawr, Llynclys, Oswestry
Williams. Rev. T. Powell, Glascoed, Aberhafesp
Williams, Rev. Evan, Bethesda, Llandyssil
Williams, Mr. W., M.A., H.M. Chief Inspector of Schools, Aberystwith
Williams, Mr. William, Council House, Llanfyllin   [3 copies]
Williams, Rev. T. E., Brynllys, Newtown
Williams, Rev. John, B.A., Moel View, Dolgelley   [2 copies]
Wills, Mr. T. F., Woodside, Newtown
Woodall, Mr. Edward, " Advertizer " Office, Oswestry
Woodhouse, Mr. James, Shrewsbury
Woosnam, Mr. George, Bryn Bank Villas, Newtown
Woosnam, Mr. Martin, Fron, Newtown
Woosnam, Mr. R. B., 29, Wolborough Street, Newton Abbot